ALSO BY ANNE TYLER

If Morning Ever Comes
The Tin Can Tree
A Slipping-Down Life
The Clock Winder
Celestial Navigation
Searching for Caleb
Earthly Possessions
Morgan's Passing
Dinner at the Homesick Restaurant
The Accidental Tourist
Breathing Lessons
Back When We Were Grownups

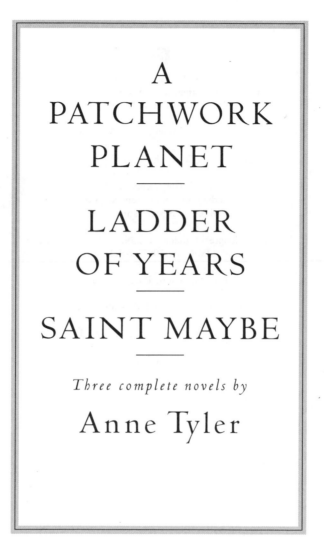

A
PATCHWORK
PLANET

———

LADDER
OF YEARS

———

SAINT MAYBE

———

Three complete novels by

Anne Tyler

bright sky press

A
PATCHWORK
PLANET

In loving memory of my husband,
Taghi Modarressi

I

I am a man you can trust, is how my customers view me. Or at least, I'm guessing it is. Why else would they hand me their house keys before they leave for vacation? Why else would they depend on me to clear their attics for them, heave their air conditioners into their windows every spring, lug their excess furniture to their basements? "Mind your step, young fellow; that's Hepplewhite," Mrs. Rodney says, and then she goes into her kitchen to brew a pot of tea. I could get up to anything in that basement. I could unlock the outside door so as to slip back in overnight and rummage through all she owns—her Hepplewhite desk and her Japanese lacquer jewelry box and the six potbellied drawers of her dining-room buffet. Not that I would. But she doesn't know that. She just assumes it. She takes it for granted that I'm a good person.

Come to think of it, I am the one who doesn't take it for granted.

On the very last day of a bad old year, I was leaning against a pillar in the Baltimore railroad station, waiting to catch the 10:10 a.m. to Philadelphia. Philadelphia's where my little girl lives. Her mother married a lawyer there after we split up.

Ordinarily I'd have driven, but my car was in the shop and so I'd had to fork over the money for a train ticket. *Scads* of money. Not to mention being some appointed place at some appointed time, which I hate. Plus, there were a lot more people waiting than I had expected. That airy, light, clean, varnished feeling I generally got in Penn Station had been crowded out. Elderly couples with matching luggage stuffed the benches, and swarms of college kids littered the floor with their duffel bags. This gray-haired guy was walking around speaking to different strangers one by one. Well-off guy, you could tell: tan skin, nice turtleneck, soft beige car coat. He went up to a woman sitting alone and asked her a question. Then he came over to a girl in a miniskirt standing near me. I had been thinking I wouldn't mind talking to her myself. She had long blond hair, longer than her skirt, which made it seem she'd neglected to put on the bottom half of her outfit. The man said, "Would you by any chance be traveling to Philadelphia?"

"Well, northbound, yes," she said, in this shallow, breathless voice that came as a disappointment.

"But to Philadelphia?"

"No, New York, but I'll be—"

"Thanks anyway," he said, and he moved toward the next bench.

Now he had my full attention. "Ma'am," I heard him ask an old lady, "are you traveling to Philadelphia?" The old lady answered something too mumbly for me to catch, and instantly he turned to the woman beside her. "Philadelphia?" Notice how he was getting more and more sparing of words. When the woman told him, "Wilmington," he didn't say a thing; just plunged on down the row to one of the matched-luggage couples. I straightened up from my pillar and drifted closer, looking toward Gate E as if I had my mind on my train. The wife was telling the man about their New Year's plans. They were baby-sitting their grandchildren who lived in New York City, she said, and the husband said, "Well, not New York City proper, dear; White Plains," and the gray-haired man, almost shouting, said, "But my daughter's counting on me!" And off he raced.

Well, *I* was going to Philadelphia. He could have asked me. I understood why he didn't, of course. No doubt I struck him as iffy, with my three-day growth of black stubble and my ripped black leather jacket and my jeans all dust and cobwebs from Mrs. Morey's garage. But still he could have given me a chance. Instead he just flicked his eyes at me and then swerved off toward the bench at the end of the room. By now he was looking seriously undermedicated. "Please!" he said to a woman reading a book. "Tell me you're going to Philadelphia!"

She lowered her book. She was thirtyish, maybe thirty-five—older than I was, anyhow. A schoolmarm sort, in a wide brown coat with a pattern like feathers all over it. "Philadelphia?" she said. "Why, yes, I am."

"Then could I ask you a favor?"

I stopped several feet away and frowned down at my left wrist. (Never mind that I don't own a watch.) Even without looking, I could sense how she went on guard. The man must have sensed it too, because he said, "Nothing too difficult, I promise!"

They were announcing my train now. ("The delayed 10:10," the loudspeaker called it. It's always "the delayed" this or that.) People started moving toward Gate E, the older couples hauling their wheeled bags behind them like big, meek pets on leashes. If the woman in the feather coat said anything, I missed it. Next I heard, the man was talking. "My daughter's flying out this afternoon for a junior semester abroad," he was saying. "Leaving from Philadelphia; the airline offers a bargain rate if you leave from Philadelphia. So I put her on a train this morning, stopped for groceries afterward, and came home to find my wife in a state. It seems our daughter'd forgotten her passport. She'd telephoned from the station in Philly; didn't know what to do next."

The woman clucked sympathetically. I'd have kept quiet myself. Waited to find out where the guy was heading with this.

"So I told her she should stay put. Stay right there in the station, I said, and I would get somebody here to carry up her passport."

A likely story! Why didn't he go himself, if this was such an emergency?

"Why don't you go yourself?" the woman asked him.

"I can't leave my wife alone that long. She's in a wheelchair: Parkinson's."

This seemed like a pretty flimsy excuse, if you want my honest opinion. Also, it exceeded what I would consider the normal quota for misfortunes. Not only a lamebrain daughter, but a wife with a major disease! I let my eyes wander toward the two of them. The woman was gazing up into the man's face, pooching her mouth out thoughtfully. The man was holding a packet. He must have pulled it from his car coat: not a manila envelope, which would have been the logical choice, but one of those padded mailers the size of a paperback book. Aha! Padded! So you couldn't feel the contents! And from where I stood, it looked to be stapled shut besides. *Watch yourself, lady,* I said silently.

As if she'd heard me, she told the man, "I hope this isn't some kind of contraband." Except she pronounced it "counterband," which made me think she must not be a schoolmarm, after all.

"No, no!" the man told her. He gave a huff of a laugh. "No, I can assure you it's not counterband."

Was he repeating her mistake on purpose? I couldn't tell. (Or maybe the word really *was* "counterband.") Meanwhile, the loudspeaker came to life again. The delayed 10:10 was now boarding. Train wheels squealed below me. "I'll do it," the woman decided.

"Oh, wonderful! That's wonderful! Thanks!" the man told her, and he handed her the packet. She was already rising. Instead of a suitcase, she had one of those tote things that could have been just a large purse, and she fitted the strap over her shoulder and lined up the packet with the book she'd been reading. "So let's see," the man was saying. "You've got light-colored hair, you're wearing a brown print coat. . . . I'll call the pay phone where my daughter's waiting and let her know who to watch for. She'll be standing at Information when you get there. Esther Brimm, her name is—a redhead. You can't miss that hair of hers. Wearing jeans and a blue-jean jacket. Ask if she's Esther Brimm."

He followed the woman through the double doors and down the stairs, although he wasn't supposed to. I was close behind. The cold felt good after the packed waiting room. "And you are?" the man was asking.

Affected way of putting it. They arrived on the platform and stopped short, so that I just about ran over them. The woman said, "I'm Sophia—" and then something like "Maiden" that I couldn't exactly hear. (The train was in place but rumbling, and passengers were clip-clopping by.) "In case we miss connections, though . . . ," she said, raising her voice.

In case they missed connections, he should put his name and phone number on the mailer. Any fool would know that much. But he seemed to have his mind elsewhere. He said, "Um . . . now, do you live in Baltimore? I mean, are you coming *back* to Baltimore, or is Philly your end destination?"

I almost laughed aloud at that. So! Already he'd forgotten he was grateful; begun to question his angel of mercy's reliability. But she didn't take offense. She said, "Oh, I'm a *long*-time Baltimorean. This is just an overnight visit to my mother. I do it every weekend: take the ten-ten Patriot Saturday morning and come back sometime Sunday."

"Well, then!" he said. "Well. I certainly do appreciate this."

"It's no trouble at all," she said, and she smiled and turned to board.

I had been hoping to sit next to her. I was planning to start a conversation—mention I'd overheard what the man had asked of her and then suggest the two of us check the contents of his packet. But the car was nearly full, and she settled down beside a lady in a fur hat. The closest I could manage was across the aisle to her left and one row back, next to a black kid wearing earphones. Only view I had was a schoolmarm's netted yellow bun and a curve of cheek.

Well, anyhow, why was I making this out to be such a big deal? Just bored, I guess. I shucked my jacket off and sat forward to peer in my seat-back pocket. A wrinkly McDonald's bag, a napkin stained with ketchup, a newspaper section folded to the crossword puzzle. The puzzle was only half done, but I didn't have a pen on me. I looked over at the black kid. He probably didn't have a pen, either, and anyhow he was deep in his music—long brown fingers tapping time on his knees.

Then just beyond him, out the window, I chanced to notice the passport man talking on the phone. Talking on the phone? Down here beside the tracks? Sure enough: one of those little cell phones you all the time see obnoxious businessmen showing off in public. I leaned closer to the window. Something here was weird, I thought. Maybe he smuggled drugs, or worked for the CIA. Maybe he was a terrorist. I wished I knew how to read lips. But already he was closing his phone, slipping it into his pocket, turning to go back upstairs. And our train was sliding out of the station.

I looked again at the woman. At the packet, to be specific.

It was resting on top of her book, which sat in her feather-print lap. (She would be the type who stayed properly buttoned into her coat, however long the trip.) Where the mailer was folded over, staples ran straight across in a nearly unbroken line. But staples were no problem. She could pry them up with, say, a nail file or a dime, and slip them out undetectably, and replace them when she was finished. *Do it,* I told her in my head. She was gazing past her seatmate, out the right-hand window. I couldn't even see her cheek now; just her bun.

Back in the days when I was a juvenile delinquent, I used to break into houses and read people's private mail. Also photo albums. I had a real thing about photo albums. The other kids who broke in along with me, they'd be hunting car keys and cigarettes and booze. They'd be tearing through closets and cabinets all around me, while I sat on the sofa poring over somebody's wedding pictures. And even when I took stuff, it was always personal stuff. This little snow globe once from a nightstand in a girl's bedroom. Another time, a brass egg that stood on scaly claw feet and opened to show a snapshot of an old-fashioned baby inside. I'm not proud of this. I'd sooner confess to jewel theft than to pocketing six letters tied up with satin ribbon, which is what I did when we jimmied the lock at the Empreys' place one night. But there you are. What can I say.

So when this Sophia woman let the packet stay untouched—didn't prod it, didn't shake it, didn't tease apart the merest corner of the flap—I felt something like, oh, almost envy. A huge wave of envy. I started wishing *I* could be like that. Man, I'd have been tearing into that packet with my bare teeth, if I'd had the chance.

The conductor came and went, and the row houses slipping by turned into factory buildings and then to matted woods and a sheet of gray water, but I was barely conscious of anything beyond Sophia's packet. I saw how quietly her hands rested on the brown paper; she was not a fidgeter. Smooth, oval nails, pale pink, and plump white fingers like a woman's in a religious painting. Her book was turned the wrong way for me to read the title, but I knew it was something worthwhile and educational. Oh, these people who prepare ahead! Who think to bring actual books, instead of dashing into a newsstand at the last minute for a *Sports Illustrated* or—worse yet—making do with a crossword puzzle that someone else has started!

It bothered me more than I liked to admit that the passport man had avoided me.

We were getting close to Wilmington, and the lady in the fur hat started collecting her things. After she left, I planned to change seats. I would wait for Sophia to shift over to the window, and then I'd sit down next to her. "Morning," I would say. "Interesting packet you've got there."

"I see you're carrying some kind of packet."

"Mind if I inquire what's in that packet?"

Or whatever. Something would come to me. But when the train stopped and the lady stood up, Sophia just turned her knees to one side to let her out. She stayed seated where she was, on the aisle, so I didn't see any natural-seeming way to make my move.

We left Wilmington behind. We traveled past miles of pipeline and smokestacks, some of them belching flames. I could tell now that it was rap music the kid beside me was listening to. He had the volume raised so high that I could hear it winding out of his earphones—that chanting and insisting sound like the voices you hear in your dreams.

"Philll-adelphia!" the conductor called.

Of course Sophia got ready too soon. We were barely in sight of the skyline—bluish buildings shining in the pale winter sunlight, Liberty Towers scalloping their way up and up and up—but she was already rising to wait in the aisle. The exit lay to the rear, and so she had to face me. I could see the pad of flesh that was developing under her chin. She leaned against her seat and teetered gently with the swaying of the car. *Critics are unanimous!* the back of her book said. The mailer was almost hidden between the book and her cushiony bosom.

I put on my jacket, but I didn't stand up yet. I waited till the train had come to a stop and she had passed me. Then I swung out into the aisle lickety-split, cutting in front of a fat guy with a briefcase. I followed Sophia so closely, I could smell the dusty smell of her coat. It was velvet, or something like velvet. Velvet always smells dusty, even when it's fresh from the cleaners.

There was the usual scuffle with that automatic door that likes to squash the passengers—Press the button, dummies!—and the usual milling and nudging in the vestibule, and then we stepped out into a rush of other people. It was obvious that Sophia knew where she was going. She didn't so much as glance around her but walked fast, coming down hard on her heels. Her heels were the short, chunky kind, but they made her as tall as I was. I had noticed that while we were standing on the train. Now she was slightly taller, because we'd started up the stairs and she was a step above me.

Even once we'd reached the waiting room, she didn't look around. Thirtieth Street Station is so enormous and echoing and high-ceilinged—a jolt after cozy Baltimore—that most people pause to take stock a moment, but not Sophia. She just went clicking along, with me a few yards to the rear.

At the Information island, only one person stood waiting. I spotted her from far across those acres of marble flooring: a girl in a denim jacket and jeans, with a billow of crinkly, electric red hair. It fanned straight out and stopped just above her shoulders. It was *amazing* hair. I was awestruck. Sophia, though, didn't let on she had noticed her. She was walking more slowly now, downright sedately, placing her toes at a slight angle outward, the way women often do when they want to look composed and genteel. Actually, she was starting to get on my nerves. Didn't that bun of hers just sum her up, I thought—the net that bound it in and the perfect, doughnut shape and the way it sat so low on her head, so matronly and drab! And Esther Brimm, meanwhile, stood burning like a candle on her stick-thin, blue-denim legs.

When we reached the island I veered right, toward a display of schedules on the counter. I heard Sophia's heels stop in front of Esther. "Esther Brimm?" she asked.

"Ms. Maynard?"

Husky, throaty voice, the kind I like.

"Your father asked me to bring you something. . . ."

I took a schedule from the rack and turned my face casually in their direction. Not till Esther said, "Right; my passport," did Sophia slip the mailer from behind her book and hold it out.

"Thanks a million," Esther said, accepting it, and Sophia said, "My pleasure. Have a good trip." Then she turned away and clicked toward the Twenty-ninth Street exit.

Just like that, I forgot her. Now I was focused on Esther. *Open it!* I told her. Instead she picked up the army duffel lying at her feet and moved off toward the phones. I meandered after her, studying my schedule. I pretended I was hunting a train to Princeton.

The phones were the unprivate kind just out in the middle of everything, standing cheek to jowl. When Esther lifted a receiver off its hook, I was right there beside her, lifting a receiver of my own. I was so near I could have touched her duffel bag with the toe of my sneaker. I heard every word she said. "Dad?" she said.

I clamped my phone to my ear and held the schedule up between us so I could watch her. This close, she was less attractive. She had that fragile, sore-looking skin you often find on redheads. "Yes," she was saying, "it's here." And then, "Sure! I guess so. I mean, it's still stapled shut and all. Huh? Well, hang on."

She put her receiver down and started yanking at the mailer's top flap. When the staples tore loose, rat-a-tat, she pulled the edges apart and peered inside—practically stuck her little freckled nose inside. Then she picked up the phone again. "Yup," she said. "Good as new."

So I never got a chance to see for myself. It could have been anything: loose diamonds, crack cocaine . . . But somehow I didn't think so. The phone call was what convinced me. She'd have had to be a criminal genius to fake that careless tone of voice, the easy offhandedness of a person who knows for a fact that she's her parents' pride and joy. "Well, listen," she was saying. "Tell Mom I'll call again from the airport, okay?" And she made a kissing sound and hung up. When she slung her duffel over her shoulder and started toward one of the gates, I didn't even watch her go.

The drill for visiting my daughter was, I'd arrive about ten a.m. and take her on an outing. Nothing fancy. Maybe a trip to the drug store, or walking her little dog in the park. Then we'd grab a bite someplace, and I'd return her and leave. This happened exactly once a month—the last Saturday of the month. Her mother's idea. To hear her mother tell it, Husband No. 2 was Superdad; but I had to stay in the picture to give Opal a sense of whatchamacallit. Connection.

But due to one thing and another—my car acting up, my alarm not going off—I was late as hell that day. It was close to noon, I figure, before I even left the station, and I didn't want to spring for a cab after paying for a train ticket. Instead I more or less ran all the way to the apartment (they lived in one of those posh old buildings just off Rittenhouse Square), and by the time I pressed the buzzer, I was looking even scruffier than my usual self. I could tell as much from Natalie's expression, the minute she opened the door. She let her eyes sort of drift up and down me, and, "Barnaby," she said flatly. Opal's little dog was dancing around my ankles—a dachshund, very quivery and high-strung.

"Yo. Natalie," I said. I started swatting at my clothes to settle them a bit. Natalie, of course, was Miss Good Grooming. She wore a slim gray skirt-and-sweater set, and her hair was all of a piece—smooth, shiny brown—dipping in and then out again before it touched her shoulders. Oh, she had been a beauty for as long as I had known her; except now that I recalled, there'd always been something too placid about her. I should have picked it up from her dimples, which made a little dent in each cheek whether or not she was smiling. They gave her a look of self-satisfaction. What I'd thought when we first met was, how could she *not* be self-satisfied? And her vague, dreamy slowness used to seem sexy. Now it just made me impatient. I said, "Is Opal ready to go?" and Natalie took a full minute, I swear, to consider every aspect of the question. Then: "Opal is in her room," she said finally. "Crying her eyes out."

"Crying!"

"She thought you'd stood her up."

"Well, I know I'm a little bit late—" I said.

She lifted an arm and contemplated the tiny watch face on the inner surface of her wrist.

"Things just seemed to conspire against me," I said. "Can I see her?"

After she'd thought that over awhile, she turned and floated off, which I took to mean yes.

I made my own way to Opal's bedroom, down a long hall lined with Oriental rugs. I waded through the dachshund and knocked on her door. "Opal?" I called. "You in there?"

No answer. I turned the knob and poked my head in.

You'd never guess this room belonged to a nine-year-old. The bedspread was appliquéd with ducklings, and the only posters were nursery-rhyme posters. By rights it should have been a baby's room, or a toddler's.

The bed was where I looked first, because that's where I figured she would be if she was crying. But she was in the white rocker by the window. And she wasn't crying, either. She was glaring at me reproachfully from underneath her eyebrows.

"Ope!" I said, all hearty.

Opal's chin stayed buried inside her collar.

I knew I shouldn't think this, but my daughter had never struck me as very appealing. She had all her life been a few pounds overweight, with a dish-shaped face and colorless hair and a soft, pink, half-open mouth, the upper lip short enough to expose her top front teeth. (I used to call her "Bunnikins" till Natalie asked me not to—and why would she have asked, if she herself hadn't noticed Opal's close resemblance to a rabbit?)

It didn't help that Natalie dressed her in the kind of clothes you see in Dick and Jane books—fussy and pastel, the smocked bodices bunching up on her chest and the puffed sleeves cutting into her arms. Me, I would have chosen something less constricting. But who was I to say? I hadn't been much of a father.

I did want the best for her, though. I would never intentionally hurt her. I walked over to where she was sitting and squatted down in front of her. "Opal-dopal," I said. "Sweetheart."

"What."

"Call off your dog. He's eating my wallet."

She started to smile but held it back. Her mother's two dimples deepened in her cheeks. The dog really was nibbling at my wallet. George Farnsworth, his name was; heaven knows why. "George Farnsworth," I said sternly, "if you're short of cash, just ask straight out for a loan, okay?"

Now I heard a definite chuckle. I took heart. "Hey, Ope, I'm sorry I'm late," I said. "First I had car trouble, see—"

"You *always* have car trouble."

"Then my alarm clock didn't go off—"

"It *always* doesn't go off."

"Well. Not always," I told her. "Then once I got to Penn Station, you'll never guess what happened. It was like a secret-agent movie. Guy is walking up to people, pulling something out of his coat. 'Ma'am,' "—I made my voice sound menacing and mysterious—" 'would you please take this package to Philadelphia for me?' "

Opal didn't speak, but I could tell she was listening. She watched me with her pinkish-gray eyes, the lashes slightly damp.

" 'Take it to my daughter in Philly; all it is is her passport,' he said, and I thought to myself, *Ha! I just bet it's her passport!* So when this one woman said she would do it, I followed her at the other end of the trip."

"You followed her?"

"I wanted to see what would happen. So I followed her to her rendezvous with the quote-unquote daughter, and then I hung around the phones while the daughter placed a call to—"

"You hung around the phones?"

I was beginning to flounder. (This story didn't have what you'd call a snappy ending.) I said, "Yes, and then—um—"

"You were only dawdling in the station all this time! It's not enough you don't look after your car right and you forget to set your alarm; then you dawdle in the station like you don't care *when* you see me!"

It was uncanny, how much she sounded like her mother. Her mother in the old days, that is—the miserable last days of our marriage. I said, "Now, hon. Now wait a sec, hon."

Which was also from those days, word for word. Some kind of reflex, I guess.

"You promised you'd come at ten," she said, "and instead you were just . . . goofing around with a bunch of secret agents! You totally lost track of where you were supposed to be!"

"In the first place," I said, "I take excellent care of my car, Opal. I treat it like a blood relative. It's not my fault if my car is older than I am. And I did not forget to set my alarm. I don't know why it didn't go off; sometimes it just doesn't, okay? I don't know why. And I honestly thought you'd like hearing about those people I was so-called goofing around with. I thought, *Man, I wish Opal could see this,* and I followed them expressly so I could tell you about it later over a burger and french fries. Wouldn't that be great? A burger and fries at Little Pete's, Ope, while I tell you my big story."

It wasn't working, though. Opal's eyes only got pinker, and for once she had her mouth tightly shut.

"Look at George Farnsworth! *He* wants to go," I said.

In fact, George Farnsworth had lost interest and was lying beside the rocker with his nose on his paws. But I said, "First we'll take George for a walk in the Square, and then we'll head over to—"

"It sounds to me," Natalie said, "as if Opal prefers to stay in."

She was standing in the doorway. Damn Oriental rugs had muffled her steps.

"Am I right, Opal?" she asked. "Would you rather tell him goodbye?"

"Goodbye?" I said. "I just got here! I just came all this way!"

"It's your decision, Opal."

Opal looked down at her lap. After a long pause, she murmured something.

"We couldn't hear you," Natalie said.

"Goodbye," Opal told her lap.

But I knew she didn't mean it. All she wanted was a little coaxing. I said, "Hey now, Ope . . ."

"Could I speak with you a minute?" Natalie asked me.

I sighed and got to my feet. Opal stayed where she was, but I caught her hidden glimmer of a glance as I turned to follow Natalie down the hall. I knew I could have persuaded her if I'd been given more time.

We didn't stop in the living room. We went on through to the kitchen, at the other end of the apartment. I guess Natalie figured my jeans might soil her precious upholstery. I had never seen the kitchen before, and I spent a moment looking around (old-fashioned tilework, towering cabinets) before it sank in on me what Natalie was saying.

"I've been thinking," she was saying. "Maybe it would be better if you didn't come anymore."

This should have been okay with me. It's not as if I enjoyed these visits. But you know how it is when somebody all at once announces you can't do something. I said, "What! Just because one Saturday I happen to run a little behind?"

Her eyes seemed to be resting slightly to the left of my left shoulder. Her face was as untroubled as a statue's.

"I'm traveling from a whole other city, for God's sake!" I told her. "A whole entirely other state! No way can you expect me to arrive here on the dot!"

"It's funny," she said reflectively. "I used to believe it was very important for Opal to keep in touch with you. But now I wonder if it might be doing her more harm than good. All those Saturdays you've come late, or left early, or canceled altogether—"

"It was only the once or twice or three times or so that I canceled," I said.

"And even when you do show up, I imagine it's started to dawn on her how you live."

"How I live! I live just fine!"

"A rented room," she mused, "an unskilled job, a bunch of shiftless friends. No goals and no ambitions; still not finished college at the age of thirty."

"Twenty-nine," I corrected her. (The one charge I could argue with.)

"Thirty in three weeks," she said.

"Oh."

There was a sudden silence, like when the Muzak stops in a shopping mall and you haven't even been hearing it but all at once you're aware of its absence. And just then I noticed, on the windowsill behind her, our old china cookie jar. I hadn't thought of that cookie jar in years! It was domed on top and painted with bars like a birdcage, and it looked so dowdy and homely, against the diamond-shaped panes. It made me lose my train of thought. The next thing I knew, Natalie was gliding out of the kitchen, and I had no choice but to follow her.

Though, in the foyer, I did say, "Well." And then, in the hall outside, I turned and said, "Well, we'll see about this!"

The door made almost no sound when she closed it.

My train home was completely filled, and stone cold to boot. Some problem with the heating system. I sat next to a Spanish-type guy who must have started his New Year's partying a tad bit early. His head kept nodding forward, and he was breathing fumes that were practically flammable. Across the aisle, this very young couple was trying to soothe a baby. The husband said, "Maybe he's hungry," and the wife said, "I just fed him." The husband said, "Maybe he's wet." I don't know why they made me so sad.

After that, it seemed all around me I saw families. A toddler peeked over his seat back, and his mother gave him a hug and pulled him down again. A father and a little girl walked toward me from the club car, the little girl holding a paper cup extremely carefully in both hands. The foreigner and I were the only ones on our own, it seemed.

The father glanced at us as he came close (at the foreigner's head bobbing and reeling, and me with my jacket collar flipped up and a wad of cottony white stuff poking out of a tear in one sleeve), and then he glanced away. It made me think of the passport man, refusing to meet my eyes. And that made me think of the woman in the feather coat. Sophia. So honorable, Sophia had been; so principled. So well behaved even when she thought nobody was looking.

Oh, what makes some people more virtuous than others? Is it something they know from birth? Don't they ever feel that zingy, thrilling urge to smash the world to bits?

Isn't it possible, maybe, that good people are just *luckier* people? Couldn't that be the explanation?

2

The company I work for is called Rent-a-Back, Inc. How I got into it is a whole other story, but basically we provide a service for people who are old or disabled. Any load you can't lift, any chore you don't feel up to, why, just call on us. Say you want your lawn chairs piled in your garage in the fall. Or your rugs rolled up and stored away in the spring. We can do that. A lot of our customers have a standing order—like, an hour a week. Others just telephone as circumstances arise. Whatever.

On the Saturday of my dud trip to Philadelphia, I came home to find a message from my boss on my answering machine. "Barnaby, it's Virginia Dibble. Could you get back to me as soon as possible? We have an urgent request for this evening."

I really liked Mrs. Dibble. She was this dainty, fluttery lady a whole lot older than my mother, but I'd seen her tote a portable toilet down two flights of stairs when we were shorthanded. So even though I wasn't in such a great mood, I dialed her number. "What's up?" I asked her.

"Oh, poor, poor Mrs. Alford," she started right in. "She needs a Christmas tree put together."

"A what?"

"An eight-foot artificial Christmas tree. It's in her attic, she says, and she needs it brought down and assembled."

"Mrs. Dibble," I said. "It's New Year's Eve."

"Oh, you have plans?"

"I mean, it's a week after Christmas. What does she want with a tree?"

"She says her seven grandchildren are stopping by for a visit. They're spending the night on their way home from skiing, and she wants the house to look cheery, she says, and not old-ladyish and glum."

"Ah."

Grandchildren ruled the world, if you judged by most of our clients.

"She needs it decorated too," Mrs. Dibble was saying. "She says she can't manage the upper branches, and if she climbed onto a step stool, she's scared she might break a hip."

Breaking a hip was what else ruled the world—the fear of it, I mean. Big bugaboo, in the circles I traveled in.

I said, "Couldn't she tell her grandchildren she did have a tree but took it down? Plenty of folks get rid of their trees on December twenty-sixth, tell her!"

But I knew what Mrs. Dibble's answer would be ("We're the muscles, not the brains," she always said); so I didn't wait to hear it. "Besides," I said, "my car is in the shop and I won't have it back until Monday."

"Oh, Martine can drive," Mrs. Dibble told me. "I thought I'd send the two of you, so as to finish that much faster. Can you do it if Martine picks you up?"

"Well," I said. "I guess."

"All the others have New Year's plans. I'll call Martine back again and tell her to come fetch you."

There were eleven full-time employees at Rent-a-Back. That meant nine people that I knew of had New Year's plans. And these were not particularly successful people. Several might even be looked upon as losers. But still, they'd found something to do with themselves on New Year's Eve.

I lived in the eastern part of the city, in the basement of a duplex out Northern Parkway. Martine lived down on St. Paul. It would take her twenty-some minutes to reach me; so I had time to fix myself a peanut butter sandwich. (My only meal all day had been a bag of chips in Penn Station.) Then I grabbed a Coke and went to eat on the patio, where I could see a sliver of the driveway. I never hung around my apartment if I could help it. It was nothing but a rec room, really, which the family above me rented out because they needed the income.

By now the sky had clouded over and darkened. When the patio lamps switched on, they made a noticeable difference, even though it couldn't have been much later than four o'clock. The patio had these tall pole lamps that were activated by motion. If anybody came near, they would all at once light up. Then after thirty seconds they shut off again. Usually, I enjoyed teasing them. I would take a step, freeze, take another step. . . . Once, when the Hardestys were gone and I was grilling steaks with this girl I'd met, I told her there was no way to make the lamps stay lit non-stop (which was a flat-out lie) and we would have to keep moving if we wanted to see what we were eating. So there we were, shifting hugely in our chairs, lifting our forks with these exaggerated gestures that the lamps would be sure to notice. Then after supper we got to making out and the lamps, of course, went dark, and we forgot about them till she stood up to pull her T-shirt off, and *whang*! they all flared on again. I laughed until my stomach hurt.

That afternoon, though, I wasn't feeling so playful. I just sat hunched over my sandwich in a shreddy mesh lawn chair, and pretty soon the lamps clicked off.

I'd finished eating by the time Martine pulled in. She was driving her boyfriend's battered red pickup, high off the ground and narrow through the eyes. I set my Coke can in a planter and came around to climb in on the passenger side. "Hey, Martine," I said. "No date for New Year's Eve?"

"He's in bed with the throwing-up flu," she said, backing into the street. "What's *your* excuse, Mr. Peanut Butter Breath?"

"I've turned against women," I told her.

"Ha!"

She shifted gears and took off.

Martine drove sitting on a cushion; that's how small she was. Heaven knows what had possessed her to sign on at Rent-a-Back. She must have weighed ninety pounds at the most—tiny little cat-faced girl with sallow skin and boxy black hair squared off above her earlobes. But tough, I have to admit. A Sparrows Point kid, from steelworking stock. Scraped sharp knuckles on the steering wheel; gigantic black nylon jacket that smelled of motor oil. "How was your trip to Philly?" she asked, and her voice had a raspy scratch to it that made me want to clear my throat.

I said, "It stunk."

"Stunk!"

"First thing wrong," I said, "was I had to take the train. Car is acting up again."

"What is it this time?"

"Steering."

"Well, it serves you right for owning an endangered species," she said.

"Tell that to my grandpa," I said. "He's the one who owned it in the first place. You think I'd go out on purpose and buy a Corvette Sting Ray? So I had to plunk down money for a train ticket. Then when I get to Philly, what does Natalie do? Sends me straight back home again. Says she's decided to stop my visits altogether."

"Why, she can't decide that!" Martine said.

"She claims I do Opal more harm than good."

"You just get ahold of your lawyer!"

"Right."

I actually didn't have a lawyer, but it seemed like too much work to explain that. Instead I slouched in my seat and watched the scenery slog by: bald brick houses, pale squares of grass, bushes strung with Christmas lights that were just now winking on.

"Anyway," I said, "her husband is a lawyer. No doubt they have some kind of fraternity or something, some secret circle she can mobilize against me. Oh, Lord. I don't know why I ever hooked up with such a woman."

"Well? Why did you?" Martine asked.

"I believe it was her hairline," I said.

Martine laughed.

"Seriously," I said. "She had this sterling-silver barrette pulling her hair straight back on top so you could see her forehead. Her clean, shiny fore-head. It kind of hypnotized me, you might say."

Martine swerved around a liquor truck that was parking at some-one's curb.

"I've got to start viewing the whole picture more," I said. "I can't go on falling for people's foreheads."

"With me, it's mouths," Martine said.

"Really."

I began chewing on a thumbnail, incidentally covering my own mouth with my fist.

"First time I met Everett, all I saw was his mouth. That curvy upper lip of his. Did I ask if he had a steady job, or whether he was the type who'd want to get married?"

I said, "Married?" and tucked both fists between my knees.

"Did I ask why he was still living with his mom, who dotes on him and serves him breakfast in bed and makes his truck payments for him when he can't come up with the money?"

"Geez, Pasko," I said. "I never figured on you getting married, exactly."

"Why not?" she asked.

"Well, I don't know. . . ."

"You think I'm not old enough? I'm twenty-six and a half!"

"Well, sure, you're *old* enough, I guess."

"Or you think I'm not frilly and girly enough? Not pretty enough? What?"

"Huh? No! Honest! I think you're very, um . . . " It didn't help that just then she sent me this crosspatch, unalluring scowl, but I said, "Very . . . attractive! Honest!"

"Everett says I remind him of a ten-year-old boy."

Everett had a point—one of the few times I'd agreed with him. I said, "Hogwash."

"When I told him I wanted lingerie for Christmas, he asked if they made black lace training bras."

I started to grin but stopped myself.

"Maybe we should both come up with some New Year's resolutions," Martine said. "Promise ourselves we won't go on acting like such saps."

"Well, maybe so," I said.

But I guess she could tell from my voice that I didn't have the heart for it. You get close to being thirty, and these resolutions start to seem kind of hopeless.

I wished Natalie hadn't felt called upon to remind me of my birthday.

Mrs. Alford lived in Mount Washington, in a white clapboard Colonial that was fairly good-sized but shabby, like most of our clients' houses.

(Anybody rich would have hired full-time help, not just Rent-a-Back. And anybody poverty-stricken couldn't afford even us.) She was watching from behind her storm door, with a cardigan clutched around her shoulders. A woman shaped like a pigeon: tidy little head and a deep, low-set pouch of a bosom. When we started up the steps she opened the door and called, "Good evening, Barnaby! Evening, Martine! Isn't it nice you could come on such short notice!"

"Oh, for you, anytime, Mrs. A.," I told her. I walked past her into the foyer and stood waiting for instructions. Her house smelled of steam heat and brothy foods and just, well, oldness. A Christmas tree wouldn't fool her grandchildren for an instant. But she was so cheerful and determined, peering up at us half blind and smiling brightly, her hair smoothly combed, her lipstick neatly applied. "The tree is in the attic, in a white box with a red lid," she said, "and the ornaments should be nearby, but I'm not sure exactly where. I haven't used them lately, because last year I went to my daughter's for Christmas, and the year before . . . Now, what did I do the year before?"

"Never fear, Mrs. A. We'll track those suckers down no matter where they are," I told her.

"Mind you don't step through the ceiling, though."

"Would we do a thing like that?"

The way Rent-a-Back operated was, we tried to send each client the same two or three workers again and again. So Martine and I already knew our way around Mrs. Alford's house. We knew how to get upstairs, and we knew more or less where the pull-down ladder was, above the second-floor hall. But I don't think either of us had ever been in her attic before. We clambered up—Martine on my heels, nimble as a monkey—into a hollow of cold air and darkness. I groped overhead till I connected with the lightbulb cord, and then all this junk sprang into view: trunks and suitcases and lamps, andirons, kitchen chairs with no seats, electric fans so outdated you could have fit a whole hand inside their metal grilles. None of it any surprise, believe me. I had toured a lot of attics in my time. I said, "Well, there's flooring in the middle, at least," and Martine said, "White box, red lid. White box, red lid," meanwhile maneuvering past a console radio, a standing ashtray, an open carton full of doorknobs. "Here it is," she said.

But I had caught sight of something else: a dress form, over by the chimney. It wasn't an ordinary dress form; not a canvas torso plumped with padding. This was a life-size wooden cutout, head and all, flat as a paper doll. The face was oval and astonished—round blue eyes, two dots for nostrils, and a pink O of a mouth—with brown corkscrew curls painted in at the edges. The arms stuck out at a slant and ended above the elbows; the legs stood in a brace arrangement that kept the figure upright. "Why! It's a Twinform," I told Martine.

"Hmm?"

"It's a Gaitlin Faithful Feminine Twinform! Invented by my great-grandfather."

Martine glanced over. She said, "Well, how would that be useful, though?"

"Listen to this," I told her. I read from the little brass plaque on the base. " 'Gaitlin Woodenworks, Baltimore, Maryland. Patent Applied For.' "

"How would you know how big around to sew your dresses?"

"It's not for sewing dresses. It's for putting together your outfit before you wear it. Like, if you're planning to go to a party or something . . . Well, it does sound kind of dumb. But once upon a time, you could find a Twinform in every bedroom. Now they've disappeared. I've never seen one in person before."

"Those old-time inventions slay me," Martine said. "People used to try so hard, seems like. Used to aim for the most roundabout method of doing things. Could you come give me a hand here, Barn?"

I turned away from the Twinform, finally, and went to help her. The Christmas tree carton was a manageable size, with holes at each end to hang on by, but it turned out to be fairly heavy. I said, "Oof!" Martine, though, didn't make a sound. (Both our girl employees behaved that way, I'd noticed—kept their breaths very even and quiet where a guy would have openly grunted.) "Better let me go first," I said when we reached the ladder, but Martine said, "What: you think I can't handle it?"

"Fine," I told her. "After you." And then had the satisfaction of watching her pretend it was no big deal when sixty pounds of Christmas tree hit her in the chest as she got halfway down.

Mrs. Alford was waiting for us in the living room—her cardigan thrown aside, her speckled hands twisting and pulling and itching to get started. "Oh, good," she said. "But what about the ornaments, I wonder?"

I said, "Half a minute, Mrs. A.," and we lowered the carton to the rug.

"You did see where they were, though," she said. "You found the boxes."

"We will; don't worry," Martine told her.

"I hope they're not in the basement, instead."

Martine and I looked at each other.

But no, they were in the attic. When we went back up, we spotted them on top of a disconnected radiator—two cardboard boxes marked *Xmas* in shaky crayon script. They weighed a lot less than the tree had. We could carry one apiece with no trouble.

As I was heading toward the ladder, I threw another glance at the Twinform. "Of course, it didn't allow for Fat Days," I told Martine, "or Short Days, or any of those other days when women take forever deciding what to wear."

Martine said, "What?" Then she said, "*I* take about two minutes deciding."

Which was abundantly obvious, I could have told her.

By the time we got back to the living room, Mrs. Alford had emptied the tree carton and heaped all the branches in a tangle on the rug. She said, "Over in that corner is where we always put it. We mustn't let it block the window, though. My husband hates for the tree to block the window."

I'd heard so much of that—the deceased coming back in present tense—I hardly noticed anymore.

Martine set up the stand, while I fanned out the branches to get them looking more lifelike. It wasn't the first time I'd put one of these together (a lot of our clients had switched to artificial), but I'd never quite adjusted to how soft the needles were. Each time I plunged my hand in among them, I felt disappointed, almost—expecting to be prickled and then failing to have it happen.

Mrs. Alford was telling us about her grandchildren. "The oldest is sixteen," she said, "and I'm sure she couldn't care less whether I have a tree or not, but the little ones are at that dinky, darling, enthusiastic stage. And they'll only be here for one night. I have to make my impression in a limited space of time, don't you see."

Then she laughed merrily so we wouldn't think she was serious, but of course she didn't fool either of us for a second. She was dead serious.

This one worker we had, Gene Rankin: he walked off the job after only three weeks. He said he couldn't stand to get so tangled up in people's lives. "Seems every time I turn around, I find myself munching cookies in some old lady's parlor," he said, "and from there it's only a step or two to the ungrateful-daughter stories and the crying jags and the offers of a grown son's empty bedroom." Mrs. Dibble told him he would get used to it, but she just said that because she didn't want to train another employee. You never get used to it.

The tree turned out to be so big that we had to pull it farther from the wall once we started hooking the lower branches on. Martine wriggled in behind it and called for what she needed. "Okay, now the red-tabbed branches. Now the yellow," and I would hand them over. Mrs. Alford went on talking. She was seated on a footstool, hugging her knees. "When the sixteen-year-old was that age," she said, "—that dinky, darling age, I mean—why, I set a sleigh and a whole team of reindeer up on top of our roof. I climbed out the attic window and strung them along the ridgepole. But I was quite a bit younger then."

"Sheesh. I've never been *that* young," I said.

I must have sounded gruffer than I'd meant to, because Martine told Mrs. Alford, "Pay no mind to Barnaby. He had a bad trip to Philly."

"Oh, was this a Philadelphia week?" Mrs. Alford asked.

"Natalie says he can't come visit anymore," Martine told her.

"Well, I'm sorry to hear that, Barnaby."

Martine crawled out from behind the tree and shucked her jacket off. Beneath it she wore overalls and a long-sleeved thermal undershirt that looked orphanish and skimpy, with the cuffs all stretched and showing her little wrists, as thin as pencils. "See if you can find some lights in one of those boxes," she told me.

But Mrs. Alford had beaten me to it. She was hauling them forth hand over hand—the old-fashioned kind of lights, with the big, dull bulbs. "It's a terrible thing, divorce," she said. "Especially when the child is caught in the middle."

I said, "I don't know that she's in the *middle*, exactly."

"He ought to talk to his lawyer," Martine said.

"Of course he ought!" Mrs. Alford said. "When my nephew and his wife split up—"

"Or go to Legal Aid."

"Oh, Legal Aid is a lovely organization!"

"Hmm," I said, making no promises.

"Or another possibility: my brother is a lawyer," Mrs. Alford told me. She hooked a scratched blue bulb onto the lowest branch. "Retired, needless to say, but still . . ."

I changed the subject. I said, "Mrs. Alford, you know that Twinform you have in your attic."

"Twinform?" she asked. She moved to the branch on her right.

"I was wondering. Did you buy it yourself? Or was it handed down through your family?"

"I'm not entirely certain what you're talking about," she said.

"That wooden person standing near your chimney. Kind of like a dress form."

"Oh, that. It was my mother's."

"Well, guess where it was manufactured," I told her. "My great-grandfather's woodenworks."

"His woodenworks, dear?"

"His shop that made wooden shoe trees and artificial limbs."

"Mercy," Mrs. Alford said.

I could see she was only being polite. She moved away from the tree and started unpacking ornaments, most of them homemade: construction-paper chains gone faded and brittle with age, pine cones glopped with red poster paint. "Someday I should get that attic cleared out," she said. "When would I use a dress form? I've never sewn a dress in my life. The most I've done is quilt a bit, and now that my eyes are going, I can barely manage that much. I've been working on a quilt of our planet for the past three years; isn't that ridiculous?"

"Oh, well, what's the hurry?" I asked. (No point explaining all over again that the Twinform wasn't meant for sewing.)

"One little measly blue planet, and it's taking me forever!"

"But here's the weird part," I said, reaching for one of the chains. It made a dry, chirpy sound, like crickets. "How the Twinform came into being was, an angel showed up and suggested it."

"An angel!" Mrs. Alford said.

"Or so my family likes to claim. They say she walked into the shop one day: big, tall woman with golden hair coiled in a braid on top of her head. Said she wanted shoe trees, but when Great-Granddad showed her a pair, she barely glanced at them. 'What women really need,' she said—these are her very words; Great-Granddad left a written account—'What women really need is a *dress* tree. A replica of their entire persons. How often have I put on a frock for some special occasion,' she said—'frock,' you notice—'only to find that it doesn't suit and must be exchanged for another at the very last moment, with another hat to match, other jewelry, other gloves and footwear?' And then she walked out."

Martine was staring at me, with her mouth a little open. Mrs. Alford said, "Really!" and hooked a modeling-clay cow onto a lower branch.

"It was the walking out that convinced them she was an angel, I believe," I said. "If she'd stayed awhile—if she'd haggled over prices, say, or bought a little something—she'd have been just another customer making chitchat. But delivering her pronouncement and then leaving, she came across as this kind of, like, oracle. She stayed in Great-Granddad's mind. Before the week was over, he'd built himself a prototype Twinform and paid a neighbor's artistic daughter to paint the face and hair on. See, you got your very own features custom painted, was the clincher."

Mrs. Alford handed me a bent cardboard star covered with aluminum foil, not one point matching any of the others. I stepped onto the footstool and propped the star against the top of the tree.

"That's the reason," I said, "after the Twinform made him rich, Great-Granddad started his Foundation for the Indigent. And that's why the Foundation has an angel on its letterhead."

Martine said, "Oh, I always thought that angel was just a *general* angel!"

"Nope, it's a very specific angel, I'll have you know," I said.

"I don't understand," Mrs. Alford said. "Are you talking about the Gaitlin Foundation?"

"Right," I said.

"Do you mean to say you're one of *those* Gaitlins?"

"Well, when they claim me, I am."

"I had no idea!"

"I'm the black sheep," I told her.

"Oh, now," Mrs. Alford said, "you could never be a black sheep."

"Just try telling my family that," I said. "My family would take it kindly if I changed my name to Smith."

"They wouldn't!"

The tree was finished, by now—all the ornaments in place, not counting a paper snowflake that Mrs. Alford was hanging on to in an absentminded way. She looked distressed but also pleased, and alert for further tidbits. (People always imagine that our family must be loaded, although if they put two and two together, they would realize the Foundation had siphoned off most of the loot.)

"He's exaggerating," Martine said. Probably she was afraid I'd bring up my criminal past, which our clients, of course, had no notion of. "Barnaby's very close to his family! Seems every time I talk to him, he's just back from seeing his grandparents."

"Those are my Kazmerow grandparents," I said. "Not Gaitlins."

"Plug in the lights, Barnaby."

"The Gaitlins I see only on major holidays," I told Mrs. Alford. "Thanksgiving. Christmas. Ever notice how closely Christmas follows Thanksgiving? Seems I've barely digested my turkey when I'm back for the Christmas goose, sitting in the same eternal chair, telling the same eternal relatives that yes, I'm still a manual laborer; still haven't found my true calling; still haven't heard from my angel yet; maybe next year."

"You have an angel too?" Mrs. Alford asked.

"All the Gaitlins have angels," I said. "They're required. My brother Jeff saw his when he was younger than I am now."

"What'd she tell him?" Martine wanted to know.

"She told him to get out of the stock market, just before Black Monday."

"Isn't that kind of . . . money-minded for an angel?"

"Yes," I said. "I've always had my doubts about her. Besides which, she was a brunette. I maintain angels are blond."

Mrs. Alford was giving me this dazed look. I said, "Don't worry, Mrs. A.; I'm not serious," and I took the snowflake from her and hung it. (It was pancake-sized, slightly crumpled, snipped from gift wrap so old that the Santas were smoking cigarettes.) "I don't think my family's serious, either, when you get right down to it," I said. "Shoot, they don't even go to church! My dad's an outright atheist! The angels are just one of those, like, insider things that help them imagine they're special. You know? I bet your family has some of those."

"Well . . . ," she said dubiously.

I bent to plug in the lights, and when I straightened up, the tree was sending out this dusty, faded glow and Mrs. Alford had her hands clasped under her chin. "Oh! How pretty!" she said.

Some of the branches were drooping—the ones where the modeling-clay animals hung. Some of the paper chains' links had sprung open. The pine cones had lost quite a few of their scales, so that they had a snaggle-toothed look. But Mrs. Alford said, "Isn't it perfect?"

I said, "It certainly is."

By the time we got back to the truck it was dark, and a chilly drizzle was falling. Martine had to switch her windshield wipers on. While she drove, I filled in the time sheets, one for her and one for me, and I tore the carbon copy off hers and stuck it in her overhead visor. Then I sat back and said, "Ah, me."

The lights from the oncoming traffic kept swinging across Martine's face, turning her skin even yellower than usual.

We passed a city bus, empty except for the driver, its windows glowing foggily like the bulbs on Mrs. Alford's tree. We passed a little strip mall, all closed for the night and eerily fluorescent, with swags of frowsy tinsel swinging in the wind.

I said, "This weather will mess up a lot of New Year's plans."

"It won't mess up mine," Martine said.

"I thought you didn't have any."

"Who told you that?"

"Didn't you say Everett was sick?"

"Yes, but I'm going to this party at my brother's. Him and his wife are throwing a party, and I said I'd help with the kids."

Martine had a whole slew of nephews that she was forever amusing— taking them to the zoo or the circus or letting them spend the night in her apartment. I don't know where she got the energy. I could never be like that. I could barely recall what my own one nephew's name was.

I said, "Ah, me," again, and this time Martine glanced over.

I said, "In Penn Station today, this guy was going around asking people to carry something to Philadelphia for him."

"Whoa! A mad bomber."

"He claimed it was a passport for his daughter," I said.

"Yeah, right."

And then . . . I don't know why I said this next thing. I'd been planning to tell the story just the way it happened, I swear. But what I said was, "So when he asked *me*, I told him yes."

"You didn't."

"I did too!" I said. (For a second, I thought she was doubting my word.) "He said I had an honest face," I said. "How could I resist?"

"For all you knew, he was planning to blow up your train."

"Well, obviously he didn't succeed," I said, "since I'm here to tell the tale. No, I'm pretty sure it was a genuine passport. Of course, I didn't actually check it out. This lady next to me, blond lady, she kept saying, 'Oh, just take a peek, why don't you? Just take a little peek!' But I wouldn't do it."

We slowed and turned into my driveway. Our headlamps lit the patio with two long spindles of mist.

"So anyway," I said.

I felt this inward kind of slumping, all at once, like, *What's the point? What's the* point? "I carried his package to Philly and gave it to his daughter," I said, "and that was that."

Martine had put the truck in neutral now, and she was facing me. For someone so small, she had an awfully large nose—an imposing nose, casting a shadow—and her eyebrows were large, too, and fiercely black, above her sharp black eyes. She said, "Hey. Barn. You want to come to my brother's?"

"Who, me?"

"You know they'd love to have you. You could help me with the treasure hunt."

"Oh," I said. "Nah. Thanks anyway."

Then I clapped her on the shoulder (little blade of bone under yards of slippery black nylon) and hopped out of the truck.

This time when the patio lamps lit up, they just annoyed me. I crossed the flagstones and went down the basement steps without stopping; unlocked my door and walked in, peeling off my jacket and dropping it to the floor, flipping on the wall switch as I headed toward the kitchen. Actually, it was more of a wet bar than a kitchen. But it did have a little under-counter fridge, and I reached inside for a beer and popped the lid. Then I turned on the TV that was sitting on top of the bar. Perky guy in a bow tie was wondering what this rain would do to the New Year's Eve fireworks. I settled on the couch to watch.

The couch was a sleeper couch, still folded out from last night, the blankets all twisted and strangled. The only other furniture was a plat-form rocker upholstered in slick red vinyl that stuck to me in the summer and turned clammy in the winter. I didn't even have a bureau—just stored my clothes on the shelves beneath the bar. My stove was a two-burner hot plate, and my bathroom was a rust-stained sink and toilet partitioned off in one corner; shower privileges upstairs. Every Saturday morning, Mimi Hardesty came tiptoeing down to do the family's laundry in the washing machine to the right of the furnace. Every evening, the Hardesty children roughhoused overhead, thumping and bumping around till the light fix-ture on my ceiling gave off little tingly whispers like a seashell.

Well, I make it sound worse than it was. It wasn't so bad. I think I was just at a low point that night. *Here I am,* I thought, *close to thirty years old and all but homeless, doing my own daughter more harm than good. Living in a world where everybody's old or sick or handicapped. Where my only friend, just about, is a girl—and even her I lie to.*

Not a useful lie, either. Just a boastful, geeky, unnecessary lie.

I think it was Mrs. Alford's fault. Or not her fault, exactly, but this job could get me down sometimes. People's pathetic fake trees and fake cheer; their muffled-sounding, overheated-smelling houses; their grandchildren whizzing through on their way to someplace better.

That employee who quit on us: Gene Rankin. He had a smart idea. He carried a kitchen timer dangling from his belt. He would set it to beeping at burdensome moments and, "Oops!" he would say to the client. "Emer-gency. Gotta go."

That was the way to do it.

• • •

How I started working for Mrs. Dibble: I was nineteen years old, fresh out of high school, looking for a summer job before I entered college. Only nobody wanted to hire me because, let's be honest, the high school I had attended was sort of more of a reform school. Not to mention that a lot of folks in the immediate area were mad at me for breaking into their houses and reading their mail. So my father asked around among his Planning Council members. (By then my father was head of the Foundation.) Eventually he persuaded this one guy, Brandon Pearson, to put me to work in his hardware chain. But I could tell Mr. Pearson had warned his staff about my evil nature. They watched my every move and they wouldn't let me near any money, even though money had never been my weakness. They gave me the most noncrucial assignments, and the manager nearly had a stroke once when he found me duplicating a house key for a customer. I guess he thought I might cut an extra copy for myself.

My second week on the job, a lady in a flowered dress came in to buy a board. Mrs. Dibble, she was, although of course I didn't know it at the time. She said she wanted this board to be two feet, two and a half inches long. So I told her I would cut it for her. I wasn't aware that a customer had to buy the whole plank. (Besides, she had these nice smile wrinkles at the corners of her eyes.) I grabbed a saw from a wall display and set to work. Made kind of a racket. Manager came running. "What's this? What's going on here?"

"Oh, he's just cutting me a teeny piece of shelving!" Mrs. Dibble sang out.

"What on earth! You weren't hired to do that," Mr. Vickers told me. "What do you think you're up to?"

That's when I should have stopped, I know. But I didn't like the tone he was using. I pretended not to hear him. Kept on sawing. When I'd finished, there was this enormous, ringing silence, and then Mr. Vickers said, clearly, "You are fired, boy."

"Oh!" Mrs. Dibble said. "Oh, no, don't fire him! It was all because I asked him to! I begged him and implored him; I pleaded on bended knee!"

But Mr. Vickers had his mind made up, I could tell. No doubt he was glad of the excuse.

I wasn't too devastated. I couldn't have stood the place much longer, anyhow. So I told Mrs. Dibble, "It's all right."

But Mrs. Dibble started burrowing in her purse. She came up with a cream-colored business card, and, "Here," she said, and she handed it to me.

RENT-A-BACK, INC., the card read. "WHEN YOUR OWN MUSCLES AREN'T QUITE ENOUGH." VIRGINIA DIBBLE, PRES.

"Your new place of employment," she told me.

"Aw," I said. "Mrs.—um—"

"All our clients are aged, or infirm, or just somehow or other in need, and what they're in need of is precisely your kind of good-heartedness."

"Ma'am—" Mr. Vickers said.

And I said, "Mrs. Dibble—"

I guess Mr. Vickers was going to say, "Ma'am, I think you should know that this boy is a convicted felon, or would have been convicted if his folks hadn't bought his way out of it."

And I was going to say, "Mrs. Dibble, I don't have a muscle to my name, if you're talking about heavy lifting."

But she didn't give either one of us the chance. "Nine a.m. tomorrow," she said, tapping the card with her index finger. "Come to this address."

Later, when she got to know me better, she told me it was my philosophical attitude that had won her. "It was the way you didn't protest at what happened," she told me. "You didn't put up any fuss. You seemed to be saying, 'Oh, all right, if that's how life works out.' I admired that. I thought it was very Zen of you." And she patted me on the arm and sent me one of her warm, wrinkly smiles.

She had no idea how she had just disappointed me. Till then, I had been telling everybody I saw—I'd told practically total strangers—that I'd been given my new job on account of my good-heartedness.

On TV, they were asking pedestrians for their New Year's resolutions. People said they had resolved to lose ten pounds, or stop smoking, or stop drinking. They'd resolved to join a gym or take up jogging. Seemed it was always something body-related. Except for this one guy—slouchy black guy in a hooded parka. He said, "Well, I just can't decide. Could be I'll start going to church again. Could be I'll apply to truckdriving school. I just can't make up my mind."

As if he were allowed no more than one resolution within a given year.

I finished my beer and set the can on the floor beside the phone. My answering machine was blinking, but I didn't expect any great messages at this hour. Unless some acquaintance was throwing a party and suddenly recollected my name. I leaned over and pressed the button.

"Barnaby," my mother said, "this is your mom and dad."

What a thrill.

"We just wanted to say Happy New Year, sweetie. Hope it's the start of good things for you—good news, good plans, a whole new beginning! Call us sometime, why don't you? Bye."

Click.

I flopped back on my bed and looked up at the ceiling. *Hope it's the end of all the trouble you've caused us,* was what she was really saying. *Hope at long, long last you're planning to mend your ways; hope you'll meet a decent girl this year and find a job we're not embarrassed to tell the neighbors about. Hope you get your instructions from your angel, finally.*

Now, why did this next thought occur to me?

I don't know, but it did.

Sophia Whatsit. Maynard. The woman on the train. Suppose Sophia Maynard was my angel.

Silly, of course. I'd been snickering at that angel stuff since I was old enough to think straight. If that was not the Gaitlins in a nutshell, I always told them: imagining they had connections even in heaven!

But still.

I saw her gold hair, her feather coat, her bun that was not so unlike (it occurred to me now) a coiled braid.

The trouble was, I seemed to be the first Gaitlin in history who didn't have a clue what my angel had wanted to tell me.

3

She was wearing the feather coat again, and boots this time instead of last week's pumps. (Overnight a light snow had fallen—that considerate kind of snow that sticks to lawns but melts on streets and sidewalks.) Would an angel wear quilted black nylon boots with white fluff around the tops? Well, sure; no reason she couldn't. And she could sit on a bench in Penn Station reading a *Baltimore Sun* too, while she was at it.

I drifted closer, pretending I wanted to look through the window behind her. The 10:10 was on time for once, according to the notice board. All I could see was a segment of bare track, but I rested one knee on the bench and set my forehead to the glass and peered down. I think she felt crowded. She gathered herself together somehow; hid behind her paper. I backed off and turned away to show I posed no threat.

Of course, if she really was my angel, she would know that on her own.

Check out what *I* was wearing: a white oxford shirt and brown corduroys. No tie (there were limits, after all), but I had exchanged my leather jacket for my one tweed sports coat and trimmed my own hair as best I could and shaved that very morning. I was so clean-shaven, my face seemed to belong to someone else. Kind of plastic-feeling. A whole new surface to it. My skin felt stretched across my bones.

When the loudspeaker called out my train, I started down to the platform ahead of all the others so she wouldn't think I was following her. And I kept my back to the stairs after I arrived. I could feel her approaching, though, like a current of air, a change of temperature in a room. Her presence, descending the steps. I fixed my eyes on a point far up the tracks.

Two young women stood nearby. Sisters, from the look of them, both dark and pretty and dressed in layers of black. The taller one was trying to convince the little one to come all the way to New York with her. The little one insisted she was getting off in Philly. I tallied up the other passengers: twenty or so, at the most. With luck, it wouldn't be hard for

Sophia to find a seat all her own. Then I would come along, nonchalant, couldn't care less. "Is this seat taken?" Or maybe not ask. Just sit, ker-plunk, looking elsewhere, before she could claim she was saving a place for a friend.

Not that she would tell an actual lie, you wouldn't think.

But just to be on the safe side.

At the end of the track our train appeared, only a dot yet but growing. I stepped closer to the edge of the platform. The man next to me wore ear-phones looped beneath his jaw instead of over his head, which made him look like the bearded version of Abraham Lincoln. Just past him, Sophia rummaged through her bag for her ticket. Never mind that it was no-where near time to have it ready.

The train drew up beside us, ding-dinging. Abe Lincoln and the two sisters entered through the door nearest me, but I walked over to where Sophia stood. Several people got off, and then a woman with a baby got on. Sophia followed her. I came next. I was too close behind and hung back, biding my time.

It was unfortunate that the car was almost empty. This way, she would wonder why I didn't sit by myself. Well, too bad. She chose a seat at her right and for one awful moment seemed about to stay on the aisle but then, with a kind of flounce, she moved over. A good thing, too, because I was holding up a whole line of people behind me. Quick as a wink, I set-tled beside her. She kept her face turned toward the window. Her news-paper was nowhere in sight. She must have stowed it in her bag.

Passengers came shuffling down the aisle, and I watched the backs of their heads once they'd passed. A kid with a Mohawk, all prickly white scalp and pierced ears. Two nuns in short navy headdresses and square coats and thick-soled shoes. An old, bent man, creeping. I was trying so hard to sit still, to keep my elbow from touching Sophia's, that I was al-most rigid. (As a rule, I twitched and jittered, jiggled a foot, drummed my fingers.) Face it: I felt kind of shy. Kind of unconfident.

Scared to death, to be honest.

The train lurched and started moving. Sophia delved into the bag at her feet and came up with a section of newspaper. It was folded open to the business page. Business! Lord above. I wondered why I was kidding my-self. Did I just not have enough to occupy my mind? Or what?

We were passing people's wintry backyards, filled with scrap lumber and rusty shovels and plastic wading pools propped on their sides, every-thing skimmed with snow. The conductor came through saying, "Tickets, please." When Sophia handed him hers, I saw that she wore a Timex watch with a wide black leather wristband.

She wouldn't have any message for me. She was merely annoyed that I'd sat down beside her; and here I was, like a fool, waiting for her to in-form me how to begin my life.

Wouldn't she laugh at me if she knew!

When Great-Granddad saw *his* angel, she lit the air of the wooden-works. *A golden dust, she dispersed, floating in the gloom,* he reported. *Lingering for an hour, at least, after she left the room.* The rhyme was intentional. He wrote up his encounter in the form of an epic poem whose scheme was A, A, A . . . till he ran out of words to rhyme with A, evidently, and then B, B, B . . . , and so forth. Not what you would call a literary masterpiece. Even so, my family treasured it. They kept it in a glass-doored bookcase in my father's study. A gray cloth ledger with maroon leather corners, containing three pages of penciled business accounts followed by seventeen pages of "A Providential Visitation, April 1898." Since then, the tradition was for *all* the Gaitlins to file reports on their angels—though Great-Granddad's was the only poem. Myself, I planned to stick to prose, when the time came. And right from paragraph one, I would stress my reliability, my solid and trustworthy nature. It's a mistake to go all misty and poetic when you're trying to convince your readers you've seen an angel.

Sophia said, "Excuse me, please."

She had her bag in both hands now, and she was perched on the edge of her seat, knees angled toward me, getting ready to rise. I said, "Oh!" and stood up and stepped into the aisle. She sidled out, bulky and wide-hipped, and started toward the front of the car. Was she leaving me? What was she doing? I sat back down and watched her bypass first one empty seat and then another; so I was partly reassured. She didn't stop at the rest room, either, but vanished through the end door. Maybe she was buying a snack. And her ticket stub was still in its overhead slot, her newspaper still in her seat. I was pretty sure she'd be returning.

I checked to see what news items she'd been reading. Plans for a merger between two banks. A growing concern over Maryland's bond rating.

She was probably some kind of financial wheeler-dealer. And I was out of my mind; and this train trip had cost me a whole lot of money for nothing, not to mention the goodwill of my best-paying customer. Mrs. Morey had wanted me to take down all her curtains for laundering today. I'd told her at the very last minute that I would be out of town. "Out of town!" she said. "You can't be out of town! This isn't a Philadelphia week; it's the first Saturday of the month!"

Oh, my life was a wide-open book to half the old ladies in Baltimore.

There was a sudden rise in the noise level, and I looked toward the front of the car and saw Sophia stepping through the door, gliding back in my direction at a stately, level pace. She hadn't left me, after all. I felt so grateful that when I noticed something in her hands, I thought for a second she was bringing me a gift. But it was only a Styrofoam cup of coffee. She paused next to me, and I jumped up, and—oh, God.

Jostled against her coffee. Spilled it all down her front.

"Geez!" I said. "I'm so—geez! I'm such an oaf!"

"That's all right," she murmured, but in a faint and reluctant tone that made it clear it was not all right. And who could blame her? Dark splotches stained the feather coat. Even her hands were wet. She shook one hand in the air, meanwhile hanging on to the cup with the other. "Allow me," I said, and I took the cup away from her—both of us still standing, braced against the swaying of the train—so that she could get a tissue out of her bag. She wiped her hands and then ducked into her seat and started dabbing at the splotches on her coat. I slid in after her. "I could kick myself," I said. Even through the Styrofoam I could tell that the coffee was hot, which made things all the worse. "I hope you didn't get burned," I told her.

She said, "No . . . ," and stopped scrubbing her coat and looked over at me. In a friendlier tone, she said, "Really. I'm fine. I should have let the counterman put a lid on, the way he wanted."

"Well, how could you have foreseen you'd be sitting next to a klutz?" I said. I passed her the cup. Then I removed the screw of soaked tissue from her hand and stuffed it into my seat pocket. "It was nerves, I guess," I told her. "I think I'm a little nervous."

"Nervous! About a train trip?"

I looked into her eyes. *Don't you know?* was the thought I sent her, but she gazed pleasantly, blankly back at me. Her eyes were blue. Her mouth was large and well shaped, lipsticked in too bright a shade of red, and the light from the window behind her gilded the powdery down along her jawline.

I said, "I'm, ah, heading up to Philly to see my little girl on not my normal visitation day."

"Oh," she said. "Well, I'm sure it will all work out."

Was this an official prophecy? No, of course not. Get a grip, Gaitlin. She took a sip of her coffee and shifted in her seat so she could pull her newspaper from beneath her. I said, "And besides!" (I was desperate. I didn't want to let the conversation die.) "Not only is it not my normal day; I'm not supposed to see her *any* day, ever again."

Her eyes came back to me. "Why is that?" she asked, finally.

"Last time I had car trouble, and I got there late, and her mother claimed it broke her heart," I said.

Then I said, "My little girl's heart, I mean. Not her mother's. Lord knows, not her mother's."

Sophia laughed. I caught the faint scent of flowers mingled with the coffee, as if she'd been chewing roses.

"So today I'm going up blind," I said. "I don't even know if Opal's going to be there."

Which was true enough, certainly. I hadn't given Opal a thought. I'd assumed that once I reached Philadelphia, I would turn around and catch the next train home. But I said, "Kids need their fathers. You can't just break off ties like that."

"You can't, indeed," she told me. "How old is she?"

"She's—um—nine? Yes, nine."

"Oh, at nine they definitely need their fathers."

"The trouble is," I said (for lack of any other subject), "I doubt my visits are anything she looks forward to. I've been seeing her once a month, is all. Last Saturday of every month. When they're that young, they can change completely in a month! Not to mention she's a girl. What do I know about girls? Do you have any daughters yourself?"

"Oh, no," Sophia said. She hesitated. Then she said, "I'm not married, actually."

I'd have been flabbergasted to hear she was, but I just said, "At least you've *been* a little girl." (Though in fact I wasn't so sure.) "You remember how it feels."

"Well, but I suspect I wasn't typical," she told me. "I was an only child. I think that tends to keep children childlike longer, don't you?"

"Opal's an only child too," I said. "Oh—sorry. My name's Barnaby Gaitlin."

"Sophia Maynard," she told me.

"Sophia, if you had your say," I said, "what would you advise a guy in my general position to do about his life?"

"I'd advise you to persevere, of course," she said.

"Persevere?"

"Why, certainly! I can guarantee that no matter what, Opal wants to keep seeing her daddy."

"Oh. Opal," I said.

Actually, Opal had never called me "daddy." "Daddy" sounded like someone else—someone who'd treat her to Shirley Temples in stodgy, flocked-wallpaper restaurants. I was starting to feel like some kind of impostor.

"But I don't have to tell you that," Sophia was saying, "because look at you!"

"Pardon?"

"You're already on your way to visit her!"

"Ah. Except that, well, this visit was really just a . . . random activity, so to speak."

"I know just what you mean," Sophia said.

"You do?"

"Sometimes intuition is our truest guiding force, don't you agree?"

"Intuition? Hmm," I said, paying close attention now.

"You can be *led* to get on a train, not even knowing why," she said.

"Is that a fact."

"And once you arrive at your ex-wife's, you're going to be led to say exactly the words that will change her mind."

"But see," I said, "I'm not sure that . . . at this point, I don't believe my family situation is the central issue anymore."

"I'm going to tell you a story," Sophia said.

I grew very still. I said, "Okay."

"Two weeks ago, I went to visit my mother. Well, I do that every week; she's elderly and she lives alone. But this time she was in such a fretful mood; so fractious. I made her some tea, and she said, 'This tea tastes moldy.' 'Moldy?' I said. 'It's a new box! How could it taste moldy?' She said, 'I don't know, but it does.' I said, 'Very well, Mother.' This was not fifteen minutes after I had got there, mind. I was still exhausted from my trip. But I said, 'Very well, Mother,' and I picked up my purse and went out to buy more tea bags. I was walking toward this little store nearby, but once I reached it, do you know what I did? I walked right past. I kept walking till I came to Thirtieth Street Station, and I hopped on a train and rode home. And all the way, I was thinking, *Heavens, what have I done?* Then something told me, *This is what you were led to do; so it must be right.* Well, my point is, that evening Mother telephoned, which she almost never does—she has that old-time attitude toward long distance—and she said, 'Sophia, I apologize. I don't know what got into me. All day I've been regretting my behavior, and I promise that when you come next week I will watch my p's and q's.' And true to her word, when I went back up last Saturday she was an entirely different person."

I couldn't figure out how this related to *me*. I said, "Well. That's very interesting."

She must have sensed my disappointment, because she said, "You think I acted terrible, don't you?"

"No, no. Not at all."

"You're shocked I would walk out on her like that."

"I'm not a bit shocked," I told her. "I know all about these aged parents. The kind that want everything done for them, and the kind you can't do a thing for, and the humble, self-denying kind, and the cranky, picky, dissatisfied kind . . . I must have seen every existing model. They're who my company deals with, mostly."

"What company is that?" Sophia asked.

"Rent-a-Back, it's called. We go around to people's houses, perform whatever chores they aren't quite up to."

"Oh! What a valuable service!"

"Well, we try," I said. (I wanted to look as good as possible.) "How about you?"

"I work in a bank. Equity loan department," she said. And while I was adjusting to this, she gave a little laugh and said, "Nothing like as helpful as what your company does!"

"Oh, I don't know," I said. "A loan can be extremely helpful."

She made a face, turning her mouth down. (She had no idea.) "And can people just telephone and you send somebody over?" she asked. "Or do they have to be on a schedule of some kind?"

"Either way. We offer both arrangements," I told her.

"Would a client be able to get her groceries carried in? Her garbage taken out to the alley? Little humdrum things like that?"

"Oh, the humdrum is our specialty," I told her. Then it dawned on me that she might have her mother in mind; so I added, "We operate just in Baltimore, though."

"I was thinking about my Aunt Grace. She's in Baltimore; and independent? You wouldn't believe how independent. But she's getting hard of hearing, and she's frail as a stick, besides; has trouble with her bones. She can break a bone in midair, if she's not careful."

"Osteoporosis," I said knowledgeably.

" 'Aunt Grace,' I tell her, 'you need a companion! Someone live-in, to fetch and haul!' But *oh*, no, no. Not Aunt Grace. 'I prefer to have my house to myself,' she says, and of course you can't really blame her."

"Yes, we see that every day," I said. Then, trying to get back to the subject, I said, "But anyhow. You believe in intuition."

"I most assuredly do." She nodded several times, cradling her coffee cup in both hands.

"You believe a person will just be led to the proper action."

"Absolutely," she told me.

I made myself keep quiet a moment. I allowed her a block of silence to fill; I put on an expression that I hoped would seem receptive. She didn't seize her chance, though. She just took a sip of her coffee. Beyond her head, bare trees skimmed past.

"So," she said, finally.

I sat up so straight, you'd think I'd been electrocuted.

But all she said was, "Tell me more about your company."

"My company," I repeated.

"How many workers does it employ? Would you call it a success?"

"Oh, yes, it's done very well," I said.

And then I gave up and just went with the flow—told her about our two newspaper write-ups and our letters from grateful clients and their relatives, their sons and daughters living elsewhere who could finally sleep at night, they said, now that we had taken over their parents' heavy lifting. Sophia kept her eyes on my face, tilting her head to one side. I could see how she would make an excellent loan officer. She had this way of appearing willing to listen all day.

I described my favorite customers—the unstoppable little black grandma whose children phoned us on an emergency basis whenever she threatened to overdo ("Come quick! Mama swears she's going to wash her upstairs windows today!"); and our "Tallulah" client, Maud May, who smoked cigarettes in a long ivory holder and drank martinis by the quart and called me "dahling." Then the weird ones. Ditty Nolan, who was only thirty-four and able-bodied as I was but couldn't face the outside world; so everything had to be brought to her. Or Mr. Shank, a lonesome and pathetic type, who took advantage of our no-task-too-small, no-hour-too-late policy to phone us in the middle of the night and ask for someone to come right away for some trifling, trumped-up job like securing a bedroom shutter that was flapping in the wind.

By the time we reached Wilmington, I'd progressed to Mrs. Gordoni, who couldn't afford our fees but needed us so badly (rheumatoid arthritis) that we would doctor her time sheet—write down a mere half hour when we'd been at her house a whole morning. "For a while, none of us knew the others were doing it," I said. "Then it all came out. Our two girl employees, Martine and Celeste: they weren't filing any hours at all for her, which is a whole lot easier to catch than just underreporting."

"Isn't that nice," Sophia said. "You don't often see that kind of heart in the business world."

"Well, I wasn't trying to brag," I said. "I mean, we generally do charge money for our labors."

"Even so," she said, and she gave me a long, serious stare and then nodded, as if we had shared a secret. But I didn't know *what* secret. And before I could say any more, the conductor walked through, announcing Philadelphia.

Still, even then, I hadn't quite lost hope for some kind of revelation. I went on weighing and considering her most casual remark, giving her every chance to redirect my course. As we stepped off the train, for instance, she said, "Notice how much faster people move, here," and I blinked and looked around me. Faster? People? Move? What was the deeper significance of that? But all I saw was the usual crowd, churning toward the stairs in the usual bobbling manner. "It always takes me by surprise, what a different atmosphere Philadelphia has from Baltimore," she said, and I said, "Atmosphere. Ah," and stumbled as I started up the steps, I was so intent on analyzing the atmosphere.

In the terminal, I stopped and faced her, wondering if her goodbye, at least, might be instructive. "Well," I said, "I enjoyed our conversation."

"Yes! Me too!" she told me. But she continued walking, and so I was forced to follow. She said, "I thought that was so fascinating about your company. Where are you headed?"

"Where am I headed," I repeated, sounding like a moron.

"Does your daughter live nearby?"

"Oh. Yes, she's off Rittenhouse Square."

"So's my mother. Shall we share a cab?"

"Well . . ."

It hadn't occurred to me that my actions would be observed at the other end of my trip. I said, "No, thanks; I—"

"Though it *is* a nice day to walk," she said.

A nice day?

We followed a group of teenagers through the Twenty-ninth Street exit, but I was dragging my heels, pondering how to get out of this. Suppose, by some horrible coincidence, Sophia's mother lived in Natalie's building! What then?

The weather did seem to have improved, I found when we reached the sidewalk. The temperature had risen some, and the sun was trying to shine. I said, "It's still kind of damp underfoot, though." I was looking toward the line of taxicabs, hoping she would change her mind and take one. But she walked right past them, and it was true she had those boots on.

On Market Street, she asked, "Are you bringing your daughter a present?"

"No," I said. I flipped my jacket collar up. (Tweed was not half as warm as leather.) "This was such a sudden decision," I said. "She's probably not even home! I should just cut my losses and grab the next train back."

"Darn," Sophia said, not appearing to hear me. "If I'd thought, we could have picked up something in the station. They have all those boutiques there."

"Well, no great loss," I told her. "I wouldn't have had the slightest idea what to get her, anyhow."

"You could have bought a stuffed animal. Something of that sort. All little girls like stuffed animals."

We veered around a man pushing a grocery cart full of rags. Sophia's pace had grown leisurely and wafting. I had a sense of being dragged backward. "When *I* was nine," she said, "my favorite toy was a stuffed raccoon named Ariadne."

"Ariadne!"

"Well, I was extremely fanciful. I liked the Greek myths and all that. It's because I was an only child. I was quite the little reader, as you might imagine."

She had the only child's elderly way of speaking too, I noticed. But I didn't point that out to her.

"My father kept forgetting Ariadne's name," she was saying. "Most often he called her Rodney. 'Sophia! Come and get Rodney! She's out here on the porch, and there's supposed to be a storm!' "

She laughed.

I looked at her then and knew, for a fact, that she was not my angel. She was an ordinary, middle-class, middle-aged bank employee with no particular life of her own, and it showed what a sorry state *my* life had come to that I could have imagined otherwise even for an instant.

If I'd had the nerve, I would have turned around then and there. Already half my Saturday had gone to waste. But it would have seemed peculiar, just wheeling and racing off with no good reason. So I dug my hands in my pockets and kept going.

I really hated this city, come to think of it—these wide, pale, bleak sidewalks littered with blowing rubbish, and the bombed-out-looking buildings.

I said, "Where does your mother live, exactly?"

"On Walnut Street," Sophia said. "How about your daughter?"

"Locust," I said.

Thank goodness.

A truck roared past, and we walked awhile without speaking before Sophia asked, "Is your ex-wife a Philadelphian?"

"No," I said, "but her husband is."

"Oh, so she's remarried."

"Right."

"That must be difficult for you."

"Difficult? Why would you say that?" I asked.

"Seeing her with someone else, I mean. I suppose inevitably there's a bit of—"

"I never give it a moment's thought," I said, and then I stopped short, at the corner of Twenty-second Street, and said, "Well, here's where I'll be—"

But Sophia turned down Twenty-second and kept walking. I had hoped she would continue east. "It must have been an amicable divorce, then," she called over her shoulder.

I said, "Oh . . . ," and took a few extra steps to catch up. "It was *sort* of amicable," I said. (No sense going into the gory details.)

"Were you very young when you married?"

"Lord, yes. I was way too young. And she was even younger. We got married on her twentieth birthday."

Then I happened to glance down the street, and who was walking toward us? Natalie. She was wearing a red coat and holding Opal's hand. It was unsettling, because I'd just had a flash of how she had looked on our wedding day: all dressed up for the registry office, so pale and prim and solemn in a red coat that was not this same one, I guess, but close enough; close enough.

She hadn't seen me yet. She was speaking to Opal, turning to look down at her, and it was Opal (gazing straight ahead) who spotted me first. Opal wrenched her hand free and cried, "Barnaby!" and ran to meet me. There was enough of a breeze so she had lost that careful, prissy look. Her hair was tumbled, her cheeks were pink, and her jacket was flying behind her. She barreled into me and threw her arms around my waist, which she wouldn't ordinarily have done. She wasn't a very *warm* child, in my limited experience. But she said, "It's not true you're stopping your visits, is it?"

"Who, me?" I asked, and I looked past her to Natalie. She approached more slowly, with a hair-thin line of puzzlement running across her forehead as she noticed Sophia. (Maybe she imagined we were together.) I said, "Hey there, Nat."

"Mom said you weren't going to come anymore," Opal told me. She grabbed hold of one of my thumbs and started tugging on it, bouncing slightly on the balls of her feet in an edgy, agitated manner I'd never noticed in her till now. "She said you'd talked it over and you'd be stopping your visits. But I knew you wouldn't do that. Would you? You'd want to keep on seeing me! Wouldn't you?"

"Well, sure I would," I said. It hadn't occurred to me that she would take this so personally. I felt kind of touched. In a funny way, I felt almost hurt. My throat got a hurtful, heavy feeling halfway down to my chest.

And Natalie must have felt the same, because she said, "Oh, honey. Of course he would! I didn't realize you would mind so much."

Then a hand arrived on my arm, so light it took a moment to register, and I turned and found Sophia smiling into my eyes. It was the most serene and radiant smile; the most *seraphic* smile. "Goodbye, Barnaby," she said, and she dropped her hand and walked away.

I never did explain her presence to Natalie. I honestly don't know what I would have said.

4

My favorite moment of the day comes before the sun is up, but conditions have to be right for it. I have to be awake then, for one thing. And the weather has to be clear, and the lights lit in my room, and the sky outside still dark. Then I switch the lights off. If I'm lucky, the sky will suddenly change to something else—a deep, transparent blue. There's almost a sound to it, a quiet sound like *loom*! as the blue swings into focus. But it lasts for only a second. And it doesn't happen that often.

It happened on my thirtieth birthday, though. I took that for a good omen. My thirtieth birthday fell on a Monday, which was garbage day for more than half our clients. I hadn't gotten around to setting out their trash cans the night before, because I'd indulged in this private little one-man birthday bash, instead. So there I was, up before dawn in spite of myself, just opening my door, which is the only place in my apartment I can even see the sky from; and I switched my lights off, and *loom*!

I decided turning thirty might not be so bad, after all. I thought maybe I could handle it. I went off to work whistling, even though I had that balsa-mouth feeling that comes from too many beers.

It was a bitter-cold day, the kind that turns your feet to stone, and after I'd dealt with the trash cans I went home and wrapped myself in a blanket and tried to get back to sleep. Only trouble was, the telephone kept ringing. I let the machine answer for me. First call, Mrs. Dibble wanted me to take the Cartwrights grocery shopping. Second call, she needed a sack of sidewalk salt run over to Ditty Nolan. Third call was my grandparents. "Barnaby, hon," my grandma said, "it's me and Pop-Pop, just wanting to wish you a—"

I leaned over the edge of the bed and picked up the phone. "Gram?" I said.

"Well, hey there! Happy birthday!"

"Thanks. Is Pop-Pop on too?"

"I'm here," he said. "Hope you got plans to celebrate."

"Oh, yeah; well, yeah," I said in this vague sort of way, because I couldn't tell if they knew about the dinner Mom was fixing. I never could be certain. Some years she invited them, but other years she thought up reasons not to. (My grandpa had driven a laundry truck till poor vision forced his retirement, and Gram still clerked in a liquor store. "God gave" them—their wording—only one child, my mother, and they were very proud of her, but the feeling didn't seem to be mutual.) I said, "Probably I'll just, you know, drop by home for dinner or something."

"That's my boy!" Gram said. "That's what I like to hear! A visit'll mean the world to them, hon."

"Yes, Gram," I said.

Then Pop-Pop asked, "How's the car doing?"

"Oh, chugging along just fine," I said. "Had to take it in and get the steering linkage tightened, but no big deal."

"Why, you could have done that yourself!" he said. "That's what *I* always did, when she was mine!"

"Maybe next time," I told him.

I'd given up trying to convince him I wasn't a born mechanic.

The way the conversation ended was, I would stop by and see them later in the week. They had a little something for me. (A book of coupons good for six take-out pizzas, I already knew. It was their standard birthday gift, and one I counted on.) Then after I hung up I called Mrs. Dibble, because my conscience had started to bother me over the Cartwrights. They tended to feel rushed when somebody else took them shopping. "So," I said. "Cartwrights' groceries, Ditty Nolan's salt. What: she's expecting snow?"

"I have no idea," Mrs. Dibble told me. "We're just the . . ."

We're just the muscles, not the brains. I said goodbye and stood up to unwind myself from my blanket.

The Cartwrights were a good example of why Rent-a-Back was so sought after. They weren't all that old—early sixties, which in this business was nothing—but Mr. Cartwright had permanently ruined his right ankle several years before while stepping off a curb in Towson. So he couldn't drive anymore, and Mrs. Cartwright had never known how and did not intend to learn, she said, at this late date. Nor could they afford a chauffeur. Rent-a-Back offered just what they needed: somebody (usually me) to drive their big old Impala to the grocery store, and unfold Mr. Cartwright's walker from the trunk when we got there, and follow behind as the two of them inched down the aisles debating each and every purchase. I could have just waited at the front of the store, but I got a kick out of listening to their discussions. Today, for instance, Mr. Cartwright expressed a desire for sauerkraut, but Mrs. Cartwright didn't feel he should have it. "You *always* think you want sauerkraut," she told him, "and then you're up half the night with indigestion and it's me who has to bring you the Tums. You know how cabbage in any form gives you indigestion."

Mr. Cartwright said he knew no such thing, but I knew it. And I knew green peppers repeated on him too, and I knew what their shoe sizes were and their grandchildren's video game preferences, and I had advised on the very coat that Mrs. Cartwright was wearing today. (It was this navy one or a gray, almost white, which I had pointed out would show the dirt.)

In the window bays near the registers I noticed big sacks of sidewalk salt, and I thought of picking one up for Ditty Nolan. But the Cartwrights might feel slighted, seeing me attend to another customer on their time. So what I did was drive them home (Mr. Cartwright next to me, Mrs. Cartwright perched in the rear but leaning forward between us to advise on traffic conditions) and carry in their groceries, and then I got in my own car and drove back to the store for salt. Then I went to Ditty Nolan's.

I don't know why Ditty Nolan was scared to go out. She hadn't always been that way, if you could believe Ray Oakley. Ray Oakley said Ditty's mother had fallen ill with some steadily downhill disease while Ditty was off in college, and Ditty came home to nurse her and never left. Even after the mother died, Ditty stayed on in the Roland Park house where she had grown up—must have had a little inheritance, or how else would she have managed? For sure, she didn't go out to work. And when I rang her doorbell, she had to check through the front window first and then undo a whole fortress of locks and sliding bolts and chains before she could let me in. "Barnaby!" she said.

She was thin and pretty and unnaturally pale, with wispy tow hair that hung to her shoulders. Her dress was more a spring type of dress—flower-sprinkled and floaty—which wasn't so unreasonable for someone who avoided all weather.

"I brought your salt," I told her.

"Oh, good," she said, stepping back. "Come on inside."

I followed her in and dropped the sack to the floor. I said, "Has there been some kind of forecast I haven't heard about?"

"Forecast?" she asked. She was wandering away to some other part of the house. Her voice came threading back to me.

"Is it supposed to snow or something?"

"Not that I know of," she said.

She returned, holding an envelope. My name was on the front. "Happy birthday," she said.

"Oh! Well, thanks."

I should have guessed: the salt was just an excuse. She knew every birthday at Rent-a-Back and never let one pass without notice. I opened the envelope and looked at the card inside. "This was really nice of you," I told her.

She waved my words away. Long, fragile hands, untouched by the sun. "What a pity you have to work today," she said. "I hope you're having a party later on."

"Just supper at my folks' house."

"Is your little girl going to join you?"

"Well, no," I said. "But look at what she sent."

From my rear jeans pocket I pulled out Opal's gift—a leather money clip, the kind you make from a kit. I hadn't put any money in (if you thought about it, it was kind of an *ironic* gift), but I liked carrying it around. "The mailman brought this Saturday," I said, "along with a handmade card with a drawing of me on the front that really did resemble me. You could even see the stitches on my blue jeans."

"Oh, isn't that sweet!" Ditty said.

"I was so tickled that I called her up long distance," I said. "Knocked her mother for a loop, as you might imagine. But I think Opal liked it that I bothered."

"I'm sure she loved it," Ditty said.

I put the money clip back in my pocket. "You want me to add the salt to your account?" I asked.

"Yes, please," she said. "And then maybe when the weather gets bad, you could come sprinkle my walks. I can't have the UPS man falling down and suing me."

Ray Oakley always claimed, every year when she gave him *his* birthday card, that she had a little crush on him. But I knew better than that. She didn't have a crush on any of us. It's just that service people were the only human beings she saw anymore.

My parents lived in Guilford, in a half-timbered, Tudor-style house with leaded-glass windows. Out front beside the gas lantern was this really jarring piece of modern sculpture: a giant Lucite triangle balanced upside down on a pole. My mother went after Culture with a vengeance.

I showed up for dinner late, hoping my brother had gotten there first; but no such luck. Mine was the only car in the driveway. So I spent some time locking my doors and double-checking the locks, studying my keys to see which pocket they should go in. Eventually I was detected, though. My father called, "Barnaby?" and I turned to find him standing on the front steps. Against the light from the hall chandelier he looked like a stretched-out question mark, with his stooped, hunched, narrow shoulders. "What's keeping you?" he asked.

"Oh, I'm just . . ."

"Come on in!"

I climbed the steps, and he stood back to let me by. He was taller than me and more graceful by far—had a Fred Astaire kind of elegance that my brother and I had totally missed out on. Nor did we get his soft fair hair or his long-chinned parchment face. My mother's genes had won every round.

"Happy birthday, son," he told me, giving my arm a squeeze just above the elbow.

"Well, thanks."

That about wrapped it up. We had nothing further to talk about. As we crossed the hall, Dad sent a desperate glance toward the second-floor landing. "Margot?" he called. "Barnaby's here! Aren't you coming down?"

"In a minute."

The living room had an expectant look, like a stage. A fire crackled in the fireplace, and somebody's symphony poured from the armoire where the stereo was hidden. Over the mantel hung more of my mother's Culture: a barn door, it could have been, taken off its hinges and framed in aluminum strips.

"Well, now," my father said.

He seized the poker and started rearranging embers.

"Which birthday is this, anyway?" he asked, finally.

"Thirtieth," I told him.

"Good grief."

"Right."

Then we heard my mother's footsteps on the stairs. "Happy birthday!" she cried, hurrying in with her arms outstretched.

"Thanks," I said, and I gave her a peck on the cheek.

She had dressed up, but in that offhand way that Guilford women do it—A-line skirt, tailored silk shirt, navy leather flats with acorns tied to the toes. Her one mistake was her hair. She dyed her hair dead black and wore it sleeked into a tight French roll. It made her look white-faced and witchy, but would I be the one to tell her? I enjoyed it. You see a woman who's reinvented herself, who's shown a kind of genius at picking up the social clues, it's a real pleasure to catch her in a blunder. I watched as she bustled about—snatching my jacket, darting off to the closet, rushing back to settle me on the couch. "We haven't seen you in ages," she said when she'd sat down next to me. Then she jumped up: cushion tilted off-center in the armchair opposite. "You're skin and bones!" she said over her shoulder. "Have you lost weight?"

"No, Mom."

"I'll bet anything you're not eating right."

"I'm eating fine," I said.

If I'd lost weight every time Mom claimed, I'd have been registering in the negative on the bathroom scale.

Now she was off to pull open a desk drawer. The woman could not sit still. Always something discontented about her, something glittery and overwrought that set my teeth on edge. "Where *is* it?" she asked, rummaging about. She came up with an envelope. "Here," she said, and she sat back down and laid it in my hand. "Your birthday present," she said.

"Well, thanks."

"Maybe you can find yourself some decent clothes."

"Maybe so," I said, not troubling to argue. I folded the envelope in two and slid it into my jeans pocket. (I didn't need to look to know it was a gift certificate from some menswear store or other, someplace Ivy League and expensive.) "Thanks to you too, Dad," I said.

"You're very welcome."

He was propping the poker against the bricks, and the sight of his thin, sensitive fingers also set my nerves on edge, and so did the music diddling about as if it couldn't decide where to go. I turned to my mother and said, "So. Are Gram and Pop-Pop coming?" Which was purely to annoy her, because I already knew the answer.

"No, they're not," she told me, brazening it out. "But your brother is, of course. And I invited Len Parrish too. He's stopping by for birthday cake after; he couldn't make it for dinner."

No surprise to me. Len was one of those boyhood friends mothers always love, but he had gone on to big doings and left me far behind. I said, "Well, I wouldn't hold my breath, if I were you."

"He told me he'd come, Barnaby. I'm sure he'll keep his word."

The doorbell rang. "Oh! Jeff!" my mother said, and she jumped up and rushed to the hall, while Dad and I exchanged relieved grins. Things would proceed more smoothly now. Not only was my brother a better conversationalist, but he had a wife and baby who would help to dilute the atmosphere. Especially the baby.

Or actually, he wasn't a baby. It shows how out of touch I was. When Jeff and Wicky entered the room, this little kid was toddling between them—a pudgy tyke in a suit like his dad's and a polka-dot bow tie. "Look at that!" I said, getting to my feet. "Walking! At his age!"

"He's *been* walking for months," Mom said. "He's nearly two, for heaven's sake."

"Happy birthday," Wicky told me, kissing the air beside my left cheek. She smelled of toothpaste. She and Jeff made a model couple—Wicky an attractive blonde in clothes that were twins to my mother's, Jeff dark and square-set and handsome in a stockbroker sort of way. He wasn't really a stockbroker; he worked at the Foundation with Dad. But he had on one of those stockbroker shirts with the pinstripes and plain white collar.

"Where'd you park?" I asked him. "You didn't park behind me, did you?"

"The birthday boy!" Jeff said, clapping me on the shoulder.

"Is your car blocking my car in?"

"Relax," he told me. "I can move it at a moment's notice."

"Damn! You *are* blocking me in!"

But he was already heading toward the cocktail cart, where Dad had started rattling ice cubes. Wicky, meanwhile, bent to scoop up my nephew. "Give your Uncle Barnaby a birthday kiss, Jape," she said, holding him out in my direction.

Jape? Oh, right: they called him J.P. Jeffrey Paul the Third. J.P. stole a peek at me and then buried his face in Wicky's shirtfront. "Silly," she said. "It's your uncle! Uncle Barnaby! How does it feel to be thirty?" she asked me.

"Feels like hell," I told her.

"Oh, it does not! Look at me: I'm thirty-three. I feel better than I did at twenty."

"Well, you probably didn't drink a case of beer last night," I told her.

"True enough," Wicky said.

"Oh, Barnaby!" Mom cried. "A whole case? You didn't!"

These little rituals were so reassuring. I could always get a rise out of Mom.

Dad was taking drink orders. Jeff wanted Scotch, and the women wanted white wine. I said, "I'll have whatever J.P. is having," because I'd been only half kidding about last night. Then I was struck by the horrible thought that J.P. might still be breast-feeding. But no, he was having ginger ale, in a plastic cup with a bunny decal. Mine came in a glass, though. Dad handed it to me with a flourish.

"So! Barnaby! How's it feel to turn thirty?" Jeff asked.

"What an original question," I said. "Did you think it up all by yourself?"

"Oh, touchy, touchy," he told me. "Don't worry, it's not a bad age. Twenty-seven was worse, as I recall."

"Twenty-seven?"

"That's when it first hit me that thirty was on the way. By the time it actually came, I'd adjusted."

Count on Jeff: he plans ahead.

The whole bunch of us were standing, like people at a cocktail party. J.P. began spitting experimentally into his bunny cup. Wicky brought forth a sheaf of Christmas photos to show Mom. (She and Jeff and J.P. had spent Christmas in South Carolina with her folks, pretty much breaking Mom's heart.) Dad and Jeff talked about, I don't know, the Deserving Poor, I guess. "Exactly," Jeff said heavily, rocking from heel to toe. "I couldn't agree with you more. Exactly."

I went over to the fireplace and considered the barn door awhile. Then I drifted into my father's study. I stood sipping my drink in front of his bookcase, pretending to be absorbed by the titles. *The Gaitlin Foundation's First Quarter-Century, 1911–1936. The Gaitlin Foundation: Fifty Years of Compassion, 1911–1961.* Dry as dust, I already knew, and dotted with black-and-white photos of Planning Council members in stiff dark suits.

On the shelf below was the ledger containing Great-Granddad's epic poem and, next to that, his son's contribution, done up by some obliging printer to look like a ledger too. Same gray cloth, same maroon leather corners, the title trimmed with spires and dangles of lace. *Light of Heaven* was the title. Grandfather must have fantasized that someone besides Gaitlins would read what he had to say, because he explained things the family already knew. *My wife, Abigail McKane Gaitlin, was exceedingly devout,* he wrote. From the sound of it, he had been visited by one of Creation's dullest angels—a sweet-faced young secretary who arrived for a job interview at a "perilous moment" in his personal life and instructed him to appreciate his wife and children, after which she vanished. Reading between the lines, I always assumed that what we had here was an instance of attempted sexual harassment in the workplace, but that could have been wishful thinking; I was so eager for some sign of colorfulness in my family. The nearest thing to a renegade that we could claim was my great-aunt Eunice, who left her husband for a stage magician fifteen years her junior. But she came home within a month, because she'd had no idea, she said, what to cook for the magician's dinners. And anyhow, Great-Aunt Eunice was a Gaitlin only by marriage.

Just look at Dad's ledger; look at Jeff's. *A Possible Paranormal Experience,* my father's contribution, described the woman who stopped him on Howard Street and asked him for a match. While he was explaining that he didn't smoke, the police arrested the gunman who'd been lurking around the next corner. (But the gunman was only Charles Murfree, the unbalanced grandson of those selfsame Murfrees who'd gone bankrupt after purchasing our Twinform patent, and he'd been stalking my family for decades, off and on. Wouldn't you say, therefore, that if not for Angel Number One, Dad never would have been endangered in the first place?) My brother called *his* report *A Tradition Repeated,* which was appropriate in view of its many redundancies. I guess he was just doing his utmost to stretch a one-sentence encounter into a respectable length. (And a fragmentary sentence, at that. "Looking mighty spooky," his angel had announced, briskly refolding the stock market page before she stepped off the elevator.)

Close behind me, Wicky said, "Stop right where you are!" I practically jumped out of my skin, till I realized she was talking to J.P. He had padded in without my noticing; he was reaching for the crystal paperweight on the desk. "Don't touch, Jape," Wicky said. "What are you up to?" she asked me.

"Oh, just browsing," I said.

She came over to stand next to me, carrying J.P. in her arms. *"A Tradition Repeated,"* I told her, gesturing toward Jeff's ledger.

I was hoping to get her reaction—her private, unvarnished views on Our Lady of the Stock Market—but she must have thought I was commenting on the whole shelf-load, because she said, "Yes, they're very inspirational, aren't they?"

Diplomatically, I took a sip of my drink. Except that the glass was empty and the ice cubes crashed into my nose.

"I feel so bad for your mom," Wicky said. "Now that angels are the latest thing, she worries you-all's will look faddish."

"You feel bad for my *mom?*" I asked. I was trying to find the connection.

"She was telling me, just the other day: 'It used to be that angels were unusual, but now they're in every bookstore; they're on every calendar and wall motto and needlepointed cushion; they're little gold pins on every lapel. Ours will be lumped right in with all those tacky newcomer angels,' she told me."

"They aren't *hers*," I said. "Mom is not even a Gaitlin! What's she all het up about?"

"Well, you know how she is."

I certainly did. If Mom had had her way, she wouldn't have merely married a Gaitlin; she'd have arranged to have a Gaitlin blood transfusion.

We went back out to the living room, where Dad and Jeff were discussing the new software they'd bought for the office. Mom headed off to the kitchen to see about dinner. J.P. wanted more ginger ale, but Wicky told him no. "It's the learning curve that worries me," Dad said, and Jeff said, "Yes, I'm very concerned about the learning curve."

The symphony on the stereo was building louder and louder, ending and ending forever. It reminded me of some huge, frantic animal crashing around the bars of its cage.

How come I always got the feeling that somebody was missing from our family table? I had thought so from the time I was little, toting up the faces at dinner every night: Mom, Dad, Jeff, me . . . It was such a pitiful showing. We didn't make enough noise; we didn't seem busy enough, embroiled enough. In the old days, I had thought we needed more kids. Two was a pretty lame amount, it seemed to me. Maybe we should have had a girl besides. I'd have liked that. It might have helped me understand women a little better. But my parents never obliged me.

Then later, when I got married, I figured Natalie would liven things up—I mean, at holiday meals and such. She didn't, though. For one thing, she was too quiet. Too demure, too well mannered; spine never touched the back of her chair. Also, she didn't last all that long. Eighteen months from wedding to bust-up. Opal was out of the picture before she got her own place setting, even. As for my sister-in-law, by the time she appeared I'd quit hoping. It's not that I had anything against her, but I had come to realize we would never be the kind of family I'd envisioned.

So there I sat at my birthday dinner, just going through the motions. "Great, you made the potato dish." That sort of thing. "Please pass the rolls." Mom had to tell her story about the New Year's Baby That Wasn't: how I had all but promised to be the very first birth of the year (name in the papers, free diaper service, six-month supply of strained spinach), but then, of course—of course!—had loafed about and procrastinated and shown up three weeks late. And that got Wicky started on Punctual-to-the-Minute J.P. We all turned, synchronized, to beam at J.P. in his high chair. "Not to imply that he was a *speedy* birth," she said. Wonderful: the Difficult Delivery Story. The rest of us were excused from inventing another topic for a good quarter hour. We fixed our eyes on her gratefully and nodded and tut-tutted.

Then I started having this problem that afflicts me every so often. I'm listening to someone talk, I'm the picture of attentiveness, and all at once I just know I'm about to burst out with something rude or disgustingly self-centered. I might say, for instance, "You think your labor pains are so interesting? Let me describe this tight feeling that's seizing up my temples." Because I did have a tight feeling. I felt overly aware of the art piece above the sideboard—actual knives and forks and spoons, bent into angular shapes and leaning out from the canvas in a threatening manner. "You wouldn't believe how my nerves are just . . . jangling!" I might have said. But apparently I didn't say it, because everyone was still nodding at Wicky.

At the end of the meal, Mom rose to clear the table, shooing away all offers of help. "I won't serve the cake just yet," she said as she set out the cream and sugar. "We'll wait for Len."

"Or go ahead without him, why don't we," I suggested.

"Oh, he'll be here by the time I get the coffee poured."

Dreamer.

While Mom was matching cups to saucers, Wicky remembered my birthday present and took it from her purse: a red silk paisley tie wrapped in red tissue. I hadn't worn a tie since Grandmother Gaitlin's funeral, but I put it on right away—knotting it around my bare neck, since my shirt didn't have a collar. "Thanks, Wicky. Thanks, Jeff," I said. "Thank you very much, J.P." Then I said, "Want to see what Opal gave me?" I dug the money clip from my pocket and passed it around. Everyone admired it. I said, "You should have seen the card that came with it. There was a really good drawing of me on the front."

"Oh," my mother said, "that child is just growing up without us! It's not fair."

"I was thinking she might come stay with me for a week or two this summer," I said. "She's getting old enough, I figure. I ought to be taking part in her life a little more."

"Stay in that basement room of yours?" Mom asked.

"Well, yes."

"I hardly think so, Barnaby. Maybe here, instead."

"There's nothing wrong with my place!"

Mom just pursed her lips and poured me a cup of coffee.

I'd been planning to mention my angel next. I mean, just jokingly. Tell how I'd half imagined she had instructed me to be more of a father. But somehow the moment had passed. A silence fell. The only sound was the clinking of spoons against cups. Finally Wicky started a story about one of her famous cooking disasters, but she interrupted herself to mop up J.P.'s spilled milk; or maybe she just lost heart. I said, "Mom? Do I get cake, or don't I?"

"Well, but what about Len?"

"Whose birthday is this, anyhow?" I asked.

"I hate to just go ahead," she said, but she stood up and went out to the kitchen. She came back with the cake held high in front of her: chocolate icing and a blaze of candles. We're not much for singing in my family, but Wicky started "Happy Birthday," and so the others raggedly joined in. "Make a wish! Make a wish!" Wicky chanted at the end. Poor Wicky; she was carrying more than her share of the burden here. Although J.P., banging his spoon on his tray, might be willing to help in a couple more years.

I blew out all the candles in one breath. (I said I'd made a wish, but I hadn't.) Then I grabbed the knife. "There's an extra plate for Len," Mom told me. "Just set a piece aside, and he can eat it when he gets here."

She was watching the path of my knife, sitting on the front two inches of her chair and coiled to spring the instant I flubbed up; but I disappointed her and cut the first slice perfectly. I sent it across to Wicky and said, "Haven't we been through this before?"

"Through what before?" Mom asked.

"Waiting for Wonder Boy and he never showed up? I seem to remember we did the same thing last year."

"I don't know why you always take that tone about him," Mom said. She waved a slice of cake on to Jeff. "You used to be inseparable, once upon a time."

"Once upon a time," I agreed.

"I believe you're jealous of his success."

"Success?" I asked. I stopped slicing the cake and looked over at her. "You call it a success, selling off fake plantation houses on streets called Foxhound Footway and Stirrup Cup Circle?"

"At least he wears a suit to work. At least he makes a decent living. At least he has a college degree."

"Well, if that's what turns you on," I told her.

She said, "Did you sign up for that course?"

"What course?"

"That night course at the college, remember? I suggested you might sign up for it and earn a few more credits."

"Oh, that," I said.

"Well, did you?"

"No."

"Why not?"

"Just never got around to it, I guess."

I handed a piece of cake to Dad. He accepted it with a pinched and disapproving expression, his gray eyes pronounced in their sockets; but it would be Mom he disapproved of, not me. He couldn't abide for people to act upset. And Mom was obviously upset. She was stripping all her rings off, a very bad sign. Setting them at the head of her place in little jingling stacks with trembling fingers: her wedding and engagement rings, Grandmother Gaitlin's dinner ring, her Mother's Day ring with its two winking red and blue birthstones. She said, "But the semester must have started already!"

I gave her a plate and said, "Probably has."

She pushed the plate away.

"Cakies, Jape-Jape!" Wicky caroled, aiming a forkful of crumbs at J.P. But J.P. was staring openmouthed at Mom, a thread of dribble spinning from his gleaming lower lip.

I cut the last slice, my own. A big one. I told my brother, "Not to be piggish or anything . . . ," and my brother rolled his eyes.

"Twelve, credits," my mother said, too distinctly. "Twelve, little, college, credits, and you could kiss Roll-a-Bat goodbye."

"Rent-a-Back," I said. I licked the frosting off a candle.

"You could buy yourself a decent suit and go to work for your father."

"Now, Margot," my father said. "If college were all that stood in his way, I'd dream up something for him to do tomorrow. Maybe he'd rather work elsewhere; have you considered that?"

"Of course he'd rather work elsewhere!" my mother cried. "Are you blind? He's spitting in your face! He's spitting in the *Foundation*'s face! He has deliberately chosen employment that has no lasting point to it, no reputation, no future, in preference to work that's of permanent significance. And he's doing it purely for spite."

I had been steadily chewing, but I couldn't let that pass. I swallowed twice (the cake might as well have been sand) and turned to my father. "It isn't spite," I told him. "It's only that I feel uneasy around do-gooders. You know? When somebody tells me he, oh, say, spent his Christmas Day volunteering in a soup kitchen, I feel this kind of inner shriveling away from him. You know what I mean?"

"Barnaby!" my mother cried. "Your own father's a do-gooder! Think what you've just said to him!"

"And who cares if my job has no future?" I asked him. He was at one end of the table and she was at the other. I could speak to him directly and shut Mom out. "I need to pay my rent and grocery bill, is all. I'm not looking to get rich."

He seemed to find this idea startling; or at any rate, he blinked. But before he could comment, I said, "Besides. I wouldn't call Rent-a-Back pointless. It serves a very useful purpose."

"Well, certainly, for a fee!" my mother said triumphantly. "For people who can pay you a fee and then die, and that's the end of it!"

J.P. was starting to make cranky, whimpering noises. Wicky rose and tried to lift him from his high chair, but he was fussing and squirming. She said, "Jeff, could you give me a hand here?"

"What am I supposed to do?"

"Can't you get his legs out from under? I shouldn't have to manage all on my own."

"You need to slide the tray off first, for God's sake," Jeff told her.

"Well, you could slide it off yourself instead of just sitting there, dammit!"

I set down my fork and turned to my mother. "I'll tell you what's really bothering you," I said. (Oh, I always did get sucked in sooner or later.) "You think a thing is worthwhile only if it makes the headlines. *Prominent Philanthropist Donates Five Hundred Thousand.* You think it's a waste of time just to carry some lady's trash out for her."

"Yes, I do," Mom said. "And it's a waste of money too. *Our* money."

"Well, I knew we'd get around to that sooner or later."

"Our eighty-seven hundred dollars," she said, "that you have never paid us back a cent of because you earn barely a subsistence wage at that so-called job of yours."

"Margot," my father said. "He doesn't have to pay us back."

"Of course he has to pay us back! It isn't your average household expense: buying off your son's burglary victims!"

"He is not required to pay us back, and you are behaving abominably!" my father said.

The silence was that sharp-edged kind that follows gunshots or shattering claps of thunder. J.P. stopped whimpering. Jeff and Wicky froze on either side of him. My mother sat very straight-backed in her seat. It was a lot more obvious now that she was just a Polish girl from Canton, scared to death Jeffrey Gaitlin might find her common.

Strange how always, at moments like these, the table finally felt full enough.

I had my brother come out with me and move his car so I could make my getaway. At first he tried to stall, saying they were about to leave themselves if I would just hold my horses. But I said, "I need to go *now*," and so he came, muttering and complaining.

"Geez, Barn," he said as he trailed me down the steps. "You take everything so personally. Mom was just being Mom; it's no big deal."

"I knew she'd bring up that money," I told him.

"If you knew, why let it bother you?"

We stopped beside my car, and I zipped my jacket. "What's our next occasion? Easter?" I asked. "Remind me to be out of town."

"You should lighten up," Jeff said. "They don't ask all that much of you."

"Only that I change into some totally other person," I told him.

"That's not true. If you made the least bit of effort; showed you cared. If you dressed a little better when you came to see them, for instance—"

"I'm dressed fine!" I glanced down at myself. "Well, so maybe the tie doesn't go. But the tie wasn't my idea, was it."

"Barnaby. You're wearing a pajama top."

"Oh," I said. "You noticed?"

I had thought it didn't look much different from a regular plaid flannel shirt.

"And both knees are poking through your jeans, and you haven't shaved in a week, I bet—"

"I did have a haircut, though," I said, hoping he would assume that meant a barber had done it.

He squinted at me and said, "When?"

"Look, pal," I said. "Could we just get a move on here? I'm freezing!"

And I strode off toward my car, which forced him to go to *his* car, sighing a big cloud of fog to show how I tried his patience. His car was one of those macho four-by-fours. You'd think he rode the range all day, herding cattle or something.

A four-by-four, and a Princeton degree, and a desk half the size of a tennis court on the top floor of the Gaitlin Foundation. None of which I wanted for myself, Lord knows. Still, I couldn't help thinking, as I unlocked my car door, how comfortable it must be to be Jeff. Things just seemed to come easier for him. Me, I'd been in trouble from adolescence on. I'd been messing up and breaking things and disappointing everyone around me, while Jeff just coolly went about his business. It's as if he were an entirely different race, a different species, more at home in the world. More blessed.

What I sometimes told myself: *I'll be that way too, as soon as my real life begins.*

But I can't explain exactly what I meant by "real life."

I slid behind the wheel, slammed my door shut, watched in my rearview mirror as Jeff backed toward the street. When I moved to start my engine, though, I heard a honk behind me. I checked in the mirror and found a sleek black Lexus just turning into the driveway and blocking Jeff's exit.

Len Parrish, after all.

I opened my door and climbed out. Jeff was rolling forward again with the Lexus following, barely tucking its tail in off the street before it had to stop short behind our two cars. "Hold it!" I called, waving both arms, but Len went ahead and doused his lights. I walked over to the Lexus. "Don't park! I have to leave!"

He lowered his window. "Nice to see you too, Gaitlin."

"You're blocking me in! I'm going. You'll have to let me by."

Instead he got out of his car. A good-looking guy, wide-shouldered and athletic, in a fitted black overcoat. He wore a broad, lazy grin, and he asked me, "How's the birthday boy?"

"Fine, but—"

"Jeff!" he said, because my brother had come to join us.

"Hello, Len," Jeff said. The two of them shook hands. (I just stood there.)

"Guess I'm a little late," Len said.

"Well, Mom's saved a piece of cake for you," Jeff told him.

"Come back inside and help me eat it, Barnaby," Len said.

"I can't," I said. "I have to be going."

"Aw, now. What's the rush?"

Here's what's funny: Len Parrish went along with me on every teenage stunt I ever pulled. He was with me the night I got caught, in fact, but he wasn't caught himself, and I never breathed a word to the police. After the helicopter buzzed us, I tried to jump from the Amberlys' sunporch roof to the limb of a maple tree. Made a little error in judgment; I'd had a puff or two of pot. Landed in the pyracantha bush below. No injuries but a few scratches, thanks again to the pot, which kept me loose-limbed as a trained paratrooper all the way down. The police got so diverted, they failed to notice Len and the Muller boys slipping out the Amberlys' back door.

I didn't blame Len in the least. I'd have done the same, in his place. But it irked me that my mother thought he was such a winner. Him in his expensive coat and velvety suede gloves. He pulled off one of the gloves now to stroke the hood of my car. In the dark, my car looked black, although it was a shade called Riverside Red. "Grit," he said. He withdrew his hand and rubbed his fingers together.

"You want to move your vehicle, Len?"

"What you need is a garage," he said. "Rent one or something. Take better care of this baby."

"I'll go see to it this instant," I told him. "Just let me out of the driveway."

"At least you ought to wash her every now and then."

I slid in behind the wheel and shut the door. Jeff returned to his car, and Len at last ambled toward the Lexus, while I watched in my mirror. The minute the driveway was clear, I shifted into reverse and backed out.

Len should try this himself, if he thought Corvettes were that great. It just so happened mine was made in 1963, the year they had a split rear window. Stupidest idea in automotive history.

I was happy enough to be leaving that I returned Len's wave very cheerfully, before I took off toward home. Now he and Mom could have their little love feast together. Shake their heads about I-don't-know-what-Barnaby-will-come-to. Cut themselves another slice of cake.

I thought of my rooftop fall again. It was possible I could have escaped, if the tippy toe of my sneaker hadn't caught on some kind of metal bracket that was sticking up from the gutter. I remembered exactly how it felt—the barely perceptible hitch as my toe and the bracket connected. I recalled the physical sensation of something happening that couldn't be reversed: that feeling, all the way down, of longing to take back my one single, simple misstep. But it was already too late, and I knew that, absolutely, even before I hit the pyracantha bush.

Eighty-seven hundred dollars. It never failed to come up at some point. Mom might say, for instance, that they planned to remodel the kitchen as soon as they could afford it; and while a stranger would find that an innocent remark, I knew better. Of course they could afford it—if they couldn't, who could?—but she wanted to make it plain that they still felt the effects of that unforeseen drain on their finances. The waste of it, the fruitlessness. The niggling dribs and drabs handed out to neighbors. Sixty dollars for a ballerina music box, which I'd thrown down a storm drain in a moment of panic. Ninety-four fifty to mend the lock on a cabinet door. The most expensive item was an ivory carving of a tiny, naked Chinese man and woman getting extremely familiar with each other. I broke it when I stuffed it between my mattress and box spring. Mr. McLeod said it was priceless but settled for six hundred, grumbling. You'd have thought he'd be embarrassed to claim ownership.

I was heading up Charles Street now, slightly above the speed limit. Racing a traffic light that turned red before I reached it, but I hooked a right onto Northern Parkway without touching the brakes.

And it wasn't only the reparation money. Get Mom wound up and she would toss in the tuition at Renascence, besides. A little harder to figure the precise amount, there. As Dad pointed out, they'd have paid for my schooling in any case. But Mom said, "Not a school like Renascence, though, with its four-to-one student-teacher ratio and its trained psychologists."

I didn't count the tuition myself; I reasoned that Renascence was their idea, not mine. First inkling I had of it was, Mom said to pack my clothes because the next day I was leaving for a special school that was perfect for me: roomy accommodations out in the country and a supervised environment. Except I heard "roomy" as "loony." ("It's perfect for you: loony accommodations.") I flipped and said I wouldn't go. Never did want to go, even after they cleared up the misunderstanding. So I couldn't be held responsible for the Renascence bill, right?

Unfortunate name, Renascence. People were always correcting my pronunciation. "Uh, don't you mean *Ren*aissance?" And nobody got reborn there, believe me—nobody I ever heard of. The aim stated on the school's letterhead was "Guiding the Gifted Young Tester of Limits," but what they should have said was "Stashing Away Your Rich Juvenile Delinquent." The only thing "special" about the place was, they kept us twelve months a year. No awkward summer vacations to inconvenience our families. Also, we had to wear suits to class. (Which explains why I favor pajama tops now.) And every time we cursed, we had to memorize a Shakespeare sonnet. Boy, that'll clean up your language in a hurry! Not to mention instilling a permanent dislike of Shakespeare.

I remember this one sonnet I learned, the first week I was at Renascence. It started out, *When, in disgrace with fortune and men's eyes* . . . I thought it was me he was talking about. I swear it just about tore me apart the moment I saw those words on the page.

Well. As I said, it was my first week. And anyhow, the guy went on to say, *Haply I think on thee,* which was certainly *not* about me. I didn't have any "thee" in my life; no way. The girls I hung out with in those days were more body mates than soul mates, and you couldn't claim that anyone in my family was my "thee."

I wondered how my family would react if I ever paid that eighty-seven hundred back. How my mother would react, to be specific. She'd probably fall over in a faint.

Sometimes I thought if I could just show her, just once and for all *show* her, I would be free of her.

I reached my apartment, finally. Switched on the lights, unzipped my jacket, punched the button on my answering machine. Mrs. Dibble needed an errand run for Miss Simmons, provided I got home before six. Too late now; so I took off my jacket and started emptying my jeans pockets. Mimi Hardesty, upstairs, left a message about an eentsy bit of laundry she wanted to do in the morning even though it wasn't a Saturday. Then Mrs. Dibble again. Never mind about Miss Simmons—she'd sent Celeste, instead—but tomorrow I should meet with a brand-new client. A Mrs. Glynn. "It was her niece who made the request," she said. "She told me you two had talked on the train. Good work, Barnaby! You must be quite a salesman. The niece says her aunt will need hours and hours; that was her exact phrase. She inquired about our weekly rates. She wants you to come to her aunt's house tomorrow evening."

Mom's envelope was made of paper so thick that it unfolded by itself as I set it on the counter. I lifted the flap and peered inside. Whoa! Not a gift certificate, but cash—a hundred dollars. Five twenties new enough to stick together slightly when I fanned them out. Well, good; I didn't need clothes, anyhow. I hadn't yet redeemed my certificate from Christmas.

I restacked the bills and fitted them into Opal's money clip. Then I stood weighing the clip in my hand, looking down at it and thinking.

Let's say I made a hundred dollars extra every week. Say I lined up this aunt of Sophia's with her hours and hours of chores; say I stopped dodging the clients I didn't care for, the assignments I didn't find convenient, and added a clear hundred dollars to my weekly income. Eighty-seven weeks, that meant. Eighty-six with the birthday money; eighty-five and eighty-four if we could count next birthday and next Christmas too.

I would hand it to Mom in cold cash: eighty-seven crisp new hundred-dollar bills. I'd slide them out of the money clip and slap them smartly on her palm.

Everybody else's angel had delivered a single message and let it go at that. Wouldn't you know, though, *my* angel seemed to be more of the nagging kind.

5

Mrs. Glynn lived on a shady street just south of Cold Spring Lane, in a brown shingle-board house with peeling green shutters. I was supposed to meet Sophia there at five-thirty, which would give her time to drive over after work; but when I pulled up early, about a quarter past, she was already waiting out front. She was leaning against the hood of her car—a silver-gray Saab. I had always thought Saab owners were shallow, but now I saw I might have been mistaken.

I parked behind her and stepped out. "Yo! Sophia," I said, and then I wondered if I should have called her Miss Maynard. Mrs. Dibble had her rules about how we addressed our clients. Except that Sophia wasn't a client, strictly speaking. And she didn't appear to mind; she just smiled and said, "Thanks for coming, Barnaby."

Today she was wearing a different coat, black wool with a Chinese type of collar. It made her hair look blonder. Also, it seemed to me she had more makeup on. This must be her loan officer outfit. I said, "I thought bankers' hours were shorter. You mean you have to work till five like everybody else?"

"Yes, alas," she told me. We started up the front steps. "It was nice of you to agree to meeting my aunt first," she said. "I need to sort of talk her into this, as I explained to your employer."

"Oh, no problem," I told her.

"Is that who she is?" Sophia asked.

"Who who is?"

"Mrs. Dibble," Sophia said. She pressed the doorbell, and a dog started yapping somewhere inside. "Is Mrs. Dibble your employer?" she asked me.

"Yes, she owns the whole company. Started it from scratch and owns it lock, stock, and barrel."

"Because I had somehow understood that the company was yours," she said.

"Mine? No way." I had to raise my voice, since the yapping was coming closer. "I'm just a peon, is all."

"Well, surely more than a peon," she said. "It must take quite a bit of skill, dealing with your older clients."

"Oh, a fair amount. Shoot, some of us have Ph.D.s, times being what they are," I said. "Not me, though, I don't mean." I was consciously trying to be truthful, so she wouldn't get any more wrong ideas. But before I could explain that I didn't even have my B.A., the front door swung open and Sophia's aunt said, "There you are!"

She was no bigger than a minute—a tiny, cute gnat of a woman with a wizened face and eyes so pouchy they seemed goggled. She wore a navy polka-dot dress that hung nearly to her ankles, although on someone else it would have been normal length, and loose, thick beige stockings and enormous Nikes. Over her forearm she carried a Yorkshire terrier, neatly folded like a waiter's napkin. "This is my doorbell," she said, thrusting him toward me. "I'd never have known you were out here if not for Tatters."

"Aunt Grace," Sophia said, "I'd like you to meet Barnaby."

"Bartleby?" her aunt said sharply.

"*Barnaby.*"

"Well, that sounds more promising. Won't you come in?"

"My aunt, Mrs. Glynn," Sophia told me, but Mrs. Glynn had already turned to lead us into her parlor. There was something about her back that let you know she was hard of hearing. And clearly the place was getting to be too much for her. The lace curtains were stiff with dust, and the walls were darker in the corners, and the air had the brownish, sweet, woolen smell that comes from a person sleeping extra-long hours in a tightly closed space.

"Sophia thinks I'm too doddery to do for myself anymore," Mrs. Glynn said. She waved us toward the couch. When she perched in a wing chair opposite, her Nikes didn't quite touch the floor. She set the dog down next to her, tidily arranging his paws. "Lately she's been after me to hire a companion. I say, 'What do I want with a companion? I'd just end up waiting on *her*, like as not, and we'd bicker and snipe at each other all day and I wouldn't know how to get rid of her.' "

"Well, there you see the value of Rent-a-Back," I told her. I was speaking in that narrower range of tone that carries well. (I had it down to a science.) "We can go about our business without a word, if you want. You can leave a key at the office, and we'll let ourselves in while you're out; be gone before you get home again."

"It's not that I'm antisocial," Mrs. Glynn said. "Am I, Sophia."

"Goodness, no, Aunt Grace. Just independent."

"Pensive? Well, I do like to have my thinking time, but—"

"*Independent,* is what I said."

"Oh. Independent. Yes."

She faced me squarely, raising her chin. "But we're not here to talk about me. We're here to talk about you. Are you a Baltimore boy, by any chance?"

"Yes, ma'am. Born and bred," I said.

"Is that right. Would I know your parents? What's your last name, anyhow?"

"Gaitlin," I told her.

"Gaitlin." She thought it over. "As in the Foundation?" she asked.

"Yes, ma'am."

"Really."

There was a pause. Sophia smoothed her skirt across her lap. Mrs. Glynn said, "Why don't you work for them, then?"

"It's a long story," I said.

"Lost art? Why is that?"

"A *long story.* Complicated."

"Aha," she said. "So you, too, are independent. Refuse to take any handouts from rich relations. Well, I don't blame you a bit, young man. Good for you!"

"Thanks," I said.

"Stand on your own two feet. Right? Now you see why I don't want a live-in companion."

"Oh, yes."

"Sophia's even offered to come stay with me herself, bless her heart," Mrs. Glynn said. She reached over to ruffle the Yorkie's bangs. He smiled, showing his tongue—a little pink dollop of a tongue like on a child's teddy bear. "I told her, 'What, and spoil a perfectly good relationship?' Sophia is my one and only niece. It's not as if I had relatives to squander."

"I thought I could live in her guest room," Sophia told me, "but Aunt Grace wouldn't hear of it."

"She'd be watching me every minute," Mrs. Glynn said. "Oh, I know: meaning the best! But trying to change what I ate or when I went to bed. Wouldn't you?" she asked Sophia fondly. "As it is, you're worse than a mother."

"It's true," Sophia said. "I'm a worrywart."

"She's a worrywart!" Mrs. Glynn announced. She came up with it so triumphantly, I was pretty sure she hadn't heard Sophia. "Pushing the multivitamins. Nagging me to exercise. Trying to make me stash my money in a bank."

"Aunt Grace distrusts banks," Sophia told me.

"Of course I distrust banks!" Mrs. Glynn said. This she seemed to have caught with no trouble, although Sophia had barely murmured it. "I lived through the Great Depression! I'd be out of my mind to trust a bank! I keep my liquid assets in the flour bin."

"There," Sophia said. "See what I mean?" she asked me. "She hasn't known a person five minutes and she tells him where she keeps her cash."

"Not just *a* person. A *nice* person, with kind brown eyes and a mouth that tips up at both ends!"

"But you'd tell anybody you met, I believe," Sophia persisted. "You think we're still in the thirties, when people left their front doors unlocked and their car keys in the ignition."

"Now, don't exaggerate," Mrs. Glynn said. "I'm very careful to lock my front door."

"When you happen to think of it!"

I could see they'd had this conversation any number of times. They were obviously enjoying themselves, each delivering her lines with an eye cocked in my direction. I said, "Well, anyhow. At Rent-a-Back, we're used to dealing with independent people. We adjust to fit our customers' needs: as much butting in as they want, or as little."

"Tell about Mr. Shank," Sophia prodded me.

"Mr. Shank?"

"How he calls in the middle of the night just because he's lonely."

"Oh," I said. I was surprised that she'd remembered. "Well, he's got the opposite problem, really—"

"Tell about Mrs. Gordoni. There's this client named Mrs. Gordoni," Sophia said to her aunt, "who can't afford to pay."

"In pain from what?" Mrs. Glynn asked.

"To pay. To pay the fees," Sophia said. "And Barnaby helps her out even so, and underreports his hours."

"I have no problem whatsoever in paying off my bills," Mrs. Glynn told me firmly.

Sophia said, "No, I didn't mean—"

"Whatever the charge, I can more than pay. And however many hours. I believe I'll start with an hour a day. After that, we'll see."

"An hour a day," I said, hunting through my pockets for my calendar. "And would that be mornings, or afternoons?"

"Afternoons, if you have them."

"Yes, ma'am. Or somebody will. Me or one of the others."

"One of the others? Wait. Wouldn't it be you who came?"

"I'll come if possible," I said.

"I'd prefer it to be you."

"Well, I'll try," I said.

"For one thing, you're left-handed," she told me.

I was, in fact, although I had no idea how she had figured that out. Sophia said, "What does left-handed have to do with it?"

"I just feel left-handers are more reliable, that's all."

Sophia made a sound somewhere between a laugh and a sigh. I said, "Yes, ma'am, I'm very reliable," as I flipped through calendar pages. "How is three o'clock?" I asked. "I have that open every weekday. Or four o'clock except for Fridays, so on Fridays we could—"

"No, I think later," Mrs. Glynn said decisively. "I think five-thirty. Could you do that?"

"Sure thing," I told her, penciling it in. Five-thirty was our slow time—dinner hour for many of the older folks. "Will you be here then? Or you want to give us a key."

"You can take a key for unexpected occurrences," she said, "but generally I'll be here. Why don't you start next Monday? By then I'll have a list written out."

She rose from her chair, and we did too. Her little dog perked up his ears and made a chortling sound. "I knew you were left-handed because you put Sophia on your right when you sat down," Mrs. Glynn told me. "My husband was left-handed. He liked to have me on his right at all times—sitting, walking, even sleeping. He said it freed his sword arm to defend me."

When she smiled up at me, the bags beneath her eyes grew bigger than ever. She had to sort of peek out over them. It made her seem mischievous and gleeful, like an elf.

Mrs. Glynn's five hours would help out quite a bit with the eighty-seven hundred, but they wouldn't be enough on their own, of course. I told Mrs. Dibble I needed more jobs. "You know Mrs. Figg? The Client from Hell? You can send me over there after all; I've changed my mind. And forget what I told you about wanting off Saturday nights."

"Hmm," Mrs. Dibble said. "Someone must be saving up for something."

I just said, "Oh, a few extra dollars would always come in handy."

For the sake of a few extra dollars, I agreed to a double trash-can route when Jay Cohen came down with mono. I spent an entire day shifting furniture for Mrs. Binney, who stood about with one finger set prettily to her chin and said, "On second thought . . ." I loaded the Winstons' station wagon at four o'clock in the morning for their annual drive to Florida. (They wouldn't let me do it the night before—scared of thieves. And of course they were the type who believed in setting off before dawn.)

I even went so far as to telephone Len Parrish, because he had mentioned needing part-time help on his newest housing development. Someone to show off the model home—just a warm body, he'd said. But not *my* warm body, evidently, because first he behaved like Mr. Important ("Barn! You caught me just as I was heading out the door! Sorry I can't chat."), and then he claimed he'd already hired someone. I didn't know whether to believe him or not. "Hey, guy," he said. "How you *doing*? How's the *car*? We should get together for a drink at some point. I'm going to give you a call."

I wondered if he planned to declare the drink on his taxes. (Not that I really expected him to call.) One time, Len had told me that just about anything he did he considered tax deductible. "Taking a trip to the beach, going to the movies . . . ," he said. "Because it gives me more experience, and I'm therefore better equipped to make informed business decisions. Heck, the way I figure it, *life* is tax deductible!"

Probably it was just as well he didn't have any work for me.

• • •

On Monday, I went to Mrs. Glynn's, bringing my canvas gloves because I didn't know what chores she had in mind. But as it turned out, her list contained only the most undemanding tasks. *Fetch all tureens and platters from tops of kitchen cabinets, replace on shelves within my reach. Move armchair from sunporch to living room.*

I was tightening the screws on a saucepan rack when Sophia showed up. I heard Tatters yapping at her. She had come straight from work, apparently. Breezed into the kitchen in her dressy black coat and asked me, "How's it going?"

"Going fine," I told her.

"I just thought I'd stop by and make sure the two of you were getting along."

"Well, we haven't had all that much to do with each other," I said. I could speak in a normal tone, because Mrs. Glynn had returned to the parlor after ushering in Sophia. "So far I've just been following what she's got on her list," I said. "But I'm not sure there's enough here to fill the whole hour."

"Oh, this is just the beginning, when she's not used to the luxury of having you around. Believe me: there's a lot to be done! I can name some things if she can't. I've been nagging her for years now to pack up my uncle's lawbooks in the sunporch."

She was watching me replace the saucepans. They were filmed with dust—Mrs. Glynn must not cook much—so I gave each one a rub with my shirtsleeve before I hung it. Then I worried that would strike Sophia as sloppy. I said, "Do you suppose she would want to run these through the dishwasher?"

"Well, maybe," Sophia said. But she didn't go ask. She said, "My ulterior motive here is to get Aunt Grace's belongings organized somewhat and then move her to an apartment. Something nearer to my place, so I could keep an eye on her. She's nearly eighty years old, after all."

I decided to give up on the dishwasher idea. I hung another pan. "Eighty, huh?" I said. "Is she actually your aunt, or is she a great-aunt?"

"No, she's my aunt. My father's sister. I was a late arrival," Sophia said. "My mother was in her forties when she had me. By now she's almost eighty herself, and I'm only thirty-six."

I was ready for the next job: fixing a loose knob on a cupboard in the pantry. I headed off to see to it, taking the screwdriver with me.

"I guess *you* think thirty-six is old," Sophia said in the pantry doorway.

"Gosh, no," I told her politely. "Not when I've been hanging out with people in their nineties." I jiggled the knob and then squatted down in front of it.

"How old are you, Barnaby?"

"I turned thirty last week."

"Oh. Well, happy birthday."

"Thanks."

"Did somebody throw you a party?"

"Just my parents had me to dinner," I said. I opened the door slightly to study the inner side of the knob.

"How about your little girl?"

"How about her."

"Did she come down for the dinner?"

"Nah. Well, she'd already given me my present, see. And besides, I knew I'd be going up there Saturday."

"Yes, I looked for you on the train," she said.

"You did?"

"I remembered you always visit her the last Saturday of the month."

"This time I drove," I said. "I generally do, if my car's not on the blink."

"Oh, you drove."

"It's cheaper."

"I should do that too, I suppose. If I weren't so nervous on interstates," she said.

I was trying to tighten a screw now, but it kept slipping away from me. Sophia was making me self-conscious. I'm not a bona fide handyman; I do these little fix-it jobs by trial and error. So I looked at her, and she must have understood, because she said, "Well. I'll let you get on with it."

Then she straightened up from the doorway and left, and a moment later I heard her out front, telling her aunt goodbye.

My second day on the job, Mrs. Glynn had me take her to the grocery store. She was a quicker shopper than the Cartwrights but a much worse back-seat driver. Although we were in my car (she'd given hers up years ago, she said), she slammed a Nike down hard every time we neared a stoplight, and she wouldn't talk at all but concentrated fiercely on the traffic.

Even in the store, conversation was tough, because the background noise made her hearing worse. When I asked her, in the canned-fruit aisle, whether she liked mandarins, she said, "I like *any* kind of instrument," and at the register she took offense when the clerk offered plastic or paper. ("*Naturally* I can pay for it, or why else would I be here?" she snapped.) But we did okay. Used up slightly more than an hour—though I didn't note the extra on my time sheet—and at the end, she told me I'd been a help. "I hate to rely on Sophia for every little thing," she said. "Not that she isn't sweet as pie about it, but *you* know."

Wednesday, I bought a new curtain rod and installed it in her dining room where the old one had started to sag. Thursday, she asked me to pack up those lawbooks of her husband's. So I drove off to the liquor store for some boxes, and when I got back, I found Sophia in the sunporch. She had her coat off and her sleeves rolled up, and she'd covered the desk with cleaning supplies—rags and a can of furniture polish. "Hello, Barnaby," she said. "I thought I'd follow along behind you and wipe off the shelves as you clear them."

"Oh, I can do that," I told her.

"I wouldn't dream of it! You're not her housekeeper, after all."

"No, but a lot of our jobs *edge over* into housekeeping," I said. "We're used to handling pretty much anything that's required. I'll be glad to wipe the shelves."

"Well, aren't you nice," she told me.

But when I returned from the car with the second load of boxes, she'd already emptied one bookshelf onto the desk and started dusting. So I gave up. She must have been one of those people who couldn't bear sitting by while other people worked—unlike her aunt, who was off in the parlor happily talking baby talk to Tatters.

"I have no idea what to do with these books once we get them packed," Sophia told me. "I suppose some charity might want them."

"I'll ask Mrs. Dibble. She keeps a Rolodex for things like that."

"Uncle George has been dead for twenty years or more, and every book he ever owned is still sitting here. I think all his clothes are still in the upstairs closet too."

"That's nothing compared to some of our clients," I said. "This one woman, Mrs. Morey: she sleeps with her husband's bathrobe laid across the foot of the bed, and he's been gone as long as I've known her."

"Oh! How sad!"

"Yeah, well."

"You must see so many sad things in this job."

"Well, quite a few," I said. I stopped to consider, bracing a carton of books against my shoulder. "On the other hand," I said, "I see quite a few happy things too. This same Mrs. Morey, for instance: she just loves her garden. Come spring, you'd think she was in heaven. She says, 'As long as I can walk out in my garden first thing every morning—take that gardener's early-morning walk, to check what's sprouted overnight and what's about to bloom,' she says, '—why, I feel I have something worth staying alive for.' "

Sophia lifted her dustcloth and turned to look at me. She said, "You're a very kindhearted person, Barnaby Gaitlin."

I said, "Me? I am?"

Of course, I no longer believed that Sophia was my angel. Not literally, at least. But still, I paid close attention whenever she told me something in that quiet, firm tone of voice.

Martine said Sophia had designs on me—that she was hanging around at her aunt's all the time in the hope I'd ask her out. I said, "She's *what*?" We were loading the books onto Martine's boyfriend's truck when she came up with this. Granted, Sophia had put in several appearances—at the moment, she was in the attic, checking for more lawbooks—but the notion of any romantic interest was absurd. I heaved a box onto the truck bed and said, "Get serious, Pasko. She's thirty-six years old."

"So?" Martine said.

"She's a . . . lady! She works in a bank!"

"We women can sense these things," Martine said knowingly. I had to laugh. (She was wearing Everett's parka today, the hood trimmed with matted fake fur, and her little face poked out of it like some sharp, quick, rodenty animal.) "I saw how she was eyeing you!" she said. "Lolling around the sunporch, getting underfoot. Asking those made-up questions in that . . . lilting way of hers. 'Ooh, Barnaby, do you think they'll all fit in one truckload?' 'Ooh, Barnaby, won't you strain your back lifting that great heavy box?' "

Sophia had asked nothing of the sort; Martine was imagining things. I said, "You're just envious, is all."

"Envious!"

"You wish *you* could act so well bred and refined."

"Like hell I do," Martine said. She started back up the front walk, calling over her shoulder, "So obvious and flirtatious is more like it."

"Sh!" I said, glancing toward the house. I caught up with her and said, "She's being a good niece; what's wrong with that? Watching out for her aunt."

"Committing her aunt to five hours a week just to have you around," Martine said.

"Now wait," I said. "I really need these extra hours, Martine."

"Well, sure, *you* need them."

Martine was the only person I'd told about my plan to pay back the eighty-seven hundred. (She'd made a bet with me that my parents wouldn't accept it—"They're not exactly poverty-stricken," she'd said—but that just showed how little she knew Mommy Dearest.) "The question is," she said now, "does the *aunt* need them?"

But before I could argue my case any further, Sophia stepped out the front door. "Guess what, Barnaby!" she called. "In the attic are boxes and boxes of books! More than there were in the sunporch, even!"

Her voice had a kind of caroling tone—a kind of, yes, lilting tone, I had to admit. And she tipped her head against the doorframe in this picturesque, inviting way and flashed me a white-toothed smile.

I felt my heart sink. I glanced over at Martine. She didn't meet my eyes; just climbed the porch steps alongside me. But I saw the smug little kink at the corner of her mouth. I heard the humming sound she made beneath her breath. "Hmm-hmm-hmm," she hummed, high-pitched and airy and innocent, clomping up the steps in her motorcycle boots.

6

On the last Saturday in February, Opal had a ballet recital. This meant I had to share my monthly visit with my mother. Mom phoned and said she'd been sent an invitation. "I'll do the driving," she told me. "I don't trust that car of yours as far as I can throw it."

"Or here's an idea," I said. "Why don't I just meet you there?"

"You mean, not ride up together?"

"Well . . ."

"Barnaby," she said. "I would hardly suppose you're in any position to buy gas when you don't need to."

Which was when I could have told her, "That's *my* business, isn't it?" so she could come back with, "Not as long as you still owe us eighty-seven hundred dollars, it isn't." For once, though, I kept quiet. I thought about Opal's money clip and I held my tongue. This seemed to throw Mom off her stride. She waited just a beat too long, and then she cleared her throat and said, "I'll pick you up at eight a.m. sharp. You be waiting out front."

I said, "Well. Okay."

"Don't make me come into that place of yours and haul you out of bed. Set your alarm clock. Promise."

"Sure thing," I told her.

I tried to look on the bright side after I hung up. At least now I'd have an ally along—or someone people would assume was my ally. Though myself, I had my doubts.

Saturday morning turned out so clear that I checked the sky for the color-change trick after I got up, but the sun had beaten me to it. And then I found I was out of instant coffee; so I had to make do with a Pepsi; and then my mother came early. I swear I would have been ready by eight, but she came five minutes before. Stalked across the patio in her brisk black wool pantsuit, all spiny-backed and indignant. "Where *are* you, Barnaby?" she asked—and this was after I'd opened the door and was standing in plain view.

"Eight o'clock, you said," I told her. "What are you doing here at five of?"

"Well, come along; don't waste more time arguing," she snapped, and she turned on her heel and marched off again. She knew she was in the wrong.

Her car was a Buick, very posh and plushy. Power windows you couldn't roll down unless *she* had turned the ignition on. She drove well, though; I had to hand her that. She slung that thing around like a grocery cart—slithered out of town and started cruising up I-95 in no time flat. "Of course, at this rate we'll hit the recital way too early," I said when we'd been traveling awhile. "We'll have to sit there making small talk with Natalie and Mr. Wonderful."

"If you didn't want her remarrying, you shouldn't have gotten divorced," Mom told me.

"Did I say I didn't want her remarrying? What do I care what she does? I'd just rather not mingle socially with the guy; that's all."

"At least we were invited," Mom said. "Oh, when I read those letters to Ann Landers, I could cry: those poor bewildered souls who lose all touch with their grandchildren after the divorce. Why should *they* have to suffer? It's no fault of theirs if their sons can't manage to sustain a serious relationship!"

"You certainly have a way with words," I told her.

"Hmm?" she asked, and she veered around a tour bus. "What did I say?" she asked me.

I kept quiet and drummed my fingers on my knees.

"I suppose it's merely your generation," Mom said in a placating tone. "Everybody in your generation seems to view marriage so lightly."

"Generation!" I said. "I don't belong to a generation!"

Oops. The trick was to dodge to one side here; resist a head-on argument. I tried for a save. "Anyhow," I said, "generations nowadays seem to change over about every three years or so, have you noticed? Why is that, I wonder."

But Mom refused to get diverted. She said, "Mind you, I don't exempt Natalie's parents. Jim and Doris Bassett were at least as much to blame as you two were, I always felt. They actively encouraged that divorce!"

I just whistled a tune through my teeth and gazed out the side window. We were crossing a body of water. It looked very broad and peaceful.

"Say what you will," Mom told me, "but at least your father and I accepted your marriage graciously. I treated Natalie like my own! That's why she still asks me to Opal's recitals and such. Even if she does send just a standard mimeographed invitation with my name filled in on the blank."

She treated Natalie *better* than her own, I wanted to say. Miss High-Class Good-Girl Natalie, the daughter of Mom's dreams. But I let it rest. I watched a train skim across a railroad bridge in the distance, and I pondered whether it really was possible, these days, to get something mimeographed.

• • •

The recital was in the basement of a church on Chestnut Street. We had the devil's own time finding parking—ended up in a space several blocks away. "Now you see why I wanted to start out early," Mom told me. She tossed the words over her shoulder as she strode ahead of me, her purse clamped in a paranoid way between her arm and her rib cage. All the women around us looked just like her, tailored and crisp, with shoes that you just knew, somehow, had cost a whole lot of money. All the men were homeless. They sat huddled under ragged blankets on top of the grates in the sidewalk, and I couldn't help thinking that I had more in common with them than with my mother.

In the church basement the women were younger, and most of them had husbands in tow. I saw no sign of Natalie or *her* husband, though— not that I tried very hard. I settled in a folding chair and made a telescope out of my program. (Which did seem mimeographed.) My mother started chattering in this chirpy, chipmunk tone she puts on when she feels ill at ease, giving me a whole rundown of an avant-garde play she'd recently dragged my father to. Maybe the sight of the stage had brought it to her mind. "First the actors came out all bundled up in down jackets," she told me, "and as the play went on they stripped off a layer of clothes, see, and then another layer, till by the last act they were down to nothing."

"They were naked?"

"It was meant to be symbolic."

"They just walked around the stage with no clothes on?"

"I promise you, it didn't seem the least bit shocking. These were just ordinary, middle-aged men and women. Some were overweight, even. Your father said he wished the move had been in the opposite direction— *adding* clothes, not taking them off."

I laughed. My mother said, "I don't know why you menfolk always have to have culture just forced down your throats."

Then here was Natalie, wearing a dark-brown dress that made you notice her brown eyes—so secretive and distinctly lidded. "Hello, Mother Gaitlin," she said. "And Barnaby," she added. "You've met Howard, I believe."

Howard stood just behind her, a silver-haired, portly man holding an enormous paper cone of sweetheart roses. He gave a deep nod that was almost a bow, and my mother said, "Yes, certainly," although I wasn't all that sure they *had* met. He and I had, of course, when it couldn't be avoided. When we accidentally crossed paths exchanging Opal or what- ever. I said, "How you doing?" and then raised my chin and squinted at the stage while Mom and Natalie took care of so-thoughtful-of-you-to- invite-us and so-good-of-you-to-come.

When we were alone again, Mom said, "That went very well, in my considered opinion."

I felt extremely tired, all at once. I saw that nothing could be said on this earth that wasn't predictable. Even the bands of sunlight slanting through the basement windows were predictable, and the milky white swirls on the green linoleum floor, and the clunky-sounding "Teddy Bears' Picnic" coming over the PA system.

And the recital: well, you can't get much more predictable than a children's ballet recital. The youngest ones were dazed and obedient, milling around in tufts of pink gauze with their eyes fixed trustingly on Madame Whosit in the wings. The middle group—Opal's group—was a bristle of gawky arms and legs struggling to form a straight line. I hadn't realized before that Opal was so big for her age. She stood a full head above the others, down at the end, where (I guessed) she was meant to be less conspicuous. When they all set their heels together and pointed their toes sideways, she was the only one with no space showing between her thighs. In each position she teetered a bit after the others had frozen, and I felt certain that the audience noticed.

But my mother said, "Wasn't that precious?" applauding with just the tips of her fingers once the piece was over.

Between acts the curtain came down, but you could see it poking out first one place and then another as children jostled behind it. It made me think of a pregnancy—Natalie's pregnant stomach, the baby's knee or elbow knobbing the plaid material of her smock.

Not so long ago, amazingly enough.

It felt like a lifetime.

The oldest girls came last and showed us how it *should* be done, but I was too tired to watch. I let the dancers in front of me turn into a blur, and when the rest of the audience clapped, I just folded my arms and studied the acoustic tiles in the ceiling.

We met down in front near the stage at the end of the show—Mom and I, Natalie and Howard, Opal still in her tutu. She was hugging the cone of roses. I said, "I didn't bring any flowers myself. I didn't have a chance to buy some. I would have, but I didn't have a chance."

Before Opal could tell me it was all right, though, Mom rushed in with, "You were the best of the bunch, honey pie!" The level stare Opal gave her struck me as disconcertingly cynical, till I remembered she always looked that way. It was a hand-me-down from Natalie—Natalie's calmness, magnified.

"I messed up on the curtsy," she said, turning to me.

"Well, if you did, nobody noticed," I told her.

"Madame Stepp's going to yell at me."

"Your dance teacher's named Madame Stepp?"

Howard gave a dry cough. "Ah . . . we had thought we might take Opal to a congratulatory lunch," he said. "You're welcome to join us, Barnaby, Mrs. Gaitlin . . ."

"Oh, I guess not," I hurried to tell him. "We should be heading back."

No one argued—not even Mom, thank heaven. "Yes," she said. "I've left poor Jeffrey holding down the fort alone!"

We stood around a moment longer, all of us no doubt picturing Dad in the throes of some kitchen emergency. (Although I knew for a fact that he spent Saturdays at the office.) Then I gave Opal's shoulder a squeeze and said, "So long, Ope. You did great. I'm sorry I didn't bring flowers." And the two of us walked out.

In the car, my mother said, "Natalie's gained some weight, don't you think?" It was her way of acting chummy—showing me she was on my side. I didn't bother answering.

"Of course, she always had that wide, smooth face," Mom went on. "Almost a *flat* face, some might say. I like a bit of an edge to a person's face, don't you?"

"He had no business taking over lunch like that," I said, all at once realizing.

"What, dear?"

"Lunch was *my* time. It's part of my Saturday visit. Then he horns in on it and makes it seem like a favor to ask us along."

"Well, I wouldn't let it upset me," Mom said, slowing for a stoplight.

"I should have said, 'Thanks, but we've already made plans to eat with Opal on her own. Reservations,' I should have said. 'Reservations for three,' so they couldn't say they'd join us. Good grief! It's not as if we're all best buddies!"

"He didn't mean any harm," Mom told me. "He seemed like a very nice man. A bit old, though, don't you agree? Is he a lot older than Natalie?"

"I wouldn't have any idea," I said.

"Of course, Natalie always did have something of a father fixation."

The light changed, but Mom didn't notice till someone behind her honked. Then she gave a start and drove on. She said, "Remember how she used to phone her father at work every day? She phoned him every morning the whole time you were married, even though you were living not twenty feet away from him."

We lived above her parents' garage—practically in their laps. Which didn't help the marriage any, believe me. Every little thing I did—take a day off from classes, say, or come home a tad bit late or not at all—they would watch and judge and comment on to Natalie. But hey, it was rent-free; don't knock it. In fact, I stayed on there after we split up, although it got kind of awkward once I started dating again. Finally her father came over and had a little talk with me; said maybe I should consider moving. I didn't make it easy for him. I said, "Your daughter was the one who walked out, Mr. Bassett. I fail to see why *I* should be dislodged from my established residence." But I did find another place, by and by. Just not the very instant he suggested it.

Now Mr. Bassett was dead of a stroke, and his widow lived in Clear-

water, Florida. Everything seemed to have changed in a flash, when I got
to looking back on it.

"Opal has Jim Bassett's eyes, have you noticed?" Mom was asking.
"His eyes were his best feature—that pale shade of gray. I was thinking after the recital; I looked at Opal and I said to myself, 'Isn't that a coincidence! Her eyes are the color of opals.' "

I pictured Mr. Bassett's eyes when I'd reminded him his daughter had
walked out. "But, Barnaby," he had said, "what actual choice did she
have?" With his upper lids crinkling, honestly perplexed. Then I pictured
Opal's eyes, so measuring and veiled.

I have a problem, sometimes, after I come away from a place. I'll start
out feeling fine, but just a few minutes later I'll get to reconsidering. I'll regret that I've said something rude, that I've disappointed people or hurt
their feelings. I'll see that I have messed up yet again, and I'll call myself
all manner of names. Freak of the week! Nerd of the herd! And I'll wish I
could rearrange my life so I'd never have to deal anymore with another
human being.

It was nearly two p.m. before I got home. Mom offered to stop for lunch
somewhere, but I said no, even though I was starving; so first thing after I
walked in the door, I made myself a sandwich. Then I checked my answering machine. Four messages.

Mrs. Dibble said, "Barnaby, I know it's a Philadelphia day, but Mrs.
Figg has the idea that you'd promised to move her husband's computer
down to their den. I told her she must be mistaken, but you know how
she is. Anyway, call me if you get back anytime soon."

Then: "Hello, Barnaby. This is Sophia, at eight-fifteen Saturday morning. Just wondered if you'd be taking the train to Philly today, by any
chance! I thought I could give you a ride to Penn Station. Oh, well! I'll try
you later, I guess."

After that, a cranky-voiced woman: "Now, how do I . . . oh, I hate
these machines!" Mrs. Figg herself, although clients were not supposed to
telephone us directly. "Where have you got to, Barnaby? You said you'd
come move my husband's computer!"

And finally Sophia again: "Just trying you one more time before I head
for the station! I guess you've decided to go by car. Well, maybe next
time." Her tone was airy and casual, with a flicker of a laugh behind her
goodbye.

I sighed and punched the Delete button.

I used to have friends to hang out with on weekends. Ray Oakley at
work, before he got married. Martine before she met Everett. Or some of
the guys from my old neighborhood, but they'd mostly moved away now,
or turned all important and busy like Len. And I hadn't dated a girl in
months. I *wanted* a girlfriend, but lately it seemed girls were getting

younger and younger. They'd begun to seem just plain silly, with their gig-gly enthusiasm and their surfer-type vocabulary and their twitchy little miniskirts.

And I never counted my clients as friends—not even the ones I liked. Clients could up and die on you.

A few years ago, when they were making a public to-do over laying the last stone at the National Cathedral, I read an interview in the paper with a guy who'd seen the *first* stone laid, in nineteen-oh-something-or-other. He said he'd been just a little boy then, and his father took him to the ceremony. That story caught my fancy, for some reason. I pictured a kid in high button shoes and a ribbon-trimmed hat, hanging on to his father's hand in a great cobbled square among crowds of cheering people. Then one by one the people started dimming. They grew pale and then trans-parent, and finally they disappeared. The father disappeared and the men in bowler hats and the women in long cloaks, until the only one left was that little boy standing all, all alone.

Sunday, I woke up late, because I'd had a bad night. I'd tossed and turned and dreamed sketchy dreams I couldn't quite remember. It was well past noon before I really got going.

The weather was gray and cold, with needles of sleet that pricked my face as soon as I stepped outside. Ice glazed my windshield. I scraped it off and let the engine warm up, and then I drove very slowly, braking as easily as possible at each intersection. Almost no other cars were on the road. The radio announcer said the sleet would continue till evening. A good thing it was a Sunday, he said, when most of us could stay home.

In Penn Station, no more than six or eight people sat far apart on the benches, buried in coats and scarves and looking grumpy.

First I checked the board. Southbound trains were due in at 1:19, 2:35, and 3:11. It was 1:07 by this time, but the 1:19 was fifteen minutes late, wouldn't you know; so I went off to the newsstand and bought myself a paper. Then I settled on a bench and started reading. When the first ar-rivals filed in, I watched both doors but I didn't stand up, because I doubted this was my train. And I was right. I didn't see anybody familiar. I went back to reading the sports section.

By 2:35 I'd finished every shred of the paper, but I held off on a return trip to the newsstand till I'd checked out the next batch of passengers. They came in at 2:43, although the board didn't warn us about the delay. (These Penn Station folks could be sneaky sometimes.) First an entire family slogged through—parents, grandparents, several kids, dressed to brave a blizzard. I set my paper aside and stood up. Next came a teenage couple in hooded jackets, toting knapsacks. And next came Sophia.

She was bareheaded—the only one who was, so far. Even in this gray light, her hair had a warm yellow glow. She didn't see me yet. She shifted her bag to her other hand, and she fastened the top button of her coat. Then she happened to glance in my direction. She came to a stop. We stood about ten feet apart. She said, "Barnaby?"

"Hi," I told her.

"How come you're traveling *today?*"

"I'm not."

"Well . . . is something wrong? Is it Aunt Grace?"

"Nothing's wrong," I told her. "I just came to drive you home."

Her mouth took on a tentative look, as if she were about to smile, but she stayed serious. She said, "My car, though."

"What about your car?"

"It's parked here in the lot."

"Never mind," I told her. "We'll pick it up tomorrow, when the sleet's stopped."

She let herself smile then. And I was smiling too. I cupped her elbow to guide her through the station. Her coat sleeve was as soft against my palm as a kitten's belly. It made me feel protective, and capable, and determined. It made me feel grown up.

7

"When I was a young slip of a thing," Sophia's aunt said, "I used to have so much trouble adjusting to a new year. We'd change from, oh, 1929 to 1930, but I'd go on writing '1929' at the tops of my letters for months, for literally months. Now, though, it's no problem whatsoever. I suppose that's because time has speeded up so, I've grown accustomed to making the switch: 1980, 1990 . . . You could tell me to date this check '2000' and I wouldn't bat an eye!"

She was sweeping the check through the air to dry it, although she'd filled it out with a ballpoint pen. I stood waiting beside her desk till she felt ready to hand it over. Apparently she was one of those clients who preferred not to pay their monthly bills by mail. (No sense wasting a stamp, they'd say, when a Rent-a-Back employee would be coming by the house.)

"You'll find out for yourself one day," she said. "Personal time works the opposite way from historical time. Historical time starts with a swoop—dinosaurs, cavemen, lickety-split!—and then slows and takes on more detail as it gets more recent: all those niggling little four-year presidential terms. But with personal time, you begin at a crawl—every leaf and bud, every cross-eyed look your mother ever gave you—and you gather speed as you go. To me, it's a blurry streak by now."

"Yes, ma'am," I said. It began to seem I would never get hold of this check. "I thought you mistrusted banks, though," I said. "How come you're not paying in cash?"

Mrs. Glynn lowered the check and peered at me over her eye pouches. All I'd done was delay things even further. "You haven't heard a word I said," she told me.

"Yes, I have! I promise! Change of dates, time speeding up, personal versus historical . . ."

"You're still so young, you can't imagine any of it will ever apply."

"Believe me, I'm not *that* young," I said.

She raised the check again, but only to blow on the signature. Then she said, "I do mistrust banks. I wouldn't dream of using one if it were up to me. However, my monthly allowance comes from my lawyer, and he insists on sending it to an account. Any money left over, it's *my* decision where I keep it."

Now she was holding the check at arm's length and studying her signature. She seemed to be having trouble placing the name. I shifted from my right foot to my left.

"The lawyer and my niece are in collusion, I believe," she told me. "Sophia's always nagging me: 'What if the house should burn down? Or what if you were robbed? Half of Baltimore knows where you stash your money.' 'Fine, then, I'll change the location,' I say, and she says, 'You are living in the past, Aunt Grace.' 'Indeed I am,' I tell her. I tell her, and I tell that lawyer too, who's young enough to be my grandson. 'You-all don't remember the Great Depression,' I say, 'when banks were falling like building blocks and grown, respectable men were sobbing in the streets.' "

If the lawyer was young enough to be her grandson, he could be Sophia's age. Were they really in collusion? Did they meet to discuss her problem aunt over drinks, over dinner, in some candlelit restaurant where I myself couldn't afford to buy her so much as a salad?

Nowadays it seemed to me that anyone in his right mind would have to want Sophia for his own.

"But here," Mrs. Glynn said, all at once passing me the check. "Tatters, say bye-bye to Barnaby."

I folded the check and slipped it into my rear jeans pocket. "Thanks, Mrs. Glynn. See you Monday," I told her, and I was out the door before she could get started on a new topic.

Down Keswick, down University Parkway, to St. Paul, and then over to Calvert. It was only the middle of March, but there'd been a burst of unseasonably warm weather—highs near eighty, the last few days—and people were jogging or walking their dogs or just standing talking on street corners, looking aimless and carefree. I felt I was back in high school. In high school, when I went out with girls, it always seemed to be spring; the girls were always wearing spring dresses, and I was in short sleeves.

Sophia lived in a solid old brick row house with wide front steps and a porch. It was just a rental, but she had fixed up the little yard as if she owned it; you could tell even now, when things weren't blooming yet. And last weekend she'd bought two window boxes and set them on the concrete railing, ready to be filled with petunias as soon as all danger of frost was past.

It was her roommate who answered the door. Wouldn't you know Sophia would have a roommate? Roommates are so wholesome. I picture them in quilted white bathrobes, their faces scrubbed and their teeth freshly brushed, although whenever I'd seen Betty she was wearing one of those pink trouser outfits that're trying not to look like a uniform. She worked in a hospital; she was some kind of pediatric health care person. A bony, spectacled woman with painfully short black hair and paper-white skin. "Sophia will be down in a minute," she told me, and then she went off somewhere and left me to my own devices. She disapproved of me, I sensed. Well, never mind.

I liked Sophia's living room—the staidness of it, the good, worn furniture handed down from relatives. When I sat in her grandfather's big recliner, it gave out a weary wheeze. Through the arched doorway I could see the dining room (claw-footed table, antique breakfront), and I knew that the kitchen, too, was comfortably old-fashioned. The upstairs I had to guess at, but I was willing to bet that she slept in a four-poster bed.

Now I heard her footsteps descending the stairs. When she walked in, I jumped up and said, "Oh! Hi!" as if she'd taken me by surprise. I don't know why I behave like such an idiot, sometimes.

"Hi," she said.

We kissed, and she stepped back.

She was wearing a navy skirt and a flowered blouse. She had this way of looking into my eyes and then quickly glancing down at her own bosom and smiling.

"Come into the kitchen," she told me. "Supper's almost ready."

The kitchen table was set for two, and the Crock-Pot on the counter gave off the smell of tomato sauce. In the mornings before she went to work, Sophia would put supper in the Crock-Pot. Then when she got home all she had to do was fix a vegetable. I don't know when the roommate ate. She never joined us, although if she happened to walk through the kitchen Sophia always offered to lay a place for her.

"How was your day?" Sophia asked, emptying a box of frozen peas into a saucepan.

"Oh, pretty good." I sat in a chrome-and-vinyl chair that must have dated from the forties. "Your Aunt Grace had me take down her storm windows," I said. "I told her it was too early, but she insisted. 'Mark my words,' I told her, 'winter will be back before next week is out,' but you know how she is. Monday, I'm putting her screens in."

"I can't imagine why she bothers," Sophia said. "She never opens her windows anyway."

"No; most of that age group doesn't. Scared of burglars."

"With her, it's she's eternally cold. You'll see: she'll be wearing a sweater in July."

I liked the thought that I'd be seeing Mrs. Glynn in July. That meant I'd be seeing Sophia too. I studied the back of her neck as she worked, and her smooth, netted bun. I hadn't seen a hair net on a bun in years, and now I wondered why; this one was so seductive. All I could think of was slipping it off, letting her hair tumble out of it.

She filled our two plates and then sat down across from me, smoothing her skirt beneath her. Her thighs, I thought, would be very pale and soft and fleshy. I stared at her like someone in a trance, till she asked me, "How's the stew?"

"Oh! Delicious," I said, although I hadn't yet tasted it.

She raised her wineglass. "To us," she said.

"To us," I repeated.

The way she served wine tickled me: one glass for each of us with each dinner, already poured beforehand. Me, I was used to drinking either not at all or far too much. This *moderation* business was a whole new approach.

Upstairs, the roommate's shoes were creaking back and forth. I heard a door slam, then a drawer bang shut. "Is she mad about something?" I asked Sophia.

Sophia shrugged, which was answer enough.

"She thinks I'm a loser, doesn't she."

"Heavens, no! Why do you say that?"

I sliced into a chunk of potato and said, "She's pointed out to you that I'm basically no more than a manual laborer. That I have the fashion sense of a Hell's Angel, and my prospects for advancement are flat zero. Right?"

Sophia flushed and looked down at her bosom again.

"Not to mention I hold the title of World's Oldest Living Undergraduate," I said. Then I said, "Hey. You didn't tell her about the Renascence School and all that, did you?"

"Certainly not," Sophia said.

Even Sophia didn't know everything; just the more dashing highlights. We were in that stage where we were formally presenting each other with our pasts: Sophia's prim, Mary-Janed childhood, my nefarious adolescence. I liked the fondly nostalgic way she said, "When I was a little girl . . . ," and she liked the fact that I'd have struck her as slightly scary if she had met me in my teens. "You were one of those boys who hung around the corner in packs," she'd surmised. "Who piled twelve deep in a car and hooted out the windows. Who smelled of cigarettes when they brushed by me on the sidewalk."

"Oh, I never cared much for cigarettes," I'd told her. "I preferred to smoke the harder stuff."

Just to see her expression of thrilled horror.

Now she said, "Betty's merely a roommate. I got her name off a bulletin board. What do I care what she thinks?"

"Actually," I said, "it's not true that I have no prospects—I mean, if I wanted prospects. I could always get a job at Dad's foundation. Does Betty know about the Foundation?"

"I believe I did happen to mention it," Sophia said.

"Also, I've held the same one job for almost eleven years," I said. "That's more than you can say for a lot of other guys."

Sophia reached across the table and laid a hand over mine. "Barnaby," she said. "It's fine. *Whatever* you do. Really."

I squeezed her fingers.

Granted, Sophia wasn't the type I'd fallen for in the past. She was luxuriously padded, and she carried herself from the hips in a settled and matronly manner. She probably weighed more than I did, in fact, but I found this sexy. It made me conscious of my own wiriness, and the springy, electric energy in the muscles of my legs. Sitting on that vinyl chair, I had all I could do not to leap up and fling myself across the table. But I stayed where I was and just smiled at her, and then I speared a cube of beef.

After supper, we moved to the living room. We settled on her sofa, surrounded by dried flower arrangements and frilled glass candy dishes, and started kissing. Once we drew apart when we heard footsteps crossing the upstairs hall, but it was a false alarm and we resumed where we'd left off. I stroked her creamy skin and I cupped her lush, heavy breasts in the circle-stitched cotton bra that I could feel through the silk of her blouse. When Betty's footsteps crossed the hall again, we had to separate in a hurry and straighten our clothes.

I told Sophia she should come to my place. She turned pink; she knew what I was asking. She said, "Well, maybe soon. Give me a little more time." I didn't push it. I almost preferred it this way for now. I left her house whistling. I imagined she'd be slipping into a quilted bathrobe exactly like her roommate's, and scrubbing her face, and brushing her teeth, and settling down for the night in her four-poster bed.

It always seemed to happen that we lost a lot of our older folks at the tail end of winter. Just when the worst of the weather was behind us, when you'd think a person would be gathering strength and looking forward to spring, why, we'd get a sudden call from a relative, or we'd find a week's worth of newspapers littering a client's lawn. During the first half of March, Mrs. Gordoni went into the hospital and didn't come out again; Mr. Quentin succumbed to whatever illness he'd been battling for the past six years (he'd never named it, and we weren't supposed to ask); and Mr. Cartwright died of a heart attack. Now I took Mrs. Cartwright shopping all on her own, and she was very different—wavery and bewildered. Funny: I had thought *he* was the dependent one in that couple. But you never know. I took her to the grocery store and she walked the aisles with this testing sort of posture, placing the balls of her feet just so, as if she were wading a creek. "Isn't it ridiculous," she told me, "how even in the face of death it still matters that the price of oranges has gone up, and an impolite produce boy can still hurt your feelings." I didn't know what to say to that. I steered her toward the dairy case.

I thought about one time when I'd driven the Cartwrights to a pharmacy and Mr. Cartwright had paused in the doorway to announce, "This used to be a pharmacy!" in his loud, impervious, hard-of-hearing voice, and the other shoppers had all raised their heads and looked around them for a second, plainly wondering what it was *now*, for heaven's sake. I don't know why he said that. Maybe he was objecting to the heaps of extraneous merchandise, the beach chairs and electric blenders pharmacies seemed to stock these days. Maybe he was just confused. At any rate, remembering the slight jolt that had rippled through the store made me smile, and Mrs. Cartwright glanced up at me just then and happened to notice. I worried she'd be offended, but instead she smiled too. "You're a good boy, Barnaby," she said.

None of my customers had the least inkling of my true nature.

Then Mrs. Beeton died—that nice black lady whose children always fussed so. First I knew of it, I telephoned to see if I should pick up any groceries on my way to her house, and her daughter was the one who answered. Said, "Hello, Barnaby!" and chatted awhile, cheery as you please. Not a clue about her mother. Finally I said, "Could I talk to Mrs. Beeton a minute?" A silence. Then she said, "Let me give you to my husband, okay?" And her husband got on the line—a man I'd never met. "My mother-in-law has passed as of yesterday morning," he told me. I guess her daughter just couldn't say the words.

I'd always admired Mrs. Beeton. She had such a sweet, chuckly face, and this attractive darker outline to her upper lip. Dirt was her personal enemy. Let her catch sight of a cobweb and she would not rest until she'd killed it dead.

And then Maud May broke her hip and had to go to a nursing home. Maud May! My Tallulah client, with her movie-star cigarette holder and her pitchers of martinis and her drawling, leathery voice. I visited her to get instructions—which plants needed watering and so forth—because she swore this was not a permanent state of affairs. "No Vegetable Villa for me," she said; that was what she called nursing homes. "I'm getting out of here if I have to crawl on my hands and knees." Then she dropped to a whisper and asked me to bring her a carton of Marlboros. "Sure thing, Ms. May," I told her. (We're the muscles, not the brains.) But I sounded cockier than I felt. She'd given me a start, lying there so helpless. Why, Maud May was my foreign correspondent, you might call it, from the country of old age. She had this way of *reporting* on it in a distant, amused tone. "I used to think old age would make me more patient," she'd told me once, "but instead I find, oh, Gawd, it's turned me into a grouch." And another time: "Everybody claims to venerate older women, but when I ask what for, they all mention things like herbal medicine, and I can't tell an herb from a mule's ass."

Now she said, "Know what this feels like, Barnaby? Feels like I'm living someone else's life. This is not the *real me*, I want to say."

"Well, of course it's not," I told her.

But I must have spoken too quickly, or too easily or something, because she jerked her head on her pillow and said, "Don't be so goddamn patronizing!"

"Ms. May," I said, "I promise you'll be out of here before you know it. What this other client was telling me just a few days ago: the older you get, the faster the time goes. By now it's all a blur, she says."

"Wrong," Maud May said firmly.

"Wrong?"

"Time has stopped dead still," she said.

Then she gave a snort and said, "No pun intended."

I took Sophia down to Canton to visit my grandparents one evening, because they'd been complaining they never saw me anymore. We sat in their tiny living room (twelve feet wide, the width of the house) and watched TV while Gram shot sideways glances at Sophia. I hadn't warned them I'd be bringing her. I didn't want to answer any questions. So Gram was having to work things out for herself, calculating Sophia's age, gauging how close together we sat. Sweetheart? Friend? Mere acquaintance? Sophia faced the TV, pretending not to notice.

We were watching a game show on what had to have been the world's largest residential television set. The only place it could fit was against the long side wall of the living room. This meant we had to line the couch on the other side wall, with our noses practically touching the screen. Pop-Pop sat at one end, so he had someplace to put his beer can. I sat next to him, Sophia next to me, and Gram on the other end. The rest of the room was filled with plaster statues of the Virgin Mary, and ceramic planters shaped like wheelbarrows and donkeys, and praying hands molded from some kind of resin, and dolls dressed like Scarlett O'Hara. Oh, and I should mention that Pop-Pop wore a V-necked undershirt that showed his scrawny white-haired chest; and Gram was in a tight tank top and baggy army-green shorts. (The thermostat was set at about eighty-five degrees, although outdoors it was winter again.) I was interested in Sophia's reaction to all this, but I couldn't tell from her profile, which was edged with blue light from the game show.

Gram said, "Sophia. Would that be an Italian name?"

"It came from a great-aunt," Sophia told her, turning briefly in her direction.

"Was your great-aunt Italian?"

"No, Scottish."

"Oh."

I knew what Gram was aiming at here. She wanted to find out whether Sophia was Catholic. She poked her headful of pink curlers forward for a moment and looked at me.

"Presbyterian," I told her.

"Oh."

She sat back again. She sighed. Oh, well, you could see her thinking, her own daughter had married Episcopal and the sky hadn't fallen in. "It's a pretty name, anyhow," she told Sophia.

"Thank you."

"I like names that end with an *a*, don't you? Or other vowels. Well, what other vowels? Most often it seems to be *a*. But wait: Margo's name ends with an *o*, for mercy's sake! Barnaby's mother. Or it used to be *o*. Then she met Barnaby's father and added a *t*."

Sophia looked at me. I told her, "Mom thought Margot with a *t* was higher-class."

"First time I saw it written that way was on the wedding invitations," Gram said. "She brought them home from the printer's and I said, 'Who's this?' She said, 'That's me.' Well, I did try to accommodate. Her daddy said it was stuff and nonsense, but I told Jeffrey the next time he came to call, 'Mar-gott will be down in a minute.' He laughed because he thought I was joking, but I was serious. I honestly assumed people pronounced the *t*."

"Watch this next contestant," Pop-Pop told me. "She knows every fact there is to know about Elvis."

"She always was a go-getter," Gram said. "Very energetic. Very brainy. She won so many prizes when she was in school! I can't imagine where that came from."

"Margot, we're talking about," I explained to Sophia. She was looking puzzled.

"Folks would ask, 'Is she a changeling?' Because Frank didn't even graduate high school, and the only reason *I* did was to fill in the time till we married. But there must be a smarty gene somewhere in our family. Look at Barnaby! He's practically an Einstein. Learned to read so young, he used to check in the child development books to see how he ought to be acting."

"I had a very promising past," I told Sophia.

She smiled and turned her eyes back to Gram. On the TV, somebody flubbed a question. The audience gave a groan, and Pop-Pop said, "Why, *I* could've answered that one!"

Gram heaved herself from the couch to fetch us a snack, and Sophia rose and followed, asking, "Can I help?" She was doing everything right. Gram ought to love her.

Now it was just me and Pop-Pop, two skinny, puny males taking up the much smaller half of the sofa. We got started on one of those man-to-man talks that are all numerals—which cable channels he was subscribing to these days, how many quarts of oil my car was burning—while in the kitchen, above the clatter of dishes, I heard Gram doing her best to figure out who Sophia was, exactly. If I cocked an ear in their direction, I could keep tabs on them while listening to Pop-Pop reel off last week's bowling scores. No, she came from Philadelphia. And yes, she had a job; she worked at Chesapeake Bank. And she rented a place on Calvert Street;

shared it with a roommate. (Gram would find the fact of the roommate reassuring—less chance we were living in sin.) And it probably *did* seem odd that a girl like her hadn't been snapped up yet by some man, but she wanted to be sure she didn't make any mistakes, because marriage was for life, she'd always felt; and in fact, she had once been engaged and another time almost engaged, but it hadn't panned out, which now she realized must have been all for the best.

Then she said, "I met Barnaby on the train to Philly a few months back"—volunteering it, without any prodding from Gram. Evidently it told Gram what she wanted to know, because when they emerged with the food, she was treating us like a couple. It was "you two" this and "you two" that, and, "Next time, the two of you will have to come for a meal."

The snack she'd fixed was a recipe she'd read about in a magazine— Bill Clinton's favorite, corn chips with a dip made of bottled salsa and Velveeta cheese melted in the microwave. She served it on a tray that showed a head-and-shoulders portrait of John F. Kennedy. "I see we're going with a presidential theme tonight," I said, and Gram jabbed an elbow into Sophia's ribs and asked, "Isn't he a cutup?"—rolling her eyes and giggling as if they shared a secret.

In the car as we were driving home, Sophia said she had liked my grandparents very much. "They liked you too," I said. I was partly proud and partly taken aback. I hadn't expected Sophia to get so *into* it, somehow. After a moment, I said, "You never told me you had been engaged."

She shrugged and said, "It didn't last long."

"Who was the guy?" I asked her.

"Oh, someone at the bank."

"And another time *almost* engaged? What happened?"

"It just didn't work out," she told me. "I'm probably too set in my ways. Too, you know. Definite. Too definite for men to feel comfortable with."

She was wearing the dressy black coat that made her hair look blonder, and the carriage of her head struck me as queenly. I said, "Well, I think definite women are great." She looked over at me and smiled. "If there's anything I'm crazy about, it's definiteness," I said.

She laughed. I got a little carried away; I said, "In fact, I've always dreamed of a having a military wife."

"Oh?" she said. "You mean a soldier?"

"No, someone whose husband's a soldier," I said. "I've seen them in the movies. They know how to do everything that needs doing. They could probably build their own houses, if they had to, and deliver their own babies. If that's not definite!"

"So . . . would this mean that you're planning to enlist?" she asked.

"Enlist! God forbid," I told her.

"Then how . . . ?"

"I only meant . . . ," I said. "Shoot, I'm just talking out loud." Which was an expression Mrs. Beeton used to use: Don't mind me; I'm just talking out loud.

Dummy.

News of all the deaths spread magically among our other clients. I've never figured out how that happens. It's not as if our people know each other, for the most part. But I could sense the agitation in just about every house I went to. Mrs. Rodney got the notion to update her will; so did Miss Simmons. Mr. Shank called on us even more often than he normally did, on even more trumped-up excuses, and one time insisted that I drive him to the emergency room, when as far as I could see there was not one thing the matter with him. I said, "What is it? Are you short of breath? Chest pains? Weak? Dizzy?" All he would say was, he felt "unusual." For the sake of his unusualness I spent three and a half hours in the Sinai Hospital waiting room, watching homemaking shows on TV. "What I like to do," this lady on one program said, "I like to place a lead crystal bowl on the credenza in my entrance hall. I fill it with tinted water and I float scented votive candles on the surface, to lend a sense of graciousness when I'm entertaining." A roomful of sick people—bleak-faced, bleary-eyed, most in threadbare clothes—stared up at her in astonishment. Mr. Shank turned out to be suffering from stress and was sent home with a prescription for some pills.

Then Mrs. Alford started sorting her belongings. That's always a worrisome sign. For a solid week she had three of us come in daily—me, Ray Oakley, and Martine. ("Two men for the real lifting," was how she put it, "and a girl so as to encourage the hiring of women.") She wanted her basement sorted, then her garage, then her attic. This was in mid-April—a busy time for us anyhow, plus it was near Easter and lots of grown children were expected home and our clients were overexcited and crabby and demanding. But Mrs. Alford couldn't wait, couldn't put it off. Each morning she met us on her front porch, or even halfway down the walk. "There you are! What kept you?" Martine didn't have the truck that week; so I had to pick her up, which once or twice made us late, and Ray Oakley was late by nature. But we're only talking minutes here. Still, Mrs. Alford would be fretting and pacing. Half the time she called Martine "Celeste," which was the name of our other female employee, and I was "Terry."

"It's Barnaby, Mrs. Alford," I said as gently as possible.

"Oh! I'm sorry! I thought your name was Terry and you played in that musical group."

Martine snickered—picturing me, I guess, at the harpsichord or something. "No, ma'am," I told Mrs. Alford. "Must be somebody else."

In my early days at Rent-a-Back, I'd have feared she was losing her marbles. But I knew, by now, that it was just anxiety. I've had an anxious client mistake me for her firstborn son; then next day, she'd be bright as a tack. I didn't let it faze me.

Sorting the basement was easy, because that was mostly stuff to be thrown out. Paint tins that no longer sloshed; mildewed rolls of leftover wallpaper; galvanized buckets so old they'd been patched with metal disks by some long-dead tinker. We crammed them all into garbage cans and hoped the city would collect them. It took us less than a day. I had time to drop Martine off and check my messages before I headed to Mrs. Glynn's.

The garage was where it got harder. Mrs. Alford's husband had left a fully stocked workbench there—the lovingly tended kind, with each tool hung on the backboard within its own painted silhouette. Mrs. Alford must have dreaded to face it, because when we showed up the next morning, she managed to get our names one hundred percent wrong. "Hello, Celeste. Hello, Roy. Hello, Terry." None of us corrected her. On her way up the back steps to the garage, she asked me, "How's the music?" and I said, "Oh, fine," because it seemed easier.

But then she wouldn't let go of it. She said, "Now, what is it you play, again?"

"The . . . tuba," I decided.

"Tuba!" She paused at the top of the steps and looked at me. One hand pitty-patting the speckled flesh at the base of her throat. "Funny," she said. "I had thought it was something stringed."

"No, it's the tuba, all right," I said, wishing I'd never begun this.

"Fancy that! A tuba in a chamber group! I hadn't heard of such a thing."

"Oh," I said. "Ah. Chamber. You hadn't?"

"But what do I know?" she asked me. "I'm such a babe in the woods when it comes to music."

"Well, that's all right, Mrs. Alford."

We walked through her backyard, where daffodils were blooming in clumps. "I haven't been to the garage in years," Mrs. Alford said. "I never go! I don't like to go." She stopped at the door, inserted a key in the lock, and turned the knob. Nothing happened. "Oh, well. I guess we can't get in, after all," she said.

"Allow me," Ray Oakley told her. He set his shoulder to the door—he was a big guy, with a giant beer belly—and gave it a shove and fell into the garage.

"Why, thank you, Roy," Mrs. Alford said, sounding not the least bit grateful.

Mr. Alford's workbench was one of those objects that seem to go on living after their owner dies. And clearly he had been a hoarder. The rows of baby-food jars on the shelves were filled with various sizes of screws in generally poor condition—some bent, some dulled, some rusted. You just knew he'd saved them for decades, even though his wife had probably begged him to get rid of them. I said, "Tell you what, Mrs. A. You go on back to the house and we'll see to this without you."

"But how will you know what to do with it all?" Mrs. Alford asked. A reasonable question. She wandered the length of the workbench, reaching up to touch a coping saw here, a claw hammer there. "My nephew, Ernie: he's very good with his hands," she told us. "I should probably give these to him."

"And the screws and things?"

"Well . . . ," she said.

"Chuck them?"

She went over to the baby-food jars. She picked one up and looked at it.

"We'll settle that," I told her. "You go on back to the house."

This time she didn't argue.

So the garage took us slightly longer, what with locating empty cartons and packing them with tools and writing *Ernie* across the top, and stuffing all the discards into trash bags. "How do people end up with so many *things*?" I asked Martine. "Look here: a bamboo rake with three prongs left to it, total."

"A rotary telephone," Martine said, "labeled *Does Not Work*." She held it up.

"I hope she's not fixing to die on us," I said.

"Why would you think that?"

"I've seen it before. It's something like when pregnant cats start hunting drawer space: old people start sorting their possessions."

"Oh, don't say that! Mrs. Alford's one of my favorites."

I had never given Mrs. Alford much thought one way or another. She didn't have the zing that, say, Maud May had. But I wouldn't want to see her die.

"Sounds to me," Ray Oakley said, "like you two are in the wrong business."

"Listen to him: Mr. Tough Guy," I told Martine.

Then on Wednesday, Ray called in sick, and we had to start the attic on our own. What Mrs. Alford wanted was, we would carry everything down to the glassed-in porch off her bedroom, where she sat in a skirted armchair, waiting to tell us what pile to put it in: Ernie's, or her daughter's, or Goodwill. "How about the Twinform?" I asked her right off.

"Pardon?"

"That mannequin-type thing," I said, because I'd already made up my mind to offer money for it if she put it in the Goodwill pile.

But she said, "Oh, I'll keep that. It reminds me of my mother."

She kept a lot. A humidor that used to be her father's, a pipe rack of her husband's, a cradle that dozens of Alfords had slept in when they were small. Each object we hauled down, she'd make us stand there holding while she told us the story that went with it. And it seemed that the more she remembered of the past, the more she forgot of the present. "Should you be lifting that, Celeste?" she asked Martine, and she mentioned twice again that Ernie was good with his hands. But when I wondered aloud how a big rolltop desk had managed to go up the attic steps in one piece, she was able to recall that it hadn't gone up in one piece. Her husband had dismantled it first. "The top half's attached to the bottom half with four brass screws under the corners," she said, and she went on to recollect that her husband and her brother-in-law had carried the two parts up in the summer of '59. "You'll find a screwdriver on my husband's workbench," she said. Then she said, "Oh, no! His tools are gone now!" and her eyes glazed over with tears.

I said, "Never mind, Mrs. A. I can dig that screwdriver out in half a second. I know just which box I put it in."

She rearranged her face into an appreciative, bright expression. "Why, thank you, Terry," she said. "Aren't you clever!" And she kept her eyes very wide so that the tears wouldn't spill over.

When we were back in the attic, Martine said, "Ray had better not be sick tomorrow, I tell you." We were struggling at the time with the top half of the desk—Martine's hair sticking out in spikes around her face—but I knew it wasn't the lifting that concerned her. We needed someone more hardhearted here, was what.

Thursday, Ray returned, greenish under the eyes and still not good for much, and we stationed him downstairs with Mrs. Alford. While he shoved items from pile to pile and listened to her stories, we did the hauling. Even then, we got waylaid a time or two. We brought down a piano bench, and Mrs. Alford wanted it placed in front of her so that she could sort the sheet music stored inside. When she lifted the lid, the smell of mice floated out. " 'I'm Always Chasing Rainbows,' " she said. She spoke so wistfully, so regretfully, that it took me a second to realize she was only quoting a song title. " 'Don't Bring Lulu.' 'You Must Have Been a Beautiful Baby.' " Once, the house key Martine wore around her wrist clinked against a metal footlocker we were carrying, and the sound must have touched off a memory in Mrs. Alford's head. Out of the blue, she said, "I used to have a wind chime made of copper circles, but then my neighbor came and told me, 'Please take down your wind chime; please. A wind chime was tinkling the whole entire time I tended my daughter's last illness, and now I can't bear to hear it.' "

We set the footlocker on the floor. "Well, of course I took it down," she said.

"Yes, ma'am," Ray said. "Ernie's pile, or your daughter's?"

Martine and I scooted back upstairs.

Friday, we found Mrs. Alford's brother eating breakfast with her—a tufty-haired, plump old man in a business suit. He'd arrived the night before for the Easter weekend. And Mrs. Alford was her merry self again, graciously introducing us all, ticking off our names perfectly. The three of us went up to the attic and finished clearing it out in no time, after which

Mrs. Alford came to the glassed-in porch and said, "This goes to Ernie, this to Valerie, this to Goodwill," zip-zip-zip. She didn't even bother sitting in her armchair. We were done by midafternoon.

I gave Martine a lift home, because she still didn't have the truck. Neither one of us talked much. I was calculating the time, wondering if I could fit some other assignment in before I went to Mrs. Glynn's. Martine was hanging her head out the window and humming to herself. Then all at once she pulled in her head and said, "Know what happened the other day? I was playing catch with my nephews in their backyard. And they were having this discussion—about my brother, I thought it was. 'He says this, he says that.' So I ask, 'What time's he due home tonight?' and they get quiet and sort of embarrassed and they look at each other and I'm thinking, *What? What'd I say?* And one of them tells me, 'Uh . . .' And the other says, 'Uh, actually, we were talking about our baseball coach.' I said, 'Oh. Sorry. I thought you meant your dad.' But it gave me this sudden picture of what it must feel like to be old. I mean, so old that people imagine you've gone dotty. I wanted to say, 'Wait! I just heard you wrong, is all. It was a natural, normal mistake to make, okay?' "

Then she hung her head out the window again, and we went back to our separate lines of thought.

Sophia and I drove up to Philadelphia on the last Saturday in April. This was my second trip to Philly since we'd started dating, but she hadn't come with me before because her mother had spent the past six weeks at a cousin's condominium in Miami. So here we were, taking our first long car ride together on a sunny blue-and-yellow morning with a little bit of a breeze, and I felt like a million dollars. Sophia did too; I could tell. She said, "I should *always* go by car! You get to see so much more countryside than you do when you take the train."

I hadn't told Sophia about watching her on the train that day. I guess I thought it would make me look sort of, I don't know, sly, the way I'd engineered our meeting afterward. And besides, I was curious to see if she would bring it up on her own. In her place, I'd have bragged about it straight off. ("Want to hear how a total stranger singled me out and approached me and entrusted me with a mission?") But she never did. Either she considered it not worth mentioning or she'd forgotten it altogether. Probably things like that happened to her all the time. She must have just taken them for granted.

A lot of our trip was spent discussing her mother, who didn't sound very likable. "Every weekend of my life," Sophia said, "she expects me to stay with her, unless of course she has plans, in which case she lets me know at the very last minute: 'Oh, by the way, don't bother coming this week,' when I've practically bought my ticket already. . . ."

She was listing her mother's physical ailments when we entered the city limits. Don't I know that kind of old lady! I drove up Broad Street and turned onto Walnut, while Sophia cataloged aches and pains and palpitations, doctor appointments, midnight phone calls ... She interrupted herself to point out her mother's apartment building, which had a green-striped awning. I double-parked in front of it. "Oh!" she said. "There's Mother now!"

Sure enough, a big-boned, white-haired woman in a sweater set and matching skirt stood twisting her hands together on the curb. "Come and say hello," Sophia told me.

I have never been the meet-the-parents type. I said, "Oh, I'd better not. I'm blocking traffic."

But Sophia was calling, "Yoo-hoo! Mother!" as she slid out of the passenger seat, leaving her door wide open behind her.

Mrs. Maynard turned, blank-faced. Then she said, "Sophia? What on earth! You came by auto? You're so late!"

While they were pressing their cheeks together, I made a lunge across the seat and tried to shut Sophia's door without being seen. But no: "I'd like to introduce you to someone," Sophia told her mother.

So I was forced to show myself. I left my engine running, though. I stepped out and rounded the front of the car and said, "How do you do. Sorry, but I'm double-parked; I really have to be going."

"This is Barnaby Gaitlin," Sophia told her mother. "My mother, Thelma Maynard."

"I said to myself," Mrs. Maynard told her, " 'Well, that's it. Sophia's met with some accident, *I* don't know what accident, and the police will have no idea that I'm her next of kin. I'll be sitting in my apartment Saturday, Sunday, Monday, without anyone to shop for me or fetch my prescriptions. I'll run out of food, run out of pills; just get weaker and weaker, and they'll find me who-can-say-how-long after, shriveled up like a prune and lying on my—' "

"Barnaby and I have been seeing quite a lot of each other," Sophia said.

Mrs. Maynard stopped speaking and looked over at me. She had one of those rectangular faces, pulled downward at the corners by two strong cords in her neck.

"How do you do," I said again. I would have shaken hands, except that she didn't hold hers out.

See why I hate meeting parents? I don't make a good first impression.

Mrs. Maynard turned back to Sophia and said, "You might at least have telephoned and warned me you'd be late. You know perfectly well what tension does to my blood pressure!"

We hadn't been *that* late. Maybe half an hour or so. But Sophia didn't bother arguing. She said, in this forthright manner, "Barnaby has become a very important part of my life."

I froze. So did her mother. She gave me another look. "Oh?" she said. Then she said, "Mr. . . . . ?"

"Gaitlin," I said.

Someone honked in the street behind me, no doubt wanting me to move my car, but I didn't turn around.

Sophia's mother asked, "Just what is your line of business, Mr. Gaitlin?"

"I'm, ah, employed by a service organization," I told her.

It came out sounding sort of smarmy, for some reason. Sophia must have thought so too, because she raised her eyebrows at me. Then she gave a sharp hitch to the shoulder strap of her bag. She said, "He works for a place called Rent-a-Back, Mother, lifting heavy objects."

"Lifting?" Mrs. Maynard asked.

I said, "Well, there's more to it than—"

"What *kind* of heavy objects?"

"Oh . . . ," I said. "In fact! I've been helping Mrs. Glynn some. Sophia's aunt. I don't know if you and she are in touch or—"

"I met him on the train a couple of months ago," Sophia broke in. "I guess you could call it a pickup."

"Pickup?" Mrs. Maynard asked faintly, at the same time that I said, "Pickup!" I stared at Sophia.

Sophia kept her gaze fixed levelly on her mother. She said, "He sat in the seat next to me, and before I knew it I had agreed to go out with him."

"Really," Mrs. Maynard said.

I wanted to explain that it hadn't been that way at all; that things had happened a good deal more inch by inch than that. But I could see what Sophia was up to here. I recognized that triumphant tilt of her chin. And I couldn't much blame her, either. With a mother like Mrs. Maynard, I'd have done the same.

Besides, the situation did work to my advantage. Because when Sophia said goodbye to me—walking me to my side of the car, ignoring the honking traffic—she kissed me on the lips and whispered, "When I get back to Baltimore, I want to come to your place."

Then she gave me a deliberate, slow smile that turned my knees weak, and she went to rejoin her mother.

8

By the end of April I'd saved eight hundred and sixteen dollars. I had
hoped to be farther along, but no matter how hard I tried, I couldn't seem
to meet my goal of a hundred extra per week. Well, at least it was a start.
I got myself a savings account and a little cardboard booklet to record all
further deposits.

For most of May I had this very lucrative short-term client—a young
guy who'd broken his leg in four places while mountain biking. He lived
alone in a two-story house, and I had to be there first thing every morning
to help him down the stairs and drive him to his law office. Then I'd pick
him up at quitting time, come back again at bedtime . . . Not to mention
the groceries he needed bought, the shirts he needed taken to the cleaner's,
and so on. When his cast was shortened to shin length and he could get
around on his own, he gave me a goodbye gift of a hundred dollars. Rent-
a-Back employees are not supposed to accept tips ever, under any conditions, and I told him that, but he said I had no choice. He said, "It's take it
now or have it come to you in the mail, which would cost me the price of
a stamp." So I took it. I confess. It would let me hit eighty-seven hundred
that much sooner.

Sophia knew I was in debt. She even knew the amount, but not the reason. (Why get into the particulars? The Chinese carving and all that.) She
was very understanding about it. She never expected me to buy her presents or take her anywhere fancy. Instead she ferried her Crock-Pot meals
to my place after work. (We'd given up on her place, now that we needed
more privacy.) First we'd go to bed and then we'd have our supper, tangled in a welter of sheets, leaning against the propped pillows that bridged
the gap between my mattress and the back of the couch. I'd be in my jeans
again, but she would stay naked, like that painting I have never understood where the men are picnicking fully dressed but the woman doesn't
have a stitch on. Me, I tend to feel kind of undefended without my
clothes, but Sophia seemed astoundingly at ease. She'd drape a napkin

across her stomach and nibble on a stewed pork chop, then wipe her fingers on the napkin and toss back the loose coils of hair streaming over one shoulder. And meanwhile, I would be asking her questions. There was so much I needed to know about her. No piece of information was too small: her favorite color, favorite crab house, favorite television show . . . I guess really I was asking, *What does it feel like, being you?*

And maybe she was asking the same. She was interested in my parents. She was curious about my brother. She wondered if he and I were anything alike. ("Not a whit," I told her.) And especially, she wanted to know about my marriage. Where had it gone wrong? Why had Natalie and I split up?

"Why'd we get together in the first place, is more to the point," I said. "A weirder combination you can't imagine. Natalie with her good-girl forehead and me fresh out of reform school."

"Oh, now," Sophia chided me. "It wasn't a reform school." But she was wearing her thrilled look, as if she hoped to be contradicted.

"Well, it was a rich-guy variation on the theme, at least," I said. "Certainly my neighbors thought as much. They pretended not to know me that whole summer after I graduated—everyone but Natalie. Natalie's family had moved in across the street while I was gone, and one afternoon I'm mowing the lawn and Natalie comes over with a pitcher and two glasses set just so on a tray. Says, 'Could I interest you in some lemonade?' Could I interest you: such a quaint way to put it. 'Why not,' I tell her, and I swig down a glass, and that might have been the end of it, except then my mother pokes her head out the door and invites us in for iced tea. As if Natalie weren't already operating her own refreshment service in the middle of our yard! Well, poor Mom; I guess the sight of a respectable girl was a little too much excitement for her. I tell Natalie, 'Cripes, let's get out of here,' and I leave the mower where it is and we walk off, just like that. So everything that happened after was my mother's fault, you might say."

"Your mother did approve of her, then," Sophia said.

"Oh, sure. Both my parents approved. It was Natalie's who objected. They'd heard stories about me, of course. Also, I was wearing my hair about halfway down my back that summer. Natalie's father called me Jesus. 'Will you and Jesus be going to the movies tonight?' This was when they were still allowing her to see me. Later, we had to sneak. I'd hired on at Rent-a-Back by then, and she would ride along on my jobs—spend the day with me while her parents thought she was swimming at their club."

"Oh, forbidden fruit! No wonder you two were attracted," Sophia said.

I was about to go on, but then a sort of hallucination stopped me in mid-breath. I swear I saw Natalie's arm, just her arm, resting on the window ledge of my car. She was waiting in the passenger seat while I was with a client. And I was stepping out the client's front door, walking down a flagstone path, heading through brilliant sunlight toward Natalie's bare, tanned arm.

Sophia said, "What happened next?"

"Oh . . . ," I said. "We got married."

"That seems awfully sudden," Sophia said.

"Well, she was about to go off to college, see. She was leaving in September."

Sophia hesitated. Then she asked, "Did you have to?"

"Have to? Oh. Have to get married. No," I said, "we didn't have to. I'm sure all the neighbors thought we did, though. To the neighbors, I was the bad guy. Natalie was 'that lovely sweet innocent Bassett girl.' It must have disappointed the hell out of them when Opal didn't come along till fourteen months after the wedding."

Sophia said, "So why . . . ?"

"But anyway!" I said. "You can imagine her parents' reaction. Mine took it more in stride. I think they hoped marriage would settle me down some. They got together with Natalie's parents and worked out all the arrangements—agreed we'd live over the Bassetts' garage and both of us would attend Towson State, and I'd keep on at Rent-a-Back in order to look like the breadwinner. Not that I really was. Our parents bankrolled just about everything. Our two mothers got into this decorating war, and pretty soon we barely had room to slither between all the furniture. And after Opal was born! They went wild. Cradles, strollers, changing tables . . . I don't know where *I* was in this. I mean, there are huge chunks of time I honestly don't remember. All at once I was standing at our front window one day, looking down at the driveway, and Natalie was buckling the baby into the car. This was a Volvo wagon her parents had given us when Opal was born. And I watched her shut the passenger door and walk around to the driver's side, and I said to myself, 'Why, great God in heaven! I seem to have married one of those station wagon mommies!' So we got divorced."

Sophia paused in the middle of licking her fingers. "Just like that?" she asked me.

"Well, no. Not instantaneously. First there was a lot of messy stuff. I admit I wasn't a model husband. Finally she took Opal and left. Didn't even warn me. Didn't even offer me a second chance. Well, you've seen Natalie. You've seen how she kind of floats along in this sealed-off, stubborn, exasperating way. Or maybe you didn't get a close enough look at her."

"No, not that close," Sophia said. "She did seem very . . . poised."

"To put it mildly," I told her. Then I said, "But why are we wasting our time on all this? Don't we have something better to do?" And I picked up our two plates and set them on the floor, and then I lifted her napkin.

Every word I had told her was true, but there was a lot I'd left out. Why we'd gotten married, for instance. I didn't tell her that I was the one who had pressed for it—that I was dying to marry, wouldn't take no for an answer, wouldn't agree to wait. I didn't tell her that at first I felt as if I'd finally come home. Hard to believe, I know; hard for even me to believe. "Did all that really take place?" I wanted to ask somebody. "Could that really have been me? How did I appear from outside? Would you say I seemed aware of my surroundings?"

The only thing I knew was, one morning I looked out the front window and thought, *Great God in heaven!* I felt as if I'd awakened from a long, drugged sleep, and the last thing I clearly remembered was Natalie bringing me lemonade. "Could I interest you?" she had asked. And I had taken a single sip and all at once found myself married to a station wagon mommy.

Sophia started catching a morning train back from Philly on Sundays so that we could see more of each other. (The roommate spent Sundays with her family in Carroll County, and we knew we'd have the house to ourselves.) I would meet the train and drive her to her place, and we'd fix a big lunch that was really a breakfast—bacon, eggs, waffles, the works. Then we would climb the stairs to her bed, which was not a four-poster, after all. It was a spool bed—same general idea. And there was a curlicued nightstand with a silk-shaded lamp on top, and a bureau with cut-glass knobs. The drawers were packed with neat, flat layers of clothing; tiny flowered sachets were tucked in all the corners. I know because I checked when she was in the bathroom. I smoothed everything down again just the way I'd found it, though. She didn't suspect a thing.

Later in the afternoon we might watch a videotape or take a walk, but we separated earlier than other days because she had her Sunday routines to follow—her stockings to rinse out, hair to shampoo, blouses to iron for the coming week. "Go, go," she would say, and I would go, grinning, and spend the evening picturing her in her quilted bathrobe, her shower rod strung with damp nylons. Even her most mundane rituals seemed dear to me, and touching.

She had two sets of friends who were married couples. All the others were single women, and I knew them only by hearsay—their latest diets or trips or boyfriend problems. The couples she introduced me to personally. She took me to the Schmidts' for supper, and the Partons were invited as well. They were okay. Nice enough, I guess. I borrowed a khaki sports coat from Joe Hardesty, because I couldn't wear my tweed anymore now that it was summer. We talked mostly about the Orioles. I think one of the husbands had had something to do with building the new stadium.

She asked me, what about *my* friends? Couldn't we double date with someone? Oh, women get so social, sooner or later. She asked about my brother and his wife. I said, "Lord God, Sofe, you don't want to spend a whole evening looking at baby pictures." She said she wouldn't mind a bit. Well, I did want to do things right this time. I said, "I know what! I'll talk to Len Parrish. Maybe we could go out with him and one of his girlfriends."

Because I couldn't think of anyone else—any of my coworkers, for instance. Martine and Everett seemed to have broken up, or so I gathered from the fact that Martine never had the truck nowadays. Not that either one of them would have been Sophia's type. Ray Oakley's wife didn't like me; she claimed I was a bad influence. My only hope was Len. Which goes to show how desperate I was.

And he knew it too. "Well, gee, pal," he said, "I'm not sure. I'm awfully busy." In the end, though, he agreed to meet for drinks. He named a bar I'd never heard of that he had discovered downtown.

This was on a Sunday night, the only night he had free, which meant that I was at Sophia's while she was choosing what to wear. She must have tried on half a dozen outfits. Each one, I said, "That looks fine," and she'd say, "No . . . ," and shuck it off again.

"It's only Len," I said, trying to reassure her. "I don't even like the guy! He's more my mom's *idea* of my friend."

"Then why are we bothering to do this?" she asked, in a voice with a teary edge to it.

"Beats me," I told her.

By the time we left, her bedroom floor was a solid mass of cast-off clothes. She had settled finally on brown slacks and some kind of long white blouse—not much different from any of the earlier get-ups, as far as I could tell.

We took her car because mine was in the shop again. I drove, and she watched for street numbers. The bar turned out to be very easy to spot: a sheet of glass for the front, with DOUGALL'S slashed carelessly across as if the sign painter had barely found the energy for the job. We heard the music even before we climbed out of the car. I started feeling old; I'd fallen behind on the music scene a long time back. And no doubt Sophia felt even older. She paused in the doorway, patting her hair. Then we braced ourselves and walked in.

Of course Len was late. Of course we had to sit alone for half an hour—me nursing a beer, she toying with the stem of her wineglass, the two of us shouting above the din about made-up topics. ("Isn't that an unusual picture over the bar!" "Oh! My. Yes.") Finally Len breezed in with this six-foot-tall girl so blond that I thought at first she was bald; not a sign of an eyebrow on her; all languorous slouch and pouting pale lips. They were both in black turtlenecks, although it was a warm June night. "Barn!" Len said, clapping me on the shoulder. "You two been waiting long? I looked for your car out front; figured you weren't here yet."

"We came in Sophia's car," I said. "Sophia, this is Len Parrish. Sophia Maynard. And . . ." I looked toward the blonde.

"Kirsten," Len said offhandedly. "Barnaby has this incredible car that's totally wasted on him," he told Kirsten as he pulled out a chair for her.

"Yes, you mentioned that," she said. She draped herself on the chair and reached idly for the drinks list that stood in the middle of the table.

Her nails were cut in U-shapes, dipping in the middle and sharp at the corners. They made me want to curl my own fingers into fists.

"So, you and Gaitlin been going out long?" Len asked Sophia, but meanwhile he was gesturing for a waiter. She said, "Oh, five months," and he looked at her blankly. Then he asked Kirsten, "What are you having?"

"A mineral water," she told him, although she was still studying the drinks list.

He ordered two, along with a snack called Wrappin's, which he swore we were going to love. Then he turned back to Sophia. "This guy's a nut; I hope you know that. Complete and utter nut," he said. "Did he tell you about his life of crime?"

"Oh, yes," she said, smiling.

"Barnaby here is the Paul Pry Burglar," Len told Kirsten.

Kirsten merely raised her nonexistent eyebrows and turned to the other side of the drinks list, but Sophia said, "The what?"

"That's the name the newspaper gave him," Len said. "People would come home and find their silver still in place, stereo still in place; but all their mail had been opened and their photo albums rifled."

I said, "Len, *she* doesn't want to hear this."

Sophia's lips were slightly parted.

"Guy was insane!" Len told her. "Love letters missing from closet shelves, locks jimmied on diaries—"

I wanted to strangle him. "Who are you to talk?" I asked him. "You were with me! It's just pure luck you weren't arrested too!"

"*I* always tracked down the liquor cabinet," Len told Sophia smugly.

I don't know why liquor should have sounded any more honorable, but right away her smile returned. I said, "Goddammit, Parrish—"

"Oh, tut-tut, Barnaby; language," he said. He told Sophia, "They sent him to a special-ed school to straighten out his evil ways and teach him not to curse."

"It wasn't special ed, for God's sake!"

"No, right, I guess it wasn't," he said. "They did make you repeat tenth grade. They must have had *some* kind of standards."

Sophia looked at me. I said, "I had played hooky the entire year before that, see."

I just wanted to dispel any suspicion that I might be mentally deficient, but Sophia read more into it. She got a softness around her eyes, and she said, "Oh, Barnaby. Had something gone wrong in your home life?"

"No, no. *I* don't know why I did it," I said irritably. By now I'd developed more of an appreciation for Kirsten. She was so plainly bored with all this, letting her gaze roam over the crowd that stood at the bar. "Thanks heaps," I told Len. "I just love digging up ancient history."

Len said, "Hmm?" and leaned back so the waiter could set his drink in front of him. Next came the Wrappin's, which turned out to be a sort of roll-your-own arrangement—miniature flour tortillas with an assortment of different fillings. Ordinarily I'm allergic to dishes with dropped *g*'s in their names, but at least these gave us something to focus on besides my unsavory character. We all sat up straighter and reached for the baby corncobs and the salsa verde. It was kind of like the activities table in kindergarten. The women fell into a separate conversation ("How long have you known Len?" I heard Sophia ask, and Kirsten said, "Um, three days? No, four."), while Len and I experimented with various fillings. The two of us got to flipping crudités off the backs of our spoons, aiming for the sauce cups. We developed an actual game with complicated rules. "No fair!" we were telling each other. "You hung on to your broccoli floret way past the legal limit; I saw you!" I enjoyed myself, in fact. You miss that kind of thing when you're not around other guys a lot. Yes, I'd say the evening ended better than it began.

Sophia thought so too, evidently. When we said good night to them, out on the sidewalk, she told Kirsten, "We should do this again." (It showed how little she knew Len Parrish. If we did do it again, it would probably be with a different girl.) And in the car, she asked, "Do you think Len liked me?"

"I'm sure he did," I told her.

Actually, I doubt he more than registered her presence. He had summed her up with a look and then dismissed her. But who cared? At that particular moment, driving up Charles with the windows down and Sophia sitting next to me, I felt completely happy.

Toward the end of July, Opal came for a week's visit to Baltimore. It was the first time she'd been allowed to do this, and judging by all the precautions taken, you would have thought she was being handed over to a serial killer or something. For starters, on the morning she was arriving I had to telephone Natalie as soon as I got out of bed, just to let her know I was really and truly awake. (The train was a super-early one, 7:52 a.m.) Then I had to phone again from Penn Station, not even waiting till we reached home, to say I'd met the train okay and Opal was safely accounted for. ("Let me speak to her," Natalie ordered, and Opal took the receiver and said, "Yes," and, "Uh-huh," and, "I guess so," all the time eyeing me narrowly, as if she were reporting on my general fitness as a father.) Also, she was required to stay at my parents' house. This was only reasonable, since I'd have had to sleep on the floor if she had stayed with me; but still I put up a fuss. "What," I had said to my mother, "you all think I live in a slum, is that it?"

"Now, Barnaby. You know you're more than welcome to move back into your old room while she's here," Mom told me. But of course, the very thought gave me the willies.

Opal seemed a lot older, suddenly. Maybe it had to do with being away from her mother. She was letting her hair grow out—it nearly reached her shoulders—and she wore a straight, dark dress, not so little-girlish as her usual clothes. I said, "Hey, Ope, you're getting to be a young lady!" She grimaced, clamping her mouth in a way that turned her dimples into parentheses, and I saw for the first time how much she resembled Natalie. Funny: Natalie was a beauty, but now I realized that she must have started out with Opal's plain, smooth face—unsettling in a child but attractive in a grown woman. Well, attractive in a child too. In fact, this Opal was . . . pretty, actually. I cleared my throat and said, "So!" Then I picked up her suitcase—molded blue Samsonite, an old person's suitcase— and we headed out to the car.

First I drove her to my parents' house. Big to-do: toast and home-squeezed orange juice, new doll propped against the pillows in the guest room. (Mom was really into this grandma business.) Then I took her to my place, because she'd never seen it before. I had cleaned it up spick-and-span and borrowed a few board games from Martine's nephews—Monopoly and Life and such—and alerted both the Hardesty kids, who were hanging out on the patio in this artificial way when we arrived. Joey was lying on a chaise longue with his ankles crossed, and Joy was jumping rope. Both of them were younger than Opal—I'd say six and eight or so; two towheaded, stick-thin kids in shorts and T-shirts—but somehow they seemed the ones in charge. Joey started shrilling questions at her ("Did you come on the train? Did you ride in the engine?"), and Joy flung aside her jump rope and executed a set of brisk, efficient cartwheels across the flagstones. Opal, meanwhile, shrank closer to my side and grew very quiet.

"I'll just take her in and show her where I live," I told the Hardestys. "Then maybe you could all have Kool-Aid here on the patio." I'd mixed up a jug already and put it in my fridge—Sophia's suggestion. Sophia had been very helpful with the preparations for this visit. The board games were her idea. She had said we needed activities, something that would let us get to know each other better. That evening she was having us to dinner, and she had canceled her weekly trip to Philly.

Every day, it seemed, I saw something new to appreciate about Sophia.

Opal didn't comment on my living quarters. I showed her all around, but she said nothing. I worried she was storing up criticisms to pass on to her mother. "I know it's not fancy," I told her, "but it's affordable. And the Hardestys are super-nice landlords."

"Where's your *bathtub*?" was all she said.

"Um, I use the shower upstairs."

"Do you have to knock on the door before you go up?"

"No," I said. I wasn't sure what she was getting at. "I just walk on in. I mean, it's only their kitchen. Then I go down the hall to the bathroom. It's no big deal."

She didn't say anything more.

I brought the Kool-Aid and three paper cups to the patio, with Opal trailing behind me, but then she said she wasn't having any. She waited till

I'd filled all three cups before she told me this. I felt a little put out, but I didn't show it. I said, "Okay. What would you like instead?" She said she wasn't thirsty. Both Hardesty kids sipped their Kool-Aid, watching Opal with round, sky-blue eyes over the rims of their cups.

After that, I took Opal to work with me. We went first to Mrs. Alford's, because today was the day her nephew was coming and I had promised to help him load his truck. He was hauling her husband's tools to his cabin in West Virginia. Mrs. Alford immediately gathered Opal under her wing. "Come see the quilt of Planet Earth that I've been working on," she said. "Come see the teeny tea set my granddaughters like to play with when they visit." Opal went willingly—too willingly, I thought—not giving me a backward glance. It seemed to me she felt more comfortable with women.

Ernie, the nephew, was a beefy, muscular guy, and we made short work of the loading. He told me most of the stuff would probably have to go elsewhere. "I live in a place the size of Aunt Jessie's kitchen," he said. "No way can I fit all this in! But she's my favorite relative. I don't want to hurt her feelings."

After Mrs. Alford's, we stopped by the Rent-a-Back office, and I introduced Opal to Mrs. Dibble and a couple of the workers who happened to be there—Ray Oakley and Celeste. Mrs. Dibble invited Opal to stay and play with the copy machine while I went on my next job, but I said, "Maybe another time"—plucking a house key from the pegboard. "We're off to visit Maud May after I pick up her mail," I said. "I figure Opal will get a kick out of her."

"Well, you come by later, then," Mrs. Dibble told Opal, and Celeste gave her a stick of sugar-free gum.

But things didn't go as well with Maud May as I had expected. First off, the nursing home had all these folks in wheelchairs lining the hall. I was used to them; I hadn't thought about how they might affect Opal. She drew so close to me that her feet stumbled into mine, and she kept one finger hooked through a belt loop on my jeans. And then Maud May was in a fractious mood. Pain, I guess. She was sitting in a chair by her bed with her shiny new walker parked alongside, and, "Who's this?" she barked when we entered the room.

"This is my daughter, Opal. Opal, this is Ms. May."

"You never told me you had a daughter."

"I told you lots of times," I said. In fact, maybe I hadn't, but I didn't want Opal to know that.

"You absolutely did not," Maud May said. "I haven't turned senile quite yet, you know. What have you brought me?"

"Mostly junk, it looks like. Bunch of catalogs and stuff. Somebody left a plant on your stoop; so I took it inside and watered it. Here's the card that came with it."

"What kind of plant?" she demanded. She accepted the card, but she didn't open it.

"Something with white flowers. I don't know. I put it in the sunporch with the others."

"Did *you* go in my house?" Maud May asked Opal.

Opal nodded, still hanging on to my belt loop.

"Did you touch anything?"

"No, she didn't touch anything. Who do you think she is?" I said. "Why would you make such an accusation?"

"Good Gawd, Barnaby, simmer down," Maud May told me. "It wasn't an accusation. I was merely inquiring."

But I was mad as hell. I tossed her mail on the nightstand and said, "So anyhow. We're leaving. What am I supposed to bring next time?"

"More cigarettes?" she asked. She was using a meeker tone of voice now. "And that plant, besides, to brighten my room?"

"Fine," I said, and I walked out, with an arm around Opal's shoulders.

In the car, I said, "Next stop is Mr. Shank. You're going to like Mr. Shank. He's lonely and he loves to see kids." My voice had a loud, fake ring to it that I couldn't seem to get rid of.

"Maybe I could just go back to Grandma's," Opal said.

"Go back *now*?"

"I could watch TV or something."

"Well," I said. "All right."

It was almost noon, anyhow. I figured we could have lunch there and she'd get her second wind.

At my parents' house, I phoned Mr. Shank to push his morning appointment up to early afternoon. Then I went out to the kitchen, where Mom and Opal were mixing tuna salad. "Barnaby Gaitlin," my mother said, "what could you have been thinking of?"

"Huh?"

"Taking a nine-year-old child to a nursing home!"

"So?" I said. "You have a problem with that?"

"She says there were people in wheelchairs everywhere she looked. *Old* people! A woman with a tube in her nose!"

"Geez, Mom," I said. "What's the big deal? We're keeping it a secret there's such a thing as old age?"

Yes, we were, evidently, because my mother threw a meaningful glance toward Opal, who kept her eyes downcast as she stirred the salad. "We'll just let Opal stay with me the rest of the day," Mom said. "I'll take her to see Gram and Pop-Pop."

"Well, I don't know what you're so het up about," I told her. But I didn't argue.

I noticed a hollow feel in my car, though, for the rest of the afternoon. It seemed that just that quickly, I'd grown accustomed to Opal's company. When I was at Mr. Shank's, I thought how she could have looked through his coin collection. And I knew she would have liked playing with Mrs. Glynn's little dog.

In the last days of my marriage, Opal was just reaching the stage where she recognized my face. I'd approach her crib, and she'd crow, "Ah!" and start wiggling all over and holding out her arms to be picked up. Then they left me. When I walked into the apartment after that, there wasn't just an absence of sound; there seemed to be an *anti*sound—a kind of, like, hole in the air.

It had been years since I had thought about that "Ah!" of hers.

Mom was miffed when I told her we'd have dinner at a friend's house. "Friend?" she asked. "What kind of friend? Male or female? You might have told me earlier. Is this a person who knows how to cook? Who'll give her fresh vegetables, and not just a Big Mac or whatnot?"

"It's someone who'll serve all the major food groups," I assured her.

"Well, I want you to know that I'll hold you to blame if Opal gets a tummyache," Mom said.

Sooner or later, I supposed, Sophia and my parents would have to meet. But I planned to put it off as long as possible.

Opal took to Sophia right away. I knew she would. Not only had Sophia gone to some trouble over the menu (Crock-Pot Chicken Drumettes and mashed potatoes, hot fudge sundaes for dessert), but she treated Opal like company: dressed up for her, in pearls and a shiny blue dress, and offered her a special fruit drink with about a dozen maraschino cherries lined up on a swizzle stick, and asked her these courteous, hostess-type questions throughout the meal. Who had Opal's favorite teacher been, so far? What kind of movies did Opal like to watch? What kind of books did she read? Opal answered gravely, sitting very straight in her chair.

As we were leaving, I told Sophia, "Thanks," and secretly squeezed her fingers. I could see the shadow where her breasts began, above her low, scooped neckline. "You coming by later?" I whispered, and she nodded and squeezed my fingers back.

I asked Opal in the car whether she'd had a good time. "Yes," she said. "That lady was nice."

"Sophia, her name is."

"She had a nice dress on."

"She liked you too," I said.

I wondered if Opal would report all this to Natalie. You never knew what a kid that age would consider worthwhile mentioning.

We fell into a pattern. Mornings, I drove over to my parents' house for breakfast, but I let Opal stay with Mom while I went out on my jobs. Then I'd stop by the house again and have lunch. This was the most I'd seen of my ancestral home in years. It wasn't so difficult, though. I guess having Opal there sort of watered the experience down some.

After lunch, I'd take Opal to my place. She never did warm to the Hardesty kids, but she would watch TV with me or play a board game. The one called Life was her favorite. I found I couldn't abide it myself. "There's no logic to it," I complained. "Look at this: the more kids you have, the more money you collect. It should work just the opposite! Children make you poorer, not richer."

Then I worried she would take that personally; she would guess I'd been less than ecstatic when Natalie learned she was pregnant. But all she said was, "I like the little plastic people." And she set her mouth in that obstinate way she had and leaned forward to spin the arrow.

I tried to keep my afternoon jobs to a minimum, so that I wouldn't burden Mom with too much baby-sitting. Not that she complained. In fact, she put up a fight when I took Opal away with me in the evenings. I took her to Sophia's for supper, and then the three of us went on an outing of some kind—down to the harbor, or one time to an Orioles game. Things like that.

On Tuesday, Martine invited Opal and me to a birthday supper for one of her nephews. (She didn't mention Sophia, who said that she could use a little catch-up time, anyhow.) We grilled hot dogs out in the yard; Martine rented the top floor of this rickety old house with a deep backyard. The nephews were all in jeans, but Opal, not knowing, had put on a party dress—one of her Dick and Jane things, with a long, flouncy sash that tied in a bow. That was okay, though, because Martine wore a party dress too. It made her look kind of bizarre. I had never seen her in anything but overalls, till now. This dress was pink, and too big for her or something, too wide at the shoulders and long in the hem. Her hair was pulled straight back off her forehead by a child's blue plastic barrette in the shape of a Scottie dog, and she was wearing lipstick the same garish pink as the dress, all wrong on that ferocious little yellow face of hers. I said, "Whoa! You look great." Which was an out-and-out lie, but her appearance was so startling that I thought it would be noticed if I didn't make some comment. Martine just said, "Thanks." I guess she thought she *did* look great.

The only other grownups were her brother and his wife, who seemed at least ten months pregnant, and Mrs. Rufus, the landlady. We all sat on folding chairs, and the kids sat in the grass. Mrs. Rufus did most of the talking, telling a string of bloodcurdling tales about childbirth. If you listened to her awhile, you marveled that the human race hadn't long ago died out. "But aren't you the cool one!" she said to the sister-in-law. "You don't even look nervous!"

"Thanks," Martine piped up. Apparently she thought Mrs. Rufus was talking to her. "I *expected* to be nervous, but actually I'm having a very good time."

Huh? Everybody stared at her a moment, and then Mrs. Rufus told how her fingers had swelled up like sausages when she was eight months along with her youngest. "We had to call in a plumber," she said, "to saw my wedding ring off with a hacksaw."

The sister-in-law said, "Ho-hum," and swallowed a yawn.

The brother had brought two six-packs of beer. Although he and I were the only ones who drank any, it somehow had a sort of rowdy effect on everyone else—a phenomenon I've observed more than once. Pretty soon Martine and the kids were playing Prisoner's Base, and Statues, and Simon Says, and a bunch of other games that I'd forgotten all about. Even Opal got involved. She loved it. By the time we left, she was as rumpled and sweaty as the nephews. Which made my mother throw a fit, of course, when I delivered her to the house. "How will I ever get those grass stains out?" she wailed. She should have seen Martine, if she thought Opal was dirty.

When I reached home I phoned Sophia, and she came over. "You smell like a new-mown lawn," she told me. I had this pleasantly tired, loose-jointed feeling. I let myself imagine how it would be if I lived this way permanently—watching my kid play with other kids in the yard, lying in bed later with a warm, sweet, generous woman.

After I'd walked Sophia to her car and turned off all the lights, I caught the sky doing its color-change trick, which is possible at night but exceedingly rare. And I hadn't even been trying! Maybe that was the secret, I thought. Let things come to you when they will, of their own accord. I went back to bed and slept like a baby.

Opal was due to leave on Friday morning. Thursday evening, therefore, we planned to have a farewell dinner. First it was going to be at my parents', but then it was switched to my brother's. (Recently, Jeff had developed some kind of fixation about hosting all family parties.) This irked my mother no end, because Wicky wasn't much of a cook. She wasn't *anything* of a cook, if you ask me. It must have been her Wasp background. Food was just a biological necessity, and a boring one, at that.

And then to make things worse, Mom took it into her head that we ought to invite Sophia. She didn't actually refer to Sophia by name. She called her "that friend that you and Opal have been seeing so much of." But she gave herself away when I said it was too short notice. "It's already Wednesday," I said, and Mom said, "Oh, I very much doubt Sophia will hold that against us."

I sent Opal a glare. Tattletale. She just gazed blandly back at me. "Shall I invite her, or will you?" Mom asked. "Which?"

I considered saying, "Neither." If I knew Mom, though, she would find a way of tracking down Sophia's number; and nothing could be worse than Mom on the phone unsupervised. I said, "I will." I wouldn't, of course. I'd say Sophia had turned out to have a previous engagement.

But I'd reckoned without Opal, who popped the question over supper that night. "Grandma wants you to come to my farewell dinner," she told Sophia.

Sophia turned from the stove, a pleased look lighting her face. "Really?" she asked me.

I shrugged.

"It's going to be at my uncle's, and Gram and Pop-Pop Kazmerow are coming too," Opal said.

"Your mother issued the invitation?" Sophia asked me.

"Well, she knows it's probably too short notice," I said.

"I'd love to come!"

I sighed.

"Would you rather I didn't?"

"These family things are such a drag, is all," I told her.

"You wouldn't think so if you were an only child," she said.

I could see there was no hope she would decline the invitation.

We went in her car, because we were the ones bringing Opal. (Mom had gone early, to try and wrestle some semblance of a meal out of Wicky's kitchen. Dad was coming directly from work.) For two days now, I'd been grousing about this whole idea, but as we were driving over I suddenly got in the spirit of things. Here we were, the three of us, traveling through a warm July night, with the fireflies flickering in the woods of Roland Park and faint, old-timey jazz playing on the radio. Sophia smelled of roses. Opal swung her heels in the back seat. And we were headed toward what was almost (if you didn't look too closely) a genuine family reunion, complete with parents and grandparents, aunt and uncle, cousins. Well, only two cousins. This was kind of a *miniature* reunion. But even so. When we drew up in front of Jeff's house, we found a huge tumble of silver balloons tied to the lamppost. Wicky's doing, clearly. Wicky was not half bad, I decided all at once.

Opal wanted to untie the balloons and bring them in with her. She seemed so impressed by them, you'd think she had never seen a balloon before. So our entrance was fairly crowded. The balloons filled the whole foyer, with the humans having to fit themselves in between them, and then Dad and Jeff arrived on our heels, and a telephone started ringing, and Pop-Pop was asking where my car was. It took several minutes before we got sorted out and seated in the living room, and by that time Sophia had somehow been introduced. *I* certainly hadn't introduced her. I was already in the doghouse for getting J.P.'s name wrong. "What's new, P.J.?" I said when he toddled over, and both Mom and Wicky said, "Who?" Like a fool, I went on with it. "P.J., old buddy! Yes, sir; it's the Peej," I babbled, till I felt the disapproval streaming toward me from across the room, and I realized I had messed up yet again.

Jeff and Wicky lived in a very nice house, old-fashioned but modernly decorated, with a long white couch that fit together in an S-curve and Japanesey low tables and such. Still, I always felt it needed something.

Maybe books, or pictures. It had this sort of blank feel. I knew my mother had given them a few paintings early in their marriage, but they had never hung them, and my dad absolutely forbade her to ask what had become of them. She said, "But it's such a waste! Especially the Rankleston, with the barbed wire and the Brillo pads. I could take it back and hang it in your study, if for some reason they don't like it." Dad didn't say what he thought of that idea, but you could guess from his expression.

It helped, at least, that there were so many of us. All the women wore their party clothes—even Gram, decked out in a bag-shaped shift with a rhinestone horseshoe pinned to the front. Pop-Pop had his shirt buttoned up to the collar, which was as dressy as he got, and Dad and Jeff and J.P. were in suits, and I had on my birthday necktie. A fairly festive-looking group, I'd say. The billow of balloons bobbing above Opal's head didn't hurt any, either.

And right from the start, Sophia was a hit. *Big* hit. Of course Gram and Pop-Pop already knew her. They showed off about that a little. "How's the bank?" Gram asked. "How's your *roommate*!" and then Pop-Pop said, "Stell brought the recipe for those nachos you liked so much." This made my mother go all alert and suspicious. She started edging closer to Sophia on the couch. "Oh?" she said. "You've had Mother's nachos? You've been to their house? Barnaby took you to visit?"—firing questions one-two-three, leaving her no room for answers. Meanwhile, Jeff was offering her a choice between white wine, Scotch, and ginger ale, and J.P. was lurching against her knees and trying to reach her pearls.

Not till we were settled around the table did Sophia manage to get a word in. Then she did a wonderful job. She made a little story of our trip to Camden Yards, and everyone came out well in it. (Opal had caught on to baseball so quickly; I'd been so patient in explaining the rules.) I kept saying, "Oh, it was nothing," and, "Just a routine game, all in all"— rolling my eyes at the other men and looking sheepish. Jeff asked me how Ripken had done. Dad asked if I had noticed any slacking off in attendance after the strike. I felt like some kind of impostor.

When I was a teenager, I would be eating dinner and all at once I'd imagine grabbing hold of the soup tureen and turning it upside down over my parents' heads. Noodles would snake down Dad's temples, and carrot disks would stud Mom's French twist. The image always set me to laughing, and then I couldn't stop. I'd be laughing so hard I was choking, spewing bits of chewed food, while the two of them sat staring at me grimly.

I don't know why that memory came back to me just at that moment.

Pop-Pop told Sophia I used to go to ball games with him as a little kid. "Him and Jeff; they'd take turns," he said. "Barnaby loved that *bugle* call! Loved it. Always used to say to me, 'Pop-Pop,' he used to say, 'aren't you glad we don't have organ music, like those poor other ball teams have?' "

It seemed everybody assumed that Sophia would be riveted by the most inconsequential mention of my name. And she did look entertained. She was smiling and nodding, forgetting to eat her canned pineapple ring.

"Just how did you two meet?" Mom asked, and my grandma, showing off again, burst in with, "They met on a train."

"On a train!"

The phrase gave me a vision of Sophia riding that train: her golden bun, her feather coat, her calm, pale hands accepting the stapled packet. My personal angel at last, I had fancied, but now that seemed an outdated concept. It was like when you're introduced to someone who reminds you of, say, an old classmate, but then later, when you know him well, you forget about the classmate altogether. Sophia was just Sophia, by this time—so familiar to me, so much a part of my life, that I couldn't imagine how she appeared to the people sitting around this table.

Except it was obvious they must like her. She was telling them in some detail now about our train ride. "He spilled coffee all over me," she told them, and they laughed and tossed me appreciative glances, as if I'd done something witty. She said, "First I was annoyed, but when I saw how nice he was, and how well-mannered—"

"Barnaby, well-mannered?" my mother said.

"Oh, he apologized endlessly and helped me clean myself up. And so then we got to talking, and he told me about his work—"

A few resigned expressions here and there, but I don't think she noticed.

"—and he described his clients so considerately, you know . . . And the clincher was that in Philly, I got a glimpse of Opal."

This was exceptionally kind of her. Just by mentioning Opal's name, sending her a wink across the table, she reminded the others that tonight was really Opal's night. I watched them all remember that. Gram, who was sitting on Opal's left, patted her hand and told her, "So *you* met Sophia before any of the rest of us, you smart little old thing!"

Opal smiled down at her plate.

"And then Barnaby asked for your phone number . . . ," Wicky suggested to Sophia.

"No, no. It was all left to me. I was the one who phoned, asking for him to come work for my aunt."

They laughed again, and Pop-Pop slapped his knee.

"Well, yes," Sophia said, laughing too. "I admit it was sort of trumped up. But Aunt Grace did need assistance, and so I didn't feel guilty about it."

"Of course not!" Gram said soothingly.

"He's been an enormous help to her—put her whole house in order again. You must be very proud to have raised such a caretaking person."

"Why, thank you, Sophia," my mother told her. "That's sweet of you to say." She glanced down the table to Dad. "It's not as if he hasn't caused us some worry, in times past."

"Oh, I know all about that," Sophia said. "But look at how he turned out!"

Everybody looked. I gave them a little wave that was something like a windshield wiper stopping in mid-arc.

In those photo albums I used to rifle, people were so consistent. They tended to assume the same poses for every shot, the same expressions. You'd see a guy on page one, some young father at the beach, standing next to his wife and baby with his arms folded across his chest and his head at a slight angle; and then on the last page, twenty years later, there he still was with his arms still folded, hair a bit thinner but head still cocked, wife still on his left, although the baby had grown taller than the father and was settled into some favorite stance of his own by now. Even the beach was the same, often. I would turn page after page, ignoring my friends. ("Gaitlin! What's keeping you, man? Look what we found upstairs!") I would set my sights on, say, one little boy and follow him through infancy, kindergarten, college. I'd see him slicing his wedding cake, and darned if he wasn't still wearing the same knotted-up scowl, or shamefaced smirk, or joyful smile.

What I'd wanted to know was, couldn't people change? Did they have to settle for just being who they were forever, from cradle to grave?

Seated at that table, the night of Opal's dinner, I felt *I* had changed. I waved a hand at my family as if I'd left them far in the distance—as if I'd become a whole other person, now that I loved Sophia.

9

Then Sophia's aunt accused me of theft.

She said I stole the cash she had been keeping in her flour bin.

"That flour bin's famous!" I said. "Everyone and his brother knows she keeps her money there. Why is she picking on *me*?"

It was Mrs. Dibble I was talking to, because did Mrs. Glynn have the decency to accuse me to my face? Oh, no. No, she went behind my back. She telephoned the office on a Sunday night in mid-August, using the after-hours number that rang in Mrs. Dibble's home. Announced right off that I had taken her money; no ifs or ands or buts. Not a question in her mind as to whether I was the culprit.

Mrs. Dibble asked her how she could be so sure. "There could be any number of explanations," Mrs. Dibble told her—or at least she claimed she'd told her, when she reported the conversation to me. I wondered what she had really said. Maybe she'd said, "Yes, that particular worker does have a history of criminal behavior."

Well, no, I decided; probably not. (It would reflect very poorly on Rent-a-Back, for one thing.)

Funny: when Mrs. Dibble broke the news to me, I felt this sudden thud of guilt, as if I might in fact have done it. I had to tell myself, *Wait. Hold on.* Why, from the first day I was hired, I had bent over backward not to meddle in our clients' private belongings. It was almost an obsession. I would go out of my way; I would ostentatiously shut a desk drawer as I passed it, and had once, while delivering a lady's diary to her hospital room, stuffed it into a grocery bag so I wouldn't be tempted to peek.

Mrs. Dibble broke the news by phone, but that wasn't her choice. First she asked if I would come see her in person. I said, "Why? What's up?"

She said, "Oh, just this and that."

"Spill it," I said.

She sighed. She said, "Now, Barnaby, I don't want you overreacting to what I'm about to tell you," and then she said Mrs. Glynn believed I'd stolen her money.

I said, "I'll go have a talk with her this minute."

"You can't. You have to promise you won't. It would only complicate matters. I just thought I should warn you first, before the police get in touch."

"The police!"

Something like a cold liquid trickled down the back of my neck.

"Do you think they're going to arrest me?" I asked.

"No, no," Mrs. Dibble said, giving a false laugh. "Arresting a person is not as easy as that! They'll probably want to question you, though, to get your side of the story."

"I hate that woman," I said.

"Now, Barnaby."

"What have I ever done to her? Why would she just up and decide it was me?"

Then I thought I knew why. I thought of how Sophia had presented me to her mother. "I guess you could call it a pickup," she'd said, with that triumphant look on her face.

She was as proud of my sins as I was of her virtues.

Mrs. Dibble was calculating aloud how I could make up for those lost hours at Mrs. Glynn's. An hour a week at Mrs. Alphonse's, she said; an hour with a man in a wheelchair over in Govans . . . She knew how hard I'd been working to save more money, she told me. But I was only half listening. I had to get hold of Sophia.

First of all, her line was busy. I tried once, tried twice, and then slammed down the receiver. Drove to her house in record time and pounded on the front door. It was after eleven o'clock by now, on a Sunday night. Normally she'd have been in bed. But all the lights were on, even the one in her room, and the footsteps I heard approaching were hard-soled and wide awake, and when she opened the door she was wearing what she'd worn that afternoon.

"Barnaby," she said.

Not surprised in the least; so I knew it must have been her aunt she was talking to on the phone.

"I didn't take that money," I said.

She pressed her cheek against the edge of the door and studied my face. She said, "Even if you did, it wouldn't change how I feel about you."

"I didn't take it, Sophia. Do you really think I'd do such a thing?"

"Of course not," she said.

Then she stepped forward and kissed me, and turned to lead me into the living room.

But after we had settled on the couch, she said, "I know you've been under some pressure, trying to pay off your debt."

"So you figured I just waltzed into a little old lady's kitchen and helped myself to eighty-seven hundred dollars."

"Twenty-nine sixty," she said.

"Pardon?"

"Two thousand, nine hundred and sixty was what she told me she had in her flour bin."

At the rear of the house, I heard the refrigerator door latch shut with a muffled, furtive sound, and then something made of glass or china clinked but was instantly hushed. Betty, trying to be discreet. No doubt they'd been discussing me before I came. ("I said all along he seemed fishy, Sophia. Didn't I have a bad feeling, way back at the beginning?")

"Level with me," I told Sophia. "Did you ever happen to mention to your aunt that I'd been in trouble with the law?"

She flushed and said nothing. She met my eyes very steadily.

"Did you?" I asked.

She said, "I might have, at some point. Maybe I did say, I don't know, you'd had some problems in the past. But I didn't mean any harm! I just wanted to show that you were an interesting person! I also said you came from a very good background. I said it was just your age or whatever, your age and circumstances, and you'd changed your ways completely and I had total faith in you."

"Well, thanks," I said.

She studied me, maybe wondering how I meant that. In fact, I wasn't sure myself. I groaned. I tipped my head back against the sofa cushions and closed my eyes.

"Barnaby," she said. She was using a tactful, delicate tone that put me instantly on guard. I opened my eyes and rolled my head in her direction. "Is it some kind of loan shark?" she asked me.

"Huh?"

"The person you owe money to."

I laughed.

"Because I know about these things, Barnaby. I see it in my business all the time: people in such deep debt they think they can't ever get out from under. Exorbitant interest rates, fees on top of fees . . . I want to help you, Barnaby. I don't have eighty-seven hundred, but I do have, let's see . . . In my savings account—"

"It's my parents," I said.

"Your parents?"

"They're the ones I owe it to."

"Well, for heaven's sake," Sophia said. "You owe eighty-seven hundred to your *parents*? And they're making you pay it back?"

"Nothing odd about that," I pointed out. "A debt's a debt."

"Yes, but your parents are so . . . affluent!"

This made me smile. It always tickles me, how people avoid the word "rich."

"I just think that's shocking," Sophia said. She was sitting very straight on the edge of the couch, practically swaybacked. "When their own son has to work weekends, even, and live in somebody's basement! That snoopy Mimi Hardesty always peeking out the window the minute I drive up, and calling down to ask if she can run a load of laundry as soon as you and I start getting intimate!"

I smiled again, but she didn't notice.

"And your clothes are practically rags," she said, "and your car is on its last legs. . . . What can your parents be *thinking* of?"

I could have calmed her down, I guess, if I'd told her about the Chinese statue and such. That would have made my parents look more reasonable. But it would have made *me* look shoddier. And besides, I enjoyed hearing somebody rail against my parents. I have to say, I took pleasure in it.

No, I was not at my best that night. I was spiteful and contrary, mean-spirited, malicious. When Sophia went out to the kitchen to get us a glass of wine, I pocketed a little porcelain bowl in the shape of a slipper that sat on her coffee table. And I didn't even like that bowl! And certainly had no use for it.

Monday, I overslept. I was supposed to run errands for Mrs. Figg, because she couldn't show her face again in half the stores in town. But I stood her up and wouldn't answer the telephone when it rang. "Barnaby, are you there?" Mrs. Dibble asked my machine. "Mrs. Figg is fit to be tied!" I just turned over and went back to sleep.

What woke me, finally, was Mimi Hardesty calling from the top of the stairs. "Barnaby?" Her voice was oddly high and childish. "There's a gentleman here to see you."

You don't often hear the word "gentleman" in everyday conversation. Especially not Mimi Hardesty's conversation. I sat up. I said, "Who is it?"

"Um, an officer. Can he come down?"

"Why, *sure,*" I said.

Meanwhile scrambling out of bed, grabbing my jeans from the floor, and hopping into them one-legged. Heavy footsteps thudded toward me. I raked desperately at my blankets. It mattered a lot, for some reason, that I should get my bed folded back into a sofa. But I had left it opened out for so long that I'd forgotten how the thing worked, and anyway, it was too late. The cop arrived at the bottom of the stairs—an older man, gray-haired, surprisingly lean considering the weight of his tread. He already had his card out to show me. Does anyone really read those cards? Not me, I can tell you. I didn't even hear his name, although he announced it in a loud, friendly voice. I looked past him to Mimi Hardesty, who was bending forward to peer at me from several steps above him. One small hand was clapped to her mouth, and her eyes were huge and perfectly round.

"Just like to ask you a couple of questions," the cop said, pocketing his card. Without glancing in Mimi's direction, he said, "Okay, ma'am."

Mimi said, "Oh! Okay," and turned to scamper upstairs. She was wearing shorts, and although the fronts of her legs were hazed with freckles, the backs were a pure, flawless white.

You notice the most ridiculous trivia during moments of stress.

But I was saying, "Have a seat," as if I weren't concerned in the least. "I can guess what you want to ask," I said. (I figured I'd be better off bringing it up before he did.) I scooped an armload of dirty laundry from the chair. "I know that one of our clients believes I stole from her."

The cop sat down and opened a spiral notebook. "So did you?" he asked mildly.

I said, "No."

He gazed at me a moment, his expression noncommittal. I wondered if that might possibly be the end of it. "Did you?" and "No," and he'd leave. But nothing's ever that easy. He had to follow protocol: take note of my name, my age, my years of employment at Rent-a-Back. Eventually I gave up and sat down on the edge of my bed. My feet were bare, which somehow put me at a disadvantage, but I worried he might think I was going for a gun if I stood up to fetch my sneakers.

I did tell him that I'd known where Mrs. Glynn kept her money. "Everybody knew," I said.

He asked, "Did you ever *see* the money?"

"No," I said. Then I said, "Hey! Do you think she could be delusional?"

But the cop just gave me a look, at that, and closed his notebook in this weary, disgusted way that made me feel about two inches tall.

When the alarm went off at the Amberlys' place, the night I was arrested, the police sent one of their helicopters putt-putting overhead. I was a little bit high. We were all a little bit high—me and Len and the Muller boys. I told the others, "Let me deal with this," and I dialed the Northern District police on the Amberlys' bedroom phone. "I wish to register a complaint," I said. "There's an extremely noisy helicopter disturbing the peace here."

The man asked what address I was at, and then he went off for a while. When he came back, he said, "Yes, sir. The helicopter is ours; we sent it out on a call."

"Well, in that case," I told him smartly, "you should know how to call it back in."

And I hung up, all dignified and haughty. Then the four of us collapsed into giggles. Then a car pulled up out front, and a flashing light revolved across the ceiling.

It was the very last moment that the world in general thought well of me.

In midafternoon, Sophia phoned. I was back in bed but not asleep. Still, I let the machine answer for me. "Barnaby, it's me," she said. "I'll try you again later. Just wanted to say hi."

"Hi," she wanted to say. "Pulled off any more grand thefts lately?"

I got up and went to pee. Ran water over my toothbrush but replaced it in the rack without brushing, as if I were still a kid trying to hoodwink my mother.

Mrs. Dibble phoned again. "Well, I don't know what's happened to you," she started out. "You are seriously disappointing me, Barnaby. Call when you get this message. Mrs. Morey wants her grill tank filled. Martine says to remind you she'll need a ride to the Alford job. Also, Mrs. Hatter would like to arrange for regular hours with you, starting tomorrow."

I couldn't even remember what Mrs. Hatter looked like, she used our services so seldom. Maybe she'd had a stroke or something. Well, tough luck. I started kicking through the clothes on the floor, trying to find my sneakers.

While I was drinking my coffee, two more people left messages. Mrs. Figg wanted me to know that I had ruined her entire morning, and Natalie asked if I could shift next weekend's visit to Sunday. It seemed Opal had been invited to a birthday party on Saturday. "I wouldn't bring it up," she said, "except the birthday girl's from the popular crowd, and it means a lot to Opal that she was included."

Yeah, right; it meant more than a visit from her own father. *Fine,* I thought. *I just won't go at all.*

By this time I was starting to feel I had died or something, listening to so many phone calls without picking up. So I grabbed my car keys and left the apartment. Went off to Mrs. Figg's to face the music.

It was hot as blazes out. I practically needed oven mitts just to work my steering wheel. I drove badly, zipping through yellow lights and honking at any pedestrian dumb enough to assume I would give him the right-of-way.

"If I'd wanted a worker who didn't show up," Mrs. Figg said when she opened the door, "someone I needed to nag about every little task, why, I could rely on my own son, for heaven's sake." She scowled into my face, pursing her raisin mouth—not an old woman, but a dried-up, drained-out one with a grudge against the universe. She went ahead and gave me her list, though, because who else could she get to do it? Most of our employees refused to deal with her anymore.

I went to the cleaner's first and picked up her husband's shirts. Ordinarily I'd have held my breath the whole time I was inside (the cancer is just swarming at you in those places), but today I took big, deep gulps of the chemical-smelling air while I waited. I wondered what Mrs. Figg had done that made her permanently unwelcome there.

At Ed's Electronics (where she had hit a salesman with her pocketbook, I happened to know), I collected her tape recorder from Repairs. Then I went to the pharmacy and the hardware, and I was done. But when I got back to Mrs. Figg's, what did she point out? The tape recorder's earphone pads were still in need of replacement. "If I'd wanted the kind of worker who did things any which way—" she began, but I was already wheeling around and stomping off. Went to Ed's Electronics again and raised such a stink, Mrs. Figg looked like a model customer by comparison. Then I drove back to her house and all but threw the pads in her face.

At Mrs. Morey's, I headed straight for the patio and unhooked the propane tank from her grill. "Wouldn't you like to see what I just persuaded to bloom?" she asked, trailing behind me, but I said only, "Mmf," and set off for my car as if I hadn't quite heard her. Got the tank filled at the gas station, reached into my pocket for my billfold, and came up with two earphone pads in a little plastic pouch. I guess they'd been clipped to the receipt and somehow worked themselves loose. Well, too late now. I tossed them in the trash bin.

At home, I found three more messages on my machine. Sophia said, "Hello, sweetie. Call me at the office, will you?" Mrs. Dibble said, "I wish you'd get in touch. Where are you?" And then Sophia again: "Barnaby, why haven't you phoned? Do you want me to bring supper tonight? Or not. I'll wait to hear."

I made myself a peanut butter sandwich and ate it standing at the bar. Then I polished off the last of the milk, drinking straight from the jug, and threw the jug in the wastebasket, even though it was the kind you were supposed to recycle. After that, I switched on the TV and watched a talk show, the outrageous type of show where everybody tries to confess to more unpleasantness than the next person. I had to sit on the bed to watch, since my chair had turned to glue in the humidity. Even my sheets felt sticky. Overhead, the Hardesty kids were carrying on a thin, shrill squabble, and their mother must have been tuned to her soaps, because at every pause in my own program, I could hear hers murmuring away.

This was the first weekday afternoon in months that I wouldn't be going to Mrs. Glynn's. The thought gave me a sort of wincing sensation. I fell back against the pillows and covered my eyes with one forearm.

I might have slept a little. When the phone rang again, the evening news was on. "Hey. Gaitlin," my machine said. (Martine's little raspy crow voice.) "Pick up, will you?"

I rolled over and reached for the receiver. I said, "What."

"Why aren't you here? It's ten till seven! You promised you'd give me a ride!"

"I did?" I said. "Where're we going?"

"Sheesh! Mrs. Alford's. We're clearing out her kitchen for the painters."

I said, "Can't you do it alone?"

"Duh, Barnaby. I don't have any wheels, remember? What's *with* you? I hope you're not hung up on that Mrs. Glynn crap."

"Oh," I said. "You heard. Great. It must be all over town."

"She's crazy; don't you think everyone knows that? Now get yourself on down here. We're running behind."

I said, "Well, okay."

It might not be a bad idea, I decided. Sophia wasn't going to wait by her phone forever. She'd come by in person, sooner or later, and I just didn't feel like facing her right at that moment.

Martine was standing out front when I pulled up—leaning against a parked car and eating pork rinds from a cellophane packet. She had on her usual overalls and what looked to be a man's sleeveless undershirt, so worn it was translucent. "At this rate, we won't finish work till midnight," she said as she got in.

I said, "You're welcome," and she said, "Oh. Thanks."

Then she slouched down in her seat and braced her boots against the dashboard and went back to eating her pork rinds. She held the packet toward me, at one point, but I shook my head.

Clearing a kitchen for painters wasn't that big a job. I could easily have done it alone. But we were dealing, I guess, with Mrs. Alford's private little affirmative action program, because her first words when she opened her door were, "Oh, I just love to see what young women can get up to nowadays!"

This evening she wore a mint-green housedress that bore an unfortunate resemblance to a mental patient's uniform. She was having one of her good spells, though, and got both our names right. "What I'd like, Martine," she said, "is, you take the small things, the pots and pans and things, and stack them in the far corner of the dining room. Barnaby, you can take the furniture and the microwave."

But Martine had to show off and grab the microwave herself. She staggered away with it, her arms straining out of her undershirt like two brown wires. I followed, with a chair in each hand, and Mrs. Alford came last, clasping a single skillet to her bosom. "You leave this to us," I told her. Already she was sounding out of breath. She said, "Oh, well, I suppose . . ." She laid the skillet on the buffet and retreated to the living room. We could hear her footsteps padding across the carpet, and a moment later, the creak, pause, creak of her rocking chair.

Before we moved the step stool, Martine climbed onto it and took down all the curtains. It was starting to get dark out, and the naked, blue-black windowpanes made the kitchen look depressing. Shadows loomed in the corners. Bare spots showed where the clock had been, and the spice rack, and the calendar. I stole a glance through the calendar after I took it down. I saw all the medical appointments—doctor this, doctor that, mammogram, podiatrist. Anything to do with her family had an exclamation mark after it. *Grandkids coming! Ernie spending night! Edward here for Labor Day!* Then I checked the times I had come, but she didn't refer to me by name. *Rent-a-Back 7 p.m.,* she wrote. And no exclamation mark.

"What're you looking at?" Martine asked. She was standing so close behind me that I jumped. I laid the calendar aside without answering.

When everything had been moved, Martine ran a dust mop around the tops of the walls, while I swept the floor. I found a dime, a red button, and a furry white pill. The pill didn't look all that intriguing, so I set it in a saucer with the dime and the button. Then we went out to the living room. Mrs. Alford was sitting in her rocker, with her hands folded—not reading, not sewing or watching TV—her face exhausted and empty. But when I cleared my throat, she instantly put on this animated expression and said, "Oh! All done? My, wasn't that speedy!" And she asked if we'd like a soft drink or something, but we told her we had to be going.

In the car, Martine got started on her favorite subject: Everett. How glad she was to be shed of him; how she couldn't imagine now what she'd ever seen in him. I wanted to discuss my own troubles, but she was rattling on so, I couldn't get a word in. She said Everett had given her every Willie Nelson tape that ever existed, given them as gifts, and now was demanding them back; and it was true she no longer listened to them, but still he shouldn't expect them returned just because she had dumped him.

"Mm-hmm," I said, and drove on.

I didn't want to see Sophia tonight. I just didn't; I wasn't sure why. I thought of her wide, gentle face and her kind smile, the way her blue eyes seemed lit from within whenever she stood in sunshine, and I got this wormy, shriveled feeling. I couldn't explain it.

"Here's an example," Martine was saying. Example of what? She'd lost me. "Say he's walking down the street and a man jumps off a roof," she said. Everett, she probably meant. "Know what he would say? He'd say, 'Hey! Why is this happening to *me*? Hey, isn't it amazing that someone should jump off a roof just as I'm passing by!' That's Everett for you. He thinks the world exists purely for his benefit. If he's not there, then nothing else is, either."

"Solipsistic," I said. I remembered the word from philosophy class.

"Right," she said, digging through her packet of pork rinds.

"Green light, now: figure it out," I told the car ahead of me. "What do we do when a light turns green? Ah. Very good."

Martine crumpled her packet and stuffed it in my ashtray. "So," she said. "Did you decide yet?"

"Huh?"

"About the truck. Yes, or no?"

"What truck?" I asked.

"Everett's truck; what else. It's a pretty good piece of machinery, you have to admit."

I didn't have the remotest opinion of Everett's truck, and I couldn't imagine why she thought I would. I put our conversation on Rewind. Came up empty. "Well, um," I said. "It's always looked fine to *me*. But face it: I'm no Mr. Goodwrench."

"You don't think it's a stupid idea, though."

"What idea is that?" I asked her.

"You and me going in on it."

"Going in on it?" I asked. "You mean, as in buying it? You and me? Buying a truck?"

"Jesus! Where have you been?"

"Sorry," I said. "I must have missed something."

We were on her block now, and I had been planning just to let her out in the street. Instead I pulled into a parking space. "I've got a lot on my mind," I told her. "Maybe it's nothing to *you* that I'm a victim of rank injustice, but—"

"What was the *point*! What have I wasted my breath for?"

She could have chosen a better moment for this. On the other hand, she was just about the last friend I had left in the world, and so I turned to face her and said, "Martine, I sincerely apologize. Run it by me again."

She sighed. "See, Everett bought that truck off a lady in Howard County—" she said.

"Howard County; yes." I tried to look as knowing as possible.

"—and he was supposed to pay for it in thirty-six monthly installments. Only he kept falling behind and his mom had to do it for him. And now he wants to move to New York, he says, where a truck wouldn't be any use to him; so he says to his mom, '*You* take the truck; I can't keep up the payments.' She says, 'When did you ever, I'd like to know? And what would I do with a truck?' And that's why she phoned me and asked if I wanted to buy it."

In the dusk, Martine was all black-and-white, like a photo. Black eyes slitted with purpose, black hair sticking out at drastic angles around her high white cheekbones.

"And you're suggesting the two of us should go in on it together," I said.

"Well, for sure I can't swing it on my own. But I can manage the installments, just barely, if you'd give his mom what she's already paid: twenty-four hundred dollars."

"Twenty-four hundred!" I said. "Martine. My total assets come to exactly half of that. And I'm still in debt to my parents, don't forget."

"Oh, well," she said, "but not if you sold off your car."

"Pardon?"

"Your car's worth thirty thousand, did you know that? I looked it up in a book."

I started laughing. I said, "My car's worth *what*?"

"They've got these books that give you the price of every used car ever made. So I went to the bookstore and, like, flipped through one, and there it was: a '63 Corvette Sting Ray coupe in excellent condition is worth thirty thousand dollars."

I was stunned. But I did think to say, "We could hardly claim my car is in excellent condition."

"Okay; so knock off a few thousand. You'd still be rolling in money. Haven't you always told me your car was a collector's item?"

"Theoretically, I suppose it is," I said. "But it was pretty well worn out way back when my Pop-Pop bought it, and you may have noticed I haven't exactly cosseted the poor thing."

"Oh! You're so negative!"

She bopped me on the kneecap with one of her fists. I said, "Hey, now." I took hold of her fist and set it back in her lap. Then I laid an arm across her shoulders. "I'm not trying to be a spoilsport here—"

"Well, you *are* one," she said, but a sort of grudging amusement had crept into her voice. She snuggled in closer under my arm and said, "Just listen a minute, okay? Let me tell you how I've got it figured."

"Go ahead," I said. It wasn't as if I had any pressing engagements.

"You would sell your car and, first off, pay back your folks. Quit your nickel-and-diming and just pay them back; be done with it. Get that Chinese statue off of your conscience once and for all. Wouldn't that feel good? Then take some more of the money and go in with me on the truck. It works out just about fifty-fifty—slightly in your favor, even—between what you'd give Everett's mom and what I would pay monthly."

"But meanwhile, I'd have no car," I told her.

"You'll have the truck then, idiot!"

"*We'll* have the truck," I reminded her. "And you'll be wanting to take it one place when I want to take it another."

"Don't we just about always go out on the same jobs together? And aren't you tired to death of trying to get your work done in a little, toy, baby-sized car that doesn't even have a rear seat?"

As she spoke, she was tracing a rip that ran across the knee of my jeans. Her fingertips hit bare skin and started coaxing at it. She said, "You could keep it at your place, if you like. And besides: we've been sharing it all along, more or less, when you stop to think."

"Well, shoot, with thirty thousand dollars, maybe I should just go on and buy each one of us a truck or two apiece," I said.

I was talking down into the top of her head, into her hair. It smelled of sweat. This got me interested, for some reason. Maybe she could tell, because she turned her face up, and next thing I knew, we were kissing. She had this very thin, hard mouth. I was surprised at how stirring that was. I wrapped both arms around her (not easy with the steering wheel in front of me), and she pressed against me, and I felt the little points of her breasts poking into my chest.

Then she drew back, and so I did too. I was relieved to see we were coming to our senses. (Or at least, partly relieved.) But what she was doing was shutting off the ignition. She dropped my keys in the cup of my hand, and her little face closed in on me again.

"You want to?" she asked me.

Her eyes had a stretched look, and she wore a peaky, excited expression that made me feel sad for her. I'd never really thought of Martine as a woman. Well, she wasn't a woman; she was just this scrappy, sharp-edged little *person*. So I said, "Oh—um—"

And yet at the same time I was reaching for her once more, as if my body had decided to go ahead without me. I had her between my palms (every rib countable inside the baggy denim), but she was leaning across me to douse the headlights. Then she tore free and climbed out of the car, all in one rough motion. I got out, too, and followed her toward the house. The porch floorboards made a mournful sound under our feet. The first flight of stairs was carpeted, but the second flight was bare, and so steep that I had to tag a couple steps below her so as not to be nicked by her boot heels as we climbed.

The instant we had reached the third floor—one large attic room full of a tweedy, dusty darkness—we were hugging again and kissing and stumbling toward her bed. Her bed had a headboard like a metal gate, white or some pale color, so tall it had to sit out a ways from the slant of the ceiling. It jangled when we landed on it. Martine breathed small, hot, bacon-smelling puffs of air into my neck while I fumbled with her overall clasps. They were the kind where you slide a brass button up through a brass figure eight. I don't think I'd worked one of those since nursery school, but it all came back to me.

"Martine," I said (whispering, though no one could have heard), "I'm sorry to say I don't have, ah, anything with me," but she said, "Never mind; I do," and she rolled away from me to rummage through her overall pockets. Then she pushed something smooth and warm and warped into my palm: her billfold. That made me even sadder, somehow. But still my body went hurtling forward on its own, and it didn't give my mind a chance to say a thing.

Not till later, at least, when everything was over.

And then it said, *What was* that *all about?*

Which Martine was probably wondering too, because already she was twisting away from me, rustling among the sheets and then rising to cross the room. A light flickered on—just the dim fluorescent light on the back of her ancient cookstove. It showed her facing me, head tilted, clutching a bedspread around her with thin bare arms. She still had her socks on. Crumpled black ankle socks. Little white pipe-cleaner shins.

"Oh, Lord," I said.

Her head came out of its tilt, and she said, "Well. I guess you want to get going."

"Yeah, I guess," I said, and I reached for my clothes. Martine turned and went off toward what must have been the bathroom, with the bedspread making a hoarse sound as it followed her across the floor planks.

I did call out a goodbye when I left, but she didn't answer.

Back when Natalie and I were still married—at the very tail end of our marriage, when things had started falling apart—I happened to be knocked down by a car after an evening class. Ended up spending several hours in the emergency room while they checked me out, but all I had was a few scrapes and bruises.

When I finally got home, about midnight, there was Natalie in her bathrobe, walking the baby. The apartment was dark except for one shaded lamp, and Natalie reminded me of some pious old painting—her robe a long, flowing bell, her head bent low, her face in shadows. She didn't speak until I was standing squarely in front of her, and then she raised her eyes to mine and said, "It's nothing to *me* anymore if you choose to stay out carousing. But how about your daughter, wondering all this time where you are? Didn't you at least give any thought to your daughter?"

Except my daughter was sound asleep and obviously hadn't noticed my absence.

I looked into Natalie's eyes—reproachful black ovals, absorbing the glow from the lamp without sending back one gleam. I said, "No, I didn't, since you ask. I was having too good a time." Then I went off to bed. I *fell* into bed, still wearing my clothes, like someone exhausted by drink and fast women.

Every now and then, I think I might have an inkling why Ditty Nolan stopped leaving her house. It may have had something to do with those years spent tending her mother. "If you make me stay home for so long, just watch: I'll stay at home forever," she said.

"If you think I'm such a villain, just watch: I'll act worse than you ever dreamed of," I said. I said it during my teens. I said it toward the end of my marriage. And I said it that whole nasty Monday, which seemed, now that I looked back, to have lasted about a month.

Back at my place, I found two more messages from Sophia and another from Mrs. Dibble. Sophia's voice was patient, without the least hint of annoyance, which made me feel terrible. Mrs. Dibble was all business. "I want you to call, Barnaby, as soon as you get in. I don't care how late it is. Use my home number."

So I called. What the hell. If she wanted to fire me, let's get it over with.

It wasn't even ten o'clock, but she must have been in bed, because she answered so immediately, in that super-alert tone people use when they don't want to let on you've wakened them. "Yes!" she said.

"It's me," I said.

"Barnaby."

A pause, a kind of shuffling noise. She must be sitting up and rearranging her pillows. "Here are your assignments for tomorrow," she said. "Mrs. Cartwright wants you to help her buy a birthday present for her niece. Mrs. Rodney needs her mower taken in for maintenance. Miss Simmons would like a window shade hung. Mr. Shank has asked for—"

"Wait," I told her. "Is this all in one day?"

"Yes," she said, and there was something unsteady in her voice—a bubble of laughter. "Package mailed for Mr. Shank, fireplace cleaned at the Brents'—"

"Fireplace?" I said. It was August. We were going through a heat wave.

The laughter grew more noticeable. "Plants moved for Mrs. Binney from the dining room to the living room—"

Mrs. Binney raised African violets, none of them over six inches tall. There was no reason on earth she should need my help to move them.

"Mrs. Portland wants you daily all next week," Mrs. Dibble said. "She's thinking of rearranging every stick of furniture she owns. The Winstons have requested—"

"What's going on here?" I asked.

"I believe they must be trying to make a point, dear heart."

I was quiet a moment. Then I said, "How did they find out?"

"How do they find out anything? Not from me, I promise."

I didn't know what to say.

"They love you, Barnaby," Mrs. Dibble told me, and now the laughter had faded. She was using a solemn, treasuring tone that embarrassed me. "It hasn't escaped their notice how you've cared for them all these years."

"So," I said. "You're not firing me?"

"Firing you!"

"Well, I know I didn't return a few of your phone calls—"

"Barnaby. I would never fire you. Did you really think I would? You're my very best worker! I tell everybody that! 'Barnaby's going to end up *owning* this company,' I say. 'You just watch: when I'm old and decrepit, it's Barnaby who'll buy me out.' "

"Who'll what?" I said.

"Oh, well, just on the installment plan or something. If only I could afford it, I'd give it to you for free! It means a lot to me to see a good man take it over."

I swallowed.

"But why are we discussing this *now*?" Mrs. Dibble asked. "For now, we have to think how you're going to manage all these assignments."

I said, "I'll find a way, Mrs. Dibble. You just leave it to me."

After I hung up, I sat there a minute, pressing my hands very tightly between my knees.

Then I phoned Sophia. I told her I was sorry. "I should have called before," I said. "I did get your messages. I've just . . . been in this mood, you know? I didn't feel all that sociable."

She said, "I understand. I understand perfectly. You don't have to explain."

"But I owe you an apology," I said. "Really. I ask your forgiveness."

"Of course I forgive you!"

Did it count if she didn't realize what she was forgiving me *for?*

Then she wanted to know if she should come over. But I thought if she came she would realize for certain, and so I said no. I said I was tired; I said I needed a shower. She didn't push it. She just said, "All right, sweetie. You get a good night's rest," and we arranged to meet the next day. I told her I was taking her out to dinner—someplace romantic.

I'd meant it when I said I was tired, but even so, I had trouble sleeping once I went to bed. I felt filled with determination. I was just about vibrating with all my plans for tomorrow.

I had to get hold of that price book. I had to sell my car and pay off my debt to my parents. And this was in addition to all those jobs for Rent-a-Back, because I couldn't let my clients down. They trusted me.

It began to seem that I really might have moved on in life.

10

"It's 'weathered and rusted,' " Len told me.

"It's 'fully drivable,' " I told him.

"It's an 'amateur restoration,' " he told me.

We were quoting from *The Collector's Automobile Prices*—the inside cover, where they explained their grading system. We were snatching the book from each other, to read aloud the phrases that supported our positions. I maintained my car qualified as Good, but Len was holding out for Poor. Secretly, I'd have been happy to settle for Adequate—the category between the two. But first I planned to put up a fight.

"If you took this to a dealer," Len told me, "he'd laugh in your face."

"Maybe I *should* take it to a dealer," I said, pretending to think it over.

A dealer would likely find about fifty things wrong with it besides what Len had already found. I knew Len was my best shot. And my bluff must have worked, because Len jumped in fast with, "Of course, no dealer would have your interests at heart the way I do."

"Or *your* interests the way *I* do," I told him. "That's why I'm giving you first refusal. You and I go back so far."

But I might have overdone it there. Len squinted at me suspiciously.

The place where I'd finally tracked him down was the Brittany Heights housing development—a series of treeless, shrubless hills out in Baltimore County. For all the snide remarks I'd made about Len's line of work, I had never actually visited any of his projects. This one was kind of eerie. Dotted about on the rolling greens, with no visible streets or driveways leading up to them and no signs of life anywhere around them, were these brand-new pastel stucco castles. They had turrets and battlements and arched front doors. The model, which we were standing in front of, flew a triangular banner from its crenellated roof. We might have strayed into a neighborhood of miniature kingdoms, all within sound of the Beltway.

"Suppose we say this," Len suggested, slapping the book shut and handing it back. "Suppose we call it Poor, but I tack on a thousand dollars for old times' sake."

The price for a Sting Ray in poor condition was forty-five hundred dollars. I shook my head.

"Two thousand?"

"Sorry," I told him. I tossed my keys up, caught them, and turned to get into the car. "Never say I didn't give you a chance," I flung back as I slid behind the wheel.

"Wait! Barn!" He grabbed hold of my door. "Where're you going?"

"Off to see the dealer," I said.

"What's your rush? We've just barely started talking here!"

"Well, hey," I told him. "You snooze, you lose." And I reached over to pull the door shut, but he wouldn't release it.

"Okay," he said. He heaved a put-upon sigh. "Just for you, then: we'll call it Adequate."

Adequate meant ten thousand dollars. I stopped hauling on my door.

Between the day we settled the price and the day I turned the keys over, about two and a half weeks passed—long enough for the red tape to be taken care of—but already it seemed to me that the car wasn't fully mine anymore. My August trip to Philly, for instance, Sophia and I made by train, because I could picture the irony of totaling on I-95 now that I had the money within my sights. And anytime I drove around town, I was more than usually aware of the salty, sun-warmed smell of the interior and the uniquely caved-in spokes of the steering wheel. I had never been a car man, never memorized all the models the way a lot of my friends had; but now I saw that a Sting Ray did have a very distinctive character. Out on the open road, it sounded like a bumblebee. Its artificial grilles and ports and vents, hinting at some barely contained explosion of power, reminded me of a boastful little kid.

I put off telling Pop-Pop. I decided I'd tell him after the fact, so that he couldn't keep me from going through with it.

On the second Saturday in September—a mild, muggy morning, overcast, the kind of day when it's hard to work up any enthusiasm—I drove to Len's garden apartment. Martine followed behind with the truck, so that I would have a ride back. Our whole transaction took place out front at the curb—Len circling the car several times, stopping to stroke a fender in this possessive, presumptuous way that got on my nerves. He was wearing his weekend outfit of polo shirt, khakis, and yachting shoes minus the socks. I couldn't abide how he combed his hair in an arrogant upward direction. And when he got in and started the engine, it seemed to me that he did it all wrong. That first little gnarly sound was missing; he wasn't gradual enough. I called out, "Careful, there—"

But Martine, lounging nearby with her hands jammed in her rear pockets, said, "Let it go, Barnaby," and so I did.

When we left she asked if I wanted to drive, but I lacked the heart for it. I sat slumped in the shotgun seat of the truck—*our* truck, for what that was worth, with its greasy vinyl upholstery and the graying white fur dice swinging from the mirror—and told Martine everything I disliked about Len Parrish. "It isn't that I blame him for letting me take the rap alone," I said. "He'd have done me no good coming forward; I understand that. But then to act so above it all! Tut-tutting with my mom about me; mentioning the Paul Pry business to Sophia. When he was in on it! When he was just as involved!"

"Let it go," Martine said again, switching her turn signal on.

"You saw how he acted this morning. So Mr. Cool, so . . . like, uncaring. I introduce you and he says, 'Uh-huh,' and doesn't even look at you; too busy gloating over the car. Doesn't even glance in your direction."

Sneakily, I glanced at her myself. She was sitting on the cushion she used for driving, one finger tapping the wheel as she waited for the light to change. Her profile was poked forward, beaky and persistent, intent on the signal overhead.

Martine and I had developed a new style of dealing with each other lately. We were careful not to touch, not even by accident, and we never quite let our eyes meet. Our tone of voice was casual and sporty. Like now: "So?" Martine said. "He's a jerk. Give it a rest, Gaitlin." And she slammed into gear and hooked a quick left turn in front of the oncoming traffic.

Maybe I should have said something. Brought things out in the open. But how would I put it, exactly? *Hey, okay; so we did something stupid. You're not going to let it change things, are you? Could we just hit the Erase button, here, and go back to the same as before?*

But I didn't say any of that, and she went on facing straight forward. She seemed to be driving with her nose. Both hands gripped the wheel; her house key dangled from the brown leather band that was looped around one wrist. I thought of something. I said, "The key."

"What key?"

"The key to the Corvette. I left it on the ring. I turned over my whole key ring, with that Chevy emblem my Pop-Pop gave me when he put the car in my name."

"So what? You'll be driving a Ford now. What do you want with a Chevrolet key ring?"

She was right. I couldn't argue with her logic. But that emblem had been with me a very long time. The plastic surface was so yellowed and dulled, you could barely make out the two crossed flags encased beneath it. At tense moments I would run my thumb across it, the way I used to stroke the satin binding of my crib blanket. I thought of Len doing that, and it killed me.

I must be more of a car man than I'd realized.

On Monday evening, I dropped by my parents' house, choosing an hour when I figured they would both be home. Sophia offered to come with me, but I had this picture in mind: me facing Mom and Dad in the entrance hall, slipping the money from Opal's clip and saying, "Here. I just stopped by to drop this off." And then I'd lay it on the flat of Mom's palm and leave. Sophia wasn't part of this picture; no offense to her. I needed to do it alone.

But these things never work out the way you imagine. First of all, it emerged that eighty-seven one-hundred-dollar bills made a stack too thick for a money clip. I had to ask the teller to fasten one of those paper bands around the middle. And then when I got to the house, my parents did not obligingly show up together at the door. (When did they ever, in fact?) Just my mother came, carrying a cordless phone and continuing with her conversation even as she let me in. "It's only Barnaby," she told the phone. "Wicky," she mouthed at me before she turned away. So I couldn't stay in the hall. I had to follow her into the living room, and settle on the couch, and wait for her to finish talking.

"Honestly," she told me as she punched the hang-up button. "I know I swore I would always get along with my daughters-in-law, but sometimes it's an effort." She turned toward the stairs and called, "Jeffrey?"

"What?" came back dimly, moments later.

"Your son is here."

"Which son?"

"The bad one," I called, just to save her the trouble.

Mom rolled her eyes at me and then came to sit in the chair to my left. She was wearing slacks and the man's white shirt she gardened in. (I had envisioned her more dressed up, somehow. Mom in her Guilford Matron outfit, Dad in his suit. Like a dollhouse couple, hand in hand in the doorway.) "How's Sophia?" she asked.

"She's fine."

"Why didn't you bring her with you?"

"Oh, well . . ."

"Sophia would never act the way Wicky does," she said. "Sophia's so considerate." And then she sailed into this tale about the birthday party Wicky was planning for Dad. "I said, 'We don't want you going to any bother, Wicky,' and she said, 'It won't be the least bit of bother,' and now I know why. Because first she told me all I had to do was show up, and then she told me, well, maybe I could make my artichoke dip, and then—"

"Whose truck is that in the driveway?" my father wanted to know. He walked into the room with a magazine suspended from one hand, his index finger marking a page. He did have his suit on still, but his tie was missing and he wore his velvet mules instead of shoes. "Red pickup," he told me. "Did *you* drive that here?"

"Yes; um . . ."

"You left your lights on."

"Well, I'll be going pretty soon," I said.

"Oh, don't hurry off!" my mother cried. "Stay for dinner! We're having shrimp salad. There's lots."

"Thanks, but I already ate," I said. "I just stopped by to—"

"Already ate? Ate dinner?" she asked. She checked her watch. "It's barely seven-thirty."

"Right."

"Goodness, Barnaby. You're so uncivilized!"

I looked at her. I said, "How do you figure that?"

"*We* always eat at eight," she said.

"Dine," I told her.

"Pardon?"

"You always *dine* at eight. Isn't that what you meant to say?"

She drew up taller in her seat. She said, "I don't see—"

"Gram and Pop-Pop dine at five-thirty, however," I said, "and what's good enough for them is good enough for me."

"Of course it is!" Dad told me. He bent to set his magazine on the coffee table, as if he'd decided the situation required his full attention. "But you could join us for cocktails," he said. "Scotch, maybe? Glass of wine?" He rubbed his hands together.

"Really I just stopped by to give you this," I said, and I picked up the denim jacket that was lying across my knees. The weather wasn't cool enough for jackets yet, but I'd needed something with roomy pockets. "Here," I said. I pulled out the brick of money and leaned forward to place it in my mother's lap.

She stared down at it. My father stopped rubbing his hands.

"I don't understand," my mother said.

"What's to understand?" I asked her.

"Well, what *is* this?" she asked.

"It's eighty-seven hundred dollars, Mom. Surely that must ring a little bell."

She glanced up at my father. He gazed off over her head, suddenly abstracted.

"But . . . is it yours?" she asked me. "Where did you get it? And in cash! Walking the streets of Baltimore with all this cash! How would you have come by such a large amount, I'd like to know?"

"No trouble at all," I told her. "Though it did make kind of a mess when the dye pack exploded."

"Seriously, Barnaby. Have you been up to something you shouldn't?"

Odd that it hadn't occurred to me she would jump to this conclusion. I made a snorting sound. I said, "Don't worry. It's legal. I sold the Corvette to Len Parrish."

"You sold the Corvette?" my father asked, suddenly coming to. "Son," he said. "Was that wise?"

I wasn't going to argue about it. I told Mom, "Feel free to count the money yourself, if you like. Make sure I didn't shortchange you."

For a moment, I thought she would do it. She picked up the bills in a gingerly way and turned them over. But then she said, "That's all right."

When they gave me the wad of cash at the bank it had seemed so bulky, but now I was struck by its slimness. For all these years, that money had loomed between us. I recalled Mom's hints and reproaches, her can't-afford-this, can't-afford-that, her self-assured air of entitlement as she inquired into my finances. I recalled my old daydream that she would cancel the debt when I married, or after my first child was born. And yet it made such an unimpressive little package! Granted, it was a lot of money—a lot for me, at least—but you'd think I could have come up with it before now.

I said, "Well, then. Are we fair and square? Everything settled?"

"I suppose," my mother said faintly.

Somehow there should have been more to this. More excitement, more relief; I don't know. I stood up. I said, "Well! Guess I'll be going."

My mother went on sitting there. It was Dad who walked me to the door.

For a month after Mrs. Glynn accused me, I had nothing to do with her. Sophia didn't, either (she was never going to speak to her again, she said), but I heard a little about her from Ray Oakley. He was the one who was going there in my place. He said she had cut her hours back to one a week, and even then he hardly saw her. "I try and steer clear of her," he told me. "I'm worried she'll say *I stole something too.*"

Me, I had pretty much let her fade from my mind. Sophia thought that was incredibly charitable of me, but it was more that I just figured things always evened out, sooner or later. Look at it this way: I might have done time in jail if I hadn't had rich parents. And even rich parents couldn't have helped if anyone had discovered I stole a Buick convertible the night of my sixteenth birthday. So when Mrs. Glynn said I did something I didn't, there was a certain justice to it.

Even losing my Corvette: a certain balance, you might say.

I was still in possession of Sophia's little porcelain slipper. I brought it back one evening and put it among some doodads on her mantel, where it didn't belong, so she would think she had simply misplaced it if she'd noticed it was missing. I didn't believe she had noticed, though. I felt artful and deft and catlike as I set the slipper soundlessly between a brass clock and a hobnail vase. I slid my hands in my jeans pockets and walked away whistling.

It wasn't entirely undeserved, Mrs. Glynn's accusing me.

Then one Friday afternoon toward the end of September, she telephoned. "Barnaby Gaitlin?" she said—pert little old-lady voice. But I knew so many old ladies, I couldn't think who she was. I said, "Yes?" in a guarded tone. When they called me direct, it was usually with a complaint.

"This is Grace Glynn."

I got very alert.

"Sophia's aunt," she reminded me.

"Yes," I said.

"How *are* you?" she asked me.

"Fine."

"Doing well?"

I waited to see what she was after.

"I was wondering," she said, after a pause. "Would you be so kind as to come to my house this evening?"

"Your house."

"Just for a little chat," she said. "It won't take long."

I said, "I guess I'll pass on that, Mrs. Glynn. Thanks anyhow."

"Please? Pretty please?"

"Sorry," I said, and I hung up.

There were limits to how charitable I was willing to be.

When the phone rang again, a few minutes later, I let the machine answer for me. But this time it was Sophia. "Barnaby, I wanted to ask if—"

I picked up the receiver. "Hi," I said. "I'm screening my calls. You'll never guess who from."

"Aunt Grace," Sophia told me.

"Oh. You knew she was calling?"

"She called me too. I just now got off the phone with her."

"What's she trying to pull?" I asked.

"She didn't say, but I guess we'll find out tonight."

"We will?"

"I told her we'd stop by."

"*I'm* not stopping by," I said.

"Oh, Barnaby. Please?"

She had a different voice from her aunt's—steadier and much lower—but the upward note at the end was the same. "I think she wants to apologize," she said.

"She didn't tell *me* she wanted to apologize."

"Well, why else would she ask us over?"

"Maybe to have me arrested," I said.

"Don't be silly. How she put it was, she wanted to 'chat.' She said, 'I know you're very cross with me, but please, please, the two of you, come for a chat.'"

"She's got some kind of ambush planned," I said. "SWAT team lying in wait for me behind her potted palm."

Sophia laughed, but dutifully, as if her thoughts were elsewhere. "How could I turn her down?" she asked. "So I said yes."

"You can't say yes on my behalf, Sophia. You had no business doing that."

"Well, but, sweetie. She's my aunt!"

I kept quiet a moment. Not to sound paranoid, but it crossed my mind that Sophia might be in on this, whatever it was. I knew she was too honorable for that, but even so, I had a little flash of doubt. Meanwhile, some other phone line seemed to be mixing in with ours—tiny distant voices I couldn't quite decipher, a woman burbling away and another woman laughing. The two of them were so lighthearted. I felt as if we'd plugged into not just another conversation but another time, simpler and more innocent; and here I was in this muddy, confused life of mine.

I told Sophia, "All right, hon. For your sake."

She said, "Oh, thank you! Thank you, Barnaby."

"But we're only staying a minute," I said.

"Of course."

"Just long enough to be polite, so things aren't awkward with your relatives."

"I understand."

Hanging up, I felt like a phony. Face it: I couldn't care less how things stood with her relatives. Underneath, my fantasy was that Mrs. Glynn really would apologize. And while she was at it, why couldn't all the others too? The Amberlys and the Royces, and Mr. McLeod with his Chinese statue. I pictured them lining up in Mrs. Glynn's parlor to say . . . what? Not that they'd wrongly accused me; that was too much to hope for. But maybe, oh, that they'd overreacted, or failed to allow for extenuating circumstances. Or that they still liked me anyhow. I don't know.

The plan was, I would drive to Sophia's after she got off work, pick her up, and then head to Mrs. Glynn's. But Martine was late bringing the truck back; she was out somewhere on a job. I had to phone Sophia and ask her to come get me. This was fine with Sophia—no doubt she preferred her Saab to my jouncing, bone-rattling truck—but it made me mad as hell. In the two weeks since I'd let the Corvette go, I'd been marooned without a ride three times and been yelled at twice when I'd marooned Martine. Also, we were stuck in a situation where we were thrown together constantly. Mrs. Dibble had always tended to pair the two of us up, for some reason, but now it was even worse. Every job assignment had to take into account that Martine and I shared a vehicle, although we lived five miles apart and couldn't stand to face each other anymore. What had I been thinking of, agreeing to such an arrangement?

And my poor little car, my little lost car. That car was my very identity—so ramshackle and rascally. I should never have let Martine talk me into selling it.

You see what I mean about my life being muddy.

Sophia arrived in her bank clothes, but I wore jeans and a stringy black sweater. No way was I dressing up for this. I climbed into the Saab, turning down her offer to let me drive. "Just gun that motor and let's get this over with," I told her.

She said, "Now, Barnaby, promise you'll be nice to her."

"Did I say I wouldn't be nice?"

"She's just a helpless old lady. Promise you won't forget that."

But as things worked out, it seemed to be Sophia who forgot.

Oh, she was congenial enough at the start. She pressed her cheek to her aunt's cheek, and she told her how pretty she looked. Mrs. Glynn wore a baggy-chested silk dress and a strand of pearls she could have jumped rope with, looped and looped again and hanging to her knees. I'd never seen her in jewelry before. Or leather pumps, either, instead of Nikes. And Tatters was yapping frantically in the pantry. The only other time I'd known him to be shut away was when the minister came to call.

"How've you been, Aunt Grace?" Sophia was asking. "How's your bursitis?" As if they were on the best of terms. It irked me some, I can tell you. When we sat down, I chose a rocker, not my usual seat beside Sophia on the couch. I tucked my hands between my knees and watched glumly as Mrs. Glynn arranged herself in her favorite chair.

"I can see just fine," she told Sophia, "except for reading. Why do you ask?"

This caused a shattered little pause, until Sophia's forehead cleared and she said, "Your bursitis, I said; not your sight."

"My bursitis. Oh. It's just lovely," Mrs. Glynn said, peculiarly. She laced her fingers together and leaned toward me. "Barnaby," she said, "I don't believe we've conversed since I discovered I was burglarized."

"No," I said, "we haven't." I felt embarrassed; Lord knows why.

"Of course, it was a *most* distressing event. Most distressing. But you know what I say: money is only money."

I'd never heard her say any such thing, but I nodded.

"In the final analysis," she said, "the human element is what counts. Wouldn't you agree?"

"Well . . ."

"You are a person my niece regards very highly. I can appreciate that. And Ray Oakley isn't half the worker that you were. I propose we let bygones be bygones."

It was while I was computing her words that Sophia's attitude changed. "If that doesn't take the cake!" she told her aunt.

"I beg your pardon?" Mrs. Glynn said.

"Let bygones be bygones? Generous of you, I must say!"

"Excuse me, dear?"

I said, "Sophia—"

"You owe Barnaby more than that, Aunt Grace. You owe him an apology. A complete and humble apology."

"Sophia, it's okay," I said.

I had never seen her like this. I felt kind of flattered. But, "We'll just put it behind us," I said. "No big deal."

"No big deal!" Sophia cried.

"Wonderful," her aunt told me. "And may I expect you to resume your regular hours?"

"No, you may *not* expect him to resume his regular hours!" Sophia cried. "Over my dead body he'll resume his regular hours!"

I said, "Hon." I turned to Mrs. Glynn. "Unfortunately, I've . . . ah, got those hours filled now," I said. "But I'm sure Ray Oakley—"

"You found the money, didn't you," Sophia told her aunt.

"What, dear?" her aunt asked quaveringly.

"You found it where you left it, and you don't have the courage to say so."

This struck me as assuming a bit too much. More likely, Mrs. Glynn had just recalled that I wasn't the only person who knew her hiding spot. I said, "In any case—"

"You are the most dishonest of all of us," Sophia told her aunt. Two scratched-looking patches of pink had risen in her cheeks. "You found that money and you won't admit it. I bet you didn't even notify the insurance company, did you?"

"On the contrary. I notified them at once," Mrs. Glynn said. "I would never commit *fraud*, for mercy's sake." She spoke very primly and evenly, somehow not moving her lips.

I stared at her.

"So there," Sophia told me, settling back in her seat.

"I don't know how I could have been so forgetful," Mrs. Glynn said. A teaspoonful of tears, it seemed, swam above each eye pouch. "I'd been listening to everybody's warnings, you know. Everybody warning me I shouldn't inform all and sundry where I kept my cash. So I took it out of the flour bin and I moved it elsewhere. Well, I'll *tell* you where: I moved it to the pocket of my winter bathrobe. Then I just . . . I don't know; I must be getting senile. I forgot! I looked inside the flour bin and I saw there was no money and I forgot I'd moved it! I hope I don't have Alzheimer's. Do you think I might have Alzheimer's? I went along for weeks not recollecting, and then this morning when the weather turned I was getting some of my woolens out of the cedar closet and I saw my winter bathrobe and I said, 'Oh, good heavens above. That's where I moved my money to!' I've been a fool, children. I've been a forgetful old fool."

"It could happen to anyone," I told her. "Don't give it another thought."

I looked over at Sophia, waiting for her to chime in, but she had this flat look on her face. "Right, Sophia?" I asked.

"Hmm?"

"We've all done things like that, right?"

"Oh, yes . . ."

"So if you've got Alzheimer's, Mrs. Glynn, I guess all the rest of us have it too."

Mrs. Glynn tried to smile, dangerously swelling the spoonfuls of tears. I said again, "Right, Sophia?"

"Right," she said after a moment.

"Well. That settles that," I said, and I stood up. "No need to show us out," I told Mrs. Glynn.

"To shout?"

"No need to *show us out*, I said."

"Oh."

I wanted to get going before she could bring up my work hours again. (I wasn't *totally* forgiving.) But Sophia stayed on the couch, still wearing that flat expression. At the door I said, "Sophia?"

She rose, finally, and so did Mrs. Glynn. They didn't kiss goodbye. "Well, Aunt Grace," was all Sophia said, "I hope next time you won't be so quick to accuse an innocent man." And she hoisted her purse strap onto her shoulder. Mrs. Glynn stood straight as a clothespin, her hands knotted tightly together.

I would have expected Sophia to act more gracious. But I felt sort of pleased that she didn't.

In the car I said, "So! Turns out you were right about why she wanted to see us."

"Yes . . . ," Sophia said. She made no move to start the engine.

I said, "How about I buy you dinner."

"Dinner?"

"What's the problem, Sofe?" I asked. "Something on your mind?"

She looked over at me. She said, "I had no idea Aunt Grace had changed her hiding place."

"Well, she'd better change it again," I said, "because already she's told at least two people where the new place is."

"And so I put the money back in the old place," Sophia went on, as if I hadn't spoken.

"What money?" I asked.

"*My* money. Two thousand, nine hundred and sixty dollars."

For a second, I misunderstood. I said, "*You* stole that money?"

Which didn't make sense, of course, since no money had been stolen, but all Sophia said was, "Me? No." She started the engine, and we pulled away from the curb.

I said, "Begin at the beginning, Sophia."

"See, I felt so responsible," she said. We arrived at an intersection, and she braked and looked over at me. "I knew Aunt Grace held me to blame for bringing you into her life. 'Well,' I said to myself, 'all right, I'll just put my own money there to replace the money she's missing.' So I took it out of my savings. I called in sick at work on a Tuesday, Aunt Grace's podiatrist day, and I let myself in with my key and put the money in the flour bin."

"But . . . how would she explain that? First her money is missing, and then it magically isn't?" I said.

"She could explain it any way she liked," Sophia said.

"And for sure the new bills would be a different denomination from the old ones. You never saw the old ones, did you? You don't know if they were tens or fifties; you don't know if they were rubber-banded, or stuffed in an envelope, or tucked away in a wallet, do you?"

"No, and I don't care, either," Sophia said. She flung her head back so recklessly that a hairpin flew out of her bun and landed in the rear seat. "All I cared about was clearing your name."

"Some criminal *you* would make," I said.

Then I saw what was bothering me. Forget the logistics; forget the question of denominations, rubber bands . . .

I said, "You believed I did it."

"No, no," Sophia said.

A car drew up behind us and honked.

"You actually believed I stole that money."

Sophia took her foot off the brake. We crossed the intersection, but on the other side she pulled over to the curb and parked. "It's not the way it looks," she said, turning to face me. "I just couldn't stand for her to suspect you; that's all."

"Well, geez, Sophia, are you going to start stashing bills every place there's been a burglary I was in the neighborhood of? That could get expensive."

"No," Sophia said, "because I don't have any more to stash. I used my whole savings account, and next month's rent besides."

I put my head in my hands.

"But, Barnaby? It's no problem. I'll just steal it back again, the next time I'm over there."

"Sure," I said, raising my head. "Unless meanwhile she goes to bake a pie or something and finds your money before you get to it."

"She won't do that. She keeps her flour in the freezer, not the flour bin," Sophia said. "I could leave it there forever!" Then she started smiling. "You know what this reminds me of?" she said. "That O. Henry story, the Christmas one. 'Gift of the Magi.' "

"How do you figure that?" I asked her.

"I mean, here I give you this gift, and it turns out you have no need of it. Still, though, it wasn't for nothing, because it proves how much I love you."

"Well," I said.

I have to admit I was touched. No one had ever done anything like that for me before.

I said, "But that story had both people giving gifts, didn't it?"

"*You* are your gift to me, Barnaby," she told me. And when she leaned close to kiss me she smelled of flowers, and her lips felt as soft as petals.

Sometimes I thought I'd been right in the first place: Sophia was my angel.

It was a tradition in my family—I mean, my own little failed *ex*-family, family in quotation marks—that Natalie would remind me when Opal's birthday was coming up. She would phone about a week ahead, no doubt doing her best to find a moment when I was out so that she could leave a message on my answering machine. "Barnaby," this year's message went, "Opal's birthday falls on the actual day of your visit this year; so you'll be able to bring your gift in person instead of mailing it. I just thought you'd like to know that."

I imagined her congratulating herself on her subtlety. "Don't act like the cad you are and forget your own daughter's birthday," she was saying, but it came out sounding all thoughtful and solicitous. I pictured her dimples denting inward with satisfaction as she hung up the phone.

Another tradition was, my gifts were always disasters. (A goldfish that died, a storybook that gave Opal nightmares, a pencil case that snapped shut on her thumb and made her cry.) So this year I asked Sophia to come shopping with me. She picked out a stuffed hedgehog—a sort of bristle ball with a button nose—and then she wrapped it for me, better than I could have done, for sure, with a satin bow and a silver gift card. On the card I wrote, *Happy birthday from Barnaby and Sophia.* Adding Sophia's name was a spur-of-the-moment decision—I'd just wanted to thank her for helping—but she looked so happy when she saw it that I was glad I'd thought of it.

We drove to Philadelphia in her Saab, with me at the wheel till we reached Locust Street. There I climbed out, and she took over. "I'll see you in three hours," she said, because she no longer spent Saturday nights at her mother's. She'd told her mother she had her own life, now, to get back to. Her mother had said, "Well, fine, then. Just don't bother coming at all, if that's how you're going to be." But Sophia came anyway, every blessed Saturday, calmly ignoring her mother's sulks and pointed remarks. Sophia was such a *sunny* person. She didn't let people get to her. I admired that. I wished I could bring her to Natalie's with me.

But as it was, I had to go it alone. Stand alone at Natalie's door like a poor relation; wait meekly for someone to answer my ring. It was Opal who answered, thank heaven. No sign of Natalie, although she must have been nearby, because Opal called, "See you, Mom!" before she let herself out.

She was wearing a rose-colored jacket, so new that I had to pluck an inspection tag from the sleeve. Beneath it she had on a lace-trimmed dress and white lace tights and patent-leather shoes. I said, "Don't you look nice," and she grimaced and said, "I had to get dressed ahead of time for my party. It's at three."

"Well, happy birthday," I said. I handed her my gift.

Then we stepped into the elevator, which was still standing there from when I'd ridden it up. Opal lifted the gift box to her ear and shook it, but she didn't open it. Used to be, she would rip right into it. Maybe she'd lost hope by now.

"Mom and Dad's present was a canopy bed," she said as we descended.

I hadn't known she called him "Dad." It gave me kind of a jolt.

"The canopy is white eyelet, and there's a ruffled spread to match."

I said, "Isn't that—" and then stopped myself from repeating the word "nice." Instead I said, "Watch your step," because we had reached the lobby.

It wasn't till we were outdoors, heading toward Rittenhouse Square, that I realized we were missing the dog. "Where's George Farnsworth?" I asked her.

"He had to go to the kennel till we're finished with the party. If there's too many kids around, he gets all excited and wees on the rug."

"How many kids will there be?" I asked.

"Twenty," she said.

"Twenty!"

"A professional magician's coming, and after that we're having a cake with a whole ballet scene on top in spun sugar."

"Well, isn't that—"

I paused at the corner of Locust and Seventeenth. I looked down at Opal and said, "Where're we going, anyhow?"

She shrugged. The weather was cold enough so I could see the puffs of her breath.

"We don't have a dog to walk," I said, "and it's too early for lunch."

"We could sit in the park," she suggested.

This seemed kind of lame, but I said, "Fine with me," and we started walking again. Opal carried her gift in both hands, like something precious. I began to feel less confident about it. Probably a stuffed animal was too childish. (My mother had suggested an opal on a chain—October's birthstone. Martine had suggested a video game, but I thought Natalie might disapprove.)

In the park, we met up with the usual crowd—unshaven men slumped on benches, rich old ladies tripping along with tiny, fussy dogs better dressed than I was. We found an empty bench, and I brushed the dead leaves off so we could sit. Opal placed her gift very precisely on her knees and started untying the bow. It was one of those rosette-shaped bows—I'd been impressed no end that Sophia knew how to make it—and Opal would have done better just slipping the whole thing off the box, but no, she had to untie it. I realized she must be just as worried as I was about how to fill the time. After she got the ribbon off, she wound it around her hand and tucked it in her pocket, and then she unstuck the card (first rolling the strip of Scotch tape into a cylinder and pocketing that too). *"Happy birthday from Barnaby and Sophia,"* she read aloud. She looked over at me. "Who's Sophia?"

"Sophia! You remember Sophia. Who cooked all those suppers when you were in Baltimore. And went with us to the Orioles game."

She studied the card a moment longer. Then she set it on the bench between us and painstakingly undid the wrapping, not once tearing it. Out came the box. She took the lid off. I realized I was holding my breath. She folded back the tissue and lifted out the hedgehog. Pathetic little critter, no bigger than my fist. "Thank you," she said, eyeing the button nose.

"Well. I didn't know what kind of thing you liked these days."

"This is fine," she told me.

"I could take it back and exchange it, if you'd rather."

"No, this is great. Really."

"Well. Okay," I said.

Opal put the hedgehog back in the box and replaced the lid. Then she picked up the gift card and looked at it again. Even turned it over to look at the other side, which was blank.

"So," she said. "Did you and Sophia, like, go halfsies on the money for this?"

"No, it was more that she helped me pick it out."

"Oh."

"You do remember her," I said.

"Sure," she said. Then she said, "I guess."

"You guess? You saw her every day of your visit, almost!"

"But I thought she was just a lady," she said.

"Just a . . . ?"

"I mean, is she, like, your *girlfriend* or something?"

"Well, yes, she is," I said. "I thought you knew that. We've been seeing each other for eight or nine months now."

"Seeing as in dating?" Opal asked.

"Didn't you realize?"

She shook her head. She wore this stony, set expression that made me uneasy.

"Ope?" I said. "Does that bother you?"

She just went on shaking her head.

"Did you not *like* Sophia, Ope?"

She said, "I liked her okay." Then she clamped her mouth tight shut again.

"So what's the problem?"

"Nothing's the problem!" she told me. She stood up, hugging the box to her chest. The wrapping paper wafted to the ground, but she seemed not to notice. "Could we go eat now?" she asked.

"Eat? Well, all right," I said.

Although it was nowhere near lunchtime yet.

I bent to retrieve the paper and tossed it into a trash bin, and then we walked out of the Square and headed toward a diner I knew of, a couple of blocks away. I figured we could order some sort of semi-lunch, semi-breakfast dish—French toast or something. I wondered what time it was. I kept trying to get a glimpse of people's watches, but everybody wore long sleeves and I didn't have any luck.

Then just as we started to cross the street, I caught sight of Natalie. She was standing on the opposite corner in her red coat and a long black scarf, and she must not have noticed that the light had changed to walk, because she was gazing off to her left. I don't know why I felt so startled. This was her neighborhood, after all. She was probably running a few last-minute errands before the birthday party. But I thought to myself, *What* is *this? She pops up everywhere*—as if she'd materialized not just once or twice but anytime I turned around, flashing in and out of view like a glimmer in a pond. I stopped short and said, "Oh! There's—!" and Opal followed my eyes and said, "Mom."

We crossed to where she stood. When she saw us, she didn't seem surprised. Natalie never seemed surprised. She surveyed me imperturbably, holding her head very level on account of the scarf, which gave her a sort of madonna-like aspect. I said, "Hi there, Nat."

"Hi," she said. Her gaze dropped to Opal. "Are you having a good time?" she asked.

"I'm cold," Opal told her.

"Cold?"

This was the first I'd heard of it, and I was about to say so if Natalie accused me of negligence. All she said, though, was, "What's in the box?"

"Barnaby gave me a hedgehog."

"Stuffed," I explained, as if I needed to. "A stuffed *toy*, I mean; not taxidermy, ha ha . . ."

"Shall I carry it home, Opal, so you won't have to lug it around?"

But Opal clutched the box tighter and said, "Maybe I could come with you."

Natalie's eyes returned to me.

I told Opal, "I thought we were having lunch at the diner."

"Yes, but I'm so cold," she said. "And besides, I've got my party dress on. I don't want to spill food on my party dress. We could maybe go next time, instead. Another time we could go! I promise!"

Natalie and I studied each other a minute longer.

"Another time. Sure," I said finally.

Then I gave Opal a little, like, cuff to the shoulder to show there were no hard feelings. But even so, when I turned to leave, she called after me, "Barnaby? You're not mad at me, are you?"

I lifted an arm as I walked and then let it flop, not looking around.

Back in the Square, I sat on a bench and stretched my legs out in front of me. It *was* cold. A woman in a plaid hat and cape was feeding the squirrels. A teenage boy loped past, and I said, "Hey, guy? You got the time?" Too late, I saw he was wearing a headset and couldn't hear me. I felt kind of foolish, with my question left hanging in the air like that.

Probably I had two hours to kill. Or two and a half, even, before I could head back to Locust, where Sophia was picking me up. I ought to go to the diner after all. Order something time-consuming. But instead I kept on sitting there, expressionless as the men on the benches all around me.

This wasn't just about Opal.

I have to say, it was Natalie who weighed more heavily on my mind.

"Could I interest you in some lemonade?" she had asked on that first afternoon, and her face had been so peaceful. Her back had been so straight; her gaze so steady. But after we'd been married awhile, she turned irritable and brisk. Any little thing I did wrong, flounce-flounce around the apartment. And I did tend to do things wrong. This weird kind of sibling rivalry set in; I can't explain it. I just had to defeat her, had to prove my own brash, irresponsible, rough-and-tumble way of life was better. And yet I'd married her because *her* way was better. Just as some people marry for money, I had married for goodness. Ironic, if you stopped to consider.

When she left me, I thought, *Well, finally!* I stopped attending classes, and I did some serious drinking, and I slept till noon or two p.m., and nobody was around to nag or look disapproving.

Now I see that I went a little crazy, even. Like, the kitchen sink in our apartment had this spray-hose attachment. If you pressed the button while the faucet was running, the faucet cut off and the hose cut on; and I remember standing there on many an occasion, pressing the button and releasing it, alternating between faucet and hose, marveling at how polite they were. The faucet stopped to let the hose talk; the hose stopped to let the faucet talk. So mannerly, so genteel. I thought, *All these years, I've underestimated the qualities of inanimate objects.*

Or the view outside my bedroom window: a big, tall spruce tree leaning over the alley. Every morning, waking up, I noticed once again that it leaned at the exact same angle as the pine tree in the highway signs—those signs showing a tree and a table to indicate a picnic ground. And every morning, I went on to wonder why the tree in those signs was tilted. Was there some special significance? Was it meant to imply protection, shelter? I mean, I thought this *every single damn everlasting morning.* You try doing that sometime. It seemed my mind got into a rut, and it wore the rut deeper and deeper, and I couldn't yank it free again.

And some nights I brought a girl home and we'd be going through the preliminaries, carrying on some artificial oh-isn't-that-interesting conversation on the couch, and she would give me this sudden puzzled look, and I'd lift a hand to my face and find my cheeks were wet. Water just pouring out of my eyes. I won't say tears, because I swear I wasn't crying. But my eyes were up to *something* or other.

So many things, it seemed, my body went ahead and did without me.

Well, that stage passed, by and by. I moved out of the apartment, developed a new routine, forgot about Natalie altogether. I'd see her when I collected Opal and when I brought Opal back, but she was never really present in my mind. Not that I was aware of, at least. Not consciously.

Here I had been thinking that the train trip where I'd first glimpsed Sophia had changed my whole existence; and in fact it had, but it was Natalie who had set that in motion. I saw that now. It was Natalie in her kitchen, her face as sealed and peaceful as the day she had offered me lemonade. *Could I interest you?* It was the cookie jar on her windowsill—that humble, chipped birdcage jar we used to be so proud of when we were kids together. Oh, once upon a time I'd had all I could ask for: a home, a loving wife, a little family of my own. A *place* in the world. How could I have thrown that away?

At Rent-a-Back, I knew couples who'd been married almost forever—forty, fifty, sixty years. Seventy-two, in one case. They'd be tending each other's illnesses, filling in each other's faulty memories, dealing with the money troubles or the daughter's suicide or the grandson's drug addiction. And I was beginning to suspect that it made no difference whether they'd married the right person. Finally, you're just with who you're with. You've signed on with her, put in half a century with her, grown to know her as well as you know yourself or even better, and she's *become* the right person. Or the only person, might be more to the point. I wish someone had told me that earlier. I'd have hung on then; I swear I would. I never would have driven Natalie to leave me.

Sophia looked so light-colored, when she arrived to pick me up. I felt a little shocked, as if I had forgotten which woman I was linked with nowadays. But also I was relieved. "Sophia!" I said. "Sweetheart!" And when she stepped out to let me slide into the driver's seat, I hugged her so hard that she laughed at me.

I told her Opal had liked the hedgehog. I didn't go into the rest of it. I certainly didn't admit that I had spent the last couple of hours sitting alone on a bench. Sophia said, "Oh, good," and pursued it no further.

One of the qualities I loved in her was her willingness to accept the surface version of things. I reached over to squeeze her knee—a bounteous, soft handful encased in slippery nylon.

Then, after we reached the highway, she sailed into this saga about shopping with her mother. "She told me she needed new bras," she said. "The only thing she won't buy through the mail. So we got into my car—never mind that she lives in the middle of downtown; she has to drive out to the suburbs—and right away it was, 'Oh, don't take this road; take that road,' and, 'Don't turn here; keep straight.' 'Mother,' I said, 'I promise I will get you there. Show some faith,' I said, but would she listen? 'That road is under repair now,' she said. 'Take the road I tell you.' I said, 'I'm sure they'll give us a detour route,' but she said, 'I don't want a detour route!' Then, when I turned anyhow, she fell into a pout. She sat there moving her lips for the rest of the ride—which was easy, incidentally. Nothing but a few traffic cones. But coming back, what did she do? Started the whole business over again. 'Don't take this road! Take that road!' "

It seemed to have escaped Sophia's notice that she could simply have followed her mother's instructions. What difference would it have made? But I didn't point that out. In this new, contented frame of mind, I just smiled to myself.

"Mother inquired after you, by the way," Sophia said.

"Hmm?"

"She said, 'How is that young man you've been seeing?' Then later she asked if I would be up for Thanksgiving, and when I said I didn't know yet, she said, 'You're welcome to bring your friend.' "

"Oh," I said. "Well. I guess I could come, if you want me to."

"I told her no," Sophia said.

This was fine with me. I said, "Whatever you decide."

"She'd be needling us every minute. Believe me."

"It sounds like our mothers have a lot in common," I said.

Which I used as yet another excuse to squeeze that handful of knee. I was thinking I'd like to get her into bed once we reached Baltimore, but Saturday afternoons could pose a problem. At my place, the Hardestys would be everywhere—kids squabbling on the patio right outside my door, Joe hammering away at some little task from his Job Jar. And Sophia's roommate had an annoying habit of cleaning house on Saturdays.

"She'd be sure to make all these not-so-subtle references to my weight," Sophia said, evidently still talking about her mother. " 'More turkey, Barnaby? I won't offer *you* any, Sophia. I know you wouldn't want the extra calories.' "

"Don't you dare lose an ounce," I told her.

There was a luscious little pouch of flesh on her inner thigh just above where her knee bent. It sprang back beneath my fingers like a ripe plum.

"With you, it would be your career," she said. "Mother's asked me three times now whether you've ever thought of other employment."

"She really *does* have a lot in common with Mom," I said.

"I tell her, 'Mother, drop it. Barnaby's very happy doing what he's doing,' I say, and she always says, 'Yes, but would his salary feed a family?' "

"It could," I said.

"It could?"

"It could if it weren't a very *hungry* family."

Sophia made a face at me.

I knew what we were creeping up on here—what we were skating around the border of. We had never, in so many words, discussed getting married; but I think lately it had been on both our minds. I said, "The way I see it, everyone has a choice: living rich and working hard to pay for it, or living a plain, uncomplicated life and taking it easy."

"Well, *you* work hard, Barnaby. You're practically a slave! Wakened up anytime Mr. Shank gets lonely, setting your alarm for crack of dawn on garbage days . . ."

"Yes, but it's the kind of work I enjoy," I said. "And at least it's not nine to five."

"Six to midnight is more like it!"

"Hey," I said, and I eased my foot on the accelerator. "Do *you* think I ought to change jobs?"

"No, no," she said.

"It sure sounds as if you do."

"I just hate to see you work such long hours," she said, "and not get better paid for it."

"I'm paid enough to live on," I said. Then I got bolder. "Maybe enough for a wife besides, if the wife was frugal."

The word "wife" hung in the air between us. It didn't really sound all that bad, after my meditations in the park.

"And face it," I said, hurrying on. (At heart, I was a coward.) "What other work could I do? I don't have any useful skills. My education's been a farce. All I've learned is trivia."

"Oh, that's ridiculous," Sophia said. "Of course you have useful skills! There's no such thing as trivia."

"There isn't?"

I had never heard that before. It struck me as so erroneous that I couldn't decide where to start attacking it. In the end, I said, "Well, here: During the Second World War, when butter was scarce in Germany, the Germans started eating their toast with the buttered side down. That way, they could use less butter and still taste it."

"Pardon?"

"But what's surprising is, when the war was over, they went back to buttered side up. You'd think they would have formed a new habit; but no, they reverted to buttered side up the very first chance they got. That's the kind of trivia I mean."

Sophia was silent. A truckful of chickens passed us—stacks and stacks of crates, strewing feathers.

"Well, anyhow," she said, finally. "One option I might suggest is, finish up your degree and then apply at my bank."

"Your bank!"

"They offer an excellent training program, with full fringe benefits while you're learning."

"I'd rather die than work in a bank," I said.

I felt Sophia's face whip toward me. I glanced over and saw how pink her cheeks were. "Well. Sorry," I said, "but—"

"It's all right for *me* to work in a bank, but you're above such things. Is that what you're saying?"

"Now, hold on, Sofe—"

"*I* can work nine to five, and scrimp and save up my earnings, which, by the way, I have lost every bit of, my entire savings account wiped out, and thirty dollars in my checking account to last till the end of the month; *I* can pay for the—"

"Wait," I said. "Surely you're not holding me to blame for that fool stunt you did with your money."

"Fool stunt? I did it to save you! I thought I was protecting you! I thought you would be grateful!"

"Why should I be grateful? I never robbed your aunt. And I certainly never asked you to cover for me."

"No," she said. And more quietly, she said, "No, you didn't. I realize that. It was my mistake. You had nothing to do with it. But I just feel, I don't know, frustrated when you talk about your plain, uncomplicated life and simple tastes, and I meanwhile am wishing for . . . oh, nothing fancy! Just to eat out a little more often, go to a play or a concert every now and then. Take a couple of trips together. But we can't! You don't make enough money, and mine is at the bottom of Aunt Grace's flour bin!"

This last sentence ended in kind of a wail. I put my arm around her, although I had to keep an eye on the road. "Hon," I said. "Look. First of all, I don't understand why that money is still at your aunt's."

"Well, I told you I haven't been back there. I'm very cross with Aunt Grace, and she knows it. I think she wasn't nearly as apologetic as she ought to have been."

"So? You have a key to her house. Slip in sometime when she's out. Slip in on her podiatrist day, or her beauty parlor day. Steal your money back again."

"Oh, I couldn't do that," Sophia said.

"Why not?"

"I'm worried she might catch me."

"You didn't let that stop you when you put it there in the first place."

"But it's different, getting caught *taking* money," she told me.

"Lord God, Sophia! Not if the money's your own!"

"There's no need to shout at me," she said gently.

Then she drew away, sliding out from under my arm.

I didn't talk anymore after that, and I barely grunted when she made some comment on the scenery. "Isn't that tree a pretty shade of yellow!" Grunt. It seemed I was my difficult, unappreciative self again. For all the good it did, I might as well not have bothered with my epiphany in the park.

These little glints of wisdom never last as long as you would expect.

Maud May had been in the nursing home for over seven months now. First it was one thing and then another. I'd begun to think she was one of those clients who go in and never come out again. Her house had taken on the faded, seedy look of a place that's been abandoned, and it gave a start and shrank back on itself whenever I walked in. The spider plant I'd been watering all this time had grown so many baby plants that some of them trailed to the floor.

But then at the end of October—Halloween, in fact—they said she was well enough to leave. I remember it was Halloween because she asked me to pick up some trick-or-treat candy before I came to collect her. "I don't want any neighbor brats soaping my windows in spite," she told me. Though how she expected to answer the door when they rang, I couldn't say. She was still exceedingly lame.

So I dropped Martine at Mrs. Cartwright's, where the two of us were scheduled to clear out the guest room, and then I went to the super-market. Halloween this year wasn't likely to amount to much. A thunder-storm had been threatening since early morning. But I bought three sacks of fun-size Almond Joys, along with the other items on Maud May's shop-ping list—the prunes and the all-bran cereal, a single grapefruit, a skinny one-quart carton of skim milk. Anyone could have told at a glance that these were an old person's groceries.

When I let myself into her house, I tried to view it through her eyes. Should that spider plant be so brownish at the tips? And how about the drawers in the sideboard: did they look *snooped into*, somehow? I hadn't snooped; I swear I hadn't; but you never know what people will imagine.

At the Silver Threads Nursing Home, Maud May was ready and wait-ing. She sat beside the reception desk in the wheelchair they always force departing patients to ride in. A jumble of belongings crowded the floor all around her. "At last!" she snapped when she saw me. "Bentham, we can go now."

Bentham was the orderly who was joking with the switchboard girl—a young black guy about seven feet tall, with a wedge-shaped hairdo. He threw one last remark over his shoulder and came to help me carry the luggage out. Suitcases, hatboxes, potted plants, a folded aluminum walker . . . We loaded them all in the back of the truck. A misty rain had started falling, and Bentham said, "Ms. May not going to be too happy about this"—meaning the fact of the open truck bed. "You want I should hunt up a tarp?" he asked.

But I said, "Never mind," because I figured things would get all the wetter while we waited. Besides, Maud May wasn't the fussy type.

She'd changed, though. I should have known. I'd certainly seen enough signs of it, over the months I'd been visiting. First off, as Bentham was wheeling her through the door, she barely acknowledged the staff's good-byes. "You're leaving us?" they asked her. "Well, you take care, now, hear?" Granted, they were most of them using a honeyed, high, thin, baby-talk voice that probably drove her nuts, but still, she could have said, "Thanks." She didn't. She gave an indifferent wave, not troubling to look back.

Then, outside, she cried, "What!" so sharply that Bentham stopped pushing her. "I'm going home in a truck?" she asked me.

"It's just a short ride, Ms. May," I said.

"What happened to your darlin' little sports car?"

"Well, I sold it."

"Good Gawd, Barnaby, you're an idiot," she said.

But already beads of rain were shining on the top of her head, and she didn't protest when Bentham started wheeling her again.

Helping her into the truck's cab caused another hitch. "Damn thing is too far off the ground," she told me. And, "Jesus! My luggage is sopping!" as she happened to glance toward the rear. Bentham *tsk*ed and hoisted her up by one elbow. I said, "At least your plants'll be watered, Ms. May." She didn't smile. After I shut her in, she sat staring straight ahead, dead-faced, and she failed to lean over and unlock the driver's-side door when I came around. I had to use my key. You see a lot of that with invalids. They start out vowing they won't depend, but then they seem to get *into* it. They turn all passive. Still, I hadn't expected it of Maud May.

"You be good, Ms. May!" Bentham called as we rolled off.

Ms. May just said, "What choice do I have?"

We didn't need our wipers at first, with the rain so light and fine, but gradually the windshield grew harder to see through. I was kind of waiting for Ms. May to mention it. I thought she would order me around in that tough-talking way she used to have. But she kept quiet, staring straight in front of her. Finally I flicked on my wipers unbidden. I said, "So! How does it feel, getting sprung?"

"Oh . . . ," she said. And then nothing more.

We reached her house, and I parked at the curb. Maud May didn't even glance toward her front door. Luckily, the rain had stopped by then. I say "Luckily" because once I'd helped her down from the truck, it took her forever to inch up the walk in her walker. Step, rest, step, rest, she went, and several times she pointedly lifted one hand or the other and wiped it on the front of her coat, although I had dried the walker off after I unloaded it. Halfway along, a neighbor came out—a pudgy-faced woman with gray hair—and she took charge of Ms. May while I brought in the luggage. "Why, Maud, you're doing wonderfully. Just wonderfully," she said, but all Ms. May would answer back was, "Huh." I kept passing them, traveling between the truck and the house, and every time, Ms. May had her head down, her eyes on her feet as they shuffled behind her walker. "Sturds," she said at one point, and the neighbor said, "What's that, dear?"

"Sturds: those klutzy, thick brown oxfords they used to make us wear at Roland Park Country Day School."

Actually, her shoes were black, not brown, but I caught her drift. Till now, she'd always worn vampish heels with sling backs and open toes. Also, she used to claim she would never be seen publicly in pants, but this morning she had on not just pants but sweatpants, elastic-waisted, cuffed bunchily at the ankles.

They'd delivered a hospital bed the day before, and it was set up in the sunporch so she wouldn't have to climb stairs. I arranged her belongings nearby where she could reach them. Then I steered her up the front steps, while the neighbor followed, hands cupped to catch her if she stumbled. "Smells musty," Ms. May said as she entered.

"We'll air it out," the neighbor assured her. "Throw open all the windows and just chase those cobwebs right out of here!"

"Well, Elaine," Ms. May said abruptly, "perhaps we'll meet again sometime. Goodbye, now."

The neighbor took on a stunned look, but she was still smiling steadily, her face very bright and determined, when she turned to leave. I told her, "Thanks a lot!" to make up for Ms. May's bad manners. "She was only trying to help," I said, once the door was shut.

"Get me onto that couch," Maud May told me, "and then go."

"Yes, ma'am," I said.

"This is the first time in seven months that some jackass fellow human won't be sharing my breathing space."

"Hey. I can dig it," I said. I felt a tad bit better, because she was starting to sound like herself.

Even so, that experience put a damper on my day. I'm telling you: don't ever get old! Before I started at Rent-a-Back, I thought a guy could just make up his mind to have a decent old age. Now I know that there's no such thing—or if once in a blue moon there is, it's a matter of pure blind luck. I must have seen a hundred of those sunporch sickrooms, stuffed wall-to-wall with hospital beds and IV poles and potty chairs. I've seen those sad, quiet widow women trudging off alone to their deaths, no one to ease them through the way they'd eased their husbands through years and years before. And if by chance the husband's the one who's survived, it's even worse, because men are not as good at managing on their own, I've come to think. They get clingy, like Mr. Shank. They tend to lack that inner gauge that tells them when they're talking too much; they're always trying to buttonhole the nearest passerby. Ask them the most offhand question; they lean back expansively and begin, "Well, now, there's a funny little story about that that I think may interest you." And, "To make a long story short," they'll say, when already they've gone on longer than God himself would have patience for. They pull this trick where they change the subject without a pause for breath—come to the end of one subject and you're thinking at last you can leave, but then they start in on the next subject; not so much as a nanosecond where you can say, "Guess I'll be going."

And those retirement watches old people consult a hundred times a day, counting off minute by minute! Those kitchen windowsills lined with medicine bottles! Those miniature servings of food, a third of a banana rewrapped in a speckly black peel and sitting in the fridge! Their aging pets: the half-bald cat, the arthritic dog creeping down the sidewalk next to his creeping owner. The reminder notes Scotch-taped all over the house: *Lawn-mowing boy is named RICHARD. Take afternoon pill with FULL GLASS OF WATER.* The sudden downward plunges they make: snappy speech one day and faltering for words not two weeks later; handsome, dignified faces all at once in particles, uneven, collapsing, dissolving.

The jar lids they can't unscrew, the needles they can't thread, the large print that's not quite large enough, even with a magnifying glass. The specter of the nursing home lurking constantly in the background, so it's, "Please don't tell my children I asked for help with this, will you?" and, "When the social worker comes, make like you're my son, so she won't think I live alone." The peculiar misunderstandings, part deafness and part out-of-syncness—insisting that someone named "Sheetrock Mom" bombed the World Trade Center, declining a visit to a tapas bar in the belief that it's a topless bar, calling free-range poultry "born-again chicken," and asking if the postpartum is blooming when what they mean is impatiens. "Don't you look youthful!" a physical therapist said once to Mrs. Alford, and she said, "Me? Useful?" and the thing that killed me was not her mishearing but the pleasure and astonishment that came over her face.

They walk down the street, and everyone looks away from them. People hate to see what the human body comes to—the sags and droops, splotches, humps, bulging stomachs, knobby fingers, thinning hair, freckled scalps. You're supposed to say old age is beautiful; that's one of those lines intended to shame whoever disagrees. But every one of my clients disagrees, I'm sure of it. You catch them sometimes watching children, maybe studying a toddler's face or his little hands, and you know they're marveling: so flawless! poreless! skin like satin! I doubt they want to be young again ("Youth is too *fraught*," was how Maud May always put it), but I'm positive not a one would turn down the chance to be, say, middle-aged.

"Fifty was nice," Mr. Shank told me once. "Fifty was great! Sixty was too. And sixty-five; I was doing good at sixty-five. But then somewhere along there . . . I don't know . . . I said to my wife, Junie—this was when Junie was still living—'Junie,' I said, 'you know? Some days I'm afraid I might commit suicide.' And Junie, she just looked at me—she was one of those *zestful* people; energetic, zestful people—and she said, 'Well, Fred, I'll tell you. Sometimes I'm afraid I might commit suicide myself.' She didn't, of course. She passed away in her sleep, God rest her. One morning I woke up and I knew without even looking; it felt like our bedroom was quieter than it ever was before. But, now, what was I saying? What point was I trying to make? Oh. If *Junie* could feel that way, such a zestful person as Junie, then I don't see as there's any hope whatsoever for the rest of us."

He said it so matter-of-factly, like someone delivering a weather report. And then turned in his chair and looked out the window, absently smoothing his kneecaps with both hands, the way he always did when he sat idle.

And Mrs. Cartwright: now, this was just the kind of thing I was referring to. The reason she wanted her guest room cleared out was, she had arranged for a live-in companion. Some woman from a classified ad. Companions generally mean a lot fewer hours for Rent-a-Back, but that's not what bothers me. It's that once they've moved in, they tend to take over. They leave their magazines lying around, and switch channels on the TV without asking, and throw out perfectly edible food, and smell up the air with strong perfume. I've heard it all! Still, it's not our place to argue. Mrs. Cartwright said she had to face the fact that she hadn't had a good night's rest since her husband died. Every little creak sounded like a footstep, she said. So we'd been called in to clear thirty years of clutter from the guest room, and the following week a total stranger was coming to keep her company.

By the time I got there, Martine had emptied the bureau and started on the closet—knitting supplies and sewing remnants and half-finished squares of needlepoint. "How was Maud May?" she asked, and I said, "Old," which made her pull her head out of the closet and give me a look. But instead of speaking, she tossed a ball of yarn at me. I dodged, and it landed squarely in the garbage can she'd set in the center of the room. "Ta-dah!" she said.

"Sure, at *that* distance," I told her. I moved the garbage can farther away and reached past her for another ball of yarn. It always soothes my mind if I can get some kind of rumpus going. And Martine was good at that; she was kind of rowdy herself. We started slam-dunking every dispensable item we came across, and maybe a few that weren't. A jar of buttons, for instance, which burst when it landed with a gratifying, hailstone sound that made me feel a whole lot better.

But then Mrs. Cartwright called out, "Children? What *was* that? Is everything all right?"

We grew very still. "Yes, ma'am," I called. "Just neatening up."

After that, I sank into a mood again.

We were dragging an unbelievably heavy footlocker out to the hall when I asked Martine, "Have you ever thought of changing jobs?"

"Why? Am I doing something wrong?"

"I mean, doesn't this job get you down? Don't you think it's kind of a *sad* job?"

She straightened up from the footlocker to consider. "Well," she said, "I know once when I was taking Mrs. Gordoni to visit her father . . . Did you ever meet her father? He'd been in some kind of accident years before and ended up with this peculiar condition where he didn't have any short-term memory. Not a bit. He forgot everything that happened from one minute to the next."

I said, "Oh, Lord."

"So he was living in this special-care facility, and I had to drive Mrs. Gordoni there once when her car broke down. And her father gave her a big hello, but then when Mrs. Gordoni stepped out to speak to the nurse, he asked me, 'Do you happen to be acquainted with my daughter? She never visits! I can't think what's become of her!' "

"See what I mean?" I said.

"*That* kind of got me down."

"Right."

"But then you have to look on the other side of it," Martine said.

"What other side, for God's sake?"

"Well, it's kind of encouraging that Mrs. Gordoni still came, don't you think? She certainly didn't get *credit* for coming, beyond the very moment she was standing in her father's view. Just for that moment, her father was happy. Not one instant longer. But Mrs. Gordoni went even so, every day of the week."

"Well," I said. Then I said, "Yeah, okay."

Martine wiped her face on the shoulder of her shirt. Her sleeves were rolled to her elbows, and her house key swung from the wide leather band that circled her wrist. It wasn't *designed* to circle her wrist. It should have been hooked to a belt loop, but since she didn't have a belt loop, she wore it like an oversized bracelet instead; and all at once I was fascinated by how she'd come up with this arrangement. The workings of her mind suddenly seemed so intricate—the wheels and gears spinning inside her compact little head.

But when she said, "What," I said, "*What* what," and bent to lift the lid of the footlocker.

Just as I had suspected, I found stacks of moldering books cramming every inch. Nothing's heavier than books. These had bleached-looking covers in shades of pink and turquoise that don't even seem to exist anymore. *Let's Bake! Fun with String. Witty Sayings of Our Presidents. The Confident Public Speaker.*

"Mrs. Cartwright?" I called. "Are you around?"

Of course she was around. She was wringing her hands at the bottom of the stairs, probably longing to come supervise if only her heart had allowed. "Yes?" she said, craning up at me.

"How about those old books in the footlocker? Shall we toss them?"

"Oh, no. My son might want them. Just put them in the basement."

Yes, and that's another thing: the possessions choking the basements and clogging the attics, lovingly squirreled away for grown children. The children say, "We don't have room. We'll never have room!" But the parents refuse to believe that the trappings of a lifetime could have so little value.

We put the footlocker on a scatter rug and slid it—a trick I'd learned my first day of employment. Martine backed down the stairs ahead of me. Mrs. Cartwright stayed planted in the foyer, tugging fretfully at her fingers as if she were pulling off gloves.

When we got back to the guest room, Martine grabbed a broom while I consulted Mrs. Cartwright's list. " 'Move nightstand in from room across hall,' " I read aloud.

"I already did that."

I stepped aside to let Martine sweep where I'd been standing. She was raising a little dust cloud—too enthusiastic with her broom. Wiry tendons flickered beneath the skin of her forearms. Really her skin was more olive-colored than yellow; or maybe that was a trick of the light. I glanced back down at Mrs. Cartwright's list. "Did you turn the mattress too?" I asked.

"Not yet," she said, "because I wasn't sure what that meant. Turn it? Turn it how?"

"Flip it to its other side," I told her. "Haven't you ever done that? It's usually part of spring cleaning."

"It isn't part of *my* spring cleaning. I've never turned a mattress in my life. Do you turn yours?"

"No, but I've done it lots of times for clients," I said.

Then—I don't know why—I started feeling embarrassed. It was something about the word "mattress." I almost wondered, for a second, if that was one of those words you shouldn't say in mixed company. (These notions hit me every so often.) I hurried on. I said, "Especially back when Mrs. Beeton was alive. About once a month, I swear, her kids would be phoning up: 'Help! Get on over to Mama's! Mama's talking again about turning her . . .' "

Maybe I should call it a pallet. Was that too much of a euphemism? Fortunately, Martine didn't seem to be listening. She had propped her broom in a corner, and she was moving toward the other side of the bed. "In fact," I told her, "that happens to be how Rent-a-Back began. I bet you didn't know that. Mrs. Dibble's mother was turning hers one day, and it got away from her. When Mrs. Dibble came to check on her that evening, she found her flat as a pancake underneath it."

Martine's eyes widened. "Dead?" she asked.

"No, no; just mad. Mrs. Dibble said, 'You should have hired a man to do that,' and her mother said, 'I can't hire a man just to turn one . . . mattress!' and Mrs. Dibble said, 'Well, I fail to see why not.' And she went home and dreamed up Rent-a-Back."

"Grab an edge, will you?" Martine asked me.

I did, finally. I heaved my side of the mattress upward and came over to the other side to help Martine support it. We were standing so close that I could hear the clink of one overall clasp when she drew in her breath. I could feel that concentrated, fierce heat she always gave off; I could smell her smell of clean sweat.

She said, "How do you get your mouth to curl up at the corners that way?"

"Practice," I said. And then, "Whoa! Look at the time." (Although there wasn't a clock to be seen.) "I promised to meet Sophia for lunch," I said. "We'd better hustle."

Martine let her end of the mattress drop. For a moment I had all the weight of it before I let mine drop too.

In the truck, she started a fight. It wasn't me who started it. She claimed that I had promised to drive her to her brother's. Her brother's wife had had a new baby. But I had promised no such thing; this was the first I'd heard of it. "How could she have a new baby?" I asked. "I seem to recollect she was pregnant just a while ago."

"She *was* pregnant just a while ago. And now she's had her baby."

"See?" I said. "This is why I should have got a car of my own. Something used, I could have bought, with the rest of my Sting Ray money. Instead I'm having to split this dratted truck."

"My heart bleeds for you," Martine said.

"Besides, a truck's a problem for old folks to climb into. It's not appropriate! That high-up seat, and Everett's silly fur dice—"

All at once, Martine reached over and swiped the dice off the mirror in one quick motion. Just snapped the string that held them, tossed the dice in the air, caught the two of them one-handed, and stuffed them into her jacket pocket.

"Satisfied?" she asked me.

"Well, hey," I said.

"You think it's easy for me, letting you keep the truck at your place? Begging you for a ride anytime I need to go somewhere? But *I* don't have any choice! I don't come from a fat-cat family! I can't just waltz out and buy myself a car if I decide a truck's not 'appropriate'!"

"You don't need to bite my head off," I said.

We had reached her house by now, and I pulled over to the curb. But Martine stayed where she was, poking her sharp yellow face into mine. "I don't know why I bother hanging out with you," she said. "You're sarcastic and moody and negative. You think just because you're good-looking you can take up with any woman you want. You think you're so understanding and sweet with those poor old-lady clients, but really you just . . . hit and run! You have no staying power! You couldn't stick around even if you tried!"

I was astounded. I said, "Huh?" I said, "Where did all *this* come from?" And when she didn't answer, I said, "You're the one who fixed it so you'd have to rely on me for your rides."

"Now, that is just exactly what I'm talking about," she said. Making no sense whatsoever.

Then she jumped out of the truck and slammed the door hard behind her.

I took off, with a screech of my tires. I went on fuming aloud as if she were still there. "Maniac," I said. "Lunatic." I asked, "Didn't I say all along this truck scheme would be a pain?"

Anyone who heard me would have thought I was demented.

13

"We are probably the only family in America eating a potluck Thanksgiving dinner," my mother said, gazing around the table.

"Oh, surely that can't be true," Gram said. "Good heavens! Many's the time, in the old days, I was asked to bring my marshmallow-yam casserole when Aunt Mary had the dinner at her house."

"That's one kind of potluck, Mother. The organized kind, where the hostess assigns a dish to each guest. But I'm talking about the other kind: catch as catch can. Pot *luck*, with the emphasis on 'luck.' Who else would be doing this?"

Mom's own dish was a redundancy; that's why she was annoyed. She had made one of her famous pumpkin chiffon pies, which turned out to be what Wicky had made too. (Using Mom's recipe. I could see how that might have been a faux pas.) Also, there was no turkey. At Jeff's insistence, he and Wicky were hosting the dinner this year, and so everybody assumed that they would supply the turkey. But they hadn't. Wicky said her oven was too small for a turkey that would feed ten people. It seemed all her efforts had gone instead into the decorations: twists of crepe paper in harvest gold and orange festooning the dining room, and an entire family of Pilgrims marching the length of the table, with lighted candlewicks sticking up out of their heads. Plus, at the start of the meal she had made us all join hands and sing "Come Ye Thankful People, Come." Except that she and Sophia were the only ones who knew the words beyond the very first line.

Our menu was: two pumpkin chiffon pies, Gram's marshmallow-yam casserole, Sophia's Crock-Pot Applesauce Cake, and a salad that Opal had tossed with a vinaigrette dressing. This was nice for Opal, because we were all so glad to see something nonsweet that her contribution was the hit of the day.

Me, I'd chosen the easy way out and brought four bottles of wine. I guess I could have complained myself, since I had specifically purchased a wine designed to complement turkey. But hey. This way, I figured, I would probably get to carry a couple of bottles home with me.

"I did inquire," my mother was saying. "I asked Wicky at least two weeks ago: 'Wicky, what *category* of food should I bring?' But, 'Oh, whatever you want,' she said. 'I'm sure it will all work out.' " Mom trilled her fingers in a breezy manner, apparently mimicking Wicky. " 'We'll each of us just *do our own thing*,' was what she told me. 'That will be much more fun, don't you feel?' "

I'd have taken umbrage, if I were Wicky, but Wicky smiled obliviously and handed J.P. a carrot disk from the salad.

"Oh, well," my grandpa said. "The important thing is, we're together. That's what Thanksgiving is all about! Everyone gathered together. Wouldn't you agree, Jeffrey?"

My father said, "Eh? Ah. Yes, indeed," and poured himself more wine. He tended to remove himself when Pop-Pop started one of his homilies.

"And we've all got our health, knock on wood. Mother's blood pressure's under control; my eyesight's no worse for the moment. Opal is with us this year, and she's turned into a young lady! J.P.'s been upped to a booster seat. . . ."

Evidently Pop-Pop was proceeding in order around the table. Some Thanksgivings he went by age, but today he began with Gram, at his left (wearing her sequined turkey T-shirt), and then himself, and then Opal and J.P. on his right—J.P. in a miniature business suit, already smeared with pumpkin.

Next came my brother, at the head of the table. "Jeff is on the road to being a stock-market millionaire," Pop-Pop said, and Jeff leaned back with a genial laugh and laced his hands across the front of his suit. The successful patriarch; that must be the image he was aiming for. I don't know why I hadn't understood that till now. The only patriarch in Jeff's acquaintance had been our Grandfather Gaitlin, a big-bellied man who'd loved a good cigar, which would explain why Jeff was nursing an imaginary paunch and letting his laugh trail off in an emphysemic wheeze. "Well, not exactly a *millionaire*," he was saying through a smoker's cough. No wonder he was so keen on hosting all family gatherings!

Pop-Pop moved on to Mom. "Margot here's the new chairwoman of the Harbor Arts Club," he said, while Mom gave a Queen Elizabeth smile, first to her left and then to her right. "And Jeffrey, of course, continues to set an example for all of us with his philanthropic activities. . . ." My father winced, bowed, and took another sip of wine.

I never could tell who, exactly, Pop-Pop was conveying his information *to*. We ourselves already knew it. God, maybe? I glanced up at the ceiling.

"Sophia, Miss Sophia, is sharing our Thanksgiving for the very first time," Pop-Pop said, "but we're hoping it won't be the last, by a long shot." Sophia flushed and directed a smile toward her bosom. She was wearing her hair drawn up high on her head today, which made her look formal and elegant.

"We credit Sophia with helping a certain young man begin to settle down," Pop-Pop said. "Speaking of who . . ." And then it was my turn.

"Didn't I always tell everyone Barnaby would be fine? He's a good, good boy," Pop-Pop said, leaning across the table to gaze earnestly into my face. "In fact, I think some might say he's found his angel. Hah? Hah?" And he sat back and looked around at the others. "Wouldn't you agree?"

But no one would take him up on that (a Kazmerow had no business tossing around the subject of the Gaitlins' angels), and so he proceeded to Wicky. "And last but not least, our charming hostess. *Nazdrowie,* Wicky!"

"To Wicky," we chimed in, raising our glasses. (All except for J.P., who was busy with a marshmallow.) Even Opal shyly held up her Pepsi can. Wicky said, "Oh, go on. I didn't do anything much!"

I saw Dad give Mom a look from under his eyebrows, warning her not to second that.

If a meal is mainly dessert, it's hard to know when it's over. Wicky got up to clear, finally, but she refused all offers of help, and so the rest of us went on sitting around the table. I saw my reserve bottles of wine rapidly disappearing. In fact, I suspected Jeff was getting tipsy. "Pass that bottle on *down!*" he said at one point, in his new, fat-man voice. "Who's hogging the bottle?" And when it turned out to be finished, he sent me for some of his own private stock from the basement. Or the "cellar," was what he called it. "Fetch me a cabernet from the cellar, will you, Barn? There's a good fellow." His accent was becoming just the teeniest bit British.

I rose obediently—I was feeling very sober and responsible, maybe on account of Pop-Pop's speech—and went through the kitchen and down the stairs to the basement. A fully stocked wooden wine rack sat next to the washing machine. I picked out the most expensive-looking cabernet I could find and climbed the stairs with it.

In the kitchen, Wicky was scraping plates. Her dress was a beige knit, cut narrow as a tube, and she was standing in a way that made her rear end look like two small, tight grapefruits nudging against the fabric. They just called out to be cupped by two hands. They *ordered* it. I got one of my irresistible urges, and I set the wine bottle on the counter and took a step closer.

My mother said, "Barnaby."

My heart stopped.

I whirled around and said, "*What?* I was just getting wine! Jeff asked me to bring up some wine."

"Yes, but I don't think we need it, do you? We've all had more than enough," Mom said.

"Oh," Wicky said, turning. "Should I be making coffee?"

"Let me do it," Mom told her. "You go out and sit awhile."

"Why, thank you. That's so nice of you!" Wicky said.

Of course, she had no idea that Mom claimed the coffee tasted more like tea when Wicky made it.

I grabbed the wine bottle and started to follow Wicky into the dining room, but Mom laid a hand on my arm "Barnaby," she said again.

"Yes, ma'am," I said. I still wasn't sure if she'd guessed what I'd had in mind for Wicky's two grapefruits.

"I want you to take this back," Mom said, and from somewhere in her clothing she brought out a folded powder-blue check.

I said, "Huh?"

"It's your money."

"What money?"

She pressed it into my hand. I think it was because it was in the form of a check that I was so slow on the uptake. First I set the wine bottle down on the counter; then I unfolded the check and peered at it for a moment. *Pay to the order of Barnaby Gaitlin, Eight thousand seven hundred and no/100 dollars.*

"Why?" I asked her.

"I've decided not to keep it."

This didn't thrill me as much as you might expect. I went on studying the check, hoping it would tell me something further. The space after *For* had been left blank. If only she had filled it in! I raised my eyes, finally.

"Why?" I asked her again.

"Oh . . . ," she said, and she turned away and reached for the percolator. "It just seemed the right course of action," she tossed over her shoulder.

"But you've always said I should pay it back."

"Oh . . ."

"You said *that* was the right course of action."

She noisily ran water into the percolator.

"You just want me to stay fixed in my accustomed role," I said. "You would feel more comfortable if I went on being indebted."

"Don't be absurd," she told me, shutting off the water.

"Now that I've repaid you, you've got nothing to hold over me."

"That's absurd. You can never repay me."

"Pardon?"

She wouldn't answer. She made a big show of measuring out the coffee.

"I just *did* repay you," I said.

She kept her lips clamped shut.

"Eighty-seven hundred dollars," I reminded her. "Every cent. In cold cash."

She wheeled on me. She said, "Do you honestly believe *money* will make up for what I went through? Visiting all our high-class neighbors, throwing myself on their mercy, pleading with them not to press charges?"

"I never asked you to do that," I said.

" 'Well, Mrs. Gaitlin, we'll need to think this over,' " she said, putting on a pinched and simpering tone of voice. " 'We'll need to give it some thought,' they told me. That insufferable Jim McLeod: 'I doubt if you fully comprehend, Mrs. Gaitlin, what a rare and valuable object that ivory happened to be.' They loved to see me beg! Upstart Margot Gaitlin. It goes to show, they were thinking: you can take the girl out of Canton, but you can't take Canton out of the . . . 'Just look at her son, if you need proof,' they said. Oh, always you were *my* son. I suppose I felt that way myself. Jeff was more related to Dad, but you were related to me. You I had to personally apologize for. You think you can repay me for that? You can never repay me. Not with eight thousand, not with eight hundred thousand! Take your money back."

"Don't you wish," I told her, and I ripped the check in two. Then I made confetti of it, ripping it again and again and letting the little pieces flutter to the floor. My mother just stared—her mouth open, a spoonful of ground coffee suspended between us.

I had imagined that we'd been shouting, but when I stormed into the dining room I realized none of the others had heard us. They were still lounging around the table, and all Jeff said when he saw me was, "Where's the wine, bro?"

"Oops," I said, and I made a U-turn into the kitchen and retrieved the bottle. It was no affair of mine how much he drank.

The Pilgrim candles were headless now, their shoulders curly-edged bowls of wax. They looked like torture victims. Wicky rose and blew them out, saying, "Let's adjourn to the living room, shall we?" By the time Mom brought in the coffee tray, I was on the couch, playing a game of cribbage with Opal. I waved the tray off without looking up, and no one thought anything of it.

Opal had learned cribbage just the day before, her first evening at my parents', but already she was good at it. I felt kind of proud of her. "Fifteen-two, a run of three for five, and his nobs for six," she said smartly. *I* never remembered to call the jack "his nobs." I said, "Way to go, Ope," and she sat back and grinned at me. With her legs tucked under her, you could see that the knees of her black tights were about to develop holes. I found that encouraging, somehow.

I had this sudden, startling thought: Would Opal get a visit from *her* angel, somewhere on down the line?

She was a Gaitlin, after all. Strange to realize that. She did have my last name and at least a few of my genes, even if they weren't obvious.

Wicky was rocking J.P. to sleep, humming something tuneless. Jeff was poking the fire. (Another patriarchal activity, I guessed.) Sophia sat next to Gram on the love seat, and Dad occupied the one remaining chair. So when Pop-Pop returned from a trip to the john, he had to nudge me down the couch a ways. "Ah, me," he said, sinking heavily into the cushions. "How's the car, Barnaby?"

"Um . . ."

As luck would have it, my mother approached him just then with the tray. "Coffee, Daddy? It's decaf."

"Now, what the hell do I want decaf for? What's the point of coffee if it don't have any kick to it?"

"Think how much better you'll sleep, though, Daddy."

"Ha," he said, but he helped himself to a cup and stirred in several spoonsful of sugar, while she waited.

"Jeffrey?" my mother said next, heading toward Dad.

"Yes, thanks. I will have some."

She bent to rest her tray on the lamp table beside him. "Barnaby won't let me give him back his money," she told him.

"Eh?" my father said.

"His eighty-seven hundred. He won't take it."

I felt Sophia glance over at me, but the others paid no attention. "Fifteen-two, fifteen-four, and a double run for twelve," Opal announced, while Jeff set aside his poker and took another swig of wine.

"I tried to give it back to him," my mother said, "but he tore up the check."

"We'll discuss this some other time, shall we?" my father said pleasantly.

"I want to get this settled, though."

"Another time, I told you."

"What other time? We hardly ever lay eyes on him!"

"Margot," my father said. "Do you suppose we could make it through one holiday without your tiresome fishwife act?"

Wicky stopped humming. There was a pause, and then my mother lifted her tray and proceeded back to the kitchen at a dignified pace. A second later, we heard the tray slamming onto a counter. A faucet started running. Dishes started clattering. Wicky looked over at Jeff, but he minutely shook his head, and so she stayed seated.

Gram cleared her throat. "Sophia, dear!" she said. "Tell us! What does *your* family do for Thanksgiving?"

Well, at least they didn't publicly demolish each other, Sophia could have said; but she told Gram, "Oh, nothing very exciting, I'm afraid. Usually, Mother's two cousins come for dinner, along with one cousin's husband. And then this year she's invited my Aunt Grace from Baltimore too."

"She's invited your Aunt Grace?" I asked.

But I don't think Sophia heard, because Gram was saying, "Isn't that lovely! And will they be serving a turkey?"

"Oh, yes. In fact, it's kind of like you-all's arrangement—a potluck— although Mother does assign specific dishes. For instance, Aunt Grace is bringing her chestnut dressing. She fixed it ahead of time, except for the baking, and I helped her onto the train with it, but Lord knows how she'll manage at the other end of the trip."

"You helped her onto the train?" I asked.

All this was news to me, I can tell you.

Sophia sent me an absentminded smile. "The cousins are in charge of the vegetables," she said, "and Cousin Dotty's husband makes the pies. He's an excellent cook, although in all other respects he's considered something of a—"

There was a crash in the kitchen, followed by the tinkling of glass. Sophia stopped short. The rest of us exchanged glances.

Gram said, "Yes, dear? Something of a . . . ?"

"Oh! Something of a . . . ne'er-do-well, I suppose. But—"

A metal object clanged so loudly that it gave off an echo, like a gong.

"Maybe I should go out there," Wicky said.

"Stay where you are, why don't you," my father told her blandly.

She sat back, drawing J.P.'s deadweight body closer against her.

Sophia looked from one of us to the other.

"Ne'er-do-well!" I said.

Sophia said, "What?"

"I haven't heard that term in ages!"

"You haven't heard . . . 'ne'er-do-well'?"

"It's almost Old English, don't you think?" I asked the room at large. I had to raise my voice to be heard above the racket from the kitchen. "It's almost something Robin Hood might have said! In fact, a lot of those bad-guy words are like that: so quaint and antiquey. 'Ruffian.' 'Knave.' 'Wastrel.' 'Scoundrel.' Ever noticed?"

No one had, apparently.

" 'Layabout.' 'Rapscallion,' " I said. " 'Scofflaw.' 'Scum of the earth.' "

" 'Beast of burden,' " Opal offered unexpectedly.

"Well, that's a *little* off the subject . . . or maybe not, come to think of it. And 'ill-gotten gains.' 'Misspent youth.' Or, let's see . . ."

" 'Besetting sins,' " my father said from his armchair.

"Right! Besetting sins. But it's not the same for good-guy words, at least not as far as I've—"

The telephone rang. We were all so relieved that every last one of us stirred as if to go answer it, but Mom picked it up in the kitchen. We could hear her intonation, if not her exact words. "Mm? Mm? Hmm-hmm-hmm."

Then she appeared in the doorway. "Barnaby," she said—her voice noncommittal, her face composed, not a hair out of place—"that was that Martine person, and she says to tell you she has the truck but she'll bring it by in the morning."

"Thanks," I said.

Pop-Pop asked, "What truck is that?"

I said, "Oh, just the, you know, work truck."

"Fool kid sold off the Sting Ray," my father told my grandpa.

"He did what?"

"Sold off the Corvette Sting Ray and bought a used Ford pickup."

Pop-Pop leaned forward on the couch to peer at me. I could feel his stare, even though I had my back to him. I turned and told him, "I was planning to mention that."

"You sold the Sting Ray?"

He was so amazed, the whites of his eyes showed all around the irises.

"Well, yes, I did," I said.

"*Why?*"

I said, "I needed the money."

"The money, son: you could have borrowed money from me! I'd have been glad to lend you money!"

"Well, see . . . the whole point was, not to be in debt anymore. Not to owe anybody."

Pop-Pop's jaw went slack.

"But, Barnaby," he said finally. "That was the only year the Corvette had a split rear window."

"Oh, *damn* that split rear window!" I said. Then I said, "Sorry." I looked around at the others. They all wore the same accusing expression— even Opal. (Or maybe I was imagining things.) "I mean," I said, "I do know what a big deal it was, Pop-Pop—"

"Shoot," Jeff said suddenly. "It broke my heart when Pop-Pop gave the Corvette to you."

"It did?" I asked.

"I would have killed for that car!"

"You would?"

I sat there a minute absorbing this, chewing the inside of my cheek. Dad, meanwhile, took over the conversation. "Of course, when I was Barnaby's age," he said, "I went out and *worked* if I needed money, but nowadays, it seems—"

"With all due respect, Dad," I told him, "you were never my age."

"Excuse me?"

"Times are different, Dad, okay? What I've experienced, you haven't. And vice versa, no doubt. So you can't compare us, is what I'm saying." I turned back to my grandpa. "I'm sorry, Pop-Pop," I told him. "Giving me that car was the best thing anyone's ever done for me, and don't think I don't know that. But I'm trying really hard to grow up now, don't you see? And I had to sell the car to get there. I hope you understand."

I could hear the rustle of Mom's apron as she wrapped her hands in it. Then Pop-Pop said, "Why, sure, son. It was yours to do what you liked with."

After that we had a fairly normal evening, but that was just because all of us were exhausted.

• • •

Sophia and I had driven over in the Saab, and we'd both assumed that I would go back to her house for the night, since the roommate was out of town. But on Jeff's front walk I said, "Why don't *you* drive, and that way you can drop me off at my place." Then I felt the need to invent too many excuses. "I have to get to work so early tomorrow, and Martine won't know where to pick me up, and besides, Opal mentioned something about breakfast. . . ."

Sophia just said, "All right," and we set off toward her car. I got the impression she was glad, even. Probably she could use a night alone herself.

Earlier it had been raining, and now the air had a damp, chilly feel. The car windows misted over before we'd gone a block. I grew extremely conscious of how closed in we were. Our breaths were too loud, and the tinny sound of Sophia's cake platter, sliding across the back seat at each turn, made our silence more noticeable.

Finally she said, "You didn't tell me your mother offered to give you back that money."

"How could I? It just now happened," I said.

"I don't see why you refused it."

I stared at her. I said, "What: you too?"

"It's eighty-seven hundred dollars, after all. Think what we could do with that."

"Well, lots. Obviously. But that's beside the point. I didn't want to worry about that money anymore."

"So you'd rather *I* worry about money."

"You? How do you figure that?"

"Well, I'm the one who couldn't buy a new outfit for Thanksgiving because my money's in the flour bin."

"So? Get it *out* of the flour bin. You said yourself you've been in touch with your aunt again."

"Oh, I knew you'd hold that against me!" she cried, swinging the car onto Northern Parkway.

I said, "Huh? Hold what against you?"

"She's my aunt, Barnaby. I don't have so many relatives that I can afford to discard a perfectly good aunt."

"Well, sure. I realize that," I told her.

"And it made me feel just awful, being on the outs with her. So I called her on the phone one day last week. I meant to tell you about it; honestly I did, but somehow it slipped my mind. I asked her how she was, and she said she had a cold. Well, what could I do? Hang up on a sick old woman? I went by to see her at lunch hour. I brought her some soup and some nose drops. I couldn't just let her fend for herself!"

"Of course you couldn't," I said.

Did she think I didn't know how these family messes operated? The most unforgivable things got . . . oh, not forgiven. Never forgiven. But swept beneath the rug, at least; brushed temporarily to one side; buried in a shallow grave. I knew all about it.

I rolled down my window a quarter of an inch, thinking it might help defog the windshield. I said, "But you still haven't gotten your money out of the flour bin."

"No."

The whistling sound from my window helped to fill the silence.

"Why not?" I asked her finally.

"Hmm?" she said. She leaned forward to swab the windshield with her palm—a mistake, but I didn't point that out.

"Why *haven't* you gotten your money?"

"Oh, it's . . . never been the right time," she said.

"Now would be a good time," I told her. "While your aunt's in Philadelphia."

"Barnaby! I can't just sneak in like a thief!"

She kept her eyes on the road while she said that. It made her indignation sound fake. All at once I found her irritating beyond endurance. I noticed how the streetlights lit the fuzz along her jawline—fur, it almost was—and how large and square and bossy her hands looked on the steering wheel. Managerial: that was the word. Wasn't that why her other romances had ended, if you read between the lines? "I'm probably too . . . definite," I seemed to remember her saying. "Too definite for men to feel comfortable with." Darn right she was too definite!

And then that lingering, doting voice she used when she spoke of herself as a child—"When I was a little girl . . ."—as if she had been more special than other little girls. And her eternal Crock-Pot dinners; oh, Lord. If I had to eat one more stewy-tasting, mixed-and-mingled, gray-colored one-dish meal, I'd croak!

And her predictability: her Sunday-night shampoos and panty-hose washing, her total lack of adventurousness. (Wasn't it a flaw, rather than a virtue, that she'd been so incurious when the passport man gave her that envelope?) Her even temper, her boring steadfastness, her self-congratulatory loyalty when she assumed I had stolen from her aunt. Here I'd been hoping she would bring me up to her level, infuse me with her goodness! Instead she had fallen all over herself rushing to protect my badness.

I said, "Sophia. Let's go get that money."

"Absolutely not," she said, and she was so prompt about it, she practically overlapped my words.

"*Why* not? If it belongs to you, why can't you?"

She said, "Don't badger me, please. It's really none of your concern what I do with my own private funds."

"In fact, it is, though," I said. "In fact, every time I turn around, you're telling me how hard your life is now that you've lost your money. You're going on and on about all the things you can't afford because your money's in the flour bin, and you know what I think, Sophia? I think you *like* to have it in the flour bin. I think you feel that as long as it's in the flour bin, I owe you something. I'm starting to suspect you have no intention of getting it back. You prefer it that I'm beholden to you for your sacrifice."

"Well, that's just simply not true," Sophia told me.

You would think she'd have raised her voice, at least, but she didn't. Her tone was low and reasonable, and she went on staring straight ahead, and she remembered to signal before she pulled into my driveway. Even that I found irritating. She was just as angry as I was; I knew it for a fact, but she'd already lost two boyfriends, and she'd promised herself she would hang on to this one no matter what a . . . ne'er-do-well he might turn out to be. Oh, I could read her like a book!

I remembered what I'd told Mrs. Alford when I was describing Great-Grandpa's visit from his angel. Angels leave a better impression, I'd said, if they don't hang around too long. Or something to that effect. If they don't hang around making chitchat and letting you get to know them.

Here is how my Pop-Pop happened to give me the Sting Ray:

I was just about to graduate from the Renascence School, and I'd been accepted at Towson State, and Dad had promised to find a summer job for me. So far he hadn't succeeded, but that's a whole other story. The point is, I was doing okay for once. My life was looking up. There was a lot of talk about clean slates and new beginnings, et cetera, et cetera.

Then, at Easter, I came home for the long weekend and got into a little trouble. Well, I'll just go ahead and say it: I locked my parents out of the house and set fire to the dining room.

I can't explain exactly how it started. How do these things *ever* start? It was your average Saturday-night supper; nothing special. My brother had brought a girlfriend. He was living on his own by then, in an apartment down on Chase Street, and he wanted us to meet this Joanna, or Joanne, or whatever her name was. But that was not the problem. The girl was innocuous enough. And my parents were putting on their happy-couple act, telling how they themselves had met and so on—my father describing Mom as lively and vivacious and "spunky" (his favorite word for her); my mother turning her eyes up to him in this adoring, First Lady manner. No problem there, either. I'd seen them do that plenty of times. Oh, I've never claimed my parents were to blame for my mistakes. My mother might lay it on a little thick—working so hard at her Guilford Matron act, wearing her carefully casual outfits and frantically dragging the furniture around before all major parties—but I realize there are far worse crimes. So, I don't know. I was just in a mood, I guess. All through supper I kept fighting off my old fear that I might burst out with some scandalous remark. It was more pronounced than usual, even. (Do you think I might have Tourette's syndrome—a mild, borderline version? I've often wondered.) But I made it through the evening. Bade Jeff and What's-her-name a civil goodbye in the front hall, watched Mom and Dad walk them to the street.

Then I locked every single door behind them and stood inside with my arms folded, listening to my parents knock and ring and shout. ("Barnaby? Barn? You've had your little joke now. Let us in now, please.") I didn't say a word. When my father stepped off the front stoop, finally, and picked his way through the azaleas to peer in the dining-room window, I snatched up the silver box of matches my mother lit her candles with and I struck a match without a thought and set fire to the curtains. They were some kind of gauzy material, and they burned lickety-split. My father said, "Call the fire department!" (He was speaking to me, I had to surmise, since who else was near a phone?) But my mother said, "No! Think of the neighbors!" and that's when I picked up a dining-room chair and sent it through the window. It felt spectacular. I can still remember the satisfaction. It made such a clean, explosive crash. Although it also provided Dad with an entryway into the house.

I didn't try to stop him. I just sort of wandered off to my room, noticing the whole while that I seemed to be behaving like a crazy man. I climbed the stairs with my hands hanging loose at my sides and my expression spacey and vacant, and I watched myself doing it or even overdoing it, the same way years ago I'd overdone my limp when I sprained my ankle once, putting everything I had into the role of a cripple.

Well, you can imagine the brouhaha. Long-distance calls to Renascence, reaming them out for sending home a dangerous individual. Telephone consultations with the headmaster and my adviser. But not my psychologist, oddly enough. I did have one, of a fair-to-middling sort; but the focus here seemed to be my criminal intent rather than my mental state. There was talk, even, of bringing in the police, although that was probably just for effect. My father went so far as to mention jail. "I saved you from jail once before, but I'm not doing it again," he said. I just kept my same vacant expression. I felt mildly interested, as if it didn't involve me. I remember reflecting on the bizarreness of jail as a punishment—like sending someone to his room, really. Just put him away! What a concept. But did it ever occur to people that getting put away could come as a relief, on occasion?

Anyhow: the next day was Easter. So we all assembled for Easter dinner—me and my folks; Jeff minus the girlfriend (I believe she'd been hastily disinvited, due to recent developments); my Grandmother Gaitlin, who was still alive at the time; and Gram and Pop-Pop Kazmerow. Of course The Event had been thoroughly discussed behind my back, and I could tell it was the only thing on anyone's mind. Much shaking of heads, much whispering in the front hall. Sidelong glances at the cardboard-covered window and the charred and blistered frame. Surreptitious sniffs of the tarry-smelling air.

Except for Pop-Pop.

He just walked straight up to me. I was standing alone in front of the unlit fireplace in the living room, feeling like a Martian, and Pop-Pop walked straight up and said, "Happy Easter, Barnaby."

"Well. Same," I said.

"It's wonderful to see you."

"It's good to see you too, Pop-Pop."

Then he reached out and put something in my hand. The Chevrolet key ring.

I said, "What's this for?"

He said, "You know about my eyesight. I shouldn't have kept on driving even as long as I have."

"But what's—?"

"I want you to have my car," he said. "She's still got a lot of miles left in her! And she's quite a machine, Barnaby. Only Corvette ever made with a split rear window."

"You're giving me the Corvette?" I asked him.

He nodded.

"You're giving it, as in *giving* it?"

"I can't think of anyone better, son," he said.

I have no idea what Jeff's face looked like at that moment. Did he, in fact, envy me? I never even glanced at him. I was staring down at the checkered flags and blinking back the tears.

This year, Mrs. Alford was planning ahead for Christmas, she told us; not waiting till the last minute to get that tree of hers trimmed. So Martine dropped me off one morning in mid-December—a cold day, but sunny enough to start melting the film of snow that had fallen overnight. I climbed the front steps and pressed the buzzer before I wiped my feet, since Mrs. Alford always took some time answering. But it was her brother who opened the door. I recognized the two clouds of white hair puffing above his ears. Had I ever known his name? I'd only met him the once.

He knew mine, though. "Why," he said. "It's Barnaby. Oh, Barnaby. How very, very kind of you to call." And he held out his hand.

I hadn't been prepared to shake hands, but I did, and then I scraped my feet on the mat a few more times to show that I was ready to head on in and get to work. But it seemed he wanted the two of us to stand talking a while longer. "I can't tell you how much this means," he said. "My sister would have been extremely touched that you stopped by."

Would have been?

Oh-oh.

"But come in! Come in! What am I thinking? Please," he said. "May I take your jacket?"

"Well . . . ah, no, thanks. I'll keep it," I said.

But I did come in. I couldn't see any way out of it, really.

"Valerie will want to meet you," the brother said, leading me through the foyer. I guessed Valerie was Mrs. Alford's daughter. We passed the dining room, where a bearded man in a bathrobe sat reading a newspaper. Next to him, a baby was pounding her high-chair tray, but the bearded man paid no attention, and when he caught sight of me he just nodded and turned a page. "Richard," the brother told me. "Valerie's husband. They left the older kids at home for now; it was such short notice. And school is still in session, of course."

"Oh, yes," I said. We were climbing the stairs to the second floor. I hoped Valerie wasn't in *her* bathrobe. I said, "It's kind of early yet. Maybe I should—"

"Nonsense. We've been up for hours," the brother said. "None of us slept very well, as you might imagine." We reached the upstairs hall, and he called, "Valerie? Val! Look who's here."

In Mrs. Alford's bedroom, a woman in baggy slacks was kneeling beside a cedar chest. She didn't resemble Mrs. Alford. She was big-boned and gawky, with tortoiseshell glasses and lank brown hair, and you could see she had been crying. She stared at me blankly, which was understandable since we had never met.

"It's Barnaby," the brother told her.

"Barnaby!" she said, and she got to her feet and came over to hug me. She smelled of cedar. "Oh, Barnaby," she said, "what'll we do without her?" When she drew away, she swiped at her nose with the back of her hand. She seemed more like an overgrown girl than a wife and mother.

"I'm sorry about your loss," I said. "Mrs. Alford was a super-nice lady."

"She thought the world of you, Barnaby. Nearly every time I phoned her, she would mention something you'd done for her or some conversation you'd had."

"I didn't even know she was sick," I said.

"Well, she wasn't, so far as anyone could tell. It was a heart attack. But I think she had some inkling, maybe. I worried all this fall, because why else did she suddenly send me those things from the attic? And her quilt: just look. She seems to have finished her quilt in a rush, after months and months of claiming she would *never* get it finished."

The quilt was draped over the edge of the chest. Valerie bent to pick it up and unfold it—a dark-blue cotton rectangle with a gaudy, multicolored circle appliquéd to the center. "Planet Earth," she said, and the brother made a clucking sound.

I'd heard about that planet quilt often, but I'd never seen it. What I had pictured was a kind of fabric map—a plaid Canada, a gingham U.S. Instead the circle was made up of mismatched squares of cloth no bigger than postage stamps, joined by the uneven black stitches of a woman whose eyesight was failing. Planet Earth, in Mrs. Alford's version, was makeshift and haphazard, clumsily cobbled together, overlapping and crowded and likely to fall into pieces at any moment.

"Pretty," I said. Because it *was* sort of pretty, in an offbeat, unexpected way.

Valerie folded it up again and smoothed it gently before she laid it in the chest.

"We're having a very small service," she said. "I'm not sure exactly when. Then afterwards, I suppose we'll need your help getting the house in shape to sell it."

"I'll be glad to help," I told her. "Just call Rent-a-Back anytime you're ready for me."

When I left, Valerie hugged me again, and the brother shook hands again at the door. "Thank you for coming," he said.

I said, "Well, I'll miss her."

It was nothing but the truth.

Of course, I had no way to get home, since Martine had driven off to mail Ditty Nolan's Christmas parcels. So I sat on the curb out front and waited for her, hugging my knees and digging my chin into my folded arms. The curb was still damp from the melted snow, and I could feel a thin line of cold seeping through the seat of my jeans.

"Oh, my! All done?" Mrs. Alford used to say when I'd finished with a job. "Doesn't that look lovely!" Her chirpy, cheery, determined voice. "Weren't you quick about it!"

And then other clients' voices—some cheery and some not, some sad, some downright cranky.

"Pasta? What's this *pasta* business? In my day we called it spaghetti."

"You'll find out soon enough, young man, it is not especially unselfish to wish on your birthday candles that your children will be happy."

"Back in Baltimore's golden age, when the streetcars were still running and downtown was still the place to go and we had four top-notch department stores all on the same one block: Hutzler's, Hochschild's, Stewart's, and Hecht's . . ."

". . . and at noon or so the phone rings, and my niece says, 'I'm waiting for Dad but he hasn't come and he said he'd be here at ten.' I say, 'Oh, now, you know how he is.' About one o'clock, she calls again; two, she calls again. 'Where can he be?' she asks me. I say, 'He'll show up; don't you worry.' Though I'm fairly worried myself, to tell the truth. Along about three-thirty, I think, *Oh!* I think, *Oh, my stars above!* Because all at once it comes to me—I can't say what brought it to mind—it comes to me that her dad had phoned me at eight o'clock that morning. 'Sis,' he'd said, 'I've been trying to reach Sue but her line is busy and I want to hit the road so you call her later on, will you, please? And tell her I've decided not to stop at her place,' he said."

Martine tapped the truck horn. I almost jumped out of my skin.

"Don't *do* that, okay?" I said, as I opened the passenger door. "A simple 'Hey, you' will suffice."

"What's up?" she asked me. She had already cut the engine. "I thought we were trimming a tree."

"Mrs. Alford died," I said.

"No!"

I hadn't meant to be so blunt about it. I settled in my seat and shut my door. "She had a heart attack," I said.

"Well, damn," Martine said. Then she started the engine again. But she drove very slowly, as if in respect. "She was one of my favorite clients," she said when we reached Falls Road.

Mine too, I realized. I wouldn't have felt that way once upon a time. It used to be that Maud May was my favorite. Maud May was so let-it-all-hang-out. But I don't know; you start to appreciate the other type of person, by and by—those ultracivilized types who keep their good humor and gracious manners even though their joints are aching nonstop and they can't climb out of their baths without help and they're not always sure what day it is. I'd be terrible at that myself.

"What are you giving Sophia for Christmas?" my mother asked on the phone.

"Oh . . . ," I said, hedging.

"Because I don't want to interfere, but if you'd ever care for a piece of your grandmother Gaitlin's jewelry—such as, say, for example, maybe perhaps a ring, perhaps, or something of that sort—you have only to ask."

"Thanks," I said, "but we've agreed not to bother with presents this year."

"Why, for goodness' sake?"

Why was a question of money, but I didn't want to say so for fear Mom would segue into the eighty-seven hundred. Instead I told her, "Just lacking in Christmas spirit, I guess."

Mom sighed. "But you do plan to bring her to dinner," she said.

"She's going up to Philly that weekend."

"To Philly? Does that mean you're going too?"

"No, I thought I'd stick around and pester you and Dad," I said.

"Oh."

"I can see you're overjoyed at the prospect."

"Well, naturally we're delighted to have you! But I was thinking her people might like to get to know you a little better."

"Evidently not," I told her.

Sophia had, in fact, invited me, but I had made up this story about how I didn't want to disappoint my parents. "For someone so down on his family," she'd said, "you certainly seem to see an awful lot of them." I told her I felt obligated, because Jeff and Wicky would be visiting Wicky's folks for Christmas and Mom was all upset about it.

Which she was, no lie, but my presence at dinner was hardly going to change that. "Christmas will be so pathetic this year!" she was saying now. "Just you and Gram and Pop-Pop. I wonder if I should invite Dad's cousin Bertha."

"You detest Cousin Bertha," I reminded her.

She said, "It's such a pity Opal's not coming."

"We'll have our turn next Christmas."

"The two of you have been getting along so well together. . . . She should start spending her summers here, don't you think? Or winters, even. We could enroll her in one of the private schools. Then for college, of course, she would go to Goucher. She could room with us, if she likes, although I suppose she'd prefer the dormitory. But dorms are so noisy! Studying in a dorm is such a struggle!"

"Mom. She's barely ten years old," I said.

She sighed again. Then she asked, "Should I invite Len Parrish?"

"I wouldn't bother."

"I could tell him to park the Corvette around the corner, where your Pop-Pop won't have to look at it."

"It's not the Corvette," I said.

"What, then?"

Someday I should get credit for all the things I *don't* say. Like, "Your hero is a sleazeball, Mom." What I told her was, "He's got other plans, I'm sure. He's a very popular guy."

"Well," she said. "All right."

This was so untypical of her—I mean, the resigned and listless tone she used—that I caught myself feeling sorry for her. I remembered what she had said at Thanksgiving: how I was more her son than Dad's, more related to her. It seemed that now I was taking that in for the very first time. Poor Mom! It hadn't been much fun loving someone as thorny as me, I bet.

So when she told me she'd better hang up because she had a hair appointment, I said, "Mom. You know what I think? I really think your hair would look great if you stopped dyeing it."

It was meant to be a kindness, but it backfired. "*You* may not like it, but all my friends say it looks lovely!" she snapped. And then she told me goodbye and slammed the receiver down.

Well, no surprise there. Just because we were related didn't mean we were any good at understanding each other.

"In the afterlife," Maud May told me, "God's got a lot of explaining to do."

"What about?" I asked. I was unpacking groceries, and she was smoking a cigarette at her kitchen table.

"Oh," she said, "children suffering, cancer, tidal waves, tornadoes . . ."

"You think those need explaining? Tornadoes just happen, man. You think God sits around aiming tornadoes at people on purpose?"

". . . old ladies breaking their hips and becoming a burden . . ."

"The most He might explain is how to *deal* with a tornado," I said. "How to accept it or endure it or whatever; how to do things right. That's what I'm going to ask about when I get to heaven myself: how to do things right."

Then I said, "Anyhow. You're not an old lady."

"Good Gawd, Barnaby, you've gone and bought those goddamned generic tea bags again!"

I looked at the box I was holding. I said, "Rats. I thought they were Twinings."

"Interesting that you imagine you'll get *into* heaven," Maud May said wryly. She blew a cloud of smoke in my direction.

"And also, you're not a burden," I added.

She inspected the end of her cigarette and then turned to stub it out. "Though who knows?" she asked the ashtray. "Nowadays, they're probably letting all kinds of people in."

Christmas fell on a Monday this year; so Friday the twenty-second was full of those last-minute chores our clients wanted seen to when guests were about to descend. Folding cots brought down from attics, wreaths hung from high-up places, major supplies of liquor hauled in. Most of this I had to handle alone, because Martine was helping out at her brother's. The new baby was in the hospital with pneumonia. I hadn't even realized new babies could *get* pneumonia. So Martine spent the first part of Friday baby-sitting her nephews, and then at three I stopped by her brother's house to collect her for a job at Mr. Shank's. Mr. Shank had taken it into his head he needed his entire guest-room furnishings exchanged with the furnishings in the master bedroom, and he needed it now, and next week or next month wouldn't do.

Only, things at Martine's brother's house were never simple. First the sister-in-law was late getting back from the hospital, and then when she did get back she was weepy and distraught, and Martine didn't want to leave her that way. So I sat in the kitchen, which was a mess, racing wind-up cars with the nephews, while Martine gave her sister-in-law rapid little pats on the back and told her everything would be fine. No mother in the world, she said, would have guessed that a tiny sniffle could go to a baby's lungs that way. And of *course* he and Jeannette would still bond; wasn't she with him in the hospital most of every day and half the night? So Jeannette brightened up and insisted on serving us fruitcake before she would let us leave. I'm a sucker for fruitcake. I like the little green things, the citrons. Why don't we ever see citrons in the produce section? What *are* citrons, anyhow? I had two slices and had just cut myself a third, when Jeannette said, "Oh, great. Hand me the breast pump, will you, Barn? I'm leaking all over the last clean blouse I own." Which reminded me in a hurry that we really ought to be going.

Martine drove, so that I could finish my fruitcake. She was still at her brother's house, mentally. She nearly ran a stop sign telling me how Jeannette was going to land in the hospital herself if she wasn't careful. "That fruitcake's the only thing I've seen her eat in the last three days," she said, "and fruitcake's not exactly what you'd call the staff of life. I tried to get her to have some breakfast this morning before she left, but she said she couldn't. I told my brother, at least she ought to be drinking fluids. You need your fluids for the breast milk."

"Must you?" I asked her. "I'm trying to eat, here."

"What'd I say? Breast milk? Big deal."

"That whole business puts me off," I told her. "I don't see how women stand it. Leaky breasts, labor pains . . ."

"Well, aren't you sensitive," Martine said. She was drifting behind a slow-moving cement truck. In her place, I would have switched lanes. "Hey," she said. "I'll let you in on a secret. There's no such thing as labor pains."

"Say what?"

"It's all a bunch of propaganda that's been spread around by women. In fact, they don't feel so much as a twinge."

"They don't?" I asked.

"They have this hormone that's an anesthetic, see, that the body releases during labor. Kind of like natural Novocain."

I laughed. For a moment, she'd had me believing her.

She glanced over at me with a glint in her eye, but her face stayed all straight lines. "Don't tell anyone else," she said. "Women have been keeping it from men for millions of years. They like for men to feel guilty."

"Ain't *that* the truth," I said. Maybe too emphatically, because she sent me another, keener glance.

We were traveling up North Charles Street now, past huge houses where electric candles lit the windows even in the daytime—pale, weak white prickles of light that struck me as depressing. I wrapped the rest of my fruitcake in my napkin. I said, "Like Sophia, for instance."

"Oh, well," Martine said. "Sophia."

She hadn't said a word against Sophia since she first found out we were dating, but I could guess what she thought of her. Or I imagined I could guess. What *did* she think of her? I studied Martine's profile. On her head was a boy's leather cap with big fleece earflaps that reminded me of mutton-chop whiskers. I said, "Like Sophia's flour-bin money, for instance."

"Flour bin?"

"The money she put in Mrs. Glynn's flour bin when I was accused of stealing."

Martine slowed for a traffic light. She said, "Sophia put money in Mrs. Glynn's flour bin."

"Right."

"Before she learned Mrs. Glynn had changed her hiding place."

"Right."

Martine was silent.

"Two thousand, nine hundred and sixty dollars," I said, as if prompting her.

Martine said, "What: is she out of her mind?"

I had this sudden feeling of relief. I almost said, "Ah," although I didn't.

"She thought you really did steal it!" she said. "She actually thought you stole it!"

"Looks that way," I agreed.

"And so then she goes and . . . Is she out of her *mind*?"

"And the thing of it is, it's still there," I said.

"What's still where?"

"The money is still in the flour bin."

"So?"

"It's, like, hanging over my head," I said. "She keeps reminding me of it. Every time she wants to buy something, it's, oh, no, she can't, because she gave up all her savings for my sake; everything she owns is sitting in the flour bin."

"Well, that's *her* problem," Martine said.

But I rode on over her words. It was all pouring out of me now. "Talk about guilt!" I said. "That money is just . . . weighing on me! But I know she could get it back if she really wanted. Anytime she visits her aunt, she has the run of the house after all. Or if she worries she'll get caught, she could go on Tuesday, her aunt's podiatrist day. Take her own key and go Tuesday, or some Friday afternoon when her aunt is having her hair done."

"What time does she have her hair done?"

"I don't know; maybe four or so, because she always used to be home again before I got there."

The light changed to green, and Martine took a violent left turn. I had to grab my door handle. I said, "Mr. Shank's house, Martine. Straight ahead."

"We're not going to Mr. Shank's," Martine told me.

"Where are we going?"

But I knew the answer to that, even before she took a right, and another left, and came to a jerky stop in front of the Rent-a-Back office.

"Back in a jiff," she said.

I sat quiet while she was gone. I looked out my side window, watched two squirrels chase each other across the remnants of snow, listened to the ticking of the engine as it cooled. Then Martine was hopping into the truck again. "Ready?" she asked, and she gave me a foxy, sharp-toothed grin and held up her left hand. Nestled in her palm was a house key, attached to one of Rent-a-Back's oval tags. *#191*, the tag read. I didn't have to be told that #191 was Grace Glynn.

When we pressed the doorbell, checking to make sure she wasn't home, I had this flash of déjà vu. In the old days, I used to check by phone. I'd phone my prospective victims and listen through a dozen rings or more. (Answering machines were not so common back then.) The feeling now was the same—that strung-up feeling where you're braced for them to be there, and then the surge of energy and purpose when you find out they're away. We lounged nonchalantly on Mrs. Glynn's front porch, in case anybody was watching, but the only sound was the dog barking. So finally Martine stepped forward and fitted the key in the lock.

It was clear from Tatters's frantic little frenzy that you could just ignore him, which we did. We walked straight through to the rear of the house while he scuttled around our ankles, making busybody sounds with his toenails.

The house had a bitter smell, as if Mrs. Glynn had recently burned some toast. On the drainboard next to the sink, a clean china cup and saucer sat upside down on a dish towel. Everything else was tidied away. I opened a cabinet: glassware. I closed it and opened another. Four white canisters in graduated sizes read TEA, COFFEE, SUGAR, FLOUR. I reached for the flour canister, and it rattled. Inside I found a pale-green mug and the handle that had broken off from it; nothing more. Martine let out a small breath next to my shoulder. Tatters sniffed my sneakers.

What if Sophia had made this whole thing up? What if she had merely *claimed* she'd stowed her money here, in order to seem noble? The thought made me instantly angry. Then I reminded myself that Sophia was not the type to lie. Even so, the anger hung on a moment, like the white spot that stays in your vision after you have looked at a too bright light.

"That's not a bin," Martine said. "It's a canister."

I said, "Okay, where's the bin, then?"

She opened a lower cabinet. Saucepans. The one next to it held cookie sheets, muffin tins, and pie plates. Not a bin in sight. I felt personally thwarted, as if Mrs. Glynn were taunting me. "I could kill that woman," I told Martine.

"Forget about it," Martine said, closing the second door. "She didn't mean any harm."

"No harm! I practically lost my job!"

"Oh, you did not," Martine said. She was checking the shelf under the sink, but that held only a trash bucket. She said, "You honestly believe Mrs. Dibble would fire you? She'd have to shut down the company. You saw how all our clients backed you up."

"Well," I said. "Yes."

I walked into the pantry. There was a bin at the head of the basement stairs—a tall metal cylinder—but that contained dry dog food. I said, "I wonder how they heard."

"Heard what?"

"That I *needed* backing up."

"Oh," Martine said. "I told them."

"You did?"

I turned to look at her. She was standing in the doorway between the pantry and the kitchen, her plaid woolen jacket buttoned wrong and the earflaps sticking up from her cap at two different angles.

I said, "Well. I guess I ought to thank you."

"What for?" she asked. "Jeepers! They're the ones you should thank. Getting on the phone like they did and volleying around."

Rallying around was what she meant, but I didn't correct her. I had this vision of a crowd of old folks on a volleyball court, keeping me up, up, up and not letting me fall, stepping forward one after the other to boost me over the net. When one of them had to leave, another would take that one's place. Even if the faces changed, the sea of upraised hands stayed constant.

So, no, I didn't correct her.

Then Martine came over to the white wooden cabinet behind me. She opened the upper door, exposing what looked to be a huge tin funnel with a crank handle. She reached into the funnel and brought out a plastic sandwich bag full of money.

I said, "Whoa!"

She handed the bag to me. It had a dusty feel from the traces of old flour clinging to it.

"How did you *do* that?" I asked her.

"This tin thing is a sifter," she explained.

"A what?"

She turned the crank, demonstrating. "You store your flour inside it," she said, "and when you go to bake something, you crank the sifter and the flour falls into this box-looking place underneath. My grandmother has almost the same kind of cabinet."

I peered into the plastic bag. I saw hundreds and a few twenties, fanning out slightly because no band or clip held them together.

Sometimes when you've been looking for an object and you find it, there's a fraction of a second where you feel a kind of . . . letdown, although that's too strong a word for it. It's like you miss the suspense of the hunt. Or something of the sort.

Then I heard the front door open.

Tatters went skittering out of the kitchen, yap-yap-yapping, and Mrs. Glynn said, "Sweetums! Did you miss me?"

Martine and I stared at each other.

"Was he a lonely boy. Was he a lonesome boy," Mrs. Glynn crooned, proceeding steadily closer. "Oh, oh, oh. I wonder what I—"

A purse or shopping bag was set down on a hard surface, but she continued moving toward us. "Maybe a cup of tea," she said. "Or hot water with some lemon; that might be more . . . My, those cabdrivers talk and talk, don't they? How he did go on! I've never understood what makes cabdrivers so . . ."

She entered the kitchen. I seemed to have run out of oxygen.

Martine said, in a normal tone, "Do you think she left a list in the parlor?"

My jaw dropped.

"Because no way would she go off and not tell us what she wanted done," Martine said, and she took a step toward the kitchen, still talking. "I bet she left a list someplace and we just have to find it, or else we could call the office and see if—"

Her voice was louder now—loud enough even for someone hard of hearing, although it had started out soft. She was letting our presence dawn on Mrs. Glynn by degrees. "Maybe Ray Oakley would know. Do you think?" she asked.

I said, "Well . . . ," and followed after her. I had no choice. I stuffed the plastic bag in my jacket pocket as we emerged from the pantry.

Mrs. Glynn was standing beside the stove, wearing this kind of flown-open expression. Both hands were pressed to her chest. She said, "Oh!" And then, "How . . .?"

"Look! There she is!" Martine told me. "Mrs. Glynn! Great to see you!"

"Why, it's . . . Barnaby," Mrs. Glynn said. "Barnaby and young . . ."

"We're just covering for Ray Oakley," Martine said. "I hope we didn't give you a scare. Ray couldn't make it today, and so he sent us instead, and when nobody answered the door—"

"But . . . today? Was he coming today?" Mrs. Glynn asked.

She had a long, drapey coat on, and her hair was screwed into those bottle-cap curls that old-lady beauty shops favor. It made her face look naked and uncertain. She said, "I don't think he was due to come *today*. Was he?"

"Well, maybe he wasn't," I said. I turned to Martine. "Do you think we made a mistake?"

"We must have," she said promptly. "Okay! Better be running along!"

"Wrong?" Mrs. Glynn asked. She stared from one of us to the other.

"Sorry about the mix-up," I said as we sidled past her. "See you, Mrs. Glynn! Bye-bye!"

And we escaped.

Before we went on to Mr. Shank's, I had Martine drive past my apartment so I could stash Sophia's money. No sense tempting fate. I ran in, leaving Martine in the truck, and hid the plastic bag behind the bar.

What had Sophia been thinking of, choosing a plastic bag? Had she wanted her aunt to know for sure that this money was a substitution?

It would serve her right if I kept it, I thought. Kept it and bought a car with it—say a used VW. One of those cute little Beetles.

No, don't worry. I wouldn't do that.

I smoothed a jumble of T-shirts over the money, and I left.

Mr. Shank, then Mrs. Portland, then Mrs. Figg. Wouldn't you know Mrs. Figg was the toughest. She wanted eight strands of Christmas lights woven around the two boxwoods beside her front door—a job that just about froze our fingers off—and then when we got done she said it looked artificial. "Artificial!" I said. "Of course it looks artificial. These are red and green and blue lightbulbs; what occurrence in nature are they supposed to imitate?"

"I mean, they're *spaced* artificially. I wanted them more random."

So Martine and I did them over. When we'd finished, Mrs. Figg said that she had no intention of paying for the extra time it took. She said anybody with half a brain would have done it right the first time. I said, "Have it your way, Mrs. Figg. Merry Christmas."

It was worth it just to see the look on her face. She hated it when someone deprived her of a good argument.

That was our last job of the day, luckily. (By now it was completely dark.) I dropped Martine at her brother's, and just as she was hopping out, I said, "Thanks for the help with, you know. The money."

"No problem," she told me, and then she slammed the door, because her sister-in-law was on the front porch, itching to get to the hospital.

This was Sophia's last night home before she left for the long Christmas weekend, and we had talked about having dinner at some not too expensive restaurant whenever I got off work. I figured that was my chance to return her money. It did occur to me, *Oh, Lord, I hope now she won't go out and buy me a Christmas present.* But I didn't want to wait till Christmas was over, because I worried about keeping that much cash around.

She was leaving a message on my machine when I walked into the apartment. ". . . and I would just like to know . . . ," she was saying.

I picked up the receiver. "Hello?"

"Barnaby," she said. "Would you please tell me what is going on?"

"Huh?"

"What were you doing at Aunt Grace's house? Why did you and that Martine person go there when you surely must have known she would be out? I couldn't believe my ears. I said to Aunt Grace, 'Who?' I said, '*Who* did you say was there?' "

I put the receiver back down.

Then I thought, *Oops.*

It was my body proceeding without me again. I didn't hang up on purpose. I almost seemed to forget that I had to keep the receiver off the hook to continue talking.

But instead of phoning her back, I grabbed the money from behind the bar and I left the house.

The night was clear enough so the stars were out—what few of them could be seen within the city limits—but as soon as I crossed the patio, the automatic lights lit up and doused them. On a hunch, I stopped walking and held still a moment. The lights clicked off, and then, sure enough, the sky did its color-change trick. *Loom!* it went, and that transparent midnight blue swung into focus. Of course, it lasted no longer than a second. After that, the blue started seeming ordinary again, and I continued on toward the truck.

I drove to Sophia's, parked in front of her house, and looked around for suspicious strangers before I got out. (The money made an obvious bulge in the right-hand side of my jacket.) Then I climbed her front steps and rang her doorbell.

An immediate, perfect silence fell. You know how sometimes your ear does something funny and there's an instant when the sound goes off? That's the kind of silence. Noises I hadn't even been aware of—mechanical hums and creaks, a murmur behind the curtains—suddenly stopped. And nobody came to the door.

I rang again. Cars hissed down the street behind me, and a faraway train whistle blew, but the house went on giving off its numb, dead silence.

If there had been a mail slot, I'd have slipped the money through it. What she had, though, was one of those black metal postboxes, the kind that doesn't lock, and I wasn't such a fool as to entrust her money to that. So I stood there awhile longer, and then I turned and left.

Probably she was watching me as I walked back to the street. She was peering out from behind her curtains to make sure I left. I felt self-conscious and stiff. I made a point of adding a carefree bounce to my step. Even after I reached the truck—after I was home again, parking in the Hardestys' driveway—I had a spied-upon feeling. When the automatic lights came on, I ducked my head. I scurried across the patio with my shoulders hunched, like a suspect on the evening news.

Okay, so she was mad at me. She was planning to make this difficult. But the nice thing about fussy people is, they have their little routines. You always know where you can find them, and when, if you want to track them down.

15

At 9:58 the next morning, she was sitting on a bench at the far end of Penn Station, gazing straight ahead. I know she saw me coming. But I couldn't read her expression until I got closer. (I was traveling through squares of sunlight; she was hardly more than a silhouette.) I arrived in front of her and stood there. She raised her chin. Her eyes were swimming in tears.

She said, "You hung up on me, Barnaby."

"I apologize for that," I told her.

A woman sharing the bench glanced over at us curiously. I sat down between her and Sophia, blocking the woman's view. "I don't know what got into me," I said.

"Nobody's ever hung up on me. Ever!"

I reached into my jacket and drew out the money, which I'd transferred to a plain white envelope for privacy's sake. (I'd thought of every possible scenario—even put a note inside, in case she refused to speak to me.) "Sophia," I said, and I cleared my throat, preparing to make my announcement.

But Sophia went right on. "I simply wasn't raised that way," she told me. "I'm sorry, but that's how I am. I was raised to be respected and treated with consideration. I was taught that I was a special, valuable person; not the kind that someone could hang up on."

I said, "See, it was only that I felt . . . interrogated, you know? On account of the tone of voice you used."

"Why wouldn't I interrogate you? You walked into my aunt's private home without her permission! Naturally I would wonder what you were doing there."

"Well, I should think it was obvious what I was doing there. I wanted to get your money back."

"Did I ask you to get my money back? Did I request your assistance? I tell you this much, Barnaby: I'd have thrown that money in your face if you brought it back!"

Then she glanced at my envelope. She said, "Is that what *this* is?" in a piercing, carrying tone that made me slide my eyes toward the other passengers. "Is that what you came to try and give me?"

I said, "Sofe—"

"Because I'm not accepting it, Barnaby. You'd have to ram it down my throat before I'd accept it."

This was a temptation, but I decided on a different tactic. I said, "*No, no, no.* Good grief, no! It's . . . something for Opal."

"Opal?"

"Her, um, Christmas present. I need for you to take it to her."

"Opal's Christmas present is in this envelope?"

"Take it, will you? Take it," I said, and I held it out to her. Right then it mattered more than anything that I get rid of it; I didn't care how. When she unclasped her hands, finally, and allowed me to lay the envelope on her palm, I felt a kind of lightness expanding inside my chest. I imagined I had been freed of an actual weight.

"You're asking me to carry this to Opal's apartment?" Sophia said, and she raised her eyes to look into mine.

"Well," I said, "or else . . . no." (I could see how that might get complicated.) "No, I want you to give it to Natalie at the train station."

"Natalie?"

"She knows you're coming. She'll meet you there."

Sophia blinked.

"She'll be . . . yes! At the Information island," I said. And then something about how this situation rhymed, so to speak, made me laugh. I said, "I can assure you it's not contraband."

A confused, slightly startled expression crossed her face, as if some string had been tugged in her memory, but she went on looking into my eyes.

"Goodbye," I said, rising.

"Wait! Barnaby? You're leaving?"

"Yes, I promised I'd help pack up Mrs. Alford's house today. Oh. Incidentally," I said. (My mind was racing now.) "If you and Natalie happen to miss connections, I did put her telephone number in the envelope. Just get it out and call her. But you shouldn't have any trouble."

She nodded, with her lips slightly parted. I turned and walked away.

Spink and Kunkle, Plumbing Specialists, the man's card read. *"Our Name Says It All."*

"Your name says it all?" I asked.

"Sure does," he said. A freckled man with reddish, fizzing hair.

" 'Spink and Kunkle' says it all?"

" 'Plumbing Specialists' says it all," he told me irritably.

"Oh."

"I'm supposed to fix a leak in the master bath."

"Right." I handed back his card, and then I turned from the door and called, "Hello?" (I had no idea how to address Mrs. Alford's daughter, never having heard her last name.) "Plumber's here!" I called.

"Oh, good." She came galumphing down the stairs. Dressed for manual labor, Valerie was gawkier than ever. She wore huge white canvas gloves that made her look like Minnie Mouse. "Thanks for stopping by on such short notice," she told the man. "We're trying to get the house ready to sell, and you know how a minor thing like a drip will scare some people away."

"Ma'am," the man said heavily, "no drip on God's green earth is minor. Believe me." He was following her up the stairs, carrying what seemed to be a doctor's bag. "If you was to put a measuring cup under that drip," he said, "you would be scandalized. Scandalized! To see how much water you're wasting."

"Well, this house belonged to my mother, you see, and somehow she never . . ."

I went back to the kitchen, where I was packing the pots and pans. Martine was doing utensils. Supposedly, we'd be finished by the end of the day, but that was just not going to happen. Valerie had already asked if we could return tomorrow. I said, "Tomorrow? Tomorrow's Sunday."

"Yes, but the next day's Christmas," she said.

So I said, "Oh, I guess I could."

I felt obliged to, really, because she had told me earlier that her mother had willed me the Twinform. "That mannequin thing in the attic," she'd explained. "I can't imagine why she thought . . . But if you don't want it, just say so. Please."

"I want it! I want it," I said.

After that, how could I refuse to come Sunday? Martine said she would come too, but only for the morning. Her brother's new baby had finally been sprung from the hospital, she said. This meant that her family would be throwing their annual carol sing, after all, and she had to help them get ready. Then she told me I was invited. "You should dress up some," she told me, "now that you have a Twinform to try out your fashion statements on."

"Right," I said. "I can't wait to see her in a coat and tie."

Underneath, though, I took my Twinform very seriously. I kept going into the foyer to check on her; I'd moved her down from the attic as soon as I learned she was mine. I pretended I was just figuring out the logistics. "If we could borrow a blanket or something," I told Martine, "and wrap her up so she doesn't rattle around the truck bed . . ."

" 'Her'?" Martine teased me. " 'She'?"

"Oh, come on, Pasko: you have to admit that face has a lot of character."

She snorted, and we went back to our packing.

Place mats, tablecloths, napkins, doilies. Tupperware and empty mayonnaise jars and plastic juice containers. Waxed paper, aluminum foil,

Saran wrap, freezer wrap. A lifetime supply of white candles. *More* than a lifetime supply, if you want to be literal about it.

Every now and then, in this job, I suddenly understood that you really, truly can't take it with you. I don't think I ordinarily grasped the full implications of that. Just look at all the possessions a dead person leaves behind: every last one, even the most treasured. No luggage is permitted, no carry-on items, not a purse, not a pair of glasses. You spend seven or eight decades acquiring your objects, arranging them, dusting them, insuring them; then you walk out with nothing at all, as bare as the day you arrived.

I told Martine, "I should find some other line of work."

"Not *that* again," she said, and she folded down the flaps on a box of cookbooks.

"It isn't natural for someone my age to go to more funerals than dinner parties."

Martine just smiled to herself.

Mrs. Alford's brother came in with an empty coffee mug. He rinsed it at the sink and placed it in the dishwasher. (Old folks almost always pre-rinse.) Then he left, slogging off with his head down, not appearing to notice us.

Overhead, the plumber was clanking pipes, and it occurred to me that the name really did say it all. *Spink!* the pipes went. *Kunkle!* In the living room, a boom box was playing alternative rock—probably the first time these walls had ever heard such a sound. "Listen to this one," a kid was saying—talking to his mother, I think. She had started packing the books. "This song comes from before their lead singer went crazy. Okay? Now, this next one . . . wait a sec. This next one is *after* he went crazy. Hear that? Can you tell the difference? Well, then, let me play it again. See, this is *before* he went crazy. This next . . ."

The bearded husband wandered into the kitchen, opened the fridge, and gazed into it. Then he closed it and wandered off. I still hadn't heard him speak. Upstairs, the baby was crying, and somebody told her, "Aw, now. Aw, now." (It sounded to me like the plumber.) I found a length of white flannel in a drawer—the kind you'd spread beneath a tablecloth for protection—and took it out to the foyer and draped it over the Twinform's shoulders. She gaped at me round-eyed, as if I'd been presumptuous.

Suppose my great-grandfather was walking down the street one day and who did he see but his angel, the woman with the golden braid. "Miss!" he'd cry. "Miss! Wait up! I never thanked you."

She would turn and say, "Me?" She'd be this average, commonplace woman, maybe even homely, maybe chapped-lipped or shiny-nosed, depending on the season. "What for?" she would ask, and he would see then that he had been mistaken—that there were no angels, after all. Or that his angels were lots of people he had never suspected.

Where, exactly, would I get hold of a gray cloth ledger with maroon leather corners?

Martine passed through the foyer, lugging a carton. "We're running out of space," she told me. "I'm going to start stacking things here." Then she said, "Yikes." She'd just about bumped into the alternative-rock kid. He veered around her, cradling his boom box in both arms. I guess his mother had finally had enough of it.

Another boy sat at the dining-room table—so far I'd counted four boys and two girls—reading a comic book. He didn't look up until I said, "Uh . . . ," because right on the carpet in front of my feet I saw a disgusting brown mess. "Is this dog do?" I asked the kid. "Or what? Is there a dog in the house? There's dog do on the rug."

"It's fate," he told me coolly.

I said, "Oh." Then I said, "Okay." I waited a moment, and finally I decided to head on into the kitchen. It wasn't till I'd cleared another shelf that I figured out he'd said, "It's fake." I grinned.

By now Sophia would be arriving in Philadelphia. She'd be clicking across the station toward the Information island, carrying the envelope and looking around for Natalie. Of course, she'd seen Natalie once before, but that was only briefly and some time ago. She would be wondering whether they'd recognize each other. Maybe she would notice a woman in a red coat, and she would think, *Her?* and then realize the woman was too plump, or too fair. (And just then the real Natalie walked across my mind—her straight, slim figure and tranquil face, her grave, brown, considering eyes.)

I fished a screwdriver out of my pocket and removed a rusted can opener from the wall above the stove. I put it in the box we had set beside the back door for trash. Mrs. Alford's brother said, "Oh! What's this?" I hadn't even heard him arrive. He bent over the box to study the can opener. "All I have at home is that hand-grip kind; nothing that hangs on a wall," he told me.

"Then why don't you take this one?" I asked. "It's only going out to the garbage."

"Yes, perhaps . . . It's a pity to throw it away, don't you think?"

"Absolutely," I told him.

He clutched the can opener to his chest and padded off. In the dining room I heard him say, "There's dog do on the rug, Johnny," but I didn't catch Johnny's answer.

Sophia would have stood waiting for several minutes now. She'd be looking to her left and her right, biting her lower lip, her eyebrows quirked in annoyance. (I pictured her in the feather coat, although more often lately she wore something beige and belted that she'd bought on sale last spring.) Maybe she would ask the Information clerk, "Has anybody been here that you've noticed—a woman who seemed to be meeting someone?"

She'd be glancing down at the envelope more and more frequently, wondering if it was time yet to get Natalie's phone number out.

The last thing left on the wall was one of those rechargeable mixers. I unhooked it and placed it in the carton of utensils. Then I unscrewed the mounting plate, and just as I was lifting it from the wall I felt the most amazing rush of happiness wash over me. I didn't know at first where it came from. I was looking at the mounting plate, is all, not thinking of anything special. I was staring at those figure-eight-shaped holes you slide over the screws. They reminded me of something. They brought to mind the brass clasps on Martine's overalls.

Martine walked back into the kitchen, dusting off her hands, and she picked up another carton. I said, "Martine?" and she said, "What," and I said, "Haply I think on thee."

"Huh?" she said.

But I could tell she knew what I meant.

Out in the dining room, Mrs. Alford's brother was demonstrating his new can opener. "Barnaby was planning to put this in the trash," he said. "Can you imagine? Why, there's years and years of use left in it!" Upstairs, the boom box was playing something noisy and disorganized. And in Philadelphia, Sophia was opening the envelope. She was staring down at the money inside and drawing a quick breath inward. She glanced around the train station. Then she unfolded my note. *Sophia,* she read, *you never did realize. I am a man you can trust.*

LADDER
OF YEARS

BALTIMORE WOMAN DISAPPEARS
DURING FAMILY VACATION

Delaware State Police announced early today that Cordelia F. Grinstead, 40, wife of a Roland Park physician, has been reported missing while on holiday with her family in Bethany Beach.

Mrs. Grinstead was last seen around noon this past Monday, walking south along the stretch of sand between Bethany and Sea Colony.

Witnesses of her departure—her husband, Dr. Samuel Grinstead, 55, and her three children, Susan, 21, Ramsay, 19, and Carroll, 15—were unable to recall any suspicious characters in the vicinity. They reported that to the best of their recollection she simply strolled away. Her failure to return was not remarked until late afternoon.

A slender, small-boned woman with curly fair or light-brown hair, Mrs. Grinstead stands 5'2" or possibly 5'5" and weighs either 90 or 110 pounds. Her eyes are blue or gray or perhaps green, and her nose is mildly sunburned in addition to being freckled.

Presumably she was carrying a large straw tote trimmed with a pink bow, but family members could not agree upon her clothing. In all probability it was something pink or blue, her husband suggested, either frilled or lacy or "looking kind of baby-doll."

Authorities do not suspect drowning, since Mrs. Grinstead avoided swimming whenever possible and professed a distinct aversion to water. In fact, her sister, Eliza Felson, 52, has alleged to reporters that the missing woman "may have been a cat in her most recent incarnation."

Anyone with knowledge of Mrs. Grinstead's whereabouts is urged to contact the Delaware State Police at once.

———

This all started on a Saturday morning in May, one of those warm spring days that smell like clean linen. Delia had gone to the supermarket to shop for the week's meals. She was standing in the produce section, languidly choosing a bunch of celery. Grocery stores always made her reflective. Why was it, she was wondering, that celery was not called "corduroy plant"? That would be much more colorful. And garlic bulbs should be "moneybags," because their shape reminded her of the sacks of gold coins in folktales.

A customer on her right was sorting through the green onions. It was early enough so the store was nearly empty, and yet this person seemed to be edging in on her a bit. Once or twice the fabric of his shirt sleeve brushed her dress sleeve. Also, he was really no more than stirring those onions around. He would lift one rubber-banded clump and then drop it and alight on another. His fingers were very long and agile, almost spidery. His cuffs were yellow oxford cloth.

He said, "Would you know if these are called scallions?"

"Well, sometimes," Delia said. She seized the nearest bunch of celery and stepped toward the plastic bags.

"Or would they be shallots?"

"No, they're scallions," she told him.

Needlessly, he steadied the roll of bags overhead while she peeled one off. (He towered a good foot above her.) She dropped the celery into the bag and reached toward the cup of twist ties, but he had already plucked one out for her. "What are shallots, anyway?" he asked.

She would have feared that he was trying to pick her up, except that when she turned she saw he was surely ten years her junior, and very good-looking besides. He had straight, dark-yellow hair and milky blue eyes that made him seem dreamy and peaceful. He was smiling down at her, standing a little closer than strangers ordinarily stand.

"Um . . . ," she said, flustered.

"Shallots," he reminded her.

"Shallots are fatter," she said. She set the celery in her grocery cart. "I believe they're above the parsley," she called over her shoulder, but she found him next to her, keeping step with her as she wheeled her cart toward the citrus fruits. He wore blue jeans, very faded, and soft moccasins that couldn't be heard above "King of the Road" on the public sound system.

"I also need lemons," he told her.

She slid another glance at him.

"Look," he said suddenly. He lowered his voice. "Could I ask you a big favor?"

"Um . . ."

"My ex-wife is up ahead in potatoes. Or not ex I guess but . . . estranged, let's say, and she's got her boyfriend with her. Could you just pretend we're together? Just till I can duck out of here?"

"Well, of course," Delia said.

And without even taking a deep breath first, she plunged happily back into the old high-school atmosphere of romantic intrigue and deception. She narrowed her eyes and lifted her chin and said, "We'll show *her*!" and sailed past the fruits and made a U-turn into root vegetables. "Which one is she?" she murmured through ventriloquist lips.

"Tan shirt," he whispered. Then he startled her with a sudden burst of laughter. "Ha, ha!" he told her too loudly. "Aren't you clever to say so!"

But "tan shirt" was nowhere near an adequate description. The woman who turned at the sound of his voice wore an ecru raw-silk tunic over black silk trousers as slim as two pencils. Her hair was absolutely black, cut shorter on one side, and her face was a perfect oval. "Why, Adrian," she said. Whoever was with her—some man or other—turned too, still gripping a potato. A dark, thick man with rough skin like stucco and eyebrows that met in the middle. Not up to the woman's standard at all; but how many people were?

Delia's companion said, "Rosemary. I didn't see you. So don't forget," he told Delia, not breaking his stride. He set a hand on her cart to steer it into aisle 3. "You promised me you'd make your marvelous blancmange tonight."

"Oh, yes, my . . . blancmange," Delia echoed faintly. Whatever blancmange might be, it sounded the way she felt just then: pale and plain-faced and skinny, with her freckles and her frizzy brown curls and her ruffled pink round-collared dress.

They had bypassed the dairy case and the juice aisle, where Delia had planned to pick up several items, but she didn't point that out because this Adrian person was still talking. "Your blancmange and then your, uh, what, your meat and vegetables and da-da-da . . ."

The way he let his voice die reminded her of those popular songs that end with the singers just absentmindedly drifting away from the microphone. "Is she looking at us?" he whispered. "Check it out. Don't make it obvious."

Delia glanced over, pretending to be struck by a display of converted rice. Both the wife and the boyfriend had their backs to her, but there was something artificial in their posture. No one could find russet potatoes so mesmerizing. "Well, she's *mentally* looking," Delia murmured. She turned to see her grocery cart rapidly filling with pasta. Egg noodles, rotini, linguine—Adrian flung in boxes at random. "Excuse me . . . ," she said.

"Oh, sorry," he told her. He stuffed his hands in his pockets and loped off. Delia followed, pushing her cart very slowly in case he meant for them to separate now. But at the end of the aisle, he paused and considered a row of tinned ravioli until she caught up with him. "The boyfriend's name is Skipper," he said. "He's her accountant."

"Accountant!" Delia said. He didn't fit the image.

"Half a dozen times, at least, he's come to our house. Sat in our actual living room, going over her taxes. Rosemary owns this catering firm. The Guilty Party, it's called. Ha. 'Sinfully Delicious Foods for Every Occasion.' Then next thing I know, she's moved in with him. She claimed she only needed a few weeks by herself, but when she phoned to say so, I could hear him coaching her in the background."

"Oh, that's terrible," Delia said.

A woman with a baby in her cart reached between them for a can of macaroni and cheese. Delia stepped back to give her room.

"If it's not too much trouble," Adrian said when the woman had moved away, "I'll just tag along while you finish your shopping. It would look sort of fishy if I left right now, all alone. I hope you don't mind."

Mind? This was the most interesting thing that had happened to her in years. "Not a bit," she told him. She wheeled her cart into aisle 4. Adrian strolled alongside her.

"I'm Adrian Bly-Brice, by the way," he said. "I guess I ought to know *your* name."

"I'm Delia Grinstead," she told him. She plucked a bottle of mint flakes from the spice rack.

"I don't believe I've ever run into a Delia before."

"Well, it's *Cor*delia, really. My father named me that."

"And are you one?"

"Am I one what?"

"Are you your father's Cordelia?"

"I don't know," she said. "He's dead."

"Oh, I'm sorry."

"He died this past winter," she said.

Ridiculously, tears filled her eyes. This whole conversation had taken a wrong turn somewhere. She squared her shoulders and pushed her cart on down the aisle, veering around an elderly couple conferring over salt substitutes. "Anyhow," she said, "it got shortened to Delia right away. Like in the song."

"What song?"

"Oh, the . . . you know, the one about Delia's gone, one more round . . . My father used to sing me to sleep with that."

"I never heard it," Adrian said.

The tune on the loudspeaker now was "By the Time I Get to Phoenix," competing with her father's gruff voice muttering "Delia's Gone" in her mind. "Anyhow!" she said again, more brightly.

They started up the next aisle: cereals on the left, popcorn and sweets on the right. Delia needed cornflakes, but cornflakes were such a *family* item, she decided against them. (What ingredients were required for blancmange?) Adrian gazed idly at sacks of butterscotch drops and rum balls. His skin had that slight tawniness that you occasionally see in fair-haired men, and it seemed almost without texture. He must not have to shave more than two or three times a week.

"I myself was named for an uncle," he said. "Rich Uncle Adrian Brice. Probably all for nothing, though. He's mad I changed my name when I married."

"You changed your name when you married?"

"I used to be Adrian Brice the Second, but then I married Rosemary Bly and we both became Bly-Brice."

"Oh, so there's a hyphen," Delia said. She hadn't realized.

"It was entirely her idea, believe me."

As if summoned up by his words, Rosemary appeared at the other end of the aisle. She tossed something into the red plastic tote basket hanging from Skipper's fist. Women like Rosemary never purchased their groceries by the cartload.

"If we went to the movie, though, we'd miss the concert," Adrian said instantly, "and you know how I've looked forward to the concert."

"I forgot," Delia said. "The concert! They'll be playing . . ."

But she couldn't think of a single composer. (And maybe he had meant some other kind of concert—a rock show, for instance. He was young enough.) Rosemary watched without a flicker of expression as Delia and Adrian approached. Delia was the first to lower her eyes. "We'll just save the movie for tomorrow," Adrian was saying. He guided her cart to the left a bit. All at once Delia felt woefully small—not dainty and petite, but squat, humble, insignificant. She didn't stand much taller than Adrian's armpit. She increased her speed, anxious to leave this image of herself behind. "They do have a Sunday matinee, don't they?" Adrian was asking.

"Of course they do," she told him, a little too emphatically. "We could go to the two o'clock showing, right after our champagne brunch."

By now she was tearing down the next aisle. Adrian had to lengthen his stride to keep up. They narrowly missed hitting a man whose cart was stacked with gigantic Pampers boxes.

In aisle 7 they zipped through the gourmet section—anchovy paste, smoked oysters—and arrived at baby foods, where Delia collected herself enough to remember she needed strained spinach. She slowed to study the rows of little jars. "Not those!" Adrian hissed. They raced on, leaving behind aisle 7 and careening into 8. "Sorry," he said. "I just thought if Rosemary saw you buying baby food . . ."

If she saw her buying baby food, she'd think Delia was just a housewife with an infant waiting at home. Ironically, though, Delia had long passed the infant stage. To suspect her of having a child that young was to flatter her. All she needed the spinach for was her mint pea soup. But she didn't bother explaining that and instead selected a can of chicken broth. "Oh," Adrian said, traveling past her, "consommé! I meant to buy some."

He dropped a tin in her cart—a fancy brand with a sleek white label. Then he wandered on, hands jammed flat in his rear pockets. Come to think of it, he reminded Delia of her first real boyfriend—in fact, her only boyfriend, not counting her husband. Will Britt had possessed this same angularity, which had seemed graceful at some moments and ungainly at others; and he had cocked his elbows behind him in just this way, like knobby, sharp wings, and his ears had stuck out a bit too. It was a relief to find that Adrian's ears stuck out. She distrusted men who were too handsome.

At the end of the aisle they looked in both directions. No telling where Rosemary might pop up next, with that carefree, untrammeled tote basket. But the coast was clear, and Delia nosed her cart toward paper goods. "What," Adrian said, "you want to buy *more?*"

Yes, she did. She had barely passed the halfway mark. But she saw his point. The longer they hung around, the greater his chances of another confrontation. "We'll leave," she decided. She started for the nearest checkout counter, but Adrian, lacing his fingers through the grid of the cart, drew it toward the express lanes. "One, two, three . . ." She counted her purchases aloud. "We can't go there! I've got sixteen, seventeen . . ."

He pulled the cart into the fifteen-item lane, behind an old woman buying nothing but a sack of dog chow. He started dumping noodle boxes onto the counter. Ah, well. Delia rummaged through her bag for her checkbook. The old woman in front of them, meanwhile, was depositing bits of small change in the cashier's palm. She handed over a penny and then, after a search, another penny. A third penny had a piece of lint stuck to it, and she plucked that away painstakingly. Adrian gave an exasperated sigh. "I forgot cat food," Delia told him. She hadn't a hope in this world that he would volunteer to go back for it; she just thought a flow of talk might settle him down some. "Seeing that dog chow reminded me, we're almost out," she said. "Oh, never mind. I'll send Ramsay for it later."

The old woman was hunting a fourth penny. She was positive, she said, that she had another one somewhere.

"Ramsay!" Adrian repeated to himself. He sighed again—or no, this time he was laughing. "I bet you live in Roland Park," he told Delia.

"Well, yes, I do."

"I knew it! Everybody in Roland Park has a last name for a first name."

"So?" she said, stung. "What's wrong with that?"

"Oh, nothing."

"It isn't even true," she said. "Why, I know lots of people who—"

"Don't take offense! I live in Roland Park myself," he said. "It's just pure luck I wasn't named . . . oh, Bennington, or McKinney; McKinney was my mother's maiden name. I bet your *husband's* mother's . . . and if we decide against the blancmange tonight we can always have it tomorrow night, don't you think?"

She felt dislocated for a second, until she understood that Rosemary must be in earshot again. Sure enough: a tote basket, still loaded, arrived on the counter behind her own groceries. By now the old woman had moved away, tottering under her burden of dog chow, and the cashier was asking them, "Plastic bags, or paper?"

"Plastic, please," Adrian said.

Delia opened her mouth to object (she generally chose paper, herself), but she didn't want to contradict Adrian in front of his wife.

Adrian said, "Delia, I don't believe you've met my . . ."

Delia turned around, already plastering a pleasantly surprised smile on her face.

"My, ah, Rosemary," Adrian said, "and her, ah, Skipper. This is Delia Grinstead."

Rosemary wasn't smiling at all, which made Delia feel foolish, but Skipper gave her an amiable nod. He kept his arms folded across his chest—short, muscular arms, heavily furred, bulging from the sleeves of his polo shirt. "Any relation to *Dr.* Grinstead?" he asked her.

"Yes! He's my . . . he was my . . . he's my husband," she said. How to explain the existence of a husband, in the present situation?

But Skipper seemed to take this in stride. He told Rosemary, "Dr. Grinstead's my mother's GP. Been treating her forever. Right?" he asked Delia.

"Right," she agreed, not having the faintest idea. Rosemary, meanwhile, went on studying her coolly. She carried her head at a deliberate tilt, accentuating the asymmetrical hairdo with its dramatic downward slant toward her chin. It was none of Delia's business, of course, but privately she thought Adrian deserved somebody more likable. She thought even Skipper deserved somebody more likable. She wished she had worn high heels this morning, and a dressier dress.

"Dr. Grinstead is just about the last man in Baltimore who makes house calls," Skipper was telling Rosemary.

"Well, only if it's absolutely essential," Delia said. A reflex: she never gave up trying to protect her husband from his patients.

Behind her, the scanner said *peep . . . peep . . . peep*, registering her groceries. The music had stopped playing several minutes back, as Delia just now noticed, and the murmuring of shoppers elsewhere in the store sounded hushed and ominous.

"That'll be thirty-three forty," the cashier announced.

Delia turned to fill in her check and found Adrian handing over the money. "Oh!" she said, preparing to argue. But then she grew conscious of Rosemary listening.

Adrian flashed her a wide, sweet smile and accepted his change. "Good seeing you," he told the other couple. He walked on out, pushing the cart, with Delia trailing behind.

It had been raining off and on for days, but this morning had dawned clear and the parking lot had a rinsed, fresh, soft look under a film of lemony sunlight. Adrian halted the cart at the curb and lifted out two of the grocery bags, leaving the third for Delia. Next came the problem of whose car to head for. He was already starting toward his own, which was evidently parked somewhere near the dry cleaner's, when she stopped him. "Wait," she said. "I'm right here."

"But what if they see us? We can't leave in two different cars!"

"Well, I do have a *life* to get back to," Delia snapped. This whole business had gone far enough, it occurred to her. She was missing her baby-food spinach and her cornflakes and untold other items on account of a total stranger. She flung open the trunk of her Plymouth.

"Oh, all right," Adrian said. "What we'll do is load these groceries very, very slowly, and by that time they'll have driven away. They didn't have so much to ring up: two steaks, two potatoes, a head of lettuce, and a box of after-dinner mints. That won't take long."

Delia was astonished at his powers of observation. She watched him arrange his bags in her trunk, after which he consumed a good half minute repositioning a small box of something. Orzo, it was—a most peculiar, tiny-sized pasta that she'd often noticed on the shelf but never bought. She had thought it resembled rice, in which case why not serve rice instead, which was surely more nutritious? She handed him the bag she was holding, and he settled that with elaborate care between the first two. "Are they coming out yet?" he asked.

"No," she said, looking past him toward the store. "Listen, I owe you some money."

"My treat."

"No, really, I have to pay you back. Only I planned to write a check and I don't have any cash. Would you accept a check? I could show you my driver's license," she said.

He laughed.

"I'm serious," she told him. "If you don't mind taking a—"

Then she caught sight of Skipper and Rosemary emerging from the supermarket. Skipper hugged a single brown paper bag. Rosemary carried nothing but a purse the size of a sandwich, on a glittery golden chain.

"Is it them?" Adrian asked.

"It's them."

He bent inside her trunk and started rearranging groceries again. "Tell me when they're gone," he said.

The couple crossed to a low red sports car. Rosemary was at least

Skipper's height if not taller, and she had the slouching, indifferent gait of a runway model. If she had walked into a wall, her hipbones would have hit first.

"Are they looking our way?" Adrian asked.

"I don't think they see us."

Skipper opened the passenger door, and Rosemary folded herself out of sight. He handed in the sack of groceries and shut the door, strode to the driver's side, slid in and started the engine. Only then did he shut his own door. With a tightly knit, snarling sound, the little car spun around and buzzed off.

"They're gone," Delia said.

Adrian closed the trunk lid. He seemed older now. For the first time, Delia saw the fragile lines etched at the corners of his mouth.

"Well," he said sadly.

It seemed crass to mention money again, but she had to say, "About the check . . ."

"Please. I owe *you*," he said. "I owe you more than that. Thanks for going along with me on this."

"It was nothing," she told him. "I just wish there'd been, oh, somebody really appropriate."

"Appropriate?"

"Somebody . . . *you* know," she said. "As glamorous as your wife."

"What are you talking about?" he asked. "Why, you're very pretty! You have such a little face, like a flower."

She felt herself blushing. He must have thought she was fishing for compliments. "Anyhow, I'm glad I could help out," she said. She backed away from him and opened her car door. "Bye, now!"

"Goodbye," he said. "Thanks again."

As if he had been her host, he went on standing there while she maneuvered out of the parking slot. Naturally she made a mess of it, knowing he was watching. She cut her wheel too sharply, and the power-steering belt gave an embarrassing screech. But finally the car was free and she rolled away. Her rearview mirror showed Adrian lifting a palm in farewell, holding it steady until she turned south at the light.

Halfway home, she had a sudden realization: she should have given him the groceries he had picked out. Good heavens—all that pasta, those little grains of orzo, and now she remembered his consommé too. Consommé madrilene: she wasn't even sure how to pronounce it. She was driving away with property that belonged to someone else, and it was shameful how pleased she felt, and how lucky, and how rich.

2

The trouble with plastic bags was, those convenient handles tempted you to carry too many at once. Delia had forgotten that. She remembered halfway across her front yard, when the crooks of her fingers began to ache. She hadn't been able to bring the car around to the rear because someone's station wagon was blocking the driveway. Nailed to the trunk of the largest oak was a rusty metal sign directing patients to park on the street, but people tended to ignore it.

She circled the front porch and picked her way through the scribble of spent forsythia bushes at the side. This was a large house but shabby, its brown shingles streaked with mildew and its shutters snaggletoothed where the louvers had fallen out over the years. Delia had never lived anywhere else. Neither had her father, for that matter. Her mother, an import from the Eastern Shore, had died of kidney failure before Delia could remember, leaving her in the care of her father and her two older sisters. Delia had played hopscotch on the parquet squares in the hall while her father doctored his patients in the glassed-in porch off the kitchen, and she had married his assistant beneath the sprawling brass chandelier that reminded her to this day of a daddy longlegs. Even after the wedding she had not moved away but simply installed her husband among her sweet-sixteen bedroom furniture, and once her children were born it was not uncommon for a patient to wander out of the waiting room calling, "Delia? Where are you, darlin'? Just wanted to see how those precious little babies were getting along."

The cat was perched on the back stoop, meowing at her reproachfully. His short gray fur was flattened here and there by drops of water. "Didn't I tell you?" Delia scolded as she let him in. "Didn't I warn you the grass would still be wet?" Her shoes were soaked just from crossing the lawn, the thin soles cold and papery-feeling. She stepped out of them as soon as she entered the kitchen. "Well, hi there!" she said to her son. He sat slumped over the table in his pajamas, buttering a piece of toast. She placed her bags on the counter and said, "Fancy finding you awake so early!"

"It's not like I had any choice," he told her glumly.

He was her youngest child and the one who most resembled her, she had always thought (with his hair the light-brown color and frazzled texture of binder's twine, his freckled white face shadowed violet beneath the eyes), but last month he had turned fifteen, and all at once she saw more of Sam in him. He had shot up to nearly six feet, and his pointy chin had suddenly squared, and his hands had grown muscular and disconcertingly competent-looking. Even the way he held his butter knife suggested some new authority.

His voice was Sam's too: deep but fine-grained, not subject to the cracks and creaks his brother had gone through. "I hope you bought cornflakes," he told her.

"Why, no, I—"

"Aw, Mom!"

"But wait till you hear why I didn't," she said. "The funniest thing, Carroll! This real adventure. I was standing in the produce section, minding my own business—"

"There's not one decent thing in this house to eat."

"Well, you don't usually want breakfast on a Saturday."

He scowled at her. "Try telling Ramsay that," he said.

"Ramsay?"

"He's the one who woke me. Came stumbling into the room in broad daylight, out all night with his lady friend. No way could I get back to sleep after that."

Delia turned her attention to the grocery bags. (She knew where this conversation was headed.) She started rummaging through them as if the cornflakes might emerge after all. "But let me tell you my adventure," she said over her shoulder. "Out of the blue, this man is standing next to me. . . . Good-looking? He looked like my very first sweetheart, Will Britt. I don't believe I ever mentioned Will to you."

"Mom," Carroll said. "When are you going to let me move across the hall?"

"Oh, Carroll."

"Nobody else I know has to room with their brother."

"Now, now. Plenty of people in this world have to room with whole families," she told him.

"Not with their boozehead college-boy brother, though. Not when there's another room, perfectly empty, right across the hall."

Delia set down the box of orzo and faced him squarely. She noticed that he needed a haircut, but this was not the moment to point that out. "Carroll, I'm sorry," she said, "but I am just not ready."

"Aunt Eliza's ready! Why aren't you? Aunt Liza was Grandpa's daughter too, and she says of course I should have his room. She doesn't understand what's stopping me."

"Oh, listen to us!" Delia said gaily. "Spoiling such a pretty day with disagreements! Where's your father? Is he seeing a patient?"

Carroll didn't answer. He had dropped his toast to his plate, and now he sat tipping his chair back defiantly, no doubt adding more dents to the linoleum. Delia sighed.

"Sweetie," she said, "I do know how you feel. And pretty soon you can have the room, I promise. But not just yet! Not right now! Right now it still smells of his pipe tobacco."

"It won't once I'm living there," Carroll said.

"But that's what I'm afraid of."

"Shoot, I'll take up smoking, then."

She waved his words away with a dutiful laugh. "Anyhow," she said. "Is your father with a patient?"

"Naw."

"Where is he?"

"He's out running."

"He's what?"

Carroll picked up his toast again and chomped down on it noisily.

"He's doing *what*?"

"He's running, Mom."

"Well, didn't you at least offer to go with him?"

"He's only running around the Gilman track, for gosh sakes."

"I asked you children; I begged you not to let him go alone. What if something happens and no one's around to help?"

"Fat chance, on the Gilman track," Carroll said.

"He shouldn't be running anyway. He ought to be walking."

"Running's good for him," Carroll said. "Look. He's not worried. His doctor's not worried. So what's your problem, Mom?"

Delia could have come up with so many responses to that; all she did was press a hand to her forehead.

These were the facts she had neglected to tell that young man in the supermarket: She was a sad, tired, anxious, forty-year-old woman who hadn't had a champagne brunch in decades. And her husband was even older, by a good fifteen years, and just this past February he had suffered a bout of severe chest pain. Angina, they said in the emergency room. And now she was terrified any time he went anywhere alone, and she hated to let him drive, and she kept finding excuses not to make love for fear it would kill him, and at night while he slept she lay awake, tensing every muscle between each of his long, slow breaths.

And not only were her children past infancy; they were huge. They were great, galumphing, unmannerly, supercilious creatures—Susie a Goucher junior consumed by a baffling enthusiasm for various outdoor sports; Ramsay a Hopkins freshman on the brink of flunking out, thanks to the twenty-eight-year-old single-parent girlfriend he had somehow acquired. (And both of them, Susie and Ramsay both, were miffed beyond belief that the family finances forced them to live at home.) And Delia's baby, her sweet, winsome Carroll, had been replaced by this rude adolescent, flinching from his mother's hugs and criticizing her clothes and rolling his eyes disgustedly at every word she uttered.

Like now, for instance. Determined to start afresh, she perked all her features upward and asked, "Any calls while I was gone?" and he said, "Why would I answer the *grown-ups'* line," not bothering to add a question mark.

Because the grown-ups buy the celery for your favorite mint pea soup, she could have told him, but years of dealing with teenagers had turned her into a pacifist, and she merely padded out of the kitchen in her stocking feet and crossed the hall to the study, where Sam kept the answering machine.

The study was what they called it, and books did line the floor-to-ceiling shelves, but mainly this was a TV room now. The velvet draperies were kept permanently drawn, coloring the air the dusty dark red of an old-time movie house. Soft-drink cans and empty pretzel bags and stacks of rented videotapes littered the coffee table, and Susie lounged on the couch, watching Saturday-morning cartoons with her boyfriend, Driscoll Avery. The two of them had been dating so long that they looked like brother and sister, with their smooth beige coloring and stocky, waistless figures and identical baggy sweat suits. Driscoll barely blinked when Delia entered. Susie didn't even do that much; just flipped a channel on the remote control.

"Morning, you two," Delia said. "Any calls?"

Susie shrugged and flipped another channel. Driscoll yawned out loud. Just for that, Delia didn't excuse herself when she walked in front of them to the answering machine. She bent to press the Message button, but nothing happened. Electronic devices were always double-crossing her. "How do I—?" she said, and then an old man's splintery voice filled the room. "Dr. Grinstead, can you get back to me right away? It's Grayson Knowles, and I told the pharmacist about those pills, but he asked if—"

Whatever the pharmacist had asked was submerged by a flood of Bugs Bunny music. Susie must have raised the volume on the TV. *Beep,* the machine said, and then Delia's sister came on. "Dee, it's Eliza. I need an address. Could you please call me at work?"

"What's she doing at work on a Saturday?" Delia asked, but nobody answered.

Beep. "This is Myrtle Allingham," an old woman stated forthrightly.

"Oh, God," Susie told Driscoll.

"Marshall and I were wondering if you-all would like to take supper with us Sunday evening. Nothing fancy! Just us folks! And do tell young Miss Susie she should bring that darlin' Driscoll. Say seven o'clock?"

Beep beep beep beep beep. The end.

"We went *last* time," Susie said, slouching lower on the couch. "Count us out."

"Well, I don't know," Driscoll said. "That crab dip she served was not half bad."

"We aren't going, Driscoll, so forget it."

"She's lonesome, is all," Delia said. "Stuck at home with her hip, no way to get around—"

Something banged overhead.

"What's that?" she asked.

More bangs. Or clanks, really. *Clank!* Clank! at measured intervals, as if on purpose.

"Plumber?" Driscoll said tentatively.

"What plumber?"

"Plumber upstairs in the bathroom?"

"I never called for a plumber."

"Dr. Grinstead did, maybe?"

Delia gave Susie a look. Susie met it blandly.

"I don't know what's come over that man," Delia said. "He's been re— what's the word?—rejuvenating, resuscitating . . ." Fully aware that neither one of them was listening, she walked on out of the room, still talking. ". . . renovating, I mean: renovating this house to a fare-thee-well. If it's about that place in the ceiling, then really you'd think . . ."

She climbed the stairs, halfway up encountering the cat, who was hurrying down in a scattered, ungraceful fashion. Vernon detested loud noises. "Hello?" Delia called. She poked her head into the bathroom off the hall. A ponytailed man in coveralls crouched beside the claw-footed tub, studying its pipes. "Well, hello," she said.

He twisted around to look at her. "Oh. Hey," he said.

"What seems to be the trouble?"

"Can't say just yet," he said. He turned back to the pipes.

She waited a moment, in case he wanted to add something, but she could tell he was one of those repairmen who think only the husband worth talking to.

In her bedroom, she sat down on Sam's side of the bed, picked up the telephone, and dialed Eliza's work number. "Pratt Library," a woman said.

"Eliza Felson, please."

"Just a minute."

Delia propped a pillow against the headboard, and then she swung her feet up onto the frilled pink spread. The plumber had progressed to the bathroom between her room and her father's. She couldn't see him, but she could hear him banging around. What information could you hope to gain from whacking pipes?

"I'm sorry," the woman said, "but we can't seem to locate Miss Felson. Are you sure she's working today?"

"She must be; she told me to call her there, and she isn't here at home."

"I'm sorry."

"Well, thanks anyway."

She hung up. The plumber was whistling "Clementine." While Delia was dialing Mrs. Allingham, he ambled into the bedroom, still whistling, and she demurely smoothed her skirt around her knees. He squatted in front of the miniature door that opened onto the pipes in the wall. *Thou art lost and gone forever,* he whistled; Delia mentally supplied the words. One tug at the door's wooden knob, and it came off in his hand. She could have told him it would. She watched with some satisfaction as he muttered a curse beneath his breath and fished a pair of pliers from his belt loop.

Seven rings. Eight. She wasn't discouraged. Mrs. Allingham walked with a limp, and it took her ages to get to the phone.

Nine rings. "Hello?"

"Mrs. Allingham, it's Delia."

"Delia, dear! How *are* you?"

"I'm fine, how are you?"

"Oh, we're fine, doing just fine. Enjoying this nice spring weather! Nearly forgot what sunshine looks like, till today."

"Yes, me too," Delia said. She was overtaken suddenly by a swell of something like homesickness; Mrs. Allingham's chipper, slightly rasping voice was so reminiscent of all the women on this street where she had grown up. "Mrs. Allingham," she said, "Sam and I would love to come for supper tomorrow night, but we can't bring the children, I'm afraid."

"Oh!" Mrs. Allingham said.

"It's just that they're so busy these days. You know how it is."

"Yes, of course," Mrs. Allingham said faintly.

"But another time, maybe! They always enjoy your company."

"Yes, well, and we enjoy theirs too."

"So we'll see you at seven tomorrow," Delia said briskly, for she could hear Sam downstairs and she had a million things to do. "Goodbye till then."

By now the plumber had the little door prized open and was peering into the bowels of the wall, but she knew better than to ask him what he'd found.

In the kitchen, Sam stood propped against a counter, taking off his mud-caked running shoes. He was telling Carroll, ". . . sort of a toboggan effect when you hit those cedar chips . . ."

"Sam, how could you go off alone like that?" Delia asked. "You knew I'd worry!"

"Hello, Dee," he said.

His T-shirt was translucent with sweat, his sharp-boned face glistened, and his glasses were fogged. His hair—that shade that could be either blond or gray, it had faded so imperceptibly—lay in damp spikes on his forehead. "Look at you," Delia scolded. "You got overheated. You went running all alone and got overheated to boot when the doctor told you a dozen times—"

"Whose car is that in the driveway?"

"Car?"

"Station wagon parked in the driveway."

"Well, doesn't it belong to a patient? No, I guess not."

"Plumber," Carroll said from behind a glass of orange juice.

"Oh, good," Sam said. "The plumber's here."

He set his shoes on the doormat and started out of the kitchen, no doubt happily anticipating one of those laconic, man-to-man discussions of valves and joints and gaskets. "Sam, wait," Delia said, for she had a pang of guilt nagging at the back of her mind. "Before I forget—"

He turned, already wary.

"Mr. Knowles phoned—something to do with his pills," she said.

"I thought he got that straightened out."

"And also, um, Mrs. Allingham. She wanted to know if we could come for—"

He groaned. "No," he said, "we can't."

"But you haven't even heard yet! A light Sunday supper, she said, and I told her—"

"I'm sure not going," Carroll broke in.

"No, I told her that; I told her you kids were tied up. But you and I, Sam, just for—"

"We can't make it," Sam said flatly.

"But I've already accepted."

He had been on the point of turning away again, but now he stopped and looked at her.

"I know I should have checked with you first, but by accident somehow I just went ahead and accepted."

"Well, then," he said, "you'll have to call her back and unaccept."

"But, Sam!"

He left.

She looked over at Carroll. "How can he be so mean?" she asked, but Carroll just raised one eyebrow in that urbane new way she suspected him of practicing in the mirror.

Sometimes she felt like a tiny gnat, whirring around her family's edges.

The linoleum was slick and chilly beneath her feet, and she would have gone back upstairs for her slippers except that Sam and the plumber were upstairs. Instead, she turned to her grocery bags and unpacked several more boxes of pasta. Maybe she could tell Mrs. Allingham that Sam had been taken ill. That was always risky, though, when you lived on the same block and could so easily be observed, hale and hearty, stepping out to collect your morning paper or whatever. She sighed and shut a cabinet door. "When did this start happening to me?" she asked Carroll.

"Huh?"

"When did sweet and cute turn into silly and inefficient?"

He didn't seem to have an opinion.

Her sister appeared in the doorway, rolling up her shirt sleeves. "Morning, all!" she announced.

"Eliza?"

There were days when Eliza seemed almost gnomish, and this was one of them. She wore her gardening clothes—a pith helmet that all but obscured her straight black Dutch-boy bob, a khaki shirt and stubby brown trousers, and boys' brown oxfords with thick, thick soles intended to make her seem taller. (She was the shortest of the three Felson sisters.) Her horn-rimmed glasses overwhelmed her small, blunt, sallow face. "I figured I'd transplant some of those herbs before the ground dried out," she told Delia.

"But I thought you were at work."

"Work? It's Saturday."

"You called from work, I thought."

Eliza looked over at Carroll. He raised that eyebrow again.

"You called and left a message on the machine," Delia said, "asking me to find an address."

"That was ten days ago, at least. I needed Jenny Coop's address, remember?"

"Then why did I just get it off the answering machine?"

"Mom," Carroll said. "You must have been playing back *old* calls."

"Well, how is that possible?"

"You didn't have the machine turned on in the first place, see, and then when you pressed the Message button—"

"Oh, Lord," Delia said. "Mrs. Allingham."

"Is there coffee?" Eliza asked her.

"Not that I know of. Oh, Lord . . ."

She went over to the wall phone and dialed Mrs. Allingham's number. "I'm snug in bed," Eliza was telling Carroll, "thinking, *Goody, Saturday morning, I can sleep till noon*—when who should come crawling through that door in the back of my closet but another one of your father's blasted repairmen."

"Mrs. Allingham?" Delia said into the phone. "This is Delia again. Mrs. Allingham, I feel like such a dummy but it seems I got my calls mixed up and it was *last* week you invited us for. And of course last week we went, and a lovely time we had too; did I write you a thank-you note? I meant to write you a thank-you note. But *this* week we're not coming; I mean I realize now that you didn't invite us for—"

"But, Delia, darlin', we'd be happy to have you this week! We'd be happy to have you any old time, and I've already sent Marshall off to the Gourmet To Go with a shopping list."

"Oh, I'm so sorry," Delia said, but then the coffee grinder started up—a deafening racket—and she shouted, "Anyhow! We'll have to invite you to our place, very soon! Goodbye!"

She replaced the receiver and glared at Eliza.

"If only coffee tasted as good as it smells," Eliza said serenely when the grinder stopped.

Sam and the plumber were descending the stairs. Delia could hear the plumber's elasticized East Baltimore vowels; he was waxing lyrical about water. "It's the most amazing substance," he was saying. "It'll burst out one place and run twenty-five feet along the underside of a pipe and commence to dripping another place, where you least expect to see it. It'll lie in wait, it'll bide its time, it'll search out some little cranny you would never think to look."

Delia placed her hands on her hips and stood waiting. The instant the two men stepped through the door, she said, "I certainly hope you're satisfied, Sam Grinstead."

"Hmm?"

"I called back poor Mrs. Allingham and canceled supper."

"Oh, good," Sam said absently.

"I broke our promise. I ducked out of our commitment. I probably hurt her feelings for all time," Delia told him.

But Sam wasn't listening. He was following the plumber's forefinger as it pointed upward to a line of blistered plaster. And Eliza was measuring coffee, so the only one who paid any heed was Carroll. He sent Delia a look of utter contempt.

Delia turned sheepishly to her grocery bags. From the depths of one she drew the celery, pale green and pearly and precisely ribbed. She gazed at it for a long, thoughtful moment. "Aren't you clever to say so!" she heard Adrian exclaim once again, and she held the words close; she hugged them to her breast as she turned back to give her son a beatific smile.

3

"Aren't you clever to say so," he had said, and, "Why, you're very pretty!" and, "You have such a little face, like a flower." Had he meant that she had such a flowerlike face, which incidentally was little? Or had its littleness been his sole point? She preferred the first interpretation, although the second, she supposed, was more likely.

Also, he had praised her marvelous blancmange. Of course the blancmange did not really exist, but still she felt a lilt of pride, remembering that he had found it marvelous.

She studied her face in the mirror when nobody else was around. Yes, maybe it did resemble a flower. If he had been referring to those flowers that seem freckled. She had always wanted to look more dramatic, more mysterious—more adult, in fact. It had struck her as unfair that she should be wrinkling around the eyes without ever losing the prim-featured, artless, triangular face of her childhood. But evidently Adrian had considered that attractive.

Unless he had been speaking out of kindness.

She checked for his name in the phone book, but he must have had an unlisted number. She kept watch for him on the streets and in the local shops. Twice in the next three days she drove back to the supermarket, on both occasions wearing the dress with the smocked, gathered front that made her seem less flat-chested. But Adrian never appeared.

And if he had, what would she have done? It wasn't that she'd fallen in love with him or anything like that. Why, she didn't even know what kind of person he was! And she certainly didn't want (as she put it to herself) "something to start up." Ever since she was seventeen, she had centered her life on Sam Grinstead. She had not so much as glanced at any other man from the moment she first met him. Even in her daydreams, she wasn't the type to be unfaithful.

Still, whenever she imagined running into Adrian, she was conscious all at once of the light, quick way she naturally moved, and the outline of her body within the folds of her dress. She couldn't remember when she had last been so aware of herself from outside, from a distance.

At home, four workmen were installing air-conditioning—another of Sam's sudden renovations. They were slicing through floors and walls; they were running huge, roaring machines; they were lugging in metal ducts and bales of what looked like gray cotton candy. Delia could lie in bed at night and gaze straight upward through a new rectangle in the ceiling to the stark bones of the attic. She pictured bats and barn swallows swooping down on her while she slept. She fancied she could hear the house groaning in distress—such a modest, mild house, so unprepared for change.

But Sam was jubilant. Oh, he could hardly fit in his patients between visits from repairmen. Electricians, plasterers, and painters streamed through his office with estimates for the many improvements he planned. A carpenter arrived for the shutters, and a man with a spray for the mildewed shingles. Twenty-two years Sam had lived here; had he felt so critical of his surroundings all along?

He had first walked into her father's waiting room on a Monday morning in July, some three weeks after her high-school graduation. Delia had been sitting in her usual place at the desk, even though it was not her usual time (she worked afternoons, mostly), because she was so eager to meet him. She and her sisters had talked of nothing else since Dr. Felson had announced his hiring. Was this person married? they had asked, and how old was he? and what did he look like? (No, he was not married, their father said, and he was, oh, thirty-two, thirty-three, and he looked fine. Fine? Well, normal; perfectly all right, their father said impatiently, for to him what counted most was whether the man could ease his workload some—take over house calls and the morning office hours.) So Delia rose early that summer day and put on her prettiest sundress, the one with the sweetheart neckline. Then she seated herself behind the spinet desk, where she ostentatiously set to work transcribing her father's notes. At nine o'clock exactly, young Dr. Grinstead stepped through the outside door, carrying a starched white coat folded over his forearm. Sunlight flashed off his clear-rimmed, serious glasses and glazed his sifted-looking blond hair, and Delia could still recall the pang of pure desire that had caused her insides to lurch as if she had leaned out over a canyon.

Sam didn't even remember that meeting. He claimed he'd first seen her when he came to dinner. It was true there had been such a dinner, on the evening of that same day. Eliza had cooked a roast and Linda had baked a cake (both advertising their housewifely skills), while Delia, the baby, still two months short of her eighteenth birthday and supposedly not even in the running, sat across from Sam and her father in the living room and sipped a grown-up glass of sherry. The sherry had tasted like liquefied raisins and flowed directly to that powerful new root of longing that branched deeper minute by minute. But Sam claimed that when he first walked in, all three girls had been seated on the couch. Like the king's three daughters in a fairy tale, he said, they'd been lined up according to age, the oldest farthest left, and like the woodcutter's honest son, he had chosen the youngest and prettiest, the shy little one on the right who didn't think she stood a chance.

Well, let him believe what he wanted. In any case, it had *ended* like a fairy tale.

Except that real life continues past the end, and here they were with air-conditioning men destroying the attic, and the cat hiding under the bed, and Delia reading a paperback romance on the love seat in Sam's waiting room—the house's only refuge, since the office and the waiting room were air-conditioned already. Her head was propped on one arm of the love seat, and her feet, in fluffy pink slippers, rested on the other. Above her hung her father's framed Norman Rockwell print of the kindly old doctor setting his stethoscope to the chest of a little girl's doll. And behind the flimsy partition that rose not quite all the way to the ceiling, Sam was explaining Mrs. Harper's elbow trouble. Her joints were wearing out, he said. There was a stupefied silence; even the electric saw fell silent. Then, "Oh, no!" Mrs. Harper gasped. "Oh, my! Oh, my heavens above! This comes as such a shock!"

A shock? Mrs. Harper was ninety-two years old. What did she expect? Delia would have asked. But Sam said, gently, "Yes, well, I suppose . . ." and something else, which Delia couldn't catch, for the saw just then started up again as if all at once recalling its assignment.

She turned a page. The heroine was touring the hero's vast estate, admiring its magnificent grounds and its tasteful "appointments," whatever those might be. So many of these books had wealthy heroes, Delia had noticed. It didn't matter about the women; sometimes they were rich and sometimes they were poor, but the men came complete with castles and a staff of devoted servants. Never again would the women they married need to give a thought to the grinding gears of daily life—the leaky basement, the faulty oven, the missing car keys. It sounded wonderful.

"Delia, dear heart!" Mrs. Harper cried, staggering out of the office. She was a stylish, silk-clad skeleton of a woman with clawlike hands, which she stretched toward Delia beseechingly. "Your husband tells me my joints have just ground themselves down to nubbins!"

"Now, now," Sam protested behind her. "I didn't say that exactly, Mrs. Harper."

Delia sat up guiltily and smoothed her skirt. She grew aware of the bunny ears on her slippers and the temptress on the cover of her book. "I'm so sorry, Mrs. Harper," she said. "Should I schedule another appointment?"

"No, he says I have to go to a specialist. A man I don't know from Adam!"

"Get her Peterson's phone number, would you, Dee?" Sam asked.

She rose and went over to the desk, scuffing along in her slippers. (Mrs. Harper herself wore sharp-toed high heels, which she kept planted on the rug in a herringbone pattern to show off her trim ankles.) Delia flipped through Rolodex cards arranged not by name but by specialty—allergy, arthritis. . . . Nowadays, this office served most often as a sort of clearing-house. Her father used to deliver babies and even performed the more elementary surgeries once upon a time, but now it was largely a matter of bee shots in the spring, flu shots in the fall; and as for childbirth, why, these patients were long past the age. They were hand-me-downs from her father, most of them. (Or even, Sam joked, from her grandfather, who had opened this office in 1902, when Roland Park was still country and no one batted an eye at running a practice out of a residence.)

She copied Dr. Peterson's number onto a card and passed it to Mrs. Harper, who examined it suspiciously before tucking it into her bag. "I trust this person is not some mere snip of a boy," she told Sam.

"He's thirty if he's a day," Sam assured her.

"Thirty! My grandson is older than that! Oh, please, can't I go on seeing you instead?" But already knowing his answer, she turned without a pause toward Delia. "This husband of yours is a saint," she said. "He's just too good to exist on this earth. I hope you realize that."

"Oh, yes."

"You make sure you appreciate him, hear?"

"Yes, Mrs. Harper."

Delia watched Sam escort the old woman to the door, and then she dropped back onto the love seat and picked up her book. "Beatrice," the hero was saying, "I want you more than life itself," and his voice was rough and desperate—uncontrolled, was the way the author put it: *uncontrolled, and it sent a thrill down her slender spine within the clinging ivory satin of her negligee.*

Maybe, instead of running into Adrian, she could just sit still and let him track her down. Maybe he was even now dwelling on his image of her and cruising the streets in search of her. Or he had looked up her address, perhaps; for he did know her last name. He was parked down the block at this very moment, hoping to catch a glimpse of her.

She took to stepping into the yard several times a day. She seized any excuse to arrange herself on the front-porch swing. Never an outdoor person, and most certainly not a gardener, she spent half an hour posed in goatskin gloves among Eliza's medicinal herbs. And after someone telephoned but merely breathed and said nothing when she answered, she jumped up at every new call like a teenager. "I'll get it! I'll get it!" When there weren't any calls, she made a teenager's bargains with Fate: *I won't think about it, and then the phone will ring. I'll go out of the room; I'll pretend I'm busy and the phone will ring for sure.* Shepherding her family

into the car for a Sunday visit to Sam's mother, she moved fluidly, sensu-
ously, like an actress or a dancer conscious every minute of being
watched.

But if someone really had been watching, think of what he would see:
the ragged disarray of Delia's home life. Ramsay, short and stonefaced
and sullen, kicking a tire in disgust; Carroll and Susie bickering over who
would get a window seat; Sam settling himself behind the wheel, pushing
his glasses higher on his nose, wearing an unaccustomed knit shirt that
made him look weak-armed and fussy. And at the end of their trip, the
Iron Mama (as Delia called her)—sturdy, plain Eleanor Grinstead, who
patched her own roof and mowed her own lawn and had reared her one
son single-handed in that spotless Calvert Street row house where she
waited now, lips clamped tight, to hear what new piece of tomfoolery her
daughter-in-law had contrived.

No, not a one of them would bear up beneath the celestial blue gaze of
Adrian Bly-Brice.

The oldest of the air-conditioning men, the one named Lysander, asked
what those hay-bunch things were doing, hanging from the attic rafters.
"Those are my sister's herbs," Delia said. She hoped to let it rest at that,
but her sister happened to be right there in the kitchen with her, stringing
beans for supper, and she told him, "Yes, I burn them in little pots around
the house."

"You set fire to them?" Lysander asked.

"Each one does something different," Eliza explained. "One prevents
bad dreams and another promotes a focused mind and another clears the
atmosphere after interpersonal strife."

Lysander looked over at Delia, raising his gray toothbrush eyebrows.

"So anyhow," Delia said hastily. "Is this job about wrapped up, do you
think?"

"This one here? Oh, no," he said. He plodded toward the sink; he had
come down to refill his thermos. Waiting for the water to run cold, he
said, "We got several more days, at the least."

"Several days!" Delia squawked. She cleared her throat. "But the noisy
part: will that be over soon? Even the cat is getting a headache."

"Now, how would you know that?" he asked.

"Oh, Delia can read a cat's mind," Eliza told him. "She's got all of us
trained in cat etiquette: what kind of voice to use with them and how to
do your eyes when you look at them and—"

"Eliza, I need those beans *now*," Delia broke in.

Too late, though: Lysander snorted as he set his thermos under the
faucet. "Me, I'll take a dog any day," he said. "Cats are too sneaky for my
taste."

"Oh, well, I like dogs too, of course," Delia said. (In fact, she was slightly afraid of dogs.) "It's just that dogs are so . . . sudden. You know?"

"But honest," Lysander said. It sounded like an accusation. "Okay if I swipe a few ice cubes?"

"Go right ahead," Delia told him.

He stood there helplessly, clasping the neck of his thermos, until she realized that he meant for her to get them. He would be one of those men who didn't know where their wives kept the spoons. She dried her hands on her apron and went to fetch the bin from the freezer.

"Last place we worked?" he said. "Putting in a new heat pump? Guy next door owned one of them attack dogs. Dog trained to attack. Lady we was working for warned us all about him."

He kept a staunch grip on his thermos while Delia tried to fit an ice cube in. It wouldn't go. She hit it with the flat of her hand (Lysander not even flinching) and, "Eek!" she cried, for the ice cube flew up in the air and then skittered across the floor. Lysander stared down at it dolefully.

"Just let me at this little devil," Delia told him, and she snatched the thermos from him and slammed it into the sink. She ran water over a second ice cube. "Aha!" she crowed, pounding it in. She started working on a third.

Lysander said, "So we're hauling in stuff from the truck one day, come to see the attack dog rounding the side of the house. Big old bristle-necked dog like a wolf, growling real deep in his throat. Lord, I thought I would die. Then out steps the lady we worked for like she had just been waiting for this. Says, '*Come* along,' and takes hold of his collar, calm-natured as you please. Walks him into the yard next door and, 'Mr. What's-it?' she calls. 'I'm about to shoot your dog dead unless you come out this minute and retrieve him.' With her voice just as clear, just as cool. That was some kind of woman, believe me."

Why was he telling this story? Was it meant to show Delia up? She dispatched the third ice cube with as little commotion as possible. For some reason, she imagined that the woman had resembled Rosemary Bly-Brice. Maybe she *was* Rosemary Bly-Brice. She wore an expression of tolerant detachment; she bent in a graceful S-curve; she hooked a single finger through the dog's spiked collar. Unexpectedly, Delia felt a rush of admiration, as if her entrancement with Adrian extended to his wife as well.

She turned off the faucet, picked up the thermos, and offered it to Lysander. "Why, looky there," Lysander said. Water was dripping rapidly from the bottom of the thermos. "Why, you've gone and broke it," he said.

Delia didn't apologize. She went on offering the thermos, wishing he would just take it and leave. In the supermarket, she recalled at that instant, she had made some reference to Ramsay, and Adrian had assumed she meant her husband. No wonder he hadn't come by yet! He'd been looking for Ramsay Grinstead, who wasn't in the phone book. Sooner or later, though, he would realize his mistake. She began smiling at the thought, and she continued holding the thermos out until Eliza, clucking, rose to fetch the mop.

In the dark the phone rang twice, and Delia woke with a start. She was reviewing her children's whereabouts even before her eyes were fully open. All three were safe in bed, she decided, but her heart went on racing anyhow.

"Hello?" Sam said. "Yes, this is Dr. Grinstead. Oh. Mr. Maxwell."

Delia sighed and rolled over. Mr. Maxwell was married to the Dowager Queen of Hypochondria.

"How long has she been experiencing this?" Sam asked. "I see. Well, that doesn't sound serious. Yes, I'm sure it *is* uncomfortable, but I doubt very much if—"

A miniature babbling sound issued from the receiver.

"Of course she does," Sam said. "I understand. All right, Mr. Maxwell—if you think it's that important, I'll come take a look."

"Oh, Sam!" Delia hissed, sitting up.

He ignored her. "See you in a few minutes, then," he was telling Mr. Maxwell.

As soon as he had replaced the receiver, Delia said, "Sam Grinstead, you are such a patsy. You know it's going to be nothing. Why can't he take her to the emergency room, if she's so sick?"

"Well, neither one of them drives anymore," Sam said mildly. He swung his feet to the floor and reached for his trousers, which lay folded over the back of the rocker. As always, he'd worn tomorrow's underwear to bed and placed tomorrow's clothes conveniently at hand.

Delia pressed a palm to her heart, which was only now settling down. Was this anything like what Sam had felt with his chest pains? She kept trying to imagine. Think of him operating a car at such a time—humming along toward a meeting and then noticing his symptoms and smoothly, composedly (she pictured) turning his wheel toward Sinai Hospital. Arranging his own admission and asking a nurse to phone Delia and break the news by degrees. ("Your husband wants you to know he'll be a tad bit later getting home than planned.") And Delia, meanwhile, had been reading *Lucinda's Lover* by the fire, without a qualm.

She switched on her lamp and climbed out of bed. Two-fifteen, the alarm clock said. Squinting against the light, Sam reached for his glasses and put them on to look at her. "Where are *you* off to?" he asked. The glasses made his face seem crisper, less vague around the eyes, as if they had corrected Delia's vision rather than his.

She drew her ruffled housecoat over her nightgown and zipped the front before she answered. "I'm coming with you," she said.

"Pardon?"

"I'll take you in my car."

"Why on earth would you do that?"

"I just want to, that's why," she said. She tied her sash very tight, in hopes her housecoat would pass for streetwear. As she stepped into her flats, she could feel him staring at her, but all she said was, "Ready?" She collected her keys from the bureau.

"Delia, are you doubting my ability to drive my own car anymore?" Sam asked.

"Oh, no! What a thought!" she told him. "But I'm awake, why not come with you? Besides, it's such a nice spring night."

He didn't look convinced, but he offered no more arguments when she led the way downstairs.

It was not a nice spring night at all. It was cool and breezy, and she wished for a sweater as soon as they stepped out the back door. Towering, luminous clouds scudded across an inky sky. But she headed toward her car at a leisurely pace, resisting the urge to hunch her shoulders against the chill. The streetlights were so bright that she could see her shadow, elongated like a stick figure in a child's drawing.

"This makes me think of Daddy," she said. She had to speak up, since Sam had walked over to his Buick to retrieve his black bag. She hoped he didn't hear the shiver in her voice. "All the house calls I used to make with Daddy, just the two of us! Seems like old times."

She slid behind her steering wheel and reached across to unlock the passenger door. The air inside the car felt refrigerated. It even smelled refrigerated—dank and stale.

"Of course, Daddy never let me drive him," she said when Sam had got in. Then she worried this would give him second thoughts, and so she added, laughing slightly, "You know how prejudiced he was! Women drivers, he always said . . ." She started the engine and turned on her lights, illuminating the double doors of the garage and the tattered net of the basketball hoop overhead. "But whenever I was still up, he'd say I could come with him. Oh, I tagged along many a night! Eliza just never was interested, and Linda was so, you know, at odds with him all the time, but I was ready at a moment's notice. I just loved to go."

Sam had heard all this before, of course. He merely settled his bag between his feet while she backed the car out of the driveway.

Once they were on Roland Avenue, she said, "In fact I ought to come with you more often, now the kids are growing up. Don't you think?" She was aware that she was chattering, but she said, "It might be kind of fun! And it's not as if you go out every night, or even every week anymore."

"Delia, I give you my word I am still capable of making the odd house call without a baby-sitter," Sam told her.

"Baby-sitter!"

"I'm strong as an ox. Stop fretting."

"I'm not fretting! I just thought it would be romantic, something the two of us could do together!" she said.

This wasn't the whole truth, but as soon as she said it she started to believe it, and so she felt a bit hurt. Sam merely sat back and gazed out the side window.

There was almost no traffic at this hour, and the avenue seemed very flat and empty, shimmering pallidly beneath the streetlights as if veiled by yellow chiffon. The newly leafed trees, lit from below, had a tumbled, upside-down look. Here and there a second-floor window glowed cozily, and Delia sent it a wistful glance as they passed.

In front of the Maxwells' house, she parked. She turned off the headlights but left the engine and the heater on. "Aren't you coming in?" Sam asked.

"I'll wait in the car."

"You'll freeze!"

"I'm not dressed for company."

"Come in, Dee. The Maxwells don't care how you're dressed."

He was right, she supposed. (And the heater hadn't even started heating yet.) She took the keys from the ignition and slid out of the car to follow him up the front walk, toward the broad, columned house where those two lone Maxwells must rattle around like dice in a cup. All the windows were blazing, and the inner door stood open. Mr. Maxwell waited just inside, a stooped, bulky figure fumbling to unhook the screen as they crossed the porch.

"Dr. Grinstead!" he said. "Thank you so much for coming. And Delia too. Hello, dear."

He wore food-stained trousers belted just beneath his armpits, and a frayed gray cardigan over a T-shirt. (He used to be such a natty dresser.) Without a pause, he turned to lead Sam toward the carpeted stairs. "It breaks my heart to see her this way," he said as they started the climb. "I'd suffer in her stead, if I could."

Delia watched after them from the foyer, and when they were out of sight she sat down on one of the two antique chairs that flanked a highboy. She sat cautiously; for all she knew, the chairs were purely for show.

Overhead the voices murmured—Mrs. Maxwell's thin and complaining, Sam's a rumble. The grandfather clock facing Delia ticked so slowly that it seemed each tick might be its last. For lack of anything better to do (she had thoughtlessly left her purse at home), she fanned her keys across her lap and sorted through them.

How many hours had she sat like this in her childhood? Perched on a chair or a bottom step, scratching at the insect bites on her bare knees or leafing through a magazine some grown-up had thrust upon her before leading her father up the stairs. And overhead that same murmur, the words never quite distinguishable. When her father spoke, all others fell silent, and she had felt proud and flattered to hear how people revered him.

The stairs creaked, and she looked up. It was Mr. Maxwell, descending by himself. "Dr. Grinstead's just examining her," he said. He inched down, clinging to the banister, and when he reached the foyer he settled with a wheeze onto the other antique chair. Because the highboy stood between them, all she saw of him was his outstretched trouser legs and his leather slippers, backless, exposing maroon silk socks with transparent heels. "He says he thinks it's a touch of indigestion, but I told him, I said, at our age . . . well, you can't be too careful, I told him."

"I'm sure she'll be all right," Delia said.

"I just thank heaven for Dr. Grinstead. A lot of those younger fellows wouldn't come out like this."

"None of them would," Delia couldn't resist saying.

"Oh, some, maybe."

"None. Believe me."

Mr. Maxwell sat forward to look at her. She found his veiny, florid face peering around the highboy.

"That Sam is just too nice for his own good," she told him. "Did you know he has angina? Angina, at age fifty-five! What could that mean for his future? If it were up to me, he'd be home in bed this very minute."

"Well, luckily it's *not* up to you," Mr. Maxwell said a bit peevishly. He sat back again and there was a pause, during which she heard Mrs. Maxwell say something opinionated that sounded like "Nee-nee. Nee-nee."

"We were Dr. Grinstead's first house call—did he ever mention that?" Mr. Maxwell asked. "Yessir: very first house call. Your dad said, 'Think you'll like this boy.' I admit we were a mite apprehensive, having relied on your dad all those years."

Sam was speaking more briskly now. He must be finishing up.

"I asked Dr. Grinstead when he came to us," Mr. Maxwell said dreamily. "I said, 'Well, young man?' He'd only been on the job a couple days by then. I said, 'Well?' Said, 'Which one of those Felson girls do you plan to set about marrying?' Pretty smart of me, eh?"

Delia laughed politely and rearranged her keys.

" 'Oh,' he said; said, 'I guess I've got my eye on the youngest.' Said, 'The oldest is too short and the middle one's too plump, but the youngest,' he said, 'is just right.' So. See there? I knew before you did."

"Yes, I guess you did," Delia said, and then Sam started down the stairs, the instruments in his black bag cheerily jingling. Mr. Maxwell rose at once, but Delia stayed seated and kept her gaze fixed on her keys. They seemed uncannily distinct—dull-finished, ill-assorted, incised with brand names as clipped and choppy as words from another language.

"Just what I . . . ," Sam was saying, and, "Nothing but a touch of . . . ," and, "Left some medication on the . . ." Then he and Mr. Maxwell were shaking hands, and he said, "Dee?" and she stood up without a word and stepped through the door that Mr. Maxwell held open.

Outside, the grass had grown white with dew and the air itself seemed white, as if dawn were not far off. Delia climbed into the car and started the engine before Sam was completely settled. "You have to feel for those folks," he said, shutting his door. "Aging all alone like that, they must dwell on every symptom."

Delia swung out into the street and drove slightly above the speed limit, concentrating, not speaking. They were nearly home before she said, "Mr. Maxwell told me they were your very first house call."

"Really?"

"The second day you worked here."

"I'd forgotten."

"He said he asked which of the Felson girls you planned to marry and you said the youngest."

"Hmm," Sam said, unzipping his bag. He checked something inside and told her, "Delia, remind me tomorrow morning to pick up more—"

" 'The oldest is too short and the middle one's too plump,' you said, 'but the youngest one is just right.' "

Sam laughed.

"Did you say that?" she asked him.

"Oh, sweetie, how would I remember after all these years?"

She pulled into their driveway and turned the engine off. Sam opened his door, but then, noticing she had not moved, he looked over at her. The little ceiling bulb cast sharp hollows in his face.

"You did say it," she told him. "I recognize the fairy-tale sound of it."

"So? Maybe I did," he said. "Gosh, Dee, I wasn't weighing every word. I might have *said* 'too short' and 'too plump,' but what I probably meant was 'too unconventional' and 'too Francophile.' "

"That's not it," Delia said.

"Why, Linda spent half the evening speaking French, remember? And when your dad made her switch to English, she still had an accent."

"You don't even know what I'm objecting to, do you?" Delia asked.

"Well, no," Sam said. "I don't."

She got out of the car and walked toward the back steps. Sam went to replace his bag in the Buick; she heard the clunk of his trunk lid.

"And Eliza!" he said as he followed her to the house. "She kept asking my opinion of homeopathic medicine."

"You arrived here that very first day planning to marry one of the Felson girls," Delia told him.

She had unlocked the door now, but instead of entering she turned to face him. He was looking down at her, with his forehead creased.

"Why, I suppose it must naturally have crossed my mind," he said. "I'd completed all my training by then. I'd reached the marrying age, so to speak. The marrying stage of life."

"But then why not a nurse, or a fellow student, or some girl your mother knew?"

"My mother?" he said. He blinked.

"You had your eye on Daddy's practice, that's why," she told him. "You thought, 'I'll just marry one of Dr. Felson's daughters and inherit all his patients and his nice old comfortable house.' "

"Well, sweetheart, I probably did think that. Probably I did. But I never would have married someone I didn't love. Is that what you believe? You believe I didn't marry for love?"

"I don't know what to believe," she told him.

Then she spun around and walked back down the steps.

"Dee?" Sam called.

She passed her car without slowing. Most women would have *driven* away, but she preferred to walk. The soles of her flats gritted against the asphalt driveway in a purposeful rhythm, reminding her of some tune she could almost name but not quite. Part of her was listening for Sam (she had a sense of perking one ear backward, like a cat), but another part was glad to be rid of him and pleased to have her view of him confirmed. *Look at that, he won't even deign to come after me.* She reached the street, turned right, and kept going. Her frail-edged shadow preceded her and then drew back and then fell behind as she traveled from streetlight to streetlight. No longer did she feel the cold. She seemed warmed from inside by her anger.

Now she understood why Sam had forgotten his actual first glimpse of her. He had prepared to meet the Felson girls as a boxed set, that was why. It had not figured in his plans to encounter an isolated sample ahead of time. What *had* figured was the social occasion that evening, with marriageable maidens one, two, and three on display on the living-room couch. She could envision that scene herself now. All it took was the proper perspective to bring it back entire: the itchy red plush cushions, the clothlike texture of her frosted sherry glass, and the fidgeting, encroaching, irritating plumpness of the middle sister, next to her.

On a branch overhead, the neighborhood's silly mockingbird was imitating a burglar alarm. "Doy! Doy! Doy!" he sang in his most lyrical voice, until he was silenced by a billow of rock music approaching from the south. Teenagers, evidently—a whole carload. Delia heard their hoots and cheers growing steadily louder. It occurred to her that even Roland Park was not absolutely safe at this hour. Also, her housecoat wouldn't fool a soul. She was running around in her nightclothes, basically. She took a sudden right turn onto a smaller, darker street and walked close to a boxwood hedge, whose shadow swallowed hers.

Sam would be back in bed now, his trousers draped over the rocking chair. And the children didn't know she was missing. With their jumbled, separate schedules, they might not know for days.

What kind of a life was she leading, if every single one of last week's telephone messages could as easily be this week's?

She walked faster, hearing the carload of music fade away behind her. She reached Bouton Road, crossed over, and turned left, and one split second later, *whomp*! she collided with someone. She ran smack against a stretch of tallness and boniness, overlaid by warm flannel. "Oh!" she said, and she recoiled violently, heart pounding, while somehow a dog became involved as well, one of those shaggy hunting-type dogs shouting around her knees.

"Butch! Down!" the man commanded. "Are you all right?" he asked Delia.

Delia said, "Adrian?"

In the half-dark he had no color, but still she recognized his narrow, distinctly cheekboned face. She saw that his mouth was wider and fuller, more sculptured, than she had been imagining, and she wondered how she could have forgotten something so important. "Adrian, it's me. Delia," she said. The dog was still barking. She said, "Delia Grinstead? From the supermarket?"

"Why, Delia," Adrian said. "My rescuer!" He laughed, and the dog grew quiet. "What are *you* doing here?"

She said, "Oh, just . . . ," and then she laughed too, glancing down at her housecoat and smoothing it with her palms. "Just couldn't sleep," she said.

She was relieved to find that he was not so well dressed himself. He wore a dark-hued robe of some kind and pale pajamas. On his feet were jogging shoes, laces trailing, no socks. "Do you live nearby?" she asked him.

"Right here," he said, and he waved toward a matted screen of barberry bushes. Behind it Delia glimpsed a porch light and a section of white clapboard. "I got up to let Butch here take a pee," he said. "It's his new hobby: waking me in the dead of night and claiming he needs to go out."

At the sound of his name, Butch sat down on his haunches and grinned up at her. Delia leaned over to give his muzzle a timid pat. His breath warmed and dampened her fingers. "I ran off with your groceries that day," she said, ostensibly to the dog. "I felt terrible about it."

"Groceries?" Adrian asked.

"Your orzo and your rotini . . ." She straightened and met his eyes. "I considered hunting up your address and bringing them over."

"Oh. Well . . . orzo? Well, never mind," he told her. "I'm just grateful you helped me out like that. You must have thought I was kind of weird, right?"

"No, not at all! I enjoyed it," she said.

"You know how sometimes you just want to, say, keep up appearances in front of someone."

"Certainly," she said. "I ought to start a business: Appearances, Incorporated."

"Rent-a-Date," Adrian suggested. "Imposters To Go."

"With blondes to pose as second wives, and football stars to take jilted girls to proms—"

"And beautiful women in black to weep at funerals," Adrian said.

"Oh, why *don't* they have such things?" Delia asked. "There's just nothing like that . . . what? Like that fury, that prideful sort of fury you feel when you've been hurt or insulted or taken for granted—"

Well. She stopped herself. Adrian was watching her with such peculiar intentness, she worried all at once that she had curlers in her hair. She nearly raised a hand to check, till she remembered she hadn't worn curlers since high school. "Goodness. I should get home," she said.

"Wait!" Adrian said. "Would you like . . . could I offer you some coffee?"

"Coffee?"

"Or tea? Or cocoa? Or a drink?"

"Well," she said, "I guess cocoa, maybe. Cocoa might be nice. I mean caffeine at this hour would probably . . . But are you sure it's not too much trouble?"

"No trouble at all," he told her. "Come on inside."

He led her to a gap in the barberry bushes. A flagstone path curved toward the house, which was one of those lace-trimmed Victorian cottages young couples nowadays found so charming. The front door was paned with lozenges of glass in sugared-almond colors impossible to see through. Delia felt a sudden pinch of uneasiness. Why, she didn't know a thing about this man! And no one else on earth had any inkling where she was.

"Usually if I'm up at this hour I'm up for good," Adrian was saying, "so I fix myself a pot of—"

"What a lovely porch!" Delia exclaimed. "Maybe we could have our cocoa out here."

"Here?"

He paused on the topmost step and looked around him. It was a depressing porch, really. The floorboards were battleship gray, and the furniture was painted a harsh bright shade of green. "Don't you think you'd be cold?" he asked.

"Not a bit," she told him, although now that she had stopped walking, it did seem cold. She stuffed both fists in the pockets of her housecoat.

He gazed down at her a moment. Then he said, "Ah. I see," and the corners of his mouth quirked upward with amusement.

"But if *you're* cold . . . ," she said, flushing.

"I understand," he said. "You can't be too careful."

"Oh, it's not that! Heavens!"

"I don't blame you in the least. We'll have our cocoa out here."

"Really," she said, "why don't I come in?"

"No, you wait here. I'll bring it out."

"Please," she said. "Please let me come in."

And because she saw that the argument would otherwise go on forever, she took one hand from her pocket and laid it on his wrist. "I want to," she said.

She wanted to come in, she meant. That was what she honestly meant, but the moment the words were out of her mouth she saw that they implied something more, and she dropped her hand and stepped back. "Or maybe . . . ," she said. "Yes, the . . . porch, why don't we have our cocoa on the . . ." And she felt behind her for a chair and sat down. The icy, uncushioned seat took her breath away for an instant, as if she had heard a piece of startling news, or glimpsed some possibility that had never crossed her mind before.

4

———

"I told Eliza when she picked us up at the airport," Linda said. "I told her, 'Well, one good thing: now that Dad's gone I won't have to share a room with you, Eliza.' Considering how she snores."

Delia said, "Yes, but—"

" 'And the twins won't have to bunk with Susie,' I said. I figured I could fit both of them in Dad's big bed with me. Then I get to the house, and guess what."

"I did plan at first for you to stay there," Delia said, "but it seemed so . . . when I walked in to put the sheets on, it seemed so . . ."

"Fine, I'll put the sheets on myself," Linda said. "I'll tell you this much: I am surely not sleeping with Eliza when there's a whole extra room going empty."

They were standing in the doorway of their father's room at that moment, gazing in on its heartbreaking neatness, the dim air laden with dust motes, the candlewick bedspread unnaturally straight on the mattress. Linda, still in her traveling clothes, had not yet lost that aura of focus and efficiency that travel gives some people. She surveyed the room without a trace of sentiment, as far as Delia could see. "You've certainly wasted no time making changes elsewhere," she said. "Air-conditioning vents every place you look, nursery men tearing out the shrubs, I don't know *what* all."

"Oh, well, that's—"

"I suppose it's what Sam Grinstead has been waiting for," Linda said. "He's finally got the house in his clutches."

Delia didn't argue. Linda sent her a quizzical glance before crossing to their father's bureau. Leaning into the mirror above it, she raked her fingers through her short brown pageboy. Then she removed her pocketbook, which she wore bandolier style, with the strap slanted over her chest—just one more of her European ways. You would never take her for American. (You would never guess she lived in Michigan, divorced from the French-literature professor who had not, after all, swooped her off to his native Paris as she'd hoped.) Her full, soft face was powdered white, her only other makeup a bloom of sticky scarlet on her lips, and although her clothes were unexceptional, she wore them with authority—those dowdy brown medium-heeled pumps, for instance, defiantly teamed with a navy suit. "But why are we standing around? No telling what Marie-Claire and Thérèse have got into," she said, and the *r*'s in her children's names were very nearly gargled. When she whisked past Delia toward the stairs, she smelled of airplane.

In the kitchen, they found Eliza making lemonade for the twins. This fall the twins would be nine years old—a long-limbed, sproutlike stage—and although they had their mother's blocky brown haircut, they resembled the professor in every other way. Their eyes were almost black, mournfully downturned; their mouths were the color of plums. They were assisting each other up a bank of glass-fronted cabinets, the first pulling the second after her once she'd reached the counter, and for mobility's sake they had tucked their old-fashioned, European-schoolgirl dresses into their underpants, which made them look all the leggier.

"As soon as your cousin Susie shows up, she'll take you to the pool," Eliza was saying. She stood at the drainboard, reaming lemons. "She promised she'd do it first thing, but I guess she must be off someplace with her boyfriend."

The mention of a boyfriend diverted them for a second. "Driscoll?" Marie-Claire asked, pausing in her climb. "Does Susie still date Driscoll?"

"She does indeed."

"Do they go to dances together? Do they kiss good night?"

"Now, that I wouldn't know," Eliza said tartly, and she bent to take a pitcher from a cupboard.

The twins had reached their goal: a jar of peppermints on the top shelf. Inch by inch, Thérèse maneuvered it through the partially opened door. (Thérèse was the uneven-featured twin, her face less balanced, less symmetrical, which made her appear slightly anxious. There was one in every set, Delia had noticed.) For a moment the jar seemed suspended, but then it arrived safely in Marie-Claire's outstretched hands. "Do Ramsay and Carroll have sweethearts too?" she asked.

"Well, Ramsey does, I'm sorry to say."

"How come you're sorry?" Thérèse asked, and Marie-Claire said, "What's wrong with her?"—the two of them so alert for scandal that Delia laughed aloud. Thérèse wheeled and said, "Are you sorry too, Aunt Delia? Do you forbid her to darken your door? Is she coming to the beach with us?"

"No, she's not," Delia said, answering only the easiest question. "The beach is just a family trip."

They were leaving for a week at the beach early the following morning, a Sunday. It had come to be an annual event. In mid-June, as soon as the schools closed, Linda arrived from Michigan and they all took off for a cottage they rented on the Delaware shore. Already the front porch was heaped with rubber rafts and badminton rackets; the freezer was stuffed with casseroles; and Sam's patients were thronging in for last-minute consultations in hopes of avoiding any contact with his backup.

"Delia, could you get the sugar?" Eliza asked. She was running water into the pitcher. "And girls, I'd like five tumblers from that cabinet to your right."

While Delia was measuring sugar, she secretly checked the clock on the wall above her. Ten minutes till four. She glanced at the twins and cleared her throat. "If Susie isn't back by the time you finish your lemonade, maybe *I* could take you to the pool," she said.

Linda said, "You?" and the twins said, in a single voice, "You hate to swim!"

"Oh, well, I wouldn't actually go in. I'd just drive you over, and then Susie could pick you up later."

Eliza clinked ice into the tumblers. Linda took a seat at the head of the table, and the twins claimed the chairs on either side of her. When Delia placed the pitcher of lemonade in front of them, Marie-Claire cried, "Ick! It's full of shreddy things!"

"Those are good for you," Linda said as she started pouring.

"And big seeds besides!"

"They won't hurt you."

"That's what *she* says," Thérèse told Marie-Claire in an ominous tone. "Really they'll take root in your stomach and grow lemon trees out your ears."

"Oh, honestly, Thérèse," Linda said.

Ignoring her, the twins gazed significantly across the table at each other. Finally Marie-Claire said, "I guess we're not thirsty after all."

"We'll just go change into our swimsuits," Thérèse added.

They scooted their chairs back and raced out of the kitchen.

"Ah, me," Linda sighed. "Sorry, Lize."

"That's all right," Eliza said stiffly.

There were times when Delia realized, for an instant, that Eliza was what they used to call an old maid. She looked so forlorn in her eccentric weekend outfit of safari suit and clunky shoes; she pulled out a chair with her head down, her chopped black hair falling forward to hide her expression, and she seated herself and folded her small hands resolutely on the table.

"Well, *I'm* thirsty!" Delia said loudly, and she sat down too and reached for one of the tumblers. From the hall she heard a series of thumps—the twins' suitcase, no doubt, being hauled up the stairs. Apparently they still planned to room with Susie, if the creaks that began overhead were any indication.

Outside the open window, a workman's bearded face popped into view.

He looked at the women, blinked, and disappeared. Delia and Linda saw him, but Eliza, who had her back to him, did not. "What is he up to, anyhow?" Linda asked.

Eliza said, "He? Who?"

"The workman," Delia explained.

"No, not the workman," Linda said. "I meant Sam. Why is he having all the shrubs torn out?"

"Well, they're old and straggly, he says."

"Can't he just cut them back or something? And central air-conditioning! This house is not the type for air-conditioning."

"I'm sure we'll appreciate it once the weather heats up," Eliza said. "Have some lemonade, Linda."

Linda took a tumbler, but she didn't drink from it. "I'd just like to know where he found the money," she said darkly. "Plus: this house is in *our* three names, not his. We're the ones Dad left it to."

Delia glanced toward the window. (She suspected the workman of lurking beneath it, absorbed as all workmen seemed to be in other people's private lives.) "Goodness!" she said. "We'd better get to the pool. Anybody want anything from Eddie's?"

"Eddie's?" Eliza asked.

"I might stop for some fruit on my way home."

"Delia, have you forgotten Sam's mother is coming to dinner? And you still have the Medicare bills to see to! Why don't I take the twins, instead, and then go to Eddie's after."

"No! Please!" Delia said. "I mean, I have plenty of time. And besides, I need to choose the fruit myself because I'm not sure what I—"

She was offering too many explanations—always a mistake. Linda didn't notice, but Eliza could read her mind, Delia sometimes thought, and she was watching Delia consideringly. "Anyhow," Delia said. "I'll see you both in a while. Okay?" And she stood up. Already she heard the twins racketing down the stairs. "Hand me my purse, will you?" she asked. Eliza was still watching her, but she reached for Delia's purse on the counter and passed it over.

In the hall, the twins were quarreling over a pair of goggles they must have liberated from the beach equipment. They wore identical skinny knit swimsuits in different colors—one red, one blue—and a red-and-blue flip-flop apiece on their long, pale, knobby feet. Neither one had a towel, but the towels were upstairs and so Delia didn't remind them. "Let's go," she told them. "I'm parked out front." From the kitchen, Linda called, "You do what the lifeguard tells you, girls, hear?"

Delia followed them across the porch, avoiding the shaft of a beach umbrella. Beside the steps, a young man in a red bandanna was hacking at the roots of an azalea bush. He straightened, wiped his face on his forearm, and gave them a grin. "Wisht *I* was going swimming," he said.

"Come with us, then," Thérèse said, but Marie-Claire told her, "Dope, you can see he's not wearing his bathing suit." They skipped ahead of Delia down the walk, chanting a routine that she remembered from her childhood:

"Well, that's life."

"*What's* life?"

"Fifteen cents a copy."

"But I only have a dime."

"Well, that's life."

"*What's* life?"

"Fifteen cents a . . ."

The weather was perfect, sunny and not too warm, but Delia's car had been sitting at the curb collecting heat all day. Both girls squealed as they slid across the backseat. "Could you turn on the air-conditioning?" they asked Delia.

"I don't have air-conditioning."

"Don't have air-conditioning!"

"Just open your windows," she told them, rolling down her own. She started the engine and pulled into the street. The steering wheel was almost too hot to touch.

You could tell it was a weekend, because so many joggers were out. And people were at work in their yards, running their mowers or their hedge trimmers, filling the air with a visible green dust that made Thérèse (the allergic one) sneeze. At Wyndhurst the traffic light changed to amber, but Delia didn't stop. She had a sense of time slipping away from her. She took the long downhill slope at a good ten miles above the speed limit, and screeched left on Lawndale and parked in the first available space. The twins were in a hurry themselves; they tore ahead of her to the gate, and even before she paid for them they had disappeared among the other swimmers.

Driving back up the hill, she kept plucking at the front of her blouse and blowing toward the damp frizz sticking to her forehead. If only she could stop by home and freshen up a bit! But she would never manage to escape her sisters a second time. She turned south, not so much as glancing northward to Eddie's. She traveled through a blessedly cool corridor of shade trees, and when she reached Bouton Road she parked beneath a maple. Before she got out, she blotted her face on a tissue from her purse. Then she walked through Adrian's front yard and climbed the porch steps and rang the doorbell.

By now the dog knew her well enough so he merely roused himself from the mat to nose her skirt. "Hi, Butch," she said. She dabbed at his muzzle ineptly, at the same time backing off a bit. The front door opened, and Adrian said, "Finally!"

"I'm sorry," she told him, stepping inside. "I couldn't get away till Linda came, and wouldn't you know her plane was late, and then of course I had to make sure that she and the children were . . ."

She was talking too much, but she couldn't seem to stop herself. These first few minutes were always so awkward. Adrian took her purse from her and set it on a chair, and she fell silent. Then he bent and kissed her. She supposed she must taste of salt. They had not been kissing for very long—at least not like this, so seriously. They had started with the breeziest peck on the cheek, pretending to be just friends; then day by day more parts of them became involved—their lips, their open mouths, their arms around each other, their bodies pressing closer until Delia (it was always Delia) drew back with a little laugh and a "Well!" and some adjustment of her clothes. "Well! Did you get much work done?" she asked now. He was looking down at her, smiling. He wore khakis and a faded blue chambray shirt that matched his eyes. Over these past few weeks of sunshine his hair had turned almost golden, so that it seemed to give off a light of its own as he stood in the dark hallway—one more detail to make her spin away abruptly and walk on into the house as if she had some business to attend to.

Adrian's house always struck her as only marginally inhabited, which was odd because until three months ago his wife had lived here too. Why, then, did the rooms have this feeling of long-term indifference and neglect? The living room, viewed from the hall, never enticed her inside. Its walls were bare except for a single bland still life above the mantel, and instead of a couch, three chairs stood at offended-looking angles to each other. The tabletops bore only what was useful—a lamp, a telephone; none of the decorative this-and-thats that would have taken the chill off.

"I finished printing out the Adwater piece," Adrian was saying. "I thought you might look it over and tell me what you think."

He was leading her up the narrow stairway and across the hall, into an area that must once have been called the conservatory or the sunroom. Now it was his office. Cloudy windows lined three walls, their sills piled high with papers. Along the fourth wall ran a built-in desk that held various pieces of computer equipment. This was where Adrian produced his newsletter. Subscribers from thirty-four states paid actual money for *Hurry Up, Please,* a quarterly devoted to the subject of time travel. Its cover was a glossy sky blue, its logo an arched wooden mantel clock on spoked wheels. Each issue contained an assortment of science fiction and nonfiction, as well as reviews of time-machine novels and time-machine movies, and even an occasional cartoon or joke. In fact, was this whole publication a joke, or was it for real? Reading the letters to the editor, Delia often wondered. Many of the subscribers seemed to believe in earnest. At least a few claimed to speak from personal experience. And she detected an almost anthropological tone to the article Adrian handed her now—an essay by one Charles L. Adwater, Ph.D., proposing that the quality known as "charisma" was merely the superior grace and dash found in visitors from the future who are sojourning in the present. *Consider,* Dr. Adwater wrote, *how easily you and I would navigate the 1940s,*

which today seems a rather naive period, by and large, and one in which a
denizen of our own decade could hope to make a considerable impact
with relatively little effort.

"Would you say the 1940s seems, or the 1940s seem?" Adrian asked.
"Either one has arguments for and against it."

Delia didn't answer. She paced the room as she read, chewing her lower
lip, squinting at draft-quality print as dotty and sparse as the scabs on an
old brier scratch. "Well . . . ," she said, and pretending absentmindedness,
she wandered out to the hall while she flipped to the second page.

Adrian followed. "In my opinion, Adwater's style is kind of stuffy," he
was saying, "but I can't suggest too many changes because he's one of the
biggest names in the field."

How would you make a name for yourself in the time-travel field? Delia
was intrigued, but only briefly. Her visit to Adrian's office was a ruse, in
fact, as even Adrian must know. It was being upstairs that mattered: roaming the second floor, the *bedroom* floor, and peeking through each doorway. Adrian slept in a drab little dressing room; he had moved there after
Rosemary left him, so Delia felt free to stroll into the master bedroom
while flipping to page three. She went over to stand near a bureau—just
trying to get more reading light from the window above it, she could argue. Behind her, Adrian straightened her collar. His fingers made a whis-
pery sound. "Why do you always wear a necklace?" he asked, very close
to her ear.

"Hmm?" she said in a small voice. She turned another page, blindly.

"You always wear a string of pearls, or a cameo, or today this heart-
shaped locket. Always something snug around your throat, and these little
round innocent collars."

"It's only habit," she said, but her thoughts were racing. Did he mean
that she looked silly, unsuited to her age?

He had never asked how old she was, and although she wouldn't have
lied to him, she didn't feel any need to volunteer the truth. When he'd told
her that he himself was thirty-two, she had said, "Thirty-two! Young
enough to be my son!"—a deliberate exaggeration, calculated to make
him laugh. She had not mentioned the ages of her children, even. Nor had
he inquired, for like most childless people, he seemed ignorant of the
enormous space that children occupy in a life.

Also, he had a slightly skewed image of her husband. She could tell
from some of his remarks that he was picturing Sam as beefy and athletic
(because he jogged) and perhaps possessed of a jealous disposition. And
Delia had not set him straight.

All it would take was bringing the two men together once—inviting
Adrian for supper, say, as a neighbor left wifeless and forced to cook for
himself—and the situation would lose all its potential for drama. Sam
would start referring to "your pal Bly-Brice," in that sardonic way of his;
the children would roll their eyes if she talked to him too long on the

phone. But Delia made no move to arrange such a meeting. She had not so much as spoken his name to anyone in her family. And when Adrian's hands left her collar to settle on both her shoulders and draw her closer, she didn't resist but tipped her head back to rest it against his chest. "You're such a little person," he said. She heard the rumble of his voice within his rib cage. "You're so little and dainty and delicate."

Compared with his wife, she supposed he meant; and the notion pulled her upright. She walked away from him, briskly realigning pages. She circled the bed (Rosemary's bed! covered with a rather seedy sateen quilt) and approached the closet. "What I want to know," she said over her shoulder, "is can you really make a living this way? Because a magazine like yours is kind of specialized, isn't it?"

"Oh, I'm not so much as breaking even," Adrian told her offhandedly. "Pretty soon I'll have to fold, I guess. Switch to something new. But I'm used to that. Before this, I published a bulletin for rotisserie-baseball owners."

The closet was filled with Rosemary's clothes—tops, then dresses, then pants, so there was an orderly progression from short to long; and they hung evenly spaced, not bunched together as in Delia's closet. According to Adrian, Rosemary had abandoned every single one of her possessions when she left. All she took was the black silk jumpsuit she was wearing and a slim black purse tucked under her arm. Why did Delia find that so alluring? This was not the first time she had stood mesmerized in front of Rosemary's closet.

"And before that," Adrian said, "I had a quarterly for *M*A*S*H* fans." He was behind her again. He reached out one finger to stroke the point of her bent elbow.

Delia said, "How've you been supporting yourself all this time?"

"Well, Rosemary had a bit of an inheritance."

She closed the closet door. She said, "Did you know that before you married her?"

"Why do you ask?"

"Lately I've been wondering if Sam married me for my father's practice," she said.

She shouldn't have told him. Adrian would look at her and think, *Yes, she is rather homely, and her elbows are chapped besides.*

But he smiled and said, "If it were me, I'd have married you for your freckles."

She went over to Rosemary's side of the bed. She knew it was Rosemary's because a blown-glass perfume bottle sat next to the lamp. First she laid Dr. Adwater's article on the nightstand, and then, as if it were the logical next step, she opened the little drawer underneath. She gazed into a clutter of manicure scissors, emery boards, and nail polish bottles.

How fitting, the name Rosemary! Rosemary was such a sophisticated herb, so sharp-tasting, almost chemical. Put too much in a recipe, and you'd swear you were eating a petroleum product. There was nothing plain about it, nothing mild or dull. Nothing freckled.

Adrian came up behind her. He turned her to face him and wrapped his arms around her, and this time she didn't move away but set her hands at his waist and strained upward to meet his kisses. He kissed her mouth, her eyelids, her mouth once more. He whispered, "Lie down with me, Delia."

Then the phone rang.

He didn't seem to hear it; he never heard it. And he never answered it. He said it was his mother-in-law, who liked him better than she liked her own daughter and was always trying to get them back together. "How do you know it's not Rosemary?" Delia once asked, and Adrian, shrugging, said, "The telephone isn't Rosemary's instrument of choice." Now he didn't flinch, didn't even tense. Delia would have felt it if he had. He kissed the curve where her neck met her shoulder, and she began to notice the bed pressing the backs of her knees. But the phone continued to ring. Ten rings, eleven. Subconsciously, she must be counting. The realization enabled her, somehow, to pull away, although she felt that she was dragging her limbs through water. "Oh, my," she said, out of breath, and she made a great business of tucking her blouse more securely into her skirt. "I really should be . . . did I leave my purse downstairs?"

He was out of breath too. He didn't speak. She said, "Yes, I remember! On the chair. I have to hurry; Sam's mother is coming to dinner."

Meanwhile she was clattering down the stairs. The extension phone in the living room was on its fourteenth ring. Its fifteenth. She reached the front hall and seized her purse and turned at the door to say, "You know we're leaving tomorrow for—"

"You never stay," he said. "You're always rushing off as soon as you get here."

"Oh, well, I—"

"What are you afraid of?"

I'm afraid of getting undressed in front of someone thirty-two years old, she did not say. She smiled up at him, falsely. She said, "I'll see you after the beach, I guess."

"Can't you ever manage a solid block of time? A whole night? Can't you tell them you're visiting one of your girlfriends?"

"I don't have a girlfriend," she said.

She really didn't, come to think of it. When she married Sam she had switched generations and left everyone behind, all her old high-school classmates. "Although it's true there's Bootsy Fisher," she said. (Whom Sam called Bootsy Officious: the thought rose out of nowhere.) "Her kids and mine used to carpool."

"Can't you say you're at Bootsy's?"

"Oh, no, I don't see how I—"

And then, because she guessed from the way his mouth seemed to soften that he was about to kiss her again, she gave him a fluttery wave and hurried out the door, nearly tripping over Butch on the mat.

Funny, she thought, as she settled herself in her car, how often lately her high-school days came to mind. It must be this dizzy, damp, rumpled feeling as she rushed home from secret meetings; her telltale flushed cheeks, the used and smushed look of her lips when she risked a glance in the rearview mirror. At a stop sign she made sure that all her buttons were buttoned, and she patted her locket into place between her collarbones. Once again she heard Adrian say, "Why do you always wear a necklace?" And then, "Lie down with me, Delia," and just as in her high-school days, she felt stirred even more by the memory than by the event itself. If she hadn't already been seated, her legs might have buckled.

Maybe she *could* say she was visiting Bootsy. Not for a whole night, of course, but for an evening. Certainly no one in her family would bother checking up on her.

She parked in the driveway, which was clear now of all cars except for Sam's. Smoke billowed from the yard on the other side of the house. He must be firing up the grill for dinner.

She followed the trail of smoke to the little flagstone rectangle beneath the office windows. Yes, there he was, peering at the grill's thermometer with his glasses raised. He still wore his shirt and tie and his suit trousers, minus his white coat. He looked so professional that Delia felt a flash of anxiety. Didn't he know everything? But when he straightened, lowering his glasses, all he said was, "Hi, Dee. Where've you been?"

"Oh, I was . . . running a few errands," she said.

She was amazed that he didn't ask why, then, she had returned empty-handed. He just nodded and tapped the thermometer with his index finger.

Climbing the steps to the kitchen door, she felt like a woman emerging from a deep, thick daytime sleep. She walked past Eliza and drifted toward the hall. "Are you going to grill the vegetables too? Or put them in the oven?" Eliza called after her.

There wouldn't be space for them on the grill. They would have to go in the oven, and she meant to say as much to Eliza but forgot, lost the words, and merely floated into the study. It was unoccupied, thank heaven. She didn't believe she could have waited till she reached the phone upstairs. She lifted the receiver, dialed Adrian's number, let his phone ring twice, and then hung up—her way of letting him know that this was not his mother-in-law. She redialed, and he answered halfway through the first ring. "Is that you?" he asked. His voice sounded urgent, intense. She sank onto a footstool and gripped the receiver more tightly.

"Yes," she whispered.

"Come back here, Delia."

"I wish I could."

"Come back and stay with me."

"I want to. I do want to," she said.

Sam's mother said, "Delia?"

Delia slammed the phone down and jumped to her feet. "Eleanor!" she cried. She thrust her hands in the folds of her skirt to hide their tremor. "I was just—I was just—"

"Sorry to barge in," Eleanor said, "but nobody answered the door." She advanced to kiss the air near Delia's ear. She smelled of soap; she was an unperfumed, unfrilled woman, sensibly clad in a drip-dry shirtdress and Nikes, with a handsome face and clipped white monkish hair. "Didn't mean to interrupt your conversation."

"No, I was just winding it up," Delia told her.

"It appears that someone has left some articles on your front porch."

"Articles?"

Delia had a fleeting vision of Dr. Adwater's article on charisma.

"Badminton sets and rafts and such, scattered all about where anyone might stumble on them."

Eleanor was the kind of guest who felt it her duty to point out alarming flaws in the household. How long had their toilet been making that noise? Did they know they had a tree limb about to come down? Delia always countered by pretending that she was a guest herself. "Imagine that!" she said. "Let me take you to Sam. He's out by the grill."

"Now, I thought you weren't going to any fuss," Eleanor told her, leading the way from the study. Instead of a purse, she had one of those belt packs, glow-in the-dark chartreuse nylon, riding in front of her stomach like some sort of add-on pregnancy. It caused her to walk slightly sway-backed, although ordinarily her posture was perfect.

"I'm only serving grilled chicken," Delia said as they crossed the hall. "Nothing complicated."

"Tinned soup would have been plenty," Eleanor said. She eyed a browning apple core centered on the newel post. "Particularly in view of all you need to do for your beach trip."

Did she mean this as a reproach? Every year, Sam suggested inviting his mother along to the beach, and every year Delia talked him out of it, which was why they always held this placatory family dinner the night before they left. It wasn't that Delia disliked his mother. She knew that Eleanor was admirable. She knew that she herself would never have coped so magnificently in Eleanor's circumstances—widowed early, forced to take a secretarial job to support herself and her young son. (And to hear Sam tell it, his father had not been much use anyhow—a weak and ineffectual, watery sort of man.) The trouble was, in Eleanor's presence Delia felt so inadequate. She felt so frivolous and spendthrift and disorganized. Their vacation was the one time she could hope to shake off that feeling.

Besides, she couldn't imagine the Iron Mama lolling on a beach towel.

"Did Linda get here?" Eleanor was asking as they entered the kitchen. "Are the twins just huge? Where are they all?"

It was Eliza, standing at the sink, who answered. "The twins are at the pool," she said. "Linda just left with Susie to fetch them home. How're you doing, Eleanor?"

"Oh, couldn't be better. Is that asparagus I see? Delia, my word, do you know what asparagus *costs*?"

"I found some on sale," Delia lied. "I'm going to roast it in the oven in this new way, really simple. No fuss," she added craftily.

"Well, if your idea of simple is asparagus and roast squab!"

"Chicken, actually."

"Just an old withered carrot would have been good enough for me," Eleanor said.

She headed for the back door, with Delia meekly shadowing her.

In the side yard, Sam was tinkering with the grill knobs. "Looks about the right temperature," he told Delia. "Hello, Mother. Good to see you."

"What's going on with the shrubbery, son?" Eleanor asked, looking past him.

"We're having it taken out," he said. "Putting in a whole new bunch of plantings."

"Why, that must cost a fortune! Couldn't you just work with what you had, for gracious sake?"

"We wanted totally new," Sam told her. (*We?* Delia thought.) "We're tired of working with what we had. Dee, believe I'm ready to start cooking."

As Delia walked toward the house, she heard Eleanor say, "Well, I don't know, son. This life of yours seems mighty rich for *my* blood, what with asparagus for dinner and grilled pheasant."

"Chicken!" Delia called back.

Eliza must have heard too, for she was grinning to herself when Delia opened the screen door. "You bring it to him," Delia told her. "I can't stand another minute."

"Oh, now, you take her too much to heart," Eliza said as she went over to the refrigerator. Eliza seemed to find Eleanor merely amusing. But then, Eliza wasn't Eleanor's daughter-in-law. She didn't have Eleanor held up before her daily as a paragon of thrift, with her professional-quality tool chest and her twelve-column budget book and her thrice-used, washed-and-dried sandwich bags.

Did it ever occur to Sam that Delia and his father might well have been kindred spirits?

She gathered up the silverware, ten of everything, and went into the dining room. Here the sounds from the yard were muted, and she could let her mind return to Adrian. She traveled around the table, doling out knives and forks and remembering the rustle of Adrian's fingers on her collar, his warm breath when he kissed her. But she could no longer truly feel the kiss, she discovered. Eleanor's interruption must have startled all feeling out of her, as in the old days when the telephone rang while she and Sam were making love and she had lost her place, so to speak, and not been able to fall back into it afterward.

She returned to the kitchen and found Eliza pondering in front of the glassware cupboard. "Which do we want?" Eliza asked her. "Iced tea or wine?"

"Wine," Delia answered promptly.

From the side yard, Eleanor's confident voice came sailing: "Have you checked the price of asparagus lately?"

"Pretty steep, is it," Sam said equably.

"Sky-high," Eleanor told him. "But that's what we're having for dinner tonight: asparagus and grilled peacock."

Eliza was the only one who laughed.

Supper was late, for one reason or another. First Linda and Susie took forever bringing the twins from the pool, and then Ramsay didn't appear till seven although he'd promised faithfully to be home by six, and when he did show up he had his girlfriend in tow and her wan and silent six-year-old daughter. This enthralled the twins, of course, but Delia was furious. It had been understood that tonight would be strictly family. However, she didn't have quite what it took to face Ramsay down in public. Seething inwardly, she scrunched two extra, mismatched place settings in among the others before she called everyone to the table.

Velma, the girlfriend, was a tiny, elfin woman with a cap of glassy hair and a pert little figure set off by trim white shorts. Delia could see what her appeal was, sort of. For one thing, when she entered the dining room she went straight to one of the orphan place settings, as if she were accustomed to existing on the edges of events. And for another, she was so inexhaustibly vivacious that even Carroll—surly Carroll—brightened in her presence, and Sam made a point of giving her the largest piece of chicken. ("Got to put some meat on your bones," he said—not his type of remark at all.) Then she endeared herself to Linda by marveling at the twins' names. "I'm crazy about things that sound French—I guess you can tell from me naming my daughter Rosalie," she said. "Shoot, I'd like to go to France. The furtherest I've been is Hagerstown a few times for hair shows."

Velma was a beautician. She worked in one of those unisex places, which was how she and Ramsay had met. He had come in for a haircut and invited her on the spot to a tea at the house of his freshman adviser. Now he sat proudly next to her, one arm resting on the back of her chair, and beamed around the table at his family. Short though he was (he took after Delia's father), he seemed manly and imposing alongside Velma.

"Although last fall I did attend a color conference in Pittsburgh," Velma was recalling. "I stayed overnight and left Rosalie with my mother."

Rosalie, perched behind the other odd plate, raised her enormous, liquid eyes and gave Velma a look that struck Delia as despairing.

"Everybody in our whole entire shop has been trained to do your colors," Velma went on. Was she speaking to Eleanor, of all people? Eleanor nodded encouragingly, wearing her most gracious expression.

"Some people ought to wear cool colors and some people ought to wear warm," Velma told her, "and they should never, ever cross over, though you'd be shocked at how many try."

"Would that be determined by temperament, dear?" Eleanor asked.

"Ma'am?"

But Eleanor was sidetracked just then by the plate that Sam was filling for her. "Oh, mercy, Sam," she said, "not such a great big helping!"

"I thought you asked for a breast."

"Well, I did, but just a little one. That one's way too big for me."

He forked another and held it up. "This okay?"

"Oh, that's huge!"

"Well, there's nothing smaller, Mother."

"Can't you just cut it in half? I could never manage to eat all that."

He put it back on the platter to cut it.

"This one lady," Velma told the others, "she was wearing pink when she came in and I'm like, 'Lady, you are so, so wrong. You should be all in cools,' I tell her, 'with the tone of skin you got.' She says, 'Oh, but that's why I head for warm.' Says, 'I go for what's my opposite.' I could not believe her. I really could not believe her."

"Sam, dear, that's about six times as much asparagus as I can possibly handle," Eleanor said.

"It's three spears, Mother. How can I give you a sixth of that?"

"I just want a half a spear, if it isn't too much trouble."

"You, now," Velma told Eliza, "you would look stunning in magenta. With your coal-black hair? That tan color doesn't do a thing for you."

"However, I'm partial to tan," Eliza said in her declarative way.

"And Susie, I bet you had your colors done already. Right? That aqua's real becoming."

"It was the only thing not in the laundry," Susie said. But she was fighting down a pleased expression around the mouth.

"I dress Rosalie in nothing but aqua, just about. She turns washed out in any other color."

"Sam, I hate to be a nuisance," Eleanor said, "but I'm going to send my plate back to you so you can take a teensy little bit of that potato salad off and give it to someone else."

"Well, why not just keep it, Mother."

"But it's much too large a helping, dear."

"Then eat what you can and leave the rest, why don't you."

"Now, you know how I hate to waste food."

"Oh, just force yourself to choke the damn stuff down, then, Mother!"

"Goodness," Eleanor said.

The telephone rang.

Delia said, "Carroll, would you answer that? If it's a patient, tell them we're eating."

Not that she imagined a patient could be so easily dissuaded.

Carroll slouched off to the kitchen, muttering something about the grown-ups' phone, and Delia took a bite of her drumstick. It was dry and stringy as old bark from being kept warm in the oven too long.

"For you, Mom," Carroll said, poking his head through the door.

"Well, see who it is and ask if I can call back."

"He says it's about a time machine."

"Oh!"

Sam said, "Time machine?"

"I'll just be a minute," Delia said, setting aside her napkin.

"Someone wants to sell you a *time* machine?" Sam asked her.

"No! Not that I know of. Or, I don't know . . ." She sank back in her seat. "Tell him we don't need a thing," she told Carroll.

Carroll withdrew his head.

It seemed to Delia that her one bite of chicken was stuck halfway down her throat. She picked up the basket of rolls and said, "Thérèse? Marie-Claire? Take one and pass them on, please."

When Carroll returned to the table, she didn't so much as glance at him. She sent the butter plate after the rolls, and only then looked up to face Eliza's steady gaze.

It was Eliza she had to watch out for. Eliza was uncanny sometimes.

"This china belonged to your great-grandmother," Linda was telling the twins. "Cynthia Ramsay, her name was. She was a famous Baltimore beauty, and the whole town wondered why she ever said yes to that short, stumpy nobody, Isaiah Felson. But he was a doctor, you see, and he promised that if she married him she would never get TB. See, just about her whole family had died of TB. So sure enough, she married him and moved out to Roland Park and stayed healthy as a horse all her days and bore two healthy children besides, one of them your grandpa. You remember your grandpa."

"He wouldn't let us roller-skate in the house."

"Right. Anyhow, your great-grandmother ordered her wedding china all the way from Europe, these very plates you are eating from tonight."

"Except for Rosalie," Marie-Claire said.

"What, sweet?"

"*Rosalie's* plate is not wedding china."

"No, Rosalie's comes from Kmart," Linda said, and she passed the butter to Eleanor, not noticing how Rosalie's eyes started growing even more liquid.

"Heavens, no butter for *me*, dear," Eleanor said.

Why had he phoned her? Delia wondered. How unlike him. He must have had something crucial to tell her. She should have taken the call.

She would go to the kitchen for water or something and call him back.

Grabbing the water pitcher, she stood up, and just then the doorbell rang. She froze. Her first, heart-pounding thought was that this was Adrian. He had come to take her away; he would no longer listen to reason. A whole scenario played itself out rapidly in her mind—her family's bewilderment as she allowed herself to be led from the house, her journey through the night with him (in a horse-drawn carriage, it seemed), and their blissful life together in a sunlit, whitewashed room on some Mediterranean shore. Meanwhile Sam was saying, "I've told them and told them . . . ," and he rose and strode out to the hall, apparently assuming that this was a patient. Well, maybe it was. Delia remained on her feet, straining to hear. One of the twins said, "*Rosalie's* napkin is plain old paper," and Delia had an urge to bat her voice away physically.

It was a woman. An elderly, querulous woman, saying something unintelligible. So. A patient after all. Delia felt more relieved than she would have expected. She said, "Well! Anybody want anything from the kitchen?" But before she could turn to go, Sam was ushering in his visitor.

Easily past seventy, doughy and wrinkled beneath her heap of dyed black curls and her plastering of red rouge and dark-red lipstick, the woman advanced on absurdly small, open-toed shoes that barely poked forth from the hem of her shapeless black dress. She was clutching a drawstring purse in both fat, ringed hands, and diamond teardrops swung from her long earlobes. All of this Delia somehow took in while at the same time registering Sam's astonished face just beyond the woman's shoulder. "Dee?" he said. "This person's saying—"

The woman asked, "Are you Mrs. Delia Grinstead?"

"Well, yes."

"I want you to leave my daughter's husband alone."

Around the table there was a sort of snapping to attention. Delia sensed it, even though she forced her eyes to remain on the woman. She said, "I can't imagine what you're talking about."

"You know who I mean! My son-in-law, Adrian Bly-Brice. Or don't you even keep track? Have you collected so many paramours you can't tell one from another?"

Somebody snickered. Ramsay. Delia felt slightly affronted by this, but she made herself focus on the issue at hand. She said, "Mrs., um, really I . . ."

She hated how little-girlish her voice came out.

"That is a happy marriage you're destroying," the old woman told her. She was stationed now at the far end of the table, just behind Sam's empty chair. She glared at Delia from underneath lashes so thickly beaded with mascara that they shaded her face like awnings. "They may have their ups and downs, like any other young couple," she said, "but they're trying to work things out, I tell you! They're dating again, has he mentioned that? Twice they've gone to dinner at the restaurant where they got engaged. They're thinking it might help if they started a baby. But every time I look out of my house, what do I find? Your car, parked across the street. You at

his front door kissing him, all over him, can't get enough of him, going up
the stairs with him to paw him at his bedroom window for all the neighbors to gawk at."

Adrian's mother-in-law lived across the street from him?

Delia felt burning hot. She sensed the others' thunderstruck expressions.

Sam said, quietly, "Delia, do you know anything about this?"

"No! Nothing!" she cried. "She's making it up! She's confused me with
somebody else!"

"Then what's this?" the old woman asked, and she started tweaking at
her purse. The drawstring was held tight by some sort of sliding clasp,
and it took her whole minutes, it seemed, to work it loose, while everybody watched in riveted silence. Delia realized she had not released a
breath in some time. She was prepared for absolutely anything to emerge
from that purse—something steamy and lurid and reeking of sex, although what would that be, precisely? But all the old woman brought
forth in the end was a photograph. "See? See?" she demanded, and she
held it up and swung slowly from left to right.

It was a Polaroid snapshot, so underexposed that it amounted to no
more than a square of mangled darkness. But not till Ramsay snickered
once again did Delia understand that she was safe.

"Now, there," Sam was saying, "don't you worry, I'm sure your
daughter is *very* happily married. . . ." In the most chivalrous fashion, he
was turning the old woman toward the door. "May I see you to your
car?" he asked.

"Oh. Well . . . yes, maybe . . . yes, maybe so," she said. She was still
fumbling with her purse, but she let him guide her out. She walked beneath the shelter of his arm in a dazed, uncertain manner that filled Delia
with sudden pity.

"Who was *that*?" Marie-Claire asked distinctly.

Ramsay said, "Oh, just somebody for your aunt Delia; you know what
a siren she is," and everybody stirred and chuckled.

It was perverse of her, she knew, but for one split second Delia actually
considered confessing, just to show them. She didn't, of course. She smiled
around the table and sat back down and placed the water pitcher on her
left. "Who's for more chicken?" she asked, and she looked brazenly into
Eliza's measuring eyes.

It was Susie's night to do the dishes, and Eleanor said she would help. She
wouldn't think of letting Delia lift a finger, she said, after that extravagant
meal. So Delia backed out of the kitchen, pretending reluctance, but instead of heading toward the porch with the others, she sped up the stairs
and into her bedroom. She shut the door behind her, sat on the edge of the
bed, and picked up the phone.

He answered almost instantly. She had braced herself to go through
that whole two-ring rigmarole, but right away he said, "Hello?"

"Adrian?"

"Oh, God, Delia, did she come?"

"She came."

"I tried to warn you. I called your house, and even after your husband answered I went ahead and—"

"My husband answered? When?"

"Wasn't that your husband?"

"Oh, Carroll. My son. At suppertime, you mean."

"Yes, and I was hoping you would . . . That was your son?"

"Yes, my younger son. Carroll."

"But he was so old."

"Old? He's not old!"

"He sounded like a grown man."

"Well, he isn't," Delia said curtly. "Adrian, why did you stand there kissing me in doors and windows when you knew your mother-in-law lived across the street?"

"So she did what she said she would, did she?"

"She came and told my family I had a 'paramour,' if that's what you mean."

"Lord, Delia, what did they say?"

"I think they just thought she was crazy or something, but . . . Adrian. She claimed you were happily married."

"Of course she did. You know she would want to believe that."

"She claimed you and Rosemary have started dating; you've gone out together twice to the restaurant where you got engaged."

"Well, that much is true."

"It is?"

"Just to talk things over; sure. We do have a lot in common, after all. A lot of shared history."

"I see."

"But it wasn't how you imagine. We met for dinner! Just to eat dinner!"

"And you're thinking of starting a baby."

"Is that what she told you?"

"Yes."

"Well, naturally it came up."

"Naturally?" Delia cried.

"I mean, Rosemary isn't getting any younger."

"No, that's right, she must be all of thirty," Delia said with some bitterness. She twined the telephone cord between her fingers. The connection was the kind with a rushing sound in the background, like long distance.

"Well, probably she's not the maternal type, though, anyhow," Adrian said cheerfully. "Weird, isn't it? The very thing that attracts you to someone can end up putting you off. When Rosemary and I first met, she was so . . . cool, I guess you'd say, so cool-mannered I was bewitched, but now I see she might be too cool to be a good mother."

"How about me?" Delia asked him.

"You?"

"What is it about *me* that attracts you but puts you off?"

"Oh, why, nothing, Delia. Why do you ask?"

"Nothing attracts you?"

"Oh! Well, maybe . . . well, when we met, you acted so fresh and sweet and childish, I mean childlike, you know? But then when we reached the point where most people would, for example, um, get more involved, you were *still* so damn sweet and childlike. Turning all flustered, saying you should leave: you'd think we were teenagers or something."

"I see," Delia said.

Adrian said, "Delia. Just how old is your son, anyway?"

"Ancient," she told him. But it was herself she was referring to.

She hung up and walked out of the room.

Downstairs, she heard water running in the kitchen, and dishes clattering, and Eleanor saying, "Susie, dear, you're not planning to *discard* that, surely." Delia crossed the hall to stand at the screen door, gazing out toward the porch. She saw no sign of the boys, who had not stayed to talk after dinner in years; no sign of Velma or Rosalie. But Sam and Linda sat sniping at each other in the swing. "Some of those azaleas were planted by our grandfather," Linda said, "not that that would be any concern of yours," and Sam said, "Or yours either, unless you plan to start sharing a little of the burden here," and Eliza, rocking in the cane rocker, said, "Oh, just quit it, both of you." The twins were twirling on the front walk beneath the pole lamp, with grass blades stuck to their skin and white moths flickering above them. They had reached that high-pitched, overwrought state that seizes children outdoors on summer evenings, and they were chanting at breakneck speed:

"*What's* life?"

"Fifteen cents a copy."

"But I only have a dime."

"Well, that's life."

"*What's* life?"

"Fifteen cents a copy."

"But I only have a dime."

5

It rained during their first evening at the beach, and their cottage roof turned out to have a leak. This was not a very fancy cottage, not an oceanfront, resort-style cottage, but a dumpy little house on the inland side of Highway 1. Delia could imagine an ordinary Delaware feed-store clerk living there until about a week ago. The kitchen sink was skirted in chintz, the living-room floor was blue linoleum squiggled to suggest a hooked rug, and all the beds sagged toward the middle and creaked at the slightest movement. Still, Sam said, they shouldn't have to endure a puddle in the upstairs hall. He phoned the rental agent at once, using the after-hours emergency number, and insisted that the problem be seen to the first thing the following morning.

"What," Linda asked him, "do you have to have your crew of work-men even on vacation?"

And Eliza said, "Let's just mop it up and forget it. It surely won't rain again while we're here, because if it does I'm going to sue God."

Delia herself said nothing. She really couldn't gather the strength.

In their own house back in Baltimore, workmen would be using the week to sand down the floors and refinish them. This meant that Delia had had to bring the cat along. (He wouldn't tolerate boarding—had nearly pined away the one time they had tried it.) Sam claimed they were sure to be evicted, since pets were expressly forbidden, but Delia told him that was impossible. How would anyone ever guess Vernon was there? For he'd been so incensed by the car trip that the instant he was set down in the cottage, he streaked to the back of a kitchen cabinet. Delia knew enough to leave him tactfully alone, but the twins wouldn't rest, and after supper they hovered at the cabinet door with a plate of leftovers, trying to coax him out. "Here, Vernon! *Nice* Vernon." His only response was that disheartening, numb silence cats seem to radiate when they're determined to keep to themselves. "Oh," Marie-Claire wailed, "what'll we do? He's going to starve to death!"

"Good riddance," Sam told her. "It's only live pets that we're not allowed."

Sam had been out of sorts all day, it seemed to Delia.

So that first evening, when they should have been taking a stroll on the beach or walking into town for ice cream, the grown-ups sat in the kerosene-smelling, poorly lighted living room, reading tattered magazines left behind by earlier tenants and listening to the pecking of the rain against the windows. The twins were still in the kitchen, badgering Vernon. Susie and the boys had borrowed the Plymouth and driven to Ocean City, which made Delia anxious because she always pictured Ocean City as a gigantic arena of bumper cars manned by drunken college students. But she tried to keep her mind on *American Deck and Patio.*

"If tomorrow isn't sunny," Linda said, "maybe we could take a little day trip out past Salisbury. I want the twins to get some sense of their heritage."

"Oh, Linda, not that damn cemetery again," Eliza said.

"Well, fine, then. Just lend me a car and I'll take them myself. That's what happened last year, as I recall."

"Yes, and last year both twins came back bored to tears and cranky. What do they care for a bunch of dead Carrolls and Webers?"

"They had a wonderful time! And I'd like to find Great-Uncle Roscoe's place too, if I can."

"Well, good hunting, is all I can say. I'm sure it's a parking lot by now, and anyhow, Mother never got along with Uncle Roscoe."

"Eliza, why do you have to run me down at every turn?" Linda demanded. "Why is it that every little thing I propose you have to mock and denigrate?"

"Now, ladies," Sam said absently, leafing through *Offshore Angler.*

Linda turned on him. She said, "Don't you 'Now, ladies' *me,* Sam Grinstead."

"Sorry," Sam murmured.

"Mr. Voice of Reason, here!"

"My mistake."

She rose in a huff and went off to check the twins. Eliza closed her *Yachting World* and stared bleakly at the cover.

Linda and Eliza were in their Day Two Mode, was how Delia always thought of it—that edgy, prickly stage after the first flush of Linda's arrival had faded. Once, Delia had asked Eliza why she and Linda weren't closer, and Eliza had said, "Oh, people who've shared an unhappy childhood rarely *are* close, I've found." Delia was surprised. Their childhood had been unhappy? Hers had been idyllic. But she refrained from saying so.

Linda returned with the twins, who were still fretting over Vernon, and Sam set aside his magazine and suggested a game of rummy. "Did you bring the cards?" he asked Delia.

She had not. She realized it the instant he asked, but made a show of rooting through the shopping bag on the coffee table. Jigsaw puzzles, Monopoly, and a Parcheesi board emerged, but no cards. "Um . . . ," she said.

"Oh, well," Sam said, "we'll play Parcheesi, then." His tone was weightily patient, which seemed worse than shouting.

At the bottom of the bag, Delia came across her current library book. *Captive of Clarion Castle,* it was called. She had started it last week and found it slow, but anything was preferable to deck plans. When Sam asked, "Are you playing too, Delia?" she said, "I think I'll go read in bed."

"Now? It's not even nine o'clock."

"Well, I'm tired," she told him. She said good night to the others and walked out with the front of her book concealed, although no one made any attempt to see the title.

Upstairs, a new ribbon of water meandered from the sodden bath mat alongside the chimney. She ignored it and proceeded to the room she was sharing with Sam. It was small and musty-smelling, with one, uncurtained window. For privacy's sake she changed into her nightgown in the dark, and then she washed up in the bathroom across the hall. Back in the bedroom, she switched on the lamp and aimed its weak yellow beam in the direction of her pillow. Then she slid under the covers, wriggled her toes luxuriously, and opened her book.

The heroine of this book was a woman named Eleanora, which unfortunately brought Eleanor to Delia's mind. Eleanora's long raven tresses and "piquant" face kept giving way to Eleanor's no-nonsense haircut and Iron Mama jawline; and when Kendall, the hero, crushed her to him, Delia saw Eleanor's judging gaze directed past his broad shoulder. Kendall was Eleanora's future brother-in-law, the younger brother of her aristocratic, suave fiancé. Impetuously, Kendall kidnapped Eleanora the first time he laid eyes on her, which happened to be about fifteen minutes before her wedding. "I will never love you! Never!" Eleanora cried, pummeling his chest with her tiny fists, but Kendall seized her wrists and waited, masterful and confident, until she subsided.

Delia closed the book, leaving one finger inside as a marker. She stared down at the couple embracing on the cover.

Not once, from the moment they met, had Adrian truly pursued her. It had all been a matter of happenstance. Happenstance had led him to ask her to pose as his girlfriend (Who else was remotely eligible? The woman with the baby? The old lady at the checkout counter?), and happenstance had brought them together again a few nights later. In addition, his every act had betrayed that he was still in love with his wife. He loved her so much that he couldn't face her on his own in the supermarket; he couldn't sleep in their bedroom after she left. But Delia, like some self-deluded teenage ninny, had chosen not to see.

And she had overlooked other clues as well—clues that revealed the very nature of his character. For instance, his behavior at that first encounter: his rearrangement of her shopping plans, his condescending reference to Roland Park names, his trendy groceries. He was not a *bad* person, surely, but his mind was on his own concerns. And he was just the least bit shallow.

In romance novels, this realization would have made her turn thankfully to the man who had been waiting in the wings all along. But in real life, when she heard Sam's step on the stairs she closed her eyes and pretended to be asleep. She felt him standing over her, and then he slipped her book from her hands and switched off the lamp and left the room.

By morning the rain had stopped and the sun was out, shining all the brighter in the washed-clean air. The whole family set off for the ocean shortly before noon—the grown-ups in Sam's Buick, the younger ones in the Plymouth with Ramsay at the wheel. Scattered puddles hissed beneath their tires as they drove across Highway 1 and threaded past the higher-priced cottages, closer to the water. When the road dead-ended, they parked and fed two meters with quarters and unloaded the day's supplies—the thermos jugs and blankets, towels, Styrofoam coolers, rafts, and beach bags. Delia carried a stack of towels, along with her straw tote stuffed so full of emergency provisions that the handles dug a furrow in her bare shoulder. She was wearing her pink gingham swimsuit with the eyelet-edged skirt, and navy canvas espadrilles, but no robe or cover-up, because she didn't care *what* Sam said, she wanted to get at least a hint of a tan.

"Watch it, girls," Linda told the twins as they lugged a cooler between them up the wooden walkway. "You're letting the bottom drag."

"It's Thérèse's fault—she's making me do all the work!"

"Am not."

"Are so."

"Didn't I tell you to take something lighter?" Linda asked them. "Didn't I offer you the blankets, or the—"

But then they crested the low, sandy rise, and there was the ocean, reminding them what they had come all this way for. Oh, every year it seemed Delia forgot. That vast, slaty, limitless sweep, that fertile, rotting, dog's-breath smell, that continual to-and-fro shushing that had been going on forever while she'd been elsewhere, stewing over trivia! She paused, letting her eyes take rest in the dapples of yellow sunlight that skated the water, and then Carroll's armload of rafts crashed into her from behind, and he said, "Geez, Mom."

"Oh, excuse me," she said. She started down the wooden steps to the beach.

There were advantages to coming so early in the season. True, the water had not had time to warm up yet, but also the beach was less crowded. Blankets were spread at civilized intervals, with space between. Only a few children splashed at the edge of the breakers, and Delia could easily count the heads that bobbed farther out.

She and Eliza unfolded a blanket and arranged themselves on it, while Sam worked an umbrella pole into the sand. Susie and the boys, however, walked a good twenty feet beyond before stopping to set up their own station. They had been keeping apart for several years now; it no longer hurt Delia's feelings. But she did always notice.

"Now, you two are not stirring from here," Linda told the twins, "until I get every inch of you covered with sunblock." She held them close, one after the other, and slathered lotion on their skinny arms and legs. As soon as she let go of them, off they raced to the young people's blanket.

Susie's radio was playing "Under the Boardwalk," which had always seemed to Delia a very lonesome song. In fact, "Under the Boardwalk" was rising from other radios as well, on other blankets, so that the Atlantic Ocean seemed to have acquired its own melancholy background music.

"Believe I'll go for a jog," Sam told Delia.

"Oh, Sam. You're on vacation!"

"So?"

He shucked off his beach robe and adjusted the leather band of his watch. (The watch was evidently part of his new exercise routine; in just what way, Delia wasn't sure.) Then he walked down to the surf, turned, and started loping northward, a lanky figure in beige trunks and gigantic white sneakers.

"At least here they have all these lifeguards who've been trained in CPR," Delia told her sisters. She folded Sam's robe and packed it away in her tote.

"Oh, he'll be fine," Eliza said. "The doctors told him to jog."

"Not to overdo, though!"

"To me he looks just the same as always," Linda said. "If you consider that a good thing." She was shading her forehead to gaze after him. "I never would have known he'd had a heart attack."

"It wasn't a heart attack! It was chest pains."

"Whatever," Linda said carelessly.

She was wearing a one-piece swimsuit held up by a center cord that encircled her neck. It made her breasts appear to droop at either side like a pair of weary eyes. Eliza, who scorned the notion of a whole separate outfit for one week of swimming per year, wore denim shorts and a black knit tank top rolled up beneath her bra.

Delia took off her shoes and dropped them into her tote. Then she lay down flat on her back, with the sun's mild warmth soaking into her skin. Gradually sounds grew fainter, like remembered sounds—the voices of other sunbathers nearby, the high, sad cries of the seagulls, the music from the radios (Paul McCartney now, singing "Uncle Albert"), and under everything, so she almost stopped hearing it, the ocean's rush, as constant and unvaried as the ocean inside a seashell.

She and Sam had come to this beach on their honeymoon. They had stayed at an inn downtown that no longer existed, and every morning, lying out here side by side with their bare, fuzzed arms just touching, they had reached such a state that, eventually, they had to rise and rush back to their room. Once even that had seemed too far, and they'd plunged into the ocean instead, out past the breakers, and she could still remember the layers of contrast—his warm, bony legs brushing hers beneath the cool, silky water—and the fishy scent of his wet face when they kissed. But the summer after that they had the baby with them (little Susie, two months old and fussy, fussy, fussy) and in later years the boys, and they had seldom managed even to stretch out on their blanket together, let alone steal back to their cottage. Eliza started coming too, and Linda before she married, and their father because he never could have kept house on his own; and Delia spent her days ankle-deep in the surf tending children, making sure they didn't drown, admiring each new skill they mastered. "Watch this, Mom." "No, watch *this*!" They used to think she was so important in their lives.

Someone's feet passed in the sand with a sound like rubbing velvet, and she opened her eyes and sat up. For a moment she felt light-headed. "Your face is burning," Eliza told her. "Better put some lotion on." She herself was sitting sensibly in the shade of the umbrella. Linda was down in the surf, braced for an incoming wave with both plump arms outflung and her hands posed as liltingly as bird wings, and the twins had returned from the other blanket and were filling buckets near Delia. Damp sand caked Marie-Claire's knees and made two circles on the empty-looking seat of Thérèse's swimsuit.

"Did Sam get back from jogging?" Delia asked Eliza.

"Not yet. Want to go for a dip?"

Delia didn't dignify that with an answer. (As everyone in her family well knew, the temperature had to be blistering, the ocean flat as glass, and not a sea nettle sighted all day before she would venture in.) Instead, she reached for her tote bag. Delving past espadrilles, Sam's robe, and her billfold, she came up with *Captive of Clarion Castle*. Eliza humphed when she saw the cover. "Guess I'll leave you to your *literature*," she told Delia. She got to her feet and set off, dusting the back of her shorts in a businesslike manner.

"Aunt Eliza, can we come too?" Marie-Claire shrilled.

"Wait for us, Aunt Liza!"

When they ran after her, they looked as skittery and high-bottomed as two little hermit crabs.

Eleanora was beginning to notice that Kendall was not the monster she had imagined. He brought trays of food to her locked tower room and let it be known he had cooked all the dishes himself. Eleanora pretended to be unimpressed, but later, after he left, she reflected on the incongruity of someone so brawny and virile stirring pots at a stove.

"Whew!" Sam said. He was back. Sweat trickled down the ridged bones of his chest, and he had the drawn, strained, gasping look that always distressed Delia after his runs. "Sam," she said, setting aside her book, "you're going to kill yourself! Sit here and rest."

"No, I have to wind down gradually," he told her. He started walking in circles around the blanket, stopping every now and then to bend over and grip his kneecaps. Drops of sweat fell from his forehead to the sand. "What have we got to drink?" he asked her.

"Lemonade, Pepsi, iced tea—"

"Iced tea sounds good."

She stood to fill a paper cup and hand it to him. He was no longer breathing so hard, at least. He drained the cup in a single draft and set it on the lid of the cooler. "Your nose is burning," he told her.

"I want to get a *little* tan."

"Melanoma is what you're going to get."

"Well, maybe after lunch I'll put on some—"

But he had already picked up Linda's bottle of sunblock. "Hold still," he said, unscrewing the cap. He started smoothing lotion across her face. It smelled like bruised peaches, an artificial, trashy smell that made her wrinkle her nose. "Turn around and I'll do your back," he told her.

Obediently, she turned. She faced inland now, where the roofs of cottages hulked beyond the sand fence. A flock of tiny dark birds crossed the blue sky in the distance, keeping a perfectly triangular formation so that they seemed connected by invisible wires. They swung around and caught the sun, and suddenly they were white, in fact almost silver, like a veil of sequins; and then they swung again, and once more they were plain black specks. Sam smoothed lotion over Delia's shoulders. It went on warm but cooled in the breeze, tingling slightly.

"Delia," he said.

"Hmm?"

"I was wondering about the old woman who came by the house Saturday night."

She grew still beneath his palm, but she felt that every one of her nerves was thrumming like a twanged string.

"I know she was, maybe, peculiar," he said. "But she had an actual photograph, and she seemed to think it really did show you and that who's-it, that what's-his-name . . ."

She had already turned toward him to deny it when he said, "That Adrian Fried Rice."

"Bly-Brice," she said.

For he had twisted the name on purpose. He always did that. The maid of honor at their wedding, Missy Pringle, he had kept referring to as Prissy Mingle. It was just like him to be so belittling! So contemptuous of her friends, with that ironic glint to his voice! Her entire marriage unrolled itself before her: ancient hurts and humiliations and resentments, theoretically forgotten but just waiting to revive at moments such as this.

"His name is Adrian, Bly, Brice," she told him.

"I see," Sam said. His face had a sheeted look.

"But that woman got it all wrong. He's nothing but an acquaintance."

"I see."

In silence, he replaced the bottle of sunblock.

"You don't believe me."

"I never said that."

"No, but you implied it."

"I surely can't be blamed for what you imagine I might have implied," Sam said. "Of course he's just an acquaintance. You're not exactly the type to have an affair. But I'm wondering how it seems to outsiders, Dee. You know?"

"No, I don't know," she said, between set teeth. "And my name is not *Dee*."

"All right," he said. "Delia. Now, why don't you just calm down."

And he leveled the air between them with both palms, in that patronizing gesture she always found so infuriating, and turned away from her and walked toward the water.

Every quarrel they had ever had, he had walked off before it was resolved. He would get her all riled up and then loftily remove himself, giving the impression that he, at least, could behave like an adult. Adult? Old man was more the case. Who else would wade into the surf in his sneakers? Who else would pat water so fastidiously on his chest and upper arms before ducking under? And check his watch, for Lord's sake, when he rose? To Delia it seemed he was timing the waves, engaging in some precise and picky ritual that filled her with irritation.

She snatched her tote bag from the blanket, spun on one bare heel, and stamped off down the beach.

More people had arrived without her noticing. Only a slender path wound among the umbrellas and canvas chairs and mesh playpens, and so after a few yards she changed course till she was marching alongside the ocean, on wet, packed sand that cooled the soles of her feet.

This part of the beach belonged to the walkers. They walked in twos, mostly: young couples, old couples, almost always holding hands or at least matching their strides. From time to time small children cut in front of them. Delia pictured a map of the entire East Coast from Nova Scotia to Florida—an irregular strip of beige sand dotted with tiny humans, a wash of blue Atlantic next to it even more sparsely dotted. She herself was a dot in motion, heading south. She would keep going till she fell off the bottom of the continent, she decided. By and by Sam would think to ask, "Have you seen Delia?" "Why, no, where could she have got to?" the others would say, but she would keep on the move, like someone running between raindrops, and they would never, ever find her.

Already, though, something was slowing her down. The first of the Sea Colony condominiums towered ahead—ugly Sea Colony with its impassive monochrome high-rises, like a settlement from an alien galaxy. She could have made her way past, but that mysterious, Star Wars hum that the buildings always emitted chilled her so that she stopped short. In her childhood, this had been grassy marshland, with a few plain-faced cottages scattered about. In her childhood, she was almost certain, she and her father had flown homemade kites right where that complex of orange plastic pyramids now shaded a modernistic sundeck. For an instant she could feel her father's blunt fingers closing over hers on the kite string. She brushed a hand across her eyes. Then she turned and started walking back.

A lifeguard slouched on his chair, surveying the bathers inscrutably from behind his dark glasses. A lardy young boy on a raft landed in the foam at Delia's feet. She stepped around him and, looking ahead, spotted her family's green-and-white umbrella and her children on their blanket just beyond. They were sitting up now, and Sam stood some distance away, still shiny after his swim. From here it didn't seem that anyone was speaking, for the children faced the horizon and Sam was studying his watch.

Just that abruptly, Delia veered inland. She left the ocean behind and picked her way around sand tunnels and forts and collections of toys. When she had traversed the wooden walkway to the road, she stopped to dust her feet off and dig her espadrilles from her tote. Sam's beach robe lay beneath them—a wad of navy broadcloth—and after a moment's consideration, she shook it out and put it on. Her shoulders were so burned by now that they seemed to give off heat.

If she had thought to get the car keys from Ramsay, she could have driven. She wasn't looking forward to that trek to the cottage. In fact, she could return for the keys right now. But then some of the others might want to come with her, and so she decided against it.

Already the ocean seemed far away and long ago, a mere whisper on this sunny paved road with its silent cottages and empty, baking automobiles and motionless rows of swimsuits on clotheslines. She cut through someone's backyard—mostly sand—and circled an enclosure of garbage cans that smelled of crab and buzzed with glittery blue flies. Then she was facing Highway 1. Traffic whizzed by so fast that she had to wait several minutes before she could cross.

On the other side of the highway, her footsteps were the loudest sound around—her stiff straw soles clopping out a rhythm. Perhaps because she'd been thinking of her father, the rhythm seemed to keep time with the song he used to sing when she was small. She stalked past screened porches, with her shoes beating out "Delia's Gone"— asking where she'd been so long, saying her lover couldn't sleep, saying all around his bed at night he kept hearing little Delia's bare feet. She especially liked that last line; she always had. Except, wasn't the other Delia dead? Yes, obviously: there was mention in the very first verse of little Delia dead and gone. But she preferred to believe the woman had simply walked out. It was more satisfying that way.

Her face felt sticky, and her shoulder hurt where the handles of her tote bag chafed her sunburn. She switched the tote to her other side. She was almost there now, anyhow. She was planning on a tall iced tea as soon as she stepped through the door, and after that a cool bath and a little private visit with her cat. It was time to lure Vernon from under her bed, where he had taken up residence at some point during the night. In fact, maybe she ought to do that first.

She smiled at a woman carrying a suitcase out of the cottage next to theirs. "Lovely beach weather!" the woman called. "Hate to leave it!"

"It's perfect," Delia said, and she rounded a van parked in the driveway and climbed her own steps.

Inside, the dimness turned her momentarily blind. She peered up the stairwell and called, "Vernon?"

"What."

She gasped.

"Somebody page me?" a man's voice asked.

He lumbered down the stairs—a chubby young man with a clipboard, dressed in jeans and a red plaid shirt. His moon-shaped face, with its round pink cheeks and nubbin nose and buttonhole mouth, reassured her somewhat, but even so she could barely draw breath to ask, "Who . . . ?"

"I'm Vernon, didn't you holler my name? I'm here about the roof."

"Oh," she said. She gave a shaky laugh and clutched her tote bag to her chest. "I was just calling my cat," she told him.

"Well, I haven't seen no cat about. Sorry if I scared you."

"You didn't scare me!"

He squinted at her doubtfully. The satiny skin beneath his eyes glistened with sweat, which made him look earnest and boyish. "Anyhow," he said. "Seems I'll need to replace that flashing up top round the chimney. I won't be doing it today, though; I got to get on back. So if those folks at the realtor's phone, tell them I'll be in touch, okay?"

"Okay," Delia said.

He waved his clipboard amiably and headed past her out the door. On the steps, he turned and asked, "How you like my vehicle?"

"Vehicle?"

"Ain't it something?"

It was, in fact. She wondered how she could have missed it. Big as a house trailer, painted a metallic bronze with a desert landscape lighting up one side, it occupied the whole driveway. "Got a microwave," Vernon was saying, "got a dinky little 'frigerator—"

"You mean it's for living in?"

"Sure, what else?"

"I thought vans would just have rows and rows of seats."

"Ain't you ever been inside a RV before? Shoot, come on and I'll show you."

"Oh, I don't know if I—"

"Come on! This'll knock your socks off."

"Well, maybe I *will* take a peek," Delia said, and she followed him, still hugging her tote bag. One section of the desert scene proved to be a sliding panel. Vernon slid it open and stood back to let her see inside. When she poked her head in she found gold shag carpeting halfway up the walls, and built-in cabinets, and a platform bed at the rear with storage drawers underneath. Two high-backed seats faced the windshield—the only sign that this was, after all, a means of transportation.

"Gosh," Delia said.

"Climb in. Get a load of my entertainment center."

"You have an entertainment center?"

"State of the art," he told her. He climbed in himself, causing the van to tilt beneath his weight, and then turned to offer a hand as big as a baseball glove. She accepted it and clambered inside. The oily, exciting smell of new carpet reminded her of airports and travel.

"Ta-daah!" Vernon said. He flung open a cabinet. "What it is," he said, "in the bottom of this here TV is a slot for a videotape, see? Integrated VCR. Evenings, I just swivel it out and watch the latest hit movies from the bed."

"You stay here all the time?"

"Just about," he said. "Well, more or less. Well, for now I do." Then he sent her a look, with his head ducked. "I'll tell you the honest truth," he said. "This van belongs to my brother."

He seemed to think the news would disappoint her deeply. He fixed her with a worried blue gaze and waited, scarcely breathing, until she said, "Oh, really?"

"I guess I kind of gave the impression it was mine," he said. "But see, my brother's off on this fishing trip, him and his wife. Left his van at our mom's house in Nanticoke Landing. Told her to watch over it and not let nobody drive it. Me is who he meant. But he's due back this afternoon and so yesterday I got to thinking. 'Well, durn,' I got to thinking. 'Here's this fully equipped RV, been setting in Mom's yard all week and I have not so much as tried that little microwave.' So last night I stayed in it, and this morning I took it out to make my estimates. Mom said she don't even want to know about it. Said not to drag her into it. But what can he do to me, right? What's he going to do to me—haul me off to jail?"

"Maybe he won't find out," Delia said.

"Oh, he'll find out, all right. Be just like him to have wrote down the mileage before he left," Vernon told her gloomily.

"You could always say you thought the battery needed charging."

"Battery. Sure."

"Does he live here? In the van, I mean?"

"Naw."

"Well, I would," Delia said. She bent to raise the seat of an upholstered bench. Just as she had expected, there was storage space underneath. She glimpsed woolens of some kind—blankets or jackets. "I would make it my year-round home," she said. "Really! Who needs a big old house and all those extra rooms?"

"Yeah, but my brother's got three kids," Vernon said.

"Have you ever seen those under-cabinet coffeemakers?" Delia asked him.

"Huh?"

She was inspecting the kitchen area now. It was a model of miniaturization, with a sink the size of a salad bowl and a two-burner stovetop. A dented metal percolator stood on one of the burners. "They have these coffeepots," she told Vernon, "that you permanently install beneath the overhang of a cabinet. So you don't waste any space."

"Is that a fact."

"Actually, there's a whole line of under-cabinet equipment. Toaster ovens, can openers . . . electric can opener you install beneath the—"

"I believe my brother just uses the hand-cranked kind," Vernon said.

"Well, if this were mine, I'd have everything under-cabinet."

"Hand-cranked don't take no space at all, to speak of."

"I'd have nothing rattling around," Delia said, "nothing interfering, so at a moment's notice I could hop behind the wheel and go. Travel with my house on my back, like a snail. Stop when I got tired. Park in whatever campground caught my fancy."

"Well, but campgrounds," Vernon said. "Mostly you'd need to reserve ahead, for a campground."

"And next morning I'd say, 'Okay! That's it for this place!' And move on."

"The rates are kind of steep too, if the campground's halfway decent," Vernon said. "Durn. Is that the time?"

He was looking at the clock above the sink. Delia was glad to see that the clock, at least, was attached to the wall. In her opinion, there was far too much loose and adrift here—not just the percolator but sloppily refolded newspapers and videotapes out of their boxes and castoff pieces of clothing. "What I can't fathom," she said, "is how you manage to drive with these things sliding all over. Wouldn't you have flying objects every time you hit a speed bump?"

"Not as I've noticed," Vernon said. "But remember this ain't my property. And speaking of which, my brother's due back in like a couple of hours so I reckon I better be going."

"I wish I could come too," Delia said.

"Yeah. Right. Well, look, it's been great talking with you—"

"Maybe I could just ride along for a little tiny part of the way," Delia said.

"When—now?"

"Just to see how it handles on the road."

"Well, it . . . handles fine on the road," Vernon said. "But I'm going inland, you know? I'm nowhere near any beaches. Going down Three eighty past Ashford, *way* past Ashford, over to—"

"I'll just ride to, um, Ashford," Delia said.

She knew she was making him nervous. He stood staring at her, his eyebrows crinkled and his mouth slightly open, his clipboard dangling forgotten from one hand. Never mind: any moment now she would let him off the hook. She would give a little coming-to-her-senses laugh and tell him that on second thought, she couldn't possibly ride to Ashford. She did have a family after all, and already they must be wondering where she was.

And yet here stood this van, this beautiful, completely stocked, entirely self-sufficient van that you could travel in forever, unentangled with anyone else. Oh, couldn't she offer to buy it? How much did such things cost? Or steal it, even—shove Vernon out the door and zoom off, careening west on little back roads where no one could ever track her.

But: "Well," she said regretfully, "I do have a family."

"Family in Ashford? Oh, in that case," Vernon said.

It took her a minute to understand. His eyebrows smoothed themselves out, and he leaned past her to slide the door shut. Then he flung his clipboard on the bench and said, "Long as you've got transportation back, then . . ."

Speechless, Delia made her way to the front. She sat in the passenger seat and perched her tote bag on her knees. Next to her, Vernon was settling behind the wheel. When he switched on the ignition, the van roared to life so suddenly that she fancied it had been jittering with impatience all this time.

"Hear that?" Vernon asked her.

She nodded. She supposed it must be the engine's vibration that caused her teeth to start chattering.

Traveling down Highway 1 toward the Maryland border, past giant beach-furniture stores and brand-new "Victorian" developments and the jumbled cafés and apartments of Fenwick Island, Delia kept telling herself that she could still get back on her own. It would mean a long walk, was all (which stretched longer moment by moment). And when they entered Ocean City, with its honky-tonk razzle-dazzle—well, Ocean City had buses, she happened to know. She could take a bus to its northernmost edge and *then* walk back. So she rode quietly, beginning to feel almost relaxed, while Vernon hunched over the wheel and steered with his forearms. He was one of those drivers who talked to traffic. "Not to pressure you or anything, fella," he said when a car ahead of him stalled, and he clucked at four teenage boys crossing the street with their surfboards. "Aren't *you*-all hotshots," he told them. Delia gazed after them. The

tallest boy wore ticking-striped shorts exactly like a pair Carroll owned—
that voluminous new fashion that billowed to mid-knee.

When her family discovered she was gone, they would be baffled.
Flummoxed. If she stayed away long enough, they would wonder if she'd
met with an accident. "Or could she have left on purpose?" Sam would at
last ask the children. "Did one of you say something? Did *I* say something? Was I mistaken to believe she wasn't the type for an affair?"

An airy sense of exhilaration filled her chest. She felt so lightweight, all
at once.

Then after they had had time to get really concerned, she would phone.
Find a booth before night fell and, "It's me," she would announce. "Just
took a little jaunt to the country; could one of you come pick me up?" No
harm done.

So when Vernon turned onto Highway 50 and started inland (talking
now about the "differential," whatever that was), she still said nothing to
stop him. The percolator clanked on the stovetop; they rattled across a
bridge she'd never seen before and entered a bleached, pale country entirely unfamiliar to her. She merely stared out the window. They passed
yellowing, papery houses set in the middle of careful lawns that appeared
to have been hand clipped, blade by blade. They flickered through leafy
woodlands. "One place he flubbed up is not opting for a CB," Vernon
said, referring evidently to his brother, but Delia was just then picturing
how Sam's lips always formed a straight line when he was angry. And it
occurred to her that what he might tell the children was, "Well, at least
we can get things done right, now she's gone."

"Besides which you will notice there's no stereo," Vernon said. "That's
my brother for you: he don't care much for music. I say there's something
lacking in a man who don't like music."

Maybe Eleanor would step in (speaking of doing things right). Oh,
Eleanor would take over gladly—plan all the menus a year in advance and
set up one of her Iron Mama budgets.

"I guess you think that's awful," Vernon said. "To pick fault with my
own brother."

Delia said, "No, no . . ."

Here and there, now, gaunt old dignified farmhouses stood at the end
of long driveways, with crops growing all around them and lightning rods
bristling on their rooftops. Imagine living in such a place! It would be so
wholesome. Delia saw herself feeding chickens, flinging corn or wheat or
whatever from her capacious country apron. First she'd have to marry a
farmer, though. You always had to begin by finding some man to set
things in motion, it seemed.

"But I'll be honest," Vernon was saying. "Me and him never have been
what you'd call close. He is three years older than me and never lets me
forget it. Keeps yammering about head of the family, when fact is he
hardly lays eyes on our family from one month to the next. *I'm* the one

takes Mom grocery shopping. *I'm* the one runs her hither and yon for her bingo nights and her covered-dish suppers and what all."

Why did everyone maintain that men were uncommunicative? In Delia's experience, they talked a blue streak, especially repairmen. And Sam was no exception. Sam communicated all too well, if you asked Delia.

She let her eyes follow a trailer park as they passed it. Each trailer was anchored by awnings and cinder-block steps and sometimes a screened extension. Whole menageries of plaster animals filled the little yards.

"Now, you take this fishing trip: know who's tending his kids? Me and Mom. Course mostly it's Mom, but time I come home from work nights, she is so wore out the rest is up to me. But don't expect Vincent to thank me. No, sir. And if he gets wind I drove his van, he'll have my head."

In her tote bag Delia had five hundred dollars of vacation money, split between her billfold and a deceptive little vinyl cosmetic kit. She could stay away overnight, if she really wanted to alarm them—take a room in some motel or even a picturesque inn. However, all she had on was her swimsuit. Oh, Lord. Her scrunchy-skirted swimsuit and her espadrilles and Sam's beach robe. But supposing she kept the robe tightly closed . . . Viewed in a certain way, it was not all that different from a dress. The sleeves were three-quarter length; the hem covered her knees. And hotels around here must be used to tourists, in their skimpy tourist outfits.

They were approaching the edge of a town now. Vernon slowed for a traffic light. He was talking about his brother's wife, Eunice. "I feel kind of sorry for her, if you really want to know," he said. "Picture being married to Vincent!"

"What town is this?" Delia asked him.

"This? Why, Salisbury."

The light changed, and he resumed driving. Delia was thinking that maybe she could just get out here. Maybe at the next red light. But the lights from then on were green, and also they had reached a residential section, very middle class and staid. And then beyond were unappealing malls, and messy commercial establishments, and somehow nothing struck her as very inviting.

"It's my belief he hits her," Vernon was saying. "Or at least, like, sort of pushes her. Anyways I know they fight a lot, because half the time when they come over she won't look him in the face."

They were riding through open country again, and Delia was beginning to fear she had missed her last chance. It was such *empty* country, so cardboard flat and desolate. She gripped her door handle and gazed at a naked dirt field in which violently uprooted trees lay every which way, their roots and branches clawing air. Unexpectedly Vernon braked, then took a sharp left onto a narrow paved road. "Three eighty," he informed her. He didn't seem to notice the clattering of the percolator behind them. "But this fishing trip they're on is supposed to be a second honeymoon."

"Honeymoon!" Delia said. She was looking at a pasture filled with rusted-out cars. Around the next curve lay a ramshackle barn halfway returned to the earth—the ridgepole almost U-shaped, the warped gray boards slumping into waist-high weeds. Every minute, she saw, she was traveling farther from civilization.

"Well, how Eunice put it to my mom," Vernon said, "she put it that her and Vincent were going off on the boat by themselves, just the two of them together."

Delia thought that a trip alone on a fishing boat would strain the best of marriages, but all she said was, "Well, I wish them luck."

"That's what I told Mom," Vernon said. He swerved around an antique tractor, whose driver was wearing what looked like a duster. "I told Mom, I said, 'Lots of luck, when her husband is Vincent the Dweeb.' "

"She should give up on him," Delia said, forgetting it was none of her business. "Especially if he hits her."

"Oh, I'm pretty sure he hits her."

Was that a brick building in the distance? Yes, and a grove of dark trees that cooled and relieved Delia's eyes, and beyond them a sparkling white steeple. She knew there must be guest accommodations here. She gathered up her tote bag and smoothed her robe around her knees.

"One time Eunice dropped by the house with a puffy place on her cheekbone," Vernon said. "And when Mom asked where she got it she said, 'I walked into a wall,' which if it had been me I could have come up with a lot better story than that."

"She should leave him," Delia said, but her mind was on the town ahead. They were passing the outskirts now—small white houses, a diner, a collection of men talking in front of a service station. "There's no point trying to mend a marriage that's got to the point of violence," she told Vernon.

Now they had reached the brick building, which turned out to be a school. DOROTHY G. UNDERWOOD HIGH SCHOOL. A street leading off just past that ended, evidently, in a park, for Delia glimpsed distant greenery and a statue of some kind. And now they were nearing the church that the steeple belonged to. Vernon was saying, "Well, I don't know; maybe you're right. Like I was telling Mom the other day, I told her—"

"I believe I'll get out here," Delia said.

"What?" he said. He slowed.

"Here is where I think I'll get out."

He brought the van to a stop and looked at the church. Two ladies in straw hats were weeding a patch of geraniums at the foot of the announcement board. "But I thought you were going to Ashford," he said. "*This* is not Ashford."

"Well, still," she said, looping the handles of her tote bag over her shoulder. She opened the passenger door and said, "Thanks for the ride."

"I hope I didn't say nothing to upset you," Vernon told her.

"No! Honest! I just think I'll—"

"Was it Eunice?"

"Eunice?"

"Vincent hitting her and all? I won't talk about it no more if it upsets you."

"No, really, I enjoyed our talk," she told him. And she hopped to the ground and sent him a brilliant smile as she closed the door. She started walking briskly in the direction they had come from, and when she reached the street where she had seen the statue she turned down it, not even slowing, as if she had some specific destination in mind.

Behind her, she heard the van shift gears and roar off again. Then a deep silence fell, like the silence after some shocking remark. It seemed this town felt as stunned as Delia by what she had gone and done.

6

———

What kind of trees lined this street? Beeches, she believed, judging by the high, arched corridor they formed. But she had never been very good at identifying trees.

Identifying the town itself, though, was easy. First she passed an imposing old house with a sign in one ground-floor window: MIKE POTTS—"BAY BOROUGH'S FRIENDLIEST INSURANCE AGENT." Then the Bay Borough Federal Savings Bank. And she was traveling down Bay Street, as she discovered when she reached the first intersection. But would the bay in question be the Chesapeake? She was fairly sure she had not come so far west. Also, this didn't have the feel of a waterside town. It smelled only of asphalt.

She found her explanation in the square. There, where scanty blades of grass struggled with plantain beneath more trees, a plaque at the base of the single bronze statue proclaimed:

ON THIS SPOT, IN AUGUST 1863,
GEORGE PENDLE BAY,
A UNION SOLDIER ENCAMPED OVERNIGHT WITH
HIS COMPANY,
DREAMED THAT A MIGHTY ANGEL
APPEARED TO HIM AND SAID,
"YE ARE SITTING IN THE BARBER'S CHAIR OF INFINITY,"
WHICH HE INTERPRETED AS INSTRUCTION
TO ABSENT HIMSELF FROM THE REMAINDER OF THE WAR
AND STAY ON TO FOUND THIS TOWNSHIP.

Delia blinked and took a step backward. Mr. Bay, a round-faced man in a bulging suit, did happen to be sitting, but his chair was the ordinary, non-barber kind, as near as she could make out, with a skirt of twisted bronze fringe. He gripped the chair's arms in a manner that squashed his fingertips; evidently he had been a nail biter. This struck Delia as comical. She gave a snuffle of laughter and then glanced over her shoulder, fearing someone had heard. But the square was empty, its four green benches uninhabited. Around the perimeter, cars cruised past, one or two at a time, and people walked in and out of the low brick and clapboard buildings, but nobody seemed to notice her.

Still, she was conscious all at once of her outfit. It wasn't so much the beach robe as the swimsuit underneath, the *feeling* of it, crumpled and bunchy and saggy. She'd give anything for some underwear. So she crossed the little square and gazed toward the row of storefronts on the other side of the street.

Clearly, modern times had overtaken the town. Buildings that must have been standing for a century—the bricks worn down like old pencil erasers, the clapboards gently rubbed to gray wood—now held the Wild Applause Video Shop, Tricia's House of Hair, and a Potpourri Palace. One place that seemed unchanged, though, was the dime store on the corner, with its curlicued red-and-gilt sign and a window full of flags and bunting.

She had been taught to buy only top-quality underwear, however else she might economize, but this was an emergency. She crossed the street and entered the dime-store smells of caramel and cheap cosmetics and old wooden floors. Apparently the notion of consolidated checkout lanes had not caught on here. At each and every counter, a clerk stood by a cash register. A floss-haired girl rang up a coloring book for a child; an elderly woman bagged a younger woman's cookie sheets. The lingerie department was staffed by a man, oddly enough; so Delia made her selections in haste and handed them over without quite raising her eyes. A plain white nylon bra, white cotton underpants. The underpants came three to a pack. Other styles could be purchased singly, but it was the pack of three that her fingers alighted on. *Just in case I'm away for more than one night,* she caught herself thinking. Then, as she counted out her money, she thought, *But I can always use them at home, of course, too. This doesn't mean a thing.*

Now she had her underclothes but no place to get into them, for she didn't see a rest room in the dime store. She went back outside, tucking her parcel into her tote, and looked up the street. Next door was Debbi's Dress Shoppe. Nineteen-forties mannequins with painted-on hair sported the latest fashions—broad-shouldered business suits or linen sheaths shaped like upside-down triangles. Not Delia's style at all, but at least she would find a changing booth here. She breezed in, trying to look purposeful, and snatched the nearest dress off a rack and hurried toward a row of compartments at the rear. "May I help you?" a woman called after her, but Delia said, "Oh, thanks, I'm only . . ." and disappeared behind a curtain.

The underwear fit, thank heaven. (She did her best to silence the rustling of the bag.) It was a relief to feel *contained* again. She folded her swimsuit into her tote. Then she reached for Sam's robe, but the sight of it gave her pause. It seemed so obviously a beach robe, all at once. She looked toward the dress she'd snatched up—a gray knit of some sort. Way too long, she could tell at a glance, but still she slipped it off its hanger and drew it over her head. The acrid smell of new fabric engulfed her. She smoothed down the skirt, zipped the side zipper, and turned to confront her reflection.

She had assumed she would resemble a child playing dress-up, for the hem nearly brushed her ankles. What she found, though, was someone entirely unexpected: a somber, serious-minded woman in a slender column of pearl gray. She might be a librarian or a secretary, one of those managerial executive secretaries who actually run the whole office from behind the scenes. "You'll find it in the Jones file, Mr. Smith," she imagined herself saying curtly. "And don't forget you're lunching with the mayor today; you'll want to take along the materials on the—"

"How're we doing in there?" the saleswoman called.

"Oh, fine."

"Can I bring you anything else to try?"

"No," Delia said. "This is perfect."

She stuffed Sam's robe into her tote and emerged from the booth to ask, "Could you just take the tags off, please? I think I'll wear it home."

The saleswoman—an overtanned blonde in a geometric black-and-white print—directed a dubious frown toward the hemline. "We do offer alterations," she said. "Would you like that shortened a bit?"

"No, thanks," Delia told her in a starchy, secretarial voice.

The saleswoman adjusted seamlessly. "Well, it certainly becomes you," she said.

Delia raised her left arm, and the woman reached for her scissors and snipped off the tags that dangled from the zipper pull.

Seventy-nine ninety-five, the dress cost, not including tax. But Delia paid without a moment's hesitation and strode out of the shop.

The momentum of her exit carried her some distance, past the dime store again and across an intersection to a row of smaller shops—a copy center, a travel agent, a florist. She noticed she walked differently now, not with her usual bouncy gait but more levelly, because of her slim skirt. *Here is the secretary, Miss X, speeding back to her office after lunch. Preparing to type up her notes for the board of directors.*

Just as a game, she started choosing her office, the same way she used to choose her house when riding througha posh neighborhood. NICHOLS & TRIMBLE FAMILY DENTISTS. But there she might have to clean teeth or something. VALUE VISION OPTICIANS. But did opticians use secretaries? EZEKIEL POMFRET, ATTORNEY. Possibly defunct, from the expressionless look of the lowered window shade. And none of these places bore a HELP WANTED sign. Not that that made any practical difference.

At the next intersection, she took a left. She passed a pet supply and an antique store, so called (its window full of Fiesta ware and aqua plastic ashtrays shaped like boomerangs). A pharmacy. Two frame houses. A mom-and-pop grocery. Then another frame house, set so close to the street that its porch floor seemed an extension of the sidewalk. Propped in the dusty front window stood a cardboard notice, ROOM FOR RENT, bracketed by limp gauze curtains.

Room for rent.

This would be, of course, a "boardinghouse." The word summoned a picture of the secretary tidying the covers on her spinsterly white bed; her fellow boarders shuffling down the hall in their carpet slippers; her ancient landlady, dressed in black, setting the dining-room table—the "board"—for tomorrow's breakfast. In the time it took Delia to cross the porch and ring the bell, she became so well entrenched that she hardly felt the need to introduce herself to the woman who appeared at the door.

"Well, hi!" the woman said. "Can I help you?"

She didn't fit Delia's vision of a landlady. She was plump and fortyish, heavily rouged, wearing a towering dessert tray of lavish golden curls and a hot-pink pantsuit. Still, she seemed to be the one in charge, so Delia said, "I'm inquiring about the room."

"Room?"

"The room for rent," Delia reminded her.

"Oh, the room," the woman said. "Well. I was hoping to rent to a man."

Was that even legal, nowadays? Delia didn't know what to say next.

"Up to last April," the woman told her, opening the baggy screen door, "I just always had men. It just always seemed to work that way. I only rent out two rooms, you know, and so I had these two men, Mr. Lamb who travels weekdays and Larry Watts who was separated. But when Larry got back with his wife last April, why, I rented his room to a woman. And did I ever regret it!"

She turned, leaving the door to Delia, and started up a flight of stairs. Uncertainly, Delia followed. She had an impression of a house that had long ago been abandoned. Ovals of lighter wallpaper showed where pictures must once have hung, and the floorboards of the upstairs hall revealed the ghost of a rug.

"Katie O'Connell, her name was," the woman said. Even so short a climb had winded her. She patted her wide pink bosom with little spanking sounds. "A Delaware girl, I believe. She came to town to work for Zeke Pomfret—Zeke had just had his dear old Miss Percy *die* on him—and so Katie needed a place to stay and I said, 'Fine,' not having the slightest inkling: 'Fine,' I told her, thinking this would be no different from renting to a man. But, oh, it was, 'Where's this, where's that, where's my fresh towels daily, where's my little bar of soap . . . ?' I am not a bed-and-breakfast, mind you. I hope you don't think I'm a bed-and-breakfast."

"Of course not," Delia said.

"I'm only renting out rooms, you know? I bought this place three years ago. Fixer-upper, they called it. I bought it after I passed my real estate exam, thought I'd fix it up and sell it, but the way the market's been doing I just never have found the money for that, and so I'm living here myself and renting out two of the rooms. But there's no meals involved; I hope you're not looking for meals. This Katie, she was, 'Oh, let me just keep this quart of milk in your fridge,' and not two shakes later she was cooking in my kitchen. Why, *I* don't even cook in my kitchen! This is a barebones operation."

Proving it, she opened the door to the right of the stairs. Delia followed her into a long, narrow room, its outside wall slanting inward under the eaves, a window at each end. A metal cot extended from beneath the front window, and a low, orange-brown bureau sat against the inside wall. There was a smell like a hornet's nest—a dry, sharp, moldering smell that came, perhaps, from the brittle-looking tan wallpaper traced with mottled roses.

"Now, Katie had drapes on these windows," the woman said, "but she took them when she left. Left last Thursday with Larry Watts; we think they went to Hawaii."

"The . . . Larry Watts who was separated?" Delia asked in confusion.

"Oh, I didn't realize you knew him. Yes, once I put it all together, I recalled he did come back for his raincoat—raincoat he'd left in the downstairs closet. That must be how they met. Next thing anyone knows, he's flown the coop, leaving that little wife of his for the second time in two years. Not to mention Zeke Pomfret needing to hunt up a whole new girl now, so soon after losing poor Miss Percy."

She flung open a door at the rear, exposing a shallow closet. Three hangers tinkled faintly. "Bathroom's off the hall, full bath with tub and shower," she said, "and you wouldn't have to share it but on weekends, when Mr. Lamb gets back from his sales trips. I stay downstairs, myself. Rent is forty-two dollars a week. You want it?"

Forty-two dollars was less than a single night in most hotels. And a hotel would not be anything like so satisfyingly Spartan. Delia said, "You mean it's all right I'm not a man?"

The woman shrugged. "No one *else* has come along," she said.

Delia walked over to the cot, which was made up with white sheets and a white woolen blanket washed bald. When she tested the mattress with one palm, it sounded the same tinny note as the hangers.

She said, "Definitely I want it."

"Well, great. I'm Belle Flint, by the way."

"I'm Delia Grinstead," Delia said, and then she wondered if she should have used an alias. But Belle seemed reassuringly uninterested. She was fluffing her curls now in the mirror over the bureau. "So," Delia said, "would I have to . . . sign a contract?"

"Contract?"

"I mean . . ."

It must be painfully apparent that she had never arranged for her own housing before. "I mean a . . . lease or something?" she asked.

"Lord, no, just pay in advance, every Saturday morning," Belle said, baring her front teeth to the mirror. "Let's see. Today's Monday. . . . Pay me thirty dollars; that'll cover this week. You plan on staying here long?"

"Oh, maybe," Delia said, deliberately vague, and she started making a to-do over digging through her tote. Belle was tilting her chin now to study the cushion of flesh beneath it. Her entire face was a cushion; she resembled one of those lush, soft flowers, a peony or a big floppy iris.

"Well, here," Delia told her, "ten, twenty . . . ," and only then did Belle turn away from the mirror. If she was surprised to receive cash, she didn't show it. She folded the bills and tucked them into her breast pocket.

"I guess you'll want to go fetch your belongings," she said, "and meantime I'll put your key on the bureau, just in case I'm out when you get back. I'm showing a house at four-thirty. You won't be bringing a lot of *stuff*, I hope."

"No, I—"

"Because this room doesn't have much storage space, and I hate for things to spill over. That's how all that happened with Larry Watts and Katie: his raincoat spilled into the downstairs closet, and so naturally he forgot it when he moved."

"I'm bringing very little," Delia said.

She would wait to come back till, say, five o'clock, when Belle was sure to be out. That way Belle wouldn't see she was really bringing nothing. It was now . . . Surreptitiously, she checked her watch. Three forty-five. Belle was clattering out of the room in her wedge-heeled sandals. "Rules are, the first floor is mine," she said, pausing in the hall, "and that includes the kitchen. Café across the street is pretty good: Rick-Rack's. There's a laundromat on East Street, and Mrs. Auburn comes Fridays to clean the rooms. We never lock the front door, but that key to your room does work, if you're the nervous type. You got all that?"

"Yes, thanks."

"And I don't suppose you'll have guests," Belle said. She gave Delia a sudden appraising look. "Men guests, that is."

"Oh! No, I won't."

"Your private life is your private life, but that forty-two dollars covers utilities for one. Sheets and towels for one, too."

"I don't even know anybody to invite," Delia assured her.

"You're not a local girl, huh?"

"Well, no."

"Me neither. Till I came here with a fella, I never heard of Bay Borough," Belle said cheerfully. "The fella didn't work out, but I stayed on anyhow."

Delia knew she should volunteer some information in exchange, but all she said was, "I guess I'll wash up before I go get my things."

"Help yourself," Belle said with a wave. And she went clomping down the stairs.

Delia waited a polite half second before stepping into the bathroom. She hadn't peed since ten o'clock that morning.

The bathroom wallpaper—seahorses breathing silver bubbles—curled at the seams, and the fixtures were old and rust-stained, but everything looked clean. First Delia used the toilet, and then she patted her face with cool water and let it air-dry. (The one towel belonged to the other boarder, she assumed.) She avoided her face in the mirror; she preferred to hang on to the image she'd seen in the changing booth. She did glance down at her dress, though, checking it for neatness, for secretarial properness. And just before walking out, she slipped her wedding ring off her finger and dropped it into her tote.

Then she made a brief return trip to her room. She didn't go inside but merely stood in the doorway, claiming it—reveling in its starkness, now that she had it completely to herself.

Clop-clop back up the street, eyes front, as if she knew where she was headed. Well, she did, more or less. Already the little town held pockets of familiar sights: the faded red soft-drink machine outside the Gobble-Up Grocery, the chipped Fiesta ware in Bob's Antiques, the stacked bags of kibble for overweight dogs in Pet Heaven. She took a right at the corner, and the green square in the distance seemed as comfortable, as well known and faintly boring, as if she had spent her childhood at the foot of Mr. Bay's fringed chair.

Ezekiel Pomfret still had his shade pulled down, but when Delia tried the door it yielded. A steep flight of stairs climbed straight ahead. A ground-floor door to the right bore, on its cloudy, pebbled glass, Ezekiel Pomfret's name once again and WILLS & ESTATES—DOMESTIC-CRIMINAL LAW. That door, too, opened when Delia tried it. She stepped into a walnut-lined room with a reception desk in the center. No one sat at the desk, she was pleased to see. No one was visible anywhere, but behind another door, this one ornately paneled, she heard a man's voice. It stopped and started, interspersed by silence, so she knew he must be talking on the phone.

She crossed to the desk, which was bare except for a telephone and a typewriter. She lifted a corner of the typewriter's gray rubber hood. Manual; not even electric. (She had worried she would find a computer.) She gave a small, testing spin to the swivel chair behind it.

Good afternoon, she would say. *I'm here to ask if* . . .

No, not *ask. Ask* was too tentative.

She reached up to pat her hair, which felt as crumbly as dry sand on the beach. (The beach! No: shoo that thought away.) She smoothed her skirt around her hips and made sure that the trim on her tote—a flashy pink bow, ridiculous—was hidden beneath her arm.

It just seemed so fateful, Mr. Pomfret, it seemed almost like a direct command, that I should learn about poor Miss Percy exactly at the moment when . . .

The voice behind the door gathered energy and volume. Mr. Pomfret must be winding up his conversation.

Like having something accidentally break my fall, does that make any sense? Like I've been falling, falling all day and then was snagged by a random hook, or caught by an outjutting ledge, and this is where I happened to land, so I was wondering whether . . .

Slam of receiver, squeak of caster wheels, heavy tread on carpet. The paneled door swung open, and a big-bellied middle-aged man in a seersucker suit surveyed her over his half-glasses. "I *thought* I heard someone," he said.

"Mr. Pomfret, I'm Delia Grinstead," she told him. "I've come to be your secretary."

At four-fifteen she returned to the dime store and bought one cotton nightgown, white, and two pairs of nylon panty hose. At four twenty-five she crossed the square to Bassett Bros. Shoe Store and bought a large black leather handbag. The bag cost fifty-seven dollars. When she first saw the price she considered settling for vinyl, but then she decided that only genuine leather would pass muster with Miss Grinstead.

Miss Grinstead was Delia—the new Delia; for after one grimacing, acidic "Ms.," that was how Mr. Pomfret had addressed her throughout their interview. It seemed apt that she should accept this compromise—the unmarried title, the married surname. Certainly the aproned, complacent sound of "Mrs." no longer applied, and yet she couldn't go back to being giggly young Miss Felson. Besides, her Social Security card said Grinstead. She had drawn it from her wallet and read off the number to Mr. Pomfret (not having had enough use of it, all these years, to know it by heart). She had told him she was relocating after burying her mother. A whole unspoken history insinuated itself in the air between them: the puttery female household, the daughter's nunnish devotion. She said she had worked in a doctor's office her entire adult life. "Twenty-two years," she told Mr. Pomfret, "and I felt so sad to leave, but I simply couldn't stay on in Baltimore with all those memories." She seemed to have been infected with Miss Grinstead's manner of speaking. She would never herself have used "simply" in casual conversation, and the word "memories" in that context had a certain mealymouthed tone that was unlike her.

If references had been called for, she was prepared to say that her employer had recently died as well. (She was killing off people right and left today.) But Mr. Pomfret didn't mention references. His sole concern was the nature of her past duties. Had she typed, had she filed, taken shorthand? She answered truthfully, but it felt like lies. "I typed all the bills and correspondence and the doctor's charts," she said. Sam's worn face rose up before her, along with his mended white coat and the paisley tie that he called his "paramecium tie." She sat straighter in her chair. "I filed and manned the phone and kept the appointment book, but unfortunately I do not take shorthand."

"Well, no matter," Mr. Pomfret said. "Neither did Miss Percy or Miss What's-her-name. I've always dreamed of having a secretary with shorthand, but I guess it's not meant to be."

There was an uncomfortable moment when he asked for her address, since she had no idea what it was. But when she mentioned Belle Flint he said, "Oh, yes, on George Street." He added, as he made a notation, "Belle's a real fun gal." That was the advantage to a small town, Delia supposed. Or the disadvantage, depending on how you looked at it.

He said she should start tomorrow; her hours were nine to five. Sorry the pay was just minimum wage, he said (sliding his eyes over subtly to gauge her reaction). Also, she was expected to brew the coffee; he hoped that wasn't a problem.

Of course it wasn't, Delia said brusquely, and she rose and terminated the interview. Her impression of Mr. Pomfret was that he was a man without any grain to him, someone benign but not especially interesting, and that was fine with her. In fact, she didn't much like him, and that was fine too. For the impersonal new life she seemed to be manufacturing for herself, Mr. Pomfret was ideal.

Her watch said twenty minutes till five, and she hadn't eaten since breakfast. Before heading back to her room, therefore, she walked to the café that Belle had recommended. It turned out to be not directly across from Belle's but a few doors farther west, next to a hardware. Still, she could see the boardinghouse from the window; so she sat in the booth that offered the best view and kept watch against Belle's return. Maybe she should have purchased a suitcase, just so she could move in openly. But it was foolish to spend money on appearances. Already her five hundred dollars had dwindled to . . . what? Mentally she tallied it up and then winced. When the waitress arrived, she confined her order to a bowl of vegetable soup and a glass of milk.

Rick-Rack's was the kind of place where she might have eaten in high school—a diner, basically, linoleum floored and tile walled, with six or eight booths and a row of stools along a Formica counter. One little redhead served the whole room, and a blue-black young man, gigantically muscled and shaven skulled, did the cooking. He was grilling a cheese sandwich for the only other customer, a boy about Ramsay's age. The smell of fried food gave Delia hunger pangs even as she was spooning her soup, but she reminded herself that soup provided more vitamins for the money, and she declined the homemade pie for dessert. She paid at the register. The cook, after wiping his hands on his apron, rang up her total without comment. Next time she'd bring something to read, she decided. She had felt awkward, munching her saltines and staring fixedly out the window.

No sign of Belle back at the house. Delia unlatched the front door and felt a thin, bare silence all around her. She climbed the stairs, thinking, *Here comes the executive secretary, returning from her lone meal to the solitude of her room.* It wasn't a complaint, though. It was a boast. An exultation.

When she opened her own door the hornet's-nest smell seemed stronger, perhaps because of the afternoon heat that had penetrated the eaves. She set her belongings on the bureau and went to raise both windows. The rear window offered a view of the tiny backyard and an alley. The front window showed the porch overhang and the buildings across the street. Delia leaned her forehead against the screen and picked out the café (B. J. "RICK" RACKLEY, PROP.) and the hardware store and a brown shingled house with the bars of a crib or a playpen visible in one upstairs window. The only sounds were soothing sounds—occasional cars swishing past and footsteps on the sidewalk.

Belle had left an old-fashioned, spindly key on the bureau, and Delia fitted it into the door and turned the lock. Then she took the tags off her new handbag, dropped her wallet inside, and hung the bag from a hook in the closet. She stowed her other purchases in the bureau. (The drawers stuck and slid out crookedly; they were cheaply made, like the house itself.) She hung Sam's beach robe on a hanger. She placed her cosmetic kit in a drawer. Her tote, with its remaining litter of sun lotions and swimsuit and rubber bands and such, she boosted onto the closet shelf. Then she closed the closet door and went over to the cot and sat down.

So.

She was settled.

She could look around the room and detect not the slightest hint that anybody lived here.

It was twilight before Belle returned. Delia heard the clunk of a car door out front, then loud heels on the porch. But neither woman called out a greeting. In fact, Delia, who had been staring into space for who knows how long, rose from the cot as soundlessly as possible, and tiptoed when she went over to collect some things from the bureau, and took care not to creak any floorboards when she crossed the hall to the bathroom.

While she waited for the shower to run warm, she brushed her teeth and undressed, putting her underwear to soak in the sink. A second towel and washcloth now hung on the other towel bar, she saw. She took the washcloth with her and stepped behind the shower curtain, which was crackly with age and slightly mildewed.

Grime and sweat and sunblock streamed off her, uncovering a whole new layer of skin. The soles of her feet, which felt ironed flat from all that walking, seemed to be drinking up water. She lifted her face to the spray and let her hair get wet. Finally, regretfully, she shut off the faucets and stepped out to towel herself dry. The new nightgown drifted airily over her scorched shoulders.

She chose not to leave her toothbrush in the holder above the sink. In-stead, she returned it to her cosmetic kit and carried everything back to her room. Her wrung-out underclothes she draped on one of the hangers in the closet. This meant she would have to keep the closet door open dur-ing the night—a blot on the room's sterility. Better that, though, than let-ting her laundry clutter the bathroom. She approved of Belle's house rules; she did not intend to "spill over."

She turned the bedcovers back and lay down, drawing up just the top sheet. The breeze from the window chilled her damp head, but not so much that she needed a blanket.

Outside, children were playing. It wasn't even completely dark yet. She lay on her back with her eyes open, keeping her mind as blank as the ceil-ing above her. Once, though, perhaps hours later, a single thought did pre-sent itself. *Oh, God,* she thought, *how am I going to get out of this?* But immediately afterward she closed her eyes, and that was how she fell asleep.

7

Baltimore Woman Disappears, Delia read, and she felt a sudden thud in her stomach, as if she'd been punched. *Baltimore Woman Disappears During Family Vacation.*

She had been checking the Baltimore newspapers daily, morning and evening. There was nothing in either paper Tuesday, nothing Wednesday, nothing Thursday morning. But the Thursday evening edition, which arrived in the vending box near the square in time for Delia's lunch hour, carried a notice in the Metro section. *Delaware State Police announced early today . . .*

She folded the paper open to the article, glancing around as she did so. On the park bench opposite hers, a young woman was handing her toddler bits of something to feed the pigeons, piece by piece. On the bench to her right, a very old man was leafing through a magazine. No one seemed aware of Delia's presence.

Mrs. Grinstead was last seen around noon this past Monday, walking south along the stretch of sand between . . .

Probably the police had some rule that people were not considered missing till a certain amount of time had passed. That must be why there'd been no announcement earlier. (Searching each paper before this, Delia had felt relieved and wounded, both. Did no one realize she was gone? Or maybe she *wasn't* gone; this whole experience had been so dreamlike. Maybe she was still moving through her previous life the same as always, and the Delia here in Bay Borough had somehow just split off from the original.)

It hurt to read her physical description: *fair or light-brown hair . . . eyes are blue or gray or perhaps green . . .* For heaven's sake, hadn't anyone in her family ever looked at her? And how could Sam have made her clothing sound so silly? *Kind of baby-doll,* indeed! She refolded the paper with a snap and then darted another glance around her. The toddler was throwing a tantrum now, a silent little stomping dance, because he'd run out of pigeon food. The old man was licking a finger to turn a page. Delia hated when he did that. Every lunch hour he came here with a magazine and licked his way clear through it, and Delia could only hope that no one else was planning to read it after him.

Like a commuter who always chooses the same seat on the train, like a guest who always settles in the same chair in the living room, Delia had managed in just three days to establish a routine for herself. Breakfast at Rick-Rack's, over the morning paper. Lunch in the square—yogurt and fresh fruit purchased earlier from the Gobble-Up Grocery. Always on the southeast park bench, always with the evening paper. Then some kind of shopping task to fill the hour: Tuesday, a pair of low-heeled black shoes because her espadrilles were blistering her heels. Wednesday, a goose-necked reading lamp. Today she had planned to look for one of those immersion coils so she could brew herself a cup of tea first thing every morning. But now, with this newspaper item, she didn't know. She felt so exposed, all at once. She just wanted to scuttle back to the office.

She dropped her lunch leavings into a wire trash basket and buried the newspaper underneath them. As a rule she left the paper on the bench for others, but not today.

The mother was trying to stuff the toddler into his stroller. The toddler was resisting, refusing to bend in the middle. The old man had finished his magazine and was fussily fitting his glasses into their case. None of the three looked at Delia when she walked past them. Or maybe they were pretending, even the toddler; maybe they'd been instructed not to alarm her. No. She gave her shoulders a shake. *Get ahold of yourself.* It wasn't as if she'd committed any crime. She decided to go on with her routine—drop by the dime store as she'd planned.

Funny how life contrived to build up layers of *things* around a person. Already she had that goosenecked lamp, because the overhead bulb had proved inadequate for reading in bed; and she kept a stack of paper cups and a box of tea bags on her closet shelf, making do till now with hot water from the bathroom faucet; and it was becoming clear she needed a second dress. Last night, the first really warm night of summer, she had thought, *I should buy a fan.* Then she had told herself, *Stop. Stop while you're ahead.*

She walked into the dime store and paused. Housewares, maybe? The old woman presiding over the cookie sheets and saucepans stood idle, twiddling her beads; so Delia approached her. "Would you have one of those immersion coils?" she asked. "Those things you put in a cup to heat up water?"

"Well, I know what you mean," the old woman said. "I can see it just as plain as the nose on your face. Electric, right?"

"Right," Delia said.

"My grandson took one to college with him, but would you believe it? He didn't read the directions. Tried to heat a bowl of soup when the directions said only water. Stink? He said you couldn't imagine the stink! But I don't have any here. Maybe try the hardware department."

"Thanks," Delia said crisply, and she moved away.

Sure enough, she found it in Hardware, hanging on a rack among the extension cords and three-prong adapters. She paid in exact change. The clerk—a gray-haired man in a bow tie—winked when he handed her the bag. "Have a nice day, young lady," he said. He probably thought he was flattering her. Delia didn't bother smiling.

She had noticed that Miss Grinstead was not a very friendly person. The people involved in her daily routine remained two-dimensional to her, like the drawings in those children's books about the different occupations. She hadn't developed the easy, bantering relationships Delia was accustomed to.

Leaving the dime store, she crossed Bay Street and passed the row of little shops. The clock in the optician's window said 1:45. She always tried her best to fill her whole lunch hour, one o'clock to two o'clock, but so far had not succeeded.

And what would she do in wintertime, when it grew too cold to eat in the square? For she was looking that far ahead now, it seemed—this Miss Grinstead with her endless, unmarked, unchanging string of days.

But in Bay Borough it was always summer. That was the only season she could picture here.

She opened Mr. Pomfret's outside door, then the pebble-paned inner door. He was already back from his own lunch, talking on his office phone as usual. *Wurlitzer, wurlitzer,* it sounded like from here. Delia shut her handbag in the bottom desk drawer, smoothed her skirt beneath her, and seated herself in the swivel chair. She had left a letter half finished, and now she resumed typing, keeping her back very straight and her hands almost level as she had been taught in high school.

Authorities do not suspect drowning, the paper had said. It hadn't occurred to her they might. *Since Mrs. Grinstead professed a*—how had they put it?—*professed an aversion to water.* Or something of the sort. Made her sound like a woman who never bathed. She slammed the carriage return more violently than was necessary. And that business about Eliza saying she'd been a cat! People must think the both of them were lunatics.

This typewriter had a stiffer action than the one in Sam's office. Her first day at work, she'd broken two fingernails. After that she had filed all her nails down blunt, which was more appropriate anyhow to Miss Grinstead's general style. Besides, it had used up twenty minutes of an evening. She was devoting a lot of thought these days to how to use up her evenings.

"Well, let's do that! We'll have to get together and do that!" Mr. Pomfret was saying, suddenly louder and heartier. Delia typed the closing ("Esquire," he called himself) and rolled the letter out of the carriage. Mr.

Pomfret burst through the door. "Miss Grinstead, when Mr. Miller shows up I'll need you in here taking notes," he said. "We're going to send a . . . What's that you've got?"

"Letter to Gerald Elliott?" Delia reminded him.

"Elliott! I met with Elliott back in . . ."

She checked the date at the top of the page. "May," she said. "May fourteenth."

"Damn."

It had come to light that Delia's immediate predecessor had stowed her more irksome chores in the filing cabinet under *Ongoing*. Anything red-inked by Mr. Pomfret had conveniently vanished. (And a great deal had been red-inked, since Katie O'Connell couldn't spell and apparently did not believe in paragraphs.) Mr. Pomfret had turned purple when Delia brought him the evidence, but Delia was secretly pleased. This way she looked so capable herself—so efficient, so take-charge. (She felt a bit like a grade-school tattletale.) Also, the retyping job amounted to a low-key training course. She would be sorry when she finished.

"Mr. Miller is due at two-thirty," Mr. Pomfret told her. He was leaning over her desk to sign the letter. "I want you to write down word for word everything he specifies."

"Yes, Mr. Pomfret."

He straightened, capping his pen, and gave her a sudden sharp look over his lizardy lower lids. Sometimes Delia carried her secretary act a bit too far, she suspected. She flashed him an insincere smile and gathered up the letter. His signature was large and sweeping, smeared on the curves. He used one of those expensive German fountain pens that leaked.

"And we'll want coffee, so you might as well fix it ahead," he told her.

"Yes, Mr.—. Certainly," she said.

She went into his office for the carafe, then took it to the sink in the powder room. When she came back he was seated at the credenza, short thighs twisted sideways, tapping once again at his computer. For he did have a computer. He had bought it sometime just recently and fallen under its spell, which might explain his failure to notice Katie O'Connell's filing methods. Theoretically, he was going to learn the machine's mysterious ways and then teach Delia, but after her first morning Delia knew she had nothing to fear. The computer would sit forever in its temporary position while Mr. Pomfret wrestled happily with questions of "backups" and "macros." Right now he was recording every dinner party he and his wife had ever hosted—guest list, menu, wines, and even seating arrangements— so their variables could be rotated into infinity. Delia gave the screen a scornful glance and circled it widely, heading for the coffeemaker at the other end of the credenza.

Water, filter, French roast. This coffeemaker was top-of-the-line: it ground its own beans. She supposed it came from one of those catalogs that weighed down the office mail. Whenever Mr. Pomfret spotted an item he liked, he had Delia place an order. ("Yes, Mr. Pomfret . . .") She called 1-800 numbers clear across the country, requesting a bedside clock that talked, a pocket-sized electronic dictionary, a black leather map case for the glove compartment. Her employer's greed, like his huge belly, made Delia feel trim and virtuous. She didn't at all mind placing the orders. She enjoyed everything about this job, especially its dryness. No one received word of inoperable cancer in a lawyer's office. No one told Delia how it felt to be going blind. No one claimed to remember Delia's babyhood.

She pressed a button on the coffeemaker, and it started grinding. "Help!" Mr. Pomfret shouted over the din. He was goggling at his computer screen, where the lines of text shivered and shimmied. For some reason, it never occurred to him that this always happened when the grinder was running. Delia left the office, closing the door discreetly behind her.

She typed another letter, this one enumerating the corporate bylaws of an accounting firm. ("Buy-laws," Katie O'Connell had spelled it.) *Pursuant to our discussion,* she typed, and *fiscal liability*, and *consent of those not in attendance.* She sacrificed speed for accuracy, as befitted Miss Grinstead, and corrected her rare mistakes with Wite-Out fluid on original and carbon both.

Mr. Miller arrived—a big, handsome, olive-skinned man with a narrow band of black hair. Delia followed him into Mr. Pomfret's office to serve their coffee and then perched on a chair, pen and pad ready. She had worried she couldn't write fast enough, but there wasn't much to write. The question was how often Mr. Miller's ex-wife could see their son, and the answer, according to Mr. Miller, was "Never," which Mr. Pomfret amended to once a week and alternate holidays, hours to be arranged at client's convenience. Then the conversation drifted to computers, and when it didn't drift back again, Delia cleared her throat and asked, "Will that be all?"

Mr. Pomfret said, "Hmm? Oh. Yes, thank you, Miss Grinstead." As she left, she heard him tell Mr. Miller, "We'll see to that right away. I'll have my girl mail it out this afternoon."

Delia settled in her swivel chair, rolled paper into the carriage, and started typing. You could have balanced a glass of water on the back of each of her hands.

The only other appointment was at four—a woman with some stock certificates belonging to her late mother—but Delia's services were not required for that. She addressed a number of envelopes and folded and inserted the letters Mr. Pomfret had signed. She sealed the flaps, licked stamps. She answered a call from a Mrs. Darnell, who made an appointment for Monday. Mr. Pomfret walked past her, cramming his arms into his suit coat. "Good night, Miss Grinstead," he said.

"Good night, Mr. Pomfret."

She sorted her carbons and filed them. She returned what was left of the Ongoing file to its drawer. She answered a call from a man who was disappointed to find Mr. Pomfret gone but would try him at home. She cleaned the coffeemaker. At five o'clock exactly she lowered all the shades, gathered the letters and her handbag, and left the office.

Mr. Pomfret had given her her own key, and she already knew the crotchets of the pebble-paned door—the way you had to push it inward a bit before it would lock.

Outside, the sun was still shining and the air felt warm and heavy after the air-conditioning. Delia walked at a leisurely pace, letting others pass her—men in business suits hurrying home from work, women rushing by with plastic bags from the Food King. She dropped her letters into the mailbox on the corner, but instead of turning left there, she continued north to the library—the next stop in her routine.

By now she had a sense of the town's layout. It was a perfect grid, with the square mathematically centered between three streets north and south of it, two streets east and west. Look west as you crossed an intersection, and you'd see pasture, sometimes even a cow. (In the mornings, when Delia woke, she heard distant roosters crowing.) The sidewalks were crumpled and given over in spots to grass, breaking off entirely when a tree stood in the way. The streets farther from the square had a tendency to slant into scabby asphalt mixed with weeds at the edges, like country highways.

On Border Street, the town's northern boundary, the Bay Borough Public Library crouched between a church and an Exxon station. It was hardly more than a cottage, but the instant Delia stepped inside she always felt its seriousness, its officialness. A smell of aged paper and glue hung above the four tables with their wooden chairs, the librarian's high varnished counter, the bookcases chockablock with elderly books. No CDs or videotapes here, no spin racks of paperback novels; just plain, sturdy volumes in buckram bindings with their Dewey decimal numbers handwritten on the spines in white ink. It was a matter of finances, Delia supposed. Nothing seemed to have been added in the last decade. Bestsellers were nowhere to be seen, but there was plenty of Jane Austen, and Edith Wharton, and various solemn works of history and biography. The children's corner gave off a glassy shine from all the layers of Scotch tape holding the tattered picture books together.

Closing time was five-thirty, which meant that the librarian was busy with her last-minute shelving. Delia could place yesterday's book on the counter without any chitchat; she could hunt down a book for today unobserved, since at this hour all the tables were empty. But what to choose? She wished this place carried romances. Dickens or Dostoyevsky she would never finish in one evening (she had an arrangement with herself where she read a book an evening). George Eliot, Faulkner, Fitzgerald . . .

She settled on *The Great Gatsby*, which she dimly remembered from sophomore English. She took it to the counter, and the librarian (a cocoa-colored woman in her fifties) stopped her shelving to come wait on her.

"Oh, *Gatsby!*" she said. Delia merely said, "Mmhmm," and handed over her card.

The card had her new address on it: 14 George Street. A dash in the space for her telephone number. She had never been unreachable by phone before.

Tucking the book in her handbag, she left the library and headed south. The Pinchpenny Thrift Shop had changed its window display, she noticed. Now a navy knit dress hung alongside a shell-pink tuxedo. Would it be tacky to buy her second dress from a thrift shop? In a town this size, no doubt everyone could name the previous owner.

But after all, what did she care? She made a mental note to come try on the dress tomorrow during lunch hour.

Taking a right onto George Street, she met up with the mother and toddler who fed the pigeons in the square. The mother smiled at her, and before Delia thought, she smiled back. Immediately afterward, though, she averted her eyes.

Next stop was Rick-Rack's Café. She glanced over at the boarding-house as she passed. No cars were parked in front, she was glad to see. With luck, Belle would be out all evening. She seemed to lead a very busy life.

Rick-Rack's smelled of crab cakes, but whoever had ordered them had already eaten and gone. The little redheaded waitress was filling salt shakers. The cook was scraping down his griddle. "Well, hey!" he said, turning as Delia walked in.

"Hello," she said, smiling. (She had nothing against simple courtesy, as long as it went no further.) She settled in her usual booth. By the time the waitress came over, she was already deep in her library book, and all she said was, "Milk and the chicken pot pie, please." Then she went on reading.

Last night she'd had soup and whole-wheat toast; the night before that, tuna salad. Her plan was to alternate soup nights with protein nights. Just inexpensive proteins, though. She couldn't afford the crab cakes, at least not till she got her first salary check.

Paying for her new shoes on Tuesday, she had wished she could use the credit card she was carrying in her wallet. If only a credit-card trail were not so easily traced! And then a peculiar thought had struck her. *Most untraceable of all,* she had thought, *would be dying.*

But of course she hadn't meant that the way it sounded.

The print in her library book was so large, she worried she had chosen something that wouldn't last the evening. She forced her eyes to travel more slowly, and when her meal arrived she stopped reading altogether. She kept the book open, though, next to her plate, in case somebody approached.

The waitress set out scalloped paper place mats for the supper crowd. The cook stirred something on the burner. Two creases traversed the base of his skull; his smooth black scalp seemed overlaid with a pattern of embroidery knots. He had made the pot pie from scratch, Delia suspected.

The crust shattered beneath her fork. And the potatoes accompanying it seemed hand mashed, not all gluey and machine mashed.

She wondered whether her family had thought to thaw the casseroles she'd packed.

"If he do come," the cook was telling the waitress, "you got to keep him occupied. Because *I* ain't going to."

"You have to be around some, though," the waitress said.

"I ain't saying I won't be around. I say I won't keep him occupied."

The waitress looked toward Delia before Delia could look away. She had those bachelor's-button eyes you often see in redheads, and a round-chinned, innocent face. "My dad is planning a visit," she told Delia.

"Ah," Delia said, reaching for her book.

"He wasn't all that thrilled when me and Rick here got married."

The waitress and the cook were married? Delia was afraid that if she started reading now, they would think she disapproved too; so she marked her place on the page with one finger and said, "I'm sure he'll accept it eventually."

"Oh, he's accepted it, all right! Or says he has. But now whenever Rick sees him, he always gets to remembering how ugly Daddy acted at the start."

"I can't stand to be around the man," Rick said sadly.

"Daddy walks into a room and Rick is like, *whap!* and his mouth slams shut."

"Then Teensy here feels the pressure and goes to talking a mile a minute, nothing but pure silliness."

Delia knew what that was like. When her sister Linda was married to the Frenchman, whom their father had detested . . .

But she couldn't tell them that. She was sitting in this booth alone, utterly alone, without the conversational padding of father, sisters, husband, children. She was a person without a past. She took a breath to speak and then had nothing to say. It was Teensy who finally broke the silence. "Well," Teensy said, "at least we've got ourselves a few days to prepare for this." And she went off to wait on a couple who had just entered.

When Delia walked out of the café, she felt she was surrounded by a lighter kind of air than usual—thinner, more transparent—and she crossed the street with a floating gait. Just inside Belle's front door she found an array of letters scattered beneath the mail slot, but she didn't pick them up, didn't even check the names on the envelopes, because she knew for a fact that none of them was hers.

Upstairs, she went about her coming-home routine: putting away her things, showering, doing her laundry. Meanwhile she kept an ear out for Belle's return, because she would have moved more quietly with someone else in the house. But she could tell she had the place to herself.

When every last task was completed, she climbed into bed with her library book. If there had been a chair she would have sat up to read, but this was her only choice. She wondered whether Mr. Lamb's room was any better equipped. She supposed she could request a chair from Belle. That would mean a conversation, though, and Delia was avoiding conversation as much as possible. Heaven forbid they should get to be two cozy, chatty lady friends, exchanging news of their workdays every evening.

She propped her pillow against the metal rail at the head of the cot and leaned back. For this first little bit, the light from outdoors was enough to read by—a slant of warm gold that made her feel pleasantly lazy. She could hear a baby crying in the house across the street. A woman far away called, "Robbie! Kenny!" in that bell-like, two-note tune that mothers everywhere fetch their children home with. Delia read on, turning pages with a restful sound. She was interested in Gatsby's story but not what you would call carried away. It would serve to pass the evening, was all.

The light grew dimmer, and she switched on the goosenecked lamp that craned over her shoulder from the windowsill. Now the children across the street, released from the supper table, were playing something argumentative outdoors. Delia heard them for a while but gradually forgot to listen, and when she thought of them again she realized they must have gone in to bed. Night had fallen, and moths were thumping against the screen. Down in the street, a car door closed; heels clopped across the porch; Belle entered the house and went directly to the front room, where she started talking on the phone. "You know it's got great resale value," Delia heard, before forgetting to listen to that as well. Later she stopped reading for a moment and heard only silence, inside and out, except for the distant traffic on 380. It was cooler now, and she felt grateful for the lamp's small circle of warmth.

She came to the end of her book, but she kept rereading the final sentence till her eyes blurred over with tears. Then she placed the book on the floor and reached up to switch the lamp off so she could sit weeping in the dark— the very last step in her daily routine.

She wept without a thought in her head, heaving silent sobs that racked her chest and contorted her mouth. Every few minutes she blew her nose on the strip of toilet paper she kept under her pillow. When she felt completely drained, she gave a deep, shuddering sigh and said aloud, "Ah, well." Then she blew her nose one last time and lay down to sleep.

It amazed her that she always slept so soundly.

The toddler wanted the pigeons to eat from his fingers. He squatted in their midst, his bulky corduroy bottom just inches from the ground, and held a crouton toward them. But the pigeons strutted around him with shrewd, evasive glances, and when it dawned on him that they would never come closer he suddenly toppled backward, not giving the slightest warning, and pedaled the air in a fury. Delia smiled, but only behind the shield of her newspaper.

Today there was no further mention of her disappearance. She wondered if the authorities had forgotten her that quickly.

She folded the Metro section and laid it on the bench beside her. She reached for the cup of yogurt at her left and then noticed, out of the corner of her eye, the woman who stood watching her from several yards away.

Her heart gave a lurch. She said, "Eliza?"

Eliza moved forward abruptly, as if she had just this second determined something.

There was no one beside her. No one behind her.

No one.

She was wearing a dress—a tailored tan shirtwaist that dated from the time when they still had a Stewart's department store. Eliza almost never wore dresses. This must be a special occasion, Delia thought, and then she thought, *Why, I am the occasion.* She rose, fumbling with her yogurt cup. "Hello, Eliza," she said.

"Hello, Delia."

They stood awkwardly facing each other, Eliza gripping a boxy leather purse in both hands, until Delia recollected the old man on the east bench. He appeared to be intent on his magazine, but that didn't fool her in the least. "Would you like to take a walk?" she asked Eliza.

"We could," Eliza said stiffly.

She was probably angry. Well, of course she was angry. Bundling her lunch things into the trash basket, Delia felt like a little girl hiding some mischief. She sensed she was blushing, too. Hateful thin-skinned complexion, always giving her away. She slung the strap of her handbag over her shoulder and set off across the square, with Eliza lagging a step behind as if to accentuate Delia's willfulness, her lack of consideration. When they reached the street, Delia stopped and turned to face her. "I guess you think I shouldn't have done this," she said.

"I didn't say that. I'm waiting to hear your reasons."

Delia started walking again. If she had known Eliza would pop up this way, she would have invented some reasons ahead of time. It was ridiculous not to have any.

"Mr. Sudler thought you were a battered wife," Eliza said.

"Who?"

"The roofer. Vernon Sudler."

"Oh, Vernon," Delia said. Yes, of course: he would have seen the newspaper.

They crossed the street and headed north. Delia had planned to visit the thrift shop, but now she didn't know where she was going.

"He phoned us in Baltimore," Eliza said. "He asked for—"

"Baltimore! What were you doing in Baltimore?"

"Why, we packed up and drove there after you left. Surely you didn't think we'd stay at the beach."

Actually, Delia *had* thought that. But she could see now it would have looked strange: everybody slathering on the suntan lotion as usual, industriously blowing air into their rafts while the policemen gave their bloodhounds a sniff of Delia's slippers.

"We thought at first you'd gone to Baltimore yourself," Eliza was saying. "You can imagine the fuss with the floor refinishers when all of us walked in. And when we didn't find you there . . . Well, thank goodness Mr. Sudler called. He called the house last night, inquiring how to get in touch with me personally, and as luck would have it I was the one who answered. So he said he could swear you hadn't been kidnapped, but he hesitated to tell the police because he believed you'd had good cause to run away. He said you got out of his van at a church that counsels battered women."

"I did?"

Delia stopped in front of the florist's shop.

"You saw their signboard and asked him to let you out, he said."

"Signboard?"

"And also there'd been some discussion, he said, something you two were discussing that made him wonder later if . . . But he wouldn't tell me your whereabouts, in case your husband was dangerous. 'Dangerous!' I said. 'Why, Sam Grinstead is the kindest man alive!' I said. But Mr. Sudler was very fixed in his mind. He said, 'I only called to tell you she's all right, and I want to say too I didn't know at the time that she was running away. She just begged me for a ride to this certain town,' he said, 'and claimed that she had family there, so I didn't see the harm.' Then he said not to tell Sam, but of course I did tell Sam; I could hardly keep it a secret. I told Sam I would come talk to you first and find out how things stood."

She waited. She was going to make Delia ask. All right. "And what did Sam say back?" Delia asked.

"He said well *naturally* I should come. He agreed completely."

"Oh."

Another wait.

"And he quite understood that I couldn't divulge which town it was till we'd talked."

"I see," Delia said.

Then she said, "But how did *you* know the town?"

"Why, because you told Mr. Sudler you had family there."

"Family. Um . . ."

"Our mother's family! In Bay Borough."

"Mother's family lives in Bay Borough?"

"Well, they used to. Maybe some still do, but nobody I would have heard of. You knew that. Bay Borough? Where Aunt Henny lived? And Great-Uncle Roscoe had his chicken farm just west of?"

"That was in Bay Borough?"

"Where else!"

"I never realized," Delia said.

"I can't imagine why not. Shoot, there's even a Weber Street— Grandmother Carroll's maiden name. I crossed it coming in from Three eighty. And a Carroll Street just south of here, if I remember correctly. Isn't there a Carroll Street?"

"Well, yes," Delia said, "but I thought that was the other Carrolls. The Declaration of Independence Carrolls."

"No, dear heart, it's our Carrolls," Eliza said comfortably. Proving her point had evidently put her in a better mood.

They started walking again, passing the dentists' office and the optician's. "In fact, I believe we're related to the man who started this town," Eliza said. "But only by marriage."

"The man . . . You mean George Bay?"

"Right."

"George Bay the deserter?"

"Well, you're a fine one to talk, might I mention."

Delia flinched.

"So I drove on over this morning," Eliza said, "and inquired anywhere I thought you might be staying. Turns out there's only one inn, not counting that sleazy little motel on Union Street. And when I didn't find you there I figured I'd keep an eye on the square, because it looked to be the kind of square that everybody in town passes through at one time of day or another."

They were abreast of Mr. Pomfret's office now. If he had returned from lunch he could glance out the front window and see her walking by. Miss Grinstead with a companion! Acting sociable! She hoped he was still in the Bay Arms Restaurant with his cronies. At George Street she steered Eliza left. They passed Pet Heaven, where a boy was arranging chew toys next to the sacks of kibble.

"Delia," Eliza said, "Mr. Sudler had it wrong, didn't he? I mean, is there some . . . problem you want to tell me about?"

"Oh, no," Delia said.

"Ah." Eliza suddenly looked almost pretty. "See there? I told him so!" she cried. "I told him I was positive you just needed a little breather. You know what the police said? When we called them, this one policeman said, 'Folks,' he said, 'I'll wager any amount she is perfectly safe and healthy.' Said, 'The most surprising number of women seem to take it into their heads to walk out during family vacations.' Did you know that? Isn't that odd?"

"Hmm," Delia said. Her feet felt very burdensome. She could just barely drag them along.

"I guess he'd had lots of experience, working in Bethany Beach and all."

"Yes, I guess he had," Delia said.

"So should we collect your things, Dee?"

"My things," Delia said. She stopped short.

"I'm parked down next to the square. Do you have any luggage?"

Something hard rose up in Delia's throat—a kind of stubbornness, only fiercer. She was taken aback by the force of it. "No!" she said. She swallowed. "I mean, no, I'm not going with you."

"Pardon?"

"I want . . . I need . . . I have a place now, I mean a job, a position, and a place to stay. See? There's where I live," Delia said, gesturing toward Belle's. The gauze curtains in the downstairs windows looked like bandages, she noticed.

"You have a house?" Eliza asked incredulously.

"Well, a room. Come see! Come inside!"

She took Eliza's elbow and drew her toward the porch. Eliza hung back, her arm as rigid as a chicken wing. "A real estate agent owns it," Delia told her as she opened the door. "A *woman* real estate agent, very nice. The rent is extremely reasonable."

"I should think so," Eliza said, gazing about.

"I work for a lawyer just around the corner. He's the only lawyer in town and he handles everything, wills, estates . . . and I have total charge of his office. I bet you didn't think I could do that, did you? You probably thought it was just because I was Daddy's daughter that I worked in the office at home, but now I'm finding . . ."

They were climbing the stairs, Delia in front. She wished Belle would hang some pictures. Either that or put up new wallpaper. "Basically this whole floor is mine," she said, "because the other boarder travels during the week. So I have a private bathroom, see?" She waved toward it. She unlocked the door to her room and walked in. "All mine," she said, setting her handbag on the bureau.

Eliza advanced slowly.

"Isn't it perfect?" Delia asked. "I know it might seem a bit bare, but—"

"Delia, are you telling me you plan to live here?"

"I do live here!"

"But . . . forever?"

"Yes, why not?" Delia said.

She kept feeling the urge to swallow again, but she didn't give in to it. "Sit down," she told Eliza. "Could I offer you some tea?"

"Oh, I . . . no, thanks." Eliza took a tighter grip on her purse. She seemed out of place in these surroundings— somebody from home, with that humble, faded look that home people always have. "Let me make sure I'm understanding this," she said.

"I could heat up the water in no time. Just have a seat on the bed."

"You are telling me you're leaving us forever," Eliza said, not moving. "You plan to stay on permanently in Bay Borough. You're leaving your husband, and you're leaving all three of your children, one of whom is still in high school."

"In high school, yes, and fifteen years old, and able to manage without me fine and dandy," Delia said. To her horror, she felt tears beginning to warm her eyelids. "Better than with me, in fact," she continued firmly. "How are the kids, by the way?"

"They're bewildered; what would you expect?" Eliza said.

"But are they doing all right otherwise?"

"Do you care?" Eliza asked her.

"Of course I care!"

Eliza moved away. Delia thought she planned to relent and take a seat, but no, she went to gaze out the front window. "Sam, as you might imagine, is just dumbfounded," she announced, with her back to Delia.

"Yes, he must wish now he'd chosen Daughter One or Two instead," Delia said.

Eliza wheeled around. She said, "Delia, what is the *matter* with you? Have you totally lost your senses? Here's this wonderful, model husband roaming the house like a zombie, and your children not knowing *what* to think, and the neighbors all atwitter, and the TV people and newspapers spreading our names across the state of Maryland—"

"It's been on TV?"

"Every station in Baltimore! Big color photograph flashing on the screen: 'Have you seen this woman?' "

"What photo did they use?" Delia asked.

"The one from Linda's wedding."

"That was years ago!"

"Well, most other times you were the one snapping the picture. We didn't have much to choose from."

"But that awful bridesmaid gown! With the shoulders that looked like the hanger was still inside!"

"Delia," Eliza said, "ever since Mr. Sudler phoned, I've been trying to figure out what could have made you walk away from us like that. Till now I'd thought you'd had it so easy. Baby of the family. Cute as a button. Miss Popularity in high school. Daddy's pet. It's true you lacked a mother, but you never seemed to notice. Well, you were only four years old when she died, and anyhow she was bedridden all your life. But now I think four years old was plenty old! Of course you noticed! You'd spent those afternoons playing in her room, for God's sake!"

"I don't remember," Delia said.

"Oh, you must. You and she had those paper dolls. You kept them in a shoe box on the floor of her closet, and every afternoon—"

"I don't remember anything about it!" Delia said. "Why do you keep insisting? I have no memory of her at all!"

"And then being Daddy's pet was kind of a mixed blessing, I guess. When he discouraged you from applying to college, took it for granted you'd come to work in the office . . . well, I wouldn't blame you for resenting that."

"I didn't resent it!"

"And then his dying: of course his dying would hit you harder than—"

"I don't see why in the world you're bringing all this up!" Delia said.

"Just hear me out, please. Dee, you know I believe that human beings live many lives."

Ordinarily, Delia would have groaned. Now, though, she was glad to see the talk veering in a new direction.

"Each life is a kind of assignment, I believe," Eliza told her. "You're given this one assigned slot each time you come to earth, this little square of experience to work through. So even if your life has been troubled, I believe it's what you're meant to deal with on this particular go-round."

"How do you know my assignment doesn't include Bay Borough?" Delia asked her.

A ripple of uncertainty crossed Eliza's forehead.

Delia said, "Eliza, um, I was wondering . . ."

"Yes?" Eliza said eagerly.

"Can you tell me if they brought the cat home from the beach?"

A mistake. Something closed over behind Eliza's eyes. "The cat!" she said. "Is that all you care about?"

"Of course it's not all I care about, but he *was* kind of skulking under furniture when I left, and I didn't know if they'd remember to—"

"They remembered," Eliza said shortly. "What for, I can't imagine. Durn creature is getting so old he snores even when he's awake."

"Old?" Delia said.

"They packed all your clothes and your casseroles too," Eliza said. "Poor Susie had to pack your—Delia? Are you crying?"

"No," Delia said in a muffled voice.

"Are you crying about the *cat*?"

"No, I said!"

Well, she knew he wasn't a kitten anymore. (Such a *merry* kitten he'd been—a kitten with a sense of humor, slinking theatrically around the forbidden houseplants and then giving her a smirk.) But she had thought of him as still in his prime, and only now did she recall how he had started pausing lately as if to assemble himself before attempting the smallest leap. How she had swatted him off the counter once this spring and he had fallen clumsily, scrabbling with his claws, landing in an embarrassed heap and then hastily licking one haunch as if he had intended to take that pose all along.

She widened her eyes to keep the tears from spilling over.

"Delia," Eliza said, "is there something you're not telling me? Does this have something to do with that . . . man back home?"

Delia didn't bother acting puzzled. She said, "No, it's not about him." Then she went to the head of the bed, causing Eliza to take a step back. She reached under her pillow for the toilet paper and blew her nose. "I must be going crazy," she said.

"No, no! You're not crazy! Just a little, oh, tired, maybe. Just a little run-down. You know what I think?" Eliza asked. "I think it took more out of you than any of us realized, tending Daddy's last illness. You're probably anemic too! What you need is plain old physical rest. A vacation on your own. Yes, this wasn't such a bad idea, coming to Bay Borough! Few more days, couple of weeks, and you'll be home again, a new woman."

"Maybe so," Delia said unsteadily.

"And that's what I'm going to tell the police. 'She just went back to our people's place for some R and R,' I'll say. Because I do have to inform them, you know."

"I know."

"And I'll have to tell Sam."

"Yes."

"And then I expect he'll want to come talk things over."

Delia pressed the toilet paper to each eye.

"I'm not very good in these situations," Eliza said. She lifted one hand from her purse and placed it on Delia's shoulder.

"You're fine," Delia told her. "It's not your fault."

She felt saddened, all at once, by the fact that Eliza was wearing lipstick. (A sugary pink, lurid against her murky skin.) Eliza never bothered with makeup, as a rule. She must have felt the need to armor herself for this visit.

"I'll have Sam bring some of your clothes with him, shall I?" she was asking.

"No, thanks."

"A dress or two?"

"Nothing."

Eliza dropped her hand.

They left the room, Eliza walking ahead, and started down the stairs. Delia said, "So how's your *gardening*?" in a forced and sprightly tone.

"Oh . . . ," Eliza said. She arrived in the downstairs hall. "You'll need money," she told Delia.

"No, I won't."

"If I'd realized you weren't coming back with me . . . I don't have very much on me, but you're welcome to what there is."

"Honest, I don't want it," Delia said. "I'm making this huge, enormous salary at the lawyer's; I couldn't believe how much when he told me." She ushered Eliza out the door. "And you know I took the vacation cash. Five hundred dollars. I feel bad enough about that."

"Oh, we managed all right," Eliza said, eyeing a fibrous area in one porch floorboard.

Delia could have walked her to her car, or at least as far as the office, but that would have meant prolonging their parting. She had left her handbag upstairs, therefore, and she stood on the porch with her arms folded, in the attitude of someone about to go back indoors. "I'm sure you *managed*," she told Eliza. "It's not that. It's just that I feel bad I didn't start out with nothing. Start out . . . I don't know. Even."

"Even?"

"Even with the homeless or something. I don't know," Delia said. "I don't know what I mean!"

Eliza leaned forward and set her cheek against Delia's. "You're going to be fine," she told her. "This little rest is going to work wonders, take my word. And meanwhile, Dee—" She was about to turn away, but one last thought must have struck her. "Meanwhile, remember Great-Uncle Roscoe's favorite motto."

"What was that?"

" 'Never do anything you can't undo.' "

"I'll bear it in mind," Delia told her.

"Uncle Roscoe may have been a grump," Eliza said, "but he did show common sense now and then."

Delia said, "Drive safely."

She stood watching after Eliza—that short, economical, energetic figure—until she disappeared down the sidewalk. Then she went back in the house for her bag.

Climbing the stairs, she thought, *But if you never did anything you couldn't undo*—she set a hand on the splintery railing—*you'd end up doing nothing at all,* she thought. She was tempted to turn around and run after Eliza to tell her that, but then she couldn't have borne saying goodbye all over again.

8

Her book that night was *The Sun Also Rises*, but she didn't manage to finish it because she kept getting distracted. It was Friday, the start of the weekend. The traffic beneath her window had a livelier, more festive sound, and the voices of passersby were louder. "Hoo-*ee*! Here we come!" a teenage boy cried out. Momentarily, Delia lost track of the sentence she was reading. Around eight o'clock someone crossed the porch—not Belle but someone in flat-soled shoes walking slowly, as if weary or sad—and she lowered her book and listened. The front door opened, he entered the house, the stairs creaked upward one step at a time. Then the doorknob across the hall gave a rattle, and she thought, *Oh. The other boarder.*

She returned to her book, but every now and then a sound would break through her concentration—a hollow cough, the sliding of metal hangers along a closet rod. When she heard the shower running, she rose and tiptoed over to her door to make sure it was locked. Then she climbed back into bed and reread the paragraph she had just finished.

An hour or so later, Belle arrived. She had a man with her. Delia heard his hearty, booming laugh—not a laugh belonging to anyone she knew. "Now, be serious!" Belle said once. The TV came on downstairs, and the refrigerator door slammed shut with a dull clunk.

Mr. Lamb turned out to be an emaciated man in his forties, with straight brown hair and sunken eyes. Delia met him in the upstairs hall as she was setting out on some errands the following morning. "Hello," she said, and passed on, having resolved in advance to keep their exchange to a minimum. But she needn't have worried. Mr. Lamb flattened his back against the wall and smiled miserably at his shoes, mumbling something unintelligible. He was probably no happier than she about having to share the bathroom.

She was looking for a bank that kept Saturday hours. She wanted to cash Friday's paycheck. The check was drawn on First Farmers', just north of the square, but she found First Farmers' closed, and so she walked on to Bay Borough Federal. It was a cool, breezy day, with dark clouds overhead that turned the air almost lilac; and this part of town, which she had not seen since the afternoon she arrived, now looked completely different to her. It looked out of date, somehow. The buildings were so faded they seemed not colored but hand tinted, like an antique photograph.

"Would you be able to cash this for me?" she asked the teller at Bay Borough Federal.

The teller—a woman in squinty rhinestoned glasses—barely glanced at the signature before nodding. "Zeke Pomfret? No problem," she said.

So Delia signed over the first real paycheck of her life and received a few crisp bills in return. She was surprised at how much the taxes and whatnot could eat away from a salary.

Weber Street, East Street. Diagonally across the square. She carried her head high and set her feet down with precision. She might have been the heroine in some play or movie. And her intended audience, of course, was Sam.

It wasn't that she looked forward to his visit, certainly. She dreaded having to explain herself; she knew how lame and contradictory all her reasons would sound to him. And yet as early as yesterday afternoon, some part of her mind had been making its devious calculations. *Let's say it's two hours to Baltimore. Eliza could get home around, oh, say, four-thirty, so Sam could be here by six-thirty. Maybe seven. Or supposing he decided to finish up at the office first, supposing he had to buy gas . . .* And then later that night: *He must be waiting for the weekend. That would be much more sensible.*

Imagine if he came upon her this minute, heading toward the library for Saturday's book. Or pausing on the way home to rummage through a table of mugs in front of Katy's Kitchenware. Or stepping out of the Pinchpenny with the navy knit dress in a bag. Imagine if he were watching from the boardinghouse porch as she rounded the corner of George Street. He would see her skimming along, wearing professional gray, entirely at ease in this town he had never laid eyes on before. He would think, *Could that really be Delia?*

Or imagine if she climbed the stairs and found him waiting at the door of her room. "Why, Sam," she would say serenely, and she would draw her keys from her handbag—so official-looking, room key and office key on Mr. Pomfret's chrome ring—and open the door and tilt her head, inviting him inside. Or he would be inside already, having persuaded Belle to admit him. He would be standing at one of the windows. He would turn and see her entering with her burdens—her library book and her tea mug and new dress—and, "Here, let me help you with those," he would say, and she would say, "Thanks. I can manage."

But he wasn't there after all, and she set her things on the bed in total silence.

• • •

She went downstairs to pay her rent. Belle was home, she could tell. She heard sounds from behind the celery-colored door leading off the hall. She knocked and Belle called, "Come in!" meanwhile squeaking something, whirring something. It was a stationary bicycle, Delia discovered when she stepped inside. Belle was pedaling madly, flushed and overheated in a pink sweat suit strewn with tiny satin bows. "Whew!" she said when she saw Delia. Her living room, like the rest of the house, seemed furnished with pieces earlier tenants had discarded. A dingy plush sofa faced the TV; the coffee table bore a loopy design of ring-shaped water stains.

"I just wanted to pay my rent," Delia told her.

"Oh, thanks," Belle said, and without slowing her pedaling she stuffed the folded bills up one sleeve. "Everything all right?"

"Yes, fine."

"Great," Belle said, and she leaned diligently over the handlebars as Delia closed the door again.

Delia planned to go next to the Gobble-Up for some lunch things, but just as she was leaving the house a young man in uniform arrived on the porch. She thought at first he was some kind of soldier; the uniform was a khaki color, and his hair was prickly short. "Miz Grinstead?" he said.

"Yes."

"I'm Chuck Akers, from the Polies."

It took her a moment to translate that.

"Think I could have a word with you?" he asked.

"Certainly," she said. She turned to lead him inside and then realized she had nowhere to take him. Her bedroom was out of the question, and she couldn't very well use Belle's living room. So she turned back and asked, "What can I do for you?" and they ended up conducting their business right there on the porch.

"You *are* Miz Cordelia F. Grinstead," he said.

"Yes."

"I understand you came here of your own free will."

"Yes, I did."

"Nobody kidnapped you, coerced you . . ."

"Nobody else had anything to do with it."

"Well, I surely wish you had thought to make that clear before you left."

"I'm sorry," she said. "Next time I will."

Next time!

She wondered when on earth she supposed that would be.

Saturday, Sunday. The elaborate filling of empty white hours, the glad pounce upon the most inconsequential task. Saturday evening she ate at home, little cartons of Chinese takeout, and she read *Daisy Miller* late into the night. Sunday breakfast was tea and a grocery-store muffin in bed, but she made an event of lunch. She ate at the Bay Arms Restaurant, a stodgy, heavily draped and carpeted establishment, where all the other tables were occupied by families in church clothes. Her inclination was to get the meal over with as fast as possible, but she forced herself to order a soup course, a main course, and a dessert, and she worked her way through all this in a measured and leisurely fashion, fixing her gaze upon a point in the middle distance.

Once Susie had announced, during a particularly feminist stage in her life, that every woman ought to learn how to dine alone in a formal restaurant without a book. Delia wished Susie could see her now.

In fact, maybe Sam would bring the children with him when he came. Maybe they would walk right into the Bay Arms; it was not impossible that they would track her down. She was wearing her new navy dress from the Pinchpenny. It looked very becoming, she thought. She requested a second cup of coffee and sat on awhile.

Out of nowhere, she longed for a cigarette, although she had not smoked since tenth grade.

When she left the restaurant she headed north to the library, planning to choose that night's reading. But the library door was locked tight and the venetian blinds were slanted shut. She should have realized the place would be closed on Sundays. Now she would have to *buy* a book—invest actual money.

In the pharmacy on George Street, she found one rack of paperbacks—mostly mysteries, a few romances. She chose a romance called *Moon Above Wyndham Moor*. A woman in a long cloak was swooning on the cover, precariously supported by a bearded man who encircled her waist with his left arm while he brandished a sword with his right. Delia hid the book in her purse after she had paid for it. Then she continued toward Belle's, taking quick, firm steps so that anybody watching would think, *That woman looks completely self-reliant.*

But there was no one watching.

She remembered how, as a child, she used to arrange herself in the front yard whenever visitors were due. She remembered one time when her great-uncle Roscoe was expected, and she had placed her doll cradle on the grass and assumed a pretty pose next to it till Uncle Roscoe stepped out of his car. "Why, looky there!" he cried. "It's little Lady Delia." He smelled of cough drops, the bitter kind. She had thought she retained no mental picture of Uncle Roscoe, and she was startled to find him bobbing up like this, shifting his veiny leather gladstone bag to his other hand so he could clamp her shoulder as they proceeded toward the house. But what had the occasion been? Why had he come to visit, wearing his rusty black suit? She suspected she would rather not know the answer.

"I was singing my doll a lullaby," she had told him in a confiding tone.

She had always been such a *false* child, so eager to conform to the grown-ups' views of her.

Moon Above Wyndham Moor was a disappointment. It just didn't seem very believable, somehow. Delia kept lowering it to stare blankly at the dim, far corners of the room. She checked to see how many pages remained. She cocked her head toward the sound of Mr. Lamb's radio. He had been playing it all weekend, though never so loudly that she could decipher the announcer's words. On the porch overhang outside, raindrops were falling one by one. She missed the noises of the family across the street. They must have closed their windows against the weather.

Is he not going to come at all, then?

On Monday morning Mr. Pomfret let her know, in a roundabout way, that he had learned the truth. "I see you have a new dress, *Mrs.* Grinstead," he said, eyeing her significantly. But she pretended not to understand, and by noon he had drifted back to "Miss." Not that she much cared. She felt oddly lackluster today. The rain didn't help. She had been forced to buy an umbrella at the pharmacy, and during lunch hour she went to the dime store and purchased an inexpensive gray cardigan made of something synthetic. Miss Grinstead's standards were slipping, it appeared. She poked her hands dispiritedly through the clingy, tubelike sleeves.

Because of the rain, she couldn't picnic on her usual park bench, and she wasn't up to the social demands of Rick-Rack's or the Bay Arms; so she took her cup of yogurt back to her room. She opened the front door, stepping over the mail, and started up the stairs. Then she halted and turned to look back at one of the envelopes on the floor.

A cream-colored envelope—or more like custard-colored, really. She knew that shade well. And she knew the name embossed in brown on the upper-left-hand corner: SAMUEL A. GRINSTEAD, M.D.

He would settle for just writing her a letter?

She stooped to pick it up. *Mrs. Delia Grinstead,* the address read (Miss Manners would be appalled). *George Street, house w/ low front porch next door to Gobble-Up Grocery. Bay Borough, Maryland.*

She took it to her room before she opened it. *Delia,* he wrote. No *Dear. Delia, it is my understanding from Eliza that . . .*

He had used the office typewriter, the one with the tipsy *e*, and he hadn't bothered to change the margins from when she'd done the bills. The body of the letter was scarcely four inches wide.

Delia, it is my understanding from Eliza that you have requested some time on your own due to various stresses including your father's recent death, etc.

Naturally, I would much rather you had forewarned us. You cannot have been unaware of the anxiety you would cause, simply strolling off down the beach like that and disappearing. ~~Do you have any idea how it feels to~~

Nor am I entirely clear on what "stresses" you are referring to. Of course I realize you and your father were close. But his death after all occurred four and a half months ago. ~~and frankly I feel~~ *Perhaps you view me as one of the stresses. If so this is regrettable but* ~~I have always tried to be a satisfactory husb~~ *vowed while I was growing up that I would be a rock for my wife and children and to the best of my belief I have fulfilled that vow* ~~and I don't understand what~~ *but if you have any complaints against me I am certainly willing to hear what they are.*

In the meantime you may rest assured that I will not invade your privacy. ~~XXXXXXXXXXXXXXXXXXXXXXXXXXXXXXXX~~ ~~XXXXXXXXXXXXXXXXXXXXXXXXXXXXXXXXXXXXXXXXXX~~ ~~XXXXXXXXXXXXXXXXXXXXXXXXXXXXX~~

Sam

He had made his first four corrections with the hyphen key—easy for Delia to read through—but the fifth was so thoroughly x-ed over that she couldn't figure it out even when she held the letter up to the light. Well, no doubt that was for the best. It was probably something even more obtuse than his other remarks, and Lord knows those were obtuse enough.

Not invade her privacy! Just sit back and give up on her, as if she were a missing pet or mitten or dropped penny!

She might have known, she reflected. All this proved was how right she had been to leave.

Her teeth were chattering, and her new sweater was no help. Instead of eating her lunch, she slipped off her shoes and climbed into bed. She lay shivering beneath the one blanket, with her jaw set against the cold and her arms wrapped around her ribs, hugging her own self tightly.

9

No wonder she'd been unable to picture winter in Bay Borough! Underneath, she realized now, she had expected Sam to come fetch her long before then. She resembled those runaway children who never, no matter how far they travel, truly mean to leave home.

So anyhow. Here she was. And the entire rest of her life was stretching out empty before her.

She took to sitting on the bed in the evenings and staring into space. It was too much to say that she was thinking. She certainly had no conscious thoughts, or at any rate, none that mattered. Most often she was, oh, just watching the air, as she used to do when she was small. She used to gaze for hours at those multicolored specks that swarm in a room's atmosphere. Then Linda had informed her they were dust motes. That took the pleasure out of it, somehow. Who cares about mere dust? But now she thought Linda was wrong. It was air she watched, an infinity of air endlessly rearranging itself, and the longer she watched the more soothed she felt, the more mesmerized, the more peaceful.

She was learning the value of boredom. She was clearing out her mind. She had always known that her body was just a shell she lived in, but it occurred to her now that her mind was yet another shell—in which case, who was "she"? She was clearing out her mind to see what was left. Maybe there would be nothing.

Often she didn't begin the night's reading till nine or nine-thirty, which meant she could no longer finish a novel in one sitting; so she switched to short stories instead. She would read a story, watch the air awhile, and read another. She would mark her page with a library slip and listen to the sounds from outdoors—the swish of cars, the chirring of insects, the voices of the children in the house across the street. On hot nights the older children slept on a second-floor porch, and they always talked among themselves until their parents intervened. "Am I going to have to *come upstairs?*" was their father's direst threat. That would quiet them, but only for a minute.

Delia wondered if Sam knew that Carroll was scheduled for tennis lessons the middle two weeks in July. You couldn't depend on Carroll to remember on his own. And did anyone recall that this was dentist month? Well, probably Eliza did. Without Eliza, Delia could never have left her family so easily.

She wasn't sure if that was something to be thankful for.

The fact was, Delia was expendable. She was an extra. She had lived out her married life like a little girl playing house, and always there'd been a grown-up standing ready to take over—her sister or her husband or her father.

Logically, she should have found that a comfort. (She used to be so afraid of dying while her children were small.) But instead, she had suffered pangs of jealousy. Why was it Sam, for instance, that everybody turned to in times of crisis? He always got to be the reasonable one, the steady and reliable one; she was purely decorative. But how had that come about? Where had she been looking while that state of affairs developed?

She read another story, which contained several lengthy nature descriptions. She enjoyed nature as much as the next person, but you could carry it too far, she felt.

And was anybody keeping an eye on Sam's health? He had that tendency, lately, to overdo the exercise. But, *It's none of my concern,* Delia reminded herself. His letter had freed her. No more need to count cholesterol grams; pointless to note that the Gobble-Up carried fat-free mayonnaise.

She called back some of the letter's phrases: *You cannot have been unaware* and *Nor am I entirely clear.* Bloodless phrases, emotionless phrases. She supposed the whole neighborhood knew he hadn't married her for love.

Again she saw the three daughters arrayed on the couch—Sam's memory, originally, but she seemed to have adopted it. She saw her father in his armchair and Sam in the Boston rocker. The two of them discussed a new arthritis drug while Delia sipped her sherry and slid glances toward Sam's hands, reflecting on how skilled they looked, how doctorly and knowing. It might have been the unaccustomed sherry that made her feel so giddy.

Just a few scattered moments, she thought, have a way of summing up a person's life. Just five or six tableaux that flip past again and again, like tarot cards constantly reshuffled and redealt. A patch of sunlight on a window seat where someone big was scrubbing Delia's hands with a washcloth. A grade-school spelling bee where Eliza showed up unannounced and Delia saw her for an instant as a stranger. The gleam of Sam's fair head against the molasses-dark wood of the rocker. Her father propped on two pillows, struggling to speak. And Delia walking south alongside the Atlantic Ocean.

In this last picture, she wore her gray secretary dress. (Not all such memories are absolutely accurate.) She wore the black leather shoes she had bought at Bassett Bros. The clothes were wrong, but the look was right— the firmness, the decisiveness. That was the image that bolstered her.

"Whenever I hear the word 'summer,' " one of the three marriageable maidens announced (Eliza, of course), "I smell this sort of melting smell, this yellow, heated, melting smell." And Linda chimed in, "Yes, that's the way she is! Eliza can smell nutmeg day at the spice plant clear downtown! Also anger." And Delia smiled at her sherry. "Ah," Sam murmured thoughtfully. Did he guess their ulterior motives? That Eliza was trying to sound interesting, that Linda was pointing out Eliza's queerness, that Delia was hoping to demonstrate the dimple in her right cheek?

The washcloth scrubbing her hands was as rough and warm as a mother cat's tongue. The squat, unhappy-looking young woman approaching Miss Sutherland's desk changed into Delia's sister. "I wish . . . ," her father whispered, and his cracked lips seemed to tear apart rather than separate, and he turned his face away from her. The evening after he died, she went to bed with a sleeping pill. She was so susceptible to drugs that she seldom took even an aspirin, but she gratefully swallowed the pill Sam gave her and slept through the night. Only it was more like *burrowing* through the night, tunneling through with some blunt, inadequate instrument like a soup spoon, and she woke in the morning muddled and tired and convinced that she had missed something. Now she thought what she had missed was her own grief. Why that rush toward forgetfulness? she asked herself. Why the hurry to leap past grief to the next stage?

She wondered what her father had been wishing for. She hadn't been able to figure it out at the time, and maybe he had assumed she just didn't care. Tears filled her eyes and rolled down her cheeks. She made no effort to stop them.

Didn't it often happen, she thought, that aged parents die exactly at the moment when other people (your husband, your adolescent children) have stopped being thrilled to see you coming? But a parent is always thrilled, always dwells so lovingly on your face as you are speaking. One of life's many ironies.

She reached for her store of toilet paper and blew her nose. She felt that something was loosening inside her, and she hoped she would go on crying all night.

In the house across the street, a child called, "Ma, Jerry's kicking me." But the voice was distant and dreamy, and the response was mild. "Now, Jerry . . ." Gradually, it seemed, the children were dropping off. Those who remained awake allowed longer pauses to stretch between their words, and spoke more and more languidly, until finally the house was silent and no one said anything more.

• • •

Independence Day had passed nearly unobserved in Bay Borough—no pa-rades, no fireworks, nothing but a few red-white-and-blue store windows. Bay Day, however, was another matter. Bay Day marked the anniversary of George Pendle Bay's famous dream. It was celebrated on the first Satur-day in August, with a baseball game and a picnic in the town square. Delia knew all about it because Mr. Pomfret was chairman of the Recre-ation Committee. He had had her type a letter proposing they replace the baseball game with a sport that demanded less space—for instance, horse-shoes. The square, he argued, was so small and so thickly treed. But Mayor Frick, who was the son and grandson of earlier mayors and evi-dently reigned supreme, wrote back to say that the baseball game was a "time-honored tradition" and should continue.

"Tradition!" Mr. Pomfret fumed. "Bill Frick wouldn't know a tradi-tion if it bit him in the rear end. Why, at the start it was *always* horse-shoes. Then Ab Bennett came back from the minors with his tail between his legs, and Bill Frick Senior got up a baseball game to make him look good. But Ab doesn't even play anymore! He's too old. He runs the lemonade stand."

Delia had no interest in Bay Day. She planned to spend the morning on errands and give the square a wide berth. But first she found everything closed, and then the peculiar weather (a fog as dense as oatmeal and al-most palpably soft) lured her to keep walking, and by the time she reached the crowd she felt so safe in her cloak of mist that she joined in.

The four streets surrounding the square were blocked off and spread with picnic blankets. Food booths lined the sidewalks, and strolling vendors hawked pennants and balloons. Even this much, though, Delia had trouble making out, because of the fog. People approaching seemed to be material-izing, their features assembling themselves at the very last instant. The effect was especially unsettling in the case of young boys on skateboards. Elated by the closed streets, they careened through the crowd recklessly, looming up entire and then dissolving. All sounds were muffled, cotton-padded, and yet eerily distinct. Even smells were more distinct: the scent of bergamot hung tentlike over two old ladies pouring tea from a thermos.

"Delia!" someone said.

Delia turned to see Belle Flint unfolding a striped canvas sand chair. She was wearing a vivid pink romper and an armload of bangle bracelets that jingled when she sat down. Delia hadn't been sure till now that Belle remembered her name; so she reacted out of surprise. "Why, hello, Belle," she said, and Belle said, "Do you know Vanessa?"

The woman she waved a hand toward was the young mother from the square. She was seated just beyond Belle on a bedspread the same color as the fog, with her toddler between her knees. "Have some of my spread," she told Delia.

"Oh, thanks, but—" Delia said. And then she said, "Yes, maybe I will," and she went over to sit next to her.

"Get a load of the picnic lunches," Belle told Delia. "It's some kind of contest; they ought to give prizes. What did you bring?"

"Well, nothing," Delia said.

"A woman after my own heart," Belle said, and then she leaned closer to whisper, "Selma Frick's brought assorted hors d'oeuvres in stacked bamboo baskets. Polly Pomfret's brought whole fresh artichokes on a bed of curried crayfish."

"Me, I'm with the teenagers," Vanessa said, handing her son an animal cracker. "I grab something from a booth whenever I get hungry."

She reminded Delia of those girl-next-door movie stars from the 1940s, slim and dark and pretty in a white blouse and flared red shorts, with shoulder-length black hair and bright-red lipstick. Her son was over-dressed, Delia thought—typical for a first child. In his corduroys and long-sleeved shirt, he looked cross and squirmy, and for good reason; Delia could feel the heat of the pavement rising through the bedspread.

"How old is your little boy?" she asked Vanessa.

"Eighteen months last Wednesday."

Eighteen months! Delia could have said. Why, she remembered that age. When Ramsay was eighteen months, he used to . . . and Susie, that was when Susie learned to . . .

Such a temptation, it was, to prove her claims to membership—the labor pains, the teething, the time when she too could have told her baby's age to the day. But she resisted. She merely smiled at the child's shimmer of blond hair and said, "I suppose he gets his coloring from his father."

"Most likely," Vanessa said carelessly.

"Vanessa's a single parent," Belle told Delia.

"Oh!"

"I have no idea who Greggie's father might be," Vanessa said, wiping her son's mouth with a tissue. "Or rather, I have a few ideas, but I could never narrow it down to just one."

"Oh, I see," Delia said, and she turned quickly toward the ball game.

Not that there was much to look at, in the fog. Apparently home plate lay in the southeast corner. It was from there she heard the *plock*! of a hit. But all she could discern was second base, which was marked by a park bench. While she watched, a runner loped up to settle on the bench, and the player already seated there rose and caught a ball out of nowhere and threw it back into the mist. Then he sat down again. The runner leaned forward with his elbows on his knees and stared intently toward home plate, although how he hoped to see that far Delia couldn't imagine.

"Derek Ames," Belle informed her. "One of our best hitters."

Delia said, "I would think the statue would get in the way."

"Oh, George plays shortstop," Belle said, giggling. "No, seriously: there's a rule. Bean the statue and you walk to first. It used to count as an automatic run till Rick Rackley moved here. But you know professional athletes: they excel at *any* sport. It got so every time Rick came to bat, he laid old Georgie low."

"Rick Rackley's a professional athlete?"

"Or was, till his knee went. Where've you been living—Mars? Of course, his game was football, but believe me, the Blues are lucky to have him on their side. That's who we're watching, in case you didn't know: the Blues versus the Grays. Blues are the new folks in town; Grays have been here all along. Whoops! That sounds to me like a homer."

Another *plock*! had broken through from the southeast corner. Delia gazed upward but saw only opaque white flannel. In the outfield, such as it was (a triangle of grass behind second base), one player called to another, "Where's it headed?"

"Damned if I know," the second player said. Then, with a startled grunt, he caught the ball as it arrived in front of him. "Got it," he called to the first man.

"You see it?"

"I caught it."

"It came down already?"

"Right."

"Bobby caught that!" the first man shouted toward home plate.

"What say?"

"He caught it," someone relayed. "Batter's out."

"He's what?"

"He's out!"

"Where is the batter?"

"*Who* is the batter?"

Vanessa fed her son another animal cracker. "Fog on Bay Day is kind of a rule here," she told Delia. "I don't believe anyone's ever once got a good look at that game. So! Delia. How do you like working for Zeke Pomfret?"

"Well . . . he's okay," Delia said. She supposed she should have expected that her job would be common knowledge.

"He's a real fine lawyer, you know. If you decide to go ahead with your divorce, you could do worse than hire Zeke."

Delia blinked.

"Yes, he did just great with my ex-boyfriend's," Belle told her. "And he got Vanessa here's brother Jip out of jail, when Jip hit a spell of bad luck once."

"I haven't given much thought to, um, divorce," Delia said.

"Well, sure! No hurry! And anyhow, my ex-boyfriend's case was totally different from yours."

What did they imagine Delia's case was? She decided not to ask.

Belle was rummaging through her big purse. She pulled forth a pale-green bottle and a stack of paper cups. "Wine?" she asked the others. "It's a screw top. Don't tell Polly Pomfret. Yes, Norton's case was so straightforward, for one thing. He'd only been married a year. In fact, we met on his first anniversary. Met at a Gamblers' Weekend Special in Atlantic City, where he'd brought his wife to celebrate. He and I just sort of . . . gravitated, you know?" She passed Delia a cup of white wine. "It helped that his wife was one of those people who end up soldered to their slot machines. So one-two-three I move to Bay Borough, and we rent a little apartment together, and Zeke Pomfret goes to work on Norton's divorce."

The wine had a metallic aftertaste, like tinned grapefruit juice. Delia cradled the cup in both hands. She said, "I'm not really planning anything that definite just yet."

"Well, of course you're not."

"I'm really feeling sort of . . . blank right now. You know?"

"Of course you are!" both women said simultaneously.

In the square, the inning must have ended. The players they had been watching vanished and new players took shape, a new second baseman floating up by degrees and solidifying on the bench.

She dreamed Sam was driving a truck across the front lawn in Baltimore and the children were playing hide-and-seek directly in his path. They were little, though; not their present-day selves. She tried to call out and warn them, but her voice didn't work, and they were all run over. Then Ramsay stood up again, holding his wrist, and Sam climbed out of the truck and he fell down and tried to get up again, fell down and tried to get up, and the sight made Delia feel as if a huge, ragged wound had ripped open in her chest.

When she woke, her cheeks were wet. She had thought she was starting to lose her habit of crying at night, but now tears flooded her eyes and she gave in to wrenching sobs. She was haunted by the picture of Ramsay in those little brown sandals she'd forgotten he'd ever owned. She saw her children lined up on the lawn, still in their younger versions before they'd turned hard-shelled and spiky, before the boys had grown whiskers and Susie bought a diary with an unpickable brass lock. Those were the children she longed for.

One evening in September, she returned from work to find several envelopes bearing her name scattered across the hall floor. She knew they must be birthday cards—she was turning forty-one tomorrow—and she could tell they were from her family because of the wordy address. *(House w/ low front porch . . .)* The first card showed a wheelbarrow full of daisies. *A BIRTHDAY WISH*, it said, and inside, *Friendship and health / Laughter and cheer / Now and through / The coming year.* The signature was just *Ramsay*, with the tail of the *y* wandering off across the page in a halfhearted manner.

She carried the rest of her mail upstairs. No sense facing this in public. *Susie*, the next card was signed. *(Heartiest Congratulations and Many*

Happy Returns.) And nothing at all from Carroll, though she riffled through the envelopes twice. Well, it was easy to see what had happened. These cards were Eliza's idea. She had coaxed and cajoled the whole family into sending them. "All I'm asking," was a phrase she would have used. Or, "No one should have to pass a birthday without . . ." But Carroll, the stubborn one, had flatly refused. And Sam? Delia opened his envelope next. A color photo of roses in a blue-and-white porcelain vase. *Barrels of joy / Bushels of glee . . .* Signed, *Sam.*

Then a letter from Linda, in Michigan. *I want you to know that I sincerely wish you a happy birthday,* she wrote. *I don't hold it against you that you absconded like that even though it did mean we had to cut short our vacation which is the twins' only chance each year to get some sense of their heritage but anyhow, have a good day.* Below her signature were Marie-Claire's and Thérèse's—a prim strand of copperplate and a left-hander's gnarly crumple.

Dear Delia, Eliza wrote, on yet another rhymed card.

> *We are all fine but we hope you'll soon be home. I am taking care of the office paperwork for now, and all three kids have started back to school.*
> *Bootsy Fisher has phoned several times and also some of the neighbors but I tell everyone you're visiting relatives at the moment.*
> *I hope you have a good birthday. I remember the night you were born as if it were just last week. Daddy let Linda and me wait in the waiting room with the fathers, and when the nurse came out she told us, "Congratulations, kids, you can form a singing trio now and go on Arthur Godfrey," and that's how we knew you were a girl. I do miss you.*
>
> Love, Eliza

Delia kept that one. The others she discarded. Then she decided she might as well discard Eliza's too. Afterward she sat on her bed a long while, pressing her fingertips to her lips.

On her actual birthday, a package arrived from Sam's mother. It was roughly the size of a book, too thick to fit through the mail slot, so it stood inside the screen door, where Delia found it when she came home. She groaned when she recognized the writing. Eleanor was known for her extremely practical gifts—a metric-conversion tape measure, say, or a battery recharger, always wrapped in wrinkled paper saved from Christmas. This time, as Delia discovered when she took the package upstairs, it was a miniature reading light on a neck cord. Well, in fact . . . , she reflected. It would probably work much better than her lamp. She tucked it under her pillow, next to her stash of toilet paper.

There was a letter too, on Eleanor's plain buff stationery:

> Dear Delia,
>   This is just a little something I thought you might find helpful. On the few occasions when I've traveled myself, the reading light has generally been miserable. Perhaps you're having the same experience. If not, just pass this along to your favorite charity. (Lately I've been most dissatisfied with Goodwill but continue to feel that Retarded Citizens is a worthwhile organization.)
>   My best wishes for your birthday.
>   Love, Eleanor

Delia flipped it over, but all she found on the back was RECYCLED PAPER RECYCLED PAPER RECYCLED PAPER running across the bottom. She had expected indignation, or at least a few reproaches.

She remembered how, when she and Sam were first engaged, she had entertained such high hopes for Eleanor. She had thought she was finally getting a mother of her own. But that was before they met. Eleanor came to supper at the Felsons', arriving directly from the Home for Wayward Girls, where she volunteered as a typing teacher twice a week. Once the introductions were over, she hardly gave Delia a glance. All she talked about was the terrible, terrible poverty endured by the wayward girls and the staggering contrast of this meal—which, by the way, was merely pot roast sprinkled with onion-soup mix and an iceberg lettuce salad. "I asked this one poor child," Eleanor said, "I asked, 'Dear, could your people buy you a typewriter so you could work from your house after the baby arrives?' And she said, 'Miss, my family's so poor they can't even afford shampoo.' " A basket of rolls appeared before her. Eleanor gazed into it, looking puzzled, and passed it on. "I don't know what made her choose that example, of all things," she said. "Shampoo."

(Why was it that so many voices came wafting back to Delia these days? Sometimes as she fell asleep she heard them nattering on without her, as if everybody she'd ever known sat around her, conversing. Like people in a sickroom, she thought. Like people at a deathbed.)

Another present Eleanor had once given her was a tiny electric steamer gadget to freshen clothes during trips. This was some years back; Delia couldn't remember what she'd done with it. But the thing was, here in Bay Borough she could have put it to use. She could have touched up her office dresses, both of which had grown somewhat puckery at the seams after repeated hand laundering. It would certainly have been preferable to buying an iron and ironing board. Oh, why hadn't she kept the steamer? Why hadn't she brought it with her? How could she have been so shortsighted, and so ungrateful?

...

She didn't answer any of the birthday cards, but etiquette demanded a thank-you note to Eleanor. *The little light is very convenient,* she wrote. *Much better than the gooJenecked lamp I've been reading by up till now. So I've moved the lamp to the bureau which means I don't have to use the ceiling bulb and therefore the room looks much softer.* In this manner she contrived to cover the entire writing area of a U.S. postcard without really saying anything at all.

The next morning, while she was dropping the card in the mailbox near the office, she was suddenly struck by the fact that Eleanor had once worked in an office. She had put her son through college on a high-school secretary's salary—no small feat, as Delia could now appreciate. She wished she had thought to mention her job in her thank-you note. But maybe Eliza had said something. "Delia's employed by a lawyer," Eliza might have said. "She handles every detail for him. You should see her all dressed up for work; if you met her on the street, you wouldn't know her."

"Is that so?" Sam would ask. (Somehow, the listener had changed from Eleanor to Sam.) "Handles everything, you say. Not mislaying important files? Not lounging around the waiting room, reading trashy novels?"

Well, she'd spent more than half her life trying to win Sam's approval. She supposed she couldn't expect to break a habit like that overnight.

October came, and the weather grew cooler. The square filled up with yellow leaves. Some nights, Delia had to shut her windows. She bought a flannel nightgown and two long-sleeved dresses—one gray pinstripe, one forest green—and she started keeping an eye out for a good second-hand coat. It was not yet cold enough for a coat, but she wanted to be prepared.

On rainy days, now, she ate lunch at the Cue Stick 'n' Cola on Bay Street. She ordered coffee and a sandwich and watched the action at the one pool table. Vanessa often wheeled her stroller in to join her. While Greggie lurched among the chair legs like a brightly colored top, Vanessa would offer Delia thumbnail sketches of the players. "See the guy breaking? Buck Baxter. Moved here eight or ten years ago. Baxter as in Baxter Janitorial Supplies, but they say his father's disowned him. No, Greggie, the man doesn't want your cookie. Now, her I don't know," she said. She meant the diminutive, dark-haired young woman who was leaning across the pool table to shoot on tiptoe, her purple canvas pocketbook still slung over her shoulder. "Must be from outside. Leave him *alone*, Greggie. And the fellow in the cowboy boots, that's Belle's ex-boyfriend, Norton Grove. Belle was out of her mind to fall for him. Fickle? That man put fickle in the dictionary."

Delia was gathering an impression of Bay Borough as a town of misfits. Almost everybody here had run away from someplace else, or been run away *from*. And no longer did it seem so idyllic. Rick and Teensy Rackley were treated very coolly by some of the older citizens; the only two gay men she knew of seemed to walk about with no one but each other; there was talk of serious drug use in the consolidated high school; and Mr. Pomfret's appointment book was crammed with people feuding over property lines and challenging drunk-driving arrests.

Still, she felt contented here. She had her comfortable routine, her niche in the general scheme of things. Making her way from office to library, from library to café, she thought that her exterior self was instructing her interior self, much like someone closing his eyes and mimicking sleep in order to persuade sleep to come. It was not that her sadness had left her, but she seemed to operate on a smooth surface several inches above the sadness. She deposited her check each Saturday; she dined each Sunday at the Bay Arms Restaurant. People nodded now when they saw her, which she took not just for greeting but for confirmation: *Ah, yes, there's Miss Grinstead, exactly where she belongs.*

Although every so often something would stab her. A song from Ramsay's Deadhead period about knock-knock-knocking on heaven's door, for instance. Or a mother and a little girl hugging each other in front of the house across the street. "She's leaving me!" the mother called mock-plaintively to Delia. "Going off to her very first slumber party!"

Maybe Delia could pretend to herself that she was back in the days before her marriage. That she didn't miss her children at all because they hadn't been born yet.

But in retrospect it seemed she had missed them even then. Was it possible there had been a time when she hadn't known her children?

Dear Delia, Eleanor wrote. (She addressed her letter to 14 George Street this time.)

> I was so pleased to get your postcard. It's good to know that my little gift came in handy, and I'm glad you're doing some reading.
> I myself find it impossible to sleep if I don't read at least a few pages first, preferably from something instructive like biography or current events. For a while after Sam's father died I used to read the dictionary. It was the only thing with small enough divisions to fit my attention span. Also the information was so definite.
> Probably Sam has been marked by losing his father at such an early age. I meant to say that in my last note but I don't believe I did. And his father never had a strong personality. He was the kind of man who let all the bathwater drain away before he got out of the tub. Maybe it would worry a boy to think he might grow up to do the same.
> I hope I haven't overstepped.
>
> Love, Eleanor

Delia didn't know what to make of that. She understood it better when the next note came, some two weeks later. *Please forgive me if you felt I sounded "mother-in-lawish" and that's why you didn't answer my letter. I had no intention of offering excuses for my son. I've always said he was forty years old when he was born, and I realize that's not easy to live with.*

Delia bought another postcard—this one the kind with a picture on it, a rectangle of unblemished white captioned *Bay Day in Bay Borough*, so there was even less space to write on. *Dear Eleanor,* she wrote. *I'm not here because of Sam, so much. I'm here because*

Then she sat back, not knowing how to end the sentence. She considered starting over, but these postcards cost money, and so she settled, finally, for *I'm here because I just like the thought of beginning again from scratch*. She signed it, *Love, Delia,* and mailed it the following morning on her way to work.

And after all, wasn't that the true reason? Truer than she had realized when she wrote it, in fact. Her leaving had very little to do with any specific person.

Unlocking the office door, she noticed the pleasure she took in the emptiness of the room. She raised the white window shades; she turned the calendar to a fresh page; she sat down and rolled a clean sheet of paper into the typewriter. It was possible to review her entire morning thus far and find not a single misstep.

Mr. Pomfret sometimes employed a detective named Pete Murphy. This was not the swaggery character Delia would have envisioned, but a baby-faced fat boy from Easton. It seemed he was hired less often to locate people than to *fail* to locate them. Whenever a will or a title search required his services, Pete would plod in, whistling tunelessly, and trill his pudgy fingers at Delia and proceed to the inner office. He never spoke to her, and he probably didn't know her name.

One rainy afternoon, though, he arrived with something bulging and struggling inside the front of his windbreaker. "Got a present for you," he told Delia.

"For me?"

"Found it out in the street."

He lowered his zipper, and a small, damp gray-and-black cat bounded to the floor and made a dash for the radiator. "Oh!" Delia said.

Pete said, "Shoot. Come out of there, you little dickens."

Beneath the radiator, silence.

"It'll never come if you order it to," Delia said. "You have to back away a bit. Turn your face away. Pretend you're not looking."

"Well, I'll let you see to that," Pete decided. He brushed cat hairs off his sleeves and started for the office.

"Me! But . . . wait! I can't do this!" Delia said. She was speaking now to Mr. Pomfret; he had come to his door to see what all the fuss was about. "He's brought a stray cat! I can't take care of a cat!"

"Now, now, I'm sure you'll think of something," Mr. Pomfret said genially. "Miss Grinstead was a cat in her last incarnation, you know," he told Pete.

"Is that a fact," Pete said. They walked into the office, and Mr. Pomfret closed the door.

For the next half hour, Delia worked with one eye on the radiator. She watched a gray-and-black tiger tail unfurl from behind a pipe, gradually fluffing as it dried. She had a sense of being under surveillance.

When Pete reemerged, she said, "Maybe the cat belongs to someone. Have you thought of that?"

"I doubt it," he told her. "I didn't see no collar." He trilled his fingers and left. When the door slammed behind him, the tail gave a twitch.

Delia rose and went to the office. "Excuse me," she said.

Mr. Pomfret said, "Hmm?" He was back at his computer already. This morning he had discovered something called Search-and-Replace that was apparently very exciting. *Tap-tap,* his fingers went, while he craned his sloping neck earnestly toward the screen.

"Mr. Pomfret, that cat is still under the radiator and I can't take it anywhere! I don't even have a car!"

"Maybe get a box from the supply closet," he said. "Damn!" He hit several keys in succession. "Just see to it, will you, Miss Grinstead? There's a good girl."

"I live in a boardinghouse!" Delia said.

Mr. Pomfret reached for his computer manual and started thumbing through it. "Who wrote this damn thing, anyhow?" he asked. "No human being, that's for sure. Look, Miss Grinstead, why don't you leave early and take the kitty wherever you think best. I'll lock up for you, how's that?"

Delia sighed and headed for the supply closet.

Pet Heaven: they might help. She emptied a carton of manila envelopes and carried it to the other room. Kneeling in front of the radiator, she placed a palm on the floor. "Tsk-tsk!" she said. She waited. After a minute, she felt a tiny wince of cold on the back of her middle finger. "Tsk-tsk-tsk!" The cat peered out at her, only its whiskers and heart-shaped nose visible. Gently, Delia curved her hand around the frail body and drew it forward.

This was hardly more than a kitten, she saw—a scrawny male with large feet and spindly legs. His fur was almost startlingly soft. It reminded her of milkweed. When she stroked him, he shrank beneath her hand, but he seemed to realize he had nowhere to run. She gathered him up and set him in the carton and folded the flaps shut. He gave a single woebegone mew before falling silent.

It was still raining, and she didn't have a free hand to open her umbrella, so she hurried along the sidewalk unprotected. The carton rocked in her arms as if it contained a bowling ball. For such a little thing, he certainly was heavy.

She rounded the corner and burst through the door of Pet Heaven. A gray-haired woman stood behind the counter, checking off a list. "You wouldn't happen to know if Bay Borough has an S.P.C.A.," Delia said.

The woman looked at her a moment, slowly refocusing vague blue eyes. Then she said, "No; the nearest one's in Ashford."

"Or any other place that takes homeless animals?"

"Sorry."

"Maybe *you'd* like a cat."

"Gracious! If I brought home another stray my husband would kill me."

So Delia gave up, for now, and bought a box of kibble and a sack of litter-box filler, the smallest size of each just to get her through one night. Then she lugged the cat home.

Belle was there ahead of her, talking on the phone in the kitchen. Delia heard her laugh. She tiptoed up the stairs, unlocked the door of her room, set the carton on the floor, and shut the door behind her. In the mirror she looked like a crazy woman. Tendrils of wet hair were plastered to her forehead. The shoulders of her sweater were dark with rain, and her handbag was spotted and streaked.

She bent over the carton and raised the flaps. Inside, the cat sat hunched in a snail shape, glaring up at her. Delia retreated, settled on the edge of her bed, looked pointedly in another direction. Eventually, the cat sprang out of the carton. He started sniffing around the baseboards. Delia stayed where she was. He ducked beneath the bureau and returned with linty whiskers. He approached the bed obliquely, gazing elsewhere. Delia turned her head away. A moment later she felt the delicate denting of the mattress as he landed on it. He passed behind her, lightly brushing the length of his body against her back as if by chance. Delia didn't move a muscle. She felt they were performing a dance together, something courtly and elaborate and dignified.

But she couldn't possibly keep him.

Then Belle's clacky shoes started climbing the stairs. Belle almost never came upstairs. But she did today. Delia threw a glance at the cat, willing him to hide. All he did was freeze and direct a wide-eyed stare toward the door. *Knock-knock.* He was smack in the center of the pillow, with his bottle-brush tail standing vertical. You couldn't overlook him if you tried.

Delia scooped him up beneath his hot little downy armpits. She could feel the rapid patter of his heart. "Just a minute," she called. She reached for the carton.

But Belle must have misheard, for she breezed on in, caroling, "Delia, here's a—" Then she said, "Why!"

Delia straightened. "I'm just trying to find a home for him," she said.

"Aww. What a honey!"

"Don't worry, I'm not keeping him."

"Oh, why not? Er, that is . . . he is housebroken, isn't he?"

"All cats are housebroken," Delia said. "For goodness' sake!"

"Well, then! Not keep this little socky-paws? This dinky little pookums?" Belle was bending over the cat now and offering him her polished fingernails to sniff. "Is it a prinky-nose," she crooned. "Is it a frowzy-head. Is it a fluffer-bunch."

"Mr. Pomfret's detective found him out in the rain," Delia said. "He just dumped him on me; nothing I could do. I mean, I knew I couldn't keep him myself. Where would I put a litter box, for one thing?"

"In the bathroom?" Belle asked. She started scratching behind the cat's ears.

"But how would he get out to use it?"

"You could leave your door cracked open, let him go in and out as he likes," Belle said. "Ooh, feel how soft! I don't know why you ever lock it, anyhow. Little town like this, who do you think's going to rob you? Who's going to creep in and ravish you?"

"Well . . ."

"Believe me, Mr. Lamb couldn't gather up the enthusiasm."

Belle stroked beneath the cat's chin, and the cat tipped his head back blissfully. He had one of those putt-putt purrs, like a Model T Ford.

"I don't know if I want my life to get that complicated," Delia said.

"Is he a complication. Is he a bundle of trouble."

Belle was holding an envelope in her free hand, Delia saw. That must be what had brought her upstairs. Eleanor's stalky print marched across the front. Delia felt suddenly overburdened. Things were crowding in on her so!

But when Belle said, "Are you going to keep this itty-bitty, or am I?" Delia said, "I am, I guess."

"Well, good. Let's call him Puffball, what do you say?"

"Hmm," Delia said, pretending to consider it.

But she had never approved of cutesy names for cats. And besides, it seemed that at some point she had already started thinking of him as George.

She was in bed that night before she got around to reading Eleanor's letter. It was more of the same: a thank you for Delia's last postcard, news of her Meals on Wheels work. *I can certainly empathize with your desire to start over!* she wrote. (That careful word, *empathize,* revealing her effort to say just the right thing.)

> And I'm relieved it's the reason you left. I had assumed it was
> Sam. I've wondered if maybe he expressly wanted a flighty wife,
> in which case you could hardly be held to blame.

But when you've finished starting over, do you picture working up to the present again and coming home? Just asking.

All my love, dear,
Eleanor

A furry paw reached out to bat the page, and Delia laid the letter aside. The cat had found a resting place next to her on the blankets. He had eaten an enormous meal and paid two visits to the makeshift litter box in the bathroom. She could tell he was beginning to feel at home.

She reached for her book—Carson McCullers—and turned to where she had stopped reading last night. She read two stories and started a third. Then she found she was growing sleepy; so she set the book on the windowsill and clicked off her little reader's light and placed it on top of the book. Light continued to shine through the partly open door, sending a rod of yellow across the floorboards. She slid downward in bed very cautiously so as not to disturb the cat. He was giving himself a bath now. He pressed against her ribs with each movement in a way that seemed accidental, but she could tell he meant to do it.

How strange it was, when you thought about it, that animals would share quarters with humans! If Delia had been out in the wilderness, if this were some woodland creature nestling so close, she would have been astounded.

She yawned and shut her eyes and pulled the blanket up around her shoulders.

One of the stories she had read tonight was called "A Tree, a Rock, a Cloud." A man in this story said people should begin by loving easier things before they worked up to another person. Begin with something less complex, he proposed. Like a tree. Or a rock. Or a cloud. The rhythm of these words kept tapping across Delia's mind: tree, rock, cloud.

First a time alone, then a casual acquaintance or two, then a small, undemanding animal. Delia wondered what came after that, and where it would end up.

10

The Sunday before Thanksgiving, Belle waylaid Delia at the bottom of the stairs. "Say, Dee," she said. "What're you doing for the holiday?"

"Oh, um . . ."

"Want to have dinner at my place?"

"Well, I'd love to," Delia said.

"I'm serving this real hokey meal: turkey and dressing, cranberry relish . . ."

"I didn't know you cooked!"

"I don't," Belle said grimly. "It's a plot. I'm trying to look domestic for this fella I've been seeing."

At the moment, she looked anything but domestic. Sunday was always a busy day at the real estate office, and she was dressed to go out in her huge purple coat, the one with the shoulders not just padded but flaring to sharp points like an alien's space suit. Lilac trousers swam beneath it, and the smell of her fruity, overripe perfume freighted the air all around her.

"Vanessa is coming with Greggie," she said. "Nice touch to invite a child, don't you think? And these out-of-towners I just sold a house to, married couple; that's always good. . . ."

"And I would help in the food department," Delia guessed.

"Oh, I'm bringing in the food from outside, just between you and me. But I was thinking you could add a little, call it, class. I need for this guy to see me as all proper and respectable. And also you could advise me on the wifely touches: the centerpiece and et cetera. You must've used to do that stuff back home, didn't you? Do you have one of those baskety things that look like a cornucopia?"

"Well, not right handy," Delia said. "But I'll be glad to do what I can."

"Great," Belle said. She toed the cat aside—he had followed Delia downstairs—and opened the front door. They stepped out into a chilly, tin-colored day. "This fella's name is Henry McIlwain, did I mention that?" she asked. "We've been dating several weeks now and I'd like to start getting more purposeful. I don't want him thinking I'm just a good-time gal! Maybe you could drop a few remarks in front of him. Something like, 'Gosh, Belle, I hope you made your famous brussels-sprout dish.' "

"You're serving him brussels sprouts?"

"I don't have any choice. It's the only green vegetable Copp Catering offers that will fit in my toaster oven."

Delia said, "How did you manage the meals when you were living with Norton?"

"We ate out. But this time I want to do things differently. Maybe while Henry's listening you could ask me for one of my recipes."

"I can hardly wait to hear how you'll answer," Delia said.

"Dinner's at one, but could you come down a bit early to help set up? And wear your gray pinstripe. Your gray pinstripe is so . . . gray; know what I mean?"

On Thanksgiving Day Delia slept late, and she idled the morning away drinking tea and reading in bed, with the cat curled up beside her. Across the hall, in Mr. Lamb's room, an announcer's voice droned steadily. This was a TV announcer, Delia had figured out; not radio. Now that she kept her door cracked open, she could hear how the music swelled and diminished without apparent reason, responding to some visual cue; and today she caught distinct phrases each time she emerged for more tea water. "The mother bear leads her cubs . . . ," she heard, and, "The female spider injects her victims . . ." Evidently Mr. Lamb was watching nature shows.

Shortly after noon, she rose and started dressing. It was a pity she didn't have a string of pearls to add a festive note, she thought. Or at least a scarf. Didn't she own a paisley scarf with gray commas around the edges? Yes, she did—back in Baltimore. She could see it lying folded in her grandmother's lacquer glove box.

She applied an extra-bright coat of lipstick, and then she leaned toward the mirror to smooth her hair. It was longer now, which made her curls look flatter and somehow calmer—very suitable for Miss Grinstead. Although when she stepped back to gauge the total effect, the person who came to mind was not Miss Grinstead at all. It was Rosemary Bly-Brice.

She turned sharply from the mirror and picked up the vase of autumn flowers she had bought the day before.

The cat came along when she left. He scampered after her down the stairs, and he tumbled around her ankles while she knocked at the living-room door. When nobody answered she tried the other door, the one to the right, and finally she turned the knob and poked her head into the dining room. "Anybody home?" she asked.

Goodness, Belle did need her services. The table—one of those long, narrow, wood-grain affairs you see at PTA bazaars—was not even spread with a cloth yet. Delia put her flowers down and walked on into the kitchen. "Belle?" she said.

Belle was leaning against the sink. Her arms were clamped across the bosom of a violently frilled white apron, and tears were streaming down her face.

"Belle? What's happened?" Delia asked.

"He's not coming," Belle said thickly.

"Your date?"

"He's back with his wife."

"I didn't know he *had* a wife."

"Well, he does."

"Oh, I'm sorry."

In fact, she was shocked, but she tried not to show it. No wonder Belle had been so eager to look respectable! Delia gave her a tentative pat, just in case she wanted consoling. She did, it turned out. She fell into Delia's arms, sobbing hotly against her neck.

"He was perfect for me!" she wailed. "He was exactly what I wanted! And then this morning he calls up and—oh, I should have known from how low he was speaking, mumbly low secretive voice like he was scared somebody might hear him—"

She drew back from Delia's embrace to snap a paper towel off the roll above the sink. Blotting first one eye and then the other, she said, " 'Belle,' he tells me, 'about today. Something's come up,' he tells me. 'Oh?' I ask. 'What's that?' Thinking maybe he couldn't start the car, or wanted to bring a friend. 'Well, it's like this,' he tells me. 'Seems like Pansy and I have gotten back together.' "

"Pansy would be his wife," Delia guessed.

"Yes, and the baby's name is Daffodil, can you believe it?"

"There's a baby?"

"And it wasn't even a springtime baby! It was born in October!"

"You're talking about . . . this *past* October?"

Belle nodded, loudly blowing her nose.

"So the baby is, what, a month old?"

"Six weeks."

"Ah."

Belle's apron was so new that the pinholes still showed from the packaging. Her hairdo was even larger than usual, and she wore the first actual dress Delia had ever seen her in—or presumably it was a dress, for her legs were visible beneath the apron, encased in nylon stockings with a frosty white sheen like the bloom on plums. But her face was a disaster— blurred lipstick and blackened eyes and gray dribbles of tears. "You'll have to get in touch with the others," she was saying as she dabbed the tears. "I can't possibly go through with dinner."

"But everything's all ready," Delia said. She was taking stock of the foil-wrapped, disposable pans covering one counter, and the plates and silver heaped on the kitchen table, and the empty serving dishes waiting to be filled. Through the oven's lighted window she could make out a brown turkey, although she wasn't able to smell it, for some reason. "That turkey looks about done," she told Belle.

"It arrived done. I'm just reheating it. I had to keep it in the fridge overnight."

"So, why not go ahead with your party? Maybe it'll cheer you up."

"Nothing could cheer me up," Belle said.

"Oh, now, you sit here and I'll see to things."

"I wish I was dead and buried," Belle said, pulling out one of the kitchen chairs. She sank into it and picked up the cat. "I'm getting too old to be jilted! I'm thirty-eight years old. It's *tiring* to keep going on first dates."

Delia didn't answer, because she was hunting a tablecloth. No telling where Belle kept her linens. This was one of those fifties kitchens with shiny bare walls and enormous white appliances and rust-specked white metal cabinets and drawers. She slid open every drawer with a clanking sound. Most were empty. Eventually she located a jumble of fabrics in the space below the sink. "Aha!" she said, shaking out a wrinkled damask cloth. She carried it into the dining room and spread it over the table, re-settling her flowers in the center. "I know you must have candlesticks," she called.

"We met last spring," Belle said. "I was the one who sold off their house. They were moving to a bigger place on account of the baby coming. And wouldn't you know it took me six months, with the market the way it's been."

Delia opened all the drawers of the apple-green bureau that served as a dining-room buffet. She found two brass candlesticks lying in a nest of extension cords, and she placed them on either side of the flowers. Meanwhile, in the kitchen, Belle had sold the house just as Daffodil arrived. "Settlement date was two days before due date," she said. "Kid was born three days later. So naturally I stopped by the hospital with a giftie; these things are tax-deductible. And there was Henry all proud and fatherly, took me down the hall to that baby window they have and showed me how smart and cute and blah-blah-blah. Well, he just got to me, you know? I stood there not hearing a word he said, watching how his mouth moved, all at once I thought, *Suppose I was to step forward and kiss him, what do you guess he'd do?*"

"Candles?" Delia asked.

"Try the broom cupboard." Belle blew her nose with a honking sound that caused the cat to spring off her lap. "And this was not even my usual style of man," she said. "He was skinny! And pale! And computerish! But there I stood, thinking, *Suppose I unbuttoned my blouse right here in front of the baby window, staring at his mouth the whole time and running the tip of my tongue across my lower lip.*"

The candles were not in the broom cupboard but on top of the refrigerator, in a yellowing white box. Even the candles were yellowed, and also a bit warped, but Delia fitted them into the holders anyway. Then she collected the dishes and silver from the kitchen table and dealt them out. Belle proceeded through the baby's colic, the new parents' cranky quarrels, her own warm-eyed, cooing sympathy. "I schemed and plotted, I lay in wait," she said. "I told him my door was always open. Two, three, four o'clock in the morning he would leave that spit-up milk and dirty-diaper smell and find me here in my spaghetti-strap nightie from Victoria's Secret."

And to think all this had been going on while Delia was sound asleep! She checked the turkey. It appeared to have caved in around the breastbone. She found the brussels sprouts in their foil pan and set them in the toaster oven at 350 degrees. There were biscuits too, but she would wait to warm those till the very last minute.

"Two weeks ago, Pansy goes back to her mom's," Belle said. "Takes Daffodil and leaves. I was in heaven. Didn't you notice I've had this radiant glow about me lately? Oh, Delia, how can you stand it, going without a love life?"

Holding a pack of paper napkins printed all over with pilgrims, Delia paused to reflect upon the question. "Well," she said, "I do miss *hugs*, I guess. But nowadays when I think about, um, the rest of it, I just feel sort of perplexed. I think, *Why did that seem like such a big deal, once upon a time?* But I suppose it's only—"

The doorbell rang.

"Oh, Lord, we didn't call off dinner," Belle said, as if she had not been sitting in the midst of Delia's preparations. "Shoot! I can't cope with this! See who's there, will you, while I try to fix my face."

As Delia walked through the dining room to the hall, she felt drab and thin and virginal, like somebody's spinster aunt fulfilling her duties.

It was Vanessa at the door. She wore a leather blazer and blue jeans, and she toted Greggie on one hip. Behind her, just stepping out of their car, were a man and a woman who must have been Belle's married couple. Delia barely had time to whisper the news to Vanessa—"Henry McIlwain's gone back to his wife"—before the couple arrived on the porch. "Why! What have we here!" the husband told Greggie. He was young, no more than thirty, but as staid as a middle-aged man, Delia thought, with his receding tuft of black hair and his long black formal overcoat. His wife was a trim, attractive brunette in a tidy red woolen suit that reminded Delia of a Barbie-doll outfit. "I'm Delia Grinstead," Delia told her. "This is Vanessa Linley—do you know each other?—and Greggie."

"We're the Hawsers," the husband said for both of them. "Donald and Melinda."

"Won't you come in?"

She planned to lead them into the living room, but when she turned she found Belle at the door of the dining room. She was showing all her teeth and adjusting the plunging neckline of a flowered, button-front dress. "Happy Thanksgiving!" she sang out. Whatever repairs she had made to her face had not done much good. Gray tracks still ran down her cheeks, and her eyes were pink and puffy. But she caroled, "So glad you could come! Step in and have a seat!"

There was nowhere to sit but around the table. "Donald, you're on my right," Belle said, "and Vanessa's on my left. I've put Greggie next to you, Vanessa. Get some phone books from the kitchen if he needs a booster. And Melinda's on the other side of Greggie."

Well, maybe this was the local custom: proceeding directly to the food. But even Vanessa seemed taken aback. And the husband (still wearing his overcoat) stood frozen in place for a moment before approaching his chair. "Are we . . . late?" he asked Belle.

"Late! Not at all!" she said, and she let out a cascade of musical laughter. "Delia, you'll sit next to—"

She broke off. "Oh!" she cried. "Delia! Honestly!"

"What's the matter?" Delia asked.

"You've gone and laid too many places!"

It was true. Delia had doled out all she'd found on the kitchen table, and that must have included a setting for Henry McIlwain. Belle gazed toward the chair at the far end, her eyes brimming over with fresh tears.

"I'm sorry," Delia told her. "We could just—"

"Run fetch Mr. Lamb," Belle ordered.

"Mr. Lamb? From upstairs?"

"Hurry, though. We're all waiting. Tell him we'll eat without him if he doesn't get down here pronto."

What they would have eaten Delia couldn't imagine, since there wasn't a morsel of food anywhere in sight. But Vanessa, returning from the kitchen with several phone books, told Delia, "Go ahead. I'll get the meal on."

Delia went out to the hall, which seemed very quiet after the bustle in the dining room. With the cat twining underfoot, she climbed the stairs and knocked on Mr. Lamb's door. "Desperately, the salmon fling themselves against the current," a stern voice announced. The door opened on a sliver of Mr. Lamb's rag-and-bone face. "Yes?" he said, and then, "Oh!" for George had somehow managed to wriggle through the crack.

Delia said, "Belle sent me up to invite you for Thanksgiving dinner."

"But it seems your animal's got into my room!"

"Sorry," Delia said. "Here, George."

She reached in for the cat, and Mr. Lamb grudgingly opened the door another few inches. Delia caught the hazelnut smell of clothes worn once and then stuffed into drawers unwashed. The television's icy light flickered in the dimness. She scooped George up and backed away.

"I've been meaning to mention the toilet arrangements under the bathroom sink," Mr. Lamb told her.

"The . . . ?"

"Couldn't your animal use the outdoors?"

"Not in the middle of the night," Delia said. She clutched George more tightly and asked, "Are you coming to dinner, or aren't you?"

"What time?"

"Um . . . now?"

"Well, I suppose I could make it," Mr. Lamb said.

He looked down at what he was wearing—a limp T-shirt, baggy dark pants—and then sadly closed the door in her face.

Delia wondered how a man so fond of nature programs could object to a harmless cat.

Downstairs, Vanessa had finished setting everything on the table— turkey, brussels sprouts, cranberry relish, mashed sweet potatoes dotted with marshmallows, all in their original pans. Still wearing her leather blazer, she was spooning the stuffing out of the turkey. Greggie lolled on the stack of phone books, sucking his thumb and watching his mother with heavy-lidded eyes. It must be naptime.

Belle was discussing Henry with the Hawsers. "What I can't figure," she was saying, "is when all this came about. Last night as of ten o'clock, everything was jim-dandy. Henry and I had a real nice dinner over in Ocean City. Then this noon on the phone—poof! He's a totally changed man."

"So his wife showed up in the morning," Donald Hawser said sagely. He had draped his coat over the back of his chair, and he was lighting the warped candles with a silver lighter. "She got out of bed this morning and, 'Here I am,' she must have said, 'away from home on Thanksgiving. A family holiday,' she said."

Delia placed the cat on the floor and sat down next to Donald. *A family holiday,* she thought, *and I'm eating a store-cooked turkey with strangers.* She felt madcap and adventurous.

" 'Here I am with my mom when I ought to be with my husband,' she said, and she packed her suitcase then and there and went back to him, but he couldn't let you know till noon because what was he going to do— excuse himself and run phone you the minute she walked in?"

"Donald has an expert opinion to offer on every subject," his wife announced with a brittle laugh.

She was sitting very tensely, her spine not touching the chair. Her hair was scrolled upward at the ends like the sound holes in a violin.

"Yes; you might call it a gift," Donald agreed, unruffled. "I'm able to envision. See, first there's the business of settling her into the house. Don't forget she has that baby with her, and a diaper bag no doubt and one of those infant car seats—"

"But he could have just turned her away!" Belle exploded. "He doesn't even love her! He told me he didn't!"

"Well, of course that's what he would claim," Donald said, leaning back expansively.

By now Vanessa was carving the turkey. Delia began passing around the other foods. The brussels sprouts were barely warm, she discovered. The sweet potatoes were refrigerator cold, but everybody took some anyhow.

"You're right," Belle said. "Oh, when will I learn? Seems this happens to me about every other week. Norton Grove was the only one who actually divorced his wife for me, and look how that ended up!"

"How *did* it end up?" Delia asked.

"He fell in love with a lady plumber who came to unstop our sink."

Donald nodded, implying he could have predicted as much.

"It's just the way Ann Landers keeps saying in her column," Belle told them. "She says a man who would leave his wife will most likely leave you, too, by and by."

"Maybe you ought to look for someone who doesn't *have* a wife," Vanessa suggested, handing her son a turkey wing.

"Yes, but it's kind of like I lack imagination. I mean, I can't seem to picture marrying a man till I see him married to someone else. Then I say, 'Why! He'd make a good husband for *me*!' "

The hallway door opened and Mr. Lamb stood on the threshold, wearing a shiny black suit that turned his skin to ashes. "Oh, God, you have guests," he said.

"Yes, Mr. Lamb, and you're one of them," Belle said. "Donald Hawser, Melinda Hawser . . . Vanessa and Greggie you've seen around, I bet. This is Horace Lamb," she told the others. She waved carelessly toward the one empty chair. "Have a seat."

"Well, I can't stay long."

"Have a *seat*, Mr. Lamb."

He entered the room with a skimming sound that made Delia glance downward. On his feet he wore the kind of backless paper slippers given out free in hospitals. "This afternoon will be sports, sports, sports," he said as he fell into his chair. "All regular programs are preempted. I'm reduced to the educational channels."

"Say!" Donald cried. "Who you going to root for?"

"Pardon? Weekday afternoons, I like to watch the soaps. Oh, I confess. I admit it. I make a point of stopping for *All My Children* every blessed day I'm on the road."

"What's your line of business, Horace? Okay if I call you Horace?"

"I sell storm windows," Mr. Lamb told him. He accepted the container of sweet potatoes and peered down into it. "This looks exceedingly rich," he said. His long front teeth were so prominent that his lips had to labor to stretch across them. His whole face seemed stretched, and too intricately hinged at the jawbone. He raised his deep-set eyes to Belle and said, "Regrettably, I'm afflicted with a touchy stomach."

"Oh, eat up, it'll do you good," Belle snapped. "We were discussing married men."

"Pardon?"

"Another problem I have is, I look at a married man and I can't believe he won't find me irresistible."

"Irresistible?"

"I'm speaking to the table at large, Mr. Lamb. Eat your dinner. I see a man with his wife, mousy boring wife who isn't even attempting to keep herself up, and I think, *Why wouldn't he prefer me instead? I'm a hell of a lot more fun, and better-looking to boot.* But it's like there's some—I don't know—some hold wives have, and I can't seem to break it. Is it a secret? Is it some secret you-all pass around among yourselves?"

She was asking Melinda Hawser, but Melinda just gave another shattered laugh and started crumbling bits of biscuit onto her plate. "Is it?" Belle asked Delia.

"Oh, no," Delia told her. "It's more like just . . . what's the word? The word from science class. Momentum?"

"Inertia," Mr. Lamb supplied.

"Right." She glanced over at him. "It's just a matter of people staying where they are."

"Well, if that's all it is," Belle said, "how come Katie O'Connell got to waltz off to Hawaii with Larry Watts? *She* must have found out the secret. Why, when Larry Watts was boarding here, he never even gave me a look! He almost seemed to be avoiding me. He acted like I was some floozy the one time I asked him downstairs for a friendly little drink!"

Her mouth collapsed, and she covered her eyes with one hand. Donald said, "Oh, now! Hey!" and Vanessa said, "Aw, Belle, don't cry," while Mr. Lamb started tugging ferociously at his nose.

"To be honest," Melinda said in a crystal voice, "I can't think what you want with a husband anyhow."

There was a pause, a kind of reconsidering among the other diners.

"Who first thought marriage up, do you suppose?" Melinda asked Greggie. He goggled at her from behind a greasy fistful of turkey wing. "Everyone pushes it so, especially the women. Your mother and your aunts and your girlfriends. Then after you're married you see how he's always so full of himself and always going on about something, always got these theories and pronouncements, always crowing over these triumphs at his business. 'I told them this,' and 'I told them that,' and you ask, 'What did they say back?' and he says, 'Oh, *you* know, but then I told them such and such, and I let them have it outright, I put it to them straight, I said . . .' And if you mention this to your mother and your aunts and so forth, 'Oh,' they say, 'marriage is a pain, all right.' 'Well, if that's the way you feel,' you want to ask them, 'why didn't you speak up before? Where were you when I was announcing my engagement?' "

"Ha. Yes," her husband said. He glanced around the table. "They're going to think you mean *our* marriage. Dear."

Everybody waited, but Melinda just speared a brussels sprout.

"Oh," Belle assured him, "we would never think that." She was sitting erect now, her tears already drying on her cheeks. "A gorgeous man like you? Of course we wouldn't." She told the others, "Donald and Melinda are customers of mine. They bought the old Meers place—lovely place. Donald's an important executive at the furniture plant."

Melinda was chewing her brussels sprout very noisily, or maybe it only seemed that way because the room was so quiet.

"*Mrs.* Meers had gone into the nursing home," Belle said, "but Mr. Meers was still living there. Took us through the house himself; taught us how to work the trash compactor. Told us, 'Here in the freezer are one hundred forty-four egg whites, no charge.' "

"Folks who made their own mayonnaise," Mr. Lamb surmised.

Belle was about to go on speaking, but she stopped and looked at him.

"I don't guess you'd be in the market for storm windows," Mr. Lamb told Donald.

"Not really," Donald said, with his eyes on his wife.

"Ah, well, I didn't think so."

"That house needs absolutely nothing," Belle said. "The Meerses kept after it every minute. And Donald here, Don . . ." She smiled at him. "Don spotted that the first time he walked through."

"Melinda and I have a *fine* marriage. Married seven years," Donald said, still watching his wife. "We were one of those recognized campus couples at our college. Went steady, got pinned: the works."

"I know the type you mean," Belle said.

"Why, Melinda's known me so long she still calls me Hawk! Hawk Hawser," he added, turning at last to meet Belle's gaze. "I was on the basketball team. Kind of a star, some people might say, though I never had the height to go professional."

"Is that right!" Belle exclaimed.

"Hawk Hawser," he repeated lingeringly.

"I believe I might've heard of you."

"Well, maybe so if you were ever in Illinois. Jerry Bingle College?"

"Jerry Bingle. Hmm."

"I played center."

"Really!"

"And midway through my senior year—"

"Marshmallow," Greggie demanded.

He didn't have the usual small child's trouble pronouncing *l*'s. He spoke very precisely and daintily. "Mama? Marshmallow!"

It was Delia, finally, who plucked a marshmallow from the sweet potatoes and reached across the table to set it on his plate. Everyone else was watching Belle. Open-mouthed and breathless, miraculously recovered, Belle stroked her topmost button with a hypnotic, circular motion and kept her damp-lashed eyes focused raptly on Donald's lips.

Sometimes Mr. Pomfret ordered Delia to go out and feed the parking meter for a client. Sometimes he snapped his fingers when he needed her. Once, he tossed her his raincoat and told her to take it down the block to the one-hour cleaner's. "Yes, Mr. Pomfret," she murmured. When she returned, she placed the receipt on his palm as smartly as a surgical nurse dealing out a scalpel.

But now she began to feel a little itch of rebellion.

"Miss Grinstead, can't you see I'm *merging*?" he demanded when she brought in some letters to sign, and she said, "Sorry, Mr. Pomfret," but neutrally, too evenly, with her expression set in granite. And back at her desk, she seethed with imaginary retorts. *You and your crummy computer! You and your "merging" and your Search-and-Destroy or whatever!*

One Friday in early December, a stooped, gray-haired man in a baseball jacket arrived without an appointment. "I'm Mr. Leon Wesley," he told Delia. "This is about my son Juval. Do you think Mr. Pomfret might have a minute for me?"

Mr. Pomfret's office door was closed—it was early morning, his time to peruse new catalogs—but when Delia inquired, he said, "Leon? Why, Leon resurfaced my driveway for me. Send him in. And make us a pot of coffee while you're at it."

It was impossible to avoid overhearing Mr. Wesley's reason for coming. He poured it out even before he was seated, speaking through the grinding of the coffee beans so Mr. Pomfret had to ask him to repeat himself. Juval, Mr. Wesley said, was scheduled to join the navy first thing after Christmas. He had a highly promising future; special interest had been taken on account of his qualifications, which seemed to involve some technical know-how that Delia couldn't quite follow. And last night, clear out of the blue, he had been arrested for breaking and entering. Caught climbing through the Hanffs' dining-room window at ten o'clock in the evening.

"The Hanffs!" Mr. Pomfret said. The Hanffs owned the furniture factory, as even Delia knew—the town's one industry. "Well, of all the doggone folks to up and burglarize," he said.

Delia went to the supply closet for more sugar, and when she came back Mr. Pomfret was still marveling at Juval's choice of victims. "I mean, here you've got Reba Hanff, who disapproves of jewelry and doesn't own a piece of silver," he said, "gives every cent of their profits to some religious honcho in India . . . What did the boy hope to steal, for God's sake?"

"And why, is what I'd like to know," Mr. Wesley said. "That's the part I can't figure. Was he in need of money? For what? He doesn't even drink, let alone take drugs. Doesn't even have a girlfriend."

"Not to mention the Hanffs own the only house alarm in all of Bay Borough," Mr. Pomfret mused.

"And with such a hotshot career ahead!" Mr. Wesley said. "You can bet that's all down the drain now. How come he went and ruined things, so close to the time he was leaving?"

"Maybe *that's* how come," Delia spoke up, setting two mugs on a tray.

"Ma'am?"

"Maybe he ruined things so he wouldn't have to leave after all."

Mr. Wesley gaped at her.

Mr. Pomfret said, "You may go now, Miss Grinstead."

"Yes, Mr. Pomfret."

"Shut the door behind you, please."

She shut the door with such conspicuous care that every part of the latch declared itself.

In regard to the establishment of a designated fund, she typed, and then Mr. Pomfret emerged from his office, stuffing his arms into his overcoat as he walked, forging a trail for Mr. Wesley. "Cancel my ten o'clock," he told Delia.

"Yes, Mr. Pomfret."

He opened the outer door, ushered Mr. Wesley through it, and then closed it and came back to stand at Delia's desk. "Miss Grinstead," he said, "from now on, please do not volunteer comments during my consultations."

She stared at him stubbornly, keeping her eyes wide and innocent.

"You're paid for your secretarial skills, not for your opinions," he said.

"Yes, Mr. Pomfret."

He left.

She knew she had deserved that, but still she felt a flare of righteous anger once he was gone. She typed rapidly and badly, flinging the carriage so hard that the typewriter kept skidding across the desk. When she called to cancel the ten o'clock appointment, her voice shook. And when she left the office at lunchtime, she picked up a Bay Borough *Bugle* so she could look for another job.

Well, not that she would actually go through with it, of course. It was just that she needed to fantasize awhile.

The weather was raw and dismal, and she hadn't brought any food with her, but she walked to the square even so because she couldn't deal with the Cue Stick 'n' Cola today. She found the park benches deserted. The statue looked huddled and dense, like a bird with all its feathers reared against the cold. She wrapped her coat around her and sat down on the very edge of one damp, chilly slat.

How satisfying it would be to announce her resignation! "I regret to inform you, Mr. Pompous . . . ," she would say. He would be helpless. He didn't even know where she kept the carbon paper.

She opened the *Bugle* and searched for the classified section. As a rule she didn't read the *Bugle*, which was little more than an advertising handout—several pages of half-price specials and extremely local news, stacked weekly in various storefronts. She flipped past a choral call for the Christmas Eve Sing on the square, a two-for-one day at the shoe store, and a progress report on the Mitten Drive. On the next-to-last page she discovered four Help Wanted ads: baby-sitter, baby-sitter, lathe operator, and "live-in woman." This town must have unemployment problems. After that came the For Sale ads. A person named Dwayne wished to sell two wedding rings, cheap. Her eyes slid back to *Live-in Woman*.

> Single father desires help w/ lively, bright, engaging, 12-yr-old son. Must be willing to wake boy in a.m., serve breakfast, see off to school, do light cleaning / errands / shopping, assist w/ homework, provide transportation to dentist / doctor / grandfather / playmates, attend athletic meets & cheer appropriate team, host groups of 11–13 yr olds, cook supper, show enthusiasm for TV sports programs / computer games / paperback war novels, be available nights for bad dreams / illness. Driver's license a must. Non-smokers only. Room, board, generous salary. Weekends & most daytimes free except school holidays / sick days / snow days. Call Mr. Miller at Underwood High 8–5 Mon–Fri.

Delia clucked. The nerve of the man! Some people wanted the moon. She rattled the paper impatiently and refolded it. You can't expect a mere hireling to serve as a genuine mother, which was really what he was asking.

She rose and placed the *Bugle* in the trash basket. So much for that.

Crossing West Street, she glanced toward the shops—Debbi's and the dime store and the florist. How about a job in sales? No, she was too quiet-natured. As for waitressing, she used to forget her own family's dessert orders in the time it took to walk to the kitchen. And she knew from her talks with Mrs. Lincoln at the library that the town was having to struggle to support even one librarian.

Actually, she reflected, passing the sterile white blinds of the Fingernail

Clinic, a hireling would in some ways be *better* than a mother—less emotionally ensnarled, less likely to cause damage. Certainly less likely to suffer damage herself. When the employer's child was unhappy, it would never occur to the live-in woman to feel personally responsible.

She turned into Value Vision and took another *Bugle* from the stack just inside the door.

"I wouldn't like for my son to think people are checking him over," Mr. Miller said. "Filing through to see if he's up to standard. That's why I asked you to come while he was out. Then if you find you're interested, you could stay on and meet him. He's eating supper at a friend's, but he'll be home in half an hour or so."

He sat across from her in a chintz armchair that he seemed to dwarf, as he dwarfed the whole overstuffed, overdecorated living room of this little ranch house on the edge of town. To Delia's surprise, he'd turned out to be someone she recognized. Joel Miller: he had consulted Mr. Pomfret several months ago on a visitation matter. She remembered admiring his undisguised baldness. Men who scorned the subterfuge of artfully draped strands of hair, she felt, conveyed an attractive air of masculine assurance; and Mr. Miller, with his large, regular features and his olive skin and loose gray suit, seemed positively serene. Underneath, though, she detected some tension. He had told her three times—contradicting the entire gist of his ad—that his son would be at school for the vast majority of every day, in essence *all* day, and that even when he was home he required not much more than a token adult in the wings. Delia had the feeling that no one else had applied for this position.

"He eats at friends' houses often, in fact," Mr. Miller was saying. "And in summer—I don't think I mentioned this—he spends two weeks at sleepaway camp. Besides which there's computer day camp, soccer clinic—"

"Summer!" Delia said. She rocked back in her chintz-padded rocking chair. Summer, with its soft, lazy afternoons, tinkling glasses of lemonade, children's peach-colored bodies in swimsuits! "Oh, Mr. Miller," she said. "The truth is, I seem to be in a changeable stage of life right now. I'm not sure I could get that . . . invested."

"And in summer I'm around more myself," Mr. Miller went on, as if she hadn't spoken. "Not the whole day, exactly—a principal doesn't have quite the same leeway his teachers do—but quite a lot."

"I probably shouldn't have come," Delia said. "A child your son's age needs continuity."

Then why did *you come?* he might reasonably have asked, but instead, poor man, he seized on her last sentence. "You sound experienced," he said. "Do you have children of your own, Miss Grinstead? Oh." The corners of his mouth jerked briefly downward. "I'm sorry. Of course not."

"Yes, I do," she told him.

"So it's *Mrs.* Grinstead?"

"I prefer 'Miss.' "

"I see."

He thought this over.

"But, so, you *are* experienced," he said finally. "That's excellent! And do you come from this area?"

Evidently he didn't keep up with Bay Borough gossip. "No, I don't," she told him.

"You don't."

She could see him reconsidering. Desperate he might be, but not foolhardy. He wouldn't want to hire an ax murderer.

"I'm from Baltimore," she volunteered at last. "I'm perfectly respectable, I promise, but I've put that part of my life behind me."

"Ah."

Oh, Lord, now he was envisioning some drama. He surveyed her with interest, his head slightly tilted.

"But!" she exclaimed. "As far as the job goes—"

"I know: you don't want it," he said sadly.

"It's nothing to do with the job itself. I'm sure your son is a very nice boy."

"Oh, he's more than nice," Mr. Miller said. "He's really, he's such a good kid, Miss Grinstead. He's wonderful! But I guess I overestimated how well we could do on our own. I thought as long as we knew how to work the washing machine . . . But things have gotten away from me."

He waved a hand toward the room in general, which puzzled Delia, because it seemed painfully neat. Fat little cushions with buttons in their middles filled the skirted couch, each one propped at a careful angle. Glossy fashion magazines lapped at mathematical intervals across the coffee table. But Mr. Miller, following her glance, said, "Oh, the *surface* I can handle. I've posted a chart in the kitchen. Each day has its special job. This afternoon we vacuumed, yesterday we dusted. But it seems there are other issues. Last weekend, for example, he asked if we could have penny soup. 'Penny soup!' I said. Sounded kind of weird to me. He said his mother used to serve it for lunch when he was little. I asked him what was in it, and it turns out he meant plain old vegetable soup. I guess they call it penny soup because it's cheap. So I said, 'Well, I can make *that*.' I heat up a tin of Campbell's, he takes one look, and what does he do? Starts crying. Twelve years old and he falls apart, kid who didn't so much as whimper the time he broke his arm. I said, 'Well, what? What did I do wrong?' He said it had to be homemade. I said, 'God Almighty, Noah.' Still, I'm not stupid. I knew this soup had some meaning for him. So I haul out a cookbook and set to work making homemade. But when he saw what I was doing, he told me to forget it. 'Just forget the whole thing,' he told me. 'I'm not hungry anyhow.' And off he went to his room, leaving me with a pile of diced carrots."

"Sliced," Delia told him.

He raised his straight black eyebrows.

"You should have *sliced* the carrots," she told him, "and also zucchini, yellow squash, new potatoes—everything coin-shaped. That's why they call it penny soup. It's nothing to do with the cost. I doubt you'd find it in cookbooks, because it's more a . . . mother's recipe, you know?"

"Miss Grinstead," Mr. Miller said, "let me show you where you'd stay if you took the job."

"No, really, I—"

"Just to look at! It's the guest room. Has its own private bath."

She rose when he did, but only because she wanted to make her escape. What had she been thinking of, coming here? It seemed she could feel within the curl of her fingers the urge to slice those vegetables as they ought to be sliced, to set the soup in front of the boy and turn away briskly (twelve was too old to cuddle) and pretend she hadn't noticed his tears. "I'm sure it's a lovely room," she said. "Somebody's going to love it! Somebody young, maybe, who still has enough . . ."

She was trailing Mr. Miller down a short, carpeted hall lined with open doors. At the last door, Mr. Miller stood back to let her see in. It was the sort of room where people were expected to spend no more than a night or two. The high double bed allowed barely a yard of space on either side. The nightstand bore a thoughtful supply of guest-type reading (more magazines, two books that looked like anthologies). The framed sampler on the wall read WELCOME in six languages.

"Large walk-in closet," Mr. Miller said. "Private bath, as I believe I've mentioned."

In another part of the house, a door slammed and a child called, "Dad?"

"Ah," Mr. Miller said. "Coming!" he called. "Now you get to meet Noah," he told Delia.

She took a step backward.

"Just to say hello," he assured her. "What harm could that do?"

She had no choice but to follow him down the hall again.

In the kitchen (cabinets the color of toffees, wallpaper printed with butter churns), a wiry little boy stood tugging off a red jacket. He had a tumble of rough brown hair and a thin, freckled face and his father's long dark eyes. As soon as they entered the room, he started talking. "Hey, Dad, guess what Jack's mother gave us for dinner! This, like, cubes of meat that you dunk into this . . ." He registered Delia's presence, flicked a look at her, and went on. ". . . dunk into this pot and then—"

"Noah, I'd like you to meet Miss Grinstead," his father said. "Should we call you Delia?" he asked her. She nodded; it hardly mattered. "I'm Joel," he said, "and this is Noah. My son."

Noah said, "Oh. Hi." He wore the guarded, deadpan expression that children assume for introductions. "So the pot is full of hot oil, I guess it is, and each of us got—"

"Fondue," his father said. "You're talking about fondue."

"Right, and each of us got our own fork to cook our meat on, with different, like, animals on the handles so we could keep straight whose was whose. Like mine was a giraffe, and guess what Jack's little sister's was?"

"I can't imagine," his father said. "Son, Delia is here to—"

"A pig!" Noah squawked. "His little sister got the pig!"

"Is that right."

"And she cried about it too, but Carrie cries about everything. Then for dessert we each had a bag of chocolate marbles, but I turned mine down. I was polite about it, though. I go to his mom, I go—"

"Said."

"Huh?"

"You *said* to his mom."

"Right, I'm all, 'Thanks a lot, Mrs. Newell, but I'm so full I guess I better pass.' "

"I thought you liked chocolate marbles," his father said.

"Are you kidding? Not after what I know now." Noah turned to Delia. "Chocolate marbles are coated with ground-up beetle shells," he told her.

"No!" she said.

"No," Mr. Miller agreed. "Where'd you get *that* information?" he asked his son.

"Kenny Moss told me."

"Well, then! If Kenny Moss said it, how can we doubt it?"

"I'm serious! He heard it from his uncle who's in the business."

"What business—tabloid newspapers?"

"Huh?"

"There are no beetle shells in chocolate marbles. Take my word for it. The FDA would never allow it."

"And guess what's in corn chips," Noah told Delia. "Those yellow corn chips? Seagull do."

"I never knew that!"

"That's what makes them so crackly."

"Noah—" his father said.

"Honest, Dad! Kenny Moss swears it!"

"Noah, Delia came to talk about keeping house for us."

Delia shot Mr. Miller a frown. He wore an oblivious, bland expression, as if he had no idea what he'd done. "Actually," she said, turning to Noah, "I was only . . . inquiring."

"She's going to think about it," Mr. Miller amended.

Noah said, "That'd be great! I've been having to fix my own school lunches."

"Horrors," his father said. "Don't let on to the child-labor authorities."

"Well, how would *you* feel? You open your lunch box: 'Gee, I wonder what I surprised myself with today.' "

Delia laughed. She said, "I should be going. It was nice to meet you, Noah."

"Goodbye," Noah said. Unexpectedly, he held out his hand. "I hope you decide to come."

His hand was small but callused. When he looked up at her, his eyes showed an underlay of gold, like sunshine filtered through brown water.

Outside the front door, Delia told his father, "I thought you didn't want him to feel people were checking him over."

"Ah," Mr. Miller said. "Yes. Well."

"I thought you were trying to spare him! Then you went and told him what I was here for."

"I realize I shouldn't have done that," Mr. Miller said. He spread one hand distractedly across his scalp, like a cap. "It's just that I wanted so badly for you to say you'd come."

"And you haven't seen my references, even! You don't know the first thing about me!"

"No, but I approve of your English."

"English?"

"It kills me to hear him speak so sloppily. 'Like' this and 'like' that, and 'I go' instead of 'I said.' It drives me bats."

"Well, of all things," Delia said. She turned to leave.

"Miss Grinstead? Delia?"

"What."

"Will you at least think it over?"

"Of course," she said.

But she knew she wouldn't.

Vanessa said Joel Miller was the most pitiful man she knew of. "Ever since his wife left, the guy has been barely coping," she told Delia.

"Isn't anyone in Bay Borough happily married?" Delia wondered.

"Yes, lots of folks," Vanessa said. "Just not who you choose to hang out with."

They were sitting in Vanessa's kitchen the following morning, a cold, sunny Saturday. Really it was her grandmother's kitchen; Vanessa and all three of her brothers lived with their father's mother. Vanessa was filling out labels with an old-fashioned steel-nibbed pen. *Highly Effective Insect Repellent,* she wrote, in hair-thin brown script on ivory paper ovals. Highly Effective was an ancient family recipe. When Vanessa had finished her daily allotment of labels, her youngest brother would glue them onto the slender glass phials in which various dried sprigs and berries bobbed mysteriously underwater. Delia found it hard to believe that people could make a living this way, but evidently the Linleys did all right. The house was large and comfortable, and the grandmother could afford to travel once a year to Disney World. Vanessa said the trick was pennyroyal. "Don't let this get around," she'd told Delia, "but insects *despise* pennyroyal. The other herbs are mostly for show."

On the floor, Greggie was building a tower with stacks of corks. After

Vanessa finished her labels, she and Delia were going to take him to visit Santa. Then Delia might do a little Christmas shopping. Or maybe not; she couldn't decide. She had always disliked Christmas, with its possibilities for disappointing her family's secret hopes, and this year would be worse than ever. Should she just, maybe, skip the whole business? Oh, why wasn't there an etiquette book for runaway wives?

Which brought her back to Mr. Miller. "How come his wife left him, does anyone know?" she asked Vanessa.

"Oh, sure; everyone knows. Here they were, together for years, sweet little boy, nice house, and one day last spring Ellie, that's his wife, found a lump in her breast. Went to the doctor and he said, yup, looked like cancer. So she came home and told her husband, 'In the time that I have left to me, I want to make the very best of my life. I want to do exactly what I've dreamed of.' And by nightfall she had packed up and gone. That was her deepest, dearest wish—did you ever hear such a thing?"

"So where is she now?"

"Oh, she's a TV weather lady over in Kellerton," Vanessa said. "The lump was nothing at all; they removed it under local anesthetic. Now Mr. Miller and Noah can turn on their TV and watch her every evening. Or you might have seen her in *Boardwalk Bulletin*. They ran a profile of her last August. Real pretty blonde? Hair like that shredded straw we pack our bottles in. Course, no one here was impressed in the slightest—person who'd leave her own child."

Delia looked down at her lap.

"All the women in town have been trying to help Mr. Miller out," Vanessa said. "Bringing pans of lasagna, taking his kid for the afternoon. But I guess by summer he realized it wasn't enough, because that's when he put the ad in the *Bugle*."

"The ad's been in since summer?"

"Right, but his neighbor tells me the onliest answers were teenaged girls from the high school. Every girl at Dorothy Underwood's got a crush on Mr. Miller. I did too; it's part of being a student there. I was a senior the first year he was principal, and I thought he was the sexiest man I'd ever laid eyes on. But of course he can't hire some airhead, so he's just kept running the ad. It never crossed my mind you'd want the job yourself."

"Well, I don't, really," Delia said. She watched Greggie start a cork train across the linoleum. His little hands reminded her of biscuits, that kind with a row of fork holes pricked on top. She had forgotten what a joy it was to rest your eyes on young children. "It's just that I'm so fed up with Mr. Pomfret," she said. "Do you suppose they have any openings at the furniture factory?"

"Oh, the furniture factory," Vanessa said, dipping her pen. "All's they ever need there is oilers. Stand all day rubbing oil into chair legs with these big mittens on your hands."

"But they must have office positions. Typist, filing clerk . . ."

"How come you're not taking the job at Mr. Miller's?"

"I don't want to just . . . step into a little boy's life like that, in case I decide to leave," Delia told her.

"Do you always up and leave a place?"

Delia wasn't sure how that question was intended. She looked at Vanessa suspiciously. "No, not always," she said.

"I mean I never heard you speak a word against Zeke Pomfret. Now you want to quit."

"He's so bossy, though. So condescending. Also, the pay is ridiculous," Delia said. "I didn't realize how ridiculous when I took the job. And he doesn't even provide health insurance! What if I got sick?"

Vanessa sat back to watch her.

"Well," Delia told her, "yes, I *do* seem to up and leave a lot."

As she spoke, she saw a lone, straight figure marching down the coastline. It was strange, the feeling of affection the image summoned up in her.

For her family's Christmas, she decided to buy nothing at all. Maybe Greggie's trip to Santa had depressed her. He had appeared to grasp the concept before they went, but once they got there he started screaming and had to be carried out. Vanessa was crushed; even the Santa looked crushed. And their shopping expedition afterward was spiritless, with Greggie hiccuping tearfully and slouching in his stroller in a brooding, insulted manner. Delia told Vanessa she thought she would call it a day. "I need to go to the laundromat anyhow," she said—a flimsy excuse.

When she got home, Belle hailed her from the living-room doorway. "You had a phone call," she said.

"I did?"

Her knees seemed to melt. She thought first of the children, then of Sam's heart.

But Belle said, "Mr. Miller from the high school. He wants you to call him back."

"Oh."

"*I* didn't know you knew Joel Miller."

Delia hadn't mentioned him to Belle because working for him would mean moving out of this house, and how could she ever do that? This house was perfect. Even Mr. Pomfret had his good points. Somehow the visit to Santa had shown her that. So she nonchalantly accepted the number Belle had scrawled on the corner of a takeout menu. Might as well get this over with. She perched on one arm of the couch and reached for the phone and dialed. Meanwhile Belle hovered in the background, supposedly absorbed with the cat. "Is you a nice little kitty. Is you a sweet little kitty," she crooned. Delia listened to the ringing at the other end of the line, letting her eyes travel gratefully over the blank white walls and bare floorboards.

"Hello?" Noah said.

She said, "This is Delia Grinstead."

"Oh, hi! I'm supposed to tell you I'm sorry."

"Sorry? For what?"

"Dad says a guy shouldn't talk about seagull do in front of ladies."

"Oh. Well—"

A man said something in the background.

"Women," Noah said.

"Excuse me?"

" 'Women,' I meant to say, not 'ladies.' "

All pretext, of course. Mr. Miller surely didn't think she would be offended by seagull do. *Or* the word "ladies." This was mere strategy. But Noah himself probably had no inkling of that, and so Delia told him, "It's quite all right."

"Kenny Moss's uncle drives a snack truck; that's how Kenny knows about the you-know-what. But Dad claims his uncle was teasing him. Dad goes, 'Right, the corn-chip factory really does take the time to send their workers out to the beach with shovels.' "

Another mutter in the background.

"Okay, 'said.' He *said*," Noah told Delia. "And on top of that he *said*"—heavy stress, meaningful pause—"he said how come it's not in the list of ingredients, if they use seagull do? Oops."

"Oh, you know those lists," Delia told him. "All those scientific terms. They can cover up just about anything with some chemical-sounding name."

"They can?"

"Why, sure! They probably call it 'dihydroxyexymexylene' or some such."

Noah giggled. "Hey, Dad," he said, his voice retreating slightly. "Delia says it probably is on the list; it's probably dihydroxy . . ."

Belle had carried the cat over to the window now. She was holding him up to the glass, which was nearly opaque with dust. And cobwebs clouded the tops of the curtains, and the philodendron plant on the sill was leggy and bedraggled. The whole room seemed drained of color, as if, already, it had slipped into the dimmest reaches of Delia's memory.

I 2

Mr. Pomfret said, "Moving on, eh," without so much as a change of expression. (You would think she was a piece of office equipment.) All he asked, he said, was that she finish out the week—tie up any dangling odds and ends. Which of course she agreed to do, even though there were no odds and ends; just the usual busywork of rat-a-tat letters and robot phone calls and Mr. Pomfret's daily sheaf of marked catalogs.

It seemed he urgently required a pair of perforated leather driving gloves. A radio antenna the size and shape of a breakfast plate. A solid-walnut display rack for souvenir golf balls.

When she turned in her office key on Friday afternoon, he told her he might wait till after New Year's to replace her. "This time," he said, "I believe I'll hire a word processor, assuming I can find one."

Delia was confused, for an instant. She pictured hiring a machine. Just try asking a machine to debate his glove size with an 800 operator! she thought. Then she realized her mistake. But still, somehow, she felt hurt, and she shouldered her bag abruptly and left without saying goodbye.

All she owned fit easily in a cardboard carton begged from Rick-Rack's. The goosenecked lamp poked its head out, though. She could have left it that way (Belle was giving her a ride), but she liked the notion of a life no larger than a single, compact box; and so she shifted things until the flaps closed securely. Then she took her coat and handbag from the bed, and she picked the carton up and walked out.

No point sending one last look backward. She knew every detail of that room by heart—every nail hole, every seam in the wallpaper, and the way the paw-footed radiator, in the furry half-light of this overcast Saturday morning, resembled some skeletal animal sitting on its haunches.

At the bottom of the stairs, she set down her load and put her coat on. She could hear Belle talking to George in the kitchen. He was staying here another week or two, just till Delia was settled. It was Delia's belief that she had to let her own smell permeate the new place first; otherwise he'd keep running back to the old place.

Mr. Miller had told her George was more than welcome. He'd been meaning to buy a cat anyhow, he said. (But notice how he'd used the word "buy," apparently unaware that true animal lovers would not be caught dead in a pet shop.)

Still buttoning her coat, she walked through the dining room to knock on the kitchen door. "Coming," Belle called. Delia returned to the hall. Upstairs, Mr. Lamb was creaking the floorboards, and his TV had started its level, fluent murmur. She wondered when he would get around to noticing she was gone. Maybe never, she thought.

It was still not too late to change her mind.

"I gave George a can of tuna," Belle said when she emerged. "That ought to keep him occupied."

"Oh, Belle, you'll spoil him."

"Nothing's too good for my whiskums! I'm hoping he'll refuse to leave me when it's time. 'No, no, Mommy!' " she squeaked. " 'I want to stay here with Aunt Belle!' "

Meanwhile she was flouncing into her winged coat, fluffing her curls, jingling her car keys. "All set?" she asked.

"All set."

They walked out to her enormous old Ford. Delia fitted her carton among a tangle of real estate signs in the trunk, and then the two of them got in the car and Belle started the engine. With the seat-belt alarm insistently dinging, they pulled away from the curb.

It was months since Delia had ridden in a car. The scenery glided past so quickly, and so smoothly! She gripped her door handle as they swung around the corner, and then *zip! zip! zip!* went the dentist, the dime store, the Potpourri Palace. In no time, they were turning onto Pendle Street and parking in the Millers' gravel driveway—a trip that had taken her at least ten minutes, walking.

"My parents live in a house like this," Belle said. She was peering through the windshield at the cut-out designs of covered wagons on the shutters. "In a suburb of York, P.A. Dee, are you sure you want to do this?"

"Oh, yes," Delia said weakly.

"You'll be nothing but a servant!"

"It's better than being a typewriter," Delia told her.

"Well, if you're going to put it *that* way."

Delia climbed out of the car, and Belle came around to help her maneuver her box from the trunk. "Thanks," Delia said. "You have my phone number."

"I have it."

"I'll let you know when's a good time to bring the cat."

"Or before then," Belle said. "Or supposing you want to move back! I'll wait a few days before I try renting your room."

They might have gone on this way forever, but at that moment Noah burst out the front door. "Delia! Hi!" he called.

"Ms. Grinstead to *you*," Belle muttered under her breath. She told Delia, "Don't you let them treat you like a peon."

Delia just hugged her and turned toward the house. How the Millers treated her was the least of her concerns, she thought. The question was how to treat *them*—what distance to maintain from this mop-headed, blue-jeaned boy. It was so easy to fall back into being someone's mother! She smiled at him as he lifted the carton from her arms. "I can manage that," she said.

"I'm *supposed* to carry your luggage. Dad told me. Don't you have anything more?" he asked. Belle was already backing the car out of the driveway.

"This is it," Delia said.

"Dad's over at the school, so I'm supposed to show you where everything is. We've got your room all made up for you. We changed the bedsheets even though they were clean."

"Oh, then why did you change them?"

"Dad said if they didn't still have their laundry smell you might think someone else had slept in them."

"I wouldn't think that," she assured him.

They walked through the living room, where the cushions lined the couch in last week's exact formation and the magazines had not varied their positions by an inch. The carpet in the hall was freshly vacuumed, though. She could see the roller marks in the nap. And when they entered the guest room, Noah placed her box on a folding luggage stand that had definitely not been there earlier. "It's new," he said, noticing her glance. "We bought it at Home 'n' Hearth."

"It's very nice."

"And lookit here," he said. On the bureau sat a tiny television set. "Color TV! From Lawson Appliance. Dad says a live-in woman always has her own TV."

"Oh, I don't need a—"

"Clock radio," Noah said, "decorator box of Kleenex . . ."

What touched her most, though, was how they'd turned the bedcovers down—that effortful white triangle. She said, "You shouldn't have." And she meant it, for the sight made her feel indebted, somehow.

She followed Noah to the closet, where he was displaying the hangers. "Three dozen matching hangers, solid plastic, pink. Not a wire one in the bunch. We had our choice between pink or white or brown."

"Pink is perfect," she told him.

Three dozen! It would disappoint them to find out how few clothes she owned.

"Now I'm supposed to leave you in private," Noah said. "But I'll be in my room if there's anything you need."

"Thank you, Noah."

"You know where my room is?"

"I can find it."

"And you're supposed to unpack and put your stuff in drawers and all."

"I'll do that," she promised.

As he left he glanced back at her doubtfully, as if he worried she wouldn't follow instructions.

Her carton looked so shabby, resting on the needlepoint webbing of the luggage stand. She walked over to it and lifted the flaps, and out floated the lonesome, stale, hornet's-nest smell of the room on George Street. Well. She took off her coat, hung it on one of the hangers. Draped her purse strap over a hook. Drew the goosenecked lamp from the box but then had nowhere to put it, for the room already contained two lamps, shaded in rigid white satin. Still holding the goosenecked lamp (with its helmet of army-green metal and the dent at its base from when the cat had knocked it over one night), she sat down limply on the edge of the bed. She had to brace her feet so as not to slide off the slick coverlet. It was one of those hotel-type beds that seem at once too springy and too hard, and she couldn't imagine getting used to it.

Elsewhere in the house she heard a door open, a set of heavy footsteps, a man's voice calling and Noah answering. She would have to rearrange her face and go join them. Any minute now, she would. But for a while she went on sitting there, clutching her homely little lamp and gathering courage.

At the rear of the house, divided from the kitchen by only a counter, lay what the Millers called the family room. Here the stuffy decorating style relaxed into something more casual. A long, low couch faced a TV, an office desk stood against one wall, and three armchairs were grouped in a corner. It was this room that became, within the next few days, Delia's territory. (She had always wanted a more modern house, without cubbies or nooks or crannies.) In the mornings, when she was through cleaning, she sat at the desk to write her grocery list. She went out for several hours then—usually on foot, even though she had a car at her disposal—but afternoons would find her puttering between family room and kitchen while Noah did his homework on the couch. Evenings, she read in one of the armchairs while Noah watched TV. Sometimes Mr. Miller watched too—or Joel, as she had to remind herself to call him—in which case she retired early with her book. She was a little shy with Mr. Miller: Joel. This was such an awkward situation, businesslike and yet at the same time necessarily intimate. But usually he had meetings to go to, or he spent the evening at his workbench in the garage. She suspected he felt the awkwardness too. He couldn't possibly have stayed away so much before she came here.

They liked plain food, plainly prepared—roast beef and broiled chicken and burgers. Noah hated vegetables but was required to eat one spoonful each night. Mr. Miller was probably no fonder of them, but he worked his way conscientiously through everything, and he always told her, "Dinner is delicious, Delia." She suspected he would have said that no matter what she served. He asked her several courteous questions at every meal (had her day gone well? was she finding what she needed?), but she sensed he didn't listen to her answers. This was a sad, sad man underneath, and sometimes even when his own son spoke there was a moment of silence before he pulled himself together to reply.

"Guess what!" Noah might say. "Kenny Moss just got a humongous golden retriever. Dad, can we get a golden retriever?"

Long pause. Clinking of china. Then finally: "There is no such word as 'humongous.'"

"Sure there is, or how come I just used it?"

And the two of them would be off on one of their arguments. Delia had never known anyone as particular about words as Joel Miller. He despised all terms that were trendy (including "trendy" itself). He refused to agree that something was "neat" unless it was, literally, tidy. He interrupted one of Noah's most animated stories with the observation that no one could be "into" mountain climbing. But he always spoke with good humor, which probably explained why Noah still ventured to open his mouth.

Fastened to Delia's bathroom door was a full-length mirror, the first she had faced in six months, outside of a changing booth; and she was startled to see how thin she had grown. Her hipbones were sharp little chips, and the tops of her dresses looked hollow. So she served herself large helpings at these suppers, and she breakfasted with Noah every morning, and she walked to Rick-Rack's each noon to dine on something hefty—even crab cakes, for she was making good money now and had nothing else to spend it on.

Rick also served pork barbecue, the vinegary kind she was partial to, as it turned out. "You know," she told him, "I never had much of a chance to try a real meal here. I knew you were a good cook, but I didn't know *how* good."

"And here you been taking your Sunday dinners at that la-di-da Bay Arms!" he said.

Was there anything about her this whole town didn't know?

After lunch, she crossed the street to pay a visit to George. He was in a snit with her for leaving. He showed up as soon as she let herself in but then turned his back pointedly and stalked off. "George?" she wheedled. No response. He marched into Belle's living room and vanished. Delia waited in the hall, and a moment later a telltale sprig of whiskers poked around the edge of the door. A nose, an ear, an accusing green eye. "Georgie-boy!" she said. He sidled out, dusting the door with his fur and seeming to hang back even as he drew close enough to let her pat him.

Why couldn't Delia's children miss her this much?

All around town the streets were festooned with bristly silver ropes and honeycombed red tissue bells. There was a wreath above Mrs. Lincoln's desk in the library. Vanessa had tied a red bow to Greggie's stroller.

The thought of spending Christmas with the Millers—poor Noah bearing the full weight of it—filled Delia with dread. But maybe they didn't celebrate Christmas. Maybe they were Jewish, or some kind of fundamentalists who frowned on pagan ritual. It was true that so far, with just a week remaining, they hadn't given a sign they knew what season this was.

Delia went out to the garage to talk to Mr. Miller. "Um, Joel?" she said.

He was measuring a board at his workbench, wearing a raveled black sweater and frayed corduroys. Delia waited for him to look up—it took a minute—and then she said, "I wanted to ask about Christmas."

"Christmas," he said. He reeled in his measuring tape.

"Do you observe it?"

"Well, yes. Normally," he said.

By "normally," he must mean when he still had his wife. This would be their first Christmas without her, after all. Delia watched the thought travel across his face, deepening the lines at either side of his mouth. But he said, "Let's see. Ah, you would get the day off, of course. Noah will be at his mother's, and some friends in Wilmington have been asking me to visit. School is closed through New Year's, so if you need more time in Baltimore—"

"I won't be going to Baltimore."

He stopped speaking.

"I just wondered how you celebrate," she told him. "Do you put up a tree? Should I take Noah shopping for gifts?"

"Gifts."

"Something for his mother, maybe?"

"Oh, God," he said, and he sank onto the high stool behind him. He clamped the top of his head with one large hand—his usual sign of distress. "Yes, certainly for his mother, and also for Nat, Ellie's father. He and Noah are pretty close. And for me, I guess; aren't we supposed to encourage that? And I should get something for him. Oh, God Almighty."

"I'll take him tomorrow," she said. She hadn't intended to plunge the man into despair.

"That's a Saturday. Your weekend."

"I don't mind."

Seated on the stool, Mr. Miller was closer to Delia's eye level. He looked across at her for a moment. He said, "Don't you have any family around? For weekend visits and such?"

"No."

It was a mark of his isolation, she thought, that he had apparently not heard so much as a whisper about her past. For all he knew, Delia had dropped from the sky. Clearly he would have liked to ask more, but in the end he just said, "Well, thanks, Delia. As far as a tree goes, I figure since Noah won't be here for the day itself, we don't need to bother."

Delia would have bothered anyhow, if it had been up to her. But she didn't argue. When she left, Mr. Miller was still slumped on his stool, staring down at the measuring tape in his hands.

She and Noah did all his Christmas shopping at the hardware store—dark, old-fashioned, wooden-floored Brent Hardware, across the street from Belle's. Noah had very definite ideas, Delia discovered. For his mother he chose a screwdriver with interchangeable shafts, because she lived alone now and would need to make her own repairs. For his grandfather, who had trouble bending, a tonglike instrument called a "grabber" that would help him retrieve dropped objects. And for his father, a device to hold a nail in position while he was hammering it in. "Dad is all the time banging his thumb," Noah told Delia. "He's not a real great carpenter."

"What is it that he builds, exactly?" Delia asked.

"Shadow boxes."

"Shadow boxes?"

For an instant she pictured Charlie Chaplin shadowboxing in baggy trunks.

"Those, like, partitioned-up wooden shelves. You know? To hang on a wall?"

"Oh, yes."

"Because my mom collects miniatures. Teeny little kitchen utensils and furniture and like that, and he used to make these shadow boxes for her to keep them in."

And now? Delia wanted to ask.

As if he had read her mind, Noah said, "Now he just piles them behind the tires in the garage."

"I see."

She couldn't tell from Noah's tone how he felt about his parents' separation. He had mentioned his mother only in passing, and this coming visit would be his first since Delia's arrival.

"I want to pick out one more thing," he told her. "You go wait outside a minute."

So he was buying her a present too. She wished he wouldn't. She would have to act appreciative; she would have to make a big show of putting whatever it was to use, not to mention the necessity of buying something for *him* that was neither more nor less serious than what he'd bought her. Oh, how had she worked her way back to this? She should have stayed at Belle's; she'd known it all along.

But Noah was so gleeful as he hustled her out the door, she couldn't help smiling.

"Will you need money?" she asked him.

"I've been saving up my allowance."

He closed the door after her and made a comic shooing motion through the glass.

She waited on the sidewalk, watching the passersby. It was hard to resist getting caught up in the spirit of things. Everyone carried shopping bags and brightly wrapped parcels. From Rick-Rack's Café, next door, the cheering smells of bacon and hot pancakes drifted into the frosty air. When Noah rejoined her, hugging his own bag, she said, "How about I buy you a soda at Rick-Rack's?"

He hesitated. "You going to put it in the book?" he asked.

He meant the little notebook Mr. Miller had given her. She was supposed to keep a record of reimbursable expenses, and Noah always worried she might shortchange herself. (He viewed her as someone *less fortunate*, which she found both amusing and slightly humiliating.) "Today it's my treat," she told him firmly, and even as he opened his mouth to protest, she was nudging him toward the café.

Rick waved a spatula in their direction; he was busy at the grill. Teensy, though, made a big fuss. "It's Delia! And Mr. Miller's boy. Look, Pop!" she chirped, turning to an old man seated at the counter. "This is Delia Grinstead! She used to live across the street! My father, Mr. Bragg," she told Delia. "He's come to stay with us awhile."

Teensy's father, Delia seemed to recall, was a snarky man who had not behaved very graciously toward his son-in-law; so she was unprepared for his timid, meek expression and wilted posture. He sat up close to his breakfast like a child. When she said, "Hello," he had to work his mouth a minute before the words formed.

"I'm having cocoa," was what he finally said.

"How nice!"

Her voice came out sounding as false as Teensy's had.

"That your boy?" he asked.

"This is . . . Noah," she told him, not bothering with a full explanation.

"Come sit here, boy."

"Oh, we'd better take a booth, with all we're carrying." Delia gestured toward Noah's shopping bag. The handles of his grandfather's grabber extended from it a good two feet.

In the rear corner booth, Mr. Lamb sat hanging his head over a bowl of cereal. Two teenage girls had a window table—Underwood students, Delia assumed, judging by how they perked up at the sight of Noah. (Already she had turned several away from the house, briskly thanking them for their plates of homemade fudge and pretending not to notice how they gazed beyond her for Joel.) One of them sang out, "Hey there, Noah!" Noah rolled his eyes at Delia.

"What can I get you?" Teensy asked, standing over their table.

"Coffee, please," Noah said.

"Coffee!"

"Can't I?" He was addressing Delia. "Dad lets me have it, sometimes on special occasions."

"Well, all right. Make that two," Delia told Teensy.

"Sure thing," Teensy said. Then she bent so close that Delia could smell her starched-fabric scent, and she whispered, "When you leave here, could you say goodbye real loud to Rick, so Pop can hear you?"

"Of course," Delia said.

"Pop can act so hurtful to him sometimes."

"I'd have said goodbye anyhow, you know that."

"I know, but . . ." Teensy flapped a hand toward her father. He still appeared harmless, the X of his suspenders curving with the hunch of his back.

Noah was one of those people who like gloating over their purchases even before they get them home. He was rustling through his bag, first pulling out the screwdriver, then burrowing to the bottom for a furtive look at something there and shooting a tucked, sly glance at Delia. When she craned across the table, pretending to be angling for a peek, he laughed delightedly and crumpled the bag shut again. His two front teeth were still new enough to seem too big for his mouth.

And see how his hair fell over his eyes—the bouncy thickness of it, the soft sheen that made her want to press it with her palm. And the tilt at the tip of his nose, the knobby cluster of little-boy warts that showed on the bend of his index finger when he gripped the mug Teensy brought him. One point of his jacket collar stuck up crookedly. The knit shirt beneath it bore scratches of ballpoint-pen ink. His jeans, she knew, were ripped at the knees, and his sneakers were those elaborate, puffy hightops that could have been designed for walking on the moon.

He was telling her a dream he'd had—something boring and impossible to follow. His teacher changed into a dog, the dog came to visit at Noah's house, which was somehow the school auditorium too, if Delia knew what he meant . . .

Delia nodded, smiling, smiling, and folded her hands tightly so as not to reach across to him. When they left, she told Rick goodbye with such feeling that her voice broke.

Belle claimed the cat had developed an eating disorder. She brought him over in a Grape-Nuts carton late Monday morning, so he could adjust to the house while Delia was the only one home. Still in the carton, he was borne directly to Delia's room and set on the floor. "It's like he's bulimic," Belle was saying. She sank onto the edge of the bed to watch him nose his way out of the carton. "The minute his bowl is half empty he starts nagging me for more; I swear I never knew a cat could plan ahead that way. And if, God forbid, he should finish every bit of it, we have this heartrending melodrama the second I walk in from work. Great yowling and wringing of paws, and as soon as I fill the bowl he staggers over all weak-kneed to eat and makes these disgusting gobbling sounds and then darned if he doesn't throw up in a corner not ten minutes after he's done."

"Oh, George, did I do this to you?" Delia asked him. He was investigating the room now, sniffling daintily at the luggage stand.

"About six times a day he goes to the cupboard and looks up at his sack of kibble, checking to make sure I'm keeping enough in stock."

"All my life," Delia said, "I've been the ideal cat-owner. I lived in one place; I had a routine. I was motionless, in fact. Now I'm flitting about like a . . . He must feel so insecure!"

She bent to stroke the black M on his forehead, while Belle gazed around her. "This room is awfully small, isn't it?" she asked. "Your old one was a whole lot bigger."

"It's okay." Delia was trying to lure George into the bathroom now. "See? Your litter box," she told him. "Store-bought; not just cardboard."

"What're you doing for Christmas, Dee?" Belle called after her.

"Oh, staying here."

"Christmas with strangers?"

"They'll be gone, at least for the day."

"That's even worse," Belle told her.

"I'm sort of looking forward to it."

George stepped into the litter box and then out again, as if demonstrating that he knew what it was.

"Come along with me to my folks'," Belle told her. "They'd be thrilled to have you."

"No, really, thanks."

"Or get Vanessa to invite you to her grandma's."

"She already did, but I said no."

"Well, granted it's kind of hectic there," Belle said. "I'm a little peeved at Vanessa these days."

"Oh? How come?"

"You know what she had the nerve to ask me?" Belle stood up to follow Delia into the hall; they were heading for the bowl of cat food in the kitchen. George wafted after them in a shadowy, indecisive way. "I was complaining about my love life," Belle said. "Can't find a man to save my soul, I told her, and she asked why I'd never thought of Mr. Lamb."

"Mr. Lamb!"

"Can you imagine? That dreary, gloomy man, that . . . Eeyore! I said, 'Vanessa, just what sort of idea do you have of me? Do you honestly believe I would date a man who's spent his entire adulthood in rented bedrooms?' I mean, think about it: no one even calls him by his first name, have you noticed? Quick: what's Mr. Lamb's first name?"

"Um . . ."

"Horace," Belle said grimly. She plunked herself at the kitchen table. "I may be single, but I'm not suicidal. What's that I see on the fridge?"

She meant Mr. Miller's map of the household. "It's to keep things in the living room the way Mrs. Miller left them," Delia said. "He's charted all the doodads, exactly where she used to set them out."

Belle leaned forward for a closer look. On the rectangle representing the mantel, tiny block letters spelled *blue vase, pine-cone candle, sandbox photo, clock.*

"Well, that's just pathetic," Belle said. "And why would he need it? What makes him think these things would go and lose themselves, for Lord's sake?"

"You wouldn't ask if you could see him around the house," Delia said. "For someone so set on order, he's awfully . . . discombobulated. He's just plain incompetent! Oh, everything's fine on the surface, but when you look in the back of a cupboard you find pans with scorched bottoms that will never come clean, dish towels with big charred holes in them . . ."

Belle was peering at the diagram of the coffee table. "*Large paperweight, small paperweight, magazines,*" she read.

"He keeps these magazines that still come to the house in her name, all about clothing styles and cellulite and such."

"Ellie Miller never had a speck of cellulite in her life," Belle said.

"A new magazine comes, he fits it in the spot where the old one was and throws the old one away."

"That's what you get for worshiping a person," Belle said. "Poor man, he thought she walked on water! In fact, she was kind of silly, but you know how the smartest men will sometimes go so gaga over silly women. I asked him to a picnic after she left, and he said, 'Oh, I'm afraid I wouldn't know anyone; thank you just the same.' This is a high-school principal we're talking about! He ought to know the whole town! But he always depended on Ellie for that. Ellie was real outgoing and social, threw these parties with themes to them like Hawaiian Luau, Wild West Bar-becue . . . and a Grade Mothers' Tea in the fall, but Joel hasn't kept that up. He just let the grade mothers flounder this year, when needless to say, every gal in town was dying to help him."

"I wish . . . ," Delia began.

She wished Sam Grinstead had felt like that about her, she'd been going to say. But she stopped herself.

"Oh, I'm sure he'll let *you* help," Belle said, misunderstanding. "You just have to do it inch by inch, you know? Pretty soon, you'll be indispensable."

"Well, yes, of course," Delia agreed.

That much she simply assumed. Already, only ten days into her stay, Mr. Miller had requested another of "her" meat loaves; he had wordlessly laid out a shirt in need of a button; he no longer left his compulsive lists of instructions on the breakfast table.

But wasn't it odd that she had assumed it? She seemed to have changed into someone else—a woman people looked to automatically for sustenance.

The cat wove around her ankles, purring. "See?" Delia told Belle. "He doesn't have an eating disorder. All he ate was a couple of kibbles, just to be polite."

"You're amazing, Dee," Belle said.

Belle had also brought Delia's mail—a package from Eleanor and a letter from Eliza. Eleanor's package contained a knitted jacket for reading in bed. Eliza's letter said she'd invited the Allinghams for Christmas dinner. *I won't press you but you know you're welcome too,* she wrote, and then she hurried on to news of Linda. *She says the twins are getting to the age where they want to spend the holidays at home, so I guess it will be just the Allinghams and us and then Eleanor too of course.* . . . The stationery gave off that faint scent of cloves (for positive thoughts) that always hung in the air of Eliza's bedroom.

Noah was very excited about the cat. He came straight home from school that day, and he flung his books any old where and raced through the house, calling, "George? George?" George, of course, hid. Delia had to explain to Noah how cats operated—that you shouldn't pursue them, shouldn't face them head-on; should do everything at a diagonal, so to speak, with a cat. "Sit at his level," she said when George finally showed himself. "Look a little sideways to him. Talk in a crooning tone of voice."

"Talk? What should I say?"

"Tell him he's beautiful. Cats love the word 'beautiful.' I guess it must be something in your tone, because they're not the least bit good at language, but if you draw out that *u* sound long and thin and twangy . . ."

"Bee-yoo-tee-ful," Noah said, and sure enough, George slitted his eyes in a sleek, self-satisfied smile.

On Christmas Eve, Delia picked Noah up at school and drove him to his mother's. The Millers' car was a Volkswagen Beetle. She didn't yet feel completely at home with the stick shift, so it was a rocky ride. Noah was nice enough not to comment. He sat forward and watched for the turnoff to Kellerton. "Most times Mom comes to get me," he said, "but her car's in the shop right now. She's had five wrecks in the last nine months."

"Five!" Delia said.

"None of them were her fault, though."

"I see."

"She's just, like, unlucky. This last time, a guy backed into her while she was looking for a parking spot. Here's where you turn."

Delia signaled and took a right onto a patchy highway that ran between fields of frozen stubble. This countryside was so flat, at least she didn't need to shift gears all that often. They were heading east, in the direction of the beaches. Mr. Miller had told her it was a half-hour drive.

"Tonight at six you want to watch WKMD," Noah said. "It's not like I'll be on it or anything, but at least you'll know I'm sitting there in the station."

It must feel eerie to see your absent mother deliver the weather report every night. Although Noah never did, to the best of Delia's knowledge. Six o'clock was *The MacNeil / Lehrer NewsHour*, which Mr. Miller watched instead.

The fields gave way to hamburger joints and used-car lots and liquor stores, implying the approach of a town, but soon Delia realized this *was* the town—this scattering of buildings flung across the farmland. Noah pointed out the television station beneath its Erector-set tower. He showed her where his mother did her grocery shopping and where she got her hair done, and then he directed her two blocks south to a low, beige-brick apartment building. "Should I come in with you?" Delia asked, parking at the curb.

"Naw. I've got a key if she's not there."

Delia was disappointed, but she didn't argue.

"When you wake up tomorrow," Noah told her as she unlocked the trunk, "look on my closet shelf and you'll find your present."

"And when you wake up, look in the inside end pocket of your duffel bag."

He grinned and took the bag from her. "So, okay," he said. "See you, I guess."

"Have a good Christmas."

Instead of hugging him, she tousled his hair. She'd been longing to do that anyhow.

By the time she got back to the house, Mr. Miller was waiting at the front window. They barely crossed paths in the doorway—Mr. Miller holding out a palm for the car keys, wishing her a Merry Christmas, saying he'd be back with Noah tomorrow evening—and then he was gone. The cat mewed anxiously and trailed Delia to her room.

On her bureau, she found a Christmas card with a check for a hundred dollars. *Season's Greetings,* the card read, followed by Mr. Miller's block print: *Just a token thank you for setting our lives back in order. Gratefully, Joel and Noah.*

That was nice of him, she thought. Also, he had shown tact in clearing out of the house when he did. It would have been a strain without Noah to serve as buffer.

She spent the afternoon on the couch, reading an extra-thick library book: *Doctor Zhivago*. The wind dashed bits of leaves against the picture windows. George slept curled at her feet. Twilight fell, and her lamp formed a nest of honey-colored light.

A few minutes before six, she took the remote control from the end table and clicked the TV on. WKMD had a one-eyed pirate advertising choice waterfront lots. Then a housewife spraying a room with aerosol. Then a deskful of newscasters—a bearded black man, a pink-faced white man, and a glamorous blonde in a business suit. Delia thought at first the blonde was Ellie Miller, till the black man called her Doris. Doris told about a bank heist in Ocean City. The robber had been dressed as Santa Claus, she said. She spoke in such a way that her lipstick never came in contact with her teeth.

Delia was disconcerted by the speed at which everything moved. She had lost the knack of watching television, it seemed. She felt her eyes had experienced an overload, and during the next round of commercials she looked away for a while.

"Now here's Ellie with the weather," the bearded man said. "So tell us, Ellie, any chance of a white Christmas?"

"Not a prayer, Dave," Ellie told him in that sporty, bosom-buddy tone that TV people affect. Her face, though, didn't match her voice. It was too soft, too open—a pretty face with a large red mouth, surprised blue eyes, and circlets of pink rouge. Her hair was silvery fluff. Her white sweater, a scoop-necked angora, seemed uncertain around the edges.

Delia rose and went to stand in front of the TV. Ellie slid weather maps along an aluminum groove. Somewhere behind that painted backdrop of marsh and improbable cattails, Noah would be sitting, but at the moment Delia wasn't thinking of Noah. She was memorizing Ellie, trying to see what lay beneath her sky-blue, doll-like stare.

"Continued cold . . . gale-force winds . . ." Delia listened with her head cocked, her fingertips supporting her cheek.

The weather was followed by sports, and Delia turned and wandered out of the family room and through the kitchen, down the hall to the master bedroom. She opened the closet door and studied the clothes hanging inside. Mr. Miller's suits straggled across the rod toward the empty space at the right. The shelf above was empty on the right as well. It appeared that Ellie, unlike Rosemary Bly-Brice, had taken everything with her when she went. Even so, Delia next pulled out each drawer in Ellie's bureau. All she found was a button, trailing a wisp of blue thread.

Back in the family room, the TV was showing the national news. It was months since she had watched the news, but she could see she hadn't missed anything: the planet was still hurtling toward disaster. She switched the TV off in midsentence and went to make her supper.

When she woke the next morning, the sun was out. Something about the hard, bright light told her it was very cold. Also, George lay nestled close under her arm, which he wouldn't do in warmer weather.

Not until she was drinking her tea did she consider the fact that it was

Christmas. Christmas, all by herself! She supposed that would strike most people as tragic, but to her the prospect was enjoyable. She liked carrying her cup through the silent house, still wearing her nightgown and beach robe, humming a snatch of "We Three Kings" with no one to hear her. In Noah's room she rooted through the top drawer for a pair of woolen socks to wear as slippers. Then she remembered he'd left her a gift, and she pulled it down from his closet shelf—a squarish shape wrapped in red foil. The tag read, *Because you don't have house-type clothes,* which puzzled her till she tore off the foil and saw a canvas carpenter's apron with pockets across the front. She smiled and slipped the neck strap over her head. Till now she'd been using the cocktail apron she'd found among the dish towels, which protected no more than the laps of her dresses.

Her gift to Noah had been a survival kit from Kemp's Kamping Store. Boys seemed to go for such things. And this kit was so ingenious—hardly bigger than a credit card, with streamlined foldout gadgets, including a magnifying lens for starting fires.

She fed George, and then she dressed and settled on the couch again with *Doctor Zhivago.* Periodically, she looked up from the book and let her eyes travel around the room. Wintry sunlight, almost white, fell across the carpet. The cat was giving himself a bath in a square of sunlight on the blue armchair. Everything had a pleasantly shallow look, like a painting.

At home they must be opening their presents now. It was nothing like the old days, when they used to rise before dawn. Now they ambled downstairs in midmorning, and they passed out presents decorously, one person at a time. Then for dinner they always had goose, a contribution from one of Sam's patients who hunted. For dessert, plum pudding with hard sauce, and they would complain it was too heavy but eat it anyhow and spend the rest of the afternoon moaning and clutching their stomachs.

Every so often it took her breath away to realize how easily her family had accepted her leaving.

Although it *did* seem acceptable, come to think of it. It seemed almost inevitable. Almost . . . foreordained. In retrospect she saw all the events of the past year—her father's death, Sam's illness, Adrian's arrival—as waves that had rolled her forward, one wave after another, closer and closer together. Not sideways, after all, but forward, for now she thought that her move to the Millers' must surely represent some kind of progress.

She had imagined that her holiday would not last nearly long enough, but when Joel and Noah turned into the driveway at dusk, she was already watching at the window. She dropped the curtain as soon as she saw the headlights, and she rushed to open the door and welcome them home.

13

Once a week, generally on Wednesday afternoons, Delia drove Noah a few miles west on Highway 50 to visit his grandfather. The old man lived in a place called Senior City—four stories of new red brick on the edge of a marshy golf course. Delia would pull up in the U-shaped drive, let Noah out, and leave, maneuvering past a fleet of gigantic Buicks and Cadillacs. She came back to collect him at the front door an hour later. It was an inconvenient length of time, just slightly too short to make returning to Bay Borough worth her while, and so she formed the habit of heading for a nearby shopping center. There she browsed in a bookstore, or picked up some treat for supper at the gourmet food store.

She was dropping Noah off one Wednesday in mid-January, when he announced that she should come in with him. "Me? What for?" she asked.

"Grandpa wants to see you."

"Well, but . . ."

She glanced down. Beneath her coat she was wearing a housedress, a dark cotton print she had bought at an after-Christmas sale. "How about next week?" she suggested.

"He asked me to bring you today. I forgot."

She pulled into one of the visitors' parking slots. "If you'd warned me, I would have dressed up," she said.

"It's only Grandpa."

"I look a mess! What's his name?"

"Nat."

"I meant his last name," she said, getting out of the car. Years of experience had taught her not to rely on children's formal introductions. "I have to call him Mister *something*."

"Everybody just says Nat."

She gave up and followed Noah past a row of Handicapped license plates. "Does he want to see me for any particular reason?" she asked.

"He says he doesn't know who to picture when I talk about you."

They approached the double doors, which slid open to admit them. The lobby was carpeted with some nubby, hard substance, probably to accommodate wheelchairs. It made a winching sound beneath their feet. On their right was a glassed-in gift shop, and through an entrance at their left Delia glimpsed a cafeteria, deserted at this hour but still giving off that unmistakable steamed-vegetable smell. Several old women waited in front of the elevators. One sat in a motorized cart, and two leaned on walkers. This was like visiting a war zone, Delia thought. But the women were elegantly coiffed and dressed, and at the sight of Noah their faces lit up in smiles. *Valiant* smiles, they seemed to Delia. She was familiar with old people's tribulations, having observed Sam's patients for so long.

The elevator opened to expose a slim, blue-haired old woman in a designer dress. "Sorry!" she caroled. "I'm going down."

"You *are* down, Pooky," the woman on the cart said. "This is the bottom floor."

"Well, you're welcome to come along for the ride, but I've pressed One, I regret to say."

"This *is* One, Pooky."

The others didn't bother to argue. They entered laboriously, most of them clinging to various surfaces for support. Noah and Delia came last. The door closed behind them, and they began rising. Meanwhile everyone beamed at Noah—even Pooky, who seemed unfazed that they were not, in fact, going down. At the second floor, a woman with a shopping bag got off. At the third floor, Noah said, "This is us," and he and Delia stepped into a long corridor. Several women followed, with metallic clanking sounds and a whirring of wheels. Pooky, however, remained on board, gazing contentedly straight ahead as the elevator door slid shut.

"She rides up and down all day sometimes," Noah told Delia.

Nothing here seemed any different from a standard apartment building, except for the handrails that ran along both walls. Blond flush doors appeared at intervals, each with a peephole at eye level. Noah stopped at the fourth door on the right. *Nathaniel A. Moffat, Photographer,* a business card read, with a Cambridge, Maryland, street address crossed out. When Noah pressed the doorbell, a single golden note sounded from within.

"Is that my favorite grandson?" a man shouted.

"Yes, it is," Noah called back.

"It's his *only* grandson," he told Delia with a giggle.

The door opened, but instead of the old man Delia had expected, a short, chunky woman stood smiling at them. She could not have been out of her thirties. She had a round apricot of a face and pink-tinted curls, and she wore an orange sweater-dress with a keyhole neckline. Her shoes were orange too—tiny, open-toed pumps, as Delia found when she checked, reflexively, for nurse shoes to explain the woman's presence. "Hi! I'm Binky," she told Delia. "Hey there, Noah. Come on in."

The living room they entered must have been as modern as the rest of the building, but Delia couldn't see beyond the furniture, which was dark and tangled, ornate, ponderously antique. Also, there was far too much of it, set far too close together, as if it had once filled several larger rooms.

For a moment Delia had trouble locating Noah's grandfather. He was rising from the depths of a maroon velvet chair with viny arms. A four-pronged metal cane stood next to him, but he moved forward on his own to shake her hand. "You're Delia," he said. "I'm Nat."

He was one of those men who look better old, probably, than they ever did young—clipped white beard, ruddy face, and a lean, energetic body. He wore a tweed sports coat and gray trousers. His handshake was muscular and brisk.

"Thank you for coming," he told her. "I wanted to get a look at this person my grandson's so taken with."

"Well, thank you for inviting me."

"Won't you give Binky your coat?"

Delia was about to tell him she would keep her coat, she could only stay a second; but then she saw that the table in front of the couch was laid for tea. There were plates of cakes, four china cups and saucers, and a teapot already steeping in a swaddling of ivory linen. Thank goodness Noah had remembered she was invited.

She handed her coat to Binky and then sat where Nat indicated, at one end of the couch. Nat reclaimed his chair, and Noah took a seat in the little rocker next to him. Binky, when she returned from the coat closet, settled on the other end of the couch and bent forward to unwrap the teapot.

"Noah always likes mint instead of plain," she told Delia. "I hope you don't mind."

"Not at all."

Noah had this tea party every time he came here, then? Delia had imagined he was, oh, playing checkers or something. She looked over at his grandfather, who nodded gravely.

"Noah's been taking tea with me since the days when he drank from a training mug," he told her. "He's the only boy in the family! We men have to stick together."

Binky handed Delia her cup and said, "So how do you like keeping house for Noah's father, Delia?"

"Oh, very much," Delia said.

"Joel's a good man," Nat said placidly. "I make it a point not to choose sides in my daughters' domestic disputes," he told Delia. "Back when they were wee little girls, I swore an oath to myself I would approve of whoever they married."

Enough of a pause hung after his words so that Delia felt pushed to ask, "And do you?"

"Oh, absolutely," he said. His chuckle, filtered through his beard, had a wheezy sound. "I love my sons-in-law to death! And they think I'm just wonderful."

"Well, you *are* wonderful," Binky told him staunchly.

He bowed from the waist. "Thank you, madam."

"Maybe not quite as wonderful as they imagine, mind you . . ."

He grimaced at her, and she gave Delia a mischievous wink.

Was this Binky a paid companion? Was she one of the daughters? But her merry face bore no resemblance to Nat's. And she didn't seem all that connected to his grandson. "Have some butter," she was telling Noah, not noticing he had nothing to put it on.

"Have some low-cholesterol vegetable-oil spread," Nat corrected her. "First I wolf down my I Can't Believe It's Not Butter," he told Delia, "and then I go wash my hair in Gee, Your Hair Smells Terrific."

Delia found this remark mystifying, but Noah tittered. His grandfather glanced over at him; his lips twitched as if he were trying not to smile. Then he turned back to Delia. "You're from Baltimore, I hear."

"Yes," she said.

"Got family there?"

"Some."

He raised his eyebrows, but she offered nothing further.

"Ninety percent of the people in this building come from Baltimore," he said finally.

"They do?"

"Rich folks, retiring to the Eastern Shore. Roland Park and Guilford folks."

Delia kept her face blank, giving no sign she had ever heard of Roland Park or Guilford.

"You surely don't suppose all those chichi ladies are locals," he said. "Lord, no. I wouldn't be here myself if I hadn't married a Murray. That's Murray as in Murray Crab Spice. You think a two-bit, hole-in-the-wall photographer could afford these exorbitant prices?"

"They're going to raise the rates again in July, I hear," Binky told him.

Delia was looking around the room. The mention of photography had alerted her to the pictures hanging everywhere—large black-and-white photos, professionally framed. "Are these your work?" she asked him.

"These? If only."

He stood, this time reaching for his cane. "These were taken by the masters," he said, stumping over to a study of a voluptuous green pepper. "Edward Weston, Margaret Bourke-White . . ." He pivoted to inspect the picture at his left—factory chimneys, lined up like notes of music. "Me, I photographed brides," he said. "Forty-two years of brides. Few golden-anniversary couples thrown in from time to time. Then I started getting my, what I call, flashbacks." He gave a downward jab with his beard. Delia thought at first he was indicating the rug. "Old boyhood polio came bouncing back on me," he said. "Thelma—that was my wife—she'd passed on by then, but she had put our names on the waiting list when they first drew up the plans for Senior City. Just why, I couldn't tell you, since she refused to budge from our big old house long after the girls were grown and gone. She always said, what if they wanted to come back for any reason? And come back they did, you know they did: all four of them rushing home at every minor crisis, just because of the very fact they had a home to rush to, if you want my honest opinion. 'Lord God, Thel,' I told her, 'we can't be rearing those girls for all time! Look at how cats do,' I told her. 'Raise up their kittens, wean them, don't know who the hell they are when they meet them in the alley a few months later. You think humans should be any different?' "

"Well, of course they should!" Binky protested, and she and Delia exchanged a smile.

But Nat hissed derisively behind his beard. "Hogwash," he told Noah. Noah merely licked a dab of frosting from his thumb. "In any event," Nat said, "I started getting these flashbacks. Times the one leg would clean give out on me, along about the end of day. Reached the point where I barely made it up the stairs some nights; I knew I couldn't go on living where I was. So I phoned the people here and said, 'Listen,' I said, 'didn't my wife put our names on your waiting list once upon a time?' And that's how I happened to end up in Senior City. Senior City: God. Abominable name."

"It seems very . . . well-organized, though," Delia said.

"Precisely. Organized. That's the word!" He spun around (there was something explosive, barely contained, about even his most painful movements) and returned to his chair. "Like files in a filing cabinet," he said, reseating himself by degrees. "We're organized on the vertical. Feebler we get, higher up we live. Floor below this one is the hale-and-hearty. Some people there go to work still, or clip their coupons or whatever it is they do; use the golf course and the Ping-Pong tables, travel south for Christmas. This floor here is for the moderately, er, challenged. Those of us who need wheelchair-height counters or perhaps a little help coping. Fourth floor is total care. Nurses, beds with railings . . . Everybody hopes to die before they're sent to Four."

"Oh, they do not!" Binky said indignantly. "It's lovely up on Four! Have a cupcake, Noah."

" 'Lovely' isn't the word that first comes to my mind," Nat told Delia. "Not that I don't applaud Senior City in theory, understand. It's certainly preferable to burdening your children. But something about the whole setup strikes me as uncomfortably, shall we say, symbolic. See, I've always pictured life as one of those ladders you find on playground sliding boards—a sort of ladder of years where you climb higher and higher, and then, *oops!*, you fall over the edge and others move up behind you. I keep asking myself: couldn't Thelma have found us a place with a few more levels to it?"

Delia laughed, and Nat sat back in his chair and grinned at her. "Well," he said, "don't let me ramble on. I'm glad we finally got to meet you, Delia. Noah's told me how much you've done for the two of them."

She recognized her cue. "It was good to meet you too," she said, rising.

"From now on, stop in and have tea whenever you come for Noah, why don't you?"

"I'll do that," she promised.

She slid her arms into the coat Binky held for her, and Noah wrangled his jacket on. "Drive carefully, now," Binky said as she opened the door. Her keyhole neckline showed a teardrop of plump, powdered pink, bisected by the tight crevice between her breasts. Was it that, or was it the memory of Nat's roguish grin, that made Delia wonder suddenly whether Binky might in fact be his girlfriend?

Joel told her he had no idea who Binky was. He hadn't realized she existed, even. "Binky? Binky who?" he asked. "What kind of a name is Binky?"

They were eating supper in the kitchen, just the two of them. Noah had accepted a last-minute invitation to the Mosses'. At first Delia had contrived to be on her feet most of the time, but finally Joel said, "Sit down, Delia," in a kindly tone that made her feel he'd seen straight through her. "Tell me how you think Noah's doing," he said.

That took about three seconds. (Noah was doing fine.) Then they had to find a new topic, and so Delia thought to mention Binky.

"How old is she, would you guess?" Joel asked.

"Oh, thirty-five, thirty-six . . ."

"So: too young to be a fellow resident. And I doubt Nat needs a nurse. What did Noah say about her?"

"He said she's just 'around.' I asked who she was, and he said, 'I don't know; someone who's just around a lot.' "

"Hmm."

"Well, anyhow," Delia said. "It's really none of my business. I can't think why I brought it up."

But then she remembered why, because they were back to an uneasy silence.

"His wife was a paragon of virtue," Joel said while he was helping himself to another roll. "Noah's grandma, that is."

"Oh, really?"

"To hear *her* tell it."

"Oh."

"I never could abide that woman. Always interfering. Nudging into our lives. Inquiring after the welfare of her gifts. 'Do you ever use the such and such?' 'How come I never see you in the so-and-so?' "

Delia laughed.

"So if this Binky is his mistress," Joel said—the bald, bold word giving Delia a slight shock—"I say more power to him. He deserves a little happiness."

"Well, I didn't mean—"

"Why not? He's only sixty-seven. If it weren't for those damn flash-backs, he'd be out sailing his boat still."

Delia hadn't known that Nat sailed, but she could easily picture it: his spiky figure all over the deck, everywhere at once.

"She liked to say she was 'there' for people," Joel was reminiscing. He must be on the subject of Noah's grandma again. "First person I ever heard say that, though Lord knows it's grown common enough since. 'I'm always *there* for my daughters,' " he mocked. "You want to ask, 'Where's that, exactly?' It's one of my least favorite terms."

Delia hoped she hadn't used it herself. She was fairly sure she had not.

"That and 'survivor,' " Joel said. "Well, unless it's meant in the literal sense."

"Survivor?"

"Nowadays you're a survivor if all you did was make it through childhood."

"Ah."

"And another word I hate is . . ."

It was lucky he held so many strong opinions. Delia wouldn't need to make conversation after all. Instead, she sat watching his mouth, that long, firm, fine-edged mouth with the distinctive notch at the center of the upper lip, and she reflected that for someone so absorbed in questions of language, he certainly didn't reveal very much.

Now when she went to the gourmet food store after dropping Noah off on Wednesday afternoons, she chose some additional item—sour French cornichons, hot-pepper jelly—and paid for it with her own money and brought it to tea at Nat's. "How did you guess I like such things?" Nat would ask. "Most people come with chocolates. Fruit preserves. Sweet stuff."

She didn't tell him it was because her father, too, had been fond of pickly foods, for something gallant and slightly flirtatious in Nat's manner suggested he didn't view himself as all that old. Often he poked fun at Senior City, as if to prove he didn't really belong there. "House of the Living Dead," he called it. He claimed to believe that the seagulls drifting above the building were vultures, and he spoke jocularly of the "poor dears" on Floor 4. And then there was his romance with Binky.

For Binky *was* his girlfriend; Delia couldn't doubt that. Three times Delia arrived for tea and found her perched on his couch, playing hostess. And the fourth time, when she was missing, Nat found it necessary to explain that she'd been called away at the last minute. Her son had chipped a tooth, he said.

"Binky has a son?" Delia asked.

"Two sons, in fact."

"I didn't know that."

"So Noah has been doing the honors today."

Delia settled on the couch, laying her coat over her arm. She watched Noah pour an unsteady stream of tea.

"I didn't even know she was married," she said.

She chose her words carefully; she didn't say *had been* married, because it could be that Binky was married still. And Nat's response left her none the wiser. "Oh, yes," was all he said. "To a dentist."

Inspired, she said, "Well, then, the chipped tooth should be no problem."

"Correct," Nat said. He sent her a glint of a look from under his tufted gray eyebrows. Then he relented. "Assuming she doesn't mind flying her son to an office in Wyoming."

"Oh."

"They're divorced."

"Oh, I see."

"*Bitterly* divorced," Nat said with some relish. "Months in court, lawyers and replacement lawyers, forty thousand dollars spent to win five thousand . . . you get the picture."

"I'm sorry to hear that."

"She ended up almost penniless, had to take a job in the Senior City gift shop."

"She works in the gift shop?"

"Well, for now."

He glanced over at Noah, who was passing around a plate of brownies at a perilous tilt. "Fact is," Nat said, "Binky and I are getting married."

Noah let the plate tilt more sharply. Delia said, "Oh! Congratulations," and bent to pick a brownie off the rug.

"Honest?" Noah asked his grandfather.

"Honest. But don't mention it to the girls yet, will you? I should have told your mom and your aunts before anyone."

"So then will you move out of here?" Noah asked.

"Afraid not, son." Nat turned to Delia. "Noah liked my old place better," he said.

"The old place had this real cool tree house out back," Noah told her.

"However, it did not have an elevator. Or a handgrip above the bathtub. Or a physical-therapy room for ancient codgers."

"You're not an ancient codger!" Noah said.

"Plus there's the little detail of my contract with Senior City," Nat told Delia. "Bit of a problem with the board of directors, as you might imagine. All my life savings are sunk in this apartment, but the minimum age of entrance is sixty-five. Binky's thirty-eight."

"And how about her sons?" Delia asked.

"Yes, that *would* have been a poser! Rock music in the cafeteria, skateboards down the halls . . . However, her sons will stay on with her parents. One is already in college, and the other's about to go. But even so, the board is having hissy fits, and then a few neighbors are mad at me too, because men are mighty scarce in these parts. Plan was, I would marry one of the residents, not some luscious babe in the gift shop."

"Well, I think you've made the perfect choice," Delia said.

She meant it, too. She had developed a liking for Binky, who edged all their conversations with a ruffle of admiring murmurs and encouraging remarks.

So when Delia stopped by the following week, she made a point of telling Binky that Nat was a lucky man.

"Well, thank you," Binky said, beaming.

"Have you set a date yet?"

"We've talked about maybe June."

"Or March," Nat amended.

Binky rounded her eyes comically at Delia. March was right around the corner; they were halfway through February. "He has no idea what goes into these things," she said.

"Oh, are you planning a big wedding?"

"Well, not *that* big, but . . . My first wedding, I eloped. I was a freshman at Washington College and wore what I'd worn to class that day. So this time I'd like all the trimmings."

"I'm going to be best man," Noah told Delia.

"You are!"

"I get to hold the ring."

"You'll come too, won't you, Delia?" Nat asked.

"If I'm invited, of course I will."

"Oh, you'll be invited, all right," Binky said, and she patted Delia's hand and gave her a dimpled smile.

But later, riding home, Noah told Delia that Binky had been crying when he got there.

"Crying! What about?"

"I don't know, but her eyes were all red. She pretended she was fine, but I could tell. And then when she was in the kitchen the phone rang and Grandpa shouted out, 'Don't answer that!' and she didn't. And he didn't either, just let it ring and ring. So finally I said, 'Want me to get it?' but he said, 'Nah, never mind.' Said, 'It's probably just Dudi.' "

"Who's Dudi?"

"One of my aunts."

"Oh." Delia thought that over. "But why wouldn't he talk to her?"

He shrugged. "Beats me," he said. "You want to watch your speedometer, Delia."

"Thanks," Delia said.

She'd been issued two tickets in the last three weeks. It was something to do with this open country, she believed. The speed just seemed to inch up on her, and before she knew it she was flying.

Back in Bay Borough, Joel was already home and waiting to hear the latest. He took a rather gleeful interest in Nat's wedding plans. "Noah's going to be best man," Delia told him as she hung up her coat.

"No kidding!" He turned to Noah. "Where are you throwing the stag party?"

"Stag party?"

"Have you thought out your toasts yet?"

"Toasts!"

"Don't you pay any attention," Delia told Noah. He was looking worried.

It occurred to her that she was bound to run into Ellie at the wedding. Scandalous that they hadn't met before; Delia was in charge of Ellie's son. What kind of mother entrusted her son to a stranger?

A couple of weeks before, passing through Nat's bedroom to use his bathroom, Delia had noticed a color photo of his daughters on the high-boy. At least she assumed they were all his daughters—Ellie and three other blondes, linking arms and laughing. Ellie was the most vivid, the one you looked at first. She wore a cream dress splashed with strawberries that matched her strawberry mouth. Her shoes, though, were not very flattering. They were ballerina flats, *black* ballerina flats, papery and klutzy. They showed the bulges of her toes. They made her ankles look thick.

Why did Delia find this so gratifying? She had nothing against Ellie; she didn't even know her. But she bent closer to the photo and spent several moments hunting other flaws. Not that she found them. And not that she would have occasion, anyhow, to point them out to Joel.

14

On a Friday morning at the tail end of February—a day so mild and sunny that she would have supposed spring was here, if she hadn't known the tricky ways of winter—Delia walked to the Young Mister Shop to exchange some pajamas for Noah. (She had bought him a pair like an Orioles uniform, not realizing that for some strange reason, Noah preferred the Phillies.) And then, because it felt so pleasant to be out in nothing heavier than a sweater, she decided to walk to the library and visit with Mrs. Lincoln awhile. So she cut across the square and started up West Street. At the florist's window she slowed to admire a pot of paperwhites, and at Mr. Pomfret's window she slid her eyes sideways to check out his new secretary. Rumor had it he was limping along with a niece of his wife's who couldn't even type, let alone run a computer. But the way the light hit the glass, Delia would have had to step closer to see inside. All she could make out was her own silhouette and another just behind, both ivy-patterned from the sprawling new plant the niece must have set on the sill. Delia increased her speed and crossed George Street.

The window display in the Pinchpenny was little girls' dresses this week; so now the two silhouettes were made up of rosebud prints and plaids. She noticed that the second silhouette was storky and gangling, mostly joints, like an adolescent boy. Like Carroll.

She turned, and there he was. He looked even more startled than she felt, if that was possible. His expression froze and he drew back sharply, hands thrust into his windbreaker pockets, elbows jutting.

She said, "Carroll?"

"What."

"Oh, *Carroll!*" she cried, and the feeling that swept through her was so wrenching, like the grip of some deep, internal fist, that she understood for the first time how terribly much she had missed him. His face might have been her own face, not because it resembled hers (although it did), but because she had absorbed its every detail over the past fifteen years—the sprinkle of starry freckles across his delicate nose, the way the shadows beneath his eyes would darken at fraught moments. (Right now they were almost purple.) He raised his chin defiantly, and so at the very last second she merely reached out to lay a hand on his arm instead of kissing him. She said, "I'm so happy to see you! How'd you get here?"

"I had a ride."

She had forgotten that his voice had changed. She had to adjust all over again. "And what are you doing on West Street?" she asked.

"I tried your boardinghouse first, but no one answered, and then I happened to see you crossing the square."

He must not have told the family he was coming, therefore. (She had sent Eliza her new address weeks ago.) She said, "Is something wrong at home? Are you all right? It's a school day!"

"Everything's fine," he said.

He was trying, unobtrusively, to step out from under her hand. He was darting embarrassed glances at passersby. Much as she hated to, she let go of him. She said, "Well, let's . . . would you like some lunch?"

"Lunch? I just had breakfast."

Yes, it was morning still, wasn't it. She felt dizzy and disoriented, almost drunk. "A Coke or something, then," she said.

"Okay."

Turning him in the direction of Rick-Rack's gave her an excuse to touch him again. She loved that hard tendon at the inside crook of his arm. Oh, she might have known it would be Carroll who finally came for her! (Her most attached child, when all was said and done—her most loving, her closest. Although she would probably have thought the same if it had been either of the other two.)

"There's so much you have to bring me up-to-date on," she told him. "How's tenth grade?"

He shrugged.

"Has your father had any more chest pains?"

"Not that I know of."

"Ramsay and Susie all right?"

"Sure."

Then what is it? she wanted to ask, but she didn't. Already she was falling back into the veiled, duplicitous manner required for teenage offspring. She led him west on George Street, very nearly holding her breath. "Is Ramsay still seeing that divorcée person? That Velma?" she said.

Another shrug. Obviously, he was.

"And how about Susie?"

"How about her."

"Has she figured out yet what she'll do after graduation?"

"Huh?" he said, looking toward a Bon Jovi poster in the record store.

He was as frustrating as ever, and he hadn't lost that habit of ostentatiously holding back a yawn each time he spoke. She forced herself to be patient. She steered him past Shearson Liquors, past Brent Hardware, and through the door of Rick-Rack's.

"Dee-babe!" Rick hailed her, lowering his copy of *Sports Illustrated.* She would have known from his greeting alone that his father-in-law was sitting at the counter. (Rick always put on a display for Mr. Bragg.) "Who's that you got with you?" he asked.

"This is my son Carroll." She told Carroll, "This is Rick Rackley."

"Hey, your son!" Rick said. "How about that!"

Carroll looked dazed. Delia felt a prickle of annoyance. Couldn't he at least act civil? "Let's sit in a booth," she said brusquely.

Teensy was nowhere in sight, so Delia took it upon herself to grab two menus from the pile on a stool. As soon as they were seated, she passed one to Carroll. "I know it's early," she said, "but you might want to try the pork barbecue sandwich. It's the North Carolina kind, not a bit sweet or—"

"Mom," Carroll whispered.

"What."

"Mom. Is that *Rick*-Rack?"

"What?"

"Rick Rackley, the football player?"

"Well, yes, I think so."

Carroll gaped at Rick, who was topping off his father-in-law's mug of coffee. He turned back to Delia and whispered, "You know Rick-Rack in person? Rick-Rack knows you?"

This was working out better than she could have hoped. She said, "Yes, certainly," in an airy tone, and then, showing off, she called, "Where's Teensy got to, Rick?"

"She's over at House of Hair," he said, setting the coffeepot back on the burner. "You-all going to have to shout your order direct to me."

"Well, is it too early to ask for pork barbecue?"

"Naw, we can do that," Rick said.

Carroll said, "I just had breakfast, Mom. I told you."

"Yes, but this is something you wouldn't want to miss," she said. "Not a drop of tomato sauce! And it comes with really good french fries and homemade coleslaw!"

She didn't know why she was making such a fuss about it. Carroll was clearly not hungry; he was still staring at Rick. But she called, "Two platters, please, Rick, and two large Cokes."

"You got it."

Mr. Bragg spun his stool around so he could study them. His thin white crew cut stood erect, giving him the look of someone flabbergasted. "Why!" he cried. "What's happened with this *boy*?"

Delia glanced toward Carroll in alarm.

"How'd he shoot up so fast?" Mr. Bragg asked. "How'd he get so big all at once?"

She wondered if the old man had somehow read her mind, but then he said, "Last Christmas he was only yea tall," and he set a palm down around the level of his shins.

"Oh," Delia said. "No, that's Noah you're thinking of."

It was common knowledge by now that Mr. Bragg was failing, which was why poor Rick and Teensy couldn't send him back wherever he came from.

"Who's Noah?" was his next question.

"Who's Noah?" Carroll echoed.

"Just the boy who . . ." She felt rattled, as if she had been caught in some disloyalty. "Just the son of my employer," she said. "So! Carroll. Tell me all that's been going on at home. Has the Casserole Harem descended? Lots of apple pies streaming in?"

"You haven't asked about Aunt Liza," Carroll told her.

"Eliza? Is she all right?"

"Well. All *right*, I guess," he said.

"What is that supposed to mean? Is she sick?"

"No, she's not sick."

"Last Christmas you were just a shrimp," Mr. Bragg called. "You and her were drinking coffee together, tee-heeing over the presents you'd bought."

"Eliza *is* still taking care of the house, isn't she?" Delia persevered.

But Carroll seemed distracted by Mr. Bragg. He said, "Who's he talking about?"

"I told you: my employer's son."

"Is that why you've got that bag with you? 'Tasteful Clothing for the Discerning Young Man'? You buy this kid clothes? You tee-hee together? And what's that you're wearing, for God's sake?"

Delia looked down. She wasn't wearing anything odd— just her Miss Grinstead cardigan and the navy print housedress. "Wearing?" she said.

"You're so, like, *ensconced*."

Two plates appeared before them, clattering against the Formica. "Ketchup, anyone?" Rick asked.

"No, thanks." She told Carroll, "Honey, I—"

"*I* would like ketchup," Carroll announced belligerently.

"Oh. Sorry. Yes, please, Rick."

Carroll said, "Have you forgotten you have a son who puts ketchup on his french fries?"

"Honey, believe me," she said, "I would never forget. Well, maybe about the ketchup, but never about—"

A plastic squirt bottle arrived, along with their Cokes in tall paper cups. "Thank you, Rick," she said.

She waited till he had left again, and then she reached across the table and touched Carroll's hand. His knuckles were grained like leather. His lips were chapped. There was something too concrete about him; she was accustomed to the misty, soft-edged Carroll of her daydreams.

"I would never forget I have children," she told him.

"Right. That's why you sashayed off down the beach and didn't once look back at them."

Someone said, "Delia?"

She started. Two teenage girls stood over their table—Kim Brewster and Marietta something. Schwartz? Schmidt? (She brought Joel home-made fudge so sweet it zinged through your temples.) "Well! Hello there!" Delia said.

"You won't tell Mr. Miller you saw us here, will you?" Kim asked. Kim was one of Delia's remedial pupils; lately, Delia had been volunteering as a math tutor over at the school. "He would kill us if he found out!"

"We're cutting class," Marietta put in. "We saw you in here and we figured we'd ask: you know how Mr. Miller's birthday is coming up."

Delia hadn't known, but she nodded. Anything to get rid of them.

"So a bunch of us are chipping in on a present, and we thought you might could tell us what to buy him."

"Oh! Well . . ."

"I mean, you know him better than anyone. He doesn't smoke, does he? Seems like a lot of gifts for guys are smokers' stuff."

"He doesn't smoke, no," Delia said.

"Not even a pipe?"

"Not even a pipe."

"He's always so, you know, distinguished and all, we think he'd look great with a pipe. Maybe we should just get him one anyways."

"No, I really think he would hate that," Delia said firmly. "Well! It was good seeing you girls."

But Kim was studying Carroll now from beneath her long silky lashes. "*You* don't go to Old Underwear," she informed him.

Carroll flushed and said, "Underwear?"

"Our high school: Dorothy Underwood," she said, snapping her gum. "You must be from out of town."

"Yeah."

"I knew we hadn't seen you around."

Delia started eating her coleslaw; she felt it would be a kindness not to look at Carroll's face. But Carroll just picked up the ketchup and squirted it thoroughly and methodically over every single one of his french fries. "Well . . . ," Kim said at last, and the two of them moved on toward an empty booth, trailing crumbs of remarks behind them. "Thanks anyhow, Dee . . . ," they said, and, "If you think of something . . ."

Delia took a sip of Coke.

"So who's the guy?" Carroll asked, setting down the ketchup with a thump.

Confused, she glanced around the café.

"The guy with the pipe, Mom. The oh-so-distinguished guy that you know so extremely-emely well."

"Oh," she said. She laughed, not quite naturally. "It's nothing like that! He's my boss."

"Right."

He pushed his plate away. "It all fits together now," he said. "No wonder you weren't home for Labor Day."

"Labor Day?"

"Dad said you'd be back by then, but I guess it's pretty clear now why you weren't."

She stared at him. "Dad said I'd be back by Labor Day?"

"He said you just needed some time to yourself and you'd come home at the end of the summer. We were counting on it. He promised. Susie thought we should go get you, but he said, 'No,' he said, 'leave her be. I guarantee she'll be here for our Labor Day picnic,' he said. And look what happened: you went back on your word."

"*My* word!" Delia cried. "That was *his* word! I didn't have a thing to do with it! And what right was it of his, I'd like to know? Who is he to guarantee when I'll be home?"

"Now, Mom," Carroll said in an undertone. He glanced furtively toward Rick. "Let's not make a big thing of this, okay? Try and calm down."

"Don't you tell me to calm down!" she cried, and at the same time she caught herself wondering exactly how often she had uttered that sentence before. *Don't you tell me to calm down!* And, *I am completely cool and collected.* But to Sam; not to Carroll. Oh, it all came back to her now: that sense of being the wrong one, the flighty, unstable, excitable one. (And the more she protested, of course, the more excitable she appeared.) She gripped the edge of the table with both hands and said, "I am completely cool and collected."

"Well, fine," Carroll told her. "I'm glad to hear it." And he picked up a red-soaked french fry and threaded it into his mouth with elaborate indifference.

I'm glad to hear it was one of Sam's favorite responses. Along with *If you say so, Dee,* and *Have it your way.* After which he might serenely turn a page, or he would start talking with the boys about some unrelated subject. Always so sure he was right; and the fact was, he *was* right, generally. When he criticized people she liked, she would suddenly notice their faults; and when he criticized Delia, she saw herself all at once as the foolish little whiffet he believed her to be. Like now, for instance: he had promised she would slink home by summer's end, and the picture of that humbled return was so convincing that she almost felt it had happened. She couldn't even *desert* properly! Had only been off in a pout, anyhow. Just needed to get it out of her system.

Although, in fact, she had not slunk home. Not by summer's end and not afterward. Not to this day. She had actually made a life for herself in a town Sam had nothing to do with.

So when Belle sailed in, calling, "Hey, Dee, I *thought* that was you I saw," Delia made a point of rising to give her a flamboyant hug.

"Belle!" she cried, and Belle (her purple-clad figure a luxurious, pillowy armful) had the grace to hug her back.

"Who's your new fella?" she asked.

"This is my son Carroll. This is Belle Flint," she told Carroll. She kept an arm around Belle's waist. "How're you *doing*, Belle?"

"Well, you're never going to guess what, not in a million years."

"What?" Delia asked, a little too enthusiastically.

"Swear you won't tell Vanessa, now. This is just between the two of us."

But the whole demonstration went for nothing, because just then Carroll stood up and pushed his way out of the booth. "So long," he mumbled, head down.

"Carroll?"

She dropped her arm from Belle's waist.

"Tomorrow night," Belle was saying, "I've asked Horace Lamb to the movies."

Horace Lamb? Delia felt an inner hitch of surprise even as she went hurrying after Carroll. He lunged out the café door. "Carroll, honey!" she called.

On the sidewalk, Teensy was mincing toward them beneath a gigantic new busby of exploding red ringlets. Carroll almost ran her down. Teensy said, "Oh!" and took a step back, reaching up to feel for her hairdo as if she feared it might have toppled off. "Delia, tell me the truth," she said. "Do you honestly think I look silly?"

"Not a bit," Delia told her. "Carroll, wait!"

Carroll wheeled, his eyebrows beetling. "Never mind me, just tend to your pals!" he said. "Orphan Annie here and Mr. Distinguished and little Tee-hee Boy and Veranda or whoever . . ."

Vanessa, Delia almost corrected him, while behind her, Teensy asked, "Delia? Is everything all right?" and Belle, in the doorway, said, "Kids. But that's just how they are, I guess."

"I *was* going to do you a favor," Carroll said.

"What, honey?"

"I *was* going to tip you off to what's going on at home, but never mind. Just never mind now," he said.

Still, he didn't turn and leave. He seemed to be suspended, teetering on the squeaky rubber soles of his gym shoes. Cannily, Delia came no closer. She stayed six or eight feet away from him, her face a mask of smoothness. "What's going on at home?" she asked him.

"Oh, nothing. Not a thing! Except that your own blood sister is making a play for your husband," he said.

"Eliza?"

"And Dad's so out of it, he just laughs it off when we tell him. But we've all noticed, me and Susie and Ramsay notice plain as day, and we can guess how it's going to end up, we bet, too."

"Eliza would never do that," Delia said, but she was trying out the notion even as she spoke. She cast her mind back to the living-room couch, the row of marriageable maidens. *Whenever I hear the word "summer," I smell this sort of melting smell.* And now it seemed that Sam sent Eliza a quick, alert, appreciative glance, as he had not done in real life. It wasn't impossible, Delia saw.

But she told Carroll, "You must be imagining things."

"Oh, what do *you* care?" Carroll burst out, and he spun around again and started running toward West Street.

"Carroll, don't go!"

She followed at a fast walk. (How far could he get, after all?) He crossed George Street, halting briefly for a mail truck, and disappeared around the corner. Delia picked up her pace. On West Street she saw him loping south, passing Mr. Pomfret, who stood in front of his office speaking with a UPS man. She raced by Mr. Pomfret herself, with her face averted; the last thing she needed just now was another acquaintance calling out her name. She lost sight of Carroll for an instant and then spotted him near the florist's. He was jogging up and down on the curb as he waited for a break in the traffic. Evidently he was headed for the square. Good: they could sit on a bench together. Catch their breath. Talk this over.

But once he'd crossed the street, he stopped at one of the cars parked along the perimeter. A gray car, a Plymouth. *Her* Plymouth. With Ramsay at the wheel. She recognized his dear, blocky profile. Carroll opened the passenger door and got in. The engine ground to life, and the car swung out into traffic.

Even then she might have run after them. They were forced to drive very slowly at first. But she stayed where she was, brought up short on the sidewalk with one hand pressed to her throat.

Ramsay had been right here in town. He had driven all these miles and then not bothered to visit her. Susie too, perhaps, although Delia had glimpsed only two heads in the Plymouth.

She deserved this, of course. There was no denying that.

She turned and retraced her steps to Rick-Rack's, all but feeling her way.

An enormous amount had happened to her, but when she reached the café Belle and Teensy were still talking out front, Kim and Marietta were blowing sultry ribbons of cigarette smoke inside, and Rick was tucking her lunch bill under the ketchup container. She counted out her money in slow motion and paid, not forgetting to leave a tip on the table. She gathered her purse and her Young Mister bag and walked out the door, through the scorched, chemical smell of Teensy's hairdo, through the clack and tumble of Belle's chatter. "Have you ever noticed," Belle was saying, "that Horace Lamb looks the eentsiest little bit like Abraham Lincoln?"

At the corner, Delia turned south. The clock in the optician's window read eleven-fifteen—nowhere near time for lunch, and yet she regretted leaving that barbecue sandwich. And the coleslaw had been superb. It was the creamy kind, with lots of celery seeds. A seed or two still lodged in her mouth, woodsy and fragrant when she bit down. She savored the taste on her tongue. She felt the most amazing hunger, all at once. She felt absolutely hollow. You would think she hadn't eaten in months.

15

For a short while after Carroll's visit, half a dozen spots around town seemed haunted by his presence. Here was the ivy-filled window where he had first appeared, here the booth at Rick-Rack's where he'd sat, here Belle's front porch where he must have spent several minutes waiting for someone to answer the door. (Had he noticed the scaly paint? The hammocking of the floorboards under his tread?) In Delia's memory he seemed not surly now but sad, his porcupine behavior merely a sign of hurt feelings. She should have taken him with her when she left, she thought. Except that then she would have had to take Susie and Ramsay too. Otherwise it would have looked like favoritism. She saw herself striding down the coastline with her retinue—the two boys' ropy wrists in her grasp, Susie scurrying to keep up. *Where we going, Mom? Hush, don't ask; we're running away from home.*

Although her children had been partly what she was running from, as it happened.

Then she reflected that after all, Carroll had not appeared ruined by her leaving. He had survived just fine, and so had his brother and sister. And she remembered Nat's philosophy: we ought to forget our grown offspring as easily as cats forget theirs. She smiled to herself. Well, maybe not *quite* as easily.

Still, wasn't it true that over the past several years, her children had turned into semistrangers—at last even her youngest? That not only had she lost her central importance to them but they, in fact, had become just a bit less overwhelmingly all-important to her?

She sat stone still, staring into space, wondering how long ago she had first begun to know that.

Then, having watched her children slip free, she turned to what remained: her husband.

If he really did remain.

In her mind's eye he sat at the breakfast table while Eliza poured his coffee. Eliza wore her tan safari dress and even a bit of rouge. She was not unattractive, from certain angles. She had that smooth, yellowish skin that didn't go all fragile with age, and the rouge turned her dark eyes bright and snappy. She would insinuate herself into Sam's routine, take over his charts and bills, provide him with hot meals and a seamlessly organized household. "Why, thanks, Eliza," Sam would say feelingly. Men were so gullible sometimes! And he had more in common with Eliza than you might suspect. Granted, Eliza claimed she was living life over and over again until she got it right, while Sam said that for his part, he meant to get it right the first time. But both of them did assume that "getting it right" was possible. Delia herself had more or less given up trying.

Besides which, there was the fact that Eliza was Delia's sister. She had Delia's small, neat bone structure and her phenomenally sound teeth, her tendency to get out of hand after eating any sugar, her habit of letting her sentences trail away unfinished. Loving Eliza would come as naturally to Sam as appreciating a song he had already heard once before.

Delia felt an impulse to jump in the car and tear off to Baltimore, but she knew how trite that was—to want a man back the instant she learned he was wanted by someone else. She made herself sit still. *This is what you asked for,* she told herself.

This other woman's maimed husband and child, this too new ranch house with its walls that thunked like cardboard when you rapped them, this thin town propped on a countryside as flat and pale as paper.

Before dawn one morning, she came sharply awake, perhaps disturbed by a dream, although no fragments of it lingered. She lay in bed recalling, for some reason, the first dinner party she'd given after she and Sam were married. He had wanted to invite two of his old classmates, along with their wives. For days she had pored over possible menus. She had refused her sisters' offers of help; she had extracted her family's promise not to show their faces during the evening. It was essential that she prove she was a grown-up. And yet from the moment the first couple arrived, she had felt herself sinking back into childhood. "Hey, Grin," the husband had said to Sam. Grin! Would she ever feel so comradely as to call Sam that herself? she had wondered, twisting her skirt. "Hi, Joe," Sam had said. "Delia, I'd like you to meet Joe and Amy Guggles." Delia had not been informed of their last name ahead of time, and in fact had never heard the name Guggles in all her life. It had struck her as funny, and she'd started laughing. She slid into helpless cascades of laughter, her breath dissolving in squeaks, her eyes streaming tears, her cheeks beginning to ache. It was like being in sixth grade again. She laughed herself boneless, while the couple watched her with kindly concern and Sam kept saying, "Delia? Honey?"

"I'm sorry," she had told them, when finally sheer embarrassment had sobered her. "I'm so sorry, really I can't think what—"

At which point, the second couple arrived. "Why, here you are!" Sam had cried in relief. "Hon, these are my oldest friends, Frank and Mia Mewmew."

Oh, Lord.

But Sam had been very understanding. After the party, he had drawn her into his arms and told her, speaking warmly into the curls on top of her head, that these things could happen to anyone.

How young he'd been, back then! But Delia hadn't realized. To her he had seemed fully formed, immune to doubt, this unassailably self-possessed man who had all but arrived on a white horse to save her from eternal daughterhood. Around his eyes faint puckers were already evident, and she had found them both appealing and alarming. *If he dies first I don't want to go on living,* she had thought. *I'll find something in Daddy's office cabinet that's deadly poison.* In those days, she could say such things, not having had the children yet. She used to picture all sorts of catastrophes, in those days. Well, later too, to be honest. Oh, she'd always been a fearful kind of person, full of hunches and forebodings. But look what happened: the night of his chest pains, she hadn't felt the slightest premonition. She had sat there reading *Lucinda's Lover,* dumb as a post. Then the phone rang.

Although the news had not come as a shock, certainly. Listening to the nurse's diplomatic wording, she had thought, *Ah, yes, of course,* while a dank, heavy sense of confirmation had solidified inside her. *First Daddy, and now Sam.* He would die and they would bury him in Cow Hill Cemetery and he would lie there alone till Delia crept up to join him, as on those nights when she stayed awake watching some silly movie and then climbed the stairs afterward and slipped between the covers and laid one arm lightly across his chest while he went on sleeping.

She sat against her headboard, jostling the cat, and switched on the clock radio. They were playing jazz, at this hour. Lots of lonesome clarinets and plinkety-plonk pianos, and after every piece the announcer stated the place it was recorded and the date. A New York bar on an August night in 1955. A hotel in Chicago, New Year's Eve, 1949. Delia wondered how humans could bear to live in a world where the passage of time held so much power.

Nat and Binky were not going to have a June wedding after all. They moved the date up to a Saturday in March. Nat said he had exercised his seniority. "I used your basic how-much-longer-have-I-got approach," he confided to Noah and Delia. "Your take-pity-on-an-old-geezer approach."

Binky adapted cheerfully to the change in plans. "This way," she told Delia, "I'm Mrs. Nathaniel Moffat three months sooner, that's all. So what if we skimp some on the frills? They're not such a very big deal." The two of them were alone in Nat's kitchen when she said this, leafing through cookbooks. (The wedding cake was one of the frills she was skimping on.) "And I do mean to be Mrs. Moffat," she said. "None of this 'Ms.' business for me! He's the first man I've ever known who's just totally, totally loved me." Then the skin around her eyes grew pink, as if she might start crying, and she turned quickly back to her cookbook.

"In that case, you ought to marry him this instant," Delia said.

"Well, I wish his daughters agreed," Binky said. "You heard Dudi cut all her hair off."

"Cut her hair off?"

"Threw a tantrum when Nat announced our engagement; ran into his bathroom, grabbed up these little scissors he trims his beard with and cut every bit of her hair off."

"Goodness," Delia said.

"And Pat and Donna refuse to come to the wedding, and when I asked Ellie to be an attendant—purely out of niceness; I've already got my sister and my nieces—she said maybe she wasn't coming either, she couldn't be sure, she might or might not, so she'd better say no. Then she went and told Nat he ought to have his lawyer draw up a prenuptial agreement. I guess they all think I'm some kind of . . . gold digger. It doesn't occur to them what an insult that is to their father, not to believe a woman might love him for his own self."

"They're just a little surprised," Delia said. "They'll get over it."

Binky shook her head, smoothing a cookbook page with her palm. "They phone him and the very first thing, 'Is *she* around?' they ask. 'She,' they call me; they never use my name if they can help it. They hardly ever come to visit. Donna says it's because I'm always here. She says I don't allow them any time alone with him, but I try to; it's just that—"

She broke off, blushing, and Delia wondered why until Binky mumbled the end of her sentence. "I do sort of, kind of like, live here now," she said.

"Well, of course," Delia hastened to say. "What do they expect?"

"Oh, well, I didn't start out to bore you with all my troubles," Binky said. "You know why I like to talk to you, Delia? You never interrupt with *your* experiences. No wonder you're so popular!"

"I'm so popular?"

"Don't be modest. Noah's told us how you're friends with half of Bay Borough."

"Good grief! I hardly know anyone," Delia said.

Although she was startled to see how her friends did add up, now that she stopped to count.

"You're not just marking time while I'm speaking," Binky said. "Not jiggling your foot till you get a chance to jump in with your life history."

"Well, it isn't as if there's a whole lot I could jump in with," Delia told her.

Last week at supper, Joel had asked what part of Baltimore Delia hailed from. "Oh," she had said, "here and there," and he had dropped the subject—or so she'd thought. But a minute later he had said, "Strange, isn't it? A person who doesn't discuss her past is automatically assumed to *have* a past, I mean more of a past than usual, something rich and exotic."

"Is that right," she had said neutrally. It had struck her as an interesting theory; she had considered it until, noticing the silence, she looked up and found his eyes on her. "What?" she had asked.

"Oh, nothing."

Then Noah had reached between them for the salt—a disruptive swoop, a lunge forward on two legs of his chair—and the moment had passed.

Driving to the wedding, Delia kept glancing in the rearview mirror. She was afraid she might have put on too much makeup. "What do you think of my lipstick?" she asked Noah.

"It's okay," he said without looking.

He had worries of his own. Periodically he wriggled his fingers between the buttons of his winter jacket, checking for the ring in his shirt pocket.

"Are you sure it's not too heavy?" she asked him.

"Hmm?"

"My lipstick, Noah."

"Nah, it's okay."

"*You* look nice," she said.

"Well, I don't know why I had to get so dressed up."

"Dressed up! You call a shirt and no tie dressed up!"

"I look like one of those yo-yos who sing in the school chorus."

"You should just be thankful Nat didn't make you buy a suit," she told him.

"And what if I drop the ring? You know my hand will shake. I'll drop the ring and it will clink real loud and roll across the floor and fall into one of those grate things, *clang-ang-ang!*, and we'll never get it back again."

"I wish I had a fancier outfit," Delia said. "I look like an old-maid aunt or something." Under her coat she was wearing her gray pinstripe. "Or at least a necklace or a locket or a string of beads."

"You're okay."

In her jewelry box back in Baltimore was a four-strand pearl choker. Fake, of course, but it would have been perfect with the pinstripe.

How long before she could say that her Baltimore things would have gone out of fashion anyway, or fallen apart or been used up even if she'd stayed? When would the things she had here become her *real* things?

She flicked her turn signal and swerved onto Highway 50. "U-u-urch!" Noah squealed, grabbing his door handle.

"Sorry." She slowed. "So," she said. "I guess I get to meet your mother, finally."

"Yup."

"She did decide to come, didn't she?"

"Last I heard she did."

Recently, Delia had found the *Boardwalk Bulletin* profile buried in the back of Noah's closet. (*Who's the gorgeous new weather wench on WKMD?* the article began.) But to look at Noah now, you wouldn't guess he spared his mother a thought. He was yawning and gazing out his window at the remains of last week's freak snowstorm. The woods were a scrawl of black against white, like an arty photograph.

A snow warning or a hurricane watch can be a matter of life and death, Ellie had told her interviewer. *It gives me a lot of warm fuzzies to know I'm making a contribution to my community.*

Delia wondered what Joel would have said about "warm fuzzies."

The red-brick cube of Senior City rose before them. Delia signaled and turned into the parking lot. "What if they want me to make a speech?" Noah was asking.

"You won't have to make a speech."

"Or what if somebody faints or something? I'm supposed to assist."

"Believe me," Delia said, "this will be a breeze."

They got out of the car and crossed the lot, which was not as well plowed as it might have been. Delia, who didn't own boots, had to hang on to Noah's arm as they picked their way around icy spots. "See?" she told him. "Already you're assisting!"

His arm was thin but fiercely strong, like a band of steel.

In the lobby, they asked an old man the way to the chapel. "Straight ahead, then left at the end of the hall," he said. "You must be going to the wedding."

They nodded.

"Well, I'll be along directly; wouldn't miss it. Everyone in the building's been invited, you know."

Delia thanked him, and they proceeded down the hall. Passing the elevators, with their gleaming metal doors, she checked her reflection. It seemed to her she looked pale and draggled, her coat a dreary, wilted shape clinging too low on her shins.

Clothes are my biggest weakness, Ellie had told *Boardwalk Bulletin. But luckily my figure's the kind that everything hangs really well on, so I don't have to spend a fortune to look good.*

At the end of the hall they turned left and entered the side door of a small chapel, carpeted wall to wall in beige and lined with sleek beige pews. Already the pews were nearly filled with elderly women and three or four widely spaced men. Most of the women wore stylish dresses; a few wore bathrobes. Several people in wheelchairs formed an extra row at the rear. Delia and Noah stood gazing about until a dark young boy in a suit approached and offered Delia his arm. "We're seating everyone helter-skelter," he told her. "Wherever we can find room."

"Well, Noah here won't need a seat. He's the best man."

"Hey there, Noah. I'm Peter. Son of the bride," the boy said. He had not inherited Binky's small, pursed features or her rosy coloring; just her easy manner of talking to people. He told Noah, "You're supposed to go through that door up front. Your grandpa's already waiting."

Noah sent Delia one last imploring glance, and she grinned at him and brushed his hair off his forehead. "Good luck," she said.

Then she let Peter escort her to one of the few remaining seats, between a woman in a brown-and-white dress and an old man fiddling with his hearing aid. The old man had the aisle seat and merely moved his bony knees to one side so she could get past. It was the woman who helped her out of her coat. "Isn't this exciting?" she asked Delia. She had a freckled, finely wrinkled face lit with a gracious expression, and a crimp of orange-sherbet hair that must once have been red. "It's our very first Senior City wedding! We don't count Paul and Ginny Mellors; they eloped. Are you a relation?"

"Just a friend."

"The board is in a tizzy, I can tell you. They want to charge Binky higher rates because she's underage. Otherwise the young folks will be *flooding* in, they claim, on account of our security and our managed health care. My name's Aileen, by the way."

"I'm Delia."

"It's nice to meet you, Delia. What I say is, hell's bells, Binky's such a lambie-pie I think we ought to pay *her*! She'll be a huge addition to our Sunday Socials."

Just then, Ellie appeared at the side entrance.

Delia knew her immediately—the tinsel hair, the pulpy red mouth. She wore a long, cream-colored coat just one shade off from her skin, and she stood poised, looking somehow stiller than ordinary women, until an usher approached. This was not Peter but his brother, evidently—someone equally dark but more stockily built. Ellie took his arm and walked toward the front, the hem of her coat swaying classily. Where would she find a seat, though? All the pews were jam-packed. The usher seemed to be informing her of this; she listened, pooching her lips and frowning. They were crossing in front of the pulpit now. On the other side, several people—mostly kitchen staff, in aprons—lined the wall, and Ellie was deposited in their midst. What a pity, Delia thought, that the one daughter who'd shown up should have to stand!

But no, another daughter was here as well—a wan, wraithlike woman who rose from her seat and edged past a row of knees to join Ellie. The second woman had fair hair too, but it was cut so brutally short that in places it seemed scraped off her skull. Behind cupped fingers, she whispered something to Ellie. Then they both turned and looked straight at Delia.

Guiltily, Delia lowered her eyes. She should have smiled at the two of them, but instead she pretended to be absorbed in conversation with Aileen. "That's Mary Lou Simms playing the organ," Aileen was saying. Delia hadn't noticed there *was* an organ, but now she heard a wispy rendition of "Blessed Assurance." From the old man on her right came a piercing whistle, something to do with his hearing aid. "Oh, and there's Reverend Merrill," Aileen said. "Isn't he striking?"

Reverend Merrill was not all that striking in Delia's opinion, but he wore his black robe with a certain flair. He strode toward the pulpit, swinging a Bible in one hand. Behind him came Nat and Noah. Nat held himself rigidly erect; he was doing without his cane today. Noah was getting so tall, Delia realized. Now that he took his position next to Nat, she could see how he had shot up, just in the few months she'd known him.

The organ slithered into the "Wedding March." Everyone looked toward the rear.

First came a stouter, plainer version of Binky—the matron of honor, in a wide blue gown, with square-cut gray hair and a broad, pleasant face. Then Binky herself, in white. She looked lovely. She was carrying pink roses and beaming joyously as she floated down the aisle. Her two nieces, as bulky as their mother, plodded behind with fistfuls of her train.

"Oh, what a vision!" Aileen said. "Did you ever see anything sweeter?" Delia's other seatmate was gnawing open a blister pack of batteries. Over by the wall, Ellie's white face blazed fixedly, but it didn't seem to be Binky she was watching.

The bridal procession reached the front, and Nat, proudly stern, gave Binky his arm and turned toward the minister.

It was a very brief ceremony—just the vows and the exchange of rings. Noah did fine. He produced the ring on cue, and he didn't drop it. But all of this Delia observed with only part of her attention, while with another part—her tensed, wary, innermost part—she was conscious every moment of Ellie Miller's unwavering stare in her direction.

All the guests were invited to Nat's apartment afterward—anybody who wanted to come. There was a great press of frail bodies milling out of the chapel. Delia offered support to arms as withered and soft as day-old balloons. She packed mothball-smelling woolens into elevators, and then, upstairs, she settled more women than she would have thought possible onto the swampy cushions of Nat's couch. They were all looking forward to Binky's cake. It seemed they *preferred* homemade, and were glad she hadn't had time to order the towering pagoda she had dreamed of. "We get store-bought in the cafeteria all the time," one woman told Delia. "Sent over from Brinhart's Bakery. Tastes like Band-Aids."

Delia looked for Ellie but didn't see her, or Dudi either. Although in this crush, people were easily missed.

She threaded her way toward Binky, who was cutting squares of sheet cake, with her train looped over her arm. "Do you think it went all right?" Binky asked. Her headpiece of pink roses slanted toward one ear like a rakish halo.

"It went perfectly," Delia said. She started distributing the cake. Nat, meanwhile, was pouring champagne, which he sent around with Binky's two sons and her nieces. They ran out of stemware and had to open a pack of disposable tumblers.

When everyone was served, Nat proposed a toast. "To my beautiful,

beautiful bride," he said, and he made a little speech about how life was not a straight line—either downward or upward, either one—but something more irregular, a zigzag or a corkscrew or sometimes a scribble. "And sometimes," he said, "you get to what you thought was the end and you find it's a whole new beginning." He raised his glass toward Binky, and his eyes were suspiciously shiny.

One of the women on the couch said Binky must have grated her own lemon zest. "I can always tell fresh-grated zest," she said. "It's no use trying to substitute that brown dust that comes in bottles." She licked crumbs off her fork in a contemplative way. Her face had gone past merely old to that stage where it seemed formed of disintegrating particles, without a single clear demarcation. Did there come a point, Delia wondered, after you'd outlived every one of your friends, when you began to believe you might be the first to escape death altogether?

She relieved Binky of her cake knife and cut more slices, which she carried around on a platter in case people wanted seconds. In the bedroom, a young woman in a nurse's white pantsuit was holding forth on various hospitals, referring familiarly to "Saint Joe" and "Holy Trin" while a circle of residents listened spellbound. Two men were playing chess in a corner; one of them asked Delia if he could take an extra piece of cake for his wife on Floor Four. Aileen, Delia's former seatmate, was nodding and smiling as a fur-stoled woman described other weddings she'd been to. "And then Lois: *she* was a lucky one! Married a man with all his major appliances, including convection oven."

Noah walked in with a glass of champagne, which he tried to hide when he saw Delia. "Give me that," she ordered.

"Aw, Delia."

She took it from him and set it on a passing tray. "By the way," she said, "where's your mother?"

"I don't know."

"She didn't come upstairs?"

He shrugged. "I guess she must have had other stuff to do," he said. Then he turned on his heel and left the room before she could comment— not that she would have been so tactless.

Binky's sister, the bearer of the tray, tut-tutted. "I saw her walk out directly after the vows," she said. "Her and her sister both. Doodoo, is that what they call her?"

"Dudi."

"All this brouhaha about *his* family's reaction! How about ours? We could have said plenty, trust me: marrying a man old enough to be her father."

"Well," Delia said, "I'm just glad she and Nat found each other."

"Yes, I suppose," the sister said, sighing.

Then Nat popped up at Delia's elbow. "Have you met my sister-in-law?" he asked her. "Bernice, my new sister-in-law. Can you imagine someone my age getting a brand-new sister-in-law?" He was exultant, his voice unsteady, his face so firm-skinned and glowing that he looked like a *pretend* old man made up for a high-school play. If he'd noticed his daughters' disappearance, it hadn't dampened his happiness.

During the drive home, Delia told Noah she thought his mother was very pretty. In fact, this was not strictly true. She had decided Ellie had a garish quality; the high contrast of her coloring went over better on TV than in person. But she wanted an excuse to mention her. All Noah said in response was, "Yeah," and he drummed his fingers and looked out the side window.

"And you looked mighty handsome up there, too," she said.

"Oh, sure."

"You don't believe me? Just watch," she teased him. "The next wedding you're in might very well be your own."

But he didn't so much as smile. "Fat chance," he said.

"What—you're not getting married?"

"Me and Dad have blown it with women," he said glumly. "There must be something about them we don't understand."

In other circumstances, she might have been amused, but now she felt touched. She glanced at him. He went on staring out the window. Finally she reached over and gave him a pat on the knee, and they rode the rest of the way without speaking.

16

———

"If x is the age Jenny is now, and y is the age she was when she went to California . . . ," Delia said.

T. J. Renfro put his head on the kitchen table.

"Now, T.J., this is not so hard! See, we know that she was three years older than the girlfriend she was visiting in California, and we know that when her girlfriend was—"

"This is not going to do me one bit of good in real life," T.J. informed her in a smothered voice.

He had the kind of haircut that seemed half finished—medium length on top but trailing long black oily strands in back. Both of his upper arms were braceleted with barbed-wire tattoos, and his black leather vest bore more zippers than you'd find in most people's entire wardrobes. Unlike Delia's other pupils, who met with her in the counseling room over at the high school, T.J. came to the house. He had been suspended till May 1 and was not allowed to set foot on school property; showed up instead at the Millers' back door every Thursday afternoon at three o'clock. Delia didn't want to know what he'd been suspended for.

She told him, "Real life is full of problems like this! Finding the unknown quantity: there's lots of times you'll need to do that."

"Like I'm really going to walk up to some chick and ask how old she is," T.J. said, raising his head, "and she's going to say, 'Well, ten years ago I was twice the age my third cousin was when . . .' "

"Oh, now, you're missing the point," Delia said.

"And how come this Jenny would visit someone three years younger anyway? That don't make sense."

The phone rang, and Delia rose to answer it.

"She probably just *claimed* she was visiting, and then hid out in some motel with her boyfriend," T.J. said.

Delia lifted the receiver. "Hello?"

Silence.

"Hello!"

Whoever it was hung up. "That's happened a lot lately," Delia said, hanging up herself. She returned to her chair.

"It's electrical backwash," T.J. told her.

"Backwash?"

"If you don't use your line awhile, it, like, develops all this pent-up power that spills out in this kind of like overflow and sets your phone to ringing."

Delia cocked her head.

"Happens at my mom's house once or twice a week," T.J. told her.

"Well, here it's been happening more on the order of once or twice a day," Delia said.

The phone rang again. She said, "See?"

"Just don't answer."

"It *kills* me not to answer."

He tipped back in his chair and studied her. The phone gave a third ring, a fourth. Then the outside door burst open and Noah tumbled in, bringing along a gust of fresh air. "Hey, T.J.," he said. He shed his school knapsack and picked up the receiver. "Hello?"

In the pause that followed, T.J. and Delia watched him closely.

"Naw, I don't guess I can," Noah said. He turned away from them. "I just can't, that's all." Another pause. "It's nothing like that, honest! Just I got all this homework and stuff. Well, I better go now. Bye." He hung up.

"Who was that?" Delia asked.

"Nobody."

He slung his knapsack over one shoulder and walked off toward his room.

T.J. and Delia looked at each other.

The next afternoon, a cool, sunny Friday, Delia went with Vanessa to a knitwear sale at Young Mister. Spring would be arriving any minute now, and Noah had outgrown all last spring's clothes. It was an excruciatingly slow trip, because Greggie was in the midst of his terrible twos and refused to ride in his stroller. He had to walk every inch of the way. Delia felt she had never seen Bay Borough in such detail—every plastic cup lid wheeling along the sidewalk, every sparrow pecking tinfoil in the gutter. They didn't start heading back until nearly three o'clock. "Oh-oh," Delia said, "look at the time. Noah will be home before I am."

"Isn't he going to his mother's?" Vanessa asked.

"Not this week."

"I thought he went every Friday."

"Well, I guess something must have come up."

They had reached the corner where they separated, and Delia said, "Bye, Greggie. Bye, Vanessa."

"So long, Dee," Vanessa said. "Let's ask Belle if she wants to get together over the weekend."

"Fine with me."

Belle was saving all her weekends for Mr. Lamb these days, but Delia had been ordered to keep that a secret.

At the grade school, children were already pouring onto the playground. Delia didn't try to find Noah, though. She knew he'd want to walk home with his friends. She sidestepped a runaway skateboard, smiled at a little girl collecting scattered papers, and politely ignored a mother and son quarreling next to their car.

But wait. The son was Noah. The mother was Ellie.

Wearing her cream-colored coat from the wedding but looking frazzled and disordered, Ellie was trying to wrestle Noah into the passenger seat. And Noah was pulling away from her, his jacket wrenched halfway off his arms. "Mom," he kept saying. "Mom. Stop."

Delia said, "Noah?"

They threw her an identical distracted stare and went on with their tussle. Ellie started mashing Noah's head down the way policemen did on TV, guiding their handcuffed suspects into squad cars.

"What's happening here?" Delia asked. She made a grab for Ellie's wrist. "Let go of him!"

Ellie flung her off so violently that she knocked Delia in the face; her sharp-stoned ring grazed Delia's forehead. Noah, meanwhile, managed to yank himself free. He stumbled several steps backward and adjusted his jacket. His knapsack was gaping open and spilling papers. (*Those* were the papers the little girl was collecting!) He wiped his fist across his nose and said, "Gee, Mom."

Ellie stood straighter, breathing harshly, glaring at him.

Reverently, the little girl presented Noah with his papers. He took them without looking at them. Now Delia saw that two of his friends were loitering nearby—Kenny Moss and a second boy, whose name she couldn't remember. They were watching but pretending not to, kicking the sidewalk. The other children, passing in groups, seemed unaware that anything was wrong.

"I just wanted you to come visit! Like always! Just a normal Friday visit!" Ellie cried. "Is that too much to ask?" She turned to Delia. "Is that so—?"

Something stopped her. Her mouth fell open.

Noah said, "Gosh!" He was staring at Delia's forehead. "Delia! Golly! You're all bloody!"

Delia raised her fingers to her forehead. They came away bright red. But she didn't feel much pain—only the least little sting at that spot in her temple where the pulse beat. She said, "Oh, it's nothing. I'll just go home and—"

But Noah's eyes were huge, and Kenny Moss said, "Holy moley!" and gripped the other boy's sleeve, and the little girl said, in an informative tone, "I pass out if I see blood."

She did seem about to pass out—her lips had an ashy pallor—and so Delia, attending to first things first, said crisply, "Don't look, then." She herself wasn't dizzy in the slightest. This was plainly one of those wounds that appear much worse than they are. However, she was concerned about her clothes. "Somewhere here . . . ," she said, hunting through her purse for a tissue. Her Young Mister bag hindered her, and she passed it to Noah, leaving sticky red fingerprints across the scrunched top. "I know I must have a—"

Soft, blossomy mounds of tissue were thrust under her chin—an offering from Ellie. "I am so, so sorry," she was saying. "It was an accident! Believe me, Delia, I never meant to harm you."

"Well, I know that," Delia said, accepting the tissues. She found it oddly flattering that Ellie called her by name. She pressed the tissues to her temple, and her pulse began to throb.

"Oh, God, we have to get you to a doctor," Ellie said.

"I don't need a doctor; goodness."

"You're no judge of that! You're not in your right mind," Ellie said. Although it was Ellie who seemed unhinged, thrusting more handfuls of tissues at her (did she carry them loose in her pockets, or what?) and shrilly ordering the others about. "Move! Give us room. Noah, you ride in back; we'll put Delia up in front."

"Isn't there a school nurse or something? Why don't we look for the nurse?" Delia asked.

But Ellie said, "You don't want to end up with a scar, do you? An ugly, disfiguring scar?"

Which was something to consider; so Delia allowed herself to be shepherded toward the front seat. Noah, who had folded the seat forward so he could climb into the rear, straightened it for Delia. When she was settled, he leaned over her shoulder to offer her a gray sweatshirt from his knapsack. "Here," he said. "You're going through those hankies like a spigot."

She would have argued (blood was so hard to launder), but it was true she had used up the tissues. She pressed the sweatshirt to her forehead and breathed in its smell of clean sweat and gym shoes. Meanwhile Ellie slid behind the wheel and started the engine. "You'll probably need stitches," she said, pulling into traffic. "Oh, lately it seems everything I touch goes galloping off in every direction! Leaves me staring after it amazed!"

"I know exactly what you mean," Delia told her. She took a peek from under the sweatshirt. Up close, Ellie seemed more likable. Her lipstick was worn to a tired outline, and her eyes sagged slightly at the outer corners.

"I'm not myself these days," Ellie said. "You hear people say that all the time, but up till now I'd assumed it was a figure of speech. Now I stand off to one side looking at myself like a whole other person, and I ask, 'What could she be *thinking* of?' "

They turned left, onto Weber Street. Delia folded the sweatshirt to a new section. She was beginning to understand why you often saw red roses planted near gray stone walls. The bloodstains looked so vivid against the sweatshirt fabric, she would have liked to show the others. But Ellie was still talking away. "I admit it was me who walked out on the marriage," she said. (Delia replayed the last few sentences, wondering if she had missed some key transition.) "You don't have to remind me! I started picturing how I'd get to heaven and God would say, 'Such a waste; I sent you into the world and you didn't even make use of it, just sat there in one spot complaining you were bored.' So I walked out. But when I saw you at the wedding, when I saw how—well, I guess I thought you'd be older and fatter and wearing a zip-front dress or something. I know I made a scene, phoning Joel like I did. . . ."

Ellie had phoned Joel?

"In fact I watched myself dialing, and I said, 'What a dumb thing to do!' But I went right on doing it. And I'd planned to be Madam Iceberg. 'I've been thinking, Joel,' I'd say. 'Perhaps you should grant me custody, now you've got a female companion.' But I guess he told you how it came out. I hear his voice, I'm like a woman possessed. 'How dare you do this to Noah! Exposing an innocent child to that tawdry little love nest you've set up!' "

Love nest! Delia was thrilled.

"And if that wasn't bad enough, then I go and drag Noah in too. I'm sorry, honey!" Ellie said, addressing the rearview mirror. But she didn't wait for Noah's reaction. "And you know how heartless kids can be. The minute you show you're upset, they pretend you don't exist. They stare right through you. They make up all these excuses why they can't come and visit you."

"Mom," Noah said.

Delia was curious to hear how he would handle this, but all he said was, "Mom, you just passed Dr. Norman's."

"Yes, I know," Ellie said. They were on Border Street now, heading toward Highway 380. "Every morning I'd wake up saying, 'Today I'll get ahold of myself. I'll just put it out of my mind,' I'd say, but there you were, regardless: this mystery woman no one knew a thing about, the very type Joel would fall for. I bet you speak perfect English too, don't you?"

"You have it all wrong," Delia said, much as she hated to. "It's not the way you—"

But Ellie was turning north on 380, and Noah broke in to ask, "Mom? Where you going?"

"There are scads of doctors in Easton," Ellie said.

"Easton!" Noah and Delia said together.

"Well, you surely don't think we could use Dr. Norman. He's right there in town! Anybody in town will believe I did this on purpose."

"Can't we just tell him you didn't?" Delia asked.

"Ha! You don't know Bay Borough like I do. People there make a scandal out of the simplest little trifle."

"Maybe a drugstore, then," Delia said. She was beginning to feel uneasy. "All I need is a bandage."

"Oh, Delia, Delia, Delia," Ellie said. "You are so naive. Sure as you live, the pharmacist would be some Underwood graduate who couldn't wait to get on the phone and start blabbing. 'Guess what!' " she mimicked. " 'Mr. Miller's demented wife tried to murder his girlfriend.' "

"I'm not his—"

"I bet *you* never say 'share,' do you?"

"Share?"

"As in communicate. As in, 'So-and-so shared his feelings with me.' Joel used to gnash his teeth when I said that. And he had this thing about putting in the objects of my verbs. 'Enjoy *what*?' he'd ask me. Or, 'Take care of *whom*? Where's the end of your sentence, Ellie?' "

Delia watched a field of dead autos slide past. In back, Noah was silent.

"Funny how men always worry ahead of time that marriage might confine them," Ellie said. "Women don't give it a thought. It's afterwards it hits them. Stuck for life! Imprisoned! Trapped forever with a man who won't let you say 'parenting.' "

She braked; they had reached the stoplight at Highway 50. While they waited for it to turn green, she started digging through her purse. "Do you have any cash?" she asked Delia. "I don't want to pay with a check. Even over in Easton, my name might ring a bell."

She was crazy, Delia decided. So far she had been able to see Ellie's side of things—had sympathized, even. But now she had a sense of panic. And besides that, her cut was starting to hurt. She imagined she could actually feel its widening mouth, the edges hardening into a permanent scar.

They would have to make a run for it, as soon as she could safely snatch Noah out of the back. Maybe when they got to the doctor's. *If* they got to the doctor's; for here they sat, on and on, at this eternal red light. "Green light, green light," she urged. She leaned forward, as if that would hurry things.

Ellie, misunderstanding, said, "Oh, sorry," and took her foot off the brake. They zoomed onto Highway 50, and an oil truck, horn blaring wildly, swerved around them and careened down the wrong side of the road. Ellie screamed. Delia was too terrified to scream. They veered onto the shoulder and bounced over a stretch of dry grass before coming to a stop.

"I thought you said the light was green!" Ellie shrieked.

"I only meant—oh, Lord," Delia said. She turned to check on Noah. "Are you all right?" she asked him.

He swallowed and then nodded.

Surreptitiously, in a movement that might have been oiled, Delia felt for her door handle. She gave it a smooth nudge downward and let the door inch open. Then she shouted, "Out, Noah! Quick!" and sprang from the car, at the same time slamming her seat forward so Noah could follow. He did, luckily. He had good reflexes. He landed almost on top of her, because she happened to step directly into some kind of hole or ditch concealed by the flattened grass. Her right ankle twisted beneath her and Noah came bruising into her shoulder, and of course she still had the sweatshirt pressed to the wound on her head, but at least they were safe.

Ellie, meanwhile, had opened her own door, causing yet another truck to honk as it passed. The bleat of the horn traveled straight through Delia's chest. All at once her heart caved in, as if only now receiving word of the danger. Why, they had run a red light! Whizzed into high-speed traffic without a glance in either direction! Her skin began to tingle with the memory of it. She imagined that her outermost surface had actually been brushed by their near miss.

"We could have been killed!" she cried, and Ellie, rushing toward her, called, "I know! I can't believe we're still alive!" She flung her arms around Delia and Noah. Noah said, "Mom," and struggled free, but Delia hugged her back. Both women were slightly teary. Ellie kept saying, "Oh, God, oh, God," and laughing and dabbing her eyes.

"Mom," Noah said again, from the sidelines. "Can we just go to Dr. Norman, please?"

"We'll tell him I bumped my head," Delia said. "He won't think a thing about it."

"Well, you're right," Ellie said. "We'll do that. Come on, if I can get up the nerve to drive again."

So they all climbed back in the car, which turned out to be a Plymouth, just a year or two newer than Delia's Plymouth; and Ellie waited till there wasn't another vehicle in sight before inching out onto the highway and executing a U-turn. Not until they were traveling back down 380 did she venture to speak, even; she was so intent on her driving. Then she asked Noah what he planned to tell his father.

Noah let a long pause develop, but finally he said, "Same thing we tell Dr. Norman, I guess. You gave us a ride home from school? Delia banged her head some way?"

"I knocked against the car door as I got in," Delia suggested.

"Oh, good," Ellie said, and her hands relaxed on the wheel.

Most likely it was Delia she had been worrying about. She must have known that Noah wouldn't tattle; he had that disconcertingly cold, stoic secretiveness you often see in children of troubled marriages.

"And in fact that's almost what happened," Ellie said. "We just got caught up in one of those, what you might call flurries of events, right? Am I right?"

"Well, of course," Delia told her.

Ellie slowed for the turn onto Border Street. "You may not believe this," she said, "but I'm a very stable person as a rule. It's just that lately, I've been under a lot of stress. Oh, working in front of the camera is way more pressure than I thought it would be! I have to watch my weight every instant, make sure I get my full eight hours' sleep, take care of my complexion. See this?" She was in the midst of parallel parking, but she paused to grab a strand of her hair. "Bleached, stripped, body-waved, color-treated . . ." She pulled the strand taut and released it. "See how it stretches out so long and thin and then just snaps, *boing*? That's not hair anymore; it's, I don't know, Silly Putty. And if only they'd give me a leave of absence till my eyebrows can grow back in!"

One tire scraped the curb. "Besides which there's my nutso sister losing her marbles over Dad's marriage," she said, "and this leak in my apartment ceiling nobody knows where from, and not to mention Dad himself. What business does he have, starting all over at his age? He's sixty-seven years old and in constant pain to boot, were you aware of that? Why do you suppose he keeps Noah's visits so short? His favorite grandchild, but any more than an hour and Dad's exhausted!"

"Oh, the poor man," Delia said. She opened the door and got out, still holding the sweatshirt to her head. Somehow the urgency of their errand had receded, she noticed. She flipped the seat forward for Noah, and he piled out after her.

"When I think how hard I worked moving him into that place!" Ellie told her, slamming her own door. "All those boxes I packed! I felt like I was sending him off to camp or something. 'Do you have the right kind of clothes for this? What will the other kids be wearing?' And now they're threatening to evict him."

"Evict him!" Delia said.

They were climbing the steps of a large frame house with a wrap-around porch. Noah led the way. Delia trailed behind because her ankle was slowing her down. She called, "I thought they said he could stay on after he married."

"That was before they found out his wife was expecting," Ellie said.

Delia halted on the top porch step and stared at her. Even Noah stared. "Expecting what?" Delia asked foolishly.

"Use your head, Delia! Why do you suppose they moved the wedding up to March?"

"Well, because . . . did they tell you this? Or are you just surmising?"

"Darn right they told me," Ellie said. "Made a big announcement of it, just last week. Dad asks Binky, 'Angel? Are you going to break the news, or am I?' and Binky says, 'Oh, you do it, honeybunch.' Don't you want to just gag? That kind of talk seems so, I don't know, fake, when it's a second marriage. So Dad clears his throat and says, 'Ellie,' he says; says, 'you're going to have a sister.' Well, I was kind of slow on the uptake. I said, 'I *already* have a sister. Several.' He said, 'I mean another sister. We're pregnant.' That's an exact quote. 'We,' he said. You can bet he didn't word it that way the first four times around."

"But . . . when is this going to happen?" Delia asked.

"September."

"September!"

Majestically, Ellie sailed through the front door. Delia stood on the porch with her mouth open. Binky had always been a rotund little person, rotund in the stomach as well, but . . . She looked over at Noah. "Did *you* know about this?" she asked.

He shook his head.

"Well," she said. "So you'll have a . . . baby aunt! Imagine!"

As she limped through the door, she heard Ellie's humorless snicker.

This was the first time Delia had been to Dr. Norman's office, although his telephone number was posted next to the Millers' kitchen phone. The instant she smelled that mixture of floor wax and isopropyl alcohol, she was overcome by a settling-in sensation—a feeling that she had returned to her rightful place; that all other places were counterfeit, temporary, foreign to her true nature. She stopped short in the foyer (stringy Oriental rug, ginger-jar lamp on a table), until Ellie took her arm and steered her toward the waiting room. "Is he in?" she asked the woman at the desk. The woman was much older than Delia and fifty pounds heavier, but still somebody Delia could identify with, seeing her fingers poised on the chrome-rimmed keys of an ancient typewriter. "We've got an emergency here!" Ellie told her.

Oh, yes, the emergency. Delia had almost forgotten. While Ellie explained the circumstances ("sharp metal corner on the . . . nothing *I* could do . . . tried to warn her but . . ."), Delia unstuck the sweatshirt from her forehead and discovered she was no longer bleeding. The bloodstains on the shirt had dried to a dull, blackish color. She glanced toward the other patients. Two women and a small girl sat watching her with interest, and she hastily clapped the sweatshirt back on her temple.

Dr. Norman was just hanging up the phone when the secretary led them in. He was a dumpy man with a flounce of white curls above his ears. "What have we here?" he asked, and he rose and came around the desk to peel away the sweatshirt with practiced fingers. His breath smelled of pipe tobacco. Delia would have liked to take hold of his hand and cradle it against her cheek. "Hmm," he said, peering. "Well, nothing you'll die of."

"Will it leave a scar?" Delia asked him.

"It shouldn't. Hard to tell for sure till I get it cleaned up."

"Of course I did everything humanly possible," Ellie warned. "Warned her over and over again. 'Watch yourself getting in, Dee,' I told her; if I told her once, I told her half a dozen times—"

Dr. Norman said, with a touch of impatience, "Yes, fine, Ellie, I understand," and Ellie shut up. "Come next door," he told Delia. He ushered her into an adjoining room. Ellie and Noah followed, which may not have been what he had intended.

This second room held an examining table upholstered in cracked black leather. Delia boosted herself nimbly onto the end of it and settled her handbag in her lap. While Dr. Norman rummaged in a metal drawer the color of condensed milk, he asked Ellie about the weather; he asked Noah about his softball team; he told Delia he had heard she was a ba-a-ad tutor.

"Bad!" Delia said.

"Good, that means." He looked up from the rubber gloves he was slipping on. "In T. J. Renfro's language, 'bad' is good, and so is 'wicked.' You teach a wicked equation, he says."

"Oh," Delia said, relieved.

Ellie, who had been studying a poster on the Heimlich maneuver, looked over at her. "You tutor at Underwood?" she asked.

"Yes."

She sniffed. "Joel must be in heaven," she said. "He was always after me to volunteer."

Dr. Norman sent Ellie a quick glance that she probably didn't notice. Then he told Noah, "Excuse me, son," and stepped around him to peer again at Delia's forehead. She stilled her swinging feet as he came close. "This'll smart some," he said, tearing open an antiseptic wipe. The keen, authoritative smell filled her with longing. *I'm really not just a mere patient,* she could have told him. *I know this office top to bottom! I know you'll sit down to supper tonight and tell your family that that Ellie Miller sure acts mighty possessive of Joel, considering they're separated. I know you'll say you finally got to meet that live-in woman of his, and depending on how discreet you are, you might even voice some suspicion as to exactly how I was injured. Don't think I'm one of those outsiders who can't see beyond the white coat!*

But of course she said nothing, and Dr. Norman swabbed her wound and then laid dots of rubbery warmth on either side of it as he tested it with his fingertips. "What you've got," he said, "is a superficial scratch across the forehead, but a fairly deep gash at the temple. No need for stitches, though, and I doubt there'll be a scar if we keep the edges together while it heals." He turned back to the cabinet. "We'll just apply a butterfly closure. This nifty type of bandage that . . ."

Yes, Delia knew what a butterfly was—had plastered more than a few onto her own children's injuries. She shut her eyes as he set it in place. Next to her she heard Noah breathing; he was leaning in close to watch. "Cool!" he said.

"Now, if you want I could prescribe a pain medication," Dr. Norman said, "but I don't believe—"

"It hardly hurts at all," Delia told him, opening her eyes. "I won't need anything."

He scrawled a note for his secretary before he showed her out, and clapped Noah on the shoulder, and said, "Ellie, always good to see your clothes hanging so well on you."

"Oh, stop," Ellie said. She told Delia, "Everybody pokes fun at this remark I made in *Boardwalk Bulletin.*"

Delia's only response was, "Oh?" because she didn't want to let on she'd read it.

"But I was misquoted!" Ellie said. "Or at least, I didn't mean it that way. What I meant was, I dress economically."

She was still going on about that—telling Noah that this skirt, for instance, had cost thirteen ninety-five at Teenage World—when they reached the reception desk, which left Delia to pay the bill. She did think Ellie might have offered. But she had planned to decline anyhow, and so she held her tongue.

Out on the porch, she folded the sweatshirt and stuffed it in her bag. Then she followed Ellie and Noah down the steps. Ellie was discussing the clothing budget of someone named Doris. Doris? Oh, yes, the anchorwoman at WKMD. "What she spends on headbands alone," Ellie said, "to say nothing of those scarves she wears to hide her scraggy neck . . ."

Delia was reflecting that she should have accepted that prescription after all, not for her forehead but for her ankle. She had completely neglected to mention twisting her ankle. She limped painfully to the car and fell with a thud into the passenger seat.

"So I guess you want to go home now," Ellie said.

"Yes, please," Delia told her.

But Ellie had been speaking to Noah. "Honey?" she said, watching his face in the rearview mirror.

"I guess," he said.

"Don't want to change your mind and visit *me?*"

"I've got this history test to study for."

Ellie's shoulders slumped. She didn't point out that he could do that anytime over the weekend.

They cruised down Weber Street, passing Copp Catering where Belle had bought Thanksgiving dinner, and the Sub Tub, where all the Underwood students headed for snacks after school. In Ellie's company, Delia felt that Bay Borough took on a different shading. It didn't look as happy as it usually did. The women walking home with their grocery bags seemed unknowingly ironic, like those plastic-faced, smiling housewives in kitchen-appliance ads from the fifties. Delia shook off the thought and turned to Ellie. "Well!" she said. "Maybe I'll run into you at your father's sometime."

"If I ever go back there," Ellie said gloomily.

"Oh, you have to go back! Why wouldn't you? He's such a pleasure to talk to."

"That's easy for you to say," Ellie said. "You're not his daughter."

She turned onto Pendle Street, braked for a jaywalking collie, and pulled into the Millers' driveway. (The glance she shot toward the front windows could have meant nothing at all.) "Bye, No-No," she said, blowing her son a kiss. "Delia, sorry again about the whatever."

"That's all right," Delia said.

Limping after Noah up the sidewalk, she remembered where she'd heard that phrase of Ellie's before. "Easy for *you*," Delia's sisters used to tell her. They said, "Naturally *you* get along with Dad. You arrived so late, is why. You don't have so much to hold against him."

But they never specified just what they held against him themselves. They hadn't been able to name it even when she asked, and she would be willing to bet that Ellie couldn't either.

When Delia changed into the shoes she wore around the house, she found that the strap of her pump had left a groove across her right instep. Her foot was so swollen, in fact, that she seemed to be wearing a *ghost* pump, pressing into her flesh. And her anklebone had become a mere dent. She doubted anything was broken, though. She could still wriggle her toes.

She drew a dishpan of cold water, added a few ice cubes, and sat down on a kitchen chair to let the ankle soak. And what else should she do for it? All those times she'd heard Sam advising his patients; you'd think she would remember. There was a mnemonic: R.I.C.E., he always told them. She tried it aloud. "Rest, ice . . ." But what was the C for? Caution? Coddling? She tried again. "Rest, ice . . ."

"Rest, ice, compression, elevation," Joel told her, setting his briefcase on the counter. "What happened to *you*? You look like a war orphan."

"Oh," Delia said, "you know that sharp corner they have on car doors . . ." Then she realized that this in no way explained her ankle. "It's just been one of those days," she finished vaguely.

He didn't pursue it. He opened an overhead cabinet and felt for something on the top shelf. "I know we have a first-aid kit," he said. "I had to take a course in—Here we go." He pulled out a gray metal tackle box. "When you're through soaking, I'll tape it."

"Oh, I'm through," Delia said. She should probably allow more time, but the ice was making her shiver. She lifted her foot and patted it dry with a dish towel. Joel bent over it. He whistled.

"Maybe you ought to get that x-rayed," he said. "Are you sure it's not broken?"

"Pretty sure. Everything works," Delia told him.

Moving aside the dishpan, he knelt and started unrolling a strip of flesh-colored elastic. Delia felt self-conscious about the puffiness of her ankle and the dead blue of her skin, but he showed no reaction. He began wrapping her foot, crisscrossing her instep, working his way upward in a series of perfectly symmetrical V's. "Oh, how neat! Tidy, I mean," Delia said. "You're very good at this."

"Part of a principal's education," Joel said. He wound the last of the bandage around her shin. Then he secured it with two metal clips the same shape as the butterfly closure on her temple. "How's that?" he asked. He took hold of her foot, as if weighing it. "Tight enough?"

"Oh, yes, it feels . . ."

It felt wonderful. Not just the bandage—although the support was a great relief—but the hand clasping her foot, the large palm warming her arch through the elastic. She wished she could push even harder against his grip. She was thirsty, it seemed, for that firmness. Till now she had never realized that the instep could be an erogenous zone.

As if he guessed, he went on kneeling there, looking into her face.

"Delia?" Noah said. "Can I invite—?"

Both of them jumped. Joel dropped her foot and stood up. He said, "Noah! I thought you were off at your mother's."

Noah stood in the doorway, frowning.

"We were just, ah, taping Delia's ankle," Joel told him. "It seems she must have sprained it."

Delia said, "Rest, ice, compression, elevation! That's the menon . . . menonom . . ." She laughed, short of breath. "Oh, Lord, I never can pronounce it."

Noah just watched her. Finally he said, "Can I invite Jack for supper?"

"Oh, of course!" she said. "Yes! Good idea!"

He looked at her a moment longer, looked at his father, then turned and walked out.

Joel wouldn't let her cook that night. He settled her on the family-room couch with her feet up and the cat in her lap, and he went off to order a pizza. Meanwhile Noah and Jack sprawled on the floor in front of the TV. Some kind of thriller was playing. During the more suspenseful scenes a piano tinkled hypnotically. Delia loosened her hold on George and leaned her head back and closed her eyes.

Behind her lids, she saw the gritty surface of Highway 50 rushing toward her. She saw the Plymouth darting across a stream of traffic, miraculously avoiding collision like a blip in a video game. She jerked awake, eyes wide and staring, shaken all over again by the narrowness of her escape.

17

The cut on Delia's forehead healed quickly, leaving just the faintest white fishhook of a scar. The sprain, though, took longer. She favored her right ankle for weeks. "This is not my actual walk," she wanted to tell passersby, for she felt, somehow, at a disadvantage—second rate, inferior. She wondered how people endured it when they knew they'd be disabled forever, like some of the residents in Senior City.

Senior City was the one place where her limp attracted no attention. She could proceed unhurriedly toward a waiting elevator, trusting the other passengers to hold it for her. When she finally stepped inside, she would find them conversing among themselves without a sign of impatience, one of them leaning absently on the Open button till Delia reminded her to release it. No longer did their own infirmities seem so apparent, either, or their wrinkles or white hair. Delia had adjusted her slant of vision over the past months.

And what a contrast Binky made! For anyone could see now that she was pregnant. By May she was in maternity clothes. By early June she was cupping her belly like an apronful of fruit as she rose from a chair. "Seems like things are *more so*, with this one," she told Delia. "When I had the boys I hardly showed till the end. I used to wear unzipped jeans and one of my husband's long-tailed shirts. But now I have to squeeze through car doors sideways and I've still got three months to go."

There was no question that this baby was unplanned. Binky said she'd been twelve weeks along before she suspected a thing—had continued proclaiming her June wedding date to all and sundry. "Then I said, 'What *is* this?' and I went to see my doctor. When he told me I was pregnant I just looked at him. He said, 'But nowadays, thirty-eight is nothing. Lots of women give birth at thirty-eight.' I said, 'How about sixty-seven?' He said, 'Sixty-seven?' I said, 'That's the age of the father.' He said, 'Oh.' Said, 'I see.' Said, 'Hmm.' "

"I view it this way," Nat told Delia. "What better place for childbirth than a retirement community? Here we have all these doctors and nurses, just standing by twiddling their thumbs on Floor Four."

Delia was horrified. She said, "You would go to Floor Four for this?"

"He's teasing," Binky told her.

"We'll turn the cardiac unit into a labor room," Nat went on impishly. "Use one of those railed hospital beds for a crib. And Lord knows these folks have got enough diapers around. Right, Noah?"

Noah grinned, but only at his teacup. He had reached that age where any talk of bodily functions was a monumental embarrassment.

"The best part is," Nat said, "whoever drew up the bylaws for Senior City never dreamed of this eventuality. All our contract says is, 'Applicants must be sixty-five before entering,' but this baby isn't an applicant. However, we did lose the Floor Two dispute. You heard we asked permission to move down to Floor Two? Now that I have Binky to look after me, I said . . . but the board said no. Said it wasn't the way the place worked. Progression was supposed to be up, they said; not down."

"Well, perhaps it's for the best," Binky told him. "Our neighbors on Three would be heartbroken to lose us, now the baby's coming."

"Yes, she certainly won't lack for sitters," Nat said dryly.

He kept insisting that the baby was a girl, even though they had chosen not to learn the sex. Girls were the only babies he'd had experience of, he said. He tried to convince Noah that *all* babies were girls but metamorphosed, some of them, into boys at about the same time their eyes darkened.

"You wouldn't believe how many old ladies are working on booties right now," he told Delia. "Little knitted slippers, socks, embroidered Mary Janes . . . Kid is going to be the Imelda Marcos of the nursery set."

Still, both Nat and Binky must have misgivings, Delia thought. How could they not? She was awed by their determined good cheer—by Binky's habit of telling people, "We couldn't be more pleased," as if prompting them; and by Nat's solicitude, even as he hobbled around as fragile and easily overturned as something constructed of Tinkertoys.

"When my first wife was dying," he told Delia one afternoon, "I used to sit by her bed and I thought, *This is her true face.* It was all hollowed and sharpened. In her youth she'd been very pretty, but now I saw that her younger face had been just a kind of rough draft. Old age was the completed form, the final, finished version she'd been aiming at from the start. *The real thing at last!* I thought, and I can't tell you how that notion colored things for me from then on. Attractive young people I saw on the street looked so . . . temporary. I asked myself why they bothered dolling up. Didn't they understand where they were headed? But nobody ever does, it seems. All those years when I was a child, longing for it to be 'my turn,' it hadn't ever occurred to me that my turn would be over, by and by. Then Binky came along. Is it any wonder I feel I've been born again?"

Binky was present when he said this, and she leaned forward and kissed his cheek. "Me too, sweetheart," she told him.

Delia grew suddenly conscious of her own separateness—of her upright posture, her elbows pressed primly against her sides in an armchair all to herself.

Then it was summer, warm and green and buzzing with cicadas after a long, cool spring. School came to an end, and Noah started sleeping late and hanging around the house with his friends and complaining of boredom. Joel switched to vacation hours and was home by midafternoon. In the maple tree out back, a woodpecker couple built themselves a nest. Delia could hear their cries from time to time—high-pitched, excited squawks that reminded her of girls'-school girls attending their first mixed party. And on Highway 50, more and more cars sped toward the beach, their rooftops spinning with bicycle wheels, their backseats stuffed with children, their rear window ledges a coagulation of sand shovels, rubber flippers, and Utz potato chip cartons.

Would Delia's family be going to the beach themselves? she wondered. It was June, after all. It was a year since she had left them, although it seemed much longer. She had, by now, done everything at least once— observed a birthday alone as well as Thanksgiving, Christmas, and New Year's. Paid her income taxes (married filing separately). Registered to vote. Taken the cat to the vet. She was a bona fide citizen of Bay Borough.

Then a letter arrived from Susie.

The envelope bore the correct address, which meant that Susie must have consulted Eliza or Eleanor. The handwriting was so rounded that *Borough* resembled a row of balloons anchored by a single string. Delia lifted the flap almost stealthily, unsealing it rather than tearing it, as if this would soften the impact of whatever waited inside.

> *Hi Mom!*
>
> *Just a quick note to fill you in! How you doing? Thanx for the graduation card! Commencement was kind of a drag but Tucky Pearson gave the most awesome party afterwards at her family's horse farm!*
>
> *Nothing special to report except Dad is being so-o-o-o difficult right now! I know you'll see my side of things so could you maybe phone him and have a talk? Don't tell him I asked you to call—just say you got a letter from me and thought you should discuss my plans. You wouldn't believe how mean he's being! Or maybe you would! Honestly Mom sometimes I don't even blame you for going! See ya!*
>
> *Luv, Susie*

Delia had a sudden sense of exhaustion. She refolded the letter and put it back in the envelope.

Well.

She couldn't phone from the house. She didn't want the call appearing on Joel's bill. Nor did she want to reverse the charges, which would give an impression of needfulness. So first she had to scrounge through her handbag and various pockets for change, and then she had to walk to the pay phone at Bay and Weber Streets, a block and a half away. She walked as fast as her ankle allowed, because if she made her call between eleven-thirty and twelve, she had a better chance of reaching Sam directly. He always broke for lunch then. Unless, in her absence, things had altered more than she had predicted.

Inside the booth—just one of those above-the-waist, partially enclosed affairs that let in every traffic sound—she lined up her coins on the shelf and then dialed the grown-ups' number. She had never called long distance from a pay phone before, and she was distressed to find that she had to wait to deposit the coins till her party answered. First the phone at the other end rang twice, then Sam said, "Dr. Grinstead," and then a recording issued instructions and Delia dropped her quarters in. *Whang! Whang!* It was humiliating—very nearly as bad as calling collect, and made worse by the fact that Sam didn't grasp what was going on. "Hello?" he kept saying. "Is anyone there?"

His deep, level voice, his habit of slanting downward even on questions. Delia said, "Sam?"

"Where are you?" he asked immediately.

He assumed this was a plea for help, she realized. He thought she was admitting defeat—calling to say, "Come get me." He must have been expecting it for months. She stood straighter. "I'm calling about Susie," she told him.

A dead silence. Then: "Oh. Susie."

"I wonder if you know what's troubling her."

"I believe my feeble brain can encompass *that* much," he said icily. "But I suppose you're going to tell me anyhow, aren't you."

"What?" Delia pressed her fingers to her forehead. "No, wait—I mean I'm honestly asking! She wrote me there was some problem, but she didn't say what it was."

"Oh," Sam said again. Another silence. "Well," he said, "this would have to do with her wedding, I suspect."

"Susie's getting married?"

"She wants to. I'm opposed."

"But—" Delia said. *But she didn't talk to me about this!* she wanted to protest. *Didn't even consult me!* Unreasonable, she knew; so she changed it to, "But Driscoll's a very nice boy. It is Driscoll, isn't it?"

"Who else," Sam said. "However, that's not the issue. She can marry whoever she chooses, of course, but I told her she'll have to live on her own for one calendar year beforehand."

"A year! Why?"

"I hate to see her jumping straight from school to marriage. From her father's house to her husband's house."

Her *father's* house? *He* hated to see? How about her mother? Oh, all right . . . but her *husband's* house?

And the biggest offense of all: what he meant was, he didn't want Susie turning out like Delia. Who had never spent so much as a night on her own before *she* married; and just look at the results.

He'd been mulling that over all year, she supposed. Arriving at his own private theory.

"But if she lives alone," Delia said, "she'll be so . . . unprotected. And also she and Driscoll might . . . I mean, what if they end up, um, sleeping together or something like that?"

"Don't you suppose they already sleep together, Delia?"

Her mouth dropped open.

A taped voice said metallically, "To continue your call, please deposit another—"

"Hold on, I'm going to try to get these charges reversed," Sam told Delia.

She didn't argue. She was trying to reassemble her thoughts. Well, no doubt they *did* sleep together. On some level, she'd probably known that. Still, she felt bereft. She pictured herself waving goodbye while Susie and Driscoll dwindled into the distance, never once looking back.

"You know she doesn't have a job yet," Sam said when he'd dealt with the operator.

"I wondered about that."

Amazing, how easy it was to fall back into this matter-of-fact, almost chatty exchange of information. The *ordinariness* of it struck her as surreal.

"She sleeps till all hours," he was saying, "and then heads off to the swimming pool. No interviews set up, no mention of careers . . ."

But if she's getting married, Delia thought. That too, though, she censored. She asked, "How about Driscoll? Does he have a job?"

"Yes, he's hired on with his father."

Delia tried to think what Driscoll's father did, but she couldn't remember. Something businessy. She said, "Well, have you and Susie talked about this? Discussed what kind of work might interest her?"

"No," Sam said.

"And where could she afford to live? I mean, if she isn't earning money yet."

"We haven't gone into that," Sam said.

"Well, golly, Sam, what *have* you gone into?"

"Nothing," Sam said. He gave a slight cough. "It appears that we're not speaking."

Delia sighed. She said, "How about Eliza? I know Susie must talk to *her.*"

"Not necessarily," Sam said.

"What do you mean?"

"I don't think they do talk, to tell the truth."

"They had a fight?"

"I'm not sure. Well, they did, I guess, but I'm not sure if it's still on or not. Actually, Eliza is out of town right now."

"Out of town!"

"She's visiting Linda awhile."

Delia digested this. She said, "Aren't you all taking your beach trip this year?"

"No, Delia," Sam told her, and the iciness was back in his voice. Delia understood his point as clearly as if he'd stated it: *Do you really imagine we'd go back to the beach, now that you've ruined it for all of us forever?*

Hastily she said, "So no one's sat Susie down and discussed her options with her."

"I fail to see how I can hold a discussion with someone who walks out of a room the instant I walk in," Sam said.

You follow her, is how, Delia wanted to tell him. *You walk out after her. What's so hard about that?* But for Sam it would be unthinkable, she knew. He wasn't a man who laid himself open to rebuff. He didn't like to plead, or bargain, or reverse himself; he had never made a mistake in all his life. (And was that why the people around him seemed to make so many?)

A delivery truck wheezed past, and she covered her free ear. "All right," she said, "here's what I propose. I'm going to write and tell her that if she wants you to pay for her wedding, she'll have to accept your conditions. And if she doesn't like those conditions, then she can pay for her own wedding. Either way, you will go along with it."

"I will?"

"You will."

"But then she might decide to marry him tomorrow."

"If she does, she does," Delia said. "That's up to her."

Sam was quiet. Delia's ankle had started to pound, but she didn't push him. Finally he said, "How about the not-speaking part?"

"How about it?"

"Could you tell her to talk all this over with me?"

"I could suggest it," she said.

"Thank you."

She felt uncomfortable in this new role. She said, "So! Everything else all right?"

"Oh, yes."

"Boys okay?"

"They're fine."

"Who's taking care of the office while Eliza's gone?"

"I am."

"Maybe *that's* a job for Susie."

"Never," he said flatly.

Another stab to the heart. *Never,* he meant, *would I let my daughter follow her mother's wretched example.* And she couldn't even argue with that. She said, "I guess I'll be going, then."

"Oh. Well. Goodbye," he said.

After she hung up, it occurred to her that on the other hand, maybe he was just saying Susie would be a disaster in the office. It was true that she was hopeless when it came to organizational matters. Unlike Delia, who had a gift for them.

Could that have been what he'd meant?

In her letter to Susie she included one request that she hadn't mentioned to Sam beforehand. *When you do get married,* she wrote, *whatever kind of wedding it may be, will you let me come? I couldn't blame you if you didn't, but . . .*

She wrote that afternoon, using the desk in the family room, choosing a time when she had the house to herself. Before she was finished, though, Joel came home. He said, "Oh, here you are." Then he stood about for a while, jingling coins deep in his pocket. At last she stopped writing and looked up at him.

"Was there something you wanted?" she asked.

"No, no," he said, and he moved away, went off to another part of the house. But as soon as she had finished the letter, he was back again. He must have heard her starting supper preparations. He stood in the kitchen doorway, once again jingling his coins. "Saw you on Weber Street today," he said.

"Weber Street?"

"Making a phone call."

"Ah."

"You know you're welcome to use the phone here," he said.

Delia had one of those flashes where she saw herself through someone else's eyes: huddling over the receiver and shielding her ear with one hand. She almost laughed. The Mystery Woman Strikes Again. She said, "Oh, well, it's just that I . . . had to call on the spur of the moment, that was all."

He waited, as if hoping for more, but she said nothing else.

Sometimes Delia noticed some detail in Joel—the play of muscles under the skin of his forearms, or the casual drape of his suit coat across his back—and she felt a pull so deep that she had to remind herself she hardly knew this man. In fact, they barely talked to each other. Ever since he'd bandaged her ankle they seemed to have grown tongue-tied and shy. And anyhow, they had Noah to think of.

Watchful, mistrustful Noah! Always lurking about, lately, scanning their faces for signs of guilt. One night when Joel and Delia came home from a Volunteer Tutors' Supper (potluck, each woman meditatively eating just her own dish, for the most part), they found him waiting at the front door with his arms clamped across his chest. "What took you so long?" he demanded. "That supper was supposed to get over at nine. It's nine forty-three, for gosh sake, and the Brookses' house is not but five minutes away!"

Well, think about it: in October he would turn thirteen. Not an easy age, as Delia knew far too well. Already there were signs. For instance, he had spurned those clothes she'd bought him this spring. And he wanted her to leave his laundry in the hall outside his room from now on, not bring it in. And one morning after his friends had slept over, he asked her, "Do you have to wear that beachy-looking cover-up at breakfast? Don't you own a bathrobe like normal people?"

Yes, it was clear where he was headed.

"He's getting so tall all at once; I went to kiss him the other day and his face was just about even with mine," Ellie said. (Often, now, the two of them talked on the phone awhile before Delia summoned Noah.) "Every time I see him, he's changed some way! He's started listening to this horrible music in the car, these singers who might as well be gossiping amongst themselves except every now and then you manage to overhear a stray word or two."

"And he says he's going to start a rock band," Delia told her. "He and Kenny Moss."

"But he doesn't play an instrument!"

"Well, *I* don't know. They've already got a name picked out: Does Your Mother Have Any Children?"

"That's a band name?"

"So he tells me."

"I don't get it," Ellie said.

"You're not supposed to, I guess. And you heard he doesn't want to go to camp this summer."

"But he loves camp!"

"He says it's babyish."

"What will he do instead, then?"

"Oh, he's going, willy-nilly," Delia told her. "Joel says he has to." She felt odd, mentioning Joel so familiarly to Ellie. She hurried on. "He's already paid the deposit, he says, and anyhow, I won't be here to tend him. I'll be on vacation."

"You will? Where?"

"Ocean City, the middle two weeks in July. Belle Flint set it up with this friend of hers who runs a motel."

"You and I should get together while you're there," Ellie told her. "Have dinner one night in my favorite restaurant. I hang out in Ocean City all the time!"

Evidently she no longer thought Delia was Joel's girlfriend. Delia wondered why. Was it seeing Delia up close that had changed her mind?

Delia felt a little bit disappointed, to be honest.

...

She dreamed she ran into Sam in front of Senior City. He was standing outside the double doors in his starched white coat, with his hands in his pockets, and she walked directly up to him and said, in her most positive tone, "At the Millers' I have a full-sized bike I built all by myself out of paper clips."

He gazed down at her thoughtfully.

"A working bike?" he asked.

"Well, no."

She woke up still squinting against the sunlight that had flashed off his glasses. He had been wearing a stethoscope, she recalled, looped across the back of his neck like a shaving towel. He hadn't worn a stethoscope since the first week he came to work for her father. It was a new-young-doctor thing to do, really, and new was what Sam had been then, in spite of his age, because he'd had to spend so long working his way through school. But he never would have given her such a stern and judging look when they were first acquainted.

Or would he?

Maybe he'd been that way from the start. Maybe Adrian had it right: what annoys you most, later on, is the very thing that attracted you to begin with.

For her trip to the beach she bought a suitcase—just a cheap one from the dime store, big enough to hold her straw tote. Belle was driving her over early Saturday morning. Noah was still home when Belle honked out front (he'd be leaving for camp around noon), and Delia gave him a quick goodbye hug, which he put up with. To Joel she said, "Don't forget to feed Vernon."

"Who's Vernon?"

She couldn't think why he asked, for a moment. Then she said, "Oh! I meant George." Silly of her: George and Vernon were not at all alike. She said, "George the *cat*!" as if it were Joel who had been confused. "Well, so long," she told him, and she rushed out the door, her suitcase knocking against her shins.

Belle wore enormous sunglasses, the upside-down kind with the earpieces hitched at the bottom. "I have the world's worst hangover," she told Delia right off. "I never want to see another drop of champagne as long as I live."

"You had champagne?"

"Did I ever. A whole entire bottle, because last night Horace proposed."

"Oh, Belle!"

"But he couldn't drink any himself because he's allergic," Belle said. "Just sat there watching *me* glug it down, following every swallow with those hound-dog eyes of his. Yes, that's the way we do things, we two. Still, it made a nice gesture. Champagne, a dozen roses, and a diamond ring: the works." She lifted her left hand from the wheel to display a tiny, winking glint. Then she pulled into the street. "Near as I can recall, I must have accepted. Think of it: Belle Lamb. Sounds like a noise in a comic book: *Blam!*" She was keeping her face expressionless behind the dark glasses, but there was something complacent and well-fed in the curve of her lips. "I guess now I'll have to go through with it," she said.

"Don't you want to go through with it?"

"Oh, well. Sure." She turned onto 380. "I do care about him. Or love him, I guess. At least, if he bangs his head climbing into my car I get this sort of clutch to my stomach. You reckon we could call that love?"

Delia was still considering this question as Belle went on. "But I can't help noticing, Dee: most folks marry just because they decide they've reached that stage. I mean, even if they don't have any particular person picked out yet. *Then* they pick someone out. It's like their marriages are arranged, same as in those foreign countries—except that here, the bride and groom are the ones who do the arranging."

Delia laughed. She said, "Well, now I don't know *what* to say. Am I supposed to congratulate you, or not?"

"Oh, well, sure," Belle said. "Congratulate me, I guess." And her left hand rose swaybacked from the wheel for a moment so she could admire her diamond.

The Mermaid's Chambers was a peeling turquoise motel on the wrong side of the highway, between a T-shirt shop and a liquor store. But Belle had got her a very good discount, and Delia wasn't planning to spend much time in her room anyhow.

Each morning, she crossed the highway carrying her tote and a motel bedspread, along with a Styrofoam cup of coffee. She rented an umbrella on the beach and settled herself amid a crowd that thickened as the day progressed—squealing children, impossibly beautiful teenagers, parents in assorted weights and ages, and stringy white grandparents. First she sat drinking her coffee as she stared out at the horizon, and then, when she had finished, she pulled a book from her tote and started reading.

Here in Ocean City she was back to romances, an average of one a day. They seemed overblown and slushy after her library books, and she read them almost without thinking about them, paying more heed to the yellow warmth soaking through her umbrella, the cries of gulls and children, the sunburned feet scrunching past her in the sand. One day, she started a book about a bride who was kidnapped by her fiancé's brother, and she realized partway through that this was what she'd been reading on *last* year's vacation. She checked the title: yes, *Captive of Clarion Castle.* She gazed toward the ocean. A mother was holding her diapered baby just above reach of the surf, and the radios all around were playing "Under the Boardwalk," and Delia fancied she caught sight of her own self strolling south alongside the festoons of sea foam.

Toward noon she would stand up and head toward the boardwalk for lunch. She ate in one or another rinky-dink café—a sandwich shop, a pizza joint—blinking away the purple spangles that swarmed across her vision in the sudden dimness. Then she returned to her umbrella and napped awhile, after which she read a bit more. Later she took a walk down the beach, just a short walk because her ankle still sent out a little blade of tenderness every time she put any weight on it. And then she went for her one swim of the day.

She spent forever submerging, like someone removing a strip of adhesive tape by painful degrees. Arms lifted fastidiously, stomach sucked in with a gasp, she advanced at a gingerly, crabwise angle so as to present the narrowest surface to the breakers. Finally, though, she was in, and not a hair on her head was dampened if she'd played her cards right. She floated far out with a smug sense of achievement, sending a lofty, amused glance shoreward whenever the swell she bobbed on crashed against the shrieking throngs in the shallows. And she always waited for the most docile wave to carry her back to land—although sometimes she misjudged and found herself knocked off her feet and churning underwater like a load of laundry.

Then she staggered onto the beach, streaming droplets and wringing out the skirt of her suit. By that time all her sunblock would have been washed off, and her face grew steadily pinker and more freckled over the course of her vacation. Her first act when she returned to her room at the end of every day was to check the mirror, and every day a more highly colored person gazed back at her. When she peeled off her swimsuit, a second suit of fish-white skin lay beneath it. In the shower her feet developed scarlet smatterings across the tops.

She lounged on the bed in Sam's beach robe and toweled her hair dry. Filed her nails. Watched the news. Later, when the moldy-smelling, air-conditioned air began to chill her, she dressed and went out to dinner—a different restaurant each night. Her Sundays at the Bay Arms stood her in good stead, and she dined alone serenely, making her way through three full courses as she surveyed the nearby tables. Then she sat on the boardwalk awhile, if she could find an empty bench. The racket of video games and rock music pummeled her from behind; in front stretched the empty black ocean, fringing itself white beneath a partly erased disk of moon.

She was back in her room by nine most nights. In bed by ten. She turned off the air conditioner and slept under just a sheet, lightly sweating in the warm air that drifted through her window.

One day was cloudy, with scattered, spitting rain, and she stayed inside and watched TV. Talk shows, mostly: a whole new world. People would say anything on television, she found. Family members who hadn't spoken in years spoke at length for the camera. Women wept in public. By the time Delia turned the set off her face ached, as if she'd attended too many social events. She went out for a walk and bought a new book to read, not a romance but something more serious and believable, about poor people living in Maine. For her walk she wore her Miss Grinstead cardigan, which clung gently to her arms and made her feel like a cherished child.

Twice she sent postcards to Noah at camp. *Nice weather, nice waves,* she wrote. That sort of thing. She bought a card for Joel too but couldn't decide what to say. In the end, she wrote Belle instead. *This was a really good idea. Thank you for setting things up for me.* Belle's friend Mineola, a dyed brunette in pedal pushers and stiletto heels, always greeted her amiably but otherwise left her alone, which suited Delia just fine.

Occasionally some jolt to the senses—a whiff of coconut oil, the grit of sand in her swimsuit seams—brought to mind the old family beach trips. She was returning her umbrella to the rental stall one afternoon when a child cried, "Ma, make Jenny carry something too!" which swept her back into that packing-up moment toward sunset each day when children beg to stay a little bit longer and grown-ups ask who's got the rafts, where's the green bucket, will somebody grab the thermos? She remembered the bickering, and the sting of carelessly kicked-up sand against burned skin, and the weighty, soft-boned weariness. She recalled each less-than-perfect detail, and yet still she would have given anything to find herself in one of those moments.

Whose sneakers are these? Someone's forgetting their sneakers! Don't come to me tomorrow whining about your sneakers!

She bought a postcard showing a dolphin, and she wrote on it, *Dear Sam and kids, Just taking a little holiday, thinking about you all.* Then it occurred to her that they might assume she was referring to this whole past year, not a mere two weeks in Ocean City; and she wasn't certain how to clarify her meaning. She tore the card in half and threw it away.

On her last night, she was supposed to meet Ellie at The Sailor's Dream. She regretted having agreed to it. Carrying on a conversation struck her all at once as a lot of work. However, canceling would have been work too, so she showed up at the appointed hour in front of the restaurant. Ellie was already standing under the awning. She wore a white halter dress shot with threads of silver, the kind of thing you'd expect to see on cruise ships, and she carried a little white purse shaped like a scallop shell. Men kept glancing over at her as they passed. "Why, Delia! *Look* at you!" she called. "Aren't you all healthy and rosy!" Delia had forgotten how good it felt to have somebody know her by name and act glad to see her coming.

The Sailor's Dream had the padded-leather atmosphere of an English gentlemen's club, but with some differences. The carpet, for instance, gave off the same mushroom smell as the one in Delia's motel room. And all the waiters were deeply tanned.

"So tell me," Ellie said as soon as they were seated. "Have you been having a good time?"

"A lovely time," Delia told her.

"Was this your first vacation by yourself?"

"Oh, yes," Delia said. "Or rather . . ."

She wasn't sure whether traveling alone to Bay Borough qualified as a vacation or not. (And if it did, when had her vacation ended and her real life begun?) She met Ellie's eyes, which were fixed on her expectantly.

"Doesn't it feel funny going swimming on your own?" Ellie asked.

"Funny? No."

"And what about eating? Have you been eating in your room all this time?"

"Goodness, no! I ate out."

"I *hate* to eat out alone," Ellie said. "You don't know how I admire you for that."

They had to stop talking to give their orders—crab imperial for Delia, large green salad hold the dressing for Ellie—but as soon as the waiter moved away, Ellie said, "Did you practice beforehand? Before you left your, ah, previous place of residence?"

"Practice?"

"Did you *use* to eat out alone?"

Delia began to see what Ellie was up to here: she was hoping to gather some tips on how to manage single life. For next she said, "I never did, myself. I never even walked down a street alone, hardly! Always had some escort at my elbow. I was awfully popular as a girl. Now I wish I'd been a little less popular. You know how long ago I first thought of leaving Joel? Three months after we were married."

"Three months!"

"But I kept thinking, *What would I do on my own, though?* Everyone would stare at me, wonder what was wrong with me."

She leaned even closer to Delia. Lowered her voice. "Dee," she said.

"Yes?"

"Did you *have* to leave?"

Delia drew back slightly.

"Like, were you in just . . . an impossible position? Had to get out? Couldn't have survived another minute?"

"Well, no," Delia said.

"I don't want to pry! I'm not asking for secrets. All I want to know is, how desperate does a person need to get before she's certain she should go?"

"Desperate? Oh, well, I wouldn't say . . . well, I'm *still* not certain, really."

"You're not?"

"I mean, it wasn't an actual decision," Delia told her.

"Take me, let's say," Ellie said. "Do you think I made a mistake? There you are in that house with my husband; do you think I was overreacting to leave him?"

"I'm not married to him, though. There's a difference."

"But you must know what he's like, by now. You know how persnick-
ety he is and how . . . right all the time and always criticizing."

"Joel, criticizing?" Delia asked. "Belle Flint says he worships you! He's
trying to keep the house exactly like you left it—hasn't anyone told you?"

"Oh, yes, *after* I left it," Ellie said. "But while I was there it was, 'Why
can't you do it this way, Ellie?' and, 'Why can't you do it that way, Ellie?'
and these big cold silent glowers if I didn't."

"Is that so," Delia said.

And just then she saw Sam standing in front of the fridge, delivering
one of his lectures on the proper approach to uncooked poultry. Sam was
so phobic about food poisoning you'd think they lived in some banana re-
public, while Joel never mentioned it. No, Joel's concerns were more endearing, she thought—his household maps and his chore charts. They so
plainly arose from a need for some sense of stability. All he was really after was *sureness*.

Or could the same be said for Sam?

Their food arrived, and the waiter flourished a pepper mill as big as a
newel post. He asked, "Would either of you like—?"

"No, no, go away," Ellie said, waving a hand. As soon as they were
alone again, she turned back to Delia. "Three months after our wedding,"
she said, "Joel went to a conference in Richmond. I said to myself, 'Free!'
I felt like dancing through the house. I almost *flew* through the house. I
played this kind of game with myself, went through all his drawers and
packed his clothes in boxes. Packed what hung in his closet too. Pretended
I lived by myself, with no one peering over my shoulder. He wasn't due
home till Wednesday, and I planned to put everything back Tuesday night
so he'd never guess what I'd done. Except he came home early. Tuesday
noon. 'Ellie?' he said. 'What *is* this?' 'Oh,' I told him, 'it's just I wanted to
picture what it would feel like to have more drawer space.' That's how
women get their reputations for ditsiness. The real reason wasn't ditsy in
the least, but who's going to tell him the real reason?"

She hadn't touched her salad. Delia plucked a piece of crab cartilage
from her tongue and set it on the side of her plate.

"In a way, the whole marriage was kind of like the stages of mourning," Ellie said. "Denial, anger . . . well, it *was* mourning. I'd go to parties
and look around; I'd wonder, did all the other women feel the same as
me? If not, how did they avoid it? And if so, then maybe I was just a cry-
baby. Maybe it was some usual state of affairs that everybody else grace-
fully put up with."

Finally she speared a lettuce leaf. She nibbled it off her fork with just her
front teeth, rabbitlike, all the while fixing Delia with her hopeful blue gaze.

"That reminds me of Melinda Hawser," Delia told her. "This woman I
met at Belle's last Thanksgiving. The way she talked, I figured she'd be divorced by Christmas! But I run into her uptown from time to time and
she's still as married as ever. Looks perfectly fine."

"Exactly," Ellie said. "So you can't help thinking, *Wouldn't I have been fine too? Shouldn't I have stuck it out?* And you get to remembering the good things. The way he loved to watch me put on my face for a party so I always felt I was doing something bewitching; or after the baby was born, when we weren't allowed to have sex for six weeks and so we just kissed, the most wonderful kisses . . ." Now the blue eyes were swimming with tears. "Oh, Delia," she said. "I *did* make a mistake. Didn't I?"

Delia looked tactfully toward a brass lamp. She said, "It's not as if you couldn't *un*make it. Jump in the car and drive back home."

"Never," Ellie said, and she dabbed beneath each eye with her napkin. "I would never give him the satisfaction," she said.

And what would have become of Delia if Ellie had answered otherwise?

Belle told Delia she hadn't missed a thing in Bay Borough, not a blessed thing. "Dead as a tomb," she said, driving languidly, one-handed. "Little fracas in town council—Zeke Pomfret wants to drop the baseball game from Bay Day this year, switch to horseshoes or something, and Bill Frick wants to keep it. But no surprises *there*, right? And Vanessa swears she's known about me and Horace all along, but I don't believe her. And we've set the wedding date: December eighteenth."

"Oh, Christmastime!" Delia said.

"I wanted an excuse to wear red velvet," Belle told her.

They left the glitter of the beaches behind and rode through plainer, simpler terrain. Delia watched shabby cottages slide by, then staid old farmhouses, then an abandoned produce stand that was hardly more than a heap of rotting gray lumber. She would never have guessed, the first time she traveled this road, that she could find such scenery appealing.

At the Millers' house, the front lawn was mowed too short and crisply edged, and each shrub stood in a circle of fresh hardwood chips. Evidently Joel had found himself with an abundance of spare time. Inside, the cat cold-shouldered her and then trailed her footsteps in a guilt-provoking way as Delia walked through the empty rooms. The house was tidy but somehow desolate, with subtle signs of bachelorhood like a huge wet dish towel instead of a proper washrag hanging over the kitchen faucet, and a thin film of grease coating the stove knobs and cupboard handles (those out-of-the-way places men never think to clean). On her bureau, a note read: *Delia—I've gone to pick up Noah. Don't fix supper; we'll all grab a bite out someplace. J.* Also, she had mail: a handwritten invitation on stiff cream paper. *Driscoll Spence Avery and Susan Felson Grinstead request your presence at their wedding, 11 a.m. Monday, September 27, in the Grinstead living room. R.S.V.P.*

What a lot could be deciphered from a couple of dozen words! For starters, the writing was Susie's (blue ink, running steeply downhill) and no parents' names were mentioned—certain proof that she was proceeding on her own. Sam must have acquiesced, though, because the wedding would take place at the house. The date was harder to figure. Why September? Why a Monday morning? And had Susie found a job or had she not?

Delia wished she could phone and ask, but she felt she didn't have the right. She would have to respond by mail, like any other guest.

Of course she planned to attend.

She looked up and met her own face in the bureau mirror—her eyes wide and stricken, her freckles standing out sharply.

When they told her that her firstborn was a girl, she had been over-joyed. Secretly, she had wished for a girl. She had planned how she would dress her in little smocked dresses; but Susie, it turned out, insisted on jeans as soon as she could talk. She had planned how they would share womanly activities (sewing, baking pies, experimenting with skincare products), but Susie preferred sports. And instead of a big white wedding, with Susie swathed in antique lace and both her parents beaming as they jointly (in the modern manner) gave her away, here Delia stood in an Eastern Shore ranch house, wondering what sort of ceremony her daughter was inviting her to.

Noah seemed to have grown two inches while he was at camp, and the macramé bracelets he wore around both wrists pointed up the new brown-ness and squareness of his hands. Also, he'd developed a habit of saying, "Are you inputting that?" in a way that already seemed to be exasperating Joel. They sat in a booth at Rick-Rack's, Joel and Noah on one side and Delia on the other, and she could observe Joel's wince even if Noah couldn't.

"Take my word for it," Joel told him finally. "I have indeed managed to grasp your meaning, but I would certainly not choose to convey that fact in computer jargon."

"Huh? So anyhow," Noah said, "at camp they made us do fifty push-ups every morning. Fifty, are you inputting that? I guess they wanted to kill us off and keep our fees for nothing. So me and Ronald went to the infirmary—"

"Ronald and I," Joel said.

"Right, and tried to get a health excuse. But the dumbhead nurse wouldn't write one. She goes, like—"

"She said."

"She said, like—"

Their food came—burgers for Noah and Joel, pork barbecue sandwich for Delia. "Thanks, Teensy," Noah said.

"Sure thing," Teensy said cheerfully.

"Mrs. Rackley to *you*," his father told him.

Noah glanced across at Delia. Delia merely smiled at him.

"Daddy's been asking where you got to these last couple of weeks," Teensy said to Delia.

"I went to Ocean City."

"Yes, I told him so, but he couldn't seem to keep it in mind. He said,

'She never even mentioned it! Just walked on out and left!' His memory's a whole lot worse lately."

"Oh, I'm sorry to hear that," Delia said.

"He says things are coming at him too fast for him to take in. And Rick tells him, just trying to be nice, tells him, 'Oh, I know exactly what you—' but Daddy says, 'Don't you poke your black self into this!' and I said, 'Daddy!'—"

Teensy broke off, glancing at Joel. "Well," she said. "I guess I better get back to work."

She slid her hands down her apron front and hurried away.

"Remarkable," Joel said.

He seemed to have no inkling that it was his impassive gaze that had sent her rushing off.

"Maybe Mr. Bragg should go live in Senior City," Noah said.

"I don't think he can afford it," Delia told him.

"Maybe they have scholarships. Or grants or something, are you in-putting that?"

Joel rolled his eyes.

"So anyhow," Noah said, picking up his burger. "Next thing, me and Ronald worked out that we'd pretend we were injured. Only we couldn't do it both at once, because it would look kind of fishy."

"You went about it all wrong," Joel told him. "Nothing good ever comes of resorting to subterfuge."

"To what?"

"Subterfuge."

"What's that?"

Joel stared across the table at Delia. His eyebrows were raised so high that his forehead resembled corduroy.

"He means something underhanded," Delia told Noah. "Something sneaky."

"Oh."

"He means you should have protested the rule openly. Or so I assume." She expected Joel to elaborate, but he was still gaping. "Is that what you meant?" she asked him.

"He doesn't know what 'subterfuge' is!" Joel said.

She took her sandwich apart and started spooning in coleslaw.

"He never heard the word 'subterfuge.' Can you believe it?"

She wouldn't answer. Noah said, "It's no big deal. Geez."

"No big deal!" Joel echoed. "Don't they teach kids anything in school these days? 'Subterfuge' is not all that arcane, for God's sake."

Delia watched Noah decide not to ask what "arcane" meant.

"Sometimes I think the language is just shrinking down to the size of a wizened little pellet," Joel told her. "Taken over by rubbish words, while the real words disappear. The other day, I discovered our cafeteria super-visor didn't know what cutlery was."

"Cutlery?" she asked.

"It seems the word has dropped out of use."

" 'Cutlery' has dropped out of use?"

"That's the only explanation I can think of. I told him we were order-ing a new supply of cutlery, and he said, 'What's that?' "

"Oh, fiddlesticks," Delia said. "*You* know what cutlery is," she told Noah.

He nodded, although he didn't risk demonstrating.

"See there? It hasn't dropped out of use! Teensy," Delia called, "could we have more cutlery, please?"

"Coming right up," Teensy said, and behind the counter they heard the rattle of knives and forks.

Delia looked triumphantly at Joel.

"Oh. Well . . . ," he said.

Noah grinned. "Way to go, Dee," he told her. And eventually even Joel started smiling.

Delia smiled too, and put her sandwich back together and gave it a pat. Underneath her breath she was making a humming sound—a thin, sweet, toneless hum, not much different from purring.

18

Binky's baby was born on Labor Day—very fitting, Nat said. He telephoned that same afternoon; he spilled the news in a swelling voice that seemed about to break. "Eight pounds, eleven ounces," he crowed. "James Nathaniel Moffat."

"James!" Delia said. "It's a boy?"

"It's a boy. Can you believe it?" He gave one of his bearded chuckles. "I'm not sure I'll know what to *do* with a boy."

"You'll do fine," Delia said. "Noah's off on a picnic right now, but he'll be thrilled when I tell him. How's Binky?"

"Couldn't be better. She just *sailed* through this, and so did James. Wait till you see him, Delia. He's got the roundest face, little pocket watch of a face, and lots of blondish hair, but Binky says . . ."

To listen to him, you would never have guessed he had been through this experience four times.

Delia had overstated when she said Noah would be thrilled. Oh, he was interested, in a mild sort of way—wanted to know who the baby looked like, and what the board of directors had said. But when Wednesday morning rolled around, he asked if he couldn't put off his regular visit. School had just reopened, and he wanted to try out for the wrestling team. Delia said, "How about we look in on the baby for just a second, and then I drop you at tryouts afterward?"

"Can't we do it tomorrow?"

"Tomorrow I have tutoring, Noah, and the day after is the Grade Mothers' Tea, and if you wait too long your grandpa's going to think you don't care. I'll phone ahead and tell him you can stay just a minute."

"Well, okay," Noah said halfheartedly.

When she picked him up at school, he was trying to elbow Jack Newell off the sidewalk, and she had to tap her horn to catch his attention. He disentangled himself, jerked open the passenger door, and fell into the car. "Hi," she told him, but he just slid down in his seat and jammed his

Phillies cap on his head. Then, out on the highway, he said, "I've got to stop doing this."

"Doing what?"

"I can't spend all my time visiting people! Mom, and Grandpa . . . I'm in the eighth grade now! I've got important activities!"

He cracked froggily on "activities," and Delia shot him a glance. His voice was about to start changing, she realized. Oh, Lord, here she was with yet another adolescent.

But all she said was, "Maybe you could switch your visits to weekends."

"Weekends I hang out with my friends! I'd miss all the fun!"

"Well, *I* don't know, Noah," she said. "Talk it over with Nat and your mom."

"And could you please drive something under ninety miles an hour? I'm not going to *live* to talk it over, riding with a maniac."

"Sorry," she said. She slowed. "Take a peek at what I found for the baby," she told him. "It's on the backseat."

He glanced back, but he didn't reach for it. "Why don't you just *tell* me what it is," he said.

"A little bitty pair of athletic shoes, not any bigger than thimbles."

"Huh."

In the old days, nothing could have stopped him from peeking at that gift.

The day was cool and cloudy, with a forecast of rain, but all they encountered during their drive was a stray drop or two on the windshield. Noah listened to a radio station where the singers screamed insults, while Delia played calmer songs in her mind—a technique she had learned with her own children. She was just starting "Let It Be" when they turned in at Senior City.

"You've got to be kidding," Noah said.

Next to the double front doors stood a four-foot-tall wooden cutout of a stork, sporting a pale-blue waistcoat and carrying a pale-blue bundle. Pale-blue balloons floated from the portico. The lobby bulletin board (which ordinarily bore cards of thanks from convalescents and sign-up sheets for bus trips to the shopping outlets in York) was plastered with color snapshots of an infant just minutes old. Three women wearing the regulation jaunty neck scarves stood peering at the photos and discussing the significance of hand size. One woman said large hands in infancy meant great height in adulthood, but another said that held true only for puppies.

In the elevator they found Pooky, taking one of her never-ending rides. Today, though, she seemed fully aware that she had reached Floor One, and she said, punching Three for them, "If you hurry you'll be in time for the burping."

"Oh, have you seen him?" Delia asked as they rose.

"Seen him twice. I was one of those in the lobby yesterday when they brought him home from the hospital. I hope that gift is not shoes."

"Well, sort of," Delia said.

"So far he's got Swedish leather clogs, inch-long flip-flops, and eentsy little motorcycle boots. And that's not even counting all we've knitted."

The elevator stopped with a lilt, and the door slid open. "I would come with you," Pooky called after them, "but I've got to get back to my apartment and finish childproofing."

It was Nat who answered when they rang the doorbell. "There you are!" he said. "Come in, come in!" He was using his cane today, but he walked rapidly and bouncily as he led them toward the bedroom. "James is just having a snack," he called over his shoulder.

"Should we wait out here?" Delia asked.

"No, no, everyone's decent. Bink, sweetheart, it's Noah and Delia."

Binky was sitting against the headboard of the bed, dressed but in her stocking feet. The receiving blanket draped over her bosom covered the baby's face, so all they could see was a fiery little ear and a fuzzy head. "Oh, look at him!" Delia whispered. It always seemed the bottom dropped out of her chest when she saw a new baby.

Noah, though, looked everywhere but. He stuck his hands in his back pockets and studied a distant corner of the bedroom till Binky, winking at Delia, asked, "Want to hold him, Noah?"

"Me?"

She removed the baby from her breast, at the same time adroitly rearranging the blanket. The baby's eyes were closed, and he made nostalgic little smacking movements with his lips, which were rosebud-shaped, tightly pursed. He did have big hands, with long, translucent fingers knotted just under his chin. "Here," Binky said, holding him out to Noah. "Just support the back of his head, like this."

Noah received him in an awkward, jumbled clump.

"He seems to be a very easy baby," Binky said as she buttoned up. "Most of the day he's slept, which is miraculous considering all the callers we've had. Your mother phoned, Noah; wasn't that nice? That was so nice. No word from the other three yet, but I hope—"

"Oh, forget it, just forget it, hon," Nat told her. "Who cares about them!" He gave an angry shake of his head, as he often did when his daughters were mentioned. "Let's go sit in the living room."

They followed him—Noah still carrying James, feeling his way with his feet—and settled amid an uncharacteristic clutter of slippers and afghans and gift boxes. Already the apartment had that rainy, sweet, baby-powder smell.

Binky unwrapped the athletic shoes and laughed and passed them to Nat, and then, at Delia's request, she brought out the baby's motorcycle boots. A present from her sons, she said; they claimed to be disgusted with her, but Peter had cut classes to deliver these in person. Then Nat reported on their ride to the hospital ("I said, 'Binky,' I said, 'didn't I say from the start we should have gone to Floor Four?' "), and Binky rehashed the birth, which all in all, she said, had been a cinch compared to her first two. ("I shouldn't discuss this in mixed company," she said, "but ever since Peter was born, I just never have known when I needed to tinkle. The best I can do is go every couple of hours, just in case.")

Noah looked downright queasy by now, so Delia stood up to collect the baby—an excuse to feel, for an instant, the limp, crumpled weight of that little body—and return him to Binky. "We have to get Noah to his tryouts," she told Binky. "Is there anything I can do for you? Grocery shopping? Errands?"

"Oh, no. Nat's taking wonderful care of me," Binky said.

Nat, Delia happened to know, felt the ache of his flashbacks most keenly when he was driving, but she couldn't point that out when he was looking so proud of himself.

Joel seemed very nervous about the Grade Mothers' Tea. He must be wishing for Ellie, Delia thought—for Ellie's clever, theme-party style of entertaining. But when she proposed phoning Ellie and asking for suggestions, he said, "Why should we do that? We're surely capable of a simple tea, for God's sake."

"Yes, but maybe—"

"All we need from Ellie is her recipe for lemon squares," he said.

"Lemon squares. I'll ask."

"The ones with the crispy glaze on top. Also her cucumber sandwiches."

"Well, *I* can make a cucumber sandwich," Delia snapped.

"Oh. Of course."

After that he let the subject drop—forced himself to drop it, no doubt. On Friday afternoon, though, he paced circles around her as she set up the party-size percolator on the dining-room buffet. "This group will be nothing but women," he told her.

"Well, so I gathered: grade mothers."

"There is a grade father, but he's away on business. It's one hundred percent women."

She went to draw the water for tea. He followed. "You do plan to help with the conversation, don't you?" he asked.

She hadn't expected to. She had envisioned herself biding her time in the kitchen, like those discreet lady housekeepers in nineteenth-century novels. She had been looking forward to it, in fact. She said, "Oh, um . . ."

"I can't do it alone, Delia."

"Well, I'll try."

But no help was needed, she found. Fourteen women showed up—two for each homeroom, minus the traveling father and a mother who couldn't get off work. All of them were acquainted, most since childhood, and they slid easily into topics so well established that they seemed to be speaking in code. "What did Jessie finally decide?"

"Oh, just what we figured all along."

"Darn!"

"Yes, but who can say—maybe this will turn out like the Sanderson girl."

"Well, that's a thought."

Delia wore her navy knit, on the assumption that teas were dressy, but the guests wore slacks or even jeans, and one had on a sweatshirt reading COMPOST HAPPENS. They all seemed unduly curious about her. They kept coming up to ask, "So how do you *like* it here? How is Noah handling all this? Has he adjusted?" When she answered, the voices nearby would trail off and others would edge closer. "Golly," one said, "Mr. Miller must be awfully glad to have you. And you help with the tutoring too! You tutor the Brewsters' youngest! Mr. Miller's always complaining he can't find enough math tutors."

Now she knew how new girls must feel on their first day at school. But she responded politely, keeping a smile on her face, holding the teapot before her like a ticket of admission. She liked Bay Borough very much, thank you, and Noah was getting on well, and she had probably learned more from her pupils than they had learned from her. The usual remarks. She could have made them in her sleep. Meanwhile Joel stood talking with two women at the other end of the room, nodding pensively and from time to time wrinkling his brow. He no longer seemed nervous. And when she approached with a plate of cookies, he said, "You're doing a fine job, Delia."

"Thank you," she said, smiling.

"It may be the best tea we've given."

"Oh! Well, the lemon squares were Ellie's, remember; Ellie was kind enough to—"

Then one of the women asked Joel what had been planned for the Fall Bazaar, and Delia escaped to the kitchen.

She straightened things up, wiped counters, put a few items in the dishwasher. The cat had taken refuge under the table, and she hauled him forth to cuddle him and scratch behind his ears. For a while she watched the minute hand of the wall clock visibly jerk forward: five-eighteen to five-nineteen to five-twenty. Time for the guests to recall that they should get home and fix supper. In fact, she could detect a certain shift in the blur of voices—the rising notes of leave-taking.

"Didn't I have a purse?"

"Has anyone seen my keys?"

And then, "Where's *Delia*? I should say goodbye to Delia."

She had to drop George and make another appearance, see them all to the door. ("It was good meeting you, too. I'd be happy to give out the recipe.") Then she returned to the dining room, and Joel unplugged the percolator while that woman who always has to stay longest (there was one at every party) fussily separated the clean spoons from the dirty ones. "Please," Delia told her, "just let them be. I've got a system." How quickly the old formulas came back to her: *I've got a system. Don't give these a thought. It won't be a bit of trouble.*

The woman was reluctant to leave and stood awhile gazing into her purse, as if searching for instructions on where to go next. She had triplets, Delia had overheard—all boys, all just starting to drive. Easy to understand why she wasn't rushing home. Finally she said, "Well, thanks, you two. This was a real treat." And darting a smile in Joel's direction, she told Delia, "Isn't he helpful! Why, if I asked *my* husband to clear, he'd think I was joking. He would just act . . . bemused and go off with his pals."

Joel waited till she was gone before he snorted. " 'Bemused'!" he echoed. "Discouraging, isn't it?"

Delia wasn't sure what he was objecting to. (At least, she thought, he hadn't seemed to notice the woman's apparent belief that they were a couple.) She carried a stack of cups to the kitchen and began fitting them into the dishwasher.

"You realize what's going to happen," Joel said. He set the percolator on the counter. "Bit by bit, more and more people will say 'bemused' in place of 'amused,' thinking it's just the twenty-dollar version, the same way they think 'simplistic' is a twenty-dollar 'simple.' And soon enough that usage will start showing up in dictionaries, without so much as a 'non-standard' next to it."

"Maybe she really did mean 'bemused,' " Delia said. "Maybe she meant her husband was puzzled; he was perplexed that she'd asked him to help."

"No, no. Nice try, Delia, but no, she meant 'amused,' all right. Everything's changing," Joel said. "It's getting so we're hardly speaking English anymore."

She looked over at him. He was winding the cord around the percolator, although it hadn't been emptied yet or washed. "Yes, I've noticed that's what bothers you, most times," she told him.

"Hmm?"

"Most times it's not grammatical errors—other than the obvious, like 'me and him.' It's the new things, the changes. 'Input' and 'I'm like' and 'warm fuzzies.' "

Joel shuddered. Too late, Delia recalled that he had never to her knowledge mentioned "warm fuzzies"—that it came from Ellie's interview. She hurried on. "But think," she said. "Probably half your own vocabulary was new not so long ago. Well, 'twenty-dollar,' for instance! These terms pop up for good reason. 'Glitch.' 'Groupie.' 'Nickel-and-diming.' 'Time-shifting.' "

"What's time-shifting?" Joel asked.

"When you record a TV program to view later. Mr. Pomfret used to say that, and I thought, *Oh, how . . . economical!* Don't you sometimes *wish* for new words? Like a word for, a word for . . ."

"Freckles," Joel said.

"Freckles?"

"Those freckles that are smaller than ordinary freckles," he said. "And paler. Like gold dust."

"And also, um, tomatoes," Delia said, too quickly. "Yes, tomatoes. You have the true kind and then you have the other kind, the supermarket kind, the same color as the gums of false teeth, and those should be given a whole separate name."

"And then," Joel told her, "that different sort of surface people take on when you really begin to see them."

She had nothing to say to that.

"They get so noticeable," Joel said. "It seems you can feel every vein and pulse underneath their skin. You think, *All at once she's become . . .* but what word would you use? Something like 'textured,' but textured to the vision, instead."

His eyes seemed a softer hue of brown now, and that long, notched mouth had grown shapelier, more tender.

"Goodness!" she said, spinning toward the door. "Is that Noah?"

Although Noah had gone to Ellie's and was not due home till bedtime. And anyhow, would be dropped off at the front of the house, not the back.

Sometimes when Delia said to herself, *Only x number of days till Susie's wedding,* she felt a clammy sense of dread. *This is going to be so embarrassing. How will I face them? It's not a situation I've been taught to handle.* But other times she thought, *Pshaw, what's so hard about a wedding? We'll have all those other people there as buffers. I can just breeze in, breeze out. Nothing to it.*

For a while she had an idea that Susie might ask her to come early, as much as several days early, to help with preparations. At least that way she wouldn't feel like a mere guest. She pounced hopefully on the mail every morning, cleared her throat before answering the phone, delayed notifying Joel of her plans till she knew how long she'd be gone. But Susie didn't ask.

And sometimes she considered not attending. What purpose would she serve? They wouldn't even miss her. A day or two after the wedding, one of them might say, "Hey! You know who didn't show up? Delia! I just now remembered."

And still other times, she fantasized that they could hardly wait to see her. "Delia!" they would cry, "Mom!" they would cry, running out onto the porch, letting the door slam behind them, flinging their arms around her.

No, cancel that. More likely they would ask, "What do you think *you're* doing here? Did you imagine you could waltz back in just as if nothing had happened?"

She should remember to bring her invitation, in case there was any question.

She broached the subject to Joel at Sunday breakfast, having waited till the very last day for word from Susie. Sunday was a good time anyhow, because Noah was there, wolfing down buckwheat pancakes; the conversation couldn't get too probing. She said, "Joel, I don't know if I mentioned or not"—knowing full well she had not—"that I'll need to take the day off tomorrow."

"Oh?" he said. He lowered his newspaper.

"I have to go to Baltimore."

"Baltimore," he said.

"Geez, Delia!" Noah said. "I promised my wrestling coach you'd give a bunch of us a ride to the meet tomorrow."

"Well, I can't," she said.

"Well, geez! *Now* what'll we do?"

"Your coach will think of something," Joel told him. "If you wanted to volunteer Delia's services, you should have asked her first." But he was keeping his eyes on Delia's face as he spoke. "Is this a, some kind of emergency?" he asked her.

"No, no, just a wedding."

"Ah."

"But it's one I'd very much like to attend, a family wedding, you know, and so I thought if you didn't mind . . ."

"Of course; not at all," Joel said. "Could I drive you to the bus station?"

"Oh, thanks, but I'm going by car," Delia said. "Baltimore's on Mr. Lamb's sales route, it turns out."

Joel probably had no idea who Mr. Lamb was, but he nodded slowly, eyes still fixed on her face.

"So!" she said. "Now, I assume I'll be back by evening. Maybe suppertime, but I can't be sure; I'm returning by bus; so I've left a chicken salad in the fridge. There's a tub of Rick-Rack's coleslaw next to it, biscuits in the bread drawer . . . But I bet I'll be back by then, anyhow."

"Should I meet your bus?"

"No; Belle's doing that. I'll call her when I get into Salisbury."

"You could call me instead."

"No, really, I have no idea when . . . it might be late at night or something. It could even be the next day; who knows?"

"The next day!" he said.

"If the reception runs very long."

"But you *are* coming back," he said.

"Well, of course."

Now Noah was watching her too. He looked up from his pancakes and opened his mouth, but then he didn't speak.

Toward noon she set out on a walk, planning to end at the Bay Arms for lunch whenever her ankle grew tired. It had rained in the morning, but now the sun was shining, and the air felt so thick and warm that she regretted wearing her sweater. She pulled it off and swung it loosely from one hand. Everywhere she looked, it seemed, she saw people she knew. Mrs. Lincoln waved to her from the steps of the A.M.E. church, and T. J. Renfro, roaring past on his Harley, called out, "What say, Teach!" and on Carroll Street she ran into Vanessa and Greggie, poking along in matching yellow slickers. "Delia! I was just about to phone you," Vanessa said. "Want to ride with me to Salisbury tomorrow?"

"Oh, I'm sorry, I can't," Delia said. "I have to go to Baltimore."

"What's in Baltimore?"

"Well," Delia said, "my daughter's getting married."

She'd told Belle this too, but nothing more, and now all at once she felt an urgent need to pour it all out. "She's marrying her childhood sweetheart and I'm so worried how to behave at the wedding but I really want to be there; her father thinks she's rushing things since she's only twenty-two years old and I say—"

"Twenty-two! How old were you when you had her: twelve?"

"Nineteen," Delia said. "I married right out of high school, practically."

Vanessa nodded, unsurprised. Well, most of the girls in Bay Borough married right out of high school, Delia supposed. And had babies at nineteen or so. And ended up mislaying their husbands somewhere along the line. Vanessa's only question was, "What'd you buy for a wedding gift?"

"I thought I'd wait to see what they needed."

"That's always smart," Vanessa said. "Greggie! Let the bug go where it wants to. That's what I did with my girlfriend," she told Delia. "I thought I'd get her a hand-held mixer but then I thought no, why not wait, and I'm so glad I did because the first time I went to visit her I saw she didn't have one single piece of Tupperware in her whole entire kitchen."

Vanessa's face, above the slicker, glowed with a fine film of sweat, and her eyes seemed very pure and clear, the whites almost blue-white. Delia suddenly felt like hugging her. She said, "Oh, I'd have loved to ride to Salisbury with you!"

"Well, another time," Vanessa said. "There's this place there we buy our barley in bulk, to make Grandma's gripe water recipe."

"Gripe water?" Delia asked.

"It's for babies. Soothes the colic and the afternoon frets and the nighttime willies."

Delia wished they made gripe water for grown-ups.

She dreamed she was in Bethany, walking down the beach. Ahead she saw a highway, a sort of narrowing and darkening of the sand until it turned to asphalt, and there sat her old Plymouth, baking in the sun. Sam encircled her upper arm to guide her toward it. He settled her inside. He shut the door gently after her and leaned through the open window to remind her to drive carefully. She woke and stared at the motes of darkness swarming above her bed.

From Noah's room she heard a repetitive dry cough, beginning sharply each time as if he'd tried first to hold it in—one of those infuriating night coughs that won't quit. For half an hour or so, she lay debating whether to get up and bring him the lozenges from the medicine cabinet. Possibly he would stop coughing on his own. Or possibly he was asleep, in which case she hated to wake him. But the cough continued, pausing and then resuming just when she thought it was finished. And then she heard the creak of a floorboard, so she knew he wasn't asleep.

She rose and went to open her door. "Noah?" she whispered.

Instantaneously, almost, Joel was standing in front of her. She couldn't see him so much as feel him, as the blind are said to feel—a tall, dense, solid shape giving off warmth, his moon-pale pajamas only gradually emerging from the dark of the windowless hall.

"Yes, Delia?" he whispered.

He had misunderstood, she realized. "Noah" and "Joel" sounded so much alike. The same thing often happened when she called one of them to the phone. She said, "I thought I heard Noah."

"I was just going to see to him," he said.

"Oh."

"I'll bring him some of those cough drops."

"All right."

But neither one of them moved.

Then he stepped forward and took her head between his hands, and she raised her face and closed her eyes and felt herself drawn toward him and enfolded, surrounded, with his lips pressing her lips and his palms covering her ears so all she could hear was the rush of her own blood.

That, and Noah's sudden cough.

They broke apart. Delia stepped back into her room and reached for her door with trembling hands and shut herself inside.

19

Mr. Lamb's car was a dull-green Maverick with one orange fender and a coat-hanger antenna. Inside, several scale-model windows filled the back seat—wood-framed, double-sashed, none more than twelve inches tall. Little girls from the neighborhood were always begging to play with them. The bottom of his trunk was paved with panes of clear plastic, so that when Delia leaned in with her suitcase, she had an impression of bending over a gleaming body of water. Mr. Lamb told her the plastic was pretty near indestructible. "Slide your suitcase right on top," he told her. "It won't do the least bit of harm. That's where our product beats anything else on the market. When I go to a house that has pets? I like to lay a square of Rue-Ray on the floor and let a dog or cat march straight across, gritching with its toenails."

Rue-Ray, Delia knew, took its name from the married couple who owned the company, Ruth Ann and Raymond Swann. They lived above their workshop on Union Street, and Mr. Lamb was their one and only salesman. She had learned all this from Belle, but still she felt like laughing at the sound of those two slurred, slippery *R*'s.

It also struck her as comical that Mr. Lamb turned out to be so talkative. Before they reached Highway 50, even, he had gone from storm windows (their noise-reduction powers) to the wedding gift he planned for Belle (a complete set of Rue-Rays, fully installed) to his philosophy of salesmanship. "The important thing to remember," he said, veering around a tractor, "is that people like to proceed through a process. A regular set of steps for every activity. For instance, the waitress wants to give you your bill before you hand her your credit card. The mechanic wants to tell all about your fuel pump before you say to go ahead and fix it. So I ask my customers, I ask, 'You notice any drafts? Northern rooms any colder than southern?' *I* know they've noticed drafts. I can hear their durn windows rattle as I'm speaking. But if I let folks kind of like describe the symptoms first—say how the baby's room is so cold at night she has to wear one of those blanket sleepers with the fold-over flaps for the hands—why, they get this sense a certain order has been followed, understand? Then I'm more apt to make the sale."

Unfortunately, he was one of those drivers who feel the need to look at the person they're talking to. He kept his muddy, deep-socketed eyes fixed on Delia, his scrawny neck twisted in his collar, while Delia glued her own eyes to the road as if to make up for it. She watched a column of cypress trees approach, then a long-dead motel as low to the ground and sprawling as a deserted chicken shed, then a strip of fog-filled woods where entire clouds seemed trapped in a web of branches. Only a few leaves here and there had developed a faint tinge of orange, and she could imagine that it was still summer—that it was last summer, even, and she had not lost the year in between.

"Many people don't realize that salesmen consider such things," Mr. Lamb was saying. "But salesmen are a very considering bunch, you'll find. I say it comes from traveling by car so much. Belle had an idea we should travel by car for our honeymoon, but I told her I just didn't know if I'd focus on her right, driving along with my own thoughts like I do."

Delia said, "Hmm." Then, because she felt she wasn't holding up her end of the conversation, she added, "*I* honeymooned by car."

"You did?"

She had startled herself; she very nearly turned to see who had volunteered this information. "I don't recall that it interfered with our focus, though," she said.

He glanced at her, and she gave an artificial cough. Probably he thought she'd meant something risqué. "Of course, my husband was not so attuned to driving as you must be," she said.

"Ah," Mr. Lamb murmured. "No, not many people are, I suppose."

Sam's car at the time had had a bench seat, and Delia had sat pressed against his side. He had driven left-handed, with his right hand resting in her lap, his fingers loosely clasping her nylon-clad knee, their steady warmth sending a flush straight through her. She coughed again and gazed out her window.

The passing houses looked arbitrarily plunked down, like Monopoly-board houses. The smaller the house, it seemed, the more birdbaths and plaster deer in the yard, the tidier the flower beds, the larger the dish antenna out back. A brown pond slid by, choked with grappling tree trunks. Then more woods. In Delia's girlhood, the very word "woods" had had an improper ring to it. "So-and-so went to the woods with So-and-so" was the most scandalous thing you could say, and even now the sight of winding, leafy paths conjured up an image of . . . Well.

Goodness, what was *wrong* with her?

She forced her thoughts back to Mr. Lamb. He seemed to be talking about dogs. He said that after he and Belle were married they might just get themselves one, and then he went into a discourse on the various breeds. Golden retrievers were sweet-natured but sort of dumb, he said, and Labs had that tendency to whap a person's knickknacks with their tails all the time, and as for German shepherds, why . . .

Gradually the scenery began to have a different feel to it. Around Easton she started noticing bookstores and European-car dealers, neither of which existed in Bay Borough, and by the time they hit Grasonville, the road had widened to six lanes that whizzed past gigantic condominiums, flashy gift shops, marinas bristling with masts.

Mr. Lamb settled finally on a collie. He said he might name it Pinocchio if it had one of those long, thin noses. They crossed the Kent Narrows bridge, high above the grassy marshland. Delia could remember when crossing the Kent Narrows could use up the better part of an hour—long enough to get out of your car and stretch your legs and buy a watermelon, if you wanted—but that was in the days of that cranky old drawbridge. Now they were beyond the narrows in no time flat and speeding through a jungle of factory outlet stores, strip malls, raw new housing developments with MODELS NOW OPEN! DESIGNER TOUCHES! And then here came the lovely, fragile twin spans of the Bay Bridge, shimmering in the distance like something out of a dream, while Mr. Lamb decided that he might let Pinocchio have one little batch of puppies before they got her fixed.

The countryside seemed so green, so lush, after the scoured pallor of the Eastern Shore. Delia was surprised when they turned onto Highway 97—a road she'd never heard of—but then she relaxed in the glide of brand-new pavement not yet bordered with commercial claptrap.

She might have been away for decades.

Mr. Lamb said Belle was scared of dogs but he thought it was all in her head. Where else could it be? Delia wondered. Not that he gave her a chance to ask. He said women just got these notions sometimes. Delia smiled to herself. It amused her to see how quickly he had come to take his happiness for granted.

On the Baltimore–Washington Parkway, the lanes were so crowded that she gathered herself inward, as if that would help their car slip through more easily. She looked ahead and saw the Baltimore skyline— smokestacks, a spaghetti of ramps and overpasses, monster storage tanks. They began to pass gray-windowed factories and corrugated-metal warehouses. Everything seemed so industrial—even the new ballpark, with its geometric strutwork and its skeletons of lights.

"Mr. Lamb, ah, Horace," she said, "I don't know where you're headed, but if you'll drop me at the train station, I can grab a taxi."

"Oh, Belle told me to drive you direct to the door."

"But it's only . . ." She checked her watch. "Not quite ten," she said, "and I don't have to be there till eleven."

"No, no, you just sit tight. Belle would never forgive me," he said.

She would have put up more of an argument, but she was afraid her voice would shake. All at once she felt so nervous. She wished she'd worn a different dress. In spite of the gloomy weather, it was warmer than she had expected, and her forest-green was too heavy. It was also too . . . Miss Grinsteadish, she realized. Luckily, though, she had brought other clothes. (She had debated which was worse: wearing the wrong thing or lugging a suitcase to a wedding, and like the most insecure schoolgirl, she had opted for the suitcase.) Maybe once she reached the house she could duck into a vacant room and change.

Mr. Lamb was asking her a question. Which street to take. She said, "Up Charles," using as few words as possible. She didn't seem to have enough air in her lungs.

How intimate this city seemed! How quaint and huddled to itself! After all those superhighways, Charles Street threaded between tall buildings like the narrowest little river in a ravine.

She opened her bag and searched for Susie's invitation. Yes, there it was, safe and sound.

Mr. Lamb was admiring the Johns Hopkins campus now. He said he had a cousin who had gone there for one semester. "Oh, really?" Delia murmured. He said he himself had not had the opportunity of a college education, although he felt he would have put it to good use. Delia wished he would stop talking. He was so irrelevant, so extraneous. She kept swallowing, but there was something in her throat that wouldn't go away.

When she told him to turn left he had to ask her to repeat herself. "Hah?" he asked, like a deaf old man. Like an irritating, deaf old man.

At a red light on Roland Avenue, a jogger ran toward them, a young woman with her long dark hair in a topknot and the fingers of her right hand delicately clasping two fingers of her left hand. A man in a tweed hacking jacket crossed with a tiny chihuahua. ("Now, there is a dog you couldn't pay me to put up with," Mr. Lamb said. "Might as well own a mosquito.") The air had a greenish, fluorescent quality, as if a storm were brewing.

She showed him where to turn next, which house to park in front of. (Was this how their house looked to strangers: so brown, so hunched, so forbidding?) She said, "I can get my things myself, if you'll just pop the trunk." But no, he had to unfold from the car, walk around to the rear, take forever hauling forth her suitcase. "Thanks! Bye!" she said, but even then she wasn't free to go. He kept on standing there, swaying slightly on his long, scuffed shoes and gazing at the house.

"We could easily manage the round one," he told her.

"Pardon?"

"The round little window up top there, what is it, over a stairs? Rue-Ray makes round windows all the time."

"Oh, good," she said, and she shook his hand, just to get him to leave. But an odd thing happened. Holding on to his bunched-twig fingers, meeting his bucktoothed, wistful smile, she unaccountably began to miss him. She felt like climbing back into the car with him and riding along for the rest of his trip.

• • •

Four vehicles stood in the driveway: Sam's Buick, a beat-up purple van, Eliza's Volvo, and a little red sports car. The mulberry tree had already started to scatter its chewed-looking leaves, and she had to step around acorns on the front walk. Evidently no one had thought to sweep.

The shutters had been repaired. The replacement louvers were a different color, though—a paler, flatter brown, as if they'd been given just a primer coat and then forgotten. There was a new sisal mat at the top of the porch steps, and a foil-wrapped pot of yellow chrysanthemums next to the door.

Knock, or walk in?

She knocked. (The doorbell would have been too much, somehow.) No answer. She knocked harder. Finally she turned the knob and stuck her head in. "Hello?"

For a house that was hosting a wedding in less than forty minutes, it didn't seem very welcoming. The front hall was empty, and so was the dining room, although (as Delia found when she advanced) the dining-room table was spread with a white tablecloth. She set down her suitcase, intending to continue into the kitchen, but just then Eliza walked through the kitchen door with a mug of something hot. She was concentrating so hard on the mug that it took her a second to see Delia. Then she said, "Oh!" and stopped short.

"I know I'm early," Delia told her.

"Oh, Delia! Thank heaven you're here!"

"What's wrong?" Delia asked. She was alarmed, of course, but also grateful to find herself in demand.

"Susie's changed her mind," Eliza called over her shoulder. She was proceeding toward the stairs.

Delia grabbed her suitcase and followed. "Changed her mind about marrying?" she asked.

"That's what she claims."

"When did this happen?"

"This morning," Eliza tossed back, starting upward. She wore a new dress, a magenta A-line Delia couldn't imagine her buying, and patent-leather shoes whose heels rang against the stair treads. "Last night she slept in her old room," she was saying, "and this morning when we got here I asked Sam, 'Where's Susie? Isn't she up yet?' and he said—"

Delia felt disoriented. Susie's *old* room? Where was her new room? And who were "we" and what place had they got there from?

There wasn't a sign of Sam. Not a sign.

They had reached the second floor now, and Eliza, holding the mug in both hands, was sidling through the partly open door of Susie's bedroom. "Look who I brought with me!" she said. Delia set her suitcase down and walked in after her.

The room itself was what she noticed first. Frilly and flowered and stuffed with chintz since the days when it had been Linda's, it was a hollow cube now, unsoftened by curtains or rugs, furnished only with a foldaway cot and an ugly, round-cornered bureau from the attic. Susie sat cross-legged in a welter of blankets, wearing striped pajamas. Surrounding her—seated on the cot as well but all dressed up, even overdressed— were Linda, Linda's twins, and a pudgy young woman Delia could almost name but not quite. They raised a flank of alerted faces when Delia entered, but Delia looked only at Susie. Susie said, "Mom?"

"Hello, dear heart."

She bent over Susie and hugged her, absorbing that unique Susie smell that was something like dill weed. Still holding on to her, she settled on the cot beside her.

"Mom, I don't want to get married," Susie said.

"Then don't," Delia told her.

"Delia Grinstead!" Linda shrilled. "We're trying to talk some sense into her, do you mind?"

Linda was wearing bifocals—a new development. The twins had grown several inches, and from their dresses— stiff, mint-colored lace that hardly touched their skinny frames—Delia suspected they might be bridesmaids. Everyone looked so detailed, so eerily distinct: she couldn't explain it. Her eyes kept returning to Susie, craving the sight of her uncombed hair and her sweetly round chin and her cushiony lower lip.

The other young woman wore mint lace too. Driscoll's sister, that's who she was. Spencer? Spence. Driscoll Spence Avery's sister, Spence Driscoll Avery. "This exact same thing happened with my cousin," Spence was saying. "You all remember my cousin Lydia. She cried the whole way down the aisle of St. David's, and now she's happy as a clam and her husband is a bigwig in D.C."

"What kills me," Susie told Delia ("kills be," was how it came out, as if earlier she had been crying), "is we just signed a two-year lease on this fancy-shmancy apartment near the harbor. I've been phoning the Realtor ever since last night, but all I get is his answering machine. I don't want to say why I'm calling, because then he might not call back. I figure if I could just reason with him . . . I left three different messages; I told him it was urgent; I said could he please get back to me immediately? But he didn't! It's after ten and he hasn't phoned and I'm stuck with that damned apartment forever!"

She was wailing now. Eliza said, "Oh, dear, oh, dear . . . have some tea, why don't you," and Linda said, "Well, for God's sake, Susie, the Realtor is the least of it!"

But Delia told Susie, "I'll take care of it. You just give me his number, and I'll keep calling till I reach him."

"Would you?" Susie asked. She jumped up, trailing blankets, and went over to the bureau. "Wait a minute, I'll find his . . . Here. Mr. Bright, his name is. Tell him I apologize and I know I said we wanted it but to please, please let me out of this if he has a shred of human decency."

"You may have to forfeit your deposit," Delia said, examining the business card Susie handed her.

"Delia! Honest to God!" Linda cried. "Could we address the issue here?"

"Well, I'm not getting married, Aunt Linda," Susie told her, "so why waste time discussing it? Has anyone seen my jeans?"

She was roaming the room now, rummaging under the cot, scooping up a T-shirt. How shiny the floor was! Delia couldn't help noticing. Then she recalled the refinishers from last year's beach trip, and she felt all the more like an outsider. She set her handbag primly on her knees, trying to take up less space. But Linda noticed her anyway. She said, "Tell her, Delia."

"Tell her what?"

"Tell her all brides go through this."

Did they? Delia hadn't. Before her own wedding, her one concern had been that Sam would die before she got to be his wife. *Groom Slain on Wedding Eve,* the papers would read, or *Tragic Accident En Route to Nuptials,* and Delia would miss her chance for perfect happiness.

She had never doubted for a moment that it *would* be perfect.

Susie was dressing now, nonchalantly facing the wall while she peeled off her pajama top and hooked a gray-seamed bra. (Accustomed to locker rooms, she evidently thought nothing of changing in public.) Her back was a beautiful butterscotch color, as sturdy as a tree trunk. She pulled her T-shirt over her head, shook her hair loose, sauntered toward a suitcase on the floor, and bent to study its contents. Everybody watched. Finally Eliza, still holding the mug, said, "Susie has a very nice wedding dress. *Don't* you, Susie. Show your mother your wedding dress."

"It's a dopey dress," Susie said, but she turned and crossed the room to fling open the closet door. White chiffon exploded forth. Both twins rose, as if pulled by strings, and floated toward the closet with their lips parted. Susie slammed the door shut again. A filmy white triangle poked through on the hinge side.

"And your veil? Show her your veil," Eliza urged.

Obediently, Susie stomped over to the wastebasket. "Here's my veil," she said, and she pulled out several tatters of gauze and a headband of white silk roses snipped into jagged shreds.

The two aunts sucked in their breaths. Spence said, "Great God Almighty!"

"Allow me to model it for you," Susie said. She clamped the headband around her neck, then let her head flop to one side and half closed her eyes and stuck out her tongue.

"Susan Grinstead!" Linda shrieked.

"So," Susie said calmly, removing the headpiece. "Driscoll and I are sitting downstairs last night, watching a movie. Folks had made this big federal case about how I ought to spend my final unwedded hours in my ancestral home.'"

"Well, how would it have *looked*?" Linda demanded.

Susie dropped the headband into the wastebasket. "So the two of us are in the study like old times," she said, "and the phone rings. It's this high-school-sounding boy; you can tell the call is taking all his courage. He clears his throat and says, 'Um, yes! Good evening. May I please speak to Courtney, please?' I tell him he has the wrong number. Not ten seconds later: *ring*! Same boy. 'Um, good evening. May I please—' 'You must have misdialed,' I tell him. So we're just getting settled again—Driscoll had rented *Nightmare on Elm Street*; he thinks it's the major motion picture of our time—when sure enough: *ring*! *ring*! Driscoll says, 'Let me handle this.' He picks up the receiver. 'Yeah?' he says. Listens a minute. Says, 'Tough luck, feller. Courtney doesn't want to have anything to do with you.' And slams the phone down."

"Oh! How mean!" Delia said involuntarily, and Eliza clucked her tongue. Then everyone looked at Driscoll's sister. "Well, sorry, Spence," Delia told her, "but really! That poor boy!"

"Yes, it *was* mean," Spence said complacently. She prinked her skirt out around her. "But that's how guys are, Sooze. What can you do?"

"It is not how guys are," Susie said. "Or if it is, all the more reason not to marry *anyone*. But for sure I'm not marrying Driscoll. And don't you defend him, Spence Avery! There is nothing you can say that will make him look good to me after that."

Thérèse said, "Couldn't he just apologize?"

"Apologize to who? Not to me; I'm not the one whose feelings he hurt. No, I see it all now," Susie said. She was drifting around the room without apparent purpose, wearing her T-shirt and pajama bottoms. She stopped in front of the mirror to yank at a handful of hair; then she continued her travels. "All these things I've been trying not to notice all this time. Like when we get ready to go out and he says, 'How do I look?' and I say, 'Fine,' he just goes, 'Thanks,' and never mentions how I look. Or when I'm telling him something that happened, he won't let me tell it my way. He always has to interrupt, to sort of . . . redirect. So I'll say, like, 'This patient of Dad's came into the shop today—' and right away he's, 'Wait a minute, you know who your dad's patients are? Isn't that a violation of confidentiality?' and, 'Now hold on, she asked for this by brand name? Or not,' and, 'What you should have told her is . . .' Till I feel like saying, 'Just shut up! Shut up! Shut up and let me get to the end of this story which I'm sorry now I ever began!' And speaking of my shop—"

What shop? Delia would have asked, except she didn't want to sound like Driscoll.

"He has never for one minute supported me on that. Oh, at the start he did because he thought it was just a whim, you know? He figured it would pass. But then when I borrowed the money from Gram—"

Eleanor had lent Susie money? (Eleanor didn't believe in lending money.) Susie must have noticed Delia's bafflement, because she said, "Oh. I've started this kind of like, business. House in a Box, I call it."

"A darling little business!" Linda chimed in.

"Got a mention in *Baltimore* magazine," Eliza said, "two and one-quarter inches long."

"I'd moved to an apartment," Susie told Delia, "after that bust-up with Dad. Me and Driscoll found a place on St. Paul Street. Well, I couldn't have afforded anything by myself. And I was looking for a job, but first I wanted to settle in, you know? Buy supplies for the kitchen and all. We had some furniture from home but no incidental stuff, skillets and stuff; didn't own so much as a spatula. So there I was, running around the stores, spending a fortune I didn't have, finding one thing one place and another thing another place. . . . I said, 'Wouldn't it be great if they sold a kitchen in a *box*? Kind of a one-stop purchase?' And that's what started me thinking. So now I've got this little showroom out past the fair-grounds; well, it's only about three feet square, but—"

"It's darling!" Linda said.

"And I sell these boxes: Kitchen in a Box, Bathroom in a Box . . . just things I buy in bulk and combine in a kit and deliver, you know? I've tacked an ad on every campus bulletin board for miles around. I'm open seven days a week and I'm slaving away like a dog; that's why I set the wedding for a Monday. Didn't want to miss the weekend shoppers. As it is, I'm closed till Friday, which I hate. But Driscoll acts like this is some kind of hobby. When he heard about Gram's loan he was, 'Oh, you wouldn't want to get in over your head, hon.' He was, 'Wouldn't want to bite off more than you can chew, now, hon.' So discouraging and dampening; he doesn't think I'm up to this. Doesn't credit me with the brains to buy a simple shower curtain for college kids and a few damn rings to hang it with."

"Now, Susie, that is just not fair," Spence told her staunchly. "He's only trying to protect you."

"Plus he leaves spat-out fruit pits all over the apartment," Susie said.

Eliza suddenly set the mug on the bureau, as if this were the last straw.

"So I stopped *Nightmare on Elm Street*," Susie said, "and I gave him back his ring and sent him packing. And then I phoned the Realtor, but I guess it was too late at night. And I'm sorry you all came for nothing, but I said to Dad, I said, 'Which is more trouble: calling off the wedding or suing for divorce?' "

"Where *is* Sam, anyhow?" Eliza wondered.

Delia was glad she hadn't had to ask that herself.

"He went to dress for the wedding," Susie said.

"But you did tell him—"

"I did tell him I'd changed my mind, but he just shut his eyes a minute and then he said he had to go dress for the wedding."

Yes, that was Sam, all right.

Delia stood up. She said, "I should get busy."

"Doing what?" Linda demanded.

"I have to phone the Realtor."

She started for the door (the nearest phone was in Eliza's room), but Linda said, "Delia, my stars! Are you just going to accept this?"

"What else can I do?" she asked. "Drag her by the hair to the altar?"

"You could reason with her, for God's sake!"

"This is not a now-or-never proposition," Delia told her. (Really she was telling Susie, who stood leaning against the bureau, watching her with interest.) "If Susie isn't sure she wants to marry Driscoll today, she can marry him tomorrow, or next week, or next year. What's the hurry?"

"*She* can say that," Linda told the others. "*She* didn't fork over an arm and a leg for three airline tickets."

Delia latched the door quietly behind her.

At the same time, Sam's door, catty-corner across the hall, swung open and he stepped forth. He was tugging down his shirt cuffs. He caught sight of her and stopped still. They were separated by the stairwell, with its varnished wooden balustrade, and so she waited where she was. He said, "Why, Delia."

"Hello, Sam."

His suit was that slim, handsome black one they had bought on sale several years ago. His face looked thinner. It was all straight lines— straight gray eyes and an arrow of a nose and a mouth that seemed *too* straight until (she knew) you saw the upward turns at the corners. His glasses happened to be slipping, the way they had a tendency to do, and when he raised a hand to adjust them he appeared to be doubting his eyesight. She said, "Didn't you know I was coming?"

"I knew," he said.

"Well . . . I guess you heard Susie's not going through with the wedding."

"She'll go through with it," he said. He rounded the balustrade—no, not to approach her (though already she had taken her first step forward to meet him), but to start down the stairs. "We'll proceed as planned," he sent back as he descended. "She'll come around."

Delia gazed down at him over the railing. She could clearly see his scalp through the fair hair on top of his head. *If I glimpsed him in a crowd, I'd say he was just another worn-out, aging man,* she thought. But she didn't really believe that.

She made herself turn away and go into Eliza's room.

Here, too, she sensed a difference. The furniture was the same, but there wasn't a single object on the bureau, and only the gaunt, old-fashioned black telephone sat on the nightstand. Had Eliza changed rooms, or what? This one had been hers from the day she was born.

I knew, he had said. *We'll proceed as planned,* he had said.

Well, no point dwelling on it. Delia propped the Realtor's card on the nightstand, lifted the receiver, and dialed.

"This is Joe Bright," a man announced thinly. "I can't come to the phone right now, but you may leave a message after the beep."

"Mr. Bright, this is Delia Grinstead calling, Susan Grinstead's mother. Could you please get back to me as soon as possible? It's very important. The number is . . ."

As she hung up, she heard the doorbell ring downstairs. "Hello, come in," Sam said, and next she heard one of those drawling, gravelly, Roland Park matron voices. Instantly, she lost all her confidence. She wasn't wearing enough makeup and her dress wasn't dressy enough, and when she looked in Eliza's mirror, her face seemed unformed and childish.

But she might have just imagined that, because when she started down the stairs (planting her feet just so and holding her head very high), everyone looked up at her with the most respectful attention. The pastor—a tweedy, shaggy man—said, "Mrs. Grinstead! What a pleasure!" and Driscoll's parents broke off their chitchat with Sam.

"It's a pleasure to see *you*, Dr. Soames," she said. (Considering she attended church only on major holidays, she was impressed that she remembered his name.) "Hello, Louise. Hello, Malcolm."

"Why, hello, Delia," Louise Avery said, as if they'd last seen each other yesterday. She was a leathery woman with a lion's mane of gold hair rearing back off her forehead. Her husband—older, smaller, crinkly-eyed—said, "I don't guess you could have brought some sunshine with you."

"Oh," Delia said, and she glanced past him toward the door. "Is it raining?" she asked.

"No, no, we're sure it will hold off till later," Louise said. "I was telling Malcolm this morning, I said, 'At least this is one good thing about a home wedding.' Can you imagine if they'd planned a big formal church affair? Or something out on the lawn?"

"No, I certainly . . . can't," Delia said.

She looked over at Sam, but he was fitting Dr. Soames's rolled umbrella into the umbrella stand, and he didn't meet her eyes.

Maybe they would just have this wedding without the bride, she thought. Was that the plan?

In the living room, all available chairs had been lined up facing the fireplace. That must be where Dr. Soames would stand. In the dining room, Linda and Eliza were setting out platters of pastries. In the kitchen, the twins were gazing enraptured at Driscoll; he was discussing the honeymoon. "I told Sooze we ought to just head to Obrycki's for crabs," he said. "Call *that* our honeymoon, in keeping with the general tone of the wedding. And she said, 'Or why not carry-out?' but in the end we settled for three days at—Oh, Miz Grinstead! Hey there!"

"Hello, Driscoll," Delia said. She was puzzled to see him looking so cheerful. He was dressed in a navy suit with a white rose in the lapel, and his face had a scrubbed, fresh, oblivious look. She said, "Ah, have you . . . talked with Susie this morning?"

"Oh, can't see the bride before the ceremony, Miz Grinstead!" he said, wagging a finger.

"Yes, but just to talk with her—talk on the phone, maybe," Delia said.

"Say! Where's those ushers of mine, Miz Grinstead? Any sign of them yet?"

"Ushers?"

"Ramsay and Carroll!"

"Well, no, I . . . gosh, I hope someone thought to wake them," she said. Neither one of the boys had yet lost the knack of sleeping till noon.

"Maybe you should give them a ring," Driscoll told her.

With her mind on wedding matters, she thought for an instant he meant the kind of ring you wear on your finger. She looked at him blankly. Then Eliza, sailing past with a three-tiered cake stand, said, "Why they need ushers anyhow, with no one but family attending and seats for not more than a dozen . . ."

"It's so these glamorous bridesmaids will have some-body's arm to hang on to," Driscoll said, winking at the twins. Marie-Claire giggled, and Thérèse sent him a solemn, worshipful stare and stood straighter inside her tepee of mint lace.

Delia gave up and left the kitchen. She would go see if Susie had decided to get married after all. Who knows, she might have. (For it was easy to believe, in such company, that she was at this moment adjusting her magically reconstructed veil.) And if so, then Delia would check on the boys, make sure they were awake and dressed.

But the boys were already downstairs, standing by the front door in their suits. They looked astoundingly grown-up—Ramsay square-jawed and almost portly now, Carroll as wiry as ever but taller, with something more carved about his face. With them were Ramsay's girlfriend, Velma, wearing an upside-down pink hollyhock of a dress that ended just below her crotch, and her little daughter (who? oh, Rosalie) in aqua. Ramsay said, "Hi, Mom," and kissed Delia's cheek, and Carroll allowed her to hug him, and Velma said, "Well, hey! How was your trip?"

"It was fine," Delia said.

So that was the way it would be, evidently. She had been settled into a convenient niche in people's minds: just another of those eccentric wives you see living year-round in an Ocean City condo or raising horses on a farm in Virginia while their husbands continue their workaday routines in Baltimore. Nobody gave it a thought.

She passed through the assembling guests, smiling and murmuring greetings. Sam's uncle Robert squeezed her hand but went on listening to Malcolm Avery rehash a recent golf game. Sam himself was helping his aunt Florence out of a black rubber raincoat that looked capable of standing on its own.

"How do we know when the ceremony starts?" someone asked at Delia's elbow.

It was Eleanor, in a gray silk shirtdress. "Oh, Eleanor!" Delia cried, and she threw her arms around Eleanor's spare figure.

"Hello, dear," Eleanor said, patting her shoulder. "How nice you came for this."

"Of course I came! How could I not?"

"I was wondering about the procession," Eleanor said smoothly. "Do they plan any kind of music? Susie has been admirably sensible about the arrangements, but how will we know when the bride walks in?"

"Eleanor, I'm not even sure there's going to be a bride," Delia said. "She claims she's reconsidered."

"Ah. Well, you'll want to go see to her, then," Eleanor said, unperturbed. "Run along; I can take care of myself, dear."

"Maybe I should go," Delia said, and she fled up the stairs.

Susie was alone now, dressed in jeans and sneakers, lounging on the cot and reading People magazine. She glanced up casually when Delia knocked on the doorframe. "Oh, hi," she said. "Are they having conniptions down there?"

"Well, they don't . . . exactly grasp the situation yet," Delia said. "Susie, should I send Driscoll up?"

"Driscoll's here?"

"He's here in his wedding suit, waiting for you to come marry him."

"Well, shoot," Susie said, lowering her magazine. "It's not like I haven't informed him in plain English."

"And his parents are here, and Dr. Soames—"

"Did you talk to the Realtor?" Susie asked.

"I left a message."

"Mom. This really, really matters. If I don't get that lease revoked, it'll be me they come after for the money, do you realize that? I'm the one who actually signed my name. And I didn't want to say this in front of Driscoll's sister, but the fact is, I am dirt poor. I'm in debt for the wedding, even—four hundred twenty-eight dollars, no thanks to that father of mine."

"What did the four hundred twenty-eight dollars go for, exactly?" Delia asked out of curiosity.

"My dress and veil and the bouquet in the fridge. Aunt Eliza's footing the bill for refreshments. Please go call Mr. Bright. If he's still not there, tell his machine it's a life-or-death situation."

"Well, all right," Delia said. "And then should I send Driscoll up?"

"He knows where to find me."

Susie went back to her magazine. Delia started to leave, but in the doorway she turned. She said, "How come the house looks so different?"

"Different?"

"All the furniture's gone from your room, and Eliza's room seems . . . unlived-in."

"Well, it is unlived-in," Susie said, flipping a page. "Nobody lives here but Dad anymore."

"What?"

"Didn't you know that?"

"*No*, I didn't know that. What happened?"

"Well," Susie said, "let me see. First Ramsay and Dad got into a fight about—no, wait. First *Eliza* and Dad got into a fight. She claimed it was because he didn't let her know he'd be late for dinner, but the real truth is, she was making a play for him, Mom, like you wouldn't believe. It was pitiful. All us kids told her so, but she was like, 'Hmm? I don't know what you're talking about,' and meanwhile there was Dad, out of it as usual, just going about his business and paying her no mind. So one day she picks a quarrel about a totally nother issue and flounces off to visit Aunt Linda, and when she comes back she announces she's leaving for good. Now she lives on Calvert Street; that's where Linda and the twins are staying for the wedding. Okay, so *then* Ramsay and Dad got into a fight, on account of Dad calling Velma 'Veronica' by accident which Velma swore he did on purpose, and Ramsay moved to Velma's in a huff; and then Carroll moved there too because he missed his curfew one night and Dad was pacing the floor and picturing him dead on the road, he said. . . . And me: you know about me. I moved out in July, just before Ramsay."

"Yes, I suppose I . . . ," Delia said abstractedly.

"So are you going to call the Realtor, Mom?"

"Oh. Right," Delia said, and after a brief pause, she walked out.

In Eliza's old room, she sat on the edge of the bed, lifted the receiver, and then stared into space.

Imagine Sam pacing the floor. Always before, it had been Delia pacing the floor, and Sam pooh-poohing her and telling her to simmer down. "How can you be so cool about this?" she used to ask him. "What have you got in your veins: ice water?" And it seemed to her that he had given a little smile at that, a gratified, sheepish little smile, as if she had paid him a compliment.

She dialed the Realtor's number again. "This is Joe Bright," the machine said. "I can't come to the . . ."

"It's Delia Grinstead again, Mr. Bright. I'd appreciate your calling me at your earliest convenience," she said. And just to oblige Susie, she added, "It's a matter of life and death. Bye."

Downstairs, the voices were a woven mass, as if people had given up on the wedding and settled for a party instead. But when she descended to join them, conversation halted for a moment and people turned expectantly. She smiled at them. She was glad now she'd worn the forest-green, with the skirt that swung so alluringly just above her ankles.

She crossed the hall to the living room, and the others followed. Probably they thought this was a signal of some kind. In fact, Carroll, killingly attractive in his usher's suit, caught up with her to offer his arm and lead her to a front seat, and a moment later Eleanor joined her, escorted by Ramsay. "Put Aunt Florence in a straight chair," Ramsay muttered to Carroll. "She says her back is acting up." Delia heard the usual audience sounds—coughs and rustling skirts. Driscoll's parents settled on the couch. Dr. Soames took his place on the hearth, smiling benignly toward the room at large and extracting a folded sheet of paper from his breast pocket.

"Bridal jitters all over now?" Eleanor whispered to Delia.

"No, um, not exactly."

Velma's colorless child chose a wing chair so big for her that her Mary Janes failed to touch the floor. A young man Delia didn't know—some relative of Driscoll's, no doubt—deposited Eliza on the love seat, and Linda plopped next to her unescorted and eased her feet out of her pumps. "Is she coming?" she mouthed when she saw Delia looking at her. Delia merely shrugged and faced front again.

Now Driscoll was standing beside Dr. Soames, fidgeting with his boutonniere. And the bridesmaids were clustered at the foot of the stairs, where the ushers joined them when the very last guest had been seated.

Sam bent over Delia. She hadn't seen him coming; she drew back slightly. "Should I put the record on?" he asked her.

"Record?"

"Is she ready?"

"Oh," she said. "Well, no, I don't believe she is."

He straightened and stared down at her. He said, "Then shouldn't you be doing something?"

"Like what?"

He didn't answer. His lips were very dry and white. Delia smoothed her skirt and sat back to observe the next development.

She had never realized before that worry could be dumped in someone else's lap like a physical object. She should have done it years ago. Why did Sam always get to be the one?

Now he turned toward the record player, which was housed in a walnut cabinet at Delia's elbow. He clicked a button, and a moment later the sound of horns flared out. Delia recognized the theme from *Masterpiece Theatre*. Privately she found the selection a bit too triumphal, and she suspected from the sniff on her right that Eleanor felt the same way. Everybody else, though, sat in a reverent hush as Sam strode from the room. Delia heard his shoes crossing the hall and crisply mounting the stairs. Why, this wedding must have been planned to duplicate her own: the father of the bride escorting the bride down the stairs and through the double doorway to the center of the living room, to a spot directly beneath the gawky brass chandelier.

But suppose the bride did not stand waiting in the upstairs hall?

The footsteps must have continued, but the music drowned them out. Or maybe Sam had stopped at the top of the stairs, just beyond the guests' view, instead of going in to talk with Susie. That was more like him. In any case, the trumpets blatted on while people smiled at one another (*Isn't this so informal and so family,* they were probably thinking), and then the footsteps started down again. But anyone could tell that no bride was keeping pace with that rapid, noisy descent.

Sam marched to a spot directly in front of Dr. Soames. Delia wondered, for an instant, whether he planned to carry on regardless—take the vows in Susie's place. But he moistened his lips and said, "Ladies and gentlemen . . ."

It was Delia who reached over and lifted the phonograph needle. That was the least she could do, she figured, since it was Sam who announced that he was sorry to have to say this, he hated to put people out like this, but the wedding had been postponed a bit.

"Postponed" was optimistic, in Delia's opinion. But people did seem to view it as the most minor readjustment in the couple's schedule. Linda announced crossly that she and the twins were reserved on a noon flight home two days from now, totally nonrefundable, which she damn well hoped Miss Susie would bear in mind. Dr. Soames, leafing through a pocket diary, muttered something about meetings, visits, Building Fund . . . but later in the week looked all right, he said; looked quite promising, in fact.

Even Driscoll's mother, who seemed more distressed than anyone, turned out to be thinking mainly of a reception she was giving after the honeymoon. "Will they be married by Saturday night, do you think?" she asked Delia. "Could you just, maybe, feel Susie out a little? We've got fifty-three of our closest friends coming; you too if you're still in town."

"Maybe Driscoll will know more when they've finished talking," Delia said. "I'll have him get in touch with you the minute he comes downstairs."

For Driscoll had at long last gone up to speak with Susie. He should have done that at the start, if you asked Delia.

The rain that had been threatening all day was falling now, and people scurried to their cars once they were out the front door. First Dr. Soames left, and then Sam's aunt and uncle with Eleanor, and Driscoll's sister with the unnamed usher, and finally Driscoll's parents. Then Eliza said, "Well! I thought that little sports car of Spence's had boxed me in for life!" and she swept out, with Linda and the twins in tow. But Ramsay and Carroll stayed on, dogging Delia's heels as she carried platters of food to the kitchen, which meant that Velma and Rosalie had to stay as well. They made themselves scarce, though, watching TV in the study. Meanwhile Sam set the living-room furniture in order, and Carroll told Delia the entire plot of a movie he and Ramsay had seen. This man, he said, had been stuck in some kind of time warp where he had to keep reliving the same one day over and over. Delia thought that with all the topics they could have been discussing, Carroll had made a mighty peculiar choice, but she just said, "Mmhmm. Mmhmm," as she flitted around the kitchen, swathing various platters in plastic wrap. Carroll followed so closely that she couldn't reverse direction without advance notice, and Ramsay wasn't far behind.

But then Sam brought in the tablecloth, bunched in a clumsy cylindrical shape, and the atmosphere changed. Carroll stumbled in his recitation. Ramsay got very busy shutting cupboard doors. Both of them seemed to be watching Delia even while they were looking away.

"Tablecloth," Sam said. He passed it to her.

Delia said, "Oh! Good! Thanks!" Then she said, "I'll just take it down to the . . . ," and she wheeled and walked through the pantry and down the basement stairs.

Not that that tablecloth had the slightest need of laundering.

At the bottom of the stairs the cat was waiting, gazing up at her intently. Vernon always escaped to the basement when there were guests. She said, "Vernon! Have you missed me?" and she bent to cup his round, soft head. "I missed you too, little one," she whispered. He was purring in that exaggerated way cats have when they want to put humans at ease.

Footsteps crossed the pantry and started down the stairs. Delia rose and went over to the washing machine. Vernon vanished into thin air. The machine was full of damp laundry, but she stuffed in the tablecloth anyhow and recklessly poured detergent on top.

Behind her, Sam cleared his throat. She turned. "Oh! Hello, Sam," she said.

"Hi."

She busied herself with the washing machine, selecting the proper cycle and rotating the dial with a zippery sound. Water started rushing; pipes clanked overhead. Outside the dust-filmed window, ivy leaves bobbed beneath the falling raindrops.

"As soon as Driscoll comes down," she said, turning again to Sam, "I'm going to call a cab, but I figured I'll wait till then so I can say goodbye to Susie."

"A cab to where?" Sam asked.

"To the bus station."

"Oh," Sam said. Then he said, "It would be silly to call a cab, with all these cars at hand. Or rather, I don't mean silly, but . . . I could drive you. Or Ramsay could, if you prefer. Ramsay's been using the Plymouth, you know."

"Oh, has he?" Delia asked. "How has it been running, anyway?"

"All right."

"No more electrical problems?"

He just looked at her.

"Well, thanks," she said. "I probably *will* ask for a lift, if it isn't too much trouble."

She left unanswered the question of who would drive her.

They went back up the stairs, Delia preceding Sam and moving with self-conscious gracefulness. The kitchen was empty now. The dining-room table had a naked look; Sam had not thought to replace the candelabra after removing the tablecloth. The hall was empty too, but they paused there a minute, gazing toward the silence overhead.

"I don't think he's going to change her mind," Delia said.

"It's only wedding-day nerves."

"I think she's serious. I think she really means this."

"You remember how she was when she was little," Sam said. "She used to get these fixations, remember? Like when she wanted to wear her cowboy pajamas to kindergarten. You said no and she came to breakfast in her underwear, but you pretended not to notice and by schooltime she'd put on a skirt."

"A skirt and her pajama tops, which I'd covered partway with a bandanna to hide the snaps," Delia said. "We compromised. There's a difference."

She was touched, though. She wasn't sure why. Maybe it was because she herself figured so prominently in his story, as if he had taken notes on what she'd done and then attempted, years later, to do the same.

She stayed in the hall a moment longer, in case he wanted to tell her anything more, but evidently he didn't. He turned away and made for the living room. Delia first smoothed her dress and adjusted her belt (not wanting to appear to chase him), and then she followed.

In the study, the lamps were unlit, and everyone sat in pewter-gray light watching TV—Velma and the boys on the couch, Rosalie on the floor between her mother's feet. They turned as Sam and Delia entered. "What's for lunch?" Carroll asked.

Delia said, "Lunch!"

"We're starving."

She checked the time. It was after one. She glanced toward Sam for some cue (the kitchen wasn't hers anymore; the household wasn't hers to feed), but he didn't help her. Then footsteps sounded overhead.

"Driscoll," Sam said.

Rosalie continued gaping at a soap opera, but the rest of them went out to the hall—Velma and the boys rising in an elaborately bored, stretching way, everyone moving slowly so as not to seem overeager. They gathered at the bottom of the stairs and watched Driscoll descend.

He looked distraught. His hair was raked and ropy, and his tie was wrenched askew. When he reached the bottom step he shook his head.

"No wedding?" Delia asked him.

"Well, I wouldn't say *no* wedding."

"What, then?"

"She says she hates me and I'm not a good person and now she sees she never loved me anyway."

"So, no wedding," Delia mused aloud.

"But if I want to change her mind, she says, I know what I should do."

"What should you do?"

"I don't know," Driscoll said.

Sam snorted and moved off toward the living room.

"Send flowers?" Velma suggested. "Send a singing telegram?"

"I don't know, I tell you. I said, 'Couldn't you give me a hint?' She said, 'It'll come to you. And if it doesn't,' she said, 'it's a sign we shouldn't get married.' "

"Send a Mylar balloon with a message printed on?" Velma pursued.

"Saying what, though?" Driscoll asked.

"Driscoll," Delia said, "I believe your mother wants to talk with you."

"Oh. Okay," he said dully.

He stood thinking a moment. Then he gave his shoulders a shake and let himself out the front door—no raincoat, no umbrella, nothing. The rain was falling so hard it was bouncing off the porch railing.

"Hire a skywriter!" Velma said after he'd gone.

"Mom," Carroll said, "could we just eat?"

"I'll fix something right away," she told him.

Might as well. Nobody else was going to do it.

Delia prepared a tray for Susie and brought it up to her room. She found her asleep on top of the covers—not all that surprising. Susie was the kind of person who retreated into sleep like a drug, losing whole days at times of emotional crisis. Oh, the *otherness* of Delia's children never failed to entrance her! She considered it a sort of bonus gift—a means of experiencing, up close, an entirely opposite way of being.

"Susie, honey," she said. Susie opened her eyes. "I thought you'd want something to eat," Delia told her.

"Thanks," Susie said, and she struggled blearily to a sitting position.

Delia placed the tray in Susie's lap. "It's all your favorites. Ginger cheesecake, Jewish-grandmother cookies . . ."

"Great, Mom," Susie said, shaking out her napkin.

"Lemon chiffon tartlets, chocolate mousse cups . . ."

Susie looked down at the tray.

"I had to use the wedding food," Delia explained. "There weren't a lot of groceries in the kitchen."

"Oh," Susie said. She said, "So is that . . . what everyone's eating?"

"Well, yes."

"They're eating up my wedding food?"

"Well . . . would you rather they didn't?"

"No, no!" Susie said too breezily. She picked up a tartlet.

Delia felt confused. She said, "Did you want us to save them? If you were planning on, um, rescheduling in the near future, why, then I suppose—"

"No, I said! It's fine."

"Well, what *are* your plans? I'm not trying to pressure you or anything, but Driscoll did mention . . . I'm just asking so I can make travel arrangements."

In the midst of taking a bite, Susie looked over at her.

"On account of my job and all," Delia explained.

"Oh, just *go*, if you're so set on it!" Susie burst out.

"That's not what I—"

"I'm amazed you came at all. You and your stupid job and your man friend and your new family!"

"Why, Susie—"

"Gallivanting off down the beach and leaving Dad just wandering the house like the ghost of someone, and your children . . . orphaned, and me setting up a whole wedding on my own without my mother!"

Delia stared at her.

"What did he *do*, Mom?" Susie demanded. "Was it him? Was it us? What was so terrible? What made you run out on us?"

"Sweetheart, no one did anything," Delia said. "It wasn't that clear-cut. I never meant to hurt you; I didn't even mean to leave you! I just got . . . unintentionally separated from you, and then it seemed I never found a way to get back again."

She knew how lame that sounded. Susie listened in silence, gazing over her tartlet, and now that letter she'd sent—the forced gaiety of all those exclamation points, the careful carelessness of *See ya!* and *Luv*—made Delia want to weep. "Honeybun," she said, "if I'd known you wanted help with the wedding, I would have done anything! Anything."

But all Susie said was, "Could you please phone the Realtor again?"

"Yes, of course," Delia said, sighing, and she bent and kissed Susie's forehead before she left.

By a process of inaction, of procrastination (much like the one that had stranded her so far from home in the first place), Delia stayed on through the afternoon, waiting for Susie to come downstairs. But time passed, and when she went back up to check, she found Susie asleep again, the tray nearly untouched on the floor beside the cot.

Sam was in his office, presumably—doing what, she had no idea, since she hadn't seen any patients arrive. The others sat in the study watching TV, and she settled on the couch next to Velma and pretended to watch too. The good thing about TV was that everyone talked around it in an unthinking, natural way; they forgot that she was listening. She learned that Carroll had gone out three times with a girl from Holland; that Ramsay's history professor had a grudge against him; that Velma had promised Rosalie a beauty-parlor manicure if she would quit biting her cuticles. It reminded Delia of her car-pool days, when she'd been privy to all the latest gossip because children don't seem to realize that drivers have ears.

Nobody mentioned Susie.

Sam came to stand in the doorway, and when she looked over at him he asked if she would like him to go get some groceries for supper. She felt absurdly pleased. She said, "Yes, why not," and then everyone started requesting specific dishes—her tarragon chicken, her ziti salad. She went out to the kitchen and made up a grocery list. She waited for Sam to invite her along when he left, but he didn't.

Eliza phoned—her second call in two hours. "Now, where is Driscoll in all this?" she asked. "Don't tell me he's just letting her be."

"It does seem that way," Delia said. She was talking on the kitchen extension, so she didn't have to lower her voice. "I don't know *what* to think," she said. "Susie's fast asleep and Driscoll's disappeared and the rest of us are just sitting here, wondering what next."

"Mark my words," Eliza said, "they'll be married before sundown tomorrow. That's what I told Linda. I said, 'You won't even have to switch your airline reservations.' How about *you*? You're not leaving yet, are you?"

"I haven't decided."

"You can't," Eliza said. "You'd only have to turn around and come back."

"You may be right," Delia said.

The real reason she couldn't leave was Susie—her sad little face above the tartlet. But she didn't tell Eliza that.

As soon as they said goodbye she called Joel, but the telephone rang and rang. They had probably gone out for supper, ignoring what she'd left for them. They were probably at Rick-Rack's. She knew what they would order, even, and the tune of their conversation—Noah's exuberant spurts of words and Joel's neutral answers. His palms cradling her head. His mouth firm but not insistent. His body tensed as if, with every move, he had been gauging her response.

After the baby, Ellie said, *we just kissed, the most wonderful kisses . . .*

Delia hung up.

When Sam came back from the grocery store, she asked him (with her head in the fridge, tossing the question over her shoulder) whether he would mind if she stayed till tomorrow.

"Why would I mind?" he said.

It wasn't a very satisfying answer. But before she could go into it further, Ramsay and Carroll trooped through—off to the video shop, they said, to rent that time-warp movie again—and Sam left the room. Delia fixed supper by herself. Everything came back to her: those weird little nipples on the cabinet knobs, the squeak of the exhaust fan above the stove. But here she was, in Miss Grinstead's forest-green dress and old-maid shoes with the strap across the instep.

Susie did appear in time for supper. She sat at the table swaddled in a blanket, looking like a little girl awakened from her nap. But she didn't refer to the wedding, and nobody else brought it up. Then afterward they all watched the movie—even Sam, his glasses glinting in the dark. Although really it was Susie they were watching. Any time Susie made a moderately humorous comment, her brothers fell all over themselves laughing, and Velma gave a hissing titter, and Rosalie sent her a deadpan, penetrating stare.

At the end of the movie Ramsay and Velma collected Rosalie and said good night, but Carroll announced that he might as well sleep over. Delia went upstairs with him to put sheets on his bed. While she was plumping his pillow she heard Susie come upstairs too, and she knew that left only Sam in the study. She didn't go back down, therefore. Instead, she returned to the linen closet for another set of sheets, and she made up the bed in Eliza's room.

Much later, flat on her back in the dark, she heard Sam's shoes on the stairs. He crossed the hall to his room without so much as a pause, and she heard his door click shut behind him.

It was ridiculous of her to feel so wounded.

20

"This sugar caster," Linda told the twins, "was a gift from your great-great-aunt, Mercy Ramsay, when her sister married Isaiah Felson in 1899."

Delia couldn't imagine how Linda knew that. The twins, however, seemed unimpressed. They were busy admiring Carroll, who was shaking the caster upside down over his bowl of cornflakes. It was eleven-thirty in the morning, and he was only now eating breakfast. Linda and the twins had had breakfast earlier, after Eliza dropped them off on her way to work. Sam, presumably, had fixed himself something before he went into his office, and Susie wasn't awake yet. It was going to be one of those days when the tail end of one person's meal ran into the start of another's from morning to night. Delia herself was just sort of munching along with every new shift.

"Mercy Ramsay was a huge concern to her parents because she never married," Linda was saying. "She had a job as a 'typewriter,' was what they called them then, at a law office down near the harbor."

Delia glanced over at her.

Carroll was shoveling in cornflakes now, and Marie-Claire appeared to be warming her hands on the sugar caster—which was not, to tell the truth, very imposing: a chesspiece-shaped urn of dulled and dented plate. Thérèse was setting an index finger here and there on the table to mash stray crystals of sugar and transfer them to her tongue.

Linda said, "In every generation of our family, there's been one girl who never married."

"This generation it'll be Thérèse," Marie-Claire said.

"Will not," Thérèse said.

"Will so."

The phone rang.

"If that's the school, I'm sick," Carroll told Delia.

"Carroll Grinstead! I refuse to fib for you," Delia said. She dumped the cat off her lap and rose to answer. "Hello?"

"Delia?" Noah said.

Delia turned away from the others. "What's wrong?" she asked, as quietly as possible.

"I've got a cold."

"Are you in bed?"

"I'm on the couch. Where'd you *get* to? Why aren't you back yet?"

"Well, I did try to telephone last night, but you were out," Delia said. "How'd you know where to call, anyway?"

"And that's another thing! You didn't leave a number! I had to phone Belle Flint and she said you'd gone to your family's so I told Information, 'Look for Grinstead,' and the first Grinstead turned out to be this lady and she said, 'Oh, that's my daughter-in-law you want,' and she had me write down the . . . But you said you'd be back yesterday!"

"Or today," Delia reminded him. "I'll probably catch a bus, oh, maybe this afternoon; I'll know more as soon as—"

"Is that the *Realtor*?" Susie called from upstairs.

Delia covered the mouthpiece of the receiver. "No, it's not!" she called back. Then she told Noah, "You just stay on the couch. I'll be home soon. Bye."

When she hung up, she turned to find everyone watching her. "Well!" she said vivaciously. "So!"

From their expressions, you would have thought she'd been caught in some crime.

Then Sam walked in, wearing his white coat. He was taking his lunch break, and here they were, still at breakfast. In fact, Linda had his chair, which she made no move to give up. "If it isn't the good doctor," she said in an acid tone.

Delia said, "Sam, what would you—?" and then she stopped. It wasn't her place, really, to offer him lunch. But he didn't seem to realize that, and he sat in Susie's usual seat and said, "Anything would be fine. Soup."

Soup must be what he lived on, because it was just about the only thing in the cupboard—his special salt-free, fat-free, taste-free brand, with a dancing heart on the label. She opened a tin of soya-milk mushroom and poured it into a saucepan.

Now he was asking Carroll why he wasn't in school. He was going about it all wrong, taking a drilling-in approach that would only raise Carroll's hackles, and Carroll was hunching belligerently over his cereal bowl. Both of them, Delia noticed—in fact, everyone in the room—had become less perceivable to her since yesterday. Already they had lost that slick exterior layer of the unaccustomed.

Sam said that the distant likelihood of a sibling's wedding was not sufficient grounds for playing hooky. "What do you know about it?" Carroll asked him. "Some of the kids in my class take off for Orioles games, for Christ's sake."

"Watch your language, young man," Sam said. Delia merely stirred the soup. She pictured Sam shifting in midair like some kind of kite or streamer, like a wind sock changing shape with changes in the wind. From one angle he was gentle and reserved and well-meaning; from another he was finicky and humorless. She remembered all at once that when she had gazed across her desk at him the morning they first met, there had been a split second when his fine-boned face had struck her as *too* fine, too priggish, and she had faltered. But then she had brushed that impression aside and forgotten it forever—or at least, until this moment.

"Please, Uncle Sam?" the twins were coaxing. Marie-Claire said, "Can't he stay home just this once? For our sakes?"

The front doorbell rang before he could answer. Everybody looked at one another, and the cat made a dash for the basement. "I'm not here," Carroll said with his mouth full. Finally Delia lowered the flame beneath the soup and went to see who it was.

In the sun-glazed windowpane at the center of the door, Driscoll Avery stood gazing off to one side and whis-tling. Whistling! Goodness. Delia opened the door and said, "Hello, Driscoll."

"Hey there, Miz G.!" he said, stepping inside. "Super weather."

It was, in fact. Autumn had moved in overnight, nippy and hard-edged, and Driscoll's cheeks glowed pink. He wore fall clothes, weekend clothes even though this was a Tuesday. Delia shut the door against the chill. "Come into the kitchen and have some breakfast," she said. "Or lunch, or whatever you're on."

"No, thanks. I just need to talk to Susie a minute."

"Well, I think she must be awake, but she hasn't come downstairs yet," Delia told him.

"Okay if I go up?"

"Oh, I don't know if she—"

"Please, Miz Grinstead. I believe now I've got it! I know how to get her to marry me."

Delia gave him a skeptical look, but he said, "All right?" and without waiting for her permission, he wheeled and bounded up the stairs.

It took real character not to listen for what happened next.

Back in the kitchen, everyone was waiting. "Well?" Linda demanded.

"That was Driscoll."

"Driscoll!" both twins said.

"He's gone up to speak with Susie."

The twins scooted their chairs away from the table. Linda said, "Stay right where you are."

"Can't we just—?"

"They'll never sort things out with you two making pests of yourselves."

Delia returned to the stove. She stirred the soup until it started dimpling, and then she poured it into a bowl—a bleak gray liquid that reminded her of scrub water. "Taupe soup," she said as she set the bowl before Sam. The phrase tickled her, and she gave a little snicker. Sam glanced at her sharply.

"Thank you, Delia," he said in his deliberate way.

The twins were badgering Linda about their bridesmaid dresses. Could they put them on right now? Could Linda iron their sashes where they'd wrinkled from before? Delia placed a spoon beside Sam's bowl, and he thanked her all over again and picked it up. "You go get your books together," he told Carroll. "A half day of school is better than none."

"I'm just waiting to hear what Driscoll says," Carroll told him.

"Driscoll has nothing to do with this."

"He does if the wedding is on again. And anyhow, I don't *have* my books. They're at Velma's place. So there."

Sam started spooning soup, ostentatiously composed.

"I've been in charge of getting my own self to school all fall," Carroll told him. "How come the minute I'm under your roof I'm treated like a two-year-old?"

"Because you're behaving like a two-year-old," Sam said.

Carroll pushed back from the table. His chair scraped across the floor, and he very nearly slammed into Driscoll, who arrived at that moment in the dining-room doorway. "Hi, all," Driscoll said.

"Driscoll!" the twins screeched. "What'd she say?" "Did she say yes?"

They should have known she hadn't. Driscoll had come back down far too soon, and if that were not enough, they could have read the bad news in his face, which was somber and no longer pink-cheeked, somehow thicker through the jaw. He gave a deep sigh and then turned and—it seemed for an instant—took his leave; but no, he was fetching a chair from the dining room. He dragged it back to the kitchen and placed it next to Carroll and sat down heavily. "She says I've got to do it myself," he said.

"Do what?"

"See, all night long I thought and thought," he said. He seemed to be addressing Delia, who had reclaimed her own seat at the end of the table. "I thought, *What is it Susie wants?* And it came to me: I had to set things straight with that kid who called on the phone. But the only person who might know his name was the girl he was trying to reach—Courtney. So this morning I started dialing every possible variation on you-all's number, looking for Courtney."

"Lord have mercy," Linda said.

"Well, it's simpler than it sounds. Turns out I had to transpose two digits, that was all. About my tenth or so try, I get Courtney's mom, I guess it was, and she tells me Courtney's at school."

"Ah," the twins said together.

"So I say, 'Well, I was supposed to drop off her history notes, so what I'll do, if you don't mind, I'll bring them by her house after school, is that okay? And could I please have that street address again?'"

"Cool," Carroll said.

Even Sam looked mildly interested. He had stopped eating his soup and was watching Driscoll, with his eyebrows raised.

"Lucky for me, the mom fell for it," Driscoll said. "Gave me their address straight off—place right here in the neighborhood." He paused, struck by a thought. "Carroll," he said, "*you* don't know any Courtneys, do you?"

"I know six or seven Courtneys," Carroll said.

"Any on Deepdene Road?"

"Not that I'm aware of."

"Well, anyhow," Driscoll said, "all I have to do now is ask her who her caller was."

"But what if she has no idea who he was?" Delia said.

"She might have *some* idea. If he's been hanging around her a lot, giving her, like, signals or something."

Sam was spooning up soup again, shaking his head.

"So next I go talk to Susie. Ask her to come with me to Courtney's after school. You know I can't do it alone! Strange guy showing up full of questions . . . Except Susie says no."

"No?" Linda echoed.

"No. Sends me straight downstairs again. Says I'll have to manage without her. Bring her the boy in person, was how she put it, if I want her to forgive me."

If you want to win the princess's hand, Delia thought to herself, because the errand did have a certain fairy-tale ring to it. She began to feel slightly sorry for Driscoll, although he himself seemed to be recovering his good spirits. "So now it's up to you, Miz G.," he said almost jauntily.

"Me!"

"Could you come with me to Courtney's after school?"

"Why, Driscoll, I—"

"I'll go!" Thérèse said.

"Me and Thérèse'll go!" Marie-Claire said.

Driscoll didn't seem to hear them. He said, "Miz Grinstead, you can't imagine what I feel like. I feel like I've got this . . . cloud in my chest! You think at first it's some snit she's having, some temporary snit, and you're mad as hell and you figure if you ignore it . . . but then it starts to get to you. You start to feel really, I guess you'd say, sad, but still mad besides and also eventually just, almost, *bored,* I mean so sick of it all, so sick of going over it and over it, sick of your own self, even; and you say to yourself, 'Well, look at it this way: you ought to be glad you're free of her. She always did act kind of irritating,' you say. But then you say, 'If she'd give me one more chance, though! I mean, how did things get so out of hand here? When did they start to go wrong that I didn't even notice?' "

Sam set down his spoon. Linda gave a sudden sigh. Delia said, "Well, I . . . well, why *don't* I come with you? I doubt I'd be much help, but certainly I could try."

"Oh, God, thank you, Miz G.," Driscoll said.

"I don't know if this will work, though," Delia told him.

"It'll work," he said, standing up. "If school lets out, say, two forty-five, three o'clock, and I come pick you up by . . ."

That wasn't what Delia had meant. She'd meant that in her opinion, Susie might reasonably refuse to marry him even after he apologized. But she changed her mind about saying so. She didn't even say goodbye to him, because just as he was leaving, the telephone rang.

This time it was Joel. He said, "Delia?"

"Yes," she said evenly. She glanced toward her family. They were all watching her—everyone but Sam, who seemed to be studying the table.

"Where *are* you?" he asked.

This was such an illogical question that she couldn't think how to answer it. She said, "Um . . ."

Where are you? Sam had asked in another phone call, months ago, and she wondered now if he had meant the question in the same way Joel did.

Then Joel, as if recollecting himself, said, "I came home to have lunch with Noah and he told me you haven't left Baltimore yet. I just thought I should find out if everything's all right."

"Oh, yes. Fine," she said.

She wished the others would resume talking, but they didn't.

"But you do plan to be back, don't you?" Joel asked. "I mean, eventually? Because I see from your closet . . . I wasn't trying to pry but I did just, so to speak, glance in your closet, and I noticed all your clothes are gone."

"They are?" she said.

"I thought you might have left for good."

"Oh, no, it's just . . . things are taking longer to finish than I expected," she told him.

Sam rose and walked out of the room.

From upstairs, Susie called, "Mom? Mom?"

"It's *not the realtor*!" Delia called back.

Joel said, "Pardon?"

"Sorry, Joel, I'd better go," she said. "See you in a while."

She hung up.

"Well, aren't *you* the popular one," Linda said.

Delia gave what she hoped was an offhand laugh and started clearing the table.

It was true, she saw when she went upstairs, that she had brought all her clothes. Well, not really all. Joel would have found enough in her bureau to reassure him, if he'd looked. But what with one thing and another—the iffy season, the dither over a wedding outfit—she had packed as if she'd be gone for days. She pictured Joel standing in front of her closet, his broad forehead creased in perplexity as he surveyed the empty hangers. Abruptly, she closed her suitcase and snapped the latches shut.

Then she crossed the hall to Sam's room. Here she had left plenty behind. How odd that when she was debating what to wear for the ceremony, she hadn't considered her old wardrobe! Or maybe not so odd—all that froufrou and those nursery pastels. She turned away. She went to her bureau and found, in the top drawer, a draggled blue hair bow, safety pins, ticket stubs, everything hazed with talcum powder. A pair of sunglasses missing one lens. A fifty-five-cent hand-lotion coupon. A torn-out photo of a fashion model in a stark, bare sliver of black. She couldn't imagine ever wearing such a style, and she studied the photo for some time before recalling that it was the model who'd caught her eye, not the dress. The sickle-shaped model with the same snooty haircut as Rosemary Bly-Brice.

Footsteps climbed the stairs, and she closed the drawer as stealthily as a thief. She turned and found Sam halting in the doorway. "Oh!" she said, and he said, "I was just—"

They both broke off.

"I thought you were seeing patients," she said.

"No, I'm through for the day."

He put his hands in his trouser pockets. Should she leave? But he was filling the doorway; it would have been awkward.

"Mostly now I keep just morning hours," he said. "I don't have a lot of patients anymore. Seems half of them have died of old age. Mrs. Harper, Mrs. Allingham . . ."

"Mrs. Allingham died?"

"Stroke."

"Oh, dear, I'm going to miss her," Delia said.

Sam very kindly did not point out that she'd lost all touch with Mrs. Allingham sixteen months ago.

His bed was made, but like most men, he seemed unable to grasp the concept of tucking a fold of spread beneath the pillows. Instead, a straight line of fabric slanted dismally toward the headboard. Just for something to do, Delia set about fixing it. She turned down the spread and whacked both pillows into shape.

"I guess you think I've destroyed your father's practice," Sam told her.

"Pardon?"

"I've run it down to a shadow of its former glory, isn't that what you're thinking?"

"It's not your fault if people die of old age," Delia said.

"It's my fault if no one new signs on, though," he said. "I lack your father's bedside manner, obviously. I tell people they have plain old indigestion; I don't call it dyspepsia. I've never been the type to flatter and cosset my patients."

Delia felt a familiar twinge of annoyance. *I would hardly consider "dyspepsia" flattery,* she could have said. And, *I don't know why you have to use that bitter, biting tone of voice any time you talk about my father.* She stalked around to the other side of the bed.

But then Sam asked, "What is that limp you've got?"

"Limp?"

"It seems to me you're favoring one foot."

"Oh, that's from a couple of months ago. It's almost healed by now."

"Sit down a minute."

She sat on the edge of the bed, and he came over to kneel in front of her and slip her shoe off. His fingertips moved across the top of her foot with a knowledgeable, deft precision that shot directly to her groin.

In her softest voice, she told him, "Your patients never minded, that *I* was aware of. They always called you a saint."

"They don't anymore," he said. He was gazing out the window while he traced a tendon, as if he expected to hear the injury rather than see it. "The other night Mrs. Maxwell phoned with one of her stomach problems, and I told her, 'If I let myself think about it, Mrs. Maxwell, I could list quite a few complaints of my own. My eyes burn and my head aches and my knee is acting up,' I said. Which of course offended her. It seems I've lost my tolerance. Or maybe I was never all that tolerant to begin with. I don't have a very . . . wide nature. I'm short on, you might call it, jollity."

The very word, in connection with Sam, made Delia smile, but he was prodding her ankle now, and he didn't notice. "Does this hurt? This?" he asked.

"A little."

She thought of how Joel had held her foot in exactly this way. But Joel's touch had felt so foreign, so separate from her—not quite real, even, it seemed as she looked back.

"I suppose that's why I married you," Sam was saying. Had she missed something? "You were extremely jolly when we met," he said. "Or more like . . . lighthearted. Now I see that I chose you for all the wrong reasons."

She drew back slightly.

"There you sat on that couch," he said, "next to your two scary sisters. Eliza preaching sea kelp and toxic doses of vitamins; Linda tossing off words like *louche* and *distingué*. But you were so shy and cute and fumbly, smiling down at your little glass eyecup of sherry. You were so wavery around the edges. You I'd be able to handle, I thought, and I never stopped to ask why I needed to believe that."

He dropped her foot and sat back on his heels. "Stand up, please," he told her. She stood. He narrowed his eyes. "It does seem there's a bit of swelling," he said. "I would guess you've torn a ligament. Ligaments can be very slow to mend. How'd you do it?"

She'd done it acting fumbly, acting wavery around the edges, but she didn't want to say so. He was continuing, anyway, with his original train of thought.

"When you left," he said, "the police were sympathetic at first. But then they figured out you'd left of your own accord, and I could see them beginning to wonder. Well, you can't blame them. I was wondering myself. I asked Eliza, when she came back from seeing you: 'Was it me? Did I have any part in it?' Maybe I hadn't phrased it right about that man friend of yours. Or I nagged too much about sunblock, or you hated how my chest hair had grayed. Or the angina; I know the angina business must have gotten tedious."

"What?" she said. "Now, that is just not fair!"

"No, no, I did go overboard for a while. Checking my pulse rate every two minutes. I think I had it in mind I was going to drop dead like my father." He rose, carefully brushing his knees even though they weren't dusty. "But Eliza said it wasn't any of those things. She said you were suffering from stress. I'm still not sure what she meant."

Nor am I entirely clear, he had written, *what "stresses" you are referring to.* Delia wished now she hadn't thrown that letter away. Had its tone, perhaps, been less cold than she had imagined? She reflected on the deletions; she recalled how they had increased near the end and how the commas had fallen away, as if he had been hurtling headlong toward his final sentence. Which he had then crossed out so thoroughly that she hadn't been able to read it.

The phone on the nightstand started ringing, but neither of them reached for it, and eventually it stopped.

"The thing of it is," he said, "you ask yourself enough questions—was it this I did wrong, was it that?—and you get to believing you did it *all* wrong. Your whole damn life. But now that I'm nearing the end of it, I seem to be going too fast to stop and change. I'm just . . . *skidding* to the end of it."

Susie called, "Mom?"

"It's like that old Jackie Gleason show on TV," Sam said. "The one that used to open with a zoom shot across a harbor toward a skyline. Was it Miami? Manhattan? That long glide across the glassy water: my picture exactly of dying. No brakes! No traction! No time to make a U-turn!"

"Mom, telephone!"

Delia didn't take her eyes from Sam's face, but Sam said, "You'd better get that."

Still she didn't move.

"The phone, Delia."

After a moment, she picked up the receiver. "Hello?" she said.

"Delia?"

"Oh, Noah."

Sam's shoulders sagged. He turned toward the window.

"Haven't you even started out yet?" Noah demanded.

"No," she said, with her eyes on Sam. He was setting his forehead against the panes now, looking down into the yard. "I won't know what my arrangements are till afternoon," she told Noah.

"But it's afternoon now, and I'm lonesome!" he said. Sickness, it seemed, had turned him into that open-faced child she'd first known.

"I've got no one taking care of me! Grandpa came but he wouldn't stay, and now I've finished the cough drops."

"Well, there's another box in the ... your grandpa? Came to Bay Borough?"

"For about a nanosecond."

"What did he want?"

"He said he was just riding around, and then he left. I told him I was sick, but what did *he* care? And Dad claims I don't even have a fever and Mom can't come till after work and also something's wrong with the television set."

"Read a book, then," she told him. "I'll be home before long. Either this evening or maybe tomorrow; tell your father, will you?"

He was in the midst of a theatrical groan when she said goodbye.

"Sorry," she told Sam. "That was just—"

But Sam said, "Well, it's obvious you have things to attend to," and he started toward the door.

"Sam?" she said.

He stopped and turned.

"It was just the little boy I'm taking care of," she told him.

"So I gathered," he said, somehow not moving his lips.

"He's sick with a cold."

"And you have to get 'home' to him."

His voice had that pinched, tight, steely quality that always made her shrivel inside, but she forced herself to say, calmly, "Well, it *is* where I happen to live."

"I may not be perfect, Delia, but at least I don't delude myself," Sam said.

"What is that supposed to mean?"

"I don't go around trying to roll the clock back," he said. "Shucking off my kids as soon as they turn difficult and hunting up a whole new, easy, *little* kid instead."

Delia stared at him. "Well, of all the preposterous theories!" she said. "What do you know about it? Maybe he's not easy at all! Maybe he's just as difficult!"

"If that's the case," he said, "you can always shuck him off too."

"I didn't shuck him off!" she shouted. "I just came for Susie's wedding and then I'm going back—and not a moment too soon, might I add. I have no intention of shucking him off!"

Sam studied her impassively. "Did I say you did?" he asked.

And while she was grabbing for words, he left the room.

One of Delia's handicaps was that when she got angry, she got teary, which always made her angrier. So there she was, banging around the kitchen and fighting back tears as she washed the dishes, while Linda followed behind, trying to console her. "There, there," she said. "*We* love you, Dee. Your blood kin loves you. Careful, that's Grandma's last soup bowl. *We'll* stand by you."

"I'm all right," Delia said, dabbing her eyes impatiently with the heel of one hand. She ran water over a sponge. It had a horrible cilantro smell, as if it had soured in the cupboard.

"You shouldn't put up with him," Linda said. "Give him the boot! Send him packing. This is our house, not Sam's. It's you who ought to be living here."

Delia had to laugh at that. "Really? On what money?" she asked. "If not for Sam, we'd have lost this place long ago. Who do you think pays the property tax? And the maintenance, and the bills for all those improvements?"

"Well, if you call uprooting every last shrub an improvement," Linda sniffed. "*I* call it high-handed! And did you know he's got plans to paint the shutters red?"

"Red?"

"Fire-engine red, is what he told Eliza. Though she says he's sort of petered out on his projects lately. But think of it! Like an old, old man with his hair dyed, that's what red shutters would look like. You notice he only started doing this after his heart attack."

"Chest pains," Delia corrected her mechanically.

Susie wandered in, dressed in her jeans and a navy pullover of Carroll's. "When's lunch?" she asked Delia.

"Lunch! Well . . ."

"A gold digger's what he is," Linda said. "He had his eye on you from the moment Daddy hired him."

"Who did?" Susie asked.

"Sam Grinstead; who do you think? He schemed to marry your mother before he ever laid eyes on her."

"He did?"

"Oh, Linda," Delia said. "If you get right down to it, I schemed to marry him, too. I sat behind that desk just pining for someone to walk in and save me."

"Save you from what?" Susie asked.

Delia ignored her. "Look at our own grandmother," she told Linda. "Marrying Isaiah to escape TB. Look at the woodcutter's honest son, marrying the princess for her kingdom!"

"Who was T.B.?" Susie demanded. "What woodcutter? What are you two *talking* about?"

Linda went over to Susie and draped an arm across her shoulders in a chummy, confiding way that made Delia feel excluded. "If your mother had half the sense you do," she told Susie, "she would kick your father out and get herself a job and move back to Baltimore."

"I already have a job," Delia said. "I have a whole life, elsewhere!"

And Bay Borough seemed to float by just then like a tiny, bright, crowded blue bubble, at this distance so veiled and misty that she wondered if she had dreamed it.

"Here's what I'm hoping," Driscoll told Delia. "When Courtney hears somebody's phoned her, she'll know right off it's got to be this guy she gave her number to. I mean, he did call you-all's house three times. So you know he didn't get the number from the phone book; he must have written it down wrong. Don't you think?"

"Well, it's possible, I suppose," Delia said. In fact, it seemed very likely, but she couldn't work up the energy to tell him so. For the past forty-five minutes they'd been standing out here in the cold. From time to time she sent a longing glance over her shoulder at Courtney's white clapboard house, but they had already rung the doorbell and no one had answered. "Driscoll," she said, "has it occurred to you that Courtney might have after-school sports? I mean, Susie used to come home in the dark, some days."

"Then we'll wait here till dark," he said.

Other students were passing—Gilman boys in their shirts and ties, and teenage girls in Bryn Mawr aqua or Roland Park Country School blue. "We should be holding up one of those signs," Delia said, "the way they do at airports."

Driscoll scowled at her.

"Couldn't you have brought Pearce for this instead?" Delia asked him.

"Your sister, for heaven's sake!"

"You mean Spence?"

"Spence. Sorry."

She gave a little laugh. He scowled harder.

"Spence is at work," he told her. "But I doubt she'd have come anyhow. She doesn't think I ought to get married."

"She doesn't!"

"Well, why is that such a shock?" he asked. "You're not the only one who's against this."

"Did I say I was against it?"

"You sure act like you are. Dragging your heels every step of the way, wishing I'd brought someone else."

"I'm just getting cold, is all," Delia told him.

"For your information, my whole family claims I'd be better off single."

Delia felt stung. She said, "Well, thanks a lot!"

"Oh, they like Susie," he said. "But, you know . . . 'Why get mixed up with those Grinsteads?' my mom is always asking."

"There's nothing wrong with Grinsteads!"

"No, well, but . . ." He followed a knot of passing schoolgirls with his eyes. "You've got to admit," he said, "you-all are so . . . you do things such a different way. Not mingling or taking part, living to yourselves like you do; and then you pretend like that's normal. You pretend like *everything's* normal; you're so cagey and smooth; you gloss things over; you don't explain."

Delia breathed again. He could have named flaws much worse, she felt, although she didn't know exactly what. "Well," she said, "those sound to me like good qualities, not bad."

"See there?" Driscoll demanded. "That's exactly what I mean!"

"Look who's talking!" Delia said. "Someone who had his wedding canceled and then showed up for it anyway! How's that for glossing over?"

"At least I didn't make believe I was nothing but a guest," Driscoll told her. "Walking in at the very last minute like the bride was some passing acquaintance."

"I would have come earlier! But nobody asked me!" she told him.

"See what I mean?" he said.

"What *do* you mean?"

A car drew up at the curb, a station wagon teeming with faces. A girl got out with an armload of books. "Thanks!" she called, and the car honked and pulled away.

"Courtney?" Driscoll asked.

The girl paused on the sidewalk. Delia had known, somehow, that Courtney would be a blonde. She was tall and slim and golden-skinned, and her clothes were just the right degree of unstudied—her blazer expertly tailored but her knee socks falling down. "Yes?" she said.

"My name is Driscoll Avery," Driscoll said, "and a couple of nights ago I believe I answered a phone call that was meant for you."

Courtney tilted her head. Her pageboy swung prettily to one side.

"Some guy called, a wrong number," Driscoll told her, "and now my fiancée is mad because I was, um, maybe a little bit rude. So I need to ask if you know who might have called you."

Courtney looked over at Delia.

"I'm his fiancée's mother," Delia explained. The word "fiancée" brought to her mind someone in a pillbox hat, nothing at all like Susie. She felt herself assuming the flat-faced, wide-eyed expression of a liar. She said, "Driscoll's telling the truth; I swear it. A boy phoned, asking for Courtney, and Driscoll said you didn't want to talk to him."

"You said *that*?" Courtney asked Driscoll. The smile was gone now. "What if it was someone I was dying to hear from?"

"Well, like who?" Driscoll said. "I mean, was there someone?"

"There's Michael Garter."

"Did you give Michael Garter your number?"

"No, but it's in the book."

"You think he's the one who called you?"

"Well, maybe. He could have. Well, sure!" She seemed to be warming to the idea. "In a couple of weeks, there's this dance?" she told Delia.

Delia said, "But you didn't actually tell him your number."

"Well, no."

"We were thinking it might be someone you'd told."

"No, but there's this big homecoming dance? And Michael Garter's this guy I know? He's the second-strongest guy in his school."

"But—" Delia began, at the same time that Driscoll said, "Well, great! Let's get moving!"

"But *was* there someone you told?" Delia asked.

"Oh, gosh, guys are always wanting my number. You know? And I give it to them, but, like, I just do it to be nice. I would never actually go out with them."

"Would you give them the *wrong* number?" Delia persisted.

"Well, sure, if they're, like, totally not of interest."

"You'd just transpose a couple of digits, say."

"I might."

"Did you do that recently?"

"Well, maybe to this guy at my Christian fellowship group."

"What's his name?"

"But I think it's more likely Michael Garter," Courtney said.

"But the name of the boy at your fellowship group . . ."

"That's Paul Cates. But he's, like, a dork. You'd know what I meant if you saw him."

"I bet anything it was Michael Garter," Driscoll said soothingly.

Courtney sent him an appreciative look.

"Well, whoever," Delia said, "you just tell Driscoll all the possibilities, and then he can track down which one it was."

"And maybe I could come along," Courtney said. "I could show you exactly where Michael Garter has football practice."

Anybody with half a brain would look for Paul Cates first. Hoping to convey that, Delia screwed up her eyes at Driscoll. "Huh?" he asked her, and then, "Ah. Does, ah, Paul Cates play football too?"

"Are you serious?" Courtney asked. "Paul Cates? Play football?"

Delia collected herself to go, hitching her handbag strap onto her shoulder. "Good hunting," she told Driscoll.

"What, you're not coming with us?"

"You'll do better by yourselves."

He opened his mouth to argue, but Courtney said, "Nice meeting you!" Delia waved and walked off.

She was glad to have some time alone. Had family life always been so cram-packed? she wondered. How had she kept her wits about her? But then she remembered she hadn't, at least not in Sam's opinion.

Skimming south on Roland Avenue, she passed Travel Arrangements, the Mercantile Bank, Eddie's Supermarket. She was careful not to look toward the other pedestrians, in case they were people she knew. Suppose they asked where she'd been all these months and what she planned to do next. Or suppose—here was a thought—she met Adrian Bly-Brice.

The funny thing was that she couldn't picture Adrian's face anymore, although she tried.

"Delia," Linda whispered at the front door, "you've got someone waiting for you."

"I do?"

Delia felt herself flush, but Linda said, "An *older* gentleman. Name of Nat?"

"Oh," Delia said.

She followed Linda through the dining room and into the kitchen. Nat was sitting at the table with Susie and the twins, but he rose to his feet when Delia entered. "There she is!" he said.

Away from Senior City, he seemed older. His hair was so white that it glittered, and he was leaning very heavily on his cane. This must be one of his flashback days. She said, "Nat? Is everything all right?"

"Oh, yes," he said, "quite all right. Hello, my dear." He gave her a courtly kiss on the cheek, prickling her with his beard. "I just happened to be tootling around in the car," he said. "Thought I'd offer you a lift back."

"Tootling around . . . Baltimore?"

"Yes, well, hither and yon."

This was puzzling, but she didn't pursue it. "That's nice of you," she said, "but I'm not sure exactly when I'll be leaving." She glanced toward Susie, who was watching her over her coffee mug. "Driscoll is still working on that telephone matter," Delia told her.

The twins nudged each other. Nat said, "Oh, I know all about that! Your sister here has filled me in. So how is it progressing? Have we located the hapless young man?"

"Well, we've narrowed the field some," Delia said. "Nat, is anything wrong at home?"

"Wrong! Why do you keep asking that?" he said. "Can't a man take a little drive on his own these days?"

Linda placed a mug of coffee on the table in front of him, and he lowered himself back onto his chair with a thud. "Thank you, my dear," he said. He set his cane aside. It stood on its four little legs in a perky, independent manner.

"Cream?" Linda asked him. "Sugar?"

"Just black, thanks." He told Delia, "You never mentioned you had a sister. And such a charming daughter! And two gorgeous nieces!"

There was something feverish about his enthusiasm, but none of the others seemed to notice. "She doesn't only got a daughter," Marie-Claire told him. "She's got two boys besides."

"Two boys!" Nat marveled. "Where does she keep them hidden?"

"Well, Carroll's hiding upstairs, on account of this fight with his dad. And Ramsay lives with his tacky girlfriend at a place we don't know the address of."

Nat shot Delia a questioning look. "Yes," she said with a laugh. "You'll have to excuse us, I'm afraid. Nobody here is on speaking terms."

"They seem to *me* to be speaking," he said reasonably.

"Oh, speaking, yes. But . . ."

She gave up and went to pour herself some coffee. Nat resumed quizzing the twins. "And do all of you live in this one big house? All except Ramsay, that is, and his tacky girlfriend?"

"Oh, no, none of us live here! Just only Uncle Sam."

"Uncle Sam! This is government property?"

The twins chortled. Thérèse said, "Silly! Uncle Sam is Aunt Delia's husband."

Delia sensed Nat's glance in her direction, but she didn't turn around, and the twins moved on to the topic of Eliza. "She burns weeds in little bowls," Marie-Claire told him. "She has a bottle called Forbearance, to smell from when she's feeling fed up."

"Where would one buy that, I wonder," Nat said wistfully.

Delia went to the silverware drawer for a spoon and found Susie all at once lounging in front of it, waiting for her, one sneakered foot cocked across the other. Her nonchalant expression didn't fool Delia for a second. "So," Susie said. "Driscoll did get hold of Courtney, sounds like."

"Yes."

"And narrowed down who the boy was, you said."

"Well, Courtney gave him a couple of possibilities."

"So I guess now he's gone to talk to them."

"He's working on it," Delia told her.

She reached toward the drawer, and Susie slid infinitesimally to one side. "Looks to me like you would have gone with him," Susie said.

"Well, you can see I'm right here," Delia snapped.

She supposed that Susie must care for Driscoll; and in that case, well, all right, they should probably get married. How simple-minded Delia had been, to take their breakup seriously! And how sage and mature and practical Susie seemed in comparison! Delia flashed her a radiant smile. Susie examined her warily.

People always talked about a mother's uncanny ability to read her children, but that was nothing compared to how children could read their mothers.

The twins were describing their bridesmaid dresses. "Big floppy bows—"

"Puffy shoulders—"

"Exact same color as Crest fluoride toothpaste."

"They must be stunning," Nat told them. "And when do you plan on wearing them?"

"Maybe tonight," Marie-Claire said, while Susie, overlapping, said, "Tomorrow."

Everyone looked at her. She met Delia's gaze defiantly. "Well, if Driscoll brings me that boy, I mean."

"But he could do that in the next five minutes!" Linda told her. "You could get married this evening, if he hurries."

"Yes, but Dr. Soames can't fit us in till ten a.m. tomorrow."

"He told you that?" Delia asked. "You talked to him? When?"

"Oh, um, just a little while ago."

"But if our flight home is tomorrow at noon," Linda said, "and the drive to the airport takes, let's see . . ."

Nat told Delia, "Sounds as if you won't be riding back with me tonight."

He spoke cheerfully enough, but Delia hadn't lost her suspicion that something was troubling him. She glanced toward the others, who were still discussing schedules, and then she said, "Nat, what brought you here? Really."

"Nothing, I tell you!"

"You just drove two hours for no reason."

"Two and a half, actually," he said. "Little backup on the bridge."

She scrutinized him. "How's the baby?" she asked.

"He's thriving."

"And Binky?"

"Healthy as a brood mare."

"Does she know you're in Baltimore?"

"I called her a few minutes ago. Your sister let me use your phone."

"And Noah has a cold, I hear," she said, still ferreting.

"The merest sniffle," Nat assured her. "I looked in on him this morning while I was driving around. Found him playing Tetris. Hardly on his deathbed, I'd say."

"It's true he didn't sound very sick," Delia said. "Maybe he just needed a day off."

"Yes," Nat said. "We could all do with a day off, from time to time."

Something bumped against the back door, and then Sam walked in bearing two bags of groceries. A long stick of French bread poked forth from one of them. "I found the ginger," he told Linda, "but they were fresh out of shallots."

"Well, never mind; we'll make do with green onions," Linda told him, taking the bags. "Is that okay, Delia?"

"Is what okay?"

"Can you make your Chinese dish using green onions?"

"I always use green onions anyhow," Delia said. "But—"

"Oh, good. Because we're going to be so many, you know, I thought you could fix your . . . Oh, Sam, you haven't met Nat, have you. Nat Moffat, this is Sam Grinstead. I certainly hope you plan to stay for supper, Nat. Delia's Chinese dish feeds an army, believe me."

"I would love to stay for supper," Nat said, to Delia's surprise. He had risen during the introductions, and now he stood holding on to the back of his chair. Sam, who must have had no idea where Nat had materialized from, wore a pleasant, slightly blank expression as they shook hands. "Good to meet you," he said.

"Good to meet *you*," Nat told him. And then he added, darting a mischievous glance at Delia, "I've heard so much about you."

This was lost on Sam, of course. He just smiled politely and asked Linda, "Have I got time for a house call before supper?"

"Ask Delia; she's the cook," Linda said.

Sam turned to Delia. "I promised Mr. Knowles I'd check on him," he said.

"You have plenty of time," she told him.

They spoke without letting their eyes meet, like people in a play, whose words are meant for the audience.

No one had to tell Delia which boy had turned out to be Courtney's caller. She knew it was Paul Cates as soon as she saw him—sweet-faced and naive, with a tousle of rust-colored curls. His jeans were a little too short for him, his sneakers too thin-soled and childish, his plaid wool jacket the kind boys wear in elementary school. He followed Driscoll over to Susie, who was perched on a stool chopping water chestnuts for Delia's Chinese dish. Behind him came Courtney, of all people. She took her place close behind Driscoll and Paul, tucking her hands into the pockets of her blazer and regarding Susie with undisguised curiosity. Susie, who had turned from the counter at their approach, looked only at Driscoll.

"Susie," Driscoll said, "this is Paul Cates." Then he faced Paul Cates and said, "Paul, I'd like to apologize. When you phoned here by accident the other night, I let you think you'd reached Courtney's house, but I was wrong, wrong, wrong."

Paul was beaming. "That's okay," he said.

Formally, Driscoll faced Susie again. "Now will you marry me?" he asked.

Susie said, "Well, I guess."

One of the twins said, "Hot dog!" and the other said, "Kiss him! Kiss him, Susie!"

Susie planted a kiss to one side of Driscoll's mouth. She told Paul, "It's nice of you to be so understanding."

"Oh, I don't mind a bit!" he said, and he sent Courtney a shining glance from under his long lashes. Courtney just surveyed him coolly and then turned back to Susie.

"And Courtney, it was nice of you to come along," Susie told her.

"No problem. Me and your brother Carroll met last spring at a party."

"Oh, really?"

"My girlfriend asked him to her birthday party; I put it all together when your fiancé told me your name."

Paul was looking less happy now; so Delia broke in and said, "Can you two stay for dinner? We're having this Chinese dish that's infinitely expandable."

"Well, I *might* could," Courtney said.

Paul said, "I'll just need to phone my mother."

"Right over here," Delia told him, and she cupped his elbow protectively as she led him toward the phone. How cruel and baffling—how tribal, almost—young girls must seem to boys! Somehow she hadn't realized that when she was a young girl herself.

"I propose a toast," Nat said. He raised his coffee mug. "To the bridal couple!"

Driscoll said, "Why, thanks"—not having the dimmest notion, of course, who this old man might be, but adapting with his usual good humor. "Hello, Ma?" Paul said into the phone, and then Carroll appeared from the dining room just as Eliza stepped through the back door; so both of them had to be filled in on the latest developments. Eliza hadn't even heard yet what Driscoll's magic task was. She kept saying, "Who? He brought who?" with her eyebrows quirked in bewilderment, her pocketbook hugged to her chest, and Courtney was sidling toward Carroll to ask, "Carroll Grinstead? I don't know if you remember me," and the twins were insisting that this time they should wear lipstick to the wedding.

Delia took her cutting board to a less populated area, and she started chopping ginger. Her Chinese dish required eleven different bowls of ingredients, most minced no bigger than matchstick heads, all lined up in a row for rapid frying. So far she had finished only bowl number four. She was thankful to be occupied, though. She chopped rhythmically, mindlessly, letting an ocean of chatter eddy around her. *Tick-tick,* the knife came down on the cutting board. *Tick-tick,* and she slid all her thoughts to one side as she slid the mounds of ginger into a bowl.

With every one of its leaves in place, the table filled the whole dining room. ("This tablecloth came from your grandma's hope chest," Linda told the twins. "The stain is where your aunt Delia set a bowl of curry. *She* doesn't give a damn; she was your grandpa's favorite; she treats these things like Woolworth things.") Twelve place settings marched the length of it—five at each side, one each at head and foot. There had been talk of inviting Eleanor, but Susie didn't want to jinx her entire marriage with thirteen at table; and no one answered the phone when they called Ramsay.

"Courtney, I'll put you in the middle here," Delia said. "Then Paul, you're next to Courtney . . ."

Courtney, however, had obviously made up her mind to sit with Carroll, which left Paul stuck between the twins; not that the twins weren't delighted. And the others remained standing while they continued a discussion they'd started in the living room—something about Mr. Knowles's tingly arm. "Didn't Daddy always say the same thing!" Eliza was exclaiming. "He used to say he wished he had a dictionary of pains. Those symptoms people came up with—'Pepsi-bubble stomach' and 'whiny argumentative back'!"

"Driscoll, you're beside Linda," Delia said, but Driscoll, feigning engrossment in the conversation, kept his face turned toward Eliza and sneakily drew out the chair beside Susie. Delia gave up. "Oh, just *sit*," she told Nat, and Nat sat down where he was, which happened to be exactly where she'd intended, at her right hand. "Help yourself to some rice," she said, passing him the bowl, and she told the others, "Everything's getting cold!"

Eliza settled at Sam's left, shaking her head at what Sam was saying. "Who knows, anyhow?" he was saying. "Maybe it's all equal: hangnail for one, cancer for another. Everything on the same level, just barely within endurance."

"Sam Grinstead, you don't believe that for a minute!" Linda squawked. "What a bizarre suggestion!"

Delia said, "Paul, will you have some rice and pass it on, please? Everybody! Sit down!"

Very suddenly, the rest of them sat. They seemed to have run out of steam, and there was a pause, during which Paul dropped the serving spoon to the table with a loud clunk. He bared all his teeth in embarrassment and picked it up.

Nat said, "Do any of you know the photographs of C. R. Savage?"

The grown-ups turned courteous, receptive faces in his direction.

"A nineteenth-century fellow," he said. "Used the old wet-plate method, I would suppose. There's a picture I'm reminded of that he took toward the end of his life. Shows his dining-room table set for Christmas dinner. Savage himself sitting amongst the empty chairs, waiting for his family. Chair after chair after chair, silverware laid just so, even a baby's high chair, all in readiness. And I can't help thinking, when I look at that photo, *I bet that's as good as it got, that day. From there on out, it was all downhill, I bet.* Actual sons and daughters arrived, and they quarreled over the drumsticks and sniped at their children's table manners and brought up hurtful incidents from fifteen years before; and the baby had this whimper that gave everybody a headache. Only just for that moment," Nat said, and his voice took on a tremor, "just as the shutter was clicking, none of that had happened yet, you see, and the table looked so beautiful, like someone's dream of a table, and old Savage felt so happy and so—what's the word I want, so . . ."

But now his voice failed him completely, and he covered his eyes with one shaking hand and bent his head. "So anticipatory!" he whispered into his plate, while Delia, at a loss, patted his arm. "I'm sorry! I'm sorry!" he said. Everyone sat dumbstruck. Then he said, "Ha!" and straightened, bracing his shoulders. "Postpartum depression, I guess this is," he said. He wiped his eyes with his napkin.

"Nat has a three-week-old baby," Delia explained to the others. "Nat, would you like—"

"Baby?" Linda asked incredulously.

Sam said, "I thought Nat was *your* friend, Linda."

"No, he's mine," Delia said. "He lives on the Eastern Shore and he's just had a baby boy, a lovely boy, you ought to see how—"

"Most irresponsible thing I've ever done in my life," Nat said hoarsely. "What could I have been thinking of? Oh, not that it was anything I planned, but . . . why did I go along with it? I believe I thought it was my chance to be a good father, finally. I know it was, or why else did I assume it was a girl? All my others were girls, you see. I must have thought I could do the whole thing over again, properly this time. But I'm just as short-tempered with James as I ever was with my daughters. Just as rigid, just as exacting. Why can't he get on a schedule, why does he have to cry at such unpredictable hours . . . Oh, the best thing I could do for that kid is toddle off to Floor Five."

"Floor Five? Oh," Delia said. "Oh, Nat! Don't even think it!" she said, patting his arm all the harder.

She should have realized at his wedding, she told herself, that someone so elated would have to end in tears, like an overexcited child allowed to stay up past his bedtime.

"Yes. Well," Sam said, clearing his throat. "It's really very common now, this more senior class of parent. Why, just last week I was reading, where was it I was reading . . ."

"The important thing to remember is, this is your assignment," Eliza said in ringing tones. She was all the way up near Sam, and she had to lean forward, bypassing a row of tactfully expressionless profiles, to search out Nat's face. "It's my belief that we're each assigned certain experiences," she said. "And then at the end of our lives—"

"*The New England Journal of Medicine!*" Sam announced triumphantly.

Nat asked Delia, "Do you have a place where I might lie down?"

"Yes, of course," she said, and she slid her chair back and handed him his cane. "Excuse us, please," she told the others.

Everyone nodded, abashed. As she and Nat crossed the hall, she could almost feel the furtive exchange of glances behind their backs.

"There's a flight of stairs," she warned Nat. "Can you manage?"

"Oh, yes, if you'll hang on to my other arm. I'm sorry, Delia. I don't know what got into me."

"You're just tired," she told him. "I hope you're not thinking of driving back tonight."

"No, I suppose I shouldn't," he said. On each stair step, his cane gave a tinny rattle, like a handful of jacks being shaken. His elbow within his tweed sleeve was nothing but knob and rope.

"I'm going to make up a bed for you," Delia told him when they reached the second floor, "and then you should call Binky and tell her you're staying over."

"All right," he said meekly. He hobbled through the door she held open and sank into a slipcovered chair.

"This used to be my father's room," Delia said. She went out to the hall closet and came back with an armload of sheets. "There's still a telephone by the bed, see? From the days when he was in practice. Even after he stopped seeing patients, he could pick up his receiver whenever Sam got a call; chime in with a second opinion. He just hated to feel left out of things, you know?"

She was babbling aimlessly as she bustled around the bed, smoothing sheets and tucking in blankets. Nat watched without comment. He might not even have been listening, for when she went to Sam's room to borrow a pair of pajamas, she returned to find him staring at the blue-black windowpanes. "In fact," she said, placing the pajamas on the bureau, "I can't tell you how often I made up his bed just the way I did tonight, while Daddy sat where you're sitting now. He liked for his sheets to be fresh off the line, oh, long after we switched to an automatic dryer. And he would sit in that chair and—"

"It's a time trip," Nat said suddenly.

"Why, yes, I suppose it is, in a way."

But he'd been talking to himself, evidently. "Just a crazy, half-baked scheme to travel backwards," he said as if she hadn't spoken, "and live everything all over again. Unfortunately, Binky's the one who's left with the consequences. Poor Binky!"

"Binky will be fine," Delia said firmly. "Now. That door right there is the bathroom. New toothbrushes on the shelf above the tub. Can I get you anything more?"

"No, thank you."

"A tray of food, maybe? You didn't touch your supper."

"No."

"Well, you be sure to call me if you need me," she said.

Then she bent to press her lips to his forehead, the way she used to do with her father all those nights in the past.

Delia was the next to go to bed. She went at nine-thirty, having struggled to keep her eyes open ever since dinner. "I am *beat*," she told the others. They were all sitting around, still—even Courtney, although Paul had been picked up by his mother at some point. "It seems this morning took place way back in prehistory," Delia told them, and then she climbed the stairs to Eliza's room, so weary that she had to haul her feet behind her like buckets of cement.

Once she was in bed, though, she couldn't get to sleep. She lay staring at the ceiling, idly stroking the curl of warm cat nestled close to her hip. Downstairs, Linda and Sam were squabbling as usual. A Mozart horn concerto was playing. Eliza said, "Why *wouldn't* he, I ask you." Wouldn't who? Delia wondered. Wouldn't do what?

She must have slept then, but it was such a fitful, shallow sleep that she seemed to remain partly conscious throughout, and when she woke again she wasn't surprised to find the house dark and all the voices stilled. She sat up and angled her wristwatch to catch the light from the window. As near as she could make out, it was either eleven o'clock or five till twelve. More likely five till twelve, she decided, judging from the quiet.

She propped her pillow and leaned back against it, yawning. Tears of boredom were already edging the corners of her eyes. It was going to be one of those nights that go on for weeks.

Let's see: if the wedding began at ten tomorrow, she supposed it would be finished by eleven. Well, say noon, to play it safe. She'd reach the bus station by half past, if she could catch a ride with Ramsay. Or with Sam. Sam had offered, after all.

She saw herself riding in the passenger seat, Sam behind the wheel. Like two of those little peg people in a toy car. Husband peg, wife peg, side by side. Facing the road and not looking at each other; for why would they need to, really, having gone beyond the visible surface long ago. No hope of admiring gazes anymore, no chance of unremitting adoration. Nothing left to show but their plain, true, homely, interior selves, which were actually much richer anyhow.

Where was she? Bus station. Catch a bus by one o'clock or so, reach Salisbury by . . .

The tears seemed not exactly tears of boredom after all. She blotted them on her nightgown sleeve, but more came.

She folded back the covers, mindful of the cat, and slid out of bed and walked barefoot toward the door. The hall was lit only by the one round window, high up. She had to more or less feel her way toward Sam's room.

Luckily, his door was ajar. No sound gave her away as she entered. But she knew, somehow, that he was awake. After all these years, of course she knew, just from that bated quality to the air. She stepped delicately across cool floorboards, then scratchy rug, then cool floorboards once again—terrain she had traveled since the day she first learned to walk. She sat with no perceptible weight upon the side of the bed that used to be hers. He was lying on his back, she saw. She could begin to sift his white face from the flocked half-dark. She whispered, "Sam?"

"Yes," he said.

"You know that letter you wrote me in Bay Borough."

"Yes."

"Well, what was the line you crossed out?"

He stirred beneath the bedclothes. "Oh," he said, "I crossed out so many lines. That letter was a mess."

"I mean the very last line. The one you put so many x's through I couldn't possibly read it."

He didn't answer at first. Then he said, "I forget."

Her impulse was to stand up and leave, but she forced herself to stay. She sat motionless, waiting and waiting.

"I think," he said finally, "that maybe it was . . . well, something like what Driscoll was wondering earlier. Was there anything that would, you know. Would persuade you to come back."

She said, "Oh, Sam. All you had to do was ask."

Then he turned toward her, and Delia slipped under the blankets and he drew her close against him. Although, in fact, he still had not asked. Not in so many words.

Long after they went to sleep, the telephone rang, and Delia resurfaced gradually. This late, it had to be a patient calling. But Sam didn't even change the rhythm of his breathing; so she inched out from under his arm to reach for the phone.

"Hello?" she said.

"Mrs. Grinstead?"

"Yes."

"It's Joe Bright."

A voice as bright as his name, wide awake and chipper at the ungodly hour of—she peered at the alarm clock. One twenty-three.

"Um . . . ," she said.

"The realtor?" he prompted.

"Oh!"

"You called me? You and your daughter? Left a whole bunch of messages?"

"Oh! Yes!" she said, but she was still floundering. "Um . . ."

"I would never phone so late except you did say it was life and death, Mrs. Grinstead, and I only now got in from out of town. Wife's mother died, spur of the moment."

"Oh, I'm sorry to hear that," she said. She sat up straighter. "Um, Mr. Bright, why I called was . . ." She shifted the phone to her other ear. "My daughter has been wanting to know," she said. "Yes . . . will she be allowed to pound nails in the walls?"

There was a silence.

"Just in case they need to hang some pictures, say, or a mirror . . . ," Delia said, trailing off.

"Nails," Mr. Bright said.

"Right."

"She wanted to know if she could pound in nails."

"Right."

"Well," Mr. Bright said. "Sure. I reckon. Long as they spackle the holes upon vacating."

"Oh, they will!" Delia said. "I can promise. Thank you, Mr. Bright. Good night."

There was another silence, and then, "Good night," he said.

Delia replaced the receiver and lay down again. She had assumed Sam was still asleep, but then she heard him give a little whisking sound of amusement. She started smiling. Outside, far downtown, a train blew past. In the house, a floorboard creaked, and a moment later a foggy cough broke from the room where Nat slept.

"It's a time trip," Nat had said.

She thought of her attempt, that afternoon, to picture Adrian. She had begun with his resemblance to her high-school boyfriend, and only now did she realize that the image she had come up with happened to be Sam's, not the boyfriend's. A younger Sam, earnest and hopeful, the day he'd first walked through the door.

It had *all* been a time trip—all this past year and a half. Unlike Nat's, though, hers had been a time trip that worked. What else would you call it when she'd ended up back where she'd started, home with Sam for good? When the people she had left behind had actually traveled further, in some ways?

Now she saw that June beach scene differently. Her three children, she saw, had been staring at the horizon with the alert, tensed stillness of explorers at the ocean's edge, poised to begin their journeys. And Delia, shading her eyes in the distance, had been trying to understand why they were leaving.

Where they were going without her.

How to say goodbye.

SAINT MAYBE

———

Contents

I

The Airmail Bowling Ball

On Waverly Street, everybody knew everybody else. It was only one short block, after all—a narrow strip of patched and repatched pavement, bracketed between a high stone cemetery wall at one end and the commercial clutter of Govans Road at the other. The trees were elderly maples with lumpy, bulbous trunks. The squat clapboard houses seemed mostly front porch.

And each house had its own particular role to play. Number Nine, for instance, was foreign. A constantly shifting assortment of Middle Eastern graduate students came and went, attending classes at Johns Hopkins, and the scent of exotic spices drifted from their kitchen every evening at suppertime. Number Six was referred to as the newlyweds', although the Crains had been married two years now and were beginning to look a bit worn around the edges. And Number Eight was the Bedloe family. They were never just the Bedloes, but the Bedloe *family*, Waverly Street's version of the ideal, apple-pie household: two amiable parents, three good-looking children, a dog, a cat, a scattering of goldfish.

In fact, the oldest of those children had long ago married and left—moved out to Baltimore County and started a family of her own—and the second-born was nearing thirty. But somehow the Bedloes were stuck in people's minds at a stage from a dozen years back, when Claudia was a college girl in bobby socks and Danny was captain of his high-school football team and Ian, the baby (his parents' big surprise), was still tearing down the sidewalk on his tricycle with a miniature license plate from a cereal box wired to the handlebar.

Now Ian was seventeen and, like the rest of his family, large-boned and handsome and easygoing, quick to make friends, fond of a good time. He had the Bedloe golden-brown hair, golden skin, and sleepy-looking brown eyes, although his mouth was his mother's, a pale beige mouth quirking upward at the corners. He liked to wear ragged jeans and plaid shirts—cotton broadcloth in summer, flannel in winter—unbuttoned all the way to expose a stretched-out T-shirt underneath. His shoes were high-top sneakers held together with electrical tape. This was in 1965, when Poe High School still maintained at least a vestige of a dress code, and his teachers were forever sending him home to put on something more presentable. (But his mother was likely to greet him in baggy, lint-covered slacks and one of his own shirts, her fading blond curls pinned scrappily back with a granddaughter's pink plastic hairbow. *She* would not have passed the dress code either.) Also, there were complaints about the quality of Ian's schoolwork. He was bright, his teachers said, but lazy. Content to slide through with low B's or even C's. It was the spring of his junior year and if he didn't soon mend his ways, no self-respecting college would have him.

Ian listened to all this with a tolerant, bemused expression. Things would turn out fine, he felt. Hadn't they always? (None of the Bedloes was a worrier.) Crowds of loyal friends had surrounded him since kindergarten. His sweetheart, Cicely Brown, was the prettiest girl in the junior class. His mother doted on him and his father—Poe's combination algebra teacher and baseball coach—let him pitch in nearly every game, and not just because they were related, either. His father claimed Ian had talent. In fact sometimes Ian daydreamed about pitching for the Orioles, but he knew he didn't have *that* much talent. He was a medium kind of guy, all in all.

Even so, there were moments when he believed that someday, somehow, he was going to end up famous. Famous for what, he couldn't quite say; but he'd be walking up the back steps or something and all at once he would imagine a camera zooming in on him, filming his life story. He imagined the level, cultured voice of his biographer saying, "Ian climbed the steps. He opened the door. He entered the kitchen."

"Have a good day, hon?" his mother asked, passing through with a laundry basket.

"Oh," he said, "the usual run of scholastic triumphs and athletic glories." And he set his books on the table.

His biographer said, "He set his books on the table."

That was the spring that Ian's brother fell in love. Up till then Danny had had his share of girlfriends—various decorative Peggies or Debbies to hang upon his arm—but somehow nothing had come of them. He was always getting dumped, it seemed, or sadly disillusioned. His mother had started fretting that he'd passed the point of no return and would wind up a seedy bachelor type. Now here was Lucy, slender and pretty and dressed in red, standing in the Bedloes' front hall with her back so straight, her purse held so firmly in both hands, that she seemed even smaller than she was. She seemed childlike, in fact, although Danny described her as a "woman" when he introduced her. "Mom, Dad, Ian, I'd like you to meet the woman who's changed my life." Then Danny turned to Mrs. Jordan, who had chosen this inopportune moment to step across the street and borrow the pinking shears. "Mrs. Jordan: Lucy Dean."

His mother, skipping several stages of acquaintanceship, swept Lucy into a hug. (Clearly more was called for than a handshake.) His father said, "Well, now! What do you know!" The dog gave Lucy's crotch a friendly sniff, while Mrs. Jordan—an older lady, the soul of tact—hastily murmured something or other and backed out the door. And Ian clamped his palms in his armpits and grinned at no one in particular.

They moved to the living room, Ian bringing up the rear. Lucy perched in an easy chair and Danny settled on its arm, with one hand resting protectively behind her loose knot of black hair. To Ian, Lucy resembled some brightly feathered bird held captive by his brown plaid family. Her face was very small, a cameo face. Her dress was scoop-necked and slim-waisted and full-skirted. She wore extremely red lipstick that seemed not gaudy, for some reason, but brave. Ian was entranced.

"Tell us everything," Bee Bedloe ordered. "Where you met, how you got to know each other—everything."

She and Ian's father had seated themselves on the sofa. (Ian's father, who had a baseball player's mild, sloping build, was pulling in his stomach.) Ian himself remained slouched against the door frame.

"We met at the post office," Danny said. He beamed down at Lucy, who smiled back at him trustfully.

Bee said, "Oh? You two work together?"

"No, no," Lucy said, in a surprisingly croaky little drawl. "I went in to mail a package and Danny was the one who waited on me."

Danny told them, "She was mailing a package to Cheyenne, Wyoming, by air. I told her it would cost twenty dollars and twenty-seven cents. You could see it was more than she'd planned on—"

"I said, 'Twenty twenty-seven! Great God Almighty!' " Lucy squawked, startling everyone.

"So I told her, 'It's cheaper by parcel post, you know. That would be four sixty-three.' 'Let me think,' she says, and moves on out of the way. Gives up her place at the counter. Stands a few feet down from me, frowning at the wall."

"I had to take a minute to decide," Lucy explained.

"Frowns at the wall for the *longest* time. Three customers go ahead of her. Finally I say, 'Miss? You ready?' But she just goes on frowning."

"I was mailing some odds and ends to my ex-husband and I wanted to be shed of them as fast as possible," Lucy said.

A little jolt passed through the room.

Bee said, "Ex-husband?"

"Half of me wanted him to get that box tomorrow, even yesterday if it could be arranged, but the other half was counting pennies. 'That's fifteen-and-some dollars' difference,' this other half was saying. 'Think of all the groceries fifteen dollars could buy. Or shoes and stuff for the children.' "

"Children?"

"What got to me," Danny said, "was how she wouldn't be hurried. How it didn't bother her what other people made of her. I mean she just stood there pondering, little bit of a person. Then finally she said, 'Well,' and straightened her shoulders and chose to spring for airmail."

"It mattered just enough, I decided," Lucy said. "It was worth it just for the satisfaction."

"If she had said parcel post I might have let her go," Danny said. "But airmail! I admired that. I asked if she'd like to have dinner."

"He was the best-looking thing I'd seen in ages," Lucy told the Bedloes. "I said I'd be thrilled to have dinner."

Bee and Doug Bedloe sat side by side, smiling extra hard as if someone had just informed them that they were being photographed.

There was this about the Bedloes: They believed that every part of their lives was absolutely wonderful. It wasn't just an act, either. They really did believe it. Or at least Ian's mother did, and she was the one who set the tone. Her marriage was a great joy to her, her house made her happy every time she walked into it, and her children were attractive and kind and universally liked. When bad things happened—the usual accidents, illnesses, jogs in the established pattern—Bee treated them with eye-rolling good humor, as if they were the stuff of situation comedy. They would form new chapters in the lighthearted ongoing saga she entertained the neighbors with: How Claudia Totaled the Car. How Ian Got Suspended from First Grade.

As for Ian, he believed it too but only after a kind of hitch, a moment of hesitation. For instance, from time to time he had the feeling that his father was something of a joke at Poe High—ineffectual at discipline, and muddled in his explanation of the more complicated algebraic functions. But Bee said he was the most popular teacher Poe had ever employed, and in fact that was true. Yes, certainly it was true. Ian knew she was right.

Or look at Claudia. The family's one scholar, she had dropped out of college her senior year to get married, and then the babies started coming so thick and so fast that they had to be named alphabetically: Abbie, Barney, Cindy, Davey . . . Where would it all end? some cynical voice inquired from the depths of Ian's mind. Xavier? Zelda? But his mother said she hoped they would progress to *double* letters—Aaron Abel and Bonnie Belinda—like items on a crowded catalog page. Then Ian saw Claudia's children as a tumbling hodgepodge heaped in a basket, and he was forced to smile.

Or Danny. Wasn't it sort of a comedown that Danny had gone to work at the post office straight out of high school, when both sides of the family as far back as anyone could remember had been teachers? ("Educators," Bee called them.) But Bee pointed out how lucky he was, knowing so early in life what he wanted and settling in so contentedly. Then Ian readjusted; he shifted gears or something and *whir*! he was rolling along with the others, impressed by Danny's good fortune.

He had always assumed he was the only one who experienced that hitch in his thoughts. He assumed it until the day Lucy arrived, when he felt his parents' hidden start at the word "ex-husband." Wait. The girl of Danny's dreams had chosen someone else before him? And was saddling him with someone else's children besides? His father looked confused. His mother's broad face developed a brittle, tight surface, like something easily broken.

Ian himself absorbed the notion with no trouble. Of course, he wanted only the best for Danny. He had worshiped Danny since infancy—the family's all-round athlete, talented in every known sport but not the least stuck up about it, unfailingly sunny-natured and patient with his little brother. But as Ian saw it, Lucy *was* the best. The ex-husband was only a minor drawback; same for the children. What mattered was that pile of black hair and those long black lashes. None of Danny's previous girls could begin to compare with this one.

But he saw how steadily his parents smiled—stony, glazed smiles as they murmured chitchat. His mother said it certainly was an unusual way for a couple to meet. His father said he'd have opted for parcel post, himself; so *he* would never have been asked to dinner, would he, heh-heh. His mother said that speaking of dinner, Lucy must stay for spaghetti. Danny said she couldn't; he was taking her to Haussner's Restaurant to celebrate their engagement. The word "engagement" sent another shock through the room; for now it was plain that, yes, Danny really was set on this. Bee said maybe later in the week, then. Lucy thanked her in her foggy, fascinating voice. They all stood up. Ian stepped away from the door frame and received his first direct glance from Lucy. She had pure gray eyes, almost silver, and up close her little nose revealed a sprinkling of freckles.

After Danny and Lucy had left, his parents returned to the living room and sat back down on the couch. Supper was more than ready, but no one mentioned eating. Ian wandered over to the upright piano in the corner. Dozens of family photos, framed in dull brass or varnished wood, stood on an ivory lace runner. Other, larger photos hung behind, nearly obscuring the flowered wallpaper that had darkened over the years to the color of a manila envelope. He studied those: his grandmother standing grimly erect beside his seated grandfather, his Great-Aunt Bess trying to master a hula hoop, Danny in a satin track uniform with a first-place ribbon hung around his neck. Whenever Danny did something he enjoyed, his face would shine with a fine sweat. Even eating made him sweat, or listening to music. And in this photograph—where he'd recently been sprinting under hot sunshine, after all, and then had the pleasure of winning besides—he gleamed; he seemed metallic. You could imagine he was a statue. Ian lightly touched the frame. (Dust felted his finger. For all her great clattery housecleaning, Bee tended to let the little things slide.) Behind him, his mother said, "Well, we've been wishing for years he'd get married."

"That's true, we have," his father said.

"And now that the draft's stepping up . . ."

"Oh, yes, the draft," his father said faintly.

"Did she mention how many children she had?"

"Not that I can recall."

"If she has lots," Bee told him, "we can mix them in with Claudia's and form our own baseball team."

She laughed. Ian turned to look at her, but he was too late. Already she had passed smoothly over to unquestioning delight, and he had missed his chance to see how she did it.

Lucy did not have lots of children after all; just two. A girl aged six and a boy aged three. She lived a couple of miles away, Danny said, in a rented apartment above a Hampden pharmacy; and she left the children with the pharmacist's wife when she went to work every day. He told Ian this later that night, when he stopped by Ian's room on his way to bed. He said she worked as a waitress at the Fill 'Er Up Café—the only job she could find that allowed her to arrange her hours around her children's. But he would soon put an end to *that*, Danny said. No working wife for Danny.

He said she had mailed that package at the request of her ex-husband. Her ex-husband was getting remarried and he wanted her to send him his things. Lucy had packed up every trace of him: the geisha girl figurine he'd won tossing darts at the fair, for instance, and the bowling ball in the red-and-white canvas bag that matched her own. Danny listed these objects in a detailed and lingering way, as if even they had fallen within the circle of his love. The bowling ball, he said, had accounted for much of the package's weight (a total of twenty-eight pounds). Lucy had also mentioned a trophy cup, which couldn't have been so very light either.

Ian tried to imagine Lucy bowling. Illogically, he pictured her in the shoes she had worn to the house—little red pumps with red cloth roses at the toes. The high heels would make tiny dimples in the glossy wood of the runway.

"She's a wonderful cook," Danny said. "Whenever I come to dinner she fixes a special meal for me and she lights new candles. Lucy feels people should always eat by candlelight. And sometimes she makes her own holders; last night it was two red apples. Wasn't that smart? She has the smartest ideas. She's good with napkins, too; she folds them into these different shapes, accordions or butterflies or wigwams, because Lucy says . . ."

Lucy says, Lucy feels, Lucy believes. She seemed almost present in the room with them. Danny lounged in the doorway with his hands in his trouser pockets, his eyes slanting slightly the way they did when something fired him up. The knot of his tie hung loose on his chest, which made him look tipsy even though he wasn't.

How did their evenings *end*? Ian wanted to ask. Did the two of them make out on her couch? Or maybe even go all the way?

Danny spoke of Lucy's knack for interior decorating, her concern for her children, her difficult past life. "Both her parents died in a car crash when she was still in her teens," he said, "and that husband of hers must not have been much, considering how far he's fallen behind on the child support. Not that she complains. She never says a word against anyone; that's not her style. I tell you, Ian, I've been looking for a woman like Lucy all my life, but I'd started to think I'd never find her. I almost thought there was something wrong with me. I'd meet these girls who seemed so pretty and so nice and then it would turn out I'd been hood-winked; they were flirts or users or constitutional liars and everyone knew it but me. Shouldn't there be some sort of training course in how to judge a woman? How are guys supposed to figure these things out? Well, some just do; it's some kind of gift, I guess. But I was starting to worry I was jinxed. Then along comes Lucy. Two weeks ago she was a total stranger, can you believe it? And yet I'm certain she's the one. She makes her own curtains and she cuts her children's hair herself. She can plant a snipped-off twig in a pot and it will turn green and start growing. When I circle her waist with my hands, my fingertips almost meet."

Ian somehow knew exactly how that would feel: her body narrowing between his palms like a slender, graceful vase.

Danny and Lucy were married a week later, in the Presbyterian church on Dober Street that the Bedloes sporadically attended. Lucy wore a rose-colored suit and a white pillbox hat with a bow. She stood in front of the minister with her arm linked through Danny's, and her feet were placed primly together so that Ian's eyes were riveted to the seams on the backs of her stockings. He had never seen seams on stockings before, if you didn't count old black-and-white movies. He wondered how she got them so straight. They looked like two fountain-pen lines drawn with the aid of a ruler.

Pathetically few guests dotted the bride's side of the church. The first pew held a couple of waitresses from the Fill 'Er Up Café, both wearing cone-shaped hairdos that made them seem the tallest people present. Behind them sat the pharmacist and his wife, with Lucy's two children huddled against the wife. Ian had met the children at a family dinner the night before, and he hadn't thought much of them. Agatha was as cloddish as her name—plain and thick, pasty-faced. Thomas was thin and dark and nimble but no more responsive to grownups. During the wedding they both gazed elsewhere—up at the vaulted ceiling, around at the pebbly pink windows—till Mrs. Myrdal leaned over and whispered sharply. Agatha was the kind of child who breathed through her mouth.

But the groom's side! First came the parents, Doug Bedloe belted in and slicked down in an unfamiliar way and Bee wearing a new striped dress from Hutzler's. Then in the second pew, a row of Daleys—Claudia and her husband, Macy, and all five of their rustling, fidgeting children, even little Ellen, although a sitter had been hired to lurk at the rear of the church just in case. Ian sat in the third pew with Cicely, holding hands. And if he turned around, he could see Danny's friends from high school and his co-workers from the post office and just about the whole neighborhood as well: the Cahns, the Crains, the Mercers, Cicely's parents and her brother Stevie, Mrs. Jordan in her bald fur stole even on this warm May day, and every last one of the foreigners—a row of tan young men wearing identical shiny black suits. The foreigners never missed a chance to attend a celebration.

The minister spoke at some length about the institution of marriage. Danny shifted his weight a few times but Lucy stayed dutifully motionless. Ian wondered why a hat like hers was called a pillbox. It looked more like a pill than a box, he thought—a big white aspirin.

Cicely squeezed his hand and Ian squeezed back, but not as hard. (She was wearing his class ring, bulky as a brass knuckle.) Distantly, he registered the bridal couple's "I do's"—Danny's so emphatic that the younger Daleys giggled, Lucy's throaty and endearing. Then Dr. Prescott pronounced them man and wife, and they kissed. It wasn't one of those show-off kisses you sometimes see at weddings. Lucy just turned and looked up into Danny's eyes, and Danny set both hands on her shoulders and bent to press his lips against hers very gently. After that they stepped back and smiled at the guests, and everyone rose and came forward to offer congratulations.

The reception was held at the Bedloes', with fancy little cakes that Bee and Claudia had been baking for days, and Doug's famous spiked punch in a plastic garbage can reserved only for that purpose, and bottled soft drinks for the children. There were more than enough children. Claudia's brood chased each other through a forest of grownups' legs. Rafe Hamnett's sexy twin ten-year-old daughters stood over by the piano, each slinging out a hip and brandishing a paper straw like a cigarette. Only Lucy's two seemed not to be enjoying themselves. They sat on a windowsill, almost hidden by the curtains on either side. At one point Cicely dragged Ian over to try and make friends with them—she was known at school for being "considerate"—but it wasn't a success. Thomas shrank against his sister and picked at a Band-Aid wrapped around his thumb. Agatha kept her arms folded and stared past them at her mother, who was offering a small hand to each guest as Danny introduced her. ("Honey, this is Melvin Cahn, who lives next door. Melvin, like you to meet the woman who's changed my life.")

Cicely asked Agatha, "Isn't it nice that you have a new uncle? Think of it: Uncle Ian."

Agatha shifted her gaze to Cicely as if it took real effort.

"Isn't that nice?" Cicely said.

Agatha finally nodded.

"She's overcome with joy," Ian told Cicely.

Cicely made a face at him. She was a pert, sweet, round-eyed girl with a bubbly head of blond curls. Today she wore a yellow shift that turned her breasts into two little upturned teacups. Ian laced his fingers through hers and said, "Let's go to your place."

"Go? I haven't said hello to your folks yet."

But she let him lead her away, past Doug Bedloe with his punch dipper poised, past her little brother with his six-gun, past the foreigners practicing their English on the front porch. "Is it not fine day," one of them said—Joe or Jim or Jack; they all had these super-American names shortened from who-knows-what. They stood back respectfully and followed Cicely with their eyes (how they admired blondes!) as Ian guided her down the steps.

Next to the curb, Danny's blue Chevy stood waiting. The bride and groom were driving to Williamsburg for their honeymoon—just a three-day trip because that was the longest Lucy felt comfortable leaving the children. Some of the neighborhood teenagers had tied tin cans to the rear bumper and chalked JUST MARRIED across the trunk. *Married!* Ian thought, and he realized, all at once, that Danny really had gone through with it. He was a husband now and would never again stop by Ian's bedroom door at night, his suit coat hooked over his thumb, to talk about the Baltimore Colts. Ian felt a rush of sorrow. But Cicely's parents wouldn't stay at the reception forever, so he said, "Let's go," and they started walking toward her house.

That summer, Ian got a job with Sid 'n' Ed's A-1 Movers—a very local sort of company consisting of a single van. Each morning he reported to a garage on Greenmount, and then he and two lean, black, jokey men drove to some shabby house where they heaved liquor cartons and furniture into the van for a couple of hours. Then they drove to some other house, often even shabbier, and heaved it all out again. Ian managed to enjoy the work because he thought of it as weight lifting. He had always been very conscious of muscles. As a small boy, admiring Danny and his friends at sports, he had focused upon their forearms—the braiding beneath the skin as they swung a bat or punched a volleyball. There, he thought, was the telling difference, more than whiskers or deep voices. And he had examined his own reedy arms and wondered if they would ever change. But when it happened he must have been asleep, for all at once two summers ago he had noticed as he was mowing the lawn—why, look at that! The ropy muscles from wrist to elbow, the distinct blue cords of his veins. He had flexed a fist and gazed down, hypnotized, till his mother hallooed from the porch and asked how long he planned to stand there.

Well, like a lot of other things, muscles had turned out to be no big deal after all. (Now he thought it might be sleeping with a girl that made the difference.) But even so, he continued to work at building himself up. He deliberately chose the heaviest pieces of furniture, pushing ahead of Lou and LeDon, who were happy to lag behind with the bric-a-brac. Then in the evenings he came home hot and sweaty and swaggery, and his mother would say, "Phew! Go take a shower before you do another thing." He stood under the shower till the water ran cold, after which he dressed in fresh jeans and a T-shirt and went off to eat dinner at Cicely's. His mother hardly cooked at all that summer. Claudia was sick as a dog with her latest pregnancy, so often as not Bee would have spent the day baby-sitting. Sometimes she said, "What, you're eating at the Browns' *again*?" But he could tell she was just as glad. She and his father would have a sandwich in front of the TV, or they'd walk over to Lipton's. She said, "Mind you don't wear out your welcome, now." Then she forgot about him.

He and Cicely twined their feet together under the table while her mother served him double portions of everything. Cicely slid a hand secretly up his thigh, and Ian rearranged his napkin and swallowed and told Mrs. Brown how much he liked her cooking. Mr. Brown was usually absent, out selling insurance to homeowners who could be reached only in the evenings, but Cicely's little brother was there—a pest and a nuisance. He would tag along after dinner, boring Ian to death with baseball questions. He hung around the two of them on the screened back porch. "*Stee*-vie!" Cicely would say, and Stevie would ask, "What? What am I doing?"

"Don't you have any friends of your own?"

"I'm not doing anything."

"Ma, Stevie's being a brat again."

"Stevie, come along inside, now," Mrs. Brown would call.

Then Stevie would leave, kicking the glider as he passed and lowering his prickly, white-blond head so no one could see his face.

Ian and Cicely had been going together since ninth grade. They were planning to get married after college, although sometimes Cicely teased him and said she'd have to see who else asked her, first. "Change the name and not the letter, change for worse and not for better," she said. But then she would move over into Ian's lap and wrap her arms around his neck. She smelled of baby powder, warm and pink. She wore pink underwear, too—a slippery pink bra with lace edges. Sometimes when they had been kissing a while she would let him unfasten the hook at the back, but he had to be careful not to tickle. She was the most ticklish person he had ever met. Things would just be getting interesting when all at once she would pull away and fall into peals of helpless laughter. Ian felt like a fool when that happened. "Oh, great. Just great," he would say, and she would say, "It's not *my* fault if your hands are cold."

"Cold? It's ninety-eight degrees out."

"That's not *my* fault."

Did other girls behave like this? He would bet they didn't. He wished she were, oh, more womanly, sometimes. More experienced. He said, "This is supposed to be a moment of romantic passion, must I remind you." He said, "We're not in kindergarten, here." Once he said, "Have you ever considered wearing stockings that have seams?" But when Cicely started laughing she just couldn't seem to stop, and all she did was shake her head and wipe the tears from her eyes.

One August afternoon, he came home from work to find a note on the hall table: *Claudia in hospital, Dad and I staying with kids.* At first he didn't think much about this. Claudia was nearly always in the hospital, it seemed to him, giving birth to one baby or another. He dropped the note in the wastebasket and climbed the stairs, with the dog panting hopefully behind him. But then while he was showering, it occurred to him that Claudia couldn't be having her baby yet. She didn't even look very pregnant yet. He'd better call his mother and find out what was wrong.

As soon as he was dressed, he bounded back downstairs to use the phone. But on the next-to-last step he heard somebody crossing the dining room. Beastie, following close on his heels, uttered a low growl. Then Lucy appeared in the doorway. "Ian?" she said.

"Oh," he said.

She wore a big white shirt of Danny's and a pair of red pedal pushers, and her hair was tied back in a red bandanna. She looked about twelve years old. "Have you talked with your mom yet?" she asked him.

"No, but she left a note. What's the matter with Claudia?"

"Oh, nothing all that serious. Just, you know, a little bleeding . . ."

Ian began studying an area slightly above her head.

"So anyway," she said, "I thought I'd fix you some supper. Ordinarily I'd invite you to our place, but we're going out so I brought something over. There's potato salad, and ham, and I've put some peas on the stove to warm up."

He didn't tell her he usually ate at Cicely's. All summer the family had tactfully left her and Danny alone, allowing them to get past the honeymoon stage, so they met only on special occasions like Bee's birthday and the Fourth of July. Lucy must not have any notion about their day-to-day lives.

He followed her through the dining room to the kitchen, where he found Thomas and Agatha sitting in two straight-backed chairs. There was something eerie about children who kept so quiet you didn't realize they were in the house. Thomas held a large, naked doll with a matted wig. Agatha's hands were folded tidily on the table in front of her. They looked at Ian with no more expression than the doll wore. Ian said, "Well, hi, gang," but neither of them answered.

He leaned against the sink and watched Lucy flitting around the kitchen. Her hair billowed halfway down her back, longer than he would have expected. She wore white sandals and her toenails were painted fire-engine red. None of the girls at school painted their nails anymore. Every-one was striving for the natural look, which all at once struck Ian as homely.

He realized she must have spoken to him. She was facing him with her head cocked. "Pardon?" he asked.

"Do you want your ham cold, or heated up?"

"Oh, um, cold is fine."

"It won't be real fancy," she said, opening the refrigerator. "Tomorrow if your mom's still busy we'll ask you to dinner. Why, you haven't been over since I painted the living room!"

"No, I guess not," Ian said.

She and Danny were renting a one-story house just north of Cold Spring Lane. So far they had hardly any furniture, but everything they did have was modern, modern, modern—black plastic and aluminum and glass. Bee claimed it would take some getting used to, but Ian loved it.

"Next week I start on the children's room," Lucy said. "I found this magazine with the best ideas! Sit down, why don't you."

He pulled out a chair and sat across from the children. A place had al-ready been laid for him with the company silver and his mother's best china. Two candlesticks from the dining room flanked a bowl of pansies. He began to feel ridiculous, like one of those rich people in cartoons who banquet all alone while a butler stands at the ready. He asked Thomas and Agatha, "Am I the only one eating?"

They gazed at him. Their eyes were a mournful shade of brown.

"How about you?" he asked Thomas's doll. "Won't you join me in a little collation?"

He caught Thomas's lips twitching—a victory. A chink of a giggle es-caped him. But Agatha remained unamused. "Her name is Dulcimer," she said reprovingly.

"Dulcimer?"

"Ian doesn't care about all that," Lucy told them.

"She used to have clothes," Agatha said, "but Thomas went and ruined them."

"I did not!" Thomas shouted.

Lucy said, "Ssh," and lit the candles.

"She used to have a dress with two pockets, but he put it in the washer and it came out bits and pieces."

"That was the washer did that, not me!"

"Now she has to go bare, because his other dolls' clothes are too little."

Ian forked up a slice of ham and looked again at Dulcimer. Her body was cloth, soiled to dark gray. Her head was pink vinyl and so were her arms and her legs, which had a wide-set, spraddled appearance. "Maybe she could wear real baby clothes," he suggested.

"Mama won't—"

"That's what I say, too!" Thomas burst out.

"Mama won't let her," Agatha continued stubbornly. There was something unswerving about her. She reminded Ian of certain grade-school teachers he had known. "Mama's got all these baby clothes she buys at Hochschild's, nightgowns and diapers and stuff Dulcimer would *love*, but Mama won't lend them out."

"Have some peas," Lucy told Ian.

"Oh, thanks, I'll just—"

"Today she bought a teeny-weeny baby hat with blue ribbons but she says if Thomas plays with it he'll get it dirty," Agatha said.

Ian looked over at Lucy, and Lucy looked back at him ruefully. She said, "Don't tell the others, will you?"

"Okay."

"I want to wait till Claudia gets out of the hospital."

"My lips are sealed," he said.

It was a pleasurable moment, sharing a secret with Lucy. The secret itself, though, he wasn't so sure of. He thought of Danny circling her waist with his hands, his fingertips nearly meeting. Couldn't he have let her stay as she was? Did everything have to keep marching forward all the time?

She said, "We ought to get going, kids."

"Well, thanks for the food," Ian told her.

"You're very welcome."

After they left he could have stopped eating—he was already late for supper at Cicely's—but he worried Lucy would find out somehow and feel hurt. So he made his way through everything, sweating in the candlelight, which was, to tell the truth, sort of uncomfortable for August. She had laid out the ham slices in a careful, scalloped design that reminded him of the patterns etched alongside the ocean. And although it would have saddened him to let the ham go to waste, it saddened him too to finish it and end up with just the empty plate.

Claudia did manage to keep her baby. In fact, she went way past her due date. Her doctor had predicted the first week in December, but things dragged on so long that Ian started betting the baby would arrive on his birthday, January 2. "Oh, please," Claudia said. "Let's hope to God you're wrong." She was big as a house and her ankles were swollen and she'd had to have her rings cut off with a hacksaw. At Christmas she was still lumbering around, and Christmas dinner was a spectacle, with Claudia and Lucy sitting elbow to elbow in their ballooning maternity smocks. Lucy turned out to be the type who carried her baby a great distance in front of her (something to do with her small frame, perhaps), so that even though she had two months to go, she looked nearly as pregnant as Claudia. She was officially a member of the family now—the honeymoon joyfully over and done with, in the Bedloes' eyes, the moment she announced her good news. Now they felt free to stop by her house more often and to invite her and Danny for potluck. Ian had almost reached the point where he could take her for granted. Although still when she turned her silvery gaze upon him he had an arrested feeling, a sense of a skipped beat in the atmosphere of the room.

One of the Bedloe traditions was that important dinners, on holidays and such, were not the usual boring assortment of meats and vegetables. Instead, Bee served their favorite course: hors d'oeuvres. Oh, there'd be a turkey at Thanksgiving, cakes for birthdays, but those were just a nod to convention. What mattered were the stuffed mushrooms, the runny cheeses, the spreads and dips and pâtés and shrimps on toothpicks. The family was secretly proud of this practice; they enjoyed watching guests' reactions. Nothing humdrum about the Bedloes! That Christmas they had oysters on the half shell, and the look of horror on Lucy's children's faces made everybody laugh. "Never mind," Danny told them. "You don't have to eat them if you don't want to."

Danny was exuberant these days. He had researched pregnancy and childbirth as if he expected to deliver the baby himself, and he kept a long scroll of possible names scrunched in his pocket. For some strange reason, he seemed very fond of Thomas and Agatha. Well, Thomas was all right, Ian supposed. He looked kind of cute in his dapper little sailor outfit. But Agatha! Really there was only so much you could do with such a child. Her frilly pink dress made her face appear all the more wooden, and her hair stood out at her jaw in a monolithic wedge. Sometimes Ian caught her giving him one of her flat stares, reminding him of that doll that Thomas was so attached to. Dulcimer. Same numb, blank face, same unseeing eyes.

They moved to the living room and settled themselves, groaning. The cat threw up an oyster behind the couch. Barney fed cracker crumbs to the goldfish, Abbie played "The First Noel" on the piano with a rhythm as ponderous as army boots, and Doug brought out his Polaroid Land camera and took pictures of them all—each photo after the first one showing somebody holding a previous photo, admiring it or grimacing or industriously coating it with fixative. Then little Cindy, who had fallen asleep in front of the fire, woke up cranky, and the dog accidentally stepped on her and made her cry. Claudia said, "That's our cue! Time to go!" and she heaved herself to her feet. They all departed at once—Claudia's family and Danny's—leaving behind a litter of torn gift wrap and mismatched mittens and oyster shells. "This was our best Christmas ever, wasn't it?" Bee asked Doug. But she always said that.

Claudia's baby came two days later—a girl. Frances, they named her. Ian said, "Well, I was *almost* right. It's almost my birthday."

"Cheer up," Bee told him. "There's always the next one."

"Next one! Good grief."

The next one of Claudia's, they both meant. It never occurred to them that *Lucy's* baby might arrive on his birthday. But that was what happened.

He had spent the evening at Ciccly's, where she and his friends threw him a party. When he got home he found his mother waiting up for him. "Guess what!" she said. "Lucy had her baby."

"What, so soon?"

"A little girl: Daphne. She's small but healthy, breathing on her own . . . Danny called about an hour ago and he was so excited he could hardly talk."

"After this he won't be fit to live with," Ian said gloomily.

"And Lucy's doing fine. Oh, won't the neighbors tease us? They'll be counting on their fingers, except in this case it's obvious that . . . you want to go with me to the hospital tomorrow?"

"I have school tomorrow," Ian said.

Besides, he had never been much interested in infants.

He didn't see the new baby for a week, in fact, what with one thing and another. Neither did Claudia, who was stuck at home with her own baby. So on Sunday, when everyone gathered at the Bedloes' for dinner, Danny made a big production of introducing his daughter. "Ta-da!" he trumpeted, and he entered the house bearing her high in both hands—a tiny cluster of crochet work. "Here she is, folks! Miss Daphne Bedloe." Lucy looked paler than usual, but she laughed as she bent to unbutton Thomas's jacket.

"Let's see her," Claudia commanded from the couch. She had constructed a kind of nest there and was nursing Franny. Ian had retreated to the other side of the room as soon as he saw Claudia fumbling under her blouse, and he made no move now to come closer. All newborns looked more or less alike, he figured. And this one might still be sort of . . . fetus-shaped. He hung back and dug his hands in his pockets and traced an arc in the rug with one sneaker.

But Danny said, "Don't you want to see too, Ian?" and he sounded so hurt that Ian had to say, "Huh? Oh. Sure." He took his hands from his pockets and approached.

Danny set her on the couch next to Claudia and started peeling off layers. First the crocheted blanket, then an inner blanket, then a bonnet. His fingers seemed too thick for the task, but finally he said, "There!" and straightened up, grinning.

What was that fairy tale? "Sleeping Beauty," maybe, or "Snow White." Skin as white as snow and hair as black as coal and lips as red as roses. So she was prettier than most other babies, yes, but still not all that interesting. Until she opened her eyes.

She opened her eyes and fixed Ian with a thoughtful, considering stare, and Ian felt a sudden loosening in his chest. It seemed she had reached out and pulled a string from somewhere deep inside him. It seemed she *knew* him. He blinked.

"Your birthday-mate," Danny was saying. "Or birthmate, or whatever they call it. Isn't she something?"

To regain his distance, Ian let his eyes slide over to Claudia. He found her looking directly into his face, meaningfully, narrowly. He couldn't think what she wanted to convey; he didn't understand her intensity. Then it came to him, as clearly as if she had spoken.

This is not a premature baby.

He was so astonished that he let his eyes slide back again, forgetting why he had glanced away in the first place. And it was true: she might be small but her cheeks were round, and her little fists were dimpled. She looked nothing like those "Life Before Birth" photos in *Life* magazine.

"Isn't she a love?" Bee asked. "Two loves," she added, blowing a kiss toward Franny. And Claudia said, "She's a beauty, Lucy."

Ian turned to study Claudia. She was smiling now. Her face—a younger, smoother version of Bee's—seemed relaxed and peaceful. The hitch had been smoothed over. Not a trace of it remained. Here was their newest member, born early but in perfect health, thank God, and everything in the Bedloe family was as wonderful as always.

Well, hold on (Ian told himself). Don't be too hasty. Daphne was no longer brand-new, after all. She'd had six whole days to catch up before he laid eyes on her. Best to put the subject right out of his mind.

But over the next few weeks it kept sidling back, somehow.

If Danny and Lucy had been going together forever, why, a seven-months baby (quote, unquote) would have been something to wink at. But they hadn't been going together forever. Nine months ago they hadn't even known each other. Lucy had not yet walked into the post office to plunk her famous package on Danny's counter. She might have been dating someone else entirely.

In school last year a senior had had to get married to a girl he swore he hardly knew. Or rather, he swore *everybody* knew her. It was Ian's first intimation of the fix a man could find himself in. Women were the ones who held the reins, it emerged. Women were up close to things. Men stood off at one remove and were forced to accept women's reading of whatever happened. Probably this was what Ian's father had been trying to tell him in that talk they'd had a few years ago, but Ian hadn't fully understood it at the time.

One night he asked Cicely, "What do you think of Lucy?"

"Oh, I just love her," Cicely said.

"Yes, but—"

"She's always so easy to talk to; she always asks me these questions that show she's been listening. Real questions, I mean. Not those who-cares questions most other grownups ask."

"Yes . . ." Ian said, because he had noticed the same thing himself.

Lucy had a grave, focused manner of looking at him. He could imagine she had been reflecting upon him seriously ever since their last meeting.

"I just think Danny is lucky to have her," Cicely said, and Ian said, "Well, yes, he is. Yes, he is lucky."

Ian had quit his job with Sid 'n' Ed's when school reopened; his mother made him. This was his senior year and she wanted him to concentrate on getting into a halfway decent college. The last thing he needed was to waste his time hauling other people's mattresses, she said.

But what she didn't seem to realize was that a person his age had to have a social life, and a social life took money. By February, he was broke. So when Lucy called and asked if he would baby-sit—a job he hated, and one he was ill equipped for besides, as youngest in his family—he didn't immediately refuse. "Well," he said, stalling, "but I don't even know how to change a diaper."

"You wouldn't have to," Lucy told him. "I would change her just before I left. And most likely she'd be sleeping; this would be afternoons."

"Oh. Afternoons."

"Just a couple of hours after school now and then. Please, Ian? I'm about to lose my mind cooped up all day. And I can't keep imposing on your mother, and Mrs. Myrdal won't come anymore and Cicely's got cheerleading practice. I just want to get out on my own a while—go shopping or take a walk with nobody hanging onto me. I'd pay you a dollar an hour."

"You would?" he said.

On the rare occasions Claudia had talked him into sitting, the pay had been fifty cents.

"And Thomas and Agatha have taken such a shine to you. They're the ones who suggested you."

"Oh, well, in that case," Ian said. "If it's a matter of popular demand . . ."

So he started walking over from school one or two afternoons a week and staying till dusk. It wasn't a job that required much work, but somehow he found it far more tiring than Sid 'n' Ed's. No wonder Lucy wanted a break! This was the coldest, grayest time of year, and the stark modern furniture that had seemed so elegant in the summer had a bleak feel in the winter. Toys and picture books covered the white vinyl couch. Sheaves of Agatha's pulpy first-grade papers lay scattered across the rug. Thomas and Agatha had the used, slightly tarnished look that even the best-tended children take on late in the day, and they pressed in upon him too closely, drilling him with questions. Was Ian ever going to play in the World Series? Did he know how to drive a car? A motorcycle? An airplane? Did he and Cicely go to many balls? (This last from Agatha, who had a big crush on Cicely.) Gradually he forgot that they had once been tongue-tied in his presence.

They clung to the belief that Ian felt a special affection for Dulcimer, and they always made a point of displaying what she was wearing that day—one or another infant outfit handed down from Daphne. "Why, Miss Dulcimer!" Ian would say. "I do believe fuzzy pink flannel is your most becoming fabric." They thought it was hilarious when he spoke to her directly. Then they might play Parcheesi—Ian's idea; all the Bedloes loved any kind of game—or he read to them, his throat aching tightly with held-back yawns as he imitated various squeaky animals.

Daphne was usually an invisible, slumbering presence, but if Lucy stayed out too long Ian might hear a tentative cry from the children's room. He would find her lying in her crib, sucking her fist and watching the door so his first impression was always that considering stare. She was the only person he knew of with navy blue eyes. He would lift her awkwardly, in a bunch, pretending not to notice the dampness seeping around the legs of her terry-cloth pajamas. He would carry her to the kitchen and set a bottle in the electric warmer. Waiting for it to heat, he breathed her smell of warm urine and something vanilla-ish—maybe just her skin. Thomas tugged at one of her terry-cloth feet. "Hey there, Daffy. Daffy-doo." Daphne squirmed and murmured into the curve of Ian's neck.

When Lucy returned, she brought a burst of cold air through the door with her. The cold seemed to lie on her surface in a sparkling film. And she was always lit up and laughing, excited by her expedition. She would hold out her arms to the children. "Were you good?" she would ask. "Did you miss me?" and she'd take the baby from Ian and nuzzle her face, nose to nose. "Guess what: I felt a couple of snowflakes. I bet we're going to have snow tonight." Balancing Daphne on her hip, she would fish in her big shoulder bag for Ian's pay—generously rounding off to the nearest dollar, sometimes even adding a tip and telling him to take Cicely someplace nice. Ian knew that she and Danny weren't rich, and he would protest but she always insisted. "Well, thanks," he'd say lamely, and she would say, "Thank *you*! You don't know how you saved my life." Her money smelled of her cologne, a tingly scent that clung to the bills for hours afterward and hung in his room when he emptied his pockets at bedtime.

One afternoon when she returned there was something distracted about her. She greeted the children absently and failed to inquire after Daphne, who was still asleep. "Ian," she said right away, "can I ask you something?"

"Sure."

"Can I ask what you think of this dress?"

She slipped her coat off, revealing a different dress from the one she had left the house in. Holding her arms out at her sides, she spun like a fashion model. Thomas and Agatha gazed at her raptly. So did Ian.

It was the most beautiful piece of clothing he had ever seen in his life. The material was a luminous ivory knit, very soft and drapey, but over her breasts and her hips it was perfectly smooth. What would you call such material? He could imagine its silkiness against his fingertips.

"Do you think Danny will mind?" Lucy asked. "I don't want him to feel I'm a spendthrift. Do you think I should take it back?"

"Oh, well, I wouldn't," Ian said. "Now that you've gone to the bother of lugging it home."

She looked down at it, doubtfully.

He told her, "That, um, what-do-you-call . . ."

That V neckline, he wanted to say, *plunging so low in the middle. And that skirt that whisks around your legs and makes that shimmery sound.*

But what he said was, "That cloth is not bad at all."

"But would you think it cost a lot?"

"Oh, only about a million," he said. "Give or take a few thousand."

"No, don't say that! That's what I was afraid of. But it didn't cost hardly anything, I promise. You want to know what it cost? Nineteen ninety-five. Can you believe it? Can you believe that's all it cost?"

Well, she did want his answer, after all. So he reached out to touch the fabric at her waist. It was so fine-spun it made his fingers feel as rough as rope. He curved his palm to cup her rib cage and he felt the warmth of her skin underneath. Then Lucy took a sharp step backward and he dropped his hand to his side.

"Oh, ah, nineteen ninety-five sounds . . . very reasonable," he said. His voice seemed to be coming from somewhere else. There was a moment of silence. All he heard was Agatha's snuffling breath.

"But anyhow!" Lucy said, and she laughed too gaily, artificially, and lifted her bag from the table. "Thanks for your opinion!" she said. Was she being sarcastic? She owed him two dollars but she paid him five. A hundred-and-fifty-percent tip. He said, "I'll bring your change next time I see you," and she said, "No, keep it. Really."

He felt mortified by that.

Walking home through the twilight, he kicked at clumps of old snow and muttered to himself. Once or twice he groaned out loud. When he entered the front hall Bee said, "Hi, hon! How was our little Daffodil?" But Ian merely brushed past her and climbed the stairs to his room.

Over the next few days—a Friday and a weekend—he didn't baby-sit; nor would he have ordinarily. He and Cicely went to a movie; he and his two best friends, Pig and Andrew, went bowling. Striding toward the foul line with the bowling ball suspended from his fingers, he thought of Lucy mailing that package to Wyoming. What kind of woman owns her own bowling ball? Not to mention the geisha girl figurine.

Really there was a great deal about Lucy that was, oh, a little bit tacky, when you came right down to it. (What a relief, to discover she wasn't flawless!) Now he recalled the grammatical slips, *It won't be real fancy* and *It didn't cost hardly anything*; the way she sometimes wore her hair down even with high heels; the fact that she had no people. He knew it wasn't her fault her parents had died, but still you'd expect a few family connections—brothers and sisters, aunts, at least cousins. And how about friends? He didn't count those two waitresses; they were just workmates. No, Lucy kept to herself, and when she went out in the afternoons she went alone and she returned alone. He envisioned her rushing in from one of her shopping trips, her cheeks flushed pink with excitement.

Funny how she never brought any parcels back.

Why, even last Thursday she'd brought no parcel, the day she came home with that dress.

She hadn't bought that dress at all. Someone had given it to her.

She wasn't out shopping. She was meeting someone.

She had asked if the dress looked expensive. Not *Do you think I paid too much?* but *Could I get away with saying I paid next to nothing?* "Can you believe it?" she had asked. (Insistently, it seemed to him now.) What she'd meant was, *Will DANNY believe it, if I tell him I bought it myself?*

He watched the bowling ball crash into the pins with a hollow, splintery sound, and a thrill of malicious satisfaction zinged through him like an electrical current.

When she phoned Monday night to ask if he could baby-sit the following afternoon, he felt confused by the realness of her. He had somehow forgotten the confiding effect of that gravelly little voice. But he was busy, he told her. He had to study for a test. She said, "Then how about Wednesday?"

He said he couldn't come Wednesday either. "Besides," he said, "baseball practice is starting soon, so I guess after this I won't be free anymore."

Lucy said, "Oh."

"Pressing athletic obligations, and all that," he said.

There was a pause. He forced himself not to speak. Instead he conjured up a picture of Danny, for whose sake he was doing this. His only brother! His dearest relative, who trusted everyone completely and believed whatever you told him.

"Well, thanks anyway," Lucy said sadly, and then she said goodbye. Ian was suddenly not so certain. He wondered if he had misjudged her. He stood gripping the receiver and he noticed how his heart ached, as if it were he, not Lucy, who had been wounded.

For Doug's birthday, Bee made his favorite hors d'oeuvres—smoked oyster log and spinach balls and Chesapeake crab spread. Claudia made a coconut cake that looked like a white shag bathmat. She and her family were the first to arrive. She had Ian come out to the kitchen with her to help put on the candles—fifty-nine of them, this year. Ian wasn't in a very good mood, but Claudia kept joshing him so finally he had to smile. You couldn't stay glum around Claudia for long; she was so funny and slap-dash and comfortable, in her boxy tan plaid shirt the same color as her skin and the maternity slacks she was wearing till she got her figure back. They ran out of birthday candles and started using other kinds—three tall white tapers and several of those stubby votive lights their mother kept for power failures. By now they had the giggles. It was almost like the old days, when Claudia wasn't married yet and still belonged completely to the family.

So Ian said, "Hey, Claude."

"Hmm?"

"You know Lucy."

"What about her?" she asked, still teary with laughter.

"*You* don't think she had that baby early. Do you?"

Her smile faded.

"Do you?" he persisted.

"Oh, Ian, who am I to say?"

"I'm wondering if somebody ought to tell Danny," he said.

"Tell him?" she said. "No, wait. You mean, talk about it? You can't do that!"

"But he looks like a dummy, Claude. He looks so . . . fooled!"

He was louder than he'd meant to be. Claudia glanced toward the door. Then she set a hand on his arm and spoke hurriedly, in an under-tone. "Ian," she said. "Lots of times, people have, oh, understandings, you might say, that outsiders can't even guess at."

"Understandings! What kind of understandings? And then also—"

But he was too late. The swinging door burst open and the children rushed in, crying, "Mom!" and "Danny and them are here, Mom." Clau-dia said, "What do you think of our cake?" She held it up, all spiky and falling apart. She was laughing again. Ian pushed past her and left the kitchen.

In the dining room, Lucy bounced the baby on her shoulder while she talked with Bee. She still had her coat on; she looked fresh and happy, and she smiled at Ian without a trace of guilt. His mother said, "Ian, hon, could you fetch the booster seats?" She was laying a notched silver fish knife next to each plate. The Bedloes owned the most specialized utensils—sugar shells and butter-pat spears and a toothy, comblike instrument for slicing angel food cake. Ian marveled that people could consider such things im-portant. "Also we'll need those bibs in the linen drawer," his mother said, but he passed on through without speaking. From the living room he heard the TV set blaring a basketball game. "Notice that young fellow on the right," his father was saying. "What's-his-name. Total concentration. What's that fellow's name?"

Ian climbed the stairs while his family's voices filled the house below him like water—just that murmury and chuckly, gliding through the rooms to form one single, level surface.

On Saturday Cicely's parents were taking a trip to Cumberland, leaving Cicely in charge of her little brother. They were planning to be gone overnight. This meant that after her brother went to bed, Cicely and Ian would be just like married people, all alone downstairs or maybe even upstairs in her bedroom with the door locked. They didn't discuss the possibilities in so many words, but Ian got the feeling that Cicely was aware of them. She said maybe he'd like to come over about eight thirty or so. (Stevie's bedtime was eight.) She wanted to cook him a really elegant dinner, she said. They would have candles, just like Lucy. Maybe Ian could dress up a little. Maybe get hold of a bottle of wine.

He preferred the taste of beer himself, but he would certainly bring wine, and also flowers. He wasn't so keen on dressing up but he would do that too, if she wanted. Anything. Anything. Would she let him stay the whole night? It didn't seem the right moment to ask. They were sitting in the school cafeteria with accordion-pleated drinking-straw wrappers whizzing around their heads.

Saturday morning he slept till noon, and as soon as he woke he phoned Cicely to see what color wine she wanted. "What *color?*" she said, sounding hurried. "Any color; I don't care."

"But aren't you supposed to—?"

"I have to go," she said. "Something's boiling over."

After he'd hung up he realized he should have asked about the flowers, too—what color flowers. Or was it only with corsages that the color mattered? This was a meal, not a prom dress. Oh, everything was all so new to him, all on a larger scale than he was used to. He worried he wouldn't know precisely what to do with her. He wished Danny were around. The only person in the house was his mother, and she was in one of her cleaning frenzies. She didn't even offer him lunch. He had to make his own—three peanut butter sandwiches and a quart of milk, which he drank directly from the carton when his mother wasn't looking.

In the afternoon he and Andrew went over to Pig Benson's house and played Ping-Pong. *Tick-tock, tick-tock,* the ball went, while Ian considered dropping a hint about tonight. Or would that be bragging? Danny had once told him that girls hate boys who kiss and tell. Also, it was possible that Pig and Andrew might do something juvenile like shine flashlights in Cicely's windows or lean on the doorbell and then run. It was *very* possible. Look at them: scuffling around the Ping-Pong table all gawky and unkempt and wild, acting years and years younger than Ian.

Although at the same time, there was something enviable about them. When he reached home, his mother was standing in front of the hall mirror in her best dress, screwing on her earrings. "Oh! Ian!" she said. "I thought you'd never get here."

"What's up?"

"You're supposed to head over to Lucy's right away. She needs you to baby-sit."

"Baby-sit? I can't baby-sit! I've got a date."

"Well, I'm sure she won't be long; she's just meeting a friend for a drink, she says. Danny's at a stag party. Goodness, look at the time, and your father's not even—"

"Mom," Ian said, following her into the living room, "you had no business volunteering me to baby-sit. I've got plans of my own, and besides I think I might spend the night at Pig's. You have way, way overstepped, Mom. And another thing. This Lucy, calling up the minute Danny's back is turned—"

"Back is turned! What are you talking about? It's Bucky Hargrove's stag party; Bucky's getting married next week."

She was plumping cushions and collecting sections of the evening paper. Her high heels gave her an unaccustomed, stalking gait, and Ian could tell she was wearing her girdle; she inhabited her dress in such a condensed manner. She stooped stiffly for a dog bone and said, "Not that I approve of such things: bunch of grown men telling dirty jokes together. So that's why I said to Lucy, 'Why, of course you should get out! Ian would be glad to sit!' I said. And don't you let on you feel otherwise, young man, or you'll be grounded for life and I mean it."

The front door opened and she spun around. "Doug?" she called.

"Here, sweetheart."

"Well, thank the Lord! You've got fifteen minutes to dress. Did you forget we were invited to the Finches'?"

When Ian passed through the hall on his way out, he sent his father a commiserating look.

It was near the end of March, that period when spring approaches jerkily and then backs off a bit. The light was hanging on longer than it had a week ago, but a raw, damp wind was moving in from the north. Ian zipped his jacket and turned up the collar. He circled a group of Waverly Street children playing hopscotch—bulkily wrapped little girls planting their feet in a no-nonsense, authoritative way down a ladder of chalked squares. He performed a polite minuet with one of the foreigners, dodging right, then dodging left, till the foreigner said, "Please to excuse me," and laughed and stepped aside. Ian nodded but he didn't stop to talk. Talking with the foreigners could tie up half the evening, what with that habit they had of meticulously inquiring after every possible relative.

By the time he reached Jeffers Street, dusk had fallen. The windows of Danny's house glowed mistily, veiled by sheer white curtains. Ian rang the doorbell and then knocked, to show he was a man in a hurry. The sooner Lucy got going the sooner she would be back, he figured.

He had expected her to look shamefaced at the sight of him. (Surely she knew she hadn't played straight, going behind his back to his mother.) But when she opened the door, she just said, "Oh, Ian! Come in. I really do appreciate this." Then Thomas and Agatha hurtled toward him from the living room, both wearing footed pajamas. "Ian!" they shouted. "Did you bring Cicely? Where's Cicely? Mama said maybe—"

"Let him catch his breath," Lucy told them. She was putting on her coat. She wore a red turtleneck and long, loose woolen pants that gave the effect of a skirt. It seemed unjust that she should be so pretty. "My friend Dot phoned at the very last minute," she said. "I know it's a Saturday night, but I thought maybe if you invited Cicely over—"

"She has to stay with her brother," Ian said bluntly. He stood in front of her with his fists in his jacket pockets. "I'm supposed to go to *her* house. I promised I'd be there at eight-thirty."

"Oh, well, that's no problem. Right now it's—" She slid back a sleeve and checked her watch. "Six forty. I'll tell Dot I have to be in early. Remember Dot? From the Fill 'Er Up Café?"

"Yeah, sure," Ian said heavily.

But she didn't seem to catch it. She was looking for something. "Now, where . . ." she said. "Has anyone seen my keys? Well, never mind. You be good, kids, hear? And you can stay up till I get back." Then she left, shutting the door behind her so neatly that Ian didn't even hear the latch click.

In the living room, Daphne sat propped in her infant seat in front of the TV. "Hey there, Daph," Ian said, shucking off his jacket. The sound of his voice sent her little terry-cloth arms and legs into unsynchronized wheeling motions. She craned around till she was looking up into his face and she gave him a lopsided smile. It was sort of flattering, really. Ian squatted to pick her up. He felt as surprised as ever by the fight in her— the wiry combativeness of such a small body. Even through the terry cloth, the heat from her tiny armpits warmed his fingers.

"Ian," Thomas said, "*why* don't you come over anymore?"

"Now we got no one," Agatha said, "and Mama called Mrs. Myrdal and begged and pleaded but Mrs. Myrdal hung up on her."

"Are you mad on account of I beat you at Parcheesi last time?" Thomas asked.

"Beat me!" Ian said. "That was just a fluke. The merest coincidence. Bring on the board and I'll prove it, you young upstart."

Thomas tittered and went off for the Parcheesi board.

While the two children were setting up the game on the rug, Ian phoned Cicely. "Hello?" she said, out of breath.

"Hi," he said. He shifted Daphne to his hip.

"Oh, Ian. Hi."

"I'm over baby-sitting at Lucy's. Just thought I'd let you know, in case you find yourself desperate for the sound of my voice or something."

"Baby-sitting! When will you be done?"

"It shouldn't take long. Lucy promised—"

"I have to go," Cicely broke in. "I'm following this recipe that says *Simmer covered, stirring constantly.* Can you figure that out? I mean, am I supposed to keep popping the cover off and popping it back on, or what? Do you suppose—"

She hung up, perhaps still talking. Ian sat down on the rug and settled Daphne on his knee.

It was true he liked all games, but Thomas and Agatha were not very challenging opponents. They employed a strategy of avoidance, fearfully clinging to the safety squares and deliberating whole minutes before venturing into open territory. Also, Thomas couldn't add. Each toss of the dice remained two separate numbers, laboriously counted out one by one. "A two and a four. One, two. One, two, three—"

"Six," Ian said impatiently. He scooped up the dice and flung them so they skittered across the board. "Eight," he said. "Ha!" Eight was what he needed to capture Agatha's man.

"No fair," she told him. "One douse went on the carpet."

"Die," he said.

Her jaw dropped.

"One *die* went on the carpet," he said. He picked up his own man.

"No fair if they don't land on the board!" she said. "You have to take your turn over."

"I should worry, I should care, only babies cry no fair," Ian singsonged. He pounded his man down the board triumphantly. "Five, six, seven—"

The phone rang.

"—eight," he said, nudging aside Agatha's man. He hoisted Daphne to his shoulder and reached up for the phone on the plastic cube table. "Hello?"

"Ian?"

"Hi, Cicely."

"On your way over, could you pick up some butter? My white sauce didn't thicken and I had to throw it out and start again, and now I don't have enough butter for the rolls."

"Sure thing," Ian said. "So how's our friend Stevie?"

"Stevie?"

"Is he getting ready for bed yet?"

"Not *now*; it's a quarter past seven."

"Oh. Right."

"Oops!" she said.

She hung up.

Ian hoped she wasn't losing sight of the important issues here. White sauce, rolls, what did he care? He just wanted to get that brother of hers out of the picture.

Daphne breathed damply into his left ear. He boosted her higher on his shoulder and turned back to the game.

They finished Parcheesi and started Old Maid. Old Maid was sort of pointless, though, because Thomas couldn't bluff. He had that sallow kind of skin that reveals every emotion; whenever he grew anxious, bruiselike shadows deepened beneath his eyes.

The game went on forever and Daphne started fussing. "She wants her bottle," Agatha said, not lifting her gaze from her cards. Ian went out to the kitchen to take her bottle from the refrigerator, and while he waited for it to warm he jounced Daphne up and down. It didn't do any good, though; he seemed to have lost his charm. All she did was fuss harder and climb higher on his shoulder, working her nosy, sharp little toes irritatingly between his ribs.

When he returned to the living room, the other two had abandoned the card game and were watching TV. He sat between them on the couch and fed Daphne while a barefoot woman sang a folk song about hammering in railroad ties. Thomas sucked his thumb. Agatha wound a strand of hair around her index finger. Daphne fell asleep halfway through her bottle and Ian rose cautiously and carried her to her crib.

At 8:15, he started getting angry. How was he supposed to make it to Cicely's by 8:30? Also he had to stop off at home beforehand—change clothes, filch some wine from the pantry. Damn, he should have seen to all that before he came here. He jiggled a foot across his knee and watched a housewife in high heels explaining that bacteria cause odors.

At 8:35, the phone rang. He sprang for it, already preparing his response. (*No*, you can't stay out longer.) "Ian?" Cicely asked. "When you come, could you bring some gravy mix?"

"Gravy mix."

"I just can't understand where I went wrong."

Ian said, "Did Stevie get to bed all right?"

"I'm going to see to that in a minute, but first this gravy! I pick up the spoon and everything in the pan comes with it, all in a clump."

"Well, don't worry about it," Ian told her. "I'll bring the mix. Meanwhile, you get Stevie into bed."

"Well . . ." Cicely said, trailing off.

"Dad's old rocker dull and gray?" two girls sang on TV. "Stain it, wax it, the Wood-Witch way!"

After he'd hung up, Ian turned to the children and asked, "Did your mother say where she was going?"

"No," Agatha said.

"Was it someplace she could walk to?"

"I don't know."

He rose and went to the front window. Beyond the gauzy curtains he saw street lamps glinting faintly and squares of soft yellow light from the neighboring houses.

There was a wet, uncorking sound behind him— Thomas's thumb popping out of his mouth. "She went in a car," Thomas said distinctly.

Ian turned.

"She went in a car with Dot," Thomas told him. "Dot lives down the

block a ways and Mama went over to her house and got herself a ride."
He replaced his thumb.

A wail floated from the children's room. Ian glanced at Agatha. A second wail, more assured.

"You didn't burp her," Agatha said serenely.

Thomas merely sent him the drugged, veiled gaze of a dedicated thumb-sucker.

From 8:40 to 9:15 Ian walked Daphne around and around the living room. Thomas and Agatha quarreled over the afghan. Thomas kicked Agatha in the shin and she started crying—unconvincingly, it seemed to Ian. She rolled her knee sock down to her thick white ankle and pointed out, "See? See there what he did?"

Ian patted the baby more rapidly and revised his plans. He would not go home first after all; they would do without the wine and butter and whatever. He would simply explain to Cicely when he got there. "I don't care about dinner," he would say, drawing her into his arms. "I care about *you.*" And they would climb the stairs together, tiptoeing past her brother's door and into—

Oh-oh.

The one thing he could not do without—the three things, in their linked foil packets—lay in the toe of his left gym shoe at the very back of his closet. There was no way he could avoid going by his house.

The phone rang again and Ian picked up the receiver and barked, "What!"

Cicely said, "Ian, where are you?"

"This goddamn Lucy," he said, not caring if the children heard. "I've a good mind to just walk on out of here."

Agatha looked up from her shin and said, "You wouldn't!"

"Everything's stone cold," Cicely said.

"Well, don't worry. The dinner's not important—"

"Not important! I've been slaving all day over this dinner! We're having flank steak stuffed with mushrooms, and baked potatoes stuffed with cheese, and green peppers stuffed with—"

"But how about Stevie? Did Stevie get to bed all right?"

"He got to bed hours ago."

Ian groaned.

"Is that all you care about?" Cicely asked. "Don't you care about my cooking?"

"Oh! Yes! Your cooking," Ian said. "I've been looking forward to it all day."

"No, don't say that! I'm afraid you'll be disappointed."

"Cicely," Ian said. "Listen. I'll be over soon no matter what. Just wait for me."

He hung up to find Thomas and Agatha eyeing him reproachfully. "What're you going to do? Leave us on our own?" Thomas asked.

"You're not babies anymore," Ian said. "You can take care of your-selves."

"*Mama* never lets us. She worries we'd get into the matches."

"Well, would you?" Ian asked him.

Thomas considered awhile. Finally he said, "We might."

Ian sighed and went back to walking Daphne.

For the next half hour or so, they played I Spy. That was the most Ian could manage with Daphne fretting in his arms. Agatha said, "I spy, with my little eye . . ." and her gaze roamed the room. Ian was conscious all at once of the mess that had grown up around them—the playing cards, the twisted afghan, the strewn Parcheesi pieces.

". . . with my little eye, as clear as the sky . . ." Agatha said, drawing it out.

"Will you just for God's sake get on with it?" Ian snapped.

"Well, I'm trying, Ian, if you wouldn't keep interrupting."

Then she had to start over again. "I spy, with my little eye . . ."

Ian thought of Lucy's gray eyes and her perfect, lipsticked mouth. The red of her lipstick was a *bitter* red, with something burnt in it. She had had things her own way every minute of her life, he suspected. Women who looked like that never needed to consider other people.

Daphne finally unknotted and fell asleep, and Ian carried her to the children's room. He lowered her into the crib by inches and then waited, holding his breath. At that moment he heard the front door open.

His first concern was that the noise would disturb Daphne. That was how thoroughly he'd been sidetracked. Then he realized he was free to go, and he headed out to tell Lucy what he thought of her.

But it wasn't Lucy; it was Danny, standing just inside the living room door and screwing up his face against the light. Ian could tell he'd had a couple of beers. He wore a loose, goofy smile that was familiar from past occasions. "Ian, fellow!" he said. "What're *you* doing here?"

"I'm going out of my mind," Ian told him.

"Ah."

"Your wife was due back ages ago, and anyhow I didn't want to come in the first place."

"Thomas!" Danny said fervently, peering toward the couch. "And Agatha!" He seemed surprised to see them, too. He told Ian, "You sure did miss a great party. Good old Bucky Hargrove!"

"Look," Ian said. "I am running late as hell and I need you to give me a lift to Cicely's house."

"Huh? Oh. Why, sure," Danny said. "Sure, Ian. Except—" He pon-dered. "Except how about the kids?" he asked finally.

"How about them?"

"We can't just leave them."

"Take them along, then," Ian said, exasperated. "Let's just *go*."

"Take Daphne, too? Where's Daphne?"

Ian gritted his teeth. The Kent cigarette song sailed out from the TV, mindless and jaunty. He turned to Agatha and said, "Agatha, you and Thomas will have to stay here and baby-sit."

She stared at him.

"Seven minutes, tops," Ian said. "Don't open the front door no matter who knocks, and don't answer the phone. Understand?"

She nodded. Thomas's eyes were ringed like a raccoon's.

"Let's go," Ian told Danny.

Danny was swaying slightly on his feet and watching Ian with mild, detached interest. "Well . . ." he said.

"Come *on*, Danny!"

Ian snatched up his jacket and gave Danny a push in the right direction. As they walked out he felt a weight slipping blessedly from his shoulders. He wondered how people endured children on a long-term basis—the monotony and irritation and confinement of them.

Outside it was much colder than before, and wonderfully quiet.

Danny bumped his head getting into the car, and he had some trouble determining which key to use. After that, though, he started the engine easily, checked sensibly for traffic, and pulled into the street. "So!" he said. "Cicely lives on Lang Avenue, right?"

"Right," Ian said. "Stop by home first, though."

"Stop by home first," Danny repeated meekly.

Ian tapped a foot against the floorboards. He felt commanding and energetic, charged up by righteous anger.

Dimly lit houses slid past them, and a dog chased the car a block or so before giving up. Danny started whistling a tune, something sort of jazzy and hootchy-kootchy. Probably they'd had a stripper at Bucky Hargrove's party, and waitresses in fishnet stockings and girls popping out of cakes and such. And Ian, meanwhile, had been warming baby bottles. He swung toward Danny sharply and said, "I might as well inform you right now that you have lost your favorite sitter for all eternity."

"Huh? What say?" Danny asked.

"I had a huge, important engagement at eight-thirty. I'm talking crucial. Lucy knew that. She swore on a stack of Bibles she'd be back in time."

"Where is she, anyhow?" Danny asked, flicking his turn signal.

"Drinking with a girlfriend. So she says."

"I didn't even know she was planning to go out."

"Her waitress friend, Dot. Is what she *claims*."

"Dot from the Fill 'Er Up Café," Danny agreed.

"Goddamnit, Danny, are you blind?" Ian shouted.

Danny's eyes widened and he looked frantically in all directions. "Blind?" he asked. "What?"

"She's out more often than she's in! Don't you ever wonder who she's with?"

"Why, no, I . . ."

"And how about that baby?"

"Baby?"

"Premature baby? Get serious. Premature baby with dimples?"

Danny opened his mouth.

"Two months early and breathing on her own, no incubator, no problems?"

"She was—"

"She was somebody else's," Ian said.

"Come again?"

"I just want to know how long you intend to be a fall guy," Ian said.

Danny turned onto Waverly and drew up in front of the house. He cut the engine and looked over at Ian. He seemed entirely sober now. He said, "What are you trying to tell me, Ian?"

"She's out all afternoon any time she can get a sitter," Ian said. "She comes back perfumed and laughing and wearing clothes she can't afford. That white knit dress. Haven't you ever seen her white dress? Where'd she get it? How'd she pay for it? How come she married you quick as a flash and then had a baby just seven months later?"

"You're talking about that dress with the kind of like crisscrossed middle," Danny said.

"That's the one."

Danny started rubbing his right temple with his fingertips. When it didn't seem he meant to say anything further, Ian got out of the car.

Inside the house, only the hall lamp was lit. His parents must still be at the Finches'. Beastie rose from the rug, yawning, and followed him up the stairs, which he climbed two steps at a time. He went directly to his room, fell to his knees in front of the closet, and rooted through the clutter for his gym shoes. Once he'd located the foil strip, he slid it into his rear pocket and stood up. Then he ducked into the bathroom. The biggest night of his life and he couldn't even stop to shower. He wet his fingers at the sink and ran them through his hair. He bared his teeth to the mirror and debated whether to brush them.

In the street below, an engine roared up. What on earth? He drew aside the curtain and peered out. It was Danny's Chevy, all right. The headlights were two yellow ribbons swinging away from the curb. The car took off abruptly, peeling rubber. Ian dropped the curtain. He turned to confront his own stunned face in the mirror.

Near the stone wall at the end of the block the brakes should have squealed, but instead the roaring sound grew louder. It grew until something had to happen, and then there was a gigantic, explosive, complicated crash and then a delicate tinkle and then silence. Ian went on staring into his own eyes. He couldn't seem to look away. He couldn't even blink, couldn't move, because once he moved then time would start rolling forward again, and he already knew that nothing in his life would ever be the same.

———

2

The Department of Reality

When the baby woke from her afternoon nap, she made a noise like singing. "La!" she called. But the only ones who heard were Thomas and Agatha. They were coloring at the kitchen table. Their crayons slowed and they looked at each other. Then they looked toward their mother's room. Nowadays their mother took naps too. She said it was the heat. She said if they would just let her be she would stay in bed from spring till fall, sleeping away this whole hot, muggy summer.

"La!" Daphne called again.

They couldn't pick her up themselves because last week Thomas had dropped her. He'd been trying to feed her a bottle and she had somehow tumbled to the floor and bumped her head. After that their mother said neither one of them could hold her anymore, which wasn't at all fair to Agatha. Agatha had turned seven this past April and she was big for her age besides. She would never have allowed Daphne to wiggle away like that.

Now Daphne was talking to herself in a questioning tone of voice, like, Where *is* everybody? Have they all gone off and left me?

Agatha's page of the coloring book had an outline of an undressed man full of veins and arteries. You were supposed to color the veins blue and the arteries red. A tiny B and R started you off and from then on you were on your own, boy. Tough luck if you slipped over onto the wrong branch accidentally and started coloring the red parts blue. It was just about the most boring picture in the world but Agatha kept at it, even when the veins narrowed to black threads and she didn't have a hope of staying inside the lines.

Thomas's page was boring too, but at least there were more shapes to it. His undressed man had different organs—pipes and beans and balloony things. He got to do that page because the coloring book was his, but then he pretended the organs didn't exist. He smeared over them every which way with a purple crayon, giving the man a suit that ended jaggedly at his wrists and bare ankles. "Now you've gone and ruined it," Agatha told him.

"I did not. I made it better."

"You're bearing down too hard, too. Look at what you did to your crayon."

He looked. Earlier he'd peeled the paper off and now the crayon curved sideways in the heat from his hand, like their mother's poor bent candles in the napkin drawer.

"I don't care," he said.

"Your last purple crayon!"

"I didn't like it anyhow," he said, "and this coloring book is stupid. Who gave me this stupid coloring book?"

"Danny gave it to you," Agatha said.

He clapped a hand over his mouth.

Danny hadn't given him the coloring book; it was Grandma Bedloe. She'd picked it up at the Pantry Pride one day when she went to buy their mother some food. But Thomas always worried that Danny was listening to them up in heaven, so Agatha said, "He bought it as a special, special present, and he hoped very much you would like it."

Thomas removed his hand and said loudly, "I do like it."

"Then why'd you mess all over it?"

"I made a mistake."

Daphne said, "Oho! Oho!"—not laughing, as you might imagine, but starting to complain. The next step would be real wailing, all sad and lost and lonely. Thomas and Agatha *hated* that. Thomas said, "Go tell Mama."

"You go."

"You're the oldest."

"I'm not in the mood."

"Last time I went, she cried," Thomas said.

"She was having a difficult day."

"Maybe this day is difficult too."

"If you go," Agatha said, "I'll give you my patent leather purse."

"I don't use a purse."

"My plastic camera?"

"Your camera's broken."

Daphne had reached the wailing stage. Agatha started feeling desperate. She said, "We could stand next to the crib, maybe. Just talk and smile and stuff."

"Okay."

They got up and went down the hall, past the closed door of their mother's room and into the children's room. It smelled of dirty diapers. Daphne was sitting in that superstraight way she had with her fingers wrapped around the crib bars, and when they came in she grew quiet and pressed her face to the bars so her little nose stuck out. She had been crying so hard that her upper lip was glassed over. She blinked and stared at them and then gave a big sloppy grin.

"Now, what is this nonsense I'm hearing?" Agatha said sternly.

She was trying to sound like Grandma Bedloe. Grownups had these voices they saved just for babies. If she'd wanted, she could have put on her mother's voice. "Sweetheart!" Or Danny's. "How's my princess?" he would ask. Used to ask. In the olden days asked.

Best to stick with Grandma Bedloe. "Who's this making such a hullabaloo?"

Daphne grinned wider, with her four new crinkle-edged teeth shining forth and her lashes all wet and sticking to her cheeks. She wore just a little undershirt, and her diaper was a brownish color—what their uncle Ian would call Not a Pretty Sight.

"Give her her pacifier," Thomas suggested.

"She gets mad if you give her a pacifier when she wants a bottle."

"Maybe she's not hungry yet."

"After her nap, she's always hungry."

Daphne looked back and forth between the two of them. It seemed to be dawning on her that they weren't going to be much help.

"Just *try* her pacifier," Thomas said.

"Well, where'd it go?"

They reached in between the bars and patted the sheet, hunting. Some places the sheet was damp, but that might have been the heat, or tears. The smell was terrible.

"Found it!" Thomas crowed. He poked the pacifier between Daphne's lips, but she spat it out again. Her chin began quivering and her eyebrows turned bright pink.

"Phooey," Thomas said. He picked up the pacifier and jammed it in his own mouth, and then he backed off till he was sitting on the edge of his bed with his arms folded tight across his chest.

"Maybe we could feed her in her crib," Agatha said.

Thomas made noisy sucking sounds.

Agatha went to the kitchen and dragged a gallon jug of milk from the refrigerator. She set the jug on the table and took a cloudy nursing bottle from the jumble of unwashed dishes next to the sink.

Daphne was back to "Oho! Oho!"

First Agatha tried pouring very, very slowly, but milk got all over the table and soaked Thomas's page of the coloring book. When she speeded up she did better. She replaced the nipple and carried the bottle down the hall, de-chilling it in her hands as she walked. Outside her mother's door she paused and listened but she didn't hear a sound. It must be a two-pill nap, or even three-pill. She went on into the children's room.

Daphne's mouth was an ugly shouting square now and she was red-faced and snotty and sweaty. Thomas had his eyes squeezed shut. "Wake up," Agatha told him roughly as she passed. She fitted the bottle between the crib bars and held it toward Daphne. "Here."

Daphne flailed out and the bottle went flying. Off popped the nipple.

Milk splashed the decal of the rabbit in pink overalls on the headboard. "Stupid!" Agatha shouted. "Stupid fat old *baby*!"

Daphne cried harder. "Help me reach this bottle," Agatha told Thomas, but Thomas had pulled his bedspread up over his head. She turned back to the bottle. It lay on its side toward the rear of the crib, and every time Daphne bounced another glug of milk would spill out onto the sheet. Finally Agatha pressed the two clamps on the railing to lower it. There was Daphne, no longer fenced in, quieting slightly and hiccuping and looking interested. There was the bottle, within easy reach. Agatha found the nipple in a fold of wet sheet and put it back on, and then she tipped the bottle toward Daphne. This time, Daphne accepted it. She drank sitting up, blinking at the first cold swallow but after that making do. One hand clutched over and over on Agatha's wrist. "Mm," she said at each gulp. "Mm. Mm." Agatha suddenly felt the most enormous thirst.

Behind her, she heard the slithering sound of Thomas coming out of his bedspread. She heard the smack as he pulled the pacifier from his mouth. "She sure does stink," he said.

She didn't answer.

"You going to change her, Agatha?"

She stood firm, cupping her elbow with her free hand. She did know how to change a diaper. She had often helped her mother—fetched the powder or the washcloth. Yes, she thought she could do it on her own. But still she didn't answer. She tossed her head to flick her hair off her face. She felt Thomas come up cautiously to stand next to her. He was twiddling the pacifier between his fingers. Just as Daphne let go of the nipple after her last gulp (*Squirrel*-oh! the nipple said), he reached over and plugged her mouth with the pacifier. Daphne went on sucking. Thomas and Agatha took a step back, but Daphne stayed quiet.

"Soose," Thomas said happily.

That was what their mother called a pacifier: soose.

Agatha took a clean diaper from the stack on the bureau. She tipped Daphne onto her back and slid the diaper beneath her. The pins were no trouble. This was going to be easy. But the poo was disgusting. She wrinkled her nose and folded the dirty diaper inward. Thomas said, "Yuck!" and went back to his bed.

She carried the diaper down the hall to the bathroom, holding it in a clump far out in front of her. She lowered it into the toilet and swished it around. All the ick started crumbling away. She flushed the toilet and swished again in clearer water, back and forth, dreamily.

Sometimes their mother said "soose" and sometimes she said "soother." Maybe they were both the same word. People here in Baltimore said "pacifier," and so did Thomas and Agatha, trying to fit in; but their mother was not from Baltimore. She was from out in the country where they used to live with their father in a metal-colored trailer. Then they all got divorced. This was when Thomas was just a baby. He couldn't even remember. And then later they moved to Baltimore in Mr. Belling's long black car. Everything was going to be wonderful, wonderful, their mother said. She got so many new clothes! Their apartment sat over a drugstore that stocked every kind of candy, and when Mr. Belling visited he sent Thomas and Agatha downstairs with a dollar bill each and they could take as long as they liked deciding. Thomas did remember Mr. Belling. He didn't like him much, though. When Mr. Belling stopped coming, Thomas asked if he could have the Baltimore Colts mug Mr. Belling used to drink his beer from, and their mother started crying. She snatched the mug from the dish drainer and slammed it against the sink until it broke in a million pieces. Thomas said, "I'm sorry! I'm sorry! I didn't *really* want it!" After that their mother had to get a job and leave them with Mrs. Myrdal, but then she met Danny. She acted more like her old self once she met Danny. On her wedding day she said it was *all* of them's wedding day. She gave Agatha a little pink rose from her bridal bouquet.

Thomas said Danny was probably their real father. Agatha knew he wasn't, though. She told Thomas their real father was nicer. In fact Danny was the nicest man she had ever known—nicer than their father, who had never had much to do with them, and certainly a whole lot nicer than Mr. Belling, with his two fat diamond rings and his puckered eyes the color of new dungarees. But she wanted Thomas to feel jealous over what she could still remember. Thomas had a terrible memory. Agatha's memory was letter-perfect; she never forgot a thing.

Thomas forgot three separate times, for instance, three different days in a row, that Danny had gone and died. Three mornings in a row he got up and said, "Do you think Danny will fix apple pancakes for breakfast?" The first day she could understand, because the news was still so fresh and neither one of them was used to it yet. So she just said, "No, did you forget? He went and died." But the second day! And the third! And those were weekdays, too. Danny would never have fixed apple pancakes on a weekday. "What's the matter with you?" she asked Thomas. "Can't you get it into your head? He had a car crash and he died." Thomas just took on a kind of closed look. He didn't seem to miss Danny as much as he missed the pancakes. It made her furious. Why did she have to be the only one who remembered? She said, "He gave Ian a ride home and we had to stay by ourselves. Not answer the phone, not open the door—"

Thomas clamped his hands over his ears.

"So when the phone rang we didn't pick it up," Agatha said. "And when the door banged we didn't unlock it."

Thomas said, "Nee-nee-nee-nee-nee!" but she rode over it. "Mama had to crawl in a window," she went on, "and she tore her sleeve and she was crying; she was worried we'd been murdered, and then the phone rang again and—"

"Shut up! Shut up! Shut up!"

She just had these urges to be evil to him. She couldn't say exactly why.

The water in the toilet was so yellow now she could hardly see the diaper, so she flushed once more. Then it felt like someone bossy and selfish reached up and grabbed the diaper away from her. She gave a little gasp and let it go. The water rose calmly higher and higher; it reached the rim. She had never guessed what a scary thing a toilet was. Thick yellow water slopped over the edge and spilled across the floor while she stood watching, horrified.

"Mama!" she shrieked finally.

Silence.

The water in the toilet slid down again.

Agatha stepped out into the hall, shaking, and went to her mother's bedroom door. She gave a tiny tap with her knuckles and then placed her ear to the door and listened.

They used to go straight in without a thought. They used to play among her bedclothes till she woke. But lately they'd stopped doing that.

(You could almost think, sometimes, that their mother wasn't there behind her face anymore.)

Agatha went on down the hall to the children's room. As she walked in, she saw Daphne roll onto her stomach and drop like a stone out of the crib. Agatha flung herself forward in a silent rush and caught her—an armload of bare-bottomed, clammy baby. She sank weak-kneed to the floor. Still busily sucking her pacifier, Daphne crawled away to a jack-in-the-box. Thomas sang to his doll, "My aunt gave me a nickel, to buy a pickle . . ."

All of a sudden, Agatha seemed to see things so clearly. Daphne's bottom was stained yellow. Thomas's shirt was splotched with food. The floor was covered with toys and dirty clothes and a cantaloupe rind on a plate beneath a cloud of fruit flies. Milk was dripping down the wall behind the crib.

She stood up and collected Daphne and staggered over to the crib with her and plopped her down. She wrestled Daphne's diaper around her, being very, very careful with the safety pins, and then she raised the railing and locked it. "Stay there," she told Daphne. "Put on a different shirt," she told Thomas.

"What shirt?"

"I don't care. Just different."

He laid Dulcimer aside, grumbling, and slid off his bed. While he was rummaging in bureau drawers, Agatha returned to the bathroom and stirred a towel through the puddle around the toilet. Then she hid the towel in the hamper. She went out to the kitchen and put the milk back into the fridge. "Chew, chew, chew, chew, chew, chewing gum," Thomas sang, while Agatha spread his coloring book on the windowsill to dry. One by one she plucked his crayons from the pool of milk on the table. They were beginning to dye the milk all different shades, lavender and pink and blue. She dumped them into the waste can under the sink.

"What are you *doing?*" Thomas asked, coming up behind her. He was wearing a green shirt now that clashed with his blue shorts, and it was buttoned wrong besides.

"Button your buttons over from scratch," Agatha told him. She unfolded a cloth and started wiping off the table.

"What did you do with my crayons?"

"They were all wet and runny."

"You can't just throw them away!"

He started rooting through the waste can. Agatha said, "Stop that! I just got everything nice again!"

"You better give me back my crayons, Agatha."

Their mother said, "Is it still daytime?"

She was standing in the doorway in her slip. Her pillow had made a mark across one cheek and she didn't have any makeup on. "I thought it was night," she said. "Is that Daphne I hear?"

"Make Agatha give me back my crayons, Mama!"

But their mother was drifting down the hall, heading toward Daphne's "Oho! Oho!"

"Stealer!" Thomas hissed at Agatha. "Crayon stealer!"

She put the wet cloth in the sink. "Sticks and stones will break my bones," she said, "but names will never—"

"You can go to jail for stealing!"

"Is this my little Daphne?" their mother said, back again with Daphne in her arms. "Is this my sweetheart?"

She sat in a kitchen chair and settled Daphne on her lap. Daphne's diaper was dry but it was so loose it pouched in front of her stomach. The table was clean but it was damp where Agatha had wiped it. Everything looked fine but just barely, like a room where you walk in and get the feeling something was rustling and whispering till half a second ago. But their mother didn't seem to notice. She stared down at Daphne with her face bare-naked and erased and pale. "Is this my Daphne?" she kept saying, "Is this my baby Daphne?" so it began to sound as if she really did wonder. "Is this her?" she asked. "Is it her? Is it?" And she looked up at Thomas and Agatha and waited for them to answer.

When the hottest part of the day was over, they got ready for their walk to the typewriter store. This was something they'd started doing just in the past few weeks, but already there was a pattern to it. Agatha liked patterns. So did Thomas. Together they hauled Daphne's stroller out of the coat closet and unfolded it. Daphne watched from the rug, flapping her arms up and down when she heard the wheels squeak. Maybe she liked patterns, too.

They went to see if their mother was ready, but she was shut up in her bathroom. When she came out, she wore her white blouse that wrapped and tied at the side and her watery flowing India skirt. She blotted her lip-stick on a tissue and asked, "How do I look?"

"You look nice," they both told her.

From the living room, Daphne made a fussy sound. Their mother sighed and picked up her bag. "Let's go," she said.

The air outdoors felt heavy and warm, but at least the sun wasn't beating down so hard anymore. Their mother walked in front, wheeling Daphne in her stroller, and Thomas and Agatha followed. Thomas's shirt was still buttoned wrong. Agatha's playsuit bunched at the crotch. She thought she and Thomas should have been dressed up too, if they were trying to make friends with the typewriter man, but that didn't seem to have crossed their mother's mind. Sometimes lately there were these holes in the way she did things, places she just fell apart. Like last night, when she got lost in the middle of what she was saying and couldn't find her way out again. "Do you believe this?" she had been saying. "That I'm back to . . . back to . . ." Then she'd just stared. It had frightened them. Thomas started crying and he flew at her with both fists. "Back to noth-ing," she had said finally. She was like a record player you had to jostle when it hit a crack. Then she'd said, "I think I'll go to bed," although it wasn't even dark outside and Daphne hadn't been put down for the night yet.

They passed the house with all the statues in the yard—elves and baby deer and a row of ducks. Agatha wished their own yard had statues, but her mother said statues were common. "Right now," she said, "the last thing I can afford is looking common." She talked a lot these days about what she couldn't afford. Danny hadn't left them well provided for.

They passed the house that said MRS. GOODE, PALMIST—FORTUNES CHEERFULLY TOLD, but their mother didn't stop. Agatha was glad. Mrs. Goode was gray all over and her parlor smelled of mothballs. They came to where the shops began, shoe repairs and laundromats. At Luckman's Pharmacy Thomas and Agatha slowed hopefully, but their mother said, "We'll go to Joyner's this time." She rotated her drugstores because she didn't want people thinking she bought too many pills. It was a pity, though. Luckman's had one of those gumball machines with plastic charms intermingled. Thomas and Agatha let their feet drag and sent a longing gaze backward.

Traffic in this area was busier, and the bus exhausts made the heat seem worse. Thomas wore a smudgy mustache of sweat. Each click of their mother's heels shot something like a little sharp paring knife straight through Agatha's head.

On Govans Road the long, low front of Rumford & Son's Office Equipment took up nearly half a block. They stood facing it across the street, waiting for the light to change. Thomas said, "Wouldn't it be nice if typewriter stores had gumball machines?"

"Well, they don't, and I don't want you asking," their mother said.

"I wasn't going to ask!"

"Just be very, very quiet, so I won't be sorry I brought you."

In the olden days, she didn't have to bring them places. She'd say, "Oh! I'm going stir-crazy, I tell you." Or, "I'm getting cabin fever." She would ask Ian or Mrs. Myrdal to baby-sit, because back then she could afford it. She would go out all afternoon and come home happy and show the children what she had picked up for them—candy bars and lollipops, sometimes even toys if they were small enough to fit in her bag. But now she had to take the three of them everywhere. She took them to her doctor, even, and when she was called inside Agatha had to watch the other two. "Can't we go back to having sitters?" Agatha would ask, already knowing the answer. The answer was, "No, we can't. Face the facts, sweetheart: we're in the Department of Reality now." Their mother's favorite thing to say. Agatha hated hearing that and she would cover her ears like Thomas, but when she took her hands away her mother would still be talking. "You think I like having you with me every single second? Think I wouldn't rather just leave on my own any time I get the notion?"

Their mother loved them, but they kept trying to make her *not* love them. That was what she told them. "You want me to walk out on you," she told them, "but I refuse to do it."

Whenever she said that, Thomas would take hold of some little part of her clothing, down near the hemline where she didn't notice.

The light turned green and they crossed the street. Their mother's heels sounded daintier now. When they stepped inside the store, cold air washed over them—lovely, cold, blowing air—and Daphne said, "Ah," which made their mother laugh. Wasn't it wonderful how quickly she could change! To laugh like that, her best little husky-throated laugh, the instant she walked through the door! And the typewriter man wasn't even listening yet, although he came over soon enough. He said, "Why, look who's here!" You could see how pleased he was. He was a blond, pale man with skin that flushed when he smiled. "What brings you out on such a hot afternoon?" he asked their mother.

"Oh, we were just taking a stroll," she said. All of a sudden she seemed bashful. "We were passing by and I said, 'Shouldn't we visit my typewriter, kids?' "

"Absolutely. You don't want it feeling neglected," he said.

He beamed down at Agatha. She gave him her biggest smile back, all teeth.

The showroom was filled with desks, and a typewriter sat on each one. Some were big complicated electrics and some were little low-slung manuals. If it were up to Agatha, they'd have a manual. Those looked easier. But her mother's was electric, with keys that chattered loudly almost before you touched them.

They had first come to this store in the spring, shortly after Danny died. Their mother had decided to be a secretary. "I have endured my very last of the Fill 'Er Up Café," she told them. "This time I want an office job." So one afternoon they had walked to Rumford's, where their mother asked a lady with squiggly hair if she could use a machine to learn to type. "Do what?" the lady said. Their mother had explained that she wanted to sit at a desk for just exactly twelve days and teach herself out of a book called *Touch Typing in Twelve Easy Lessons*, and she promised that all three children would be as quiet as mice. "Hon," the lady said, "this is not a secretarial college."

"Well, don't you think I know that?" their mother cried. "But how do you suppose I could manage a *real* secretarial college? How do you expect me to pay? Who would watch my children?"

"Hon—"

"This is all I've got to go on, don't you understand? I need to find a job of some kind, I need to find employment!"

Then the typewriter man came over. "What seems to be the trouble here?" he asked, and the lady looked relieved and said, "This is Mr. Rumford, the owner. *He* can tell you," and she walked away. Mr. Rumford had been much more sympathetic. Not that he let their mother carry out her plan (he was really just the owner's *son*, he said, and his father would have a conniption), but he admired her spunk and he suggested that she rent, instead. She could rent from this very store and practice in the privacy of her home. Their mother said, "Oh! I never thought of that," and she took a Kleenex from her pocket and blew her nose.

"Know what I recommend?" the man had said. "An electric. Look at those pretty fingernails! You don't want to ruin your nails, now, do you?"

Their mother tried to smile.

"A manual, you have to pound down hard," he told her. "That's why you see those professional stenographers with their squared-off, ugly, short fingernails."

Agatha hid her own hands behind her back. Her mother looked up into the typewriter man's eyes. She said, "But wouldn't an electric be more expensive?"

"Pennies a day! Just pennies."

"And heavy, too. I mean an electric must weigh a lot more. And I'm not . . . I'm all on my own. I don't have anyone to carry things."

"Tell you what," he said. "I'll bring it by myself, after work."

"You would do that?"

"It'll be my pleasure," he told her. "Let me show you the machine I have in mind." And off he went, leading them through the rows of desks.

The machine he had in mind was a blue metal hulk with a cord so thick that when he brought it that evening, the only outlet they could plug it into was the one behind the refrigerator. He had to move the refrigerator and pull the kitchen table over so the cord would reach, and then he was red in the face and their mother made him sit down and have a beer. While he was drinking his beer, he showed her the special features—the electric return and the keys that would repeat. "This is just so nice of you," their mother told him. "I know *Mrs.* Rumford must be having to keep your supper warm."

"I'd be mighty surprised if she was," he said. "We're in the process of a divorce." Then he placed her fingers in the right position on the keys—what he called "home base"—and taught her to type *a sad mad lad,* which made her laugh. When he left he gave her his card so she could call him with any questions.

That night she whizzed through the first five lessons in a single sitting. Agatha woke in the dark to hear the clacking of the keys, and when she came out to the kitchen her mother said, "See how far I've gone! At this rate I'll be an expert in no time." Agatha went back to bed and slept better than she had in weeks.

The next morning the kitchen table was covered with sheets of typing—*pat rat sat hat* and *pop had a top.* Agatha poured Coca-Cola into a glass and added a spoonful of instant coffee (her mother's favorite way to get herself going) and carried it into the bedroom. Her mother was asleep in her slip with an arm hanging over the edge of the mattress, so it looked like one of those times when she would have trouble waking. But she opened her eyes at just the clink of the glass on the nightstand and she thanked Agatha very clearly. She spent that morning on Lessons Six through Eleven while Agatha, who this once was allowed to skip school, watched over Thomas and Daphne. Lesson Twelve was not important, their mother decided. That was only numerals, which she could go on doing hunt-and-peck unless she had to work for an accountant or something, which she certainly wasn't planning on. She was planning to work for one of the downtown law firms, something at a nice front desk with flowers in a vase, she said, where she would answer the phone in a la-de-da voice and type letters clickety-click while the clients sat in the waiting room waiting. She demonstrated how she would look—nose raised snootily in the air and fingers tripping smartly as if the keys were burning hot. She was still in her bathrobe but you could see she was going to be perfect.

Around lunchtime that day they walked to Cold Spring Lane and bought a newspaper. They used to have home delivery but now they couldn't afford it. Once she was hired, their mother said, they'd have home delivery again and they would sit around the breakfast table reading their horoscopes before she went to her office. Agatha had a thought. She said, "But Mama, who's going to *stay* with us?"

"We'll work that out when we come to it," her mother said, tipping the stroller up onto a curb.

"Work it out how?"

"We'll manage, Agatha. All right?"

"You wouldn't just leave us on our own, would you?"

"Have I ever, ever left you on your own?"

Agatha opened her mouth but then closed it. Thomas looked over at her. His eyes filled with tears.

"Stop it," Agatha told him.

He stood in the middle of the sidewalk and his face crumpled up.

"What in the world?" their mother asked. She turned to stare at him.

"He's just . . . feeling sad," Agatha explained. She didn't want to remind her about Danny.

At home, their mother had spread the paper across the coffee table and circled every secretarial ad—dozens of them. The problem, she said, was not finding a job but choosing which one. "If I'd known how easy this was I'd have done it years ago," she said. Then during Daphne's nap she took the paper off to the bedroom telephone. For a while her voice murmured: "Da-dah? Da-da-dah? Da-de-*dah*-da . . ." Finally a long quiet spell. Thomas and Agatha looked at each other. They were watching soap operas with the sound turned off. Thomas took his thumb out of his mouth and said, "Go see."

So Agatha went to tap at the door. No answer. She turned the knob and peered through the crack. Her mother was sitting against the headboard with the telephone on her lap. She was staring into space.

"Mama?" Agatha said.

"Hmm?"

"Did you find a job?"

"Agatha, do you have to keep pestering me? Isn't there any place in this house where I can be private?"

"Maybe there'll be something tomorrow," Agatha said.

"Well, even if there is," her mother said, "I'll lose out the minute I tell them the truth. These people just *want* you to lie. They practically *beg* you to lie. 'I've got thirty years' experience,' they want me to say. Even though I'm not but twenty-five."

"Should I bring you a Coke, Mama?"

"No, just let me get on with this. I'm going to try a couple more."

Now what they heard from the living room was louder and firmer, though still no easier to make out. "*Dah*-da. *Dah*-da-da." And when she came to stand in the doorway, she was smiling. "Well," she said, "I've set up an interview."

They could tell it was something they should hug her for.

That evening she practiced her typing—little rushes of clacks separated by pauses when she had to make capital letters. She let Agatha phone Passenger Pizza even though they couldn't afford it. And the next morning she took them to stay at Grandma Bedloe's while she went to her interview. Grandma Bedloe said, "Doesn't Agatha have school today?" but their mother said, "Her head was hurting." She gave Agatha one of her secret looks—not a wink but more of a twinkle, without a single muscle moving. Then off she went to the bus stop, wearing the rose-colored suit she had married Danny in. Grandma Bedloe said, "She is way overdressed." This worried Thomas, you could tell. His thumb homed in to his mouth and he glanced at Agatha. But Agatha had seen how perky their mother looked spiking down the front steps with her hair flouncing over her shoulders, so she wasn't concerned. Anyhow, of all people to talk! Grandma Bedloe in her slacks and a man's plaid shirt, with the skin beneath her eyes grown so loose and droopy and pleated since Danny died.

When their mother came back, she was walking more slowly. "How'd it go, dear?" Grandma Bedloe asked.

"Fine," their mother said.

"You got the job?"

"We'll have to see."

"When will they let you know?"

"It may be a while," their mother said, and she didn't seem to move her lips as she spoke.

She wouldn't stay for lunch. She said she had to get Daphne home for her bottle. "This is why I think your Aunt Claudia's so smart to breast-feed," Grandma Bedloe told the children, and their mother spun around from settling Daphne in her stroller and said, "Well, I *don't* breast-feed. All right? I never breast-fed a one of them and I don't intend to start now!"

Grandma Bedloe said, "Why! Lucy? All I meant was—"

"*Some* people can let themselves get saggy and baggy but I don't have that luxury. I can't afford to take anything for granted in this life, I've learned. If there's one thing I've learned, it's that. You think I enjoy this? Watching my weight and painting my nails, never letting my guard down, always on the lookout for split ends?"

"Split ends?"

"Oh, forget it. Thanks for keeping the children," their mother said, and she took hold of the stroller and pushed it through the door.

On the way home, she wouldn't talk. Or she talked, but only to herself. "Snob!" she whispered once. She stalked behind the stroller awhile and then whispered, "Conceited!" Agatha thought at first she meant Grandma Bedloe (who had never acted like a snob that she knew of and was not a bit conceited). But then their mother said, "Just tell me what *words per minute* have to do with anything!" So Agatha knew it must be someone at the interview.

At home, their mother left Daphne in her stroller in the middle of the kitchen while she phoned the typewriter man. "You can come and fetch this machine of yours," she started right in. "Pick it up and haul it back, I'll be glad to see the last of it. What? This is Lucy Bedloe. You brought me a Smith-Corona day before yesterday."

He must have said something. She paused. Unsmiling, she made a short laughing sound. "Oh, really. What a thing to say," she said.

Another pause.

Another laugh, this time a real one.

"You surely know how to brighten up a person's mood," she said.

Then she sat down on a kitchen chair and told him about her awful morning, this woman in charge of hiring who'd acted so uppity and hoity-toity . . . So anyhow, she said. Would he please come and get his machine? She should have realized she wasn't the type for an office.

He came after work and he stayed for supper. She made him an omelet. She set two of the least bent candles in the center of the table. "This is delicious," he said after his first mouthful.

She said, "Oh, no, really, you caught me without any groceries. You should see what I usually fix."

What she usually fixed was Kellogg's Corn Flakes, but Agatha knew she didn't mean it as a lie. It was more like a politeness. Trying to help her out, Thomas and Agatha kept their eyes on their plates and ate extra neatly.

He took the typewriter away with him when he left, but he told their mother not to feel discouraged. "Want to know what I think?" he asked. "I think someone's going to jump at the chance to hire a gal like you. All you got to do is bide your time—that and keep your skills up. Sure you don't want to hang onto this machine?"

"I can't afford it," she said.

"Tell you what: I'll hold it for you. You liked this model, didn't you? I'll hold it in the showroom a while in case you change your mind."

"Well, that's very thoughtful," she said.

So now she had her own machine at Rumford & Son's, which they went regularly to visit. And at first she really did type on it. She sat down at the desk and showed the man she still remembered her *pat rat sat hat.* But then she started just *talking* about her typewriter. She asked how it was getting along without her and he said it looked mighty lonesome and she laughed and changed the subject. Today, for instance, she discussed the weather. She said how some people had all the luck, working in an air-conditioned building; how at home she slept with nothing to cool her off but a fan; how she had to slide out of her negligee halfway through every night on account of the heat. She scooted the stroller a few inches forward, a few inches backward, forward, backward, over and over, speaking in her slow, scrapy voice and every so often laughing when the typewriter man said something funny.

Thomas crawled under a desk and told Agatha it was his house. The typewriter on top was so little and cute that Agatha started punching the keys. She had to punch really hard because it wasn't electric, and Thomas complained about the noise. He said, "This is *my* house. You go somewhere else." Agatha pretended not to hear. She typed *agatha dean 7 years old baltimore md usa.* Thomas shouted, "Stop that racket on my roof!" and reared up and bumped his head. When their mother heard him crying she broke off her conversation and turned. "Oh, Thomas," she said, "now what?" But the typewriter man didn't seem cross. He said, "Why, what's this? Two customers in need of my assistance," and he helped Thomas out from under the desk. "Something I can show you, sir? Some question I can answer?"

Thomas stopped crying and rubbed the top of his head. "Well," he said. He thought a moment. He said, "You know how people have those blood veins one in each arm?"

"Blood veins, ah . . ."

"So how come any place you prick will bleed? Wouldn't you think there'd be places that don't?"

"Ah, well . . ."

"I apologize for this," their mother said. "They promised they'd behave. Come on, children, I'm taking you home."

"No, Mama! *I* behaved!" Agatha said. She didn't want to leave the air-conditioning.

But her mother said, "Nice talking with you, Murray."

"Hurry back, okay?" the man said, and he walked them to the door. Agatha could tell he was sorry to see them go.

Out on the sidewalk their mother started humming. She hummed "Ramblin' Rose" while they waited for the traffic light, and she took them to Joyner's Drugstore for Lifesavers. Just trailed her fingers across the candy counter, brush-brush, nothing to it, and dropped the two rolls in her bag. Then she twinkled her eyes at Thomas and Agatha. They giggled and she instantly looked elsewhere as if she'd never met them.

While she collected her prescription, Agatha rocked the stroller because Daphne was starting to fuss. Thomas dawdled up and down the aisles, hunting dropped coins. At Luckman's he'd once found a nickel and put it in the gumball machine, but all he got back was gum. He'd been hoping for a set of silver plastic handcuffs the size of finger rings.

The pharmacist saw them to the door, saying, "Still hot out there?" Thomas and Agatha smiled up at him, remembering to look attractive— Thomas not sucking his thumb, Agatha not letting her mouth flop open— but their mother said, "Mmhmm," and wheeled the stroller on through without a glance. You never could be sure, with her, who you had to be nice to and who you didn't.

Standing at the front window and holding back the curtain, Agatha watched for the first star. In the summertime she had to be alert, because the sky stayed light for so long that the stars would more or less *melt* into view. Agatha knew all about it. She waited at this window every night. Sometimes Thomas waited too, but he wasn't nearly so faithful. Also he said his wishes aloud, no matter how often she warned him not to. And he wished for definite objects—toys and candy and such—as if the sky were one big Sears, Roebuck Christmas catalog. "Star light, star bright, first star I see tonight . . . I wish for a front-end loader with real rubber treads on it."

Agatha, on the other hand, wished silently, and not even in words. She wished in a strong wash of feeling, instead. *Let everything turn out all right,* was the closest she could put it. Or, no, *Let us be safe.* But that was not exactly it either.

She looked from the sky to the street and saw Ian and Grandma Bedloe coming up the sidewalk. Ian carried a picnic basket covered with a red-checked cloth, and Grandma Bedloe carried a cake tin. Agatha loved Grandma Bedloe's cakes. She made one last sweeping search for her star and then gave up and ran to answer the doorbell.

"Hello, dearies," Grandma Bedloe said, and she kissed Agatha first and then Thomas. It was just since Danny died that she'd started kissing them. It was just since Danny died that she'd dried out so and shortened, and begun to move so stiffly. But the stiffness was rheumatism, she said: her knees acting up. A matter of humidity.

"See what we brought you!" she told them. "Devil's food cake and fried chicken. Where's your mother?"

"She's having a nap."

"A nap?"

She glanced over at Ian. He wore his most faded jeans and a plain white T-shirt; he must have just got off work. Agatha thought he resembled those handsome teenaged hoodlums on TV. She wished the girls at school could see her once in his company, but it never seemed to happen.

"I hope you haven't had supper yet," Grandma Bedloe said. "Has your mother started anything cooking? How long has she been in her nap? Does she usually nap at this hour?"

Each question brought her further into the house. She pressed forward, passing Thomas and Agatha, heading for the kitchen, where she set the cake tin on the table and turned to look around her. "Oh, my, I'd say she *hasn't* started cooking," she said. "Goodness. Well. Try and make space for that basket on the counter, Ian. Agatha, dear, shall I put a few of these dishes to soak while you wake your mother?"

"Or we could eat without her," Agatha said. "We could let her rest."

"No, no, I'm sure she'd want—where's Daphne?"

"In her crib," Agatha said.

"She's napping too?"

"No, she's just . . . Mama just set her there a while."

"Well, let's go get her!" Grandma Bedloe said. "We can't leave our Daphne all alone, now!" And off she went, with Thomas and Agatha following.

In the children's room, Daphne poked her nose between the crib bars and cooed. "Hello, sweetness," Grandma Bedloe told her. She picked her up and said, "Somebody's sopping." Then she looked at the supplies lined against the footboard—a filled nursing bottle, a plate of darkening banana slices, and one of the breadsticks Daphne liked to teethe on. "What *is* all this?" Grandma Bedloe asked. "Her lunch? Her supper? How long has she been in here?"

"Just a teensy while," Agatha said. "Honest. She just did get put down."

"Well, I'm going to change her diaper and dress her in some nicer little clothes," Grandma Bedloe said. (It was true that Daphne's undershirt didn't seem very fresh.) "You and Thomas go start your suppers."

So they went back to the kitchen, where Ian was unpacking the basket. He didn't ask what parts of the chicken they preferred. Agatha had been going to say the keel, a word she'd heard last week at a fast-food place. "I'll have the keel, please." Whatever that was. She figured it might make Ian stop and notice her. But he served each of them a drumstick without a word and went to the refrigerator for milk. He filled two glasses and thought a minute and then bent forward and sniffed. Then he took both glasses to the sink and poured them out. Agatha pinched a piece of crust off her drumstick and placed it in her mouth, meanwhile waiting to see what other drink he would offer. But he didn't offer anything. He just pulled out a chair and sank down onto it.

"Aren't you going to eat too?" Thomas asked him.

But he must not have been listening.

"Ian? You can have our mama's share. I bet she won't be hungry."

"Thanks," Ian said after a pause. But he didn't reach into the basket.

Grandma Bedloe was talking to Daphne. "Now, doesn't that feel better?" she was saying. "Let's go show Mommy." She knocked on their mother's bedroom door. They heard her turn the knob and walk in. "Oh, Mom-mee! Look who's come to see you, Mommy."

Their mother gave one of her sleep-moans.

"Lucy?" Grandma Bedloe said. "Are you all right, dear?"

Poor Grandma Bedloe. She didn't know their mother had to wake on her own. Finally she came back to the kitchen, carrying Daphne in a white knit romper that showed off her curly black hair. "Does your mother tend to sleep like that till morning?" she asked.

Agatha said, "Oh, no." She was glad to be able to tell the truth. "She'll get up again! Don't worry! She wakes up after dark and then she's awake all night, just about."

Grandma Bedloe settled Daphne on her hip. She said, "I certainly hope . . ." Then she said, "I wouldn't blame her a bit, understand . . ." Finally she said, "Tell me, Agatha, do you think she might be taking a little too much to drink?"

"Drink?"

"I mean, alcohol? A beer or two, or wine?"

"No," Agatha said.

"I hope you don't mind my asking. And you know I wouldn't blame her. We all like a little cocktail now and then!"

"Mama doesn't," Agatha said.

"Well, that's something," Grandma Bedloe said with a sigh.

Then she started pestering Thomas to eat his chicken. She claimed he was skinny as a sparrow. Come to think of it, he *was* kind of skinny. But she was wrong about the cocktails. Their mother never drank at all. She said drinking made her say things.

She also said that dead people don't really leave us; they just stop weighing anything. But Agatha didn't know who was right there, her mother or Grandma Bedloe, because when she'd asked Grandma Bedloe why they had needed six people to carry Danny's coffin, Grandma Bedloe said, "What do you mean?" Agatha said, "Couldn't just one person do it? With just the tips of his fingers?" Grandma Bedloe said, "Why, Agatha, he was a full-grown man. He weighed a hundred and seventy pounds." Then she had turned all teary and Grandpa Bedloe told her, "There, hon. There, hon."

"He used to say he was getting a paunch, and he'd have to start watching what he ate," Grandma Bedloe wept. "He never dreamed how little time he had! He could have eaten anything he wanted!"

"There, honeybee."

Now it occurred to Agatha that what had weighed so much was the coffin itself. Maybe that was why they'd needed six people.

After supper Grandma Bedloe tidied the kitchen while Ian played Parcheesi with Thomas and Agatha. He held Daphne on his knee and gazed down at the board with a sort of puzzled expression. When Thomas miscounted on purpose, he didn't even notice. "Cheater!" Agatha told Thomas. "He's cheating, Ian."

"Really?" Ian said.

"He should be up in front of you where you could take him off next move."

"Really," Ian said.

He had been a lot more fun in the olden days.

When Grandma Bedloe had finished the dishes she came to stand in the doorway, wearing a flowered apron of their mother's that Agatha had forgotten about. "Ian," she said, "I cannot in all good conscience walk out and leave these children on their own like this."

Ian shook the dice in one cupped hand and spilled them across the board: a four and a six. "You hear me, Ian?" his mother asked.

Agatha watched their faces, hoping. They could stay, she wanted to tell them. Or they could take the three of them home with them. But then what about their mother?

"Maybe you could bring her too," she suggested to Grandma Bedloe.

"Bring who, dear?"

"Maybe you could bring us all to your house. Mama too."

Ian moved one man four spaces. Then he reached toward another man.

"If you wrap her in a blanket, she can walk pretty good," Agatha said. "Stir coffee into her Coca-Cola and make her drink it and then hold her hand; she can walk anywhere you want her to."

Ian's fingers stopped in midair. He and Grandma Bedloe looked at each other.

Just at that moment, footsteps creaked in the hall and here came their mother, tying the sash of her kimono. It was the shiny gray kimono she hardly ever wore, not her usual bathrobe, so she must have known there were visitors. Also her hair was brushed. It puffed around her shoulders and down her back, dark and cloud-shaped, so her face stood out brightly. She gave them all her best smile. "Oh! Mother Bedloe. And Ian," she said. "This is so embarrassing! Caught napping in the shank of the evening! But I took the children on a long, long walk this afternoon and I guess I must have worn myself out."

Grandma Bedloe and Ian studied her. Thomas and Agatha held very still.

Then Grandma Bedloe said, "Why, my heavens! Pushing a stroller, on a day like today! Of *course* you're worn out. You just sit yourself down and let me bring you some supper."

Agatha let go of her breath. Thomas was smiling too, now. He had a smile like their mother's, sort of dipping at the center, and he looked relieved. And Grandma Bedloe was moving toward the kitchen, and Ian reached again for his Parcheesi piece. *Everyone* was relieved.

So why did Agatha suddenly feel so anxious?

It was past their bedtime but their mother hadn't noticed yet. She was perched on a stool in the kitchen, reading a cookbook and munching one of the drumsticks Grandma Bedloe had left on the counter. "Beef Goulash," she read out. "Beef with Pearl Onions. Beef Crescents. Agatha, what was that beef dish Grandma Bedloe told us about?"

"I don't remember," Agatha said, switching to a yellow crayon.

"It was rolled up in Bisquick dough."

"I remember she talked about it but I don't remember the name."

"Bisquick dough sprinkled with herbs of some kind. She had it at their neighbors'."

"Maybe you could call and ask her."

"I can't do that. She'd want to know who I was making it for."

Her mother set down the drumstick and wiped her fingers on a paper towel before turning another page. "Beef à la Oriental," she read out.

"Couldn't you just say you were making it for the typewriter man?"

"These things are touchy," her mother said. "You wouldn't understand."

That hurt Agatha's feelings a little. She scowled and kicked her feet out. By mistake, she kicked Thomas. He was drowsing over a plastic cup of grapefruit juice. He opened his eyes and said, "Stop."

"Always serve a man red meat," her mother told Agatha. "Remember that for the future."

"Red meat," Agatha repeated dutifully.

"It shows you think of them as strong."

"What if you served them fish?"

"Men don't like fish."

"They like chicken, though."

"Well, yes."

"If you served them chicken, would they think you thought they were scared?"

"Hmm?" her mother said.

Thomas said, "Mama, Agatha kicked me." But his eyes were closing again.

"Well, here goes," their mother said, and she reached for the phone.

"You're calling Grandma Bedloe?" Agatha asked.

"No, silly, I'm calling Mr. Rumford."

She dialed in that special way she had, very fast and zippy. She must know the number by heart. She had called two earlier times that Agatha was aware of—one morning while he was at work, just to make sure he didn't have anyone else; and then one evening, hanging up when he answered. Also they'd gone in person to see where he lived. They'd ridden the bus out to Ruxton in the company of nothing but colored maids; they'd peered through the window at his red brick house. "Deserted," their mother had said in a pleased, flat voice. "And no one has tended those shrubs in ages." Then they rattled back to town all by themselves, having left the maids behind.

"Hello?" their mother said into the receiver.

Her forehead was suddenly creased.

"Hello, is this . . . who is this?"

She listened. She said, "You mean the, um, the *wife* Mrs. Rumford?"

Then she said, "Sorry." And hung up.

Thomas said, "Agatha kicked me, Mama."

Their mother closed the cookbook and stared down at it. She stroked the cover, the golden letters stamped into the cloth.

"Mama?"

"We'd better go to bed," Agatha told Thomas.

"You're not the boss of me!"

"It's time, Thomas," she said, and she made her voice very hard.

He slid off his chair and followed her out of the kitchen.

In the children's room, Daphne was asleep. They undressed in the dark, using the light from the hallway. Thomas wanted his cowboy pajamas but Agatha couldn't find them. She said he'd have to wear his airplane pajamas instead. He climbed into them without an argument, staggering around the room as he tried to fit his feet through. Then he said he had to pee. "Use Mama's bathroom," Agatha told him.

"What for?"

"Just do."

She'd kept him away from the other one all evening. She worried the toilet would flood again.

She lay down in bed and pulled the covers up and listened to her mother moving around the house. Every sound meant something: the TV clicking on and then off, a drawer in the living room opening and then closing, the clang of a metal ashtray on the coffee table. Their mother smoked only when she was upset, holding the cigarette in some wrong-looking way with her fingers sticking out too straight. Agatha heard the scrape of a match, the pushed, tired sound of her breath whooshing forth.

Where were the pills? The popping of the lid off the pill bottle?

At least when she took pills she didn't fidget around like this.

Thomas appeared in the doorway—a black-and-gray shape against the yellow light. He crossed not to his own bed but to Agatha's. She had more or less expected that. She grumbled but she slid over to make room. His hair smelled like sugar browning in a saucepan. He said, "She didn't come kiss us good night."

"Later she'll come."

"I want her to come now."

"*Later,*" Agatha said.

"She didn't read us a story, either."

"I'll tell you one."

"Reading's better."

"Well, Thomas! I can't read in the dark, can I?"

Sometimes she noticed how much she sounded like her mother. Same sure tone, same exasperated answers. Although she failed to resemble her in any other way. At a family dinner last winter Grandma Bedloe had said, "What a pity Agatha didn't inherit Lucy's bone structure."

"Once upon a time," she told Thomas, "there was a poor servant girl named Cinderella."

"Not that one."

"Once upon a time a rich merchant had three daughters."

"Not that one either. I want 'Hansel and Gretel.' "

This was no surprise to Agatha. (He liked things that rhymed. *Nibble, nibble, like a mouse, who is nibbling at my house?*) But Agatha hated "Hansel and Gretel." There wasn't any magic to it—no fairy godmothers, or frogs turning into princes. "How about 'Snow White'?" she asked. "That's got *Mirror, mirror, on the wall . . .*"

"I want 'Hansel and Gretel.' "

She sighed and resettled her pillow. "All right, have it your way," she said. "Once upon a time Hansel and Gretel were taking a walk—"

"That's not how it starts!"

"Who's telling this: you or me?"

"First there's their parents! And dropping breadcrumbs on the path! And the birds eat all the crumbs and Hansel and Gretel get lost!"

"Keep your voice down!" Agatha hissed.

Daphne slept on, though. And in the living room their mother's footsteps continued. Pace, pace. Swish of kimono. Pace, pace.

The night after Danny's funeral, she had paced till morning. (Back then she didn't have her pills yet.) The next day when Agatha got up she found the ashtray heaped with nasty-smelling butts and her mother asleep on the couch. Danny's picture stood on the coffee table nearby—the one she usually kept on her bureau. He was laughing under a beach umbrella. His eyes were dark and curly and full of kindness.

Agatha never thought about Danny anymore.

"I have to pee," Thomas whispered.

"What, again?"

He slid out of bed and hitched up his pajama bottoms. "It was too much grapefruit juice," he said.

Agatha leaned against her pillow and folded her arms and watched him go. The cigarette smoke from the living room made her nose feel crinkly inside. Wasn't it strange how dead butts smelled so dirty, but lighted cigarettes smelled exciting and promising.

Something nagged at her mind, a bothersome thought she couldn't quite get hold of. Then she noticed what she was hearing: the flushing of the toilet. Oh, no. She threw back her covers and started out of bed.

Too late, though. Thomas shrieked, "Mama! Mama!" and their mother cried, "Thomas?" Her bare feet came rushing down the hall. Her kimono made a crackling sound like fire.

Agatha decided to stay where she was.

"Oh, my God," her mother said. "Oh, my Lord in heaven."

She must be standing in the bathroom doorway. Her voice echoed off the tiles.

"What did you put down that toilet?" she asked.

"Nothing! I promise! I just flushed and the water poured everywhere!"

"Oh, my Lord above."

Agatha wondered if the toilet was still running. She couldn't hear it. She imagined the house flooding silently with the murky yellow water from Daphne's diaper.

"Just *go*, will you?" their mother said. "Go back to bed and stay there. And don't you dare use this toilet again till I can get hold of a plumber, hear?"

The word "plumber" sounded so knowledgeable. Yes, of course: there was a regular, normal person to take charge of this situation, and that meant it must happen to other people too. Agatha pulled her covers up. She watched Thomas enter the room and trudge to his own bed. He walked like an old man, huddled together across the back of his neck. He lay down and reached for Dulcimer and hugged her to his chest.

It wasn't like him to be so quiet. Maybe he had guessed the toilet was Agatha's fault.

She said, "Thomas?"

No answer.

"Thomas, is the water still spilling over?"

"Doe," he said, and the stopped-up sound of his voice told her he was crying.

"You want to come sleep in my bed?"

"Doe."

In the hall she heard their mother's bare feet heading toward her bedroom, and then a pause and then hard shoes clopping out again—or maybe boots. Something big and heavy. Clop-clop toward the kitchen, clop-clop back down the hall. The swabbing of a mop across the bathroom floor. Well, so. It would all be taken care of.

Agatha relaxed and let her eyes fall shut. She might even have slept a few minutes. She saw sleep-pictures floating behind her lids—a black cat hissing and then Ian rattling his dice and all at once flinging them into her face and causing her to start. Her eyes flew open. The lights were still on, and the radio was playing a Beatles song. Ice cubes clinked in a glass. The cloppy footsteps came down the hall, and there was her mother outlined in the doorway. From the ankles up she was thin and fragile, but on her feet she wore two huge shoes from Danny's closet. She came over to Agatha's bed, shuffling slightly so the shoes wouldn't fall off. "Are you awake?" she whispered.

Agatha said, "Yes."

She realized that Thomas must not be. His breathing had grown very slow.

Her mother sat on the edge of the bed. In one hand she held a glass of Coke and in the other her brown plastic pill bottle, uncapped. Probably that was what had rattled in the dream; not Ian's dice after all. She tipped the bottle to her mouth and swallowed a pill and then took a sip of Coke. She said, "Do you believe this? Do you believe a person would just have to fend for herself in this world?"

"Won't the plumber come help?" Agatha asked.

"Everything is resting on my shoulders."

"Maybe Grandma Bedloe knows a plumber."

"It's Howard Belling all over again," her mother said, which was confusing because, for a second, Agatha thought she meant that the plumber was Howard Belling. "It's the same old story. Unattached, they tell you. Separated, they tell you—or soon about to be. And then one fine morning they're all lovey-dovey with their wives again. How come other people manage to have things so permanent? Is it something I'm doing wrong?"

"No, Mama, *you* didn't do anything wrong," Agatha said.

Her mother tipped another pill into her mouth and took another swallow of Coke. The ice cubes sounded like wind chimes. She raised one foot, her ankle just a stem above the clumsy shoe. Agatha thought of "Clementine." *Herring boxes without topses, sandals were for . . .*

"No wonder men aren't afraid of things!" her mother said. "Would *you* be afraid, if you got to wear gigantic shoes like these?"

Yes, even then she would be, Agatha thought. But she didn't want to say so.

Her mother bent to kiss her good night, brushing her face with the soft weight of her hair, and then she rose and left. Her shoes clopped more and more faintly and her ice cubes tinkled more distantly. Agatha closed her eyes again.

She tried to ride away on the beat of rhymed words—*herring boxes without topses* and *Johnny over the ocean, Johnny over the sea, Johnny broke a milk bottle, blamed it on me.*

Nibble, nibble, like a mouse, she thought. *Who is nibbling at my house?*

She kept repeating it, concentrating. *Nibble, nibble* . . . She fixed all her thoughts upon it. *Like a mouse* . . . But no matter how hard she tried, she couldn't push back the picture that kept forming behind her lids. Hansel and Gretel were wandering through the woods alone and lost, holding hands, looking all around them. The trees loomed so tall overhead that you couldn't see their tops, and Hansel and Gretel were two tiny specks beneath the great dark ceiling of the forest.

3

The Man Who Forgot How to Fly

In his ninth-grade biology class, Ian had watched through a microscope while an amoeba shaped like a splash approached a dot of food and gradually surrounded it. Then it had moved on, wider now and blunter, distorted to accommodate the dot of food within.

As Ian accommodated, over and over, absorbing the fact of Danny's death.

He would see it looming in his path—something dark and stony that got in the way of every happy moment. He'd be splitting a pizza with Pig and Andrew or listening to records with Cicely and all at once it would rise up in front of him: *Danny is dead. He died. Died.*

And then a thought that was even worse: *He died on purpose. He killed himself.*

And finally the most horrible thought of all: *Because of what I told him.*

He learned to deal with these thoughts in order, first things first. *All right, he's dead. I will never see him again. He's in Pleasant Memory Cemetery underneath a lilac bush. He won't be helping me with my fast ball. He hasn't heard I got accepted at Sumner College. Trees that were bare when he last saw them have bloomed and leafed without him.*

It felt like swallowing, to take in such a hard set of truths all at one time.

And then he would tackle the next thought. But that was more of a struggle. *Maybe it was an accident,* he always argued.

He smashes headlong into a wall by ACCIDENT? A wall he knew perfectly well was there, a wall that's stood at the end of that street since before he was born?

Well, he'd been drinking.

He wasn't drunk, though.

Yes, but, you know how it is . . .

Face it. He really did kill himself.

And then finally the last thought.

No, never the last thought.

Sometimes he tried to believe that everyone on earth walked around with at least one unbearable guilty secret hidden away inside. Maybe it was part of growing up. Maybe if he went and confessed to his mother she would say, "Why, sweetheart! Is that all that's bothering you? Listen, every last one of us has caused *somebody*'s suicide."

Well, no.

But if he told her anyway, and let her get as angry as she liked. If he said, "Mom, you decide what to do with me. Kick me out of the house, if you want. Or disown me. Or call the police."

In fact, he wished she *would* call the police. He wished it were something he could go to prison for.

But if he told his mother she would learn it was a suicide, and everyone assumed it was an accident. Driving under the influence. Too much stag party. That was the trouble with confessing: it would make him feel better, all right, but it would make the others feel worse. And if his mother felt any worse than she did already, he thought it would kill her. His father too, probably. This whole summer, all his father had done was sit in his recliner chair.

Once his mother asked, "Ian, you don't suppose Danny was depressed or anything, do you?"

"Depressed?"

"Oh, but what am I saying? He had a new baby! And a lovely new wife, and a whole new ready-made family!"

"Right," Ian said.

"Of course, there could have been *little* problems. Some minor snag at work, maybe, or a rocky patch in his marriage. But nothing out of the ordinary, don't you agree?"

"Well, sure," Ian told her.

Was that all it had been? A rocky patch? Had Ian overreacted?

He saw how young he was, how inexperienced, what a shallow, ignorant *boy* he was. He really had no idea what would be considered out of the ordinary in a marriage.

On Sundays when the family gathered, he sent Lucy sidelong glances. He noticed she was growing steadily paler, like one of his father's old Polaroid photos. He wanted to believe Danny's death hadn't touched her, but there she sat with something still and stricken in her face. Her children quarreled shrilly with Claudia's children, but Lucy just sat straight-backed, not appearing to hear, and smoothed her skirt over and over across her lap.

Privately Bee told the others, "I wish she had someone to go to. Relatives, I mean. Of course we'd miss her but . . . if she had someone to tend the children so she could get a job, for instance! I know *I* ought to offer—"

Doug said, "Don't even consider it."

"Well, I'm their grandma! Or one of them's grandma. But lately I've been so tired and my knees are acting up and I don't see how I could handle it. I know I ought to, though."

"Don't give it a moment's consideration."

Did Lucy ever think, *If only I hadn't gone out with Dot that night?* Did she think, *If only Dot's car hadn't broken down?*

For it *was* Dot she'd gone out with. And the car *had* broken down, someplace on Ritchie Highway. That much emerged at the funeral, which Dot had attended all weepy and disbelieving.

Did Lucy ever think, *If only I had been a faithful wife?*

No, probably not, for Ian couldn't shake off the feeling that he was the one she blamed. (At the very least, he'd made Danny drive him home that night.) He was almost positive that she slid her eyes reproachfully in his direction as she smoothed her skirt across her lap. But Ian looked elsewhere. He made a point of looking elsewhere.

Only Cicely knew the whole story. He had told her after the first time they ever made love. Lying next to her in her bed (her parents had gone to a Memorial Day picnic, taking her little brother with them), he had thought, *Danny will never know I've finally slept with a girl.* His eyes had blurred with tears and he had turned abruptly and pressed his hot, wet face into Cicely's neck. "I'm the one who caused Danny's accident," he blurted out. But the thing was, she wouldn't accept it. It was like some physical object that she kept batting away. "Oh, no," she kept saying. "No, that's silly. You didn't do anything. Lucy didn't do anything. Lucy was a *perfect* wife. Danny knew you didn't mean it."

He should have said, "Listen. You have to believe this." But her skin was so soft, and her neck smelled of baby powder, and instead of speaking he had started making love again. He had felt ashamed even then at how easily he was diverted.

Or here was something more shameful than that: In the emergency room that awful night, when the doctors said there was no hope, Ian had thought, *At least now Cicely can't stay mad at me for missing our dinner date.*

Despicable. Despicable. He ground his teeth together any time he recalled it.

That summer he worked again for Sid 'n' Ed's A-1 Movers. Lou had been fired for bleeding all over some lady's sofa after he sat on his own whiskey flask; but LeDon was still there, along with a new man named Brewster, a rough-and-tough, prune-colored type who didn't have two words to say from one day to the next. That was fine with Ian. He felt grateful just for someplace to escape to, some hard labor to throw himself into.

One move he helped with was obviously upward, from a tiny house in Govans to a much nicer one in Cedarcroft. Workers were swarming around the new place, patching the roof and resodding the lawn and measuring for window screens. In the kitchen he found a man installing wooden cabinets, and he stood watching as one was fitted precisely into place. The man plucked nails out of nowhere. (Maybe he had a mouthful, like Bee with her sewing pins. His back was turned so Ian couldn't tell.) He hammered them in with quick rat-a-tats. And he didn't act the least self-conscious, not even when Ian said, "Looks good." In fact, he didn't bother answering. Or maybe he hadn't heard. Ian said, loudly, "Nice piece of work."

Then he understood that the man was deaf. It was something about his head—the way he held it so steady, not troubling to keep alert for any sounds. Ian stepped forward and the man glanced over at him. He had a square-jawed, deeply lined face and a bristly gray crewcut. "Looks good," Ian repeated, and the man nodded briefly and returned to his hammering.

Ian felt a twist of envy. It wasn't just the work he envied, although that was part of it—the all-consuming task that left no room for extraneous thoughts. It was the notion of a sealed-off world. A world where no one traded speech, and where even dreams, he supposed, were soundless.

He dreamed Danny stood in the doorway jingling a pocketful of change. "I nearly forgot," he told Ian. "I owe you."

Ian caught his breath. He said, "Owe me?"

"I never paid you for baby-sitting that evening. What was it—three dollars? Five?"

Ian said, "No, please," and backed away, holding up his palms. He woke to hear his own voice saying, "No. No. Please."

His parents drove him to school on a hot day in September. Cicely had already left for her own school, near Philadelphia, but since that was just an hour from Sumner College there had not been any big farewell scene. In fact, they were planning on meeting that weekend. And Andrew was close by too, at Temple. But none of Ian's friends were attending Sumner, and he was glad. He liked the idea of making a new beginning. His mother said, "Oh, I hope you won't be lonesome!" but Ian almost hoped he would be. He saw himself striding unaccompanied across the campus, a mysterious figure dressed all in black. "Who *is* that person?" girls would ask. Although he didn't actually own anything black, come to think of it. Still, he had his plans.

They dropped his belongings at the freshman dorm, where the only sign of his roommate was a khaki duffel bag and a canvas butterfly chair printed to resemble a gigantic hand. (At least Ian assumed the chair was his roommate's. All the other furniture was blond oak.) Then they walked over to the Parents' Reception. Ian was in favor of skipping the reception and so was his father, but his mother insisted.

At the college president's house they were given three paper cups of 7-Up with orange sherbet floating foamily on top, and they stood in a clump by a blond oak table trying to make conversation with each other. "Quite a crowd," his father said, and his mother said, "Yes, isn't it!" Ian started eating spice cookies from a plate on the table. He ate one after the other, frowning and chewing intently as if he could have made many interesting comments if only his mouth weren't full. "Are these all parents of freshmen, do you suppose?" his father asked. "Well, maybe some are transfers' parents," his mother said.

She stood among these ruffly people in her ordinary navy dress, and her shoes were plain flat pumps because of her knees. Without high heels she seemed downtrodden, Ian noticed, like somebody's maid. And his father's suit was rucked up around his calves with static cling or something. He had the crazy appearance of a formally attired man standing shin-deep in ocean breakers. Ian swallowed a sharp piece of cookie and felt it hurting all the way down his throat, all the way to his chest where it lodged and wouldn't go away. He wanted to say, "Take me back to Baltimore! I'll never complain again, I promise." But instead he joined in the small talk, and he noticed that his voice had the same determined upward slant as his mother's.

They left the reception without having spoken to another soul, and they walked together to the parking lot. The family car looked dusty and humble. Ian opened the door for his mother, but she was used to opening her own door and so she got in his way and he stepped on her foot. "Sorry," he said. "Well . . ." She kissed his cheek and slid hurriedly inside, not looking at him. His father gave him a wave across the roof of the car. "Take care of yourself, son."

"Sure thing," Ian said.

He stood with his palms clamped in his armpits and watched them drive off.

His roommate was a zany, hooting, clownish boy named Winston Mills. Not only was the hand-shaped chair his, but also a bedspread made from an American flag, and a beer stein that tinkled out "How Dry I Am" when you lifted it, and a poster for a movie called *Teenage Robots*. The other boys thought he was weird, but Ian liked him. He liked the fact that Winston never had a serious discussion or asked a serious question. Instead he told the entire plots of movies Ian had never heard of—werewolf movies and Japanese westerns and monster movies where the zippers showed clearly between the scales—or he read aloud in a falsetto voice from a collection of syrupy "love comics" he'd found at a garage sale, meanwhile lolling in his butterfly chair with the huge pink fingers curving up behind him.

Ian dreamed Danny drove onto the quad in his Chevy, which didn't have so much as a dented fender. He leaned out his window and asked Ian, "Don't you think I knew? Don't you think I knew all along?" And Ian woke and thought maybe Danny *had* known. Sometimes people just chose not to admit a thing, not even to themselves. But then he realized that was immaterial. So what if he'd known? It wasn't till he'd been told point-blank that he'd felt the need to take action.

As far as Ian could see, college was not much different from high school. Same old roots of Western civilization, same old single-cell organisms. He squinted through a microscope and watched an amoeba turn thin and branchy, curve two branches around a black dot, thicken to a blob and drift on. His lab partner was a girl and he could tell she liked him, but she seemed too foreign. She came from someplace rural and said "ditten" instead of "didn't." Also "cooten": "I cooten find my notebook anywhere." He lived for the weekends, when Cicely rode out to Sumner on a tiny, rattling train and they hung around his dorm in the hope that Winston might leave for one of his movies at some point. Supposedly Cicely was bunking with the older sister of a girl she knew from home, but in fact she shared Ian's narrow bed where late at night—silently, almost motionlessly, all but holding their breaths—they made love over and over again across the room from Winston's snoring shape.

He called home collect every weekend; that was easier than his parents' trying to call him. But the Wednesday before Halloween his mother phoned, reaching him purely by chance as he was passing through the dorm between classes. "I hate to bother you," she said, "but I thought you'd want to know. Honey, it's Lucy."

"Lucy?"

"She died."

He noticed that a sort of whirring silence seemed to be traveling down the corridor. He said, "She what?"

"We think it was pills."

He swallowed.

"Ian?"

Oh, God, he thought, *how long will I have to pay for just a handful of tossed-off words?*

"Are you all right, Ian?"

"Sure," he said.

"We got a call from Agatha last night. She told us, 'Mama keeps sleeping and won't wake up.' Well, you know that could have meant anything. Of course I made plans to get right over there but I did say, 'Oh, sweetie, I bet she's just tuckered out,' and that's when Agatha said, 'She wouldn't even wake for breakfast.' I said, 'Breakfast?' I said, 'This morning?' Ian, would you believe it, those children had been on their own since the night before when she put them to bed. Then she went to bed herself and just, I don't know, I mean there's no sign she did it on purpose but when we walked in she was flat on her back and breathing so slowly, just a breath here and another breath there, and this pill bottle sat on her nightstand totally empty. There wasn't any letter though or anything like that. So it *couldn't* have been on purpose, right? But why would she take even one of those pills? Our family's never held with sleeping pills. I always say, get up and scrub the floors if you can't sleep! Do some reading! Improve your mind! Anyhow, we called the ambulance and they took her to Union Memorial. She had gone on too long, though. If they'd got to her right away, well, maybe; but she'd been lying there a whole night and a day and there wasn't much they could do. She died this noon without ever regaining consciousness."

Can't we just back up and start over? Couldn't I have one more chance?

"Ian?" his mother was saying. "Listen, don't breathe a word to the children."

He found his voice from somewhere. He said, "They don't know yet?"

"No, and we're not ever going to tell them."

Maybe the shock had sent her around the bend. He said, "They're going to have to find out sometime. How will you explain it when she doesn't come home from the hospital?"

Or when she fails to show up for Thomas's high-school graduation or Agatha's wedding, he thought wildly, and he almost laughed.

"I mean we're not going to tell them they might have saved her," his mother said. "If they'd phoned earlier, I mean. They'd feel so guilty."

He leaned against the wall and briefly closed his eyes.

"So we've set the funeral for Friday," his mother said, "assuming her people agree to it. Did she ever happen to tell you who her people were?"

"She didn't have any. *You* know that."

"Well, distant relatives, though. Isn't it odd? I don't believe she once mentioned her maiden name."

"Lucy . . . Dean," Ian said. "Dean was her name."

"No, Dean would have been her first husband's name."

"Oh."

"There must be cousins or something, but the children couldn't think who. We said where could we reach their daddy, then? They didn't have the slightest idea."

"He lives in Cheyenne, Wyoming," Ian said. As clearly as if he'd been present, he saw Lucy heaving her package onto the post office counter. She looked up into Danny's face and asked in her little cracked voice how much it would cost to airmail a bowling ball to Wyoming.

"Your father has already called every Dean in the Cheyenne directory," his mother said, "but he came up empty. Now all we have to rely on is someone maybe seeing the obituary."

Two boys were walking down the corridor. Ian turned so he was facing the other way.

"Ian? Are you there?"

"I'm here."

"I told your father I wasn't going to phone you. I said, why interrupt your studies? But he thought maybe you could come on account of the children. Well, goodness, *I* can handle the children but they're so . . . the baby hasn't slept since she got here. And Thomas just sits around hugging that doll of his, and Agatha's being, oh, Agatha; you know how she is. Somehow I just never have felt like those two's grandma. Isn't that awful? They can't help it! But somehow ... and your sister's all tied up with Davey's measles ..."

Ian could guess what this was leading to. He felt suddenly burdened.

"So your father said maybe you could come help out a few days."

"I'll catch the next Greyhound," he said.

He rode to Baltimore that evening on a nearly empty bus, staring at his own reflection in the window. His eyes were deep black hollows and he appeared to have sharper cheekbones than he really did. He looked stark and angular, bitterly experienced. He wondered if there was any event, any at all, so tragic that it could jolt him out of this odious habit of observing his own reaction to it.

His father met him at the terminal. Neither of them knew yet how they were supposed to greet each other after long separations. Hug? Shake hands? His father settled for clapping him on the arm. "How was the trip?" he asked.

"Pretty good."

Ian hoisted his knapsack higher on his shoulder and they walked through the crowd, dodging people who seemed to have set up housekeeping there. They threaded between stuffed laundry bags and take-out food cartons; they stepped over the legs of a soldier asleep on the floor. Outside, Howard Street looked very bustling and citified after Sumner.

"So," his father said, once they were seated in the car. "I guess you heard the news."

"Right."

"Terrible thing. Terrible."

"How're the kids?" Ian asked him.

"Oh, they're okay. Kind of quiet, though."

They entered the stream of traffic and drove north. The evening was still warm enough for car windows to be open, and scraps of songs sailed past—"Monday, Monday" and "Winchester Cathedral" and "Send Me the Pillow That You Dream On." Ian's father said, "Your mom put me to work this afternoon hunting Lucy's relatives. I don't know if she told you."

"She told me you tried calling Cheyenne."

"Yes, well. No luck. And I stopped by the Fill 'Er Up Café—remember the Fill 'Er Up? Where Lucy used to work? I was hoping to find those two waitresses from the wedding. But the owner said one had walked out on him and the other moved south a couple of months ago. So then I went through Lucy's drawers, thinking there'd be, oh, an address book, say, or some letters. Didn't find a thing. Hard to figure, isn't it? This is what we've come to, now that people phone instead of writing."

"Maybe there just *aren't* any relatives," Ian told him.

"Well, in that case, what'll we do with the children?"

"Children."

"The older two have their father, of course. Soon as we track him down. But I suppose it's expecting too much that he would raise the little one as well."

"Well, naturally," Ian said. "She isn't even kin!"

"No, I guess not," his father said. He sighed.

"He doesn't even keep in touch with the two that are!"

"No."

"Couldn't you and Mom, maybe . . ."

"We're too old," his father said. He turned up Charles Street.

"You're not old!"

"We've just reached that time in our lives, Ian, when I think we deserve a rest. And your mother's not getting around so good lately; I don't know if you've noticed. Doc Plumm says this thing in her knees is arthritis. Can't exactly picture her chasing after a toddler."

"Yes, but—"

"Never mind, I'm sure we'll come up with someone or other," his father said, "once we find that ex-husband."

Then he went back to deploring how no one wrote letters these days. Pretty soon, he said, this country's mail service would be canceled for lack of interest. Turn all the post offices into planters, he said, and his lips twisted into one of his wry smiles before he recollected himself and grew serious again.

At home, Beastie nosed Ian's palm joyfully and lumbered after him into the living room, where his mother was walking Daphne up and down. She kissed him hello and then handed him the baby, who was too near sleep to do more than murmur. "Oh, my legs!" Bee said, sinking onto the couch. "That child has kept me on my feet all evening."

Thomas sat at the other end of the couch with his doll clutched to his chest, her yellow wig flaring beneath his chin like a bedraggled sunflower. Agatha sat in an armchair. She surveyed Ian levelly and then returned to her picture book. Both of them wore pajamas. They had the moist, pale, chastened look of children fresh from their baths.

"Have you eaten yet?" Ian's mother asked him. "I fed the children early because I didn't know."

"I can find something."

"Oh. Well, all right."

Daphne had gained weight, or maybe it was her sleepiness that made her feel so heavy. She drooped over Ian's shoulder, giving off a strong smell of apple juice.

"Your father's been through . . . various drawers," his mother said. She glanced toward Agatha. Evidently Lucy's name was not supposed to be spoken. "He didn't find a thing."

"Yes, he told me."

Agatha turned a page of her book. Ian's father crossed to the barometer on the wall and tapped the glass.

"Ian, dear," his mother said, "would you mind very much if I toddled off to bed?"

"No, go ahead," Ian said, although he did feel a bit hurt. After all, this was his first visit home.

"It's been such a long day, I'm just beat. The older two are sleeping in Danny's room, and I've set up the Port-a-Crib in your room. I hope Daphne won't disturb you."

"I'll be okay."

"He looks downright domestic, in fact," his father said, and he gave a snort of laughter. Doug belonged to an era when the sight of a man holding a baby was considered humorous. He liked to say he'd changed a diaper only once in all his life, back when Bee had the flu and Claudia was an infant. The experience had made him throw up. Everyone always chuckled when he told this story, but now Ian wondered why. He felt irked to see his father drift behind Bee toward the stairs, although *his* knees were not arthritic and he might easily have stayed to help. "Night, son," he said, lifting an arm.

"Good night," Ian said shortly.

He sat on the couch next to Thomas. Daphne instantly made a chipped sound of protest, and he stood up and started walking again.

"Ian," Agatha said, "will you read us a story?"

"I can't right now. Daphne won't let me sit down."

"She will if you sit in a rocking chair," Agatha said.

He tried it. Daphne stirred, but as soon as he began rocking she went limp again. He wondered why his mother hadn't thought of this—or why Agatha hadn't informed her.

Agatha was pulling up a footstool so she could sit next to him. Her eyes were lowered and her plain white disk of a face seemed complete in itself, ungiving. "Get a chair, Thomas," she ordered. Thomas slid off the couch and dragged over the miniature rocker from the hearth. It took him awhile because he never let go of Dulcimer.

The book Agatha placed on Ian's lap dated from his childhood. *The Sad Little Bunny,* it was called. It told about a rabbit who got lost on a picnic and couldn't find his mother. Ian wondered about reading this story under these particular circumstances, but both children listened stolidly— Thomas sucking his thumb, Agatha turning the pages without comment. First the rabbit went home with a friendly robin and tried to live in a tree, but he got dizzy. Then he went home with a beaver and tried to live in a dam, but he got wet. Ian had never realized what a repetitive book this was. He swallowed a yawn. Tears of boredom filled his eyes. The effort of reading while rocking made him slightly motion-sick.

On the last page, the little rabbit said, "Oh, Mama, I'm so glad to be back in my own home!" The picture showed him in a cozy, chintz-lined burrow, hugging an aproned mother rabbit. Reading out the words, Ian noticed how loud they sounded—like something tactless dropped into a shocked silence. But Agatha said, "Again."

"It's bedtime."

"No, it's not! What time is it?"

"Tell you what," he said. "You get into your beds, and then I'll read it once more."

"Twice," Agatha said.

"Once."

What did this remind him of? The boredom, the yawns . . . It was the evening of Danny's death, revisited. He felt he was traveling a treadmill, stuck with these querulous children night after night after night.

In the morning the minister came to discuss the funeral service. He was an elderly, stiff, formal man, and Bee seemed flustered when Ian led him into the kitchen. "Oh, don't look at all this mess!" she said, untying her apron. "Let's go into the living room. Ian can feed the children."

But Dr. Prescott said, "Nonsense," and sat down in a kitchen chair. "Where's *Mr.* Bedloe?" he asked.

Bee said, "Well, I know it sounds heartless, but he had to take the day off yesterday and of course tomorrow's the funeral so . . . he went to work."

"Is that good?" Dr. Prescott asked Daphne. She was squirting a piece of banana between her fingers and then smearing it across her high-chair tray.

"It's not that he doesn't mourn her. Really, he feels just dreadful," Bee said. "Ian, could you fetch a cloth, please? But substitute teachers are so hard to get hold of—"

"Yes, life must go on," Dr. Prescott said. "Isn't that right, young Abigail."

"Agatha," Bee corrected him. "It's Claudia's girl who's named Abigail."

"And will the children be attending the service?"

"Oh, no."

"Sometimes it's valuable, I've learned."

"We think they'll have a *fine* time staying here with Mrs. Myrdal," Bee said. "Mrs. Myrdal used to sit with them when they lived above the drugstore and she knows all their favorite storybooks."

She beamed across the table at Agatha. Agatha gazed back at her without a trace of a smile.

Dr. Prescott said, "Agatha, Thomas, I realize all that's happened must be difficult to understand. Perhaps you'd like to ask me some questions."

Agatha remained expressionless. Thomas shook his head.

Ian thought, *I would! I would!* But it wasn't Ian Dr. Prescott had been addressing.

He'd remembered to bring his suit but he had forgotten a tie, so he had to borrow one of his father's for the funeral. Standing in front of his mirror, he slid the knot into place and smoothed his collar. When the doorbell rang, he waited for someone to answer. It rang again and Beastie gave a worried yap. "Coming!" Ian called. He crossed the hall and sprinted downstairs.

Mrs. Myrdal had already opened the front door a few inches and poked her head in. Her hat looked like a gray felt potty turned upside down. Ian said, "Hi. Come on in."

"I worried I was late."

"No, we're just getting ready."

He showed her into the living room, where she settled on the sofa. She was one of those women who grow quilted in old age—her face a collection of pouches, her body a series of squashed mounds. "My, it's finally getting to be fall," she said, removing her sweater. "Real nip in the air today."

"Is that so," Ian said. He was hanging about in the doorway, wondering whether it was rude to leave.

"And how are those poor children bearing up?" she asked him.

"They're okay."

"I couldn't get over it when your mother called and told me. Those poor little tots! And I understand your parents won't be keeping them."

"No, we're trying to find some relatives," Ian said.

"Well, it's a shame," Mrs. Myrdal said.

"I don't guess *you* know of any relatives."

"No, dear, your mother already asked me. I told her, I said, 'I'm sorry, but I wouldn't have an inkling.' Although just between you and me, I'm pretty near positive that Lucy was, well, not from Baltimore."

"Ah."

"You could sort of tell, you know," she said. "I always sensed it, even before we had our falling out. You heard we'd fallen out, I suppose."

"Not in so many words," Ian said.

"Well!" Mrs. Myrdal said. She folded her sweater caressingly. "One time we went downtown together and I caught her shoplifting."

"Shoplifting?"

"Bold as you please. Swiped a pure silk blouse off a rack and tucked it into the stroller where her innocent baby girl lay sleeping. I was so astounded I just didn't do a thing. I thought I must have misunderstood; I thought there must be *some* explanation. I followed along behind her thinking, 'Now, Ruby, don't go jumping to conclusions.' On we march, past the scarf counter. Whisk! Red-and-tan Italian scarf scampers into her bag. I know I should have spoken but I was too amazed. My heart was racing so I thought it had riz up in my throat some way, and I worried we'd be arrested. We could have been, you know! We could have been hauled off to jail like common criminals. Well, luckily we weren't. But next time she phoned I said, 'Lucy, I'm busy.' She said, 'I just wanted to ask if you could baby-sit.' 'Oh,' I said, 'I don't believe I care to, thank you.' She knew why, too. She didn't let on but she had to know. Couple of times she asked again, and each time I turned her down."

Ian ducked his head and busied himself patting Beastie.

"Not that I wished her ill, understand. I was sorry as the next person to hear about her passing."

From the stairs came the sound of footsteps and his mother's voice saying, ". . . juice in that round glass pitcher and—" She arrived in the doorway with the baby propped on her hip. Thomas and Agatha were shadowing her. "Oh! Mrs. Myrdal," she said. "I didn't hear you come in."

Mrs. Myrdal rose and reached out in that fumble-fingered, greedy manner that old ladies take on around babies. "Would you look at how this child has grown!" she said. "Remember Mrs. Moo-doe, darlin'?" She accepted Daphne in a rumpled bunch and cocked her head at the other two. "Thomas and Agatha, I'd never have known you!"

"Now, we shouldn't be long," Bee told her. "It's going to be a very simple . . . Ian, where's your father got to?"

Ian said, "Um . . ."

"Isn't this just like him! Check the basement, will you? Mrs. Myrdal, the tea bags are in the . . ."

Ian went out to the kitchen. He thought, *She was only shoplifting.* He crossed the pantry and started down the basement steps. *She wasn't meeting some man, she was shoplifting.* He called, "Dad?"

"Down here."

That dress was not a present from her lover after all.

His father was tinkering at his workbench. Wearing his good dark suit, his hair still showing the comb lines, he bent over the lamp from the attic bedroom. "Are we set to go?" he asked without turning.

Why, even I have been known to shoplift. Me and Pig and Andrew, back in fifth grade. It's nothing. Or next to nothing.

"Ian?"

He looked at his father.

"Are we set to go?"

"Yes," Ian said after a moment.

"Well, then."

His father switched off the light above the bench. He started toward the stairs. He halted next to Ian and said, "Coming?"

"Yes."

They climbed the stairs.

Oh, God, this is the one last little dark dot I can't possibly absorb.

In the hall, his mother was putting on her hat. "Why is it," she asked his father, "that the minute everyone's ready, you choose to disappear?"

"I was just looking at that lamp, sweetheart."

The three of them left the house and walked to the car. Ian felt bruised all down the front of his body, as if he'd been kicked.

• • •

The last time he'd been in this church was for Danny's funeral—and before that, for Danny's wedding. When he stood on the sidewalk looking up at Dober Street Presbyterian, all his thoughts were gathered toward his brother. He could almost believe that Danny had been left behind here, in this peaked stone building with the louvered steeple.

Inside, his parents stopped to greet Mrs. Jordan while Ian continued down the aisle. He passed Aunt Bev and her husband, and Cousin Amy, and a couple of the foreigners from the neighborhood. He caught sight of Cicely's blond curls gleaming like fresh pine shavings, and he slid in next to her and took hold of her hand, which turned out to contain a knob of damp Kleenex. Her lashes and her cheeks were damp too, he saw when she smiled at him. She had told him when he telephoned that she wouldn't think of not coming to this, even though it meant a two-hour train ride. She just needed to say goodbye, she told him. She had always thought Lucy was special.

The organ started playing softly, and Dr. Prescott entered through a side door and took a seat behind the pulpit. Below the pulpit lay the casket, pearly gray, decorated with a spray of white flowers. The sight of it made Ian feel cold. Something like a cold blade entered his chest and he looked away.

Now the others were filing down the aisle—his father solemn and sheepish, his mother wearing an expression that seemed less grief-stricken than disappointed. "I'm not angry; just disappointed," she used to tell Ian when he misbehaved. (What would she say now, if she knew what he had done?) Behind came Claudia and Macy with Abbie, who was evidently considered old enough now for funerals. She had on her first high heels and wobbled slightly as she followed the others into a pew. This wasn't the front pew but the one just behind. Maybe the front pew was reserved for Lucy's blood relations, if any showed up.

But none did. The organ music dwindled away, Dr. Prescott rose and announced a prayer, and still no one arrived to fill that empty pew.

The prayer was for the living. "We know Thy daughter Lucy is safely by Thy side," Dr. Prescott intoned, "but we ask Thee to console those left behind. Comfort them, we pray, and ease their pain. Let Thy mercy pour like a healing balm upon their hearts."

Like a healing balm. Ian pictured something white and semi-liquid—the bottle of lotion his mother kept by the kitchen sink, say—pleasantly scented with almonds. Could the balm soothe not just grief but guilt? Not just guilt but racking anguish over something impulsively done that could not be undone?

Ordinarily indifferent to prayers (or to anything else even vaguely religious), Ian listened to this one yearningly. He leaned forward in his seat as if he could ride the words all the way to heaven. He kept his eyes tightly shut. He thought, *Please. Please. Please.*

In the pews around him he heard a rustling and a creaking, and he opened his eyes and found the congregation rising. Struggling to his feet, he peered at the hymnbook Cicely held in front of him. ". . . with me," he joined in belatedly, "fast falls the eventide . . ." His voice was a creak. He fell silent and listened to the others—to Cicely's clear soprano, Mrs. Jordan's plain, true alto, Dr. Prescott's rich bass. "The darkness deepens," they sang, "Lord, with me abide!" The voices ceased to be separate. They plaited themselves into a multistranded chord, and now it seemed the congregation was a single person—someone of great kindness and compassion, someone gentle and wise and forgiving. "In life, in death, O Lord," they finished, "abide with me." And then came the long, sighed "Amen." They sat down. Ian sat too. His knees were trembling. He felt that everything had been drained away from him, all the grief and self-blame. He was limp and pure and pliant as an infant. He was, in fact, born again.

Through the burial in Pleasant Memory Cemetery and the car trip home, through the flurry of reclaiming the children, setting up the coffeepot, and greeting the guests who stopped by afterward, Ian wandered in a dreamlike state of mind. He traveled around the living room with a plate of butterscotch brownies, failing to notice it was empty till his brother-in-law pointed it out. "Earth to Ian," Macy said, guffawing, and then Mrs. Jordan relieved Ian of the plate. Cicely came up from behind and slipped a hand into his. "Are you all right?" she asked him.

"Yes, fine," he said.

Her fingertips were soft little nubbins because she bit her nails. Her breath gave off the metallic scent of Coca-Cola. Mrs. Jordan's craggy face had a hinged and plated look, like an armadillo hide. Everything seemed very distinct, but also far away.

"It's been too much," Mrs. Jordan told Cicely. "Just too much to take in all at once. First Danny, and now Lucy!" She turned to draw one of the foreigners into the conversation; he was hovering hopefully nearby. "Why, I remember the day they announced their engagement!" she said. "Remember, Jim?"

"Jack," the foreigner said.

"Jack, I was there when he brought her home. I'd come over to borrow the pinking shears and in they walked. Well, I knew right away what was what. Pretty little thing like that, who *wouldn't* want to marry her?"

"Woe betide you," Jack told Ian.

"Um . . ."

"O lud lud! Please to accept my lamentations."

This must be the foreigner who was so devoted to *Roget's Thesaurus*. Bee was always quoting choice remarks. Mrs. Jordan gave him a speculative stare. "I suppose in your culture, Lucy wouldn't have lasted even this long," she said. "Don't they throw themselves on their husband's pyre or something?"

"Pyre?"

"And now I reckon Doug and Bee will have to take on those poor children," she told Ian.

Ian said, "Well, actually—"

"Just look at that little one. Did you ever see anything so precious?"

Ian followed her gaze. In the doorway to the hall, Daphne stood rocking unsteadily. Her dazzling white shoes—hard-soled and ankle-high—no doubt helped to keep her upright; but still, standing alone at ten months was quite an accomplishment, Ian suspected. Was this the first time she'd tried it? He thought of all the fuss that would have been made ordinarily— the applause and the calls for a camera. But Daphne went unnoticed, a frail, wispy waif in an oversized dress, looking anxiously from face to face.

Then she spotted Ian. Her eyes widened. She grinned. She dropped to the floor and scuttled toward him, expertly weaving between the grownups' legs and pausing every now and then to wrench herself free from the hem of her dress. She arrived at his feet, took hold of his trousers and hauled herself to a standing position. When she beamed up at him, she had to tip her head so far back she nearly fell over.

Ian bent and lifted her into his arms. She nestled against his shoulder. "Oh, the darling," Mrs. Jordan said. "Why, she's crazy about you! Isn't she, Ian? Isn't she? Ian?"

He couldn't explain why the radiance left over from church fell away so suddenly. The air in the room seemed dull and brownish. Mrs. Jordan's voice sounded hollow. This child was far too heavy.

Back in school, he kept trying to recapture that feeling he'd had at the funeral. He hummed "Abide with Me" under his breath. He closed his eyes in hopes of summoning up the congregation's single, melting voice, the soft light from the pebbled windows, the sense of mercy and forgiveness. But nothing came. The bland brick atmosphere of Sumner College prevailed. Biology 101 progressed from nematodes to frogs, and King John repudiated the Magna Carta, and Ian's roommate dragged him to see *Devil-Women from Outer Space.*

At night, Danny stood at the blackboard in front of Ian's English class. "This is a dream," he announced. "The word 'dream' comes from the Latin word *dorimus*, meaning 'game of chance.' " Ian awoke convinced that there had been some message in this, but the harder he worked to decipher it, the farther away it drifted.

He phoned home Saturday afternoon and learned that Mrs. Jordan, of all people, had cleverly uncovered the name of Lucy's ex-husband. "What she did," Bee told Ian, "was sit Agatha down beside her and run through a lot of everyday, wife-ish remarks. She said, 'Don't forget the garbage,' and, 'Suppertime!' and, 'You're late.' Her theory was, the name would sort of swim into Agatha's memory. She thought Thomas was too young to try it on. But all at once Thomas pipes up, 'You're late with the check again, Tom!' he said. Just out of nowhere!"

"Well, that would make sense," Ian said. "So Thomas must be Tom Junior."

"I said to Jessie Jordan, I said, 'Jessie,' I said, 'you're amazing.' Really I don't know what I'd have done without her, these past few days. Or *any* of the neighbors. They've all been so helpful, running errands for me and taking the children when my legs are bad . . ."

What she was saying, it seemed to Ian, was, "See what you've gone and done? See how you've ruined our lives?" Although of course she didn't mean that at all. She went on to say the Cahns, next door, had lent her their sitter, and the foreigners had brought over a pot of noodle soup with an aftertaste resembling throw-up. "People have been just lovely," she said, "and Cicely's mother called to say—"

"But what about Thomas Senior?" Ian broke in.

"What about him?"

"Did you look for him in the Cheyenne phone book?"

"Oh, we'd already called all the Deans in Cheyenne, but now we have a name to give the officials. They ought to be able to track *something* down—driver's license, marriage license . . . I remember Lucy said once he'd remarried."

That night Ian dreamed that Lucy sat in her living room among bushel baskets of mail—letters and fliers and magazines. Then Danny walked in and said, "Lucy? What is this?"

"Oh," she said, "I just can't open them anymore. Since you died it seems I haven't had the heart."

"But this is terrible!" he cried. "Your bulks and your flats I could understand, but first-class, Lucy! First-class envelopes lying untouched!"

"Then talk to Ian," she said in a wiry, tight voice.

"Ian?"

"Ian says I'm not a bit first-class," she said, and her mouth turned down at the corners, petulant and spiteful looking.

Ian awoke and blinked at the crack of light beneath the door. Winston was snoring. Someone's radio was playing. He heard the scrape of a chair down the hall and carefree, unthinking laughter.

Sunday morning he rode into town on the college's little blue church bus. Most of the passengers were students he'd never laid eyes on before, although he did recognize his lab partner, dressed in a hard-surfaced, voluminous gray coat. He pretended not to see her and proceeded toward the long seat at the rear, where he settled between two boys with haircuts so short and suits so tidy that they might have stepped out of the 1950s.

Really this was a sort of *losers'* bus, he realized, and he had an impulse to jump off while he still could. But then the senior class secretary boarded—a poised, attractive girl—and he felt reassured. He rode through the stubbled farmlands with his eyes fixed straight ahead, while the boy on his left fingered a rosary and the boy on his right whispered over a Bible.

At the courthouse square in Sumner, the bus stopped and everyone disembarked. Ian chose to follow the largest group of students, which included the senior class secretary and also a relatively normal-looking freshman named Eddie something whom he'd seen around the dorm. He and Eddie fell into step together, and Eddie said, "You on your way to Leeds Memorial?"

"Well, yeah, I guess so."

Eddie nodded. "It's not too bad," he said. "I go every week on account of my grandmother's paying me."

"Paying you?"

"If I don't miss a Sunday all year I get a check for a hundred bucks."

"Gosh," Ian said.

Leeds Memorial was a stately brick building with a white interior and dark, varnished pews. The choir sounded professional, and they sang the opening hymn on their own while the congregation stayed seated. Maybe that was why Ian didn't have much feeling about it. It was only music, that was all—something unfamiliar, classical-sounding, flawlessly performed. Maybe the whole church had to be singing along.

The theme of the day was harvest, because they were drawing close to Thanksgiving. The Bible reading referred to the reaping of grain, and the sermon had to do with resting after one's labors. The pastor—a slouching, easygoing, just-one-of-the-guys type with a sweater vest showing beneath his suit coat—counseled his listeners to be kind to themselves, to take time for themselves in the midst of the hurly-burly. Ian felt enormous yawns hollowing the back of his throat. Finally the organist began thrumming out a series of chords, and the sermon came to an end and everyone rose. The hymn was "Bringing in the Sheaves." It was a simpleminded, seesawing sort of tune, Ian felt, and the collective voice of the congregation had a note of fluty gentility, as if dominated by the dressed-up old ladies lining the pews.

Walking back to the bus, Eddie asked if he'd be coming every Sunday. Ian said he doubted it.

His Thanksgiving vacation was fractious and disorganized; Lucy's children had still not been claimed. By now they had moved in upon the household in full force. Their toys littered the living room, their boats and ducks crowded the bathroom, and Daphne's real crib—much larger than the Port-a-Crib—cramped his bedroom. He was alarmed at how haggard his mother looked, and how heavy and big-bellied. The waistband of her slacks was extended with one of those oversized safety pins women once decorated their kilts with. And the holiday dinner she served was halfhearted—no hors d'oeuvres, not even beforehand, and the turkey unstuffed and the pies store-bought. Even the company seemed lacking. Claudia snapped at her children, Macy kept drifting away from the table to watch a football game on TV, and the foreigners had to leave before dessert in order to meet the plane of a new arrival. All in all, it was a relief to have the meal over with.

He tried to help with the children as much as possible. He played endless games of Parcheesi; he read and reread *The Sad Little Bunny*. And he rose at least once each night to rock Daphne back to sleep, sometimes nodding off himself in the process. Often he had the feeling that she was rocking *him*. He would wake to find her coolly studying his face in the dark, or even prying up one of his lids with her chubby, sticky fingers.

Ironically, it was during this vacation that Cicely told him she might be pregnant. In the middle of a movie called *Georgy Girl*, which concerned a young woman who was tiresomely, tediously fond of infants, she clutched a handful of his sleeve and whispered that she was two weeks late. "Late for what?" he asked, which for some reason made her start crying. Then he understood.

They walked out on the movie and drove around the city. Ian kept inventing other possibilities. She was tense about her exams, maybe, or it was all that traveling back and forth on the train, or—"I don't know! How would I know? *Some* damn reason!" he said, and she said, "You don't have to shout! It was your fault as much as it was mine! Or more, even; way more. You're the one who talked me into it."

This wasn't entirely accurate. Still, on some deeper level it seemed he deserved every word she hurled at him. He saw himself as a plotter and a predator, sex-obsessed; Lord, there were days when thoughts of sex with anyone—it didn't have to be Cicely—never left his mind for a moment. And now look: here was his rightful penance, marriage at eighteen and a job bagging groceries in the A&P. He drew a breath. He said, "Don't worry, Ciss. I'll take care of you."

They were supposed to stop by Andrew's after the movie, but instead he drove her home. "I'll call you tomorrow," he said, and then he went on to his own house and climbed the stairs to his room, where he found Daphne sitting upright and holding out her arms.

By the time he returned to school on Sunday evening, he had almost persuaded Cicely to see a doctor. What he hoped for (although he didn't say it) was a doctor who could offer her a magic pill or something. There must be such a pill. Surely there was. Maybe it was some common cold remedy or headache tablet, available on open shelves, with NOT TO BE TAKEN DURING PREGNANCY imprinted on the label—a message in code for those who needed it. But if he mentioned this to Cicely she might think he didn't want to marry her or something, when of course he did want to and

had always planned to. Just not yet, please, God. Not when he'd never
even slept with a *dark*-haired girl yet.

He flinched at the wickedness of this thought, which had glided so
smoothly into his mind that it might have been there all along.

In Biology 101 on Tuesday, his lab partner said she'd noticed him on
the church bus. She wondered if he'd like to attend the Wednesday Night
Youth Group at her place of worship. "Oh, I'm sorry, I can't," he said instantly. "I've got a paper due."

"Well, maybe another time, then," she said. "We always have such fun!
Usually they show a movie, something nice and clean with no language."

"It does sound like fun," he said.

He meant that sincerely. He ached, all at once, for a blameless life. He
decided that if Cicely turned out not to be pregnant, *they* would start living like that. Their outings would become as wholesome as those pictures
in the cigarette ads: healthy young people laughing toothily in large, impersonal groups, popping popcorn, taking sleigh rides.

But on Thursday, when Cicely phoned to tell him she'd got her period,
what did he do? He said, "Listen. You have to go on the pill now. You
know that." And she said, "Yes, I've already made an appointment." And
that weekend they picked up where they had left off, although Cicely still
had her period and really it was sort of complicated. He had to rinse all
the bedclothes the following morning, and as he stood barefoot in the
dormitory bathroom watching the basin fill with pink water, he felt weary
and jaded and disgusted with himself, a hopeless sinner.

Christmas fell on a Sunday that year. Ian didn't get home till Friday evening; so Saturday was a hectic rush of shopping for gifts. Only on Christmas Eve did he have a chance to look around and realize the state of the
household. He saw that although a good-sized tree had been erected in the
living room, no one had trimmed it; the box of decorations sat unopened
on the piano. The swags of evergreen were missing from the banister, the
front door bore no wreath, and the house had a general air of neglect. It
wasn't just relaxed, or folksy, or happy-go-lucky; it was dirty. The kitchen
smelled of garbage and cat box. The last two remaining goldfish floated
dead in their scummy bowl. None of the gifts had been wrapped yet, and
when the children asked to hang their stockings it emerged that all the
socks were in the laundry.

"Well, I'm sorry," Bee said, "but one person or another has been sick
the last two weeks running and I just haven't had a minute. So I'm sorry.
Hang something else, instead. Hang grocery bags. Hang pillowcases."

"Pillowcases!" Thomas said dolefully.

"Don't worry," Ian told him. "I'll do a wash tonight. You go on to bed
and I'll hang your stockings later."

So that evening was spent in the basement, more or less. Ian found the
hampers so overstuffed and moldy that he guessed the laundry had not

been seen to in some time, and he decided to take care of the whole lot. Also he put himself in charge of gift wrapping. While his mother sat at the dining room table sipping the sherry he'd poured her, he swaddled everything ineptly in plain tissue. (She had not thought to buy Christmas paper.) He wrapped even the gifts meant for him—a couple of shirts, a ski jacket—pretending to pay them no heed. Periodically he left his work to run downstairs to the basement and start another load of laundry. The scent of detergent and fresh linens gradually filled the house. It wasn't such a bad Christmas Eve after all.

"Remember Christmas in the old days?" his mother asked. "When we got everything ready so far ahead? Presents sat under the tree for weeks! Homemade, most of them. Lord, you children made enough clay ashtrays to cover every surface, and none of us even smokes. But this year I just couldn't get up the spirit. Seems like ever since this happened with your brother I've been so . . . unenthusiastic."

Ian didn't know what to say to that. He made a big business of tying a bow on a package.

"And remember all the hors d'oeuvres at Christmas dinner?" she asked. "This year I'll be doing well to throw a piece of meat in the oven."

"Maybe we should go to a restaurant," Ian said.

"A restaurant!"

"Why not?"

"Let's hope we haven't come to *that*," his mother said.

In the living room they heard a sharp grunt—his father, asleep in his recliner chair.

But as it turned out, Christmas Day was not so different that year from any other. Mrs. Jordan came, along with the foreigners. The children contributed their share of excitement (Claudia's six and Lucy's three, combined), and Doug's Polaroid Land camera flashed, and the cat made choking sounds behind the couch. It was disconcerting, in a way. Last Christmas Daphne hadn't been born yet; nor had Franny. Now here sat Daphne chewing a wad of blue tissue while Franny stirred her fists through Agatha's jigsaw puzzle. They both seemed so accustomed to being here. And Danny and Lucy had completely vanished. Something was wrong with a world where people came and went so easily.

The day after Christmas, Sid at the movers' phoned to see if Ian could help out over vacation. Their man Brewster had left them in the lurch, he said. Ian told him he'd be glad to help. School would not reopen till mid-January and he could use the extra cash. So Tuesday morning, he reported to the garage on Greenmount.

LeDon was delighted to see him. That Brewster fellow, he said, had just up and walked away in the middle of a job. "He say, 'See you round, LeDon.' I say, 'Hey, man, you ain't *ditching* me.' He say, 'All day long I'm ditching you,' and off he go. Well, he weren't never what you call real friendly."

They were moving an old lady from a house to an apartment—lots of old-lady belongings, bowlegged furniture and mothballed dresses and more than enough china to stock a good-sized restaurant. Her son, who was overseeing the move, had some kind of fixation about the china. "Careful, now! That's Spode," he would say as they lifted a crate. And, "Watch out for the Haviland!" LeDon rolled his eyes at Ian.

Then at the new place, they found out the kitchen was being remodeled and they had to set the china crates in the living room. "What the hell?" the son said. "This was supposed to be finished three days ago." He was talking to the cabinetmaker—the deaf man Ian had come across last summer, as it happened. "How much longer?" the son asked him. Any fool could see it would be *way* longer; the kitchen was nothing but a shell. The cabinetmaker, not looking around, measured the depth of a counter with a steel measuring tape. The son laid a hand on the man's forearm. The man turned slowly, gazed a moment at the son's hand, and then lifted his eyes to his face. "HOW . . . LONG!" the son shouted, exaggerating his lip movements.

The cabinetmaker considered, and then he said, "Two weeks."

"Two weeks!" the son said. He dropped his hand. "What are you building here, Noah's ark? All we need is a few lousy cupboards!"

The cabinetmaker went on about his business, measuring the counter's length now and the height of the empty space above it. Surely he must have known the son was speaking to him, but he seemed totally absorbed in what he was doing. Once again, Ian envied the man his insular, impervious life.

On New Year's Eve Pig Benson threw a big, rowdy party, but Ian didn't go. Cicely was baby-sitting her brother and it was her last night home. (Her college worked on a different schedule from Ian's.) So they set all the clocks an hour ahead and tricked Stevie into going to bed early, and then they snuck upstairs to her room, where Ian unintentionally dozed off. He was awakened by church bells ringing in the New Year, which meant her parents could be expected at any moment. As soon as he'd dressed, he slipped downstairs and into the frosty, bitter night. He walked home half asleep while bells pealed and firecrackers popped and rockets lit the sky. What optimism! he found himself thinking. Why did people have such high hopes for every New Year?

He practiced saying the date aloud: "Nineteen sixty-seven. January first, nineteen sixty-seven." Monday was his birthday; he'd be nineteen years old. Daphne would be one. He shivered and pulled his collar up.

That night he dreamed Danny came driving down Waverly Street in Sumner College's blue church bus. He stopped in front of home and told Ian, "They've given me a new route and now I get to go anywhere I like."

"Can I ride along?" Ian asked from the sidewalk.

"You can ride along after you learn Chinese," Danny told him.

"Oh," Ian said. Then he said, "Chinese?"

"Well, I like to call it Chinese."

"Call what Chinese?"

"You understand, Chinese is not what I really mean."

"Then what *do* you mean?" Ian asked.

"Why, I'm talking about . . . let us say . . . Chinese," Danny said, and he winked at Ian and laughed and drove away.

When Ian woke, Daphne was crying, and the room seemed moist as a greenhouse from her tears.

Agatha's school reopened Tuesday, and Thomas's nursery school Wednesday. This should have lightened Bee's load, but still she looked exhausted every evening. She said she must have a touch of the flu. "Ordinarily I'm strong as a horse!" she said. "This is only temporary, I'm positive."

Ian asked, "What's the word on Tom Dean, Senior? Any sign of him?"

"Oh," his mother said, "I guess we'll have to give up on Tom Dean. It doesn't seem he exists."

"Then what'll you do with the children?"

"Well, your father has some ideas. He's pretty sure from something Lucy once mentioned that she came from Pennsylvania. Maybe her first marriage was recorded there, he says, in which case—"

"You're stuck with them, aren't you," Ian said.

"Pardon?"

"You're stuck with those children for good."

"Oh, no," she told him. "I'm certain we'll find somebody sooner or later. We'll just have to. We'll have to!"

"But what if you don't?" Ian asked her.

Her face took on a flown-apart, panicked look.

Two of the children weren't even Bedloes, and he wondered if it occurred to his parents that those two could simply be made wards of the state, or whatever—popped into some kind of foster home or orphanage. But he suspected that with Daphne, they wouldn't feel free to do that. Daphne was their dead son's child, and an infant besides. She wasn't already formed, as the other two were. She hadn't yet reached the knobby-kneed, scabby stage that only a mother could love; she was still full of dimples, still tiny and beguiling.

Thomas, on the other hand, could cause a serious puncture wound if he accidentally poked you with his elbow. Holding him on your lap was like holding a bunch of coat hangers. Which didn't prevent his trying to climb up there, heaven knows. He had the nuzzling, desperate manner of a small dog starved for attention, which unfortunately lessened his appeal; while Agatha, who managed to act both sullen and ingratiating, came across as sly. Ian had seen how grownups (even his mother, even his earth-mother sister) turned narrow-eyed in Agatha's presence. It seemed that only Ian knew how these children felt: how scary they found every waking minute.

Why, being a child at all was scary! Wasn't that what grownups' nightmares so often reflected—the nightmare of running but getting nowhere, the nightmare of the test you hadn't studied for or the play you hadn't rehearsed? Powerlessness, outsiderness. Murmurs over your head about something everyone knows but you.

He finished moving a family into a row house on York Road and went home from there on foot, passing a series of shabby stores. The job had run unusually late. It was after seven on a dismal January evening, and most places had closed. One window, though, glowed yellow—a wide expanse of plate glass with CHURCH OF THE SECOND CHANCE arching across it in block letters. Ian couldn't see inside because the paper shade was lowered. He walked on by. Behind him a hymn began. "Something something something lead us . . ." He missed most of the words, but the voices were strong and joyful, overlaid by a single tenor that rose above the rest.

He paused at the intersection, the arches of his sneakers teetering on the curb. He peered at the DON'T WALK sign for a moment. Then he turned and headed back to the church.

A shopkeeper's bell jingled when he opened the door. The singers looked around—some fifteen or twenty people, standing in rows with their backs to him—and smiled before they looked away again. They were facing a tall, black-haired man in a tieless white shirt and black trousers. The pulpit was an ordinary store counter. The floor was green linoleum. The lights overhead were long fluorescent tubes and one tube flickered rapidly, giving Ian the impression that he had a twitch in his eyelid.

"Blessed Jesus! Blessed Jesus!" the congregation sang. It was a tender, affectionate cry that sounded personally welcoming. Ian found his way to an empty spot beside a woman in a white uniform, a nurse or a waitress. Although she didn't look at him, she moved closer and angled her hymnal so he could follow the words. The hymnal was one of those pocket-sized pamphlets handed out free at public sing-alongs. There wasn't any accompaniment, not even a piano. And the pews—as Ian realized when the hymn came to an end and everyone sat down—were plain gray metal folding chairs, the kind you'd see at a bridge game.

"Friends," the minister said, in a sensible, almost conversational tone. "And guests," he added, nodding at Ian. All over again, the others turned and smiled. Ian smiled back, maybe a little too broadly. He had the feeling he was their first and only visitor.

"We have reached that point in the service," the minister said, "when any person here is invited to step forward and ask for our prayers. No request is too great, no request is trivial in the eyes of God our Father."

Ian thought of the plasterer who'd repaired his parents' bathroom ceiling. NO JOB TOO LARGE OR TOO SMALL, his panel truck had read. He brushed the thought away. He watched a very fat young woman heave herself to her feet just in front of him. The width of her sprigged, summer-weight skirt, when she finally reached a standing position, completely blocked his view of the minister. "Well, Clarice as you may have heard is down real bad with her blood," she said breathily. "We had thought that was all behind her but now it's come on back, and I asked what I could do for her and she says, 'Lynn,' says, 'take it to Wednesday Night Prayer Meeting, Lynn, and ask them for their prayers.' So that's just what I'm doing."

There was a silence, during which she sat down. As soon as she left Ian's line of vision, he realized the silence was part of the program. The minister stood with both palms raised, his face tipped skyward and his eyelids closed and gleaming. In his shirtsleeves, he seemed amateurish. His cuffs had slipped down his forearms, and his collar, Ian saw, was buttoned all the way to the neck, in the fashion of those misfits who used to walk around high school with slide rules dangling from their belts. He wasn't so very old, either. His frame was lanky as a marionette's and his wrist bones boyishly knobby.

Ian was the only one sitting erect. He bowed his head and squinted at the billow of sprigged skirt puffing out the back of the fat woman's chair.

"For our sister Clarice," the minister said finally.

"Amen," the congregation murmured, and they straightened.

"Any other prayers, any other prayers," the minister said. "No request is beyond Him."

On the other side of Ian's neighbor, a gray-haired woman rose and placed her purse on her seat. Then she faced forward, gripping the chair in front of her. "You all know my son Chuckie was fighting in Vietnam," she said.

There were nods, and several people turned to look at her.

"Well, now they tell me he's been killed," she said.

Soft sounds of dismay traveled down the rows.

"Tell me he got killed jumping out of a plane," she said. "You know he was a paratrooper."

More nods.

"Monday night these two soldiers came, all dressed up."

"Ah, no," they said.

"I told them I had thought he'd be safe. I said he'd been jumping so *long* now, looked to me like he'd learned how to stay alive up there. Soldier says, 'Yes, ma'am,' he says. 'These things happen,' he says. Says Chuckie was a, what do you call, fluke accident. Forgot to put his parachute on."

Ian blinked.

"Forgot!" his neighbor marveled in a voice like a dove.

" 'Forgot!' I said. 'How could that be?' This soldier tells me, it's the army's considered opinion that Chuckie had just jumped so often, he'd stopped thinking about it. So up he comes to that whatever, that door where they jump out of, the whole time making smart remarks so everybody's laughing—you remember what a card he was—and gives a little kind of like salute and steps into empty air. It's not till then the fellow behind him says, 'Wait!' Says, 'Wait, you forgot your—' "

"Parachute," Ian's neighbor finished sadly.

"So I don't ask your prayers for Chuckie after this; I ask for me," the woman said. For the first time, her voice was unsteady. "I'm just about sick with grief, I tell you. Pray for me to find some deliverance."

She sat down, fumbling behind her for her purse. The minister lifted his palms and the room fell silent.

Could you really forget your parachute?

Well, maybe so. Ian could see how it might have come about. A man to whom jumping was habit might imagine that floating in space was all his own doing, like flying. Maybe it had slipped his mind he *couldn't* fly, so in the first startled instant of his descent he supposed he had simply forgotten how. He may have felt insulted, betrayed by all he'd taken for granted. *What's the big idea here?* he must have asked.

Ian pictured one of those animated films where a character strolls off a cliff without noticing and continues strolling in midair, perfectly safe until he happens to look down and then his legs start wheeling madly and he plummets.

He gave a short bark of laughter.

The congregation swiveled and stared at him.

He bowed his head, cheeks burning. The minister said, "For our sister Lula."

"Amen," the others said, mercifully facing forward again.

"Any other prayers, any other prayers . . ."

Ian studied the sprigged skirt while shame slammed into him in waves. He had said and done heedless things before but this was something new: to laugh out loud at a mother's bereavement. He wished he could disappear. He wanted to perform some violent and decisive act, like leaping into space himself.

"No prayer is unworthy in the eyes of our Creator."

He stood up.

Heads swiveled once again.

"I used to be—" he said.

Frog in his throat. He gave a dry, fake-sounding cough.

"I used to be good," he said. "Or I used to be not bad, at least. Not evil. I just *assumed* I wasn't evil, but lately, I don't know what's happened. Everything I touch goes wrong. I didn't mean to laugh just now. I'm sorry I laughed, Mrs. . . ."

He looked over at the woman. Her face was lowered and she seemed unaware of him. But the others were watching closely. He had the sense they were weighing his words; they were taking him seriously.

"Pray for me to be good again," he told them. "Pray for me to be forgiven."

He sat down.

The minister raised his palms.

The silence that followed was so deep that Ian felt bathed in it. He unfolded in it; he gave in to it. He floated on a fluid rush of prayers, and all the prayers were for his pardon. How could God not listen, then?

When Ian was three or four years old, his mother had read him a Bible story for children. The illustration had showed a Roman soldier in full armor accosting a bearded old man. "Is that God?" Ian had asked, pointing to the soldier; for he associated God with power. But his mother had said, "No, no," and continued reading. What Ian had gathered from this was that God was the other figure, therefore—the bearded old man. Even after he knew better, he couldn't shake that notion, and now he imagined the congregation's prayers streaming toward someone with long gray hair and a floor-length, Swedish-blue robe and sturdy bare feet in leather sandals. He felt a flood of gratitude to this man, as if God were, in literal truth, his father.

"For our guest," the minister said.

"Amen."

It was over too suddenly. It hadn't lasted long enough. Already the minister was saying, "Any other prayers, any other prayers . . ."

There weren't any.

"Hymn sixteen, then," the minister said, and everyone stirred and rustled pages and stood up. They were so matter-of-fact; they were smoothing skirts, patting hairdos. Ian's neighbor, a stocky, round-faced woman, beamed at him and tilted her hymnal in his direction. The hymn was "Leaning on the Everlasting Arms." The minister started it off in his soaring tenor:

"What a fellowship, what a joy divine,
Leaning on the everlasting arms . . ."

This time Ian sang too, although really it was more of a drone.

When the hymn was finished, the minister raised his palms again and recited a benediction. "Go ye now into the world and bear witness to His teachings," he said. "In Jesus' name, amen."

"Amen," the others echoed.

Was that *it*?

They started collecting coats and purses, buttoning buttons, winding scarves. "Welcome!" Ian's neighbor told him. "How did you find out about us?"

"Oh, I was just walking by . . ."

"So many young people nowadays don't give half enough thought to their spiritual salvation."

"No, I guess not," Ian said.

All at once he felt he was traveling under false pretense. Spiritual salvation! The language these places used made him itch with embarrassment. (Blood of the Lamb, Died for Your Sins . . .) He looked yearningly behind him, where the first people to leave were already sending a slap of cold air into the room. But his neighbor was waving to the minister. "Yoo-hoo! Reverend Emmett! Come and meet our young person!"

The minister, already choosing a path between the knots of worshipers, seemed disconcertingly jubilant. His smile was so wide that his teeth looked too big for his mouth. He arrived in front of Ian and shook his hand over and over. "Wonderful to have you!" he said. (His long, bony fingers felt like dried beanpods.) "I'm Reverend Emmett. This is Sister Nell, have you introduced yourselves?"

"How do you do," Ian said, and the other two waited so expectantly that he had to add, "I'm Ian Bedloe."

"We use only first names in our place of worship," Reverend Emmett told him. "Last names remind us of the superficial—the world of wealth and connections and who came over on the *Mayflower*."

"Really," Ian said. "Ah. Okay."

His neighbor laid a hand on his arm and said, "Reverend Emmett will tell you *all about it*. Nice meeting you, Brother Ian. Good night, Reverend Emmett."

"Night," Reverend Emmett said. He watched as she swirled a navy cape around her shoulders (so she was, after all, a nurse) and sidled out the other end of the row. Then he turned back to Ian and said, "I hope your prayer was answered this evening."

"Thanks," Ian said. "It was a really . . . interesting service."

Reverend Emmett studied him. (His skin was an unhealthy shade of white, although that could have been the fluorescent lighting.) "But your prayer," he said finally. "Was there any response?"

"Response?"

"Did you get a reply?"

"Well, not exactly."

"I see," Reverend Emmett said. He watched an aged couple assist each other through the door—the very last to leave. Then he said, "What was it that you needed forgiven?"

Ian couldn't believe his ears. Was this even legal, inquiring into a person's private prayers? He ought to spin on his heel and walk out. But instead his heart began hammering as if he were about to do something brave. In a voice not quite his own, he said, "I caused my brother to, um, kill himself."

Reverend Emmett gazed at him thoughtfully.

"I told him his wife was cheating on him," Ian said in a rush, "and now I'm not even sure she was. I mean I'm pretty sure she did in the past, I know I wasn't *totally* wrong, but . . . So he drove into a wall. And then his wife died of sleeping pills and I guess you could say I caused that too, more or less . . ."

He paused, because Reverend Emmett might want to disagree here. (Really Lucy's death was just indirectly caused by Ian, and maybe not even that. It might have been accidental.) But Reverend Emmett only rocked from heel to toe.

"So it looks as if my parents are going to have to raise the children," Ian said. Had he mentioned there were children? "Everything's been dumped on my mom and I don't think she's up to it—her or my dad, either one. I don't think they'll ever be the same, after this. And my sister's busy with her own kids and I'm away at college most of the time . . ."

In the light of Reverend Emmett's blue eyes—which had the clean transparency of those marbles that Ian used to call ginger-ales—he began to relax. "So anyhow," he said, "that's why I asked for that prayer. And I honestly believe it might have worked. Oh, it's not like I got an answer in plain English, of course, but . . . don't you think? Don't you think I'm forgiven?"

"Goodness, no," Reverend Emmett said briskly.

Ian's mouth fell open. He wondered if he'd misunderstood. He said, "I'm *not* forgiven?"

"Oh, no."

"But . . . I thought that was kind of the point," Ian said. "I thought God forgives everything."

"He does," Reverend Emmett said. "But you can't just say, 'I'm sorry, God.' Why, anyone could do that much! You have to offer reparation—concrete, practical reparation, according to the rules of our church."

"But what if there isn't any reparation? What if it's something nothing will fix?"

"Well, that's where Jesus comes in, of course."

Another itchy word: Jesus. Ian averted his eyes.

"Jesus remembers how difficult life on earth can be," Reverend Emmett told him. "He helps with what you can't undo. But only after you've *tried* to undo it."

"Tried? Tried how?" Ian asked. "What would it take?"

Reverend Emmett started collecting hymnals from the chair seats. Apparently he was so certain of the answer, he didn't even have to think about it. "Well, first you'll need to see to those children," he said.

"Okay. But . . . see to them in what way, exactly?"

"Why, raise them, I suppose."

"Huh?" Ian said. "But I'm only a freshman!"

Reverend Emmett turned to face him, hugging the stack of hymnals against his concave shirt front.

"I'm away in Pennsylvania most of the time!" Ian told him.

"Then maybe you should drop out."

"Drop out?"

"Right."

"Drop out of college?"

"Right."

Ian stared at him.

"This is some kind of test, isn't it?" he said finally.

Reverend Emmett nodded, smiling. Ian sagged with relief.

"It's God's test," Reverend Emmett told him.

"So . . ."

"God wants to know how far you'll go to undo the harm you've done."

"But He wouldn't really make me follow through with it," Ian said.

"How else would He know, then?"

"Wait," Ian said. "You're saying God would want me to give up my education. Change all my parents' plans for me and give up my education."

"Yes, if that's what's required," Reverend Emmett said.

"But that's crazy! I'd have to be crazy!"

" 'Let us not love in word, neither in tongue,' " Reverend Emmett said, " 'but in deed and in truth.' First John three, eighteen."

"I can't take on a bunch of kids! Who do you think I am? I'm nineteen years old!" Ian said. "What kind of a cockeyed religion *is* this?"

"It's the religion of atonement and complete forgiveness," Reverend Emmett said. "It's the religion of the Second Chance."

Then he set the hymnals on the counter and turned to offer Ian a beatific smile. Ian thought he had never seen anyone so absolutely at peace.

"I don't understand," his mother said.

"What's to understand? It's simple," Ian told her. "What you mean is, you don't approve."

"Well, of course she doesn't approve," his father said. "Neither one of us approves. No one in his right mind would approve. Here you are, attending a perfectly decent college which you barely got into by the skin of your teeth, incidentally; you've had no complaints about the place that your mother or I are aware of; you're due back this Sunday evening to begin your second semester and what do you up and tell us? You're dropping out."

"I'm taking a leave of absence," Ian said.

They were sitting in the dining room late Friday night—much too late to have only then finished supper, but Daphne had developed an earache and what with one thing and another it had somehow got to be nine P.M. before they'd put the children in bed. Now Bee, having risen to clear the table, sank back into her chair. Doug shoved his plate away and leaned his elbows on the table. "Just tell me this," he said to Ian. "How long do you expect this leave of absence to last?"

"Oh, maybe till Daphne's in first grade. Or kindergarten, at least," Ian said.

"Daphne? What's Daphne got to do with it?"

"The reason I'm taking a leave is to help Mom raise the kids."

"Me?" his mother cried. "I'm not raising those children! We're looking for a guardian! First we'll find Lucy's people and then I know there'll be someone, some young couple maybe who would just love to—"

"Mom," Ian said. "You know the chances of that are getting slimmer all the time."

"I know nothing of the sort! Or an aunt, maybe, or—"

Doug said, "Well, he's got a point, Bee. You've been running yourself ragged with those kids."

Contrarily, Ian felt a pinch of alarm. Would his father really let him go through with this?

His mother said, "And anyway, how about the draft? You'll be drafted the minute you leave school."

"If I am, I am," Ian told her, "but I don't think I will be. I think God will take care of that."

"Who?"

"And I do plan to pay my own way," he said. "I've already found a job."

"Doing what?" his father asked. "Moving poor folks' furniture?"

"*Building* furniture."

They peered at him.

"I've made arrangements with this cabinetmaker," Ian said. "I've seen him at work and I asked if I could be his apprentice."

Student, was the way he'd finally put it. Having sought out the cabinetmaker in that apartment full of china crates and mothballs, he had plunged into the subject of apprenticeship only to be met with a baffled stare. The man had sat back on his heels and studied Ian's lips. "Apprentice," Ian had repeated, enunciating carefully. "Pupil."

"People?" the man had asked. Two furrows stitched themselves across his leathery forehead.

"I already have some experience," Ian said. "I used to help my father in the basement. I know I could build a kitchen cabinet."

"I dislike kitchens," the man said harshly.

For a moment, Ian thought he still hadn't made himself clear. But the man went on: "They're junk. See this hinge." He pointed to it—an ornately curlicued piece of black metal, dimpled all over with artificial hammer marks. "My real work is furniture," he said.

"Fine," Ian told him. What did he care? Kitchen cabinets, furniture, it was all the same to him: inanimate objects. Something he could deal with that he couldn't mess up. Or if he did mess up, it was possible to repair the damage.

"I have a workshop. I make things I like," the man said. He spoke like anyone else except for a certain insistence of tone, a thickness in the consonants, as if he had a cold. "These kitchens, they're just for the money."

"That's okay! That's fine! And as for money," Ian said, "you could pay me minimum wage. Or lower, to start with, because I'm just an apprentice. Student," he added, for he saw now that it was the uncommon word "apprentice" that had given him trouble. "And any time you have to do a kitchen, you could send me instead."

He knew he had a hope, then. He could tell by the wistful, visionary look that slowly dawned in the man's gray eyes.

But were his parents impressed with Ian's initiative? No. They just sat there blankly. "It's not brute labor, after all," he told them. "It's a craft! It's like an art."

"Ian," his father said, "if you're busy learning this . . . art, how will you help with the kids?"

"I'll work out a schedule with my boss," Ian said. "Also there's this church that's going to pitch in."

"This what?"

"Church."

They tilted their heads.

"There's this . . . it's kind of hard to explain," he said. "This church sort of place on York Road, see, that believes you have to really do something practical to atone for your, shall we call them, sins. And if you agree to that, they'll pitch in. You can sign up on a bulletin board—the hours you need help, the hours you've got free to help others—"

"What in the name of God . . . ?" Bee asked.

"Well, that's just it," Ian said. "I mean, I don't want to sound corny or anything but it *is* in the name of God. 'Let us not love in—' what—'in just words or in tongue, but in—' "

"Ian, have you fallen into the hands of some *sect*?" his father asked.

"No, I haven't," Ian said. "I have merely discovered a church that makes sense to me, the same as Dober Street Presbyterian makes sense to you and Mom."

"Dober Street didn't ask us to abandon our educations," his mother told him. "Of course we have nothing against religion; we raised all of you children to be Christians. But *our* church never asked us to abandon our entire way of life."

"Well, maybe it should have," Ian said.

His parents looked at each other.

His mother said, "I don't believe this. I do not believe it. No matter how long I've been a mother, it seems my children can still come up with something new and unexpected to do to me."

"I'm not doing this to *you*! Why does everything have to relate to *you* all the time? It's for me, can't you get that into your head? It's something I have to do for myself, to be forgiven."

"Forgiven what, Ian?" his father asked.

Ian swallowed.

"You're nineteen years old, son. You're a fine, considerate, upstanding human being. What sin could you possibly be guilty of that would require you to uproot your whole existence?"

Reverend Emmett had said Ian would have to tell them. He'd said that was the only way. Ian had tried to explain how much it would hurt them, but Reverend Emmett had held firm. Sometimes a wound must be scraped out before it can heal, he had said.

Ian said, "I'm the one who caused Danny to die. He drove into that wall on purpose."

Nobody spoke. His mother's face was white, almost flinty.

"I told him Lucy was, um, not faithful," he said.

He had thought there would be questions. He had assumed they would ask for details, pull the single strand he'd handed them till the whole ugly story came tumbling out. But they just sat silent, staring at him.

"I'm sorry!" he cried. "I'm *really* sorry!"

His mother moved her lips, which seemed unusually wrinkled. No sound emerged.

After a while, he rose awkwardly and left the table. He paused in the dining room doorway, just in case they wanted to call him back. But they didn't. He crossed the hall and started up the stairs.

For the first time it occurred to him that there was something steely and inhuman to this religion business. Had Reverend Emmett taken fully into account the lonely thud of his sneakers on the steps, the shattered, splintered air he left behind him?

The little lamp on his desk gave off just enough light so it wouldn't wake Daphne. He leaned over the crib to check on her. She had a feverish smell that reminded him of a sour dishcloth. He straightened her blanket, and then he crossed to the bureau and looked in the mirror that hung above it. Back-lit, he was nothing but a silhouette. He saw himself suddenly as the figure he had feared in his childhood, the intruder who lurked beneath his bed so he had to take a running leap from the doorway every night. He turned aside sharply and picked up the mail his mother had set out for him: a *Playboy* magazine, an advertisement for a record club, a postcard from his roommate. The magazine and the ad he dropped into the wastebasket. The postcard showed a wild-haired woman barely covered by a white fur dress that hung in strategic zigzags around her thighs. (*SHE-WOLVES OF ANTARCTICA! In ViviColor!* the legend read.) *Dear Ian, How do you like my Christmas card? Better late than never. Kind of boring here at home, no Ian and Cicely across the room oh-so-silently hanky-pankying . . .* He winced and dropped the card on top of the magazine. It made a whiskery sound as it landed.

He saw that he was beginning from scratch, from the very ground level, as low as he could get. It was a satisfaction, really.

That night he dreamed he was carrying a cardboard moving carton for Sid 'n' Ed. It held books or something; it weighed a ton. "Here," Danny said, "let me help you," and he took one end and started backing down the steps with it. And all the while he and Ian smiled into each other's eyes.

It was the last such dream Ian would ever have of Danny, although of course he didn't know that at the time. At the time he woke clenched and anxious, and all he could think of for comfort was the hymn they had sung in the Church of the Second Chance. "Leaning," they sang, "leaning, leaning on the everlasting arms . . ." Gradually he drifted loose, giving himself over to God. He rested all his weight on God, trustfully, serenely, the way his roommate used to rest in his chair that resembled the palm of a hand.

4

Famous Rainbows

Holy Roller, their grandma called it. Holy Roller Bible Camp. She shut a cupboard door and told Thomas, "If you all went to *real* camp instead of Holy Roller, you wouldn't have to get up at the crack of dawn every day. And I wouldn't be standing here half asleep trying to fix you some breakfast."

But it wasn't the crack of dawn. Hot yellow bands of sunshine stretched across the linoleum. And she didn't look half asleep, either. She already had her hair combed, fluffed around her face in a curly gray shower-cap shape. She was wearing the blouse Thomas liked best, the one printed like a newspaper page, and brown knit slacks stretched out in front by the cozy ball of her stomach.

One of the words on her blouse was VICTORY. Another was DISASTER. Thomas hadn't even started second grade yet but he was able to read nearly every word you showed him.

"If you all went to Camp Cottontail like the Parker children you wouldn't have to leave till nine A.M.," his grandma said, inching around the table with a stack of cereal bowls. "An air-conditioned bus would pick you up at the doorstep. But oh, no. *Oh*, no. That's too simple for your uncle Ian. Let's not do it the easy way, your uncle Ian says."

What Ian had really said was, "Camp Cottontail costs eighty dollars for a two-week session." Thomas had heard the whole argument. "Eighty dollars per child! Do you realize what that comes to?"

"Maybe Dad could make a bit extra teaching summer school," their grandma had told him.

"Dream on, Mom. You really think I'd let him do that? Also, Camp Cottontail doesn't take three-year-olds. Daphne would be home all day with little old *you*."

That was what had settled it. Their grandma had the arthritis in her knees and hips and sometimes now in her hands, and chasing after Daphne was too much for her. Daphne just did her in, Grandma always said. Dearly though she loved her.

She shook Cheerios into Thomas's bowl and then turned toward the stairs. "Agatha!" she called. "Agatha, are you up?"

No answer. She sighed and poured milk on top of the Cheerios. "You get started on these and I'll go give her a nudge," she told Thomas. She walked stiffly out of the kitchen, calling, "Rise and shine, Agatha!"

Thomas laid his spoon flat on top of his cereal and watched it fill with milk and then sink.

Now here came his grandpa and Ian, with Daphne just behind. Ian wore his work clothes—faded jeans and a T-shirt, his white cloth carpenter cap turned around backward like a baseball catcher's. (Grandma just despaired when her men kept their hats on in the house.) He'd dressed Daphne in her new pink shorts set, and she was pulling the toy plastic lawn mower that made colored balls pop up when the wheels turned.

"The way I figure it," Ian was saying, "we'd be better off moving the whole operation to someplace where the lumber could be stored in the same building. But Mr. Brant likes the shop where it is. So I'm going to need the car all day unless you . . ."

Thomas stopped listening and took a mouthful of cereal. He watched Daphne walk around and around Ian's legs, with the lawn mower bobbling behind her. "This is what I'm bringing to Sharing Hour," she announced, but Thomas was the only one who heard her. "Ian? This is what I'm—"

"You should bring something fancier," Thomas told her.

"No! I'm bringing this!"

"Remember yesterday, what Mindy brought?"

Mindy had brought an Egyptian beetle from about a million years ago, pale blue-green like old rain spouts. But Daphne said, "I don't care."

"*Lots* of people have plastic lawn mowers," Thomas told her.

She pretended not to hear and walked in tighter and tighter circles around Ian's blue denim legs.

Once Daphne had her mind made up, nothing could change it. Everyone always joked about that. But Thomas worried she would look dumb in front of Bible camp. It was such a small camp that all the children were jumbled together, the three-year-olds in with the seven-year-olds like Thomas and even Agatha's age, the ten-year-olds; even ten-year-old Dermott Kyle. Dermott Kyle would be sure to laugh at her. Thomas watched her round-nosed white sandals taking tiny steps and he started getting angry at her just thinking about it.

Then Ian bent over and scooped her up, lawn mower and all. He said, "What's your breakfast order, Miss Daph?" and she giggled and told him, "Cinnamon toast."

That Daphne was too ignorant to worry.

When Agatha came downstairs she looked puffy-eyed and dazed. She never woke up easily. Their grandma hobbled around her, trying to get her going—pushing the Cheerios box across the table to her and offering other kinds when Agatha shook her head. "Cornflakes? Raisin bran?" she said. Agatha rested her chin on her fist and her eyes started slowly, slowly drooping shut. "Agatha, *don't* go back to sleep."

"She'll be fine once she hits fresh air," Ian said. He was standing by the toaster, waiting for Daphne's toast to pop up. He'd set Daphne on the counter next to him where she swung her feet and banged her heels against the cupboard doors beneath her.

"She'd be even finer if she could sleep till a decent hour," their grandma told him. "Why, they're having to get up earlier in summer than in winter! Poor child can barely keep her eyes propped open."

"She ought to be in Camp Cottontail," their grandpa said suddenly. Everyone had forgotten about him. He was scrambling himself some eggs at the stove. "Camp Cottontail comes to the house for them about nine o'clock or so; I've seen the bus in the neighborhood."

"Wasn't I just saying that? While Holy Roller, on the other hand—"

"It's not Holy Roller, Mom. Please," Ian told her. "It's Camp Second Chance. And it's sponsored by my church and it's free of charge. Not to mention it offers the kids a little grounding for their lives."

Their grandma looked up at the ceiling and let out a long, noisy breath.

"When I was seventeen," their grandpa said from the stove, "I volunteered to be a counselor at my church's camp out in western Maryland. That's because I was in love with this girl who taught archery there. Marie, her name was. I can see her still. She wore this leather cuff on her wrist so the bowstring wouldn't thwack her. Every night I prayed and prayed for her to love me back. I said, 'God, if you'll do this one thing for me I'll believe in you forever and I'll never ask another favor.' But she preferred the lifeguard and they started going out together. After that, why, me and God just never have been that chummy."

"God and I," Grandma murmured automatically.

"I mean I still go to church on holidays and such, but I don't feel quite the same way about it."

Ian said, "Well, what does that prove? Good grief! You act as if it proves something. But all it proves is, you didn't know what was best for you. You were asking for a girl who wasn't right for you."

Their grandpa just shrugged, but their grandma said, "Oh, Lord, it's too early in the day for this," and she dropped heavily into a chair.

Agatha's eyes were closed now and Daphne had stopped swinging her feet. The dog lay next to the sink like a rumpled floor mat. Only Ian seemed to have any pep. He plucked the toast from the toaster, flipping it a couple of times so it wouldn't burn his fingers. As he turned to bring it to the breakfast table, he gave Thomas a quick little wink and a smile.

While Ian was driving them to camp he said, "You mustn't take it too seriously when your grandma and grandpa talk that way. They've had some disappointments in their lives. It doesn't mean they don't believe deep down."

"I know that," Thomas said, but Agatha just stared out the side window. She always got grumpy and embarrassed when talk of religion came up. Thomas suspected she was not a true Christian. He knew for a fact that she hated going to Camp Second Chance. Even the name, she said, made it seem they were settling for something; and what sort of camp has just a backyard, above-ground, corrugated plastic pool you have to fill with a garden hose? But she said this privately, only to Thomas. Neither one of them would have hurt Ian's feelings for the world.

Ian dropped them off at Sister Myra's house in a rush; he was running late. "Morning, Brother Ian!" Sister Myra called from her front door, and he said, "Morning, Sister Myra. Sorry I can't stop to talk." Then he drove away, leaving them on the sidewalk. Sister Myra lived in a development called Lullaby Acres where no trees grew, and it was hotter than at home. Thomas could feel a trickle of sweat starting down between his shoulder blades.

"My, don't you three look spiffy," Sister Myra said, opening the screen door for them. She was a plump, smiley-faced woman with a frizz of sand-colored curls. "What's that you got with you, sweetheart?" she asked Daphne.

"This here is my lawn mower."

"Well, bring it on in where it's cool."

It wasn't just cool; it was cold. Sister Myra's house was air-conditioned. Thomas thought air-conditioning was wonderful, even if it did mean they tended to stay inside as much as possible. Today, for instance, no one at all was playing in the brownish backyard around the swimming pool. Everybody was down in the basement rec room, which felt like a huge refrigerator. Dermott Kyle and Jason were lining up dinky plastic Bible figures in two rows across the indoor-outdoor carpet, making believe one row was ranchers and the other was cattle rustlers. Three girls were dressing dolls in a corner, and the Nielsen twins were helping Sister Myra's daughter Beth put today's memory verse on the flannelboard: *As the hart* . . . and then a word that Thomas couldn't figure out. He hoped the verse was a short one. Dermott Kyle had asked yesterday for *Jesus wept*, and it made the other campers laugh till Sister Myra pointed out how sad He must have been for our sins.

"We have three more people to wait for," Sister Myra said. "Mindy and the Larsons. Then we can begin. You all stay here with Sister Audrey while I go up and watch for the others."

Sister Audrey was sitting on a child's stool way too small for her. She was a big, soft, pale teenager in tight cutoffs and a tank top that showed her bra straps. When she heard her name she smiled around the room and hugged her potato-looking bare knees, but nobody smiled back. They were scared to death of Sister Audrey. She was helping out at Bible camp because she'd had a baby when she wasn't married and put it in a Dempster Dumpster and now she was atoning for her sin. They weren't supposed to know that, but they did. They discussed the details amongst themselves in whispers: how the baby had been wrapped in a towel (or Dermott said a grocery bag), how a janitor heard it peeping, how a police car took it where somebody grown could adopt it. Sister Audrey smiled at them hopefully while they clustered in the doll corner and rehashed this information. "Doesn't anybody want me to read them a story?" she called, but they weren't about to get that close to her; no, sirree.

Sister Myra came back downstairs with Mindy and one of the Larsons, Johnny. Kenny was home with the earache, she said. "Something for us to mention in our prayers," she told them, and she clapped her hands. "All right, campers! Gather round! Everybody pull up a chair!"

Some of the chairs were little wooden ones, painted in nursery-school colors. Others were regular folding chairs, and all the boys fought for those so they wouldn't look sissy. Especially Thomas. He couldn't bear to have Dermott Kyle mistake him for one of the babies.

"Our Lord in Heaven," Sister Myra said, "we thank you for another beautiful day. We thank you for these innocent, unsullied souls gathered in your name, and we ask for Kenny Larson's recovery if it be thy will. Now we're going to offer up our sentence prayers as we do every morning at this time."

That last part was spoken more to the campers than to God, Thomas felt. Surely God knew by now they offered up sentence prayers every morning. He must know what they were going to say, even, since most of them just repeated what they'd said on other mornings. The girls said thank-yous—"Thank You for the trees and flowers," and such. (With Agatha, it was, "Thanks for the family," in a mumbling, furry tone of voice.) The boys were more likely to make requests. "Let the Orioles win tonight" was commonest. ("If it be Thy will," Sister Myra always added in a hurry.) The only exception was Dermott Kyle, who said, "Thank You for air-conditioning." That always got a laugh. Thomas usually asked for good swimming weather, but today he prayed for Kenny Larson's earache to go away. For one thing, Kenny was his best friend. Also Thomas liked to come up with some different sentence now and then, and this one made Sister Myra nod approvingly.

Sister Audrey offered the closing sentence. "Dear God," she said, "look down upon us and understand us, we humbly beg in Jesus' name. Amen."

Some of the boys nudged each other at that, because she probably meant He should understand about the Dempster Dumpster. But then they caught Sister Myra's frown and so they put on their blankest faces and started gazing around the room and humming.

After Devotions came Sharing Hour. In school they called it Show and Tell. You didn't have to bring anything to Sharing Hour if you didn't want to, and most of the boys didn't. Also what you brought didn't have to be religious, although of course it was always nice if it was. It could be just some belonging you'd been blessed with that you wanted others to share the joy of. Sister Myra's daughter Beth, for instance, brought a beautiful silver whistle that used to be her cousin Rob's from Boy Scout camp. But when it came time to let others share the joy of it, she refused. She said she didn't want people blowing it and passing on their germs. "Well, honestly, Beth," Sister Myra said, looking cross, but Beth said, "I got a right! I don't have to put up with all and sundry's summer colds!" She was a skinny stick of a girl who never seemed that healthy anyway. Her nose was always red, and her braids were the pale, pinkish color of transparent eyeglass frames. Sister Myra sighed and said, "Anybody else?"

Daphne stood up so hard that her chair fell over backward. (You were supposed to raise your hand.) "Well, I have this," she announced, and she held the toy lawn mower over her head. All the girls said, "Aw!" They thought she was cute. Then the boys, Dermott and the nine-year-olds, said, "Awww," making fun of the girls, but you could tell they didn't mean any harm. They were smiling, and Daphne smiled back at them. Then she showed how the colored balls popped up when she pushed the lawn mower across the carpet. She *was* cute, Thomas realized. She was darling, with her springy black curls as thick as the wig on a doll and her face very small and lively. He felt suddenly proud of her, and also, for some reason, a little bit sad.

"Thank you, sweetheart," Sister Myra said. "Any other sharers?"

Agatha raised her hand. Thomas looked over at her; she hadn't mentioned she was bringing something. She stood up and rooted through her front pocket, knotting her mouth because she was kind of fat for her shorts and it was hard to get her fist around whatever it was. Finally she pulled out something round and clear. "A mustard seed," she said.

Sister Myra said, "A what, hon?"

"A mustard seed in a plastic ball, like what Reverend Emmett talked about yesterday at Juice Time."

"Oh, yes: 'If ye have faith as a grain of mustard . . .' " Sister Myra said. She held out her hand, and Agatha let the object drop into her palm. "Why, I remember these! We wore them on chains back in high school. We bought them at Woolworth's jewelry counter."

"It used to be my mother's," Agatha said.

Thomas's mouth fell open.

"My mother's dead now, and I don't know what church she belonged to. But when Reverend Emmett showed us those mustard seeds at Juice Time I thought, '*That's* what that is! That round ball in my mother's box.' "

Their mother's jewelry box, she meant, the cloth-covered box Agatha kept her barrettes in; and she was evil, evil to show other people something from the mysterious bottom drawer. Hadn't she made Thomas cross his heart and hope to die if he told anyone their mother's things were hidden there? She wouldn't even let him tell Daphne, because Daphne might tell the grownups and then the grownups would go through their mother's papers and figure out a way to ship Thomas and Agatha off to strangers, keeping Daphne for themselves since Daphne was the only true Bedloe. Agatha had warned him a dozen times, and now look: here she was, speaking of "my" mother, of how "I" don't know what church she belonged to, while their mother's private mustard seed traveled from hand to hand like something ordinary. From Sister Myra's cushiony palm to Beth's wiry, freckled claw to Dermott Kyle's not-very-clean fist, and by the time it reached Thomas he believed he caught the smell of sweat. He held it up by its tiny gold ring and studied it at eye level. (He was no more familiar with it than the others were, since Agatha guarded that box so jealously.) Had the plastic been this scratched and clouded even before the others handled it? If so, then it was because of his mother's touch; her actual fingers had rubbed off the shine. Her actual eyes had looked upon that white glint of a seed.

He didn't really remember their mother, to tell the truth. When he tried to picture her, he had the vaguest recollection of following some red high-heeled shoes down a sidewalk and then looking up to discover they belonged to the wrong lady. "Mama!" he had cried in a panic, and there'd been a flurry of footsteps, a low, soft laugh . . . but he couldn't put together what she'd looked like. It seemed that whenever he tried he came up with a sort of *general* mother, the kind you imagine when someone reads out the word "mother" in a storybook. He'd asked Agatha once, "Did she used to have a station wagon, maybe? I think I remember a car pool, a lady in the car pool at my nursery school—"

But Agatha said, "What are you talking about? She didn't even know how to drive!"

"I must've mixed her up with someone else," he said.

But the car-pool lady stayed on in his mind—someone like other children had, waiting for him in a brown station wagon with wood-grained panels on the sides and a rear compartment full of tennis-ball cans and lacrosse sticks.

"The best thing is, Agatha's brought us something having to do with our faith," Sister Myra said. "She listened to what Reverend Emmett talked about at Juice Time and then she brought something related to that. Very nice, Agatha."

Agatha nodded and sat down in her chair. When Thomas passed the mustard seed to Jason, he felt he was parting with a piece of himself, like an arm.

The Bible verse for the day came from the Forty-second Psalm: *As the hart panteth after the water brooks* . . . First Sister Myra explained what it meant. "Does everyone know what a hart is? Anyone? Anyone at all?" Then she helped them memorize it, breaking the verse into phrases that they repeated after her. This was all in preparation for the Bible Bee, which was a kind of spelldown that happened every Friday. Sometimes they competed against other camps—last week, Lamb of God from Cockeysville. Lamb of God had won.

After Bible Verse it was time for Morning Swim. The girls changed upstairs in Beth's room and the boys changed in the workshop off the rec room. They met in the backyard. At first the sun felt wonderful, soaking into Thomas's chilled skin, and then all at once it felt too hot, *way* too hot, so that he was glad to race the others to the pool and clamber up the three wooden steps and drop into the lukewarm water. Sister Myra was the lifeguard. She stood hip-deep with her swimsuit skirt floating out around her and tried to make the boys stop splashing the girls. Sister Audrey watched the baby pool, which was an inflatable rubber dish nearby. She wore her same tank top and cutoffs and didn't even remove her flip-flops but sat high and dry in a folding chair she'd dragged out, smiling or else squinting at the little ones as they sailed their toy boats and poured water from their tin buckets.

Jason said the Dumpster had been parked behind the stadium, but Dermott said Mondawmin Mall.

After their swim they sat down for lunch at two redwood picnic tables on the patio. That way they didn't drip across Sister Myra's floors; they'd be dry before they'd finished eating. It was Mindy's turn to ask the blessing (not a chance Dermott Kyle would get another turn, not after last time!), and then they had bologna sandwiches and milk. Dessert was little foil packets of salted peanuts because Sister Myra's husband worked for a company that made airplane meals and he got a special discount. By now they'd used up all their energy and they were quieter. Daphne fell asleep with her head on the table halfway through her sandwich. Thomas pumped a mouthful of milk from one cheek to the other to hear the swishing sound. Dermott asked, dreamily, "Does *everybody* see flashes of white light while they're chewing tinfoil?"

Still in their swimsuits, they were herded downstairs (Daphne sagging over Sister Myra's shoulder), where they unrolled their blankets from home and stretched out on the floor for their naps. Sister Myra sat in a chair above them and read aloud from the Bible-story book with its queerly lightweight paper and orange drawings: "The Boy Jesus in the Temple," today. (How rude He was to his parents! But there must be some excuse for it that Thomas was still too young to understand.) The idea was, the little ones would sleep and the older ones would just rest and listen to the story. Thomas always meant to just rest, but Sister Myra's low voice mingled with the creaks overhead where Sister Audrey was clearing away lunch, and next thing he knew the others were rolling their blankets and Reverend Emmett had arrived for Juice Time.

Reverend Emmett was tall and thin and he never seemed to get hot, not even in his stiff white shirt and black trousers. All the children loved him.

Well, all except Agatha. Agatha said his Adam's apple was too big. But the others loved him because he acted so bashful with them. A grownup, scared of children! He said, "How are our campers today? Enjoying this beautiful weather?" and when somebody (Mindy) finally said, "Yup," he practically fell apart. "Oh! Wonderful!" he said, all flustered and delighted. Then he sat down on one of the nursery-school chairs so his knees jutted nearly to his chin, and the others settled on the floor in a circle while Sister Myra and Sister Audrey passed out paper cups of apple juice. Reverend Emmett took a cup himself. (In his long, bony fingers, it looked like a thimble.) He said, "Thank you, Sister Audrey," and he smiled so happily into her face you would think he'd never heard of the Dempster Dumpster. Sister Audrey blushed and backed away and stepped on one of the Nielsen twins' hands, but since she was wearing her flip-flops it must not have hurt much. The twin only blinked and went on staring at Reverend Emmett.

Sometimes Reverend Emmett talked about Jesus and sometimes about modern days. Thomas liked modern days best. He liked hearing about the Church of the Second Chance: how it had started out meeting in Reverend Emmett's garage where the floor was still marked with oil stains from Reverend Emmett's Volkswagen. Or even before that: how Reverend Emmett, an Episcopal seminarian and the son of an Episcopal minister, had gradually come to question the sham and the idolatry—for what was kneeling before a crucifix but idolatry?—and determined to found a church without symbols, a church without baptism or communion where only the *real* things mattered and where the atonement must be as real as the sin itself, where for instance if you broke a playmate's toy in anger you must go home immediately and fetch a toy of your own, of as good or better quality, and give it to that playmate for keeps and then announce your error at Public Amending on Sunday. Or how Reverend Emmett's fiancée had dumped him and his father had called him a crackpot although his mother, the smart one in the family, had seen the light at once and could even now be observed attending Second Chance every Sunday in her superficial Episcopal finery, her white gloves and netted hat. But that was all right, Reverend Emmett said. To condemn a person for fancy dress was every bit as vain as condemning her for humble dress. It's only the inside that counts.

Today he talked about how meaningful it was that he should come for these chats of theirs at Juice Time. "This way," he told them, "it's a period of spiritual nourishment as well as physical." Then he put it more simply for the little ones. "You don't get just apple juice, you get the juice of heavenly knowledge besides." He said, "How lucky you are, to have both at once! Most children have to choose one at a time—either nourishment for the soul or nourishment for the body."

"Isn't there anything else?" Agatha wanted to know.

"Excuse me?"

But she shrugged and picked at a cuticle.

"And even young as you are, you can still bear witness," Reverend Emmett said. "You can live in such a way that people will ask, 'Who *are* those children? And what is the secret of their joy?' That's what 'bearing witness' means, in our faith—not empty words or proselytizing. Those cigarette smokers and coffee addicts and sugar fiends in their big expensive churches, contributing to the Carpet Fund and sipping their communion wine which we all know is an artificial stimulant—'Why are those children so *blessed*?' they'll ask. For you are blessed, my little ones. Someday you'll appreciate that. You're luckier than you realize, growing up in a church that cares for you so."

Then he took a small brown bottle out of his trouser pocket and said it came from Kenny Larson's doctor. He said all the campers had to have eardrops before they went in Sister Myra's pool again.

Next came Crafts, where they made framed scripture plaques from drinking straws. And after that, Song Time, where they sang, "I've got the peace-that-passeth-understanding down in my heart, down in my heart . . ." as fast as possible in hopes that someone's tongue would get twisted, but nobody's did. And then Afternoon Swim, the longest single period of the day. Thomas thought maybe Sister Myra had lost all her zip by then and just let them go on swimming because it was easiest. During their nap she had changed back into her skirt and blouse (probably for Reverend Emmett's visit, even though clothes were not supposed to matter), and she didn't bother getting into her swimsuit again but sat on a chair next to the pool with her skirt pulled up above her knees and her face tipped back to catch the sun. Still, you couldn't put a thing past her. "No dunking allowed, Dermott Kyle!" she called, although Dermott was barely beginning to move in Mindy's direction and Sister Myra's eyes were closed. Her face was so freckled that it had a spattered look, as if someone had thrown handfuls of beige spangles at her.

Thomas knew how to swim—Ian had taught him last summer—but he hated getting his head wet. He swam straining out of the water, his arms flailing wildly and splashing too much. Agatha swam a slow, steady breaststroke like an old person. Her gaze was fixed and her chin stayed just under the surface, so that she looked obstinate. Dermott Kyle, naturally, was wonderful at every stroke there was and also claimed to be able to dive, although he couldn't prove it because Sister Myra didn't have a diving board.

In the baby pool, Sister Audrey stood ankle-deep and bent over with her hands in the water. Johnny Larson was emptying a sprinkling can on top of Percy's head. Daphne was . . . Thomas couldn't see Daphne. He waded toward the edge of his own pool to check, and that's when he realized that the thing in Sister Audrey's hands was Daphne's little blue-flowered body.

Later, he couldn't remember how he got out of the water so fast. It almost seemed he was lifted straight up. Then he was running, with the sharp, stubbly grass pricking his bare feet, and then he was flying through the air as level as a Frisbee and belly flopping into the baby pool where Daphne lay on her stomach, smiling, making splashy little pretend-swim motions while Sister Audrey supported her.

He grabbed hold of Daphne anyway. (It seemed he'd been wound with a key and had to follow through with this.) He struggled to his feet, staggering a bit, hanging onto her even though she squirmed and protested. "You leave her alone," he told Sister Audrey. Sister Audrey stared at him; her mouth was partway open. Thomas hauled Daphne out of the pool, dumped her in a heap, brushed off his hands all businesslike, and then strode back to the big pool.

As soon as he was in the water, the others crowded around him asking, "What'd she do? What happened?" Sister Myra looked confused. (For once, she had missed something.) Thomas said, "I just don't like her messing with my little sister, is all." He set his jaw and gazed beyond them, over toward the baby pool. Sister Audrey was standing on dry ground now. She was concentrating on stepping back into her flip-flops, and something about her lowered head and her meek, blind smile made Thomas's stomach all at once start hurting. He turned away. "Boy, you were *out* of here," Dermott Kyle said admiringly.

"Oh, well, you do what you got to do," Thomas told him.

Toweled dry and dressed, their swimsuits hanging on the line outdoors and their hair still damp, they gathered for Devotions. Sister Myra said, "Dear Lord, thank You for this day of fellowship and listen now to our silent prayers," and then she left a long, long space afterward. Silent prayers were sort of like Afternoon Swim; you had the feeling she was too worn out to make the effort anymore. *Everyone* was worn out. Still, Thomas tried. He bowed his head and closed his eyes and prayed for his mother in heaven. He knew she was up there, watching over him. And he knew his prayers were being heard. Hadn't he prayed for Ian not to go to Vietnam that time? And the draft notice came anyhow and Thomas had blamed God, but then the doctors found out Ian had an extra heartbeat that had never been heard before and never given a moment's trouble since, and Thomas knew his prayer had been answered. He'd stood up at Public Amending the following Sunday and confessed how he had doubted, but everyone was so happy about Ian that they just smiled at him while he spoke. He had felt he was surrounded by loving feelings. Afterward, Reverend Emmett said he thought Thomas had not really sinned, just shown his ignorance; and he was confident it would never happen again. And sure enough, it hadn't.

"In Jesus' name, we pray. Amen," Sister Myra said.

They all rustled and jostled and pushed each other, glad to be moving again.

It was Agatha's turn to sit in front, but Ian said they should all three sit in back because he was picking up Cicely on the way home. "She's coming for supper," he told them. "It's a state occasion: Aunt Claudia's birthday. Remember?"

No, they hadn't remembered, even though they'd spent last evening making a birthday card. Daphne said, "Oh, goody," because that meant all the cousins would be there. Thomas and Agatha were glad, too—especially on account of Cicely. They both thought Cicely was as pretty as a movie star.

Ian asked Daphne what the day's Bible verse had been. Daphne said, "Um . . ." and looked down into her lap. She was sitting in the middle, with her legs sticking straight out in front of her and the lawn mower resting across her knees.

"Agatha?" Ian called back, turning onto Charles Street.

Agatha sighed. "As the hart panteth after the water brooks," she said flatly, "so panteth my soul after Thee, O God."

She mumbled the word "God," so she almost didn't say it at all, but Ian appeared not to notice. "Good for you," he said. "And what did Reverend Emmett talk about?"

Agatha didn't answer, so Thomas spoke up instead. "Juice," he said.

"Juice?"

"How we get juice for the soul and juice for the body, both at once, in Bible camp."

"Well, that's very true," Ian said.

"It's very dumb," Agatha said.

"Pardon?"

"Besides," she said, "isn't 'juice' a bad word?"

"I beg your pardon?"

"It just has that sound to it, somehow, like maybe it could be."

"I don't know what you're talking about," Ian said. They had reached a red light, and he was able to glance over his shoulder at her. "Juice? What?"

"And that pool is full of germs; I think everybody pees in it," Agatha said. "And Sister Audrey makes the sandwiches so far ahead they're all dried out before we get to eat them. And anyhow, what's she doing in a children's camp? A person who'd put a baby in a Dempster Dumpster!"

By now, those words were like some secret joke. Thomas giggled. Ian looked at him in the rearview mirror.

"You're laughing?" he asked.

Thomas got serious.

"You think Sister Audrey is funny?"

A driver behind them honked his horn; the light had turned green. Ian didn't seem to hear. "She's just a kid," he told Thomas. "She's not much older than you are, and had none of your advantages. I can't believe you would find her situation comical."

"Ian, cars are getting mad at us," Agatha said.

Ian sighed and started driving again.

I'm just a kid too, Thomas wanted to tell him. *How would I know what her situation is?*

They took a left turn. Daphne sucked her thumb and slid her curled index finger back and forth across her upper lip, the way she liked to do when she was tired. Thomas kept his eyes wide open so no one would see the tears. He wished he had his grandma. Ian was his favorite person in the world, but when you were sad or sick to your stomach who did you want? Not Ian. Ian had no soft nooks to him. Thomas tipped his head back against the seat and felt his eyes growing cool in the breeze from the window.

On Lang Avenue, with its low white houses and the sprinklers spinning under the trees, Ian parked and got out. He climbed the steps to Cicely's porch, meanwhile taking off his cap. "Ooh," Agatha said. "He's got horrible hat-head." Thomas had never heard the phrase before, but he saw instantly what she meant. All around Ian's shiny brown hair the cap had left a deep groove. "He looks like a goop," Agatha said. That was her way of comforting Thomas, he knew. It didn't really help much, but he tried to smile anyhow.

When Cicely came to the door, she was wearing bell-bottom jeans and a tie-dyed T-shirt. A beaded Indian headband held back her long messy waterfall of curls. First she stood on her toes and gave Ian a kiss. (All three of them watched carefully from the car. For a while now they had been worrying that Cicely didn't like Ian as much as she used to.) Then she waved at them and started down the porch steps. Ian followed, clamping his cap back on.

Daphne took her thumb out of her mouth. "Hi, Cicely!" she called.

"Well, hey, gang," Cicely said. "How we doing?" She opened the door on the passenger side and slid across to the middle of the front seat. The car filled with the moldy smell of the perfume she'd started wearing.

Ian got in on the driver's side and asked, "Have a good day at work?"

"Great," Cicely said. (This summer she worked part-time at a shop where they made leather sandals.) She moved over very close to him and brushed a wood shaving off his shoulder. "How was *your* day?"

"Well, we got a new order," Ian said.

"Right on!"

He pulled into traffic and said, "This woman came all the way from Massachusetts with a blanket box, her great-grandfather's blanket box. Asked if we knew how to make one just like it, using the same methods. Exactly the kind of thing Mr. Brant likes best."

Cicely made a sort of humming noise and nestled in against him.

"Soon as she left Mr. Brant told me, 'Go call those kitchen people.' People who wanted an estimate on their kitchen cabinets. 'Call and cancel,' he said. Cicely hon, stop that, please."

"Stop what?" she asked him, in a smiling voice.

"You know what."

"I'm not doing anything!" she said. She sat up straight. She slid over to her side of the car and set her face toward the window. "Mr. Holiness," she muttered to a fire hydrant.

"Pretty soon we may give up kitchens altogether," Ian said, turning down Waverly. He parked at the curb and cut the engine. "We'll build nothing but fine furniture. Custom designs. Old-style joinery."

Cicely wasn't listening. All three of them sitting in back could tell that, just from the way she kept her face turned. But Ian said, "We might hire another worker, too. At least, Mr. Brant's thinking about it. I said, 'Good, hire several, and give me a raise while you're at it,' and he said he might do it. 'I won't be a single man forever,' I told him." Ian glanced over at Cicely when he said that, but Cicely was still looking out the window.

It was amazing, how he could talk on like that without realizing. When even they realized! Even little Daphne, sucking her thumb and watching Cicely with round, anxious eyes!

Thomas all at once felt so angry at Ian that he jumped out of the car in a rush and slammed the door loudly behind him.

Their grandma said they had to change clothes at once, this instant, because Aunt Claudia was arriving at five-thirty and they looked as if they'd spent the day rolling in a barnyard. She told Ian to run Daphne a bath, and she said, "Clean shirts for the other two! And clean shorts for Thomas. Hair combed. Faces washed."

But the minute Ian's back was turned, Thomas followed Agatha up the narrow, steep wooden stairs to the attic. He trailed her into the slanty-ceilinged attic bedroom that was hers and Daphne's, that used to be Aunt Claudia's when she was a girl at home. "Agatha," he said, putting on a fake frown, "do you think we should've bought Aunt Claudia a present? Maybe a card will be too boring."

What he was after, of course, was a glimpse of their mother's jewelry box. He knew Agatha had to open it to return the mustard seed.

"You heard what Grandma said," Agatha told him. "A handmade card means more than anything. What are you in my room for?"

"But she gives *us* presents," Thomas said. He sat on her bed and swung his feet. "Maybe we should've made her something bigger, a picture for her wall or something."

"I mean it, Thomas. You're trespassing in my private room."

"It's Daphne's room, too," Thomas said. "Daphne would be glad to have me here."

"Get out, I tell you."

"Agatha, can't I just watch you put the mustard seed away?"

"No, you can't."

"She wasn't only *your* mama, you know."

"Maybe not," Agatha said, "but you don't keep secrets good."

"I do so. I didn't tell about the jewelry box, did I?"

"You told our father's name, though," Agatha said, screwing up her eyes at him.

"That just slipped out! And anyway, I was little."

"Well, who knows what'll slip out next time?"

"Agatha, I implore you," he said, clasping his hands. "How about I look at the picture and nothing else?"

"You'll get it dirty."

"How about I hold it by the edges, sitting here on the bed? I won't ask to look at anything else, honest. I won't even peek inside the box."

She thought it over. She had taken the mustard seed from her pocket and he could see it glimmering between her fingers, so close he could have touched it.

"Well, okay," she said finally.

"You'll let me?"

"But just for a minute."

She crossed to the closet, which was only more attic—the lowest part of the attic, where the ceiling slanted all the way down. It didn't even have a door to shut. Thomas would have been scared to sleep near so much darkness, but Agatha wasn't scared of anything, and she stepped inside as bold as you please and knelt on the floor. He heard the box's bottom drawer slide open, and then the clink of the mustard seed against other clinky things—maybe the charm bracelet Agatha had let him sleep with once when he was sick, with the tiny scissors charm that could really cut paper and the tiny bicycle charm that could really spin its wheels.

She came back out, holding the picture by one corner. "Don't you dare get a speck of dirt on it," she said. He took it very, very gently between the flat of his hands, the way you'd take an LP record. The crinkly edges felt like little teeth against his palms.

It was a color photograph, with JUN 63 stamped on the border. A tin house trailer with cinder blocks for a doorstep. A pretty woman standing on the cinder blocks—black hair puffing to her shoulders, bright lipstick, ruffled pink dress—holding a scowly baby (him!) in nothing but a diaper, while a smaller, stubbier Agatha wearing a polka-dot playsuit stood alongside and reached up to touch the baby's foot.

If only you could climb into photographs. If only you could take a running jump and land there, deep inside! The frill at his mother's neckline must have made pretzel sounds in his ear. Her bare arms must have stuck to his skin a little in the hot sunshine. His sister must have thought he was cute, back then, and interesting.

It was spooky that he had no memory of that moment. It was like talking in your sleep, where they tell you in the morning what you said and you ask, "*I* did? *I* said that?" and laugh at your own crazy words as if they'd come from someone else. In fact, he always thought of the baby in the photo as a whole other person—as "he," not "I"—even though he knew better. "Why were you hanging onto his foot?" he asked now.

"I forget," Agatha said, sounding tired.

"You don't remember being there?"

"I remember! I remember everything! Just not why I was doing that with your foot."

"Where was our father?"

"Maybe he was taking the picture."

"You don't know for sure?"

"Of course I do! I know. He was taking our picture."

"Maybe you've forgotten, too," Thomas said. "Maybe these aren't even us."

"Of course they're us. Who else would they be? I remember our trailer and our yellow mailbox, and this dirt road or driveway or something with grass and flowers in the middle. I remember this huge, enormous rainbow and it started in the road and bent all the way over our house."

"What! Really? A rainbow?" Thomas said. He had an amazing thought. He got so excited he slid off the bed, not forgetting to be careful of the picture. "Then, Agatha!" he said. "Listen! Maybe that's how we could find where we used to live."

"What do you mean?"

"We could ask for the trailer with the rainbow."

She gave him a look. He could see he'd walked into something, but he didn't know what.

"Well, they must have maps of things like that," he said. "Don't they? Maps that show where the really big, really famous rainbows are?"

"Thomas," Agatha said. She rolled her eyes. Clearly it was almost more than she could manage to go on dealing with him. "For gosh sake, Thomas," she said, "rainbows don't just sit around forever. What do you think, it's still there waiting for us? Get yourself a brain someday, Thomas."

Then she took hold of the picture—with her fingers right on the colored part!—and pulled it out of his hands and carried it back to the closet.

"Thomas?" Ian called from the second floor. "Are you cleaned up?"

"Just about."

He would never know as much as Agatha did, Thomas thought while he was clomping down the stairs. He would always be left out of things. People would forever be using words he'd never heard of, or sharing jokes he didn't get the point of, or driving him places they hadn't bothered to tell him about; or maybe (as they claimed) they *had* told him, and he had just forgotten or been too little to understand.

• • •

"Last night I dreamed a terrible dream," Aunt Claudia said at dinner. "I think it had something to do with my turning thirty-eight."

She was twisted around in her seat, feeding baked potato to Georgie in his high chair. Over her shoulder she said, "I opened the door to the broom cupboard and this burglar jumped out at me. I kept trying to call for help but all I managed was this pathetic little whimper and then I woke up."

"How does that relate to turning thirty-eight?" her husband asked her.

"Well, it's scary, Macy. Thirty-eight sounds so much like forty. Forty! That's middle-aged."

She didn't look middle-aged. She didn't have gray hair or anything. Her hair was brown like Ian's, cut almost as short, and her face was smooth and tanned. Her clothes weren't middle-aged, either: jeans and a floppy plaid shirt. Whenever Georgie got hungry she would tuck him right under her shirt without unbuttoning it and fiddle with some kind of snaps or hooks inside and then let him nurse. Thomas thought that was fascinating. He hoped it would happen this evening.

"You know what I believe?" she asked now, wiping Georgie's mouth with a corner of her napkin. "I believe what I was trying to do was, teach myself how to scream."

Grandpa said, "Why, hon, I would think you'd already know how."

"I was speaking figuratively, Dad. Here I am, thirty-eight years old and I've never, I don't know, never *said* anything. Everything's so sort of level all the time. Tonight, for instance: here we sit. Nice cheerful chitchat, baseball standings, weather forecast, difficult ages eating in the kitchen . . ."

By "difficult ages," she meant the older children—ten to fifteen, Agatha to Abbie. The "biggies," Grandma called them. The people with exciting things to say. Thomas could hear them even from the dining room. Cindy was telling a story and the others were laughing and Barney was saying, "Wait, you left out the most important part!"

Here in the dining room, there *were* no important parts. Just dull, dull conversation among the grownups while the "littlies" secretly fed their suppers to Beastie under the table. Cicely was holding up a pinwheel biscuit and carefully unwinding it. Ian kept glancing over at her, but she didn't seem to notice.

"Well, Claudia," Grandma said, "would you prefer it if we moaned and groaned and carried on?"

"No, no," Claudia said, "I don't mean that exactly; I mean . . . oh, I don't know. I guess I'm just going through the middle-aged blues."

"Nonsense, you're nowhere near middle-aged," Grandma told her. "What an idea! You're just a slip of a girl still. You still have your youth and your wonderful life and everything to look forward to." She raised her wineglass. Thomas could tell her arthritis was bad tonight because she used both hands. "Happy birthday, sweetheart," she said.

Macy and Grandpa raised their glasses, too, and Cicely set aside the biscuit to raise hers. Ian, who didn't drink, held up his water tumbler. "Happy birthday," they all said.

"Well, thanks," Claudia told them.

She thought a moment, and then she said, "Thank you very much," and smiled around the table and took a sip from her own glass.

The cake was served in the living room, so they could all sing "Happy Birthday" together. But really just the grownups and the little ones sang. The difficult ages seemed to think singing was beneath them, so after the first line Thomas didn't sing either. Then just as Claudia was blowing out the candles, Mrs. Jordan arrived from across the street along with two of the foreigners. The foreigners brought a third foreigner named Bob who apparently used to live with them. Bob greeted Thomas by name but Thomas didn't remember him. "You were only so much high," Bob told him, setting his palm about six inches above the floor. "You wore little, little sneakers and your mother was very nice lady."

"My mother?" Thomas asked. "Did you know her?"

"Of course I knew her. She was very pretty, very kind lady."

Thomas was hoping to hear more, but Mrs. Jordan came over then and started filling Bob in on all the neighborhood news: how Mr. Webb had finally gone to be dried out and the newlyweds had had a baby and Rafe Hamnett's sexy twin daughters were making life a living hell for his girlfriend. Thomas wandered off finally.

His grandma was passing the cake around on her big tole tray. She served the grownups first. She said, "Macy, cake? Jim, cake?" She offered some to Ian, too, but of course he said no. (At church they didn't approve of sugar, as Grandma surely knew by now.) She thinned her lips and passed on. "Jessie? You'll have cake."

Ian asked Cicely, "What do you say to a movie after this?"

"Well, I kind of like made plans with some friends from school," Cicely told him.

"Oh."

"Melanie and them from school."

"Okay."

"I'd ask you along except it's, you know, like all just college talk about people you never heard of."

"That's okay," Ian said.

Thomas hooked his fingers into one of Ian's rear pockets. He slid his thumb back and forth across the puckery seam at the top. What did this remind him of? Daphne sucking her thumb, that was it. Curling her index finger across her upper lip. He leaned his head against Ian's side, and Ian put his arm around him. "I should get to bed early anyhow," he was telling Cicely. "Rumor has it tomorrow's another workday."

Now Grandma was offering her tray to the children. She said, "Thomas? Cake?"

"No, thanks."

"No birthday cake?" she asked. She put on a look of surprise.

"Sugar is an artificial stimulant," he reminded her.

He expected her to argue like always, but he didn't expect she'd get angry. Ian was the one she seemed angry with, though. She turned toward Ian sharply and said, "Really, Ian! He's just a little boy!"

"Sure. He's free to make up his own mind," Ian said.

"Free, indeed! It's that church of yours again."

"Excuse me. Mrs. Bedloe?" Cicely said. "Maybe Thomas is just listening to his body. Processed sugar is a poison, after all. No telling what it does to your body chemistry."

"Well, everybody in this room eats sugar and I don't exactly notice them keeling over," Grandma said.

"Me, now," Cicely said, "I've started using nonpasteurized honey whenever possible and I feel like a whole new person."

"But honey is a stimulant, too," Thomas told her.

Ian said, "Thomas. Hey, sport. Maybe if we just—"

"Do you hear that?" Grandma asked Ian. "Do you hear how he's been brainwashed?"

"Oh, well, I wouldn't—"

"It's not enough that you should fall for it yourself! That you'd obey their half-wit rules and support their maniac minister and scandalize the whole neighborhood by trying to convert the Cahns."

"I wasn't trying to convert them! I was having a theoretical discussion."

"A theoretical discussion, with people who've been Jewish longer than this country's been a nation! Oh, I will never understand. Why, Ian? Why have you turned out this way? Why do you keep doing penance for something that never happened? I *know* it never happened; I *promise* it never happened. Why do you persist in believing all that foolishness?"

"Bee, dear heart," Grandpa said.

Now Thomas noticed how still the room had grown. Maybe Grandma noticed too, because she stopped talking and two pink spots started blooming in her cheeks.

"Bee," Grandpa said, "we've got a crew of hungry kids here wondering if you plan on coming their way."

The others made murmury laughing sounds, although Thomas didn't see anything so funny. Then Grandma quirked the corners of her mouth and raised her chin. "Why! I certainly doo-oo!" she said musically, and off she sailed with her cake.

The frosting was caramel. Thomas had checked earlier. His grandma made the best caramel frosting in Baltimore—rich and deep and golden, as smooth as butter when it slid across your tongue.

Daphne went off at nine, kicking up a fuss in Ian's arms because the cousins were still there, but Thomas and Agatha got to stay awake till the last of the guests had said good night—almost ten-thirty, which was way past their normal bedtime.

"Don't forget your baths!" Ian called after them as they climbed the stairs, but Thomas was too sleepy for a bath and he fell into bed in his underwear, leaving his clothes in a heap on the floor. He shut his eyes and saw turquoise blue, the color of Sister Myra's swimming pool. He heard the clatter of china downstairs, and the rattle of silver, and the slow, dancy radio songs his grandma liked to listen to while she did the dishes. (She would be washing and Ian would be clearing away and drying; she always said the hot water felt so good on her finger joints.) "Where do you want these place mats?" Ian called. Loud announcers' voices interrupted each other in the living room; Grandpa was hunting baseball scores on TV. ". . . never saw Jessie Jordan so gossipy," Grandma said, and someone shouted, "BEEN IN A BATTING SLUMP SINCE MID-JUNE—"

"Could you turn that down?" Grandma called.

Then Thomas must have slept, because the next thing he knew the house was silent and he had a feeling the silence had been going on a long time. There wasn't even a cricket chirping. There wasn't even a faraway truck or a train whistle. The only sounds were those scraps of past voices that float across your mind sometimes when there's nothing else to listen to. "Thank you, Sister Audrey," Reverend Emmett said, and Grandma said, "Why, Ian? Why?"

Thomas should have told her why. He knew the answer, after all. Or, at least, he thought he did. The answer is, you get to meet in heaven. They'll be waiting for you there if you've been careful to do things right. His mother would be waiting in her frilly pink dress. She would drive her station wagon to the gate and she'd sit there with the motor idling, her elbow resting on the window ledge, and when she caught sight of him her face would light up all happy and she would wave. "Thomas! Over here!" she would call, and if he didn't spot her right away she would honk, and then he would catch sight of her and start running in her direction.

5

People Who Don't Know the Answers

After Doug Bedloe retired, he had a little trouble thinking up things to do with himself. This took him by surprise, because he was accustomed to the schoolteacher's lengthy summer vacations and he'd never found it hard to fill them. But retirement, it seemed, was another matter. There wasn't any end to it. Also it was given more significance. Loaf around in summer, Bee would say he deserved his rest. Loaf in winter, she read it as pure laziness. "Don't you have someplace to go?" she asked him. "Lots of men join clubs or something. Couldn't you do Meals on Wheels? Volunteer at the hospital?"

Well, he tried. He approached a group at his church that worked with disadvantaged youths. Told them he had forty years' experience coaching baseball. They were delighted. First he was supposed to get some training, though—spend three Saturdays learning about the emotional ups and downs of adolescents. The second Saturday, it occurred to him he was tired of adolescents. He'd been dealing with their ups and downs for forty years now, and the fact was, they were shallow.

So then he enrolled in this night course in the modern short story (his daughter's idea). Figured *that* would not be shallow, and short stories were perfect since he never had been what you would call a speed reader. It turned out, though, he didn't have a knack for discussing things. You read a story; it's good or it's bad. What's to discuss? The other people in the class, they could ramble on forever. Halfway through the course, he just stopped attending.

He retreated to the basement, then. He built a toy chest for his youngest grandchild—a pretty decent effort, although Ian (Mr. Artsy-Craftsy) objected to particleboard. Also, carpentry didn't give him quite enough to think about. Left a kind of empty space in his mind that all sorts of bothersome notions could rush in and fill.

Once in a while something needed fixing; that was always welcome. Bee would bring him some household object and he would click his tongue happily and ask her, "What did you *do* to this?"

"I just broke it, Doug, all right?" she would say. "I deliberately went and broke it. I sat up late last night plotting how to break it."

And he would shake his head, feeling gratified and important.

Such occasions didn't arise every day, though, or even every week. Not nearly enough to keep him fully occupied.

It had been assumed all along that he would help out more with the grandkids, once he'd retired. Lord knows help was needed. Daphne was in first grade now but still a holy terror. Even the older two—ten and thirteen—took quite a lot of seeing to. And Bee's arthritis had all but crippled her and Ian was running himself ragged. They talked about getting a woman in a couple of days a week, but what with the cost of things . . . well, money was a bit tight for that. So Doug tried to lend a hand, but he turned out to be kind of a dunderhead. For instance, he saw the kids had tracked mud across the kitchen floor and so he fetched the mop and bucket with the very best of intentions, but next thing he knew Bee was saying, "Doug, I swan, not to sweep first and swabbing all that dirty water around . . ." and Ian said, "Here, Dad, I'll take over." Doug yielded the mop, feeling both miffed and relieved, and put on his jacket and whistled up the dog for a walk.

He and Beastie took long, long walks these days. Not long in distance but in time; Beastie was so old now she could barely creep. Probably she'd have preferred to stay home, but Doug would have felt foolish strolling the streets with no purpose. This gave him something to hang onto—her ancient, cracked leather leash, which sagged between them as she inched down the sidewalk. He could remember when she was a puppy and the leash grew taut as a clothesline every time a squirrel passed.

For no good reason, he pictured what it would look like if Bee were the one walking Beastie. The two of them hunched and arthritic, a matched set. It hurt to think of it. He had often seen such couples—aged widows and their decrepit pets. If he died, Bee would *have* to walk Beastie, at least in the daytime when the kids weren't home. But of course, he was not about to die. He had always kept in shape. His hair might be gray now but it was still there, and he could fit into trousers he'd bought thirty years ago.

A while back, though, their family doctor had told him something unsettling. He'd said, "Know what I hate? When a patient comes in and says, 'Doc, I'm here for a checkup. Next month I hit retirement age and I've planned all these great adventures.' Then sure as shooting, I'll find he's got something terminal. It never fails."

Well, Doug had avoided *that* eventuality. He just hadn't gone for a checkup.

And anyhow, planned no great adventures.

The trouble was, he was short on friends. Why had he never noticed before? It seemed he'd had so many back in high school and college.

If Danny had lived, maybe he would have been a friend.

Although Ian was nice company too, of course.

It was just that Ian seemed less . . . oh, less related to him, somehow. Maybe on account of that born-again business. He was so serious and he never just goofed off the way Danny used to do or sat around shooting the breeze with his dad. Didn't even have a girlfriend anymore; that pretty little Cicely had faded clear out of the picture. She had found someone else, Doug supposed. Not that Ian had ever said so. That was the thing: they didn't talk.

Danny used to talk.

Walking Beastie past the foreigners' house one unseasonably mild day in February, Doug noticed someone lying face down on the roof. Good Lord, what now? They lived the strangest lives over there. This fellow was sprawled parallel to the eaves, poking some wire or electrical cord through an upstairs window. Doug paused to watch. Beastie groaned and thudded to the ground. "Need help?" Doug called.

The foreigner raised his head. In that peremptory way that foreigners sometimes have, he said, "Yes, please to enter the house and accept this wire."

"Oh. Okay," Doug said.

He let Beastie's leash drop. She wasn't going anywhere.

He had been in the foreigners' house several times, because they gave a neighborhood party every Fourth of July. ("Happy your Independence Day," one of them had once said. "Happy *yours*," he'd answered before he thought.) He knew that the window in question belonged to the second-floor bathroom, and so he crossed the hall, which was totally bare of furniture, and climbed the stairs and entered the bathroom. The foreigner's face hung upside down outside the window, his thick black hair standing straight off his head so that he looked astonished. "Here!" he called.

Darned if he hadn't broken a corner out of a pane. Not a neatly drilled hole in the wood but a jagged triangle in the glass itself. A wire poked through—antenna wire, it looked like. Doug pulled on it carefully so as not to abrade it. He reeled it in foot by foot. "Okay," the foreigner said, and his face disappeared.

Doug hadn't thought to wonder how the man had got up on the roof in the first place. All at once he was down again, brushing off his clothes in the bathroom doorway—a good-looking, stocky young fellow in a white shirt and blue jeans. You could always tell foreigners by the way they wore their jeans, so neat and proper with the waist at the actual waistline, and in this man's case even a crease ironed in. Jim, was that his name? No, Jim was from an earlier batch. (The foreigners came and went in rotation, with their M.D.'s or their Ph.D.'s or their engineering degrees.) "Frank?" Doug tried.

"Fred."

They were always so considerate about dropping whatever unpronounceable names they'd been christened with. Or not christened, maybe, but—

"Please to tie the wire about the radiator's paw," Fred told him.

"What is it, anyhow?"

"It is aerial for my shortwave radio."

"Ah."

"I attached it to TV antenna on chimney."

"Is that safe?" Doug asked him.

"Maybe; maybe not," Fred said cheerfully.

Doug wouldn't have worried, except these people seemed prone to disasters. Last summer, while hooking up an intercom, they had set their attic on fire. Doug wasn't sure how an intercom could start a fire exactly. All he knew was, smoke had begun billowing from the little eyebrow window on the roof and then six or seven foreigners had sauntered out of the house and stood in the yard gazing upward, looking interested. Finally Mrs. Jordan had called the fire department. What on earth use would they have for an intercom anyway? she had asked Bee later. But that was how they were, the foreigners: they just loved gadgets.

Fred was walking backward now, playing out the wire as he headed across the hall. From the looks of things, he planned to let it lie in the middle of the floor where it would ambush every passerby. "You got any staples?" Doug asked, following.

"Excuse me?"

"Staples? U-shaped nails? Electrical staples, insulated," Doug went on, without a hope in this world. "You tack the wire to the baseboard so it doesn't trip folks up."

"Maybe later," Fred said vaguely.

Meanwhile leading the wire directly across the hall and allowing not one inch of slack.

In Fred's bedroom, gold brocade draped an army cot. A bookcase displayed folded T-shirts, boxer shorts, and rolled socks stacked in a pyramid like cannonballs. Doug managed to take all this in because there was nothing else to look at—not a desk or chair or bureau, not a mirror or family photo. A brown plastic radio sat on the windowsill, and Fred inserted the wire into a hole in its side.

"Looks to me like you might've brought the wire in *this* window," Doug told him.

But Fred shrugged and said, "More far to fall."

"Oh," Doug said.

Presumably, Fred was not one of the engineering students.

Fred turned on the radio and music started playing, some Middle Eastern tune without an end or a beginning. He half closed his eyes and nodded his head to the beat.

"Well, I'd better be going," Doug said.

"You know what means these words?" Fred asked. "A young man is telling farewell to his sweetheart, he is saying to her now—"

"Gosh, Beastie must be wondering where I've got to," Doug said. "I'll just see myself out, never mind."

He had thought it would be a relief to escape the music, but after he left—after he returned home, even, and unsnapped Beastie's leash—the tune continued to wind through his head, blurred and wandery and mysteriously exciting.

A couple of days later, the foreigners tried wiring the radio to speakers set strategically around the house. The reason Doug found out about it was, Fred came over to ask what those U-shaped nails were called again. "Staples," Doug told him, standing at the door in his slippers.

"No, no. Staples are for paper," Fred said firmly.

"But the nails are called staples too. See, what you want is . . ." Doug said, and then he said, "Wait here. I think I may have some down in the basement."

So one thing led to another. He found the staples, he went over to help, he stayed for a beer afterward, and before long he was more or less hanging out there. They always had some harebrained project going, something he could assist with or (more often) advise them not to attempt; and because they were students, keeping students' irregular hours, he could generally count on finding at least a couple of them at home. Five were currently living there: Fred, Ray, John, John Two, and Ollie. On weekends more arrived—fellow countrymen studying elsewhere—and some of the original five disappeared. Doug left them alone on weekends. He preferred late weekday afternoons, when the smells of spice and burnt onions had already started rising from Ollie's blackened saucepans in the kitchen and the others lolled in the living room with their beers. The living room was furnished with two webbed aluminum beach lounges, a wrought-iron lawn chair, and a box spring propped on four stacks of faded textbooks. Over the fireplace hung a wrinkled paper poster of a belly dancer drinking a Pepsi. A collapsible metal TV tray held the telephone, and the wall above it was scribbled all over with names and numbers and Middle Eastern curlicues. Doug liked that idea—that a wall could serve as a phone directory. It struck him as very practical. He would squint at the writing until it turned lacy and decorative, and then he'd take another sip of beer.

These people weren't much in the way of drinkers. They appeared to view alcohol as yet another inscrutable American convention, and they would dangle their own beers politely, forgetting them for long minutes; so Doug never had more than one. Then he'd say, "Well, back to the fray," and they would rise to see him off, thanking him once again for whatever he'd done.

At home, by comparison, everything seemed so permanent—the rooms layered over with rugs and upholstered furniture and framed pictures. The grandchildren added layers of their own; the hall was awash in cast-off jackets and schoolbooks. Bee would be in the kitchen starting supper. (How unadorned the Bedloes' suppers smelled! Plain meat, boiled vegetables, baked potatoes.) And if Ian was back from work he'd be occupied with the kids—sorting out whose night it was to set the table, arbitrating their disputes or even taking part in them as if he were a kid himself. Listen to him with Daphne, for instance. She was nagging him to find her green sweater; tomorrow was St. Patrick's Day. "Your green sweater's in the wash," he said, and that should have been the end of it—would have been, if Bee had been in charge. But Daphne pressed on, wheedling. "Please? Please, Ian? They'll make fun of me if I don't wear something green."

"Tell them your eyes are the something green."

"My what? My eyes? But they're blue."

"Well, if anybody points that out, put on this injured look and say, 'Oh. I've always liked to *think* of them as green.' "

"Oh, Ian," Daphne said. "You're such a silly."

He was, Doug reflected. And a sucker besides. For sure enough, later that night he heard the washing machine start churning.

Most days Ian took the car, but Tuesdays he caught the bus to work so Doug could drive Bee to the doctor. She had to go every single week. Doug knew that doctor's waiting room so well by now that he could see it in his dreams. A leggy, wan philodendron plant hung over the vinyl couch. A table was piled with magazines you would have to be desperate to read—densely printed journals devoted to infinitesimal research findings.

Two other doctors shared the office: a dermatologist and an ophthalmologist. One morning Doug saw the ophthalmologist talking with a very attractive young woman at the receptionist's desk. The receptionist must have proposed some time or date, because the young woman shook her head and said, "I'm sorry, I can't make it then."

"Can't make it?" the doctor asked. "This is surgery, not a hair appointment. We're talking about your eyesight!"

"I'm busy that day," the young woman said.

"Miss Wilson, maybe you don't understand. This is the kind of problem you take care of *now*, you take care of *yesterday*. Not next week or next month. I can't state that too strongly."

"Yes, but I happen to be occupied that day," the young woman said.

Then Bee came out of Dr. Plumm's office, and Doug didn't get to hear the end of the conversation. He kept thinking about it, though. What could make a person defer such crucial surgery? She was meeting a lover? But she could always meet him another day. She'd be fired from her job? But no employer was *that* hard-hearted. Nothing Doug came up with was sufficient explanation.

Imagine being so offhand about your eyesight. About your life, was what it amounted to. As if you wouldn't have to endure the consequences forever and ever after.

Wednesday their daughter dropped by to help with the heavier cleaning. She breezed in around lunchtime with a casserole for supper and a pair of stretchy gloves she'd heard would magically ease arthritic fingers. "Ordinary department-store gloves, I saw this last night on the evening news," she told Bee. "You're lucky I got them when I did; I went to Hochschild's. Don't you know there'll be a big rush for them."

"Yes, dear, that was very nice of you," Bee said dutifully. She already owned gloves, medically prescribed, much more official than these were. Still, she put these on and spread her hands out as flat as possible, testing. She was wearing one of Ian's sweatshirts and baggy slacks and slipper-socks. In the gloves, which were the dainty, white, lady's-tea kind, she looked a little bit crazy.

Claudia filled a bucket in the kitchen sink and added a shot of ammonia. "Going to tackle that chandelier," she told them. "I noticed it last week. A *disgrace!*"

Probably it was Ian's housekeeping she was so indignant with—or just time itself, time that had coated each prism with dust. She wasn't thinking how it sounded to waltz into a person's home and announce that it was filthy. Doug cast a sideways glance at Bee to see how she was taking it. Her eyes were teary, but that could have been the ammonia. He waited till Claudia had left the kitchen, sloshing her bucket into the dining room, and then he laid a hand on top of Bee's. "Peculiar, isn't it?" he said. "First you're scolding your children and then all at once they're so smart they're scolding *you.*"

Bee smiled, and he saw that they weren't real tears after all. "I suppose," he went on more lightly, "there was some stage when we were equals. I mean while she was on the rise and we were on the downslide. A stage when we were level with each other."

"Well, I must have been on the phone at the time," Bee said, and then she laughed.

Her hand in the glove felt dead to him, like his own hand after he'd slept on it wrong and cut off the circulation.

The foreigners set their car on fire, trying to install a radio. "*I* didn't know radios were flammable," Mrs. Jordan said, watching from the Bedloes' front porch. Doug was a bit surprised himself, but then electronics had never been his strong point. He went over to see if he could help. The car was a Dodge from the late fifties or maybe early sixties, whenever it was that giant fins were all the rage. Once the body had been powder blue but now it was mostly a deep, matte red from rust, and one door was white and one fender turquoise. Whom it belonged to was unclear, since the foreigner who had bought it, second- or third-hand, had long since gone back to his homeland.

John Two and Fred and Ollie were standing around the car in graceful poses, languidly fanning their faces. The smoke appeared to be coming from the dashboard. Doug said, "Fellows? Think we should call the fire department?" but Fred said, "Oh, we dislike to keep disturbing them."

Hoping nothing would explode, Doug reached through the open window on the driver's side and pulled the first wire his fingers touched. Almost immediately the smoke thinned. There was a strong smell of burning rubber, but no real damage—at least none that he could see. It was hard to tell; the front seat was worn to bare springs and the backseat had been removed altogether.

"Maybe we just won't have radio," John Two told Ollie.

"We never had radio before," Fred said.

"We were very contented," John Two said, "and while we traveled we could hear the birds sing."

Doug pictured them traveling through a flat green countryside like the landscape in a child's primer. They would be the kind who set off without filling the gas tank first or checking the tire pressure, he was certain. Chances were they wouldn't even have a road map.

One morning when he came downstairs he found Beastie dead on the kitchen floor, her body not yet stiff. It was a shock, although he should have been prepared for it. She was sixteen years old. He could still remember what she'd looked like when they brought her home—small enough to fit in her own feed dish. That first winter it had snowed and snowed, and she had humped her fat little body ecstatically through the drifts like a Slinky toy, with a dollop of snow icing her nose and snowflakes on her lashes.

He went upstairs to wake Ian. He wanted to get her buried before the children saw her. "Ian," he said. "Son."

Ian's room still looked so boyish. Model airplanes sat on the shelves among autographed baseballs and high-school yearbooks. The bedspread was printed with antique cars. It could have been one of those rooms that's maintained as a shrine after a young person dies.

Danny's room, on the other hand, had been redecorated for Thomas. Not a trace of Danny remained.

"Son?"

"Hmm."

"I need you to help me bury Beastie."

Ian opened his eyes. "Beastie?"

"I found her this morning in the kitchen."

Ian considered a moment and then sat up. When Doug was sure he was awake, he left the room and went downstairs for his jacket.

Beastie had not been a large dog, but she weighed a lot. Doug heaved her onto the doormat and then dragged the mat outside and down the back steps. Thump, thump, thump—it made him wince. The mat left a trail in the sparkling grass. He backed up to the azalea and dropped the corners of the mat and straightened. It was six thirty or so—too early for the neighbors to be about yet. The light was nearly colorless, the traffic noises sparse and distant.

Ian came out with his windbreaker collar turned up. He had both shovels with him. "Good thing the ground's not frozen," Doug told him.

"Right."

"This is probably not even legal, anyhow."

They chipped beneath the sod, trying as best they could not to break it apart, and laid it to one side. A breeze was ruffling Beastie's fur and Doug kept imagining that she could feel it, that she was aware of what they were doing. He made his mind a blank. He set up an alternating rhythm with Ian, hacking through the reddish earth and occasionally ringing against a pebble or a root. In spite of the breeze he started sweating and he stopped to take off his jacket, but Ian kept his on. Ian didn't look hot at all; he looked chilly and pale, with that fine white line around his lips that meant he had his jaw set. For the first time, Doug thought to wonder how this was hitting him. "Guess you'll miss her," he said.

"Yes," Ian said, still digging.

"Beastie's been around since you were . . . what? Eight or so, or not even that."

Ian nodded and bent to toss a rock out of the way.

"We'll let the kids set some kind of marker up," Doug told him. "Plant bulbs or something. Make it pretty."

It was all he could think of to offer.

They ended up cheating a bit on the grave—dug more of an oval than a rectangle, so they had to maneuver to get her into it. She fit best on her side, slightly curled. When Doug saw her velvety snout against the clay, tears came to his eyes. She had always been such an undemanding dog, so accommodating, so adaptable. "Ah, God," he said, and then he looked up and realized Ian was praying. His head was bowed and his lips were moving. Doug hastily bowed his own head. He felt as if Ian were the grownup and he the child. It had been years, maybe all the years of his adulthood, since he had relied so thankfully on someone else's knowledge of what to do.

The two younger children came down with chicken pox—first Daphne and then Thomas. Everybody waited for Agatha to get it too but she must have had it earlier, before they knew her. Daphne was hardly sick at all, but Thomas had a much worse case and one night he woke up delirious. Doug heard his hoarse, startled voice, oddly bright in the darkness— "Don't let them come! Don't let their sharp hooves!"—and then Ian's steady "Thomas, old man. Thomas. Tom-Tom."

In that short-story course, Doug had read a story about an experiment conducted by creatures from outer space. What the creatures wanted to know was, could earthlings form emotional attachments? Or were they merely at the mercy of biology? So they cut a house in half in the middle of the night, and they switched it with another half house in some totally different location. Tossed the two households together like so many game pieces. This woman woke up with a man and some children she'd never laid eyes on before. Naturally she was terribly puzzled and upset, and the others were too, but as it happened the children had some kind of illness, measles or something (maybe even chicken pox, come to think of it), and so of course she did everything she could to make them comfortable. The creatures' conclusion, therefore, was that earthlings didn't discriminate. Their family feelings, so called, were a matter of blind circumstance.

Doug couldn't remember now how the story had ended. Maybe that *was* the end. He couldn't quite recollect.

In the dark, Bee's special white arthritis gloves glowed eerily. She lay on her side, facing him, with the gloves curled beneath her chin. The slightest sound used to wake her when their own three children were little—a cough or even a whimper. Now she slept through everything, and Doug was glad. It was a pity so much rested on Ian, but Ian was young. He had the energy. He hadn't reached the point yet where it just plain didn't seem worth the effort.

Ian invited his parents to a Christian Fellowship Picnic. "To a what?" Doug asked, stalling for time. (Who cared what it was called? It was bound to be something embarrassing.)

"Each of us invites people we'd like to join in fellowship with," Ian said in that deadly earnest way he had. "People who aren't members of our congregation."

"I thought that church of yours didn't believe in twisting folkses' arms."

"It doesn't. We don't. This is only for fellowship."

They were watching the evening news—Doug, Bee, and Ian. Now Bee looked away from a skyful of bomber airplanes to say, "I've never understood what people mean by 'fellowship.'"

"Just getting together, Mom. Nothing very mysterious."

"Then why even say it? Why not say 'getting together'?"

Ian didn't take offense. He said, "Reverend Emmett wants us to ask, oh, people we care about and people who wonder what we believe and people who might feel hostile to us."

"We're not hostile!"

"Then maybe you would qualify for one of the other groups," Ian said mildly.

Bee looked at Doug. Doug pulled himself together (he had a sense of struggling toward the surface) and said, "Isn't it sort of early for a picnic? We're still getting frost at night!"

"This is an indoor picnic," Ian told him.

"Then what's the point?"

"Reverend Emmett's mother, Sister Priscilla, has relatives out in the valley who own a horse farm. They're in Jamaica for two weeks and they told her she could stay in the house."

"Did they say she could throw a church picnic in the house?"

"We won't do any harm."

Bee was still looking at Doug. (She wanted him to say no, of course.) The bombers had given way to a moisturizer commercial.

"Well, it's nice of you to think of us, son," Doug said, "but—"

"I've invited Mrs. Jordan, too."

"Mrs. Jordan?"

"Right."

"*Jessie* Jordan?"

"She's always wanting to know what Second Chance is all about."

This put a whole different light on things. How could they refuse when a mere neighbor had accepted? Drat Jessie Jordan, with her lone-woman eagerness to go anywhere she was asked!

And then she had the nerve to make out she was being so daring, so rakish. On the way to Greenspring Valley (for they did end up attending, taking their own car which was easier on Bee's hips than the bus), Mrs. Jordan bounced and burbled like a six-year-old. "Isn't this exciting?" she said. She was dressed as if headed for a Buckingham Palace garden party—cartwheel hat ringed with flowers, swishy silk dress beneath her drab winter coat. "You know, there are so many alternative religions springing up these days," she said. "I worry I'll fall hopelessly behind."

"And wouldn't *that* be a shame," Bee said sourly. She wore an ordinary gray sweat suit, not her snazzy warm-up suit with the complicated zippers; so her hands must be giving her trouble today. Doug himself was dressed as if for golfing, carefully color-coordinated to compensate for what might be misread as sloppiness on Bee's part. He kept the car close behind Second Chance's rented bus. Sometimes Daphne's little thumbtack of a face bobbed up in the bus's rear window, smiling hugely and mouthing elaborate messages no one could catch. "*What* did she say? What?" Bee asked irritably.

"Can't quite make it out, hon."

They traveled deeper and deeper into country that would be luxurious in the summer but was now a vast network of bare branches lightly tinged with green. Pasturelands extended for miles. The driveway they finally turned into was too long to see to the end, and the white stone house was larger than some hotels. "Oh! Would you look!" Mrs. Jordan cried, clapping her hands.

Doug didn't like to admit it, but he felt easier about Second Chance now that he saw such a substantial piece of property connected to it. He wondered if the relatives were members themselves. Probably not, though.

They parked on the paved circle in front. Passengers poured from the bus—first the children, then the grownups. Doug fancied he could tell the members from the visitors. The members had a dowdy, worn, slumping look; the visitors were dressier and full of determined gaiety.

It occurred to him that Bee could be mistaken for a member.

Carrying baskets, coolers, and Thermos jugs, everyone followed Reverend Emmett's mother up the flagstone walk. They entered the front hall with its slate floor and center staircase, and several people said, "Ooh!"

"Quite a joint," Doug murmured to Bee.

Bee hushed him with a look.

They crossed velvety rugs and gleaming parquet and finally arrived in an enormous sun porch with a long table at its center and modern, high-gloss chairs and lounges set all about. "The conservatory," Reverend Emmett's mother said grandly. She was a small, finicky woman in a matched sweater set and a string of pearls and a pair of chunky jeans that seemed incongruous, downright wrong, as if she'd forgotten to change into the bottom half of her outfit. "Let's spread our picnic," she said. "Emmett, did you bring the tablecloth?"

"I thought you were bringing that."

"Well, never mind. Just put my potato salad here at this end."

Reverend Emmett wore a sporty polo shirt, a tan windbreaker, and black dress trousers. (He and his mother belonged in Daphne's block set, the one where you mismatch heads and legs and torsos.) He put a covered bowl where she directed, and then the others laid out platters of fried chicken, tubs of coleslaw, and loaves of home-baked bread. The table— varnished so heavily that it seemed wet—gradually disappeared. Streaky squares of sunlight from at least a dozen windows warmed the room, and people started shedding their coats and jackets. "Dear Lord in heaven," Reverend Emmett said (catching Doug with one arm half out of a sleeve), "the meal is a bountiful gift from Your hands and the company is more so. We thank You for this joyous celebration. Amen."

It was true there was something joyous in the atmosphere. Everyone converged upon the food, clucking and exclaiming. The children turned wild. Even Agatha, ponderously casual in a ski sweater and stirrup pants, pushed a boy back with shy enthusiasm when he gave her a playful nudge at the punch bowl. The members steered the guests magnanimously toward the choice dishes; they took on a proprietary air as they pointed out particular features of the house. "Notice the leaded panes," they said, as if they themselves were intimately familiar with them. The guests (most as suspicious as Doug and Bee, no doubt) showed signs of thawing. "Why, this is not bad," one silver-haired man said—the father, Doug guessed, of the hippie-type girl at his elbow. Doug had hold of too much dinner now to shake hands, but he nodded at the man and said, "How do. Doug Bedloe."

"Mac McClintock," the man said. "You just visiting?"

"Right."

"His son is Brother Ian," the hippie told her father. "I just think Brother Ian is so faithful," she said to Doug.

"Well . . . thanks."

"My daughter Gracie," Mac said. "Have you met?"

"No, I don't believe we have."

"We've met!" Gracie said. "I'm the one who fetched your grandchildren from school every day when your wife was in the hospital."

"Oh, yes," Doug said. He didn't have the faintest memory of it.

"I fetched the children for Brother Ian and then Brother Ian closed up the rat holes in my apartment."

"Really," Doug said.

"My daughter lives in a slum," Mac told him.

"Now, Daddy."

"She makes less money than I made during the Depression and then she gives it all to this Church of the Second Rate."

"Second Chance! And I do not; I tithe. I don't have to do even that, if I don't want to. It's all in secret; we don't believe in public collection. You act like they're defrauding me or something."

"They're a church, aren't they? A church'll take its people for whatever it can get," Mac said. He glanced at Doug. "Hope that doesn't offend you."

"Me? No, no."

"Want to hear what I hate most about churches? They think they know the answers. I really hate that. It's the people who *don't* know the answers who are going to heaven, I tell you."

"But!" his daughter said. "The minute you say that, you see, you yourself become a person who knows the answers."

Mac gave Doug an exasperated look and chomped into a drumstick.

Bee was sitting on a chaise longue with her legs stretched out, sharing a plate with Daphne. She was the only guest who seemed to have remained outside the gathering. Everyone else was laughing, growing looser, circulating from group to group in a giddy, almost tipsy way. (Although of course there wasn't a bit of alcohol; just that insipid fruit punch.) Reverend Emmett was holding forth on his inspiration for this picnic. "I felt led," he told a circle of women. He had the breathless look of an athlete being interviewed after a triumph. "I was listening to one of our brothers a couple of weeks ago; he said he wished he could share his salvation with his parents except they never would agree to come to services. And all at once I felt led to say, 'Why should it be services? Why not a picnic?' "

The women smiled and nodded and their glasses flashed. (One of them was Jessie Jordan, looking thrilled.) An extremely fat young woman threaded her way through the crowd with a plastic garbage bag, saying, "Plates? Cups? Keep your forks, though. Dessert is on its way."

What could they serve for dessert if they didn't believe in sugar? Fruit salad, it turned out, in little foil dishes. Thomas carried one of the trays around. When he came to Doug he said, "Grandpa? Are you having a good time?"

"Oh, yes."

"Are you making any friends?"

"Certainly," Doug said, and he felt a sudden wrench for the boy's thin, anxious face with its dots of old chicken-pox scars. He took a step closer to Mac McClintock, although they'd run out of small talk some minutes ago.

The women were clearing the table now, debating leftovers.

"It seems a shame to throw all this out."

"Won't you take it home?"

"No, you."

"Law, I couldn't eat it in a month of Sundays."

"We wouldn't want to waste it, though."

Reverend Emmett's mother said, "Mr. Bedloe, we all think so highly of Brother Ian."

"Thank you," Doug said. This was starting to remind him of Parents' Night at elementary school. He swallowed a chunk of canned pineapple, which surely contained sugar, didn't it? "And you must be very proud of *your* son," he added.

"Yes, I am," she said. "I look around me and I see so many people, so many redeemed people, and I think, 'If not for Emmett, what would they be doing?' "

What *would* they be doing? Most would be fine, Doug supposed—his own son among them. Lord, yes. But in all fairness, he supposed this church met a real need for some others. And so he looked around too, following Sister What's-Her-Name's eyes. What he saw, though, was not what he had expected. Instead of the festive throng he had been watching a few minutes ago, he saw a spreading circle of stillness that radiated from the table and extended now even to the children, so that a cluster of little girls in one corner allowed their jack ball to die and the boys gave up their violent ride in the glider. Even Bee seemed galvanized, an orange section poised halfway to her parted lips.

"It's the table," a woman told Reverend Emmett's mother.

"The—?"

"Something's damaged the surface."

Reverend Emmett's mother thrust her way through the circle of women, actually shoving one aside. Doug craned to see what they were talking about. The table was bare now and even shinier than before; someone had wiped it with a damp cloth. It looked perfect, at first glance, but then when he tilted his head to let the light slant differently he saw that the shine was marred at one end by several distinct, unshiny rings.

"Oh, *no*," Reverend Emmett's mother breathed.

Everyone started speaking at once: "Try mayonnaise."

"Try toothpaste."

"Rub it down with butter."

"Quiet! Please!" Reverend Emmett's mother said. She closed her eyes and pressed both hands to her temples.

Reverend Emmett stood near Doug, peering over the others' heads. (Above the collar of his jaunty polo shirt, his neck looked scrawny and pathetic.) "Perhaps," he said, "if we attempted to—"

"Shut up and let me *think*, Emmett!"

Silence.

"Maybe if I came back tomorrow," she said finally, "with that cunning little man from Marx Antiques, the one who restores old . . . he could strip it and refinish it. Don't you suppose? But the owners are due home Tuesday, and if he has to strip the whole . . . but never mind! I'll tell him to work round the clock! Or I'll ask if . . ."

More silence.

Ian said, "Was it soaped?"

Everyone turned and looked for him. It took a minute to find him; he was standing at the far end of the room.

"Seems to me the finish is some kind of polyurethane," he said, "and if those rings are grease, well, a little soap wouldn't do any harm and it might even—"

"Soap! Yes!" Reverend Emmett's mother said.

She went herself to the kitchen. While she was gone, the fat young woman told Doug, "Brother Ian works with wood every day, you know."

"Yes, I'm his father," Doug said.

She said, "Are you really!"

Reverend Emmett's mother came back. She held a sponge and a bottle of liquid detergent. They parted to let her through and she approached the table and bent over it. Doug was too far away to see what she did next, but he heard the sighs of relief. "Now dry it off," someone suggested.

A woman whipped a paisley scarf from her neck and offered that, and it was accepted.

"Perfect," someone said.

This time when he craned, Doug saw that the rings had vanished.

Right away the congregation started packing, collecting coats and baskets. Maybe they would have anyhow, but Doug thought he detected a sort of letdown in the general mood. People filed out meekly, not glancing back at the house as they left it. (Doug imagined the house thinking, *Goodness, what was all THAT about?*) They crossed the columned front porch with their heads lowered. Doug helped Bee into the car. "Coming?" he asked Mrs. Jordan.

"Oh, I'm going to ride in the bus," she said. She alone seemed undampened. "Wasn't Ian the hero, though!"

"Sure thing," Doug said.

He watched her set off toward the bus with one hand clamping down her cartwheel hat.

Driving home, he made no attempt to stay with the others. He left the bus behind on the Beltway and breezed eastward at a speed well above the legal limit. "So now we've been to a Christian Fellowship Picnic," he told Bee.

"Yes," she said.

"I wonder if it'll become a yearly event."

"Probably," she said.

Then she started talking about Danny. How did she get from the picnic to Danny? No telling. She started kneading the knuckles of her right hand, the hand that looked more swollen, and she said, "Sometimes I have the strangest feeling. I give this start and I think, 'Why!' I think, 'Why, here we are! Just going about our business the same as usual!' And yet so much has changed. Danny is gone, our golden boy, our first baby boy that we were so proud of, and our house is stuffed with someone else's children. You know they *all* are someone else's. You know that! And Ian is a whole different person and Claudia's so bustling now and our lives have turned so makeshift and second-class, so second-string, so second-fiddle, and everything's been lost. Isn't it amazing that we keep on going? That we keep on shopping for clothes and getting hungry and laughing at jokes on TV? When our oldest son is dead and gone and we'll never see him again and our life's in ruins!"

"Now, sweetie," he said.

"We've had such extraordinary troubles," she said, "and somehow they've turned us ordinary. That's what's so hard to figure. We're not a special family anymore."

"Why, sweetie, of course we're special," he said.

"We've turned uncertain. We've turned into worriers."

"Bee, sweetie."

"Isn't it amazing?"

It was astounding, if he thought about it. But he was careful not to.

The weather began to grow warmer, and Doug raised all the windows and lugged the summer clothing down from the attic for Bee. Across the street, the foreigners came out in their shirtsleeves to install an electric garage-door opener they'd ordered from a catalog. Doug found this amusing. A door that opened on its own, for a car that could barely *move* on its own! Of course he kept them company while they worked, but the door in question was solid wood and very heavy, potentially lethal, and he'd just as soon not be standing under it when calamity struck. He stayed several feet away, watching Ollie teeter on a kitchen chair as he screwed something to a rafter overhead. Then when Doug got bored he ambled inside with the two who were less mechanically inclined, leaving Ollie and Fred and John Two to carry on. He refused a beer (it was ten in the morning) but accepted a seat by the window, where a light breeze stirred the tattered paper shade.

From here the garage was invisible, since it lay even with the front of the house, but he could see Fred standing in the drive with the pushbutton control in both hands, pressing hard and then harder. Doug grinned. Fred leaned forward, his face a mask of straining muscle, and he bore down on the button with all his might. You didn't have to set eyes on the door to know it wasn't reacting. Meanwhile Ollie walked out to the street and climbed into the car and started the engine, and John Two removed a brick from under the left rear wheel. Optimistic of them; Doug foresaw a good deal more work before the garage would be ready for an occupant. Through the open window he heard the croupy putt-putt as the car turned in and rolled up the drive and sat idling. "In another catalog," John One was saying, "we have seen remarkable invention: automatic yard lights! That illuminate when dark falls! We plan to send away for them immediately."

"I can hardly wait," Doug said, and then he twisted in his chair because he thought he noticed someone emerging from his own house, but it was only shrubbery stirring in the breeze.

He was a touch nearsighted, and the mesh of the window screen seemed more distinct to him than what lay beyond it. What lay beyond it—home— had the blocky, blurred appearance of something worked in needlepoint, each tiny square in the screen filled with a square of color. Not only was there a needlepoint house but also a needlepoint car out front, a needlepoint swing on the porch, a needlepoint bicycle in the yard. His entire little world: a cozy, old-fashioned sampler stitched in place forever.

The best thing about the foreigners, he decided, was how they thought living in America was a story they were reading, or a movie they were watching. It was happening to someone else; it wasn't theirs. Good Lord, not even their names were theirs. Here they spoke lines invented by other people, not genuine language—not the language that simply *is*, with no need for translation. Here they wore blue denim costumes and inhabited a Hollywood set complete with make-believe furniture. But when they went back home, there they'd behave as seriously as anyone. They would fall in love and marry and have children and they'd agonize over their children's problems, and struggle to get ahead, and practice their professions soberly and efficiently. What Doug was witnessing was only a brief holiday from their real lives.

He was pleased by this notion. He thought he'd examine it further later on—consider, say, what happened to those foreigners who ended up *not* going home. The holiday couldn't last forever, could it? Was there a certain moment when the movie set turned solid? But for now, he didn't bother himself with all that. He was happy just to sit here, letting some of their Time Out rub off on him.

Then Ollie turned toward the house and called, "Come see!" and for courtesy's sake, Doug rose and followed Ray and John One to the yard. Other neighbors were here too, he realized. It looked like a party. He joined them and stood squinting in the sunshine, smiling at the foreigners' car which sat half inside the garage and half out like a crumpled beer can, with the door bisecting it neatly across the middle.

6

Sample Rains

Every Saturday morning, the Church of the Second Chance gathered to perform good works. Sometimes they went to an ailing member's place and helped with the cleaning or the fixing up. Sometimes they went to some stranger. Today—a warm, sunny day in early September—they met at the little house where Reverend Emmett lived with his widowed mother. Reverend Emmett was not a salaried minister. His sole means of support was a part-time counseling job at a private girls' school. So when his house needed painting (as it sorely did now, with the old paint hanging in ribbons off the clapboards), all his flock pitched in to take care of it.

Ian brought the three children, dressed in their oldest clothes. Thomas and Daphne loved Good Works but Agatha had to be talked into coming. At fifteen she was balky and resentful, given to fits of moody despair. Ian never could decide: should he force her to participate for her own good? Or would that just alienate her further? This morning, though, he'd had an easier time than usual. He suspected her of harboring a certain furtive interest in the details of Reverend Emmett's private life.

The house was a one-story cottage, more gray than white, lying in a modest neighborhood east of York Road. By the time Ian and the children arrived, several members of the congregation were already setting out paint cans and brushes. Mrs. Jordan (Sister Jessie now, but Ian found it hard to switch) was spreading a dropcloth over the boxwoods, and Reverend Emmett was perched on a ladder wire-brushing the porch overhang. Ian grabbed a ladder of his own and went to take the shutters down. Reverend Emmett's mother came out in high heels and an aqua knit dress and asked if there was any little thing she could do, but they all said no. (What *could* they say? Her cardigan draped her shoulders so genteelly, with the sleeves turned back a precise two inches.)

Partway through the job, someone Ian didn't know was sent to assist him. This was a cadaverously thin man in his thirties with a narrow ribbon of beard like Abraham Lincoln's. Ian glanced at him curiously (their

591 / Saint Maybe

church didn't see many guests), and the man said, "I'm Eli Everjohn. Bertha King's son-in-law; we're visiting from over Caro Mill."

"Ian Bedloe," Ian said.

He could see now who the man's wife must be—the strawberry blonde who did resemble Sister Bertha, come to think of it, scraping clapboards with the children. She seemed much too pretty for such a knobby, gangling husband. This Eli handled tools at a remove. He handled his own *hands* at a remove, as if operating one of those claw arrangements where you try to scoop up prizes. His task was to take the hinges off the shutters and stow them in a bucket, which should have been easy enough; but the screwdriver seemed to confound him and he let it slip so many times that the screw heads were getting mangled. "Tell you what," Ian said, setting down a shutter. "I'll see to this and you can have my job."

"Oh, I couldn't do that!" the man said. "I'm scared of heights."

Heights? The highest shutter was eight feet off the ground. But Ian didn't point that out.

Eli raised one arm to wipe his forehead, waving the screwdriver dangerously close to Ian's face. "At *my* church, we don't mess with such as this," he said. "We visit door to door instead."

"What church is that?"

"Holy House of the Gospel."

"I guess I never heard of it."

"We're much stricter than you-all are," Eli said. "We would never for instance let our women wear the raiment of men."

Ian glanced at Eli's wife. Sure enough, she wore a dress—a rosebudded, country-looking dress that was interfering seriously with her attempts to mount a step stool.

"We don't play cards neither, nor dance, and we're more mindful of the appearance of evil," Eli said. "Why, yesterday my mother-in-law got a prescription filled at a pharmacy that sells liquor! Walked right into a place that sells liquor without a thought for how it might look! And you don't have no missionary outreach, neither."

Ian was starting to feel defensive. He said, "We believe our *lives* are our missionary outreach."

"Now, that's just selfish," Eli said. "To look at someone living in the shadow of eternal damnation and not try and change his ways: that's selfish."

Ian spun on his heel and went to fetch another shutter.

When he came back, though, Eli resumed where he had left off. "And if we did mess with house painting, we'd have prayed beforehand," he said. His screwdriver slashed uselessly across a screw. "We pray before each task. We believe that whatever work we undertake is God's work; I am an arrow shot by God to do His handiwork."

He did look something like an arrow: straight and smooth, a sharp cowlick sticking up on the crown of his head.

"What exactly *is* your work?" Ian asked him, hoping to change the subject.

"I'm a private detective."

This was so unexpected that Ian laughed. Eli scowled. "What's funny about that?" he said.

"Detective?" Ian said. "You mean, like solving murders and mysteries and such?"

"Well, it's more like tailing husbands to motel rooms. But that's the Lord's business too! Believe me."

"If you say so," Ian told him.

"What do you do, brother?"

"I'm a carpenter," Ian said.

"Our Savior was a carpenter."

"Well, yes."

"Nothing to be ashamed of."

"Who said I was ashamed?"

"Those your kids you came with?"

"Yes."

"You look kind of young to have kids that old."

"Really I'm just their uncle," Ian said. "My parents and I take care of them."

"I would've thought you were nothing but a college boy."

"No, no."

"You married?"

"No."

"A bachelor."

"Well, yes. A . . . bachelor," Ian said.

Eli bent over a hinge again. Ian watched for a minute and then turned back to his ladder.

But the next time he brought down a shutter, he said, "So you've never found a missing person, or anything like that."

"Depends on what you call missing," Eli said. "Sure, I've found a few husbands here and there. Usually they're just staying with a girlfriend, though, that everybody except their wives knows the name and address of."

"I see," Ian said.

He leaned the shutter against a sawhorse. He studied it. Not looking at Eli, he said, "Say a person had been missing a long time. Five or six years, say. Maybe seven or eight. Would the trail be too cold for you to follow?"

"What? Naw," Eli said. "Bound to be *something* he left behind. People are so messy. That's been my experience. People leave so much litter wherever they go to."

He rotated one forearm and examined the inside of his wrist. A dribble of dusty blood ran downward from his palm. "Somebody special you had in mind?" he asked.

"Not really," Ian said.

He brushed a dead leaf from a louver. He cleared his throat. He said, "Those kids I'm taking care of: their father is missing, I guess you could say. The father of the older two."

"Is that so," Eli said. "Ducking his child support, huh?"

"Child support? Oh. Right," Ian said.

"Boy, I hate those child-support guys," Eli said. "Or, no, not hate. Forget hate. The Bible cautions us not to hate. But I . . . pity them, yes, I surely do pity those child-support guys. You'd never get *me* to raise one of them's kids."

"Oh, they're really like my own now," Ian said.

"Even so! Here you are sitting home with three young ones and he's off enjoying his self."

"I don't mind," Ian said.

He didn't want to go into the whole story. In fact, he couldn't remember now why he'd brought it up in the first place.

He was supervising the children's homework at the kitchen table when he heard a wailing sound outdoors. He said, "Was that a baby?"

No one answered. They were too busy arguing. Thomas was telling Daphne that when *he* was in third grade, a plain old wooden pencil had been good enough for him. Daphne had no business, he said, swiping his personal ballpoint pen. Daphne said, "Maybe what *you* wrote in third grade wasn't worth a pen." Then Agatha complained they'd made her lose her train of thought. Thanks to them, she would have to start this whole equation over again.

"Was that a baby crying?" Ian asked.

They barely paused.

"Hey," Thomas said to the others. "Want to hear something disgusting?"

"No, what?"

Ian crossed the kitchen and opened the screen door. It was light enough still so he could make out the clothesline poles and the azalea bushes, and the stockade fence that separated the backyard from the alley.

"In science class, my teacher? Mr. Pratt?" Thomas said. "He stands at the blackboard, he tells us, 'By the time I've finished teaching this lesson, microscopic portions of my mouth will be *all over this room.*' "

"Eeuw!" Daphne and Agatha said.

Just inside the gate, which had not been completely closed in years, sat a minuscule patch of darkness, a denser black than the fence posts. This patch stirred and glinted in some way and uttered another thin wail.

"Kitty-kitty?" Ian called.

He stepped outside, shutting the screen door behind him. Yes, it was definitely a cat. When he approached, it teetered on the brink of leaving but finally stood its ground. He bent to pat its head. He could feel the narrow skull beneath fur so soft that it made almost no impression on his fingertips.

"Where's your owner, little cat?" he asked.

But he thought he knew the answer to that. There wasn't any tag or collar, and when he ran a hand down its body he could count the ribs. It staggered weakly beneath his touch, then braced itself and started purring in a rusty, unpracticed way, pressing its small face into the cup of his palm.

As it happened, the Bedloes had no pets at that particular moment. They had never replaced Beastie, and the latest of their cats had disappeared a few months ago. So this new little cat had come to the right people. Ian let it spend a few minutes getting used to him, and then he picked it up and carried it back inside the house. It clung to him with needle claws, tense but still conscientiously purring. "See what I found in the alley," he told the children.

"Oh, look!" Daphne cried, slipping out of her chair. "Can I hold it, Ian? Can I keep it?"

"If no one comes to claim it," Ian said, handing it over.

In the light he saw that the cat was black from head to foot, and not much more than half grown. Its eyes had changed to green already but its face was still the triangular, top-heavy face of a kitten. Thomas was lifting its spindly tail to see what sex it was, but the cat objected to that and climbed higher on Daphne's shoulder. "Ouch!" Daphne squawked. "Thomas, quit! See what you made it do?"

"It's a girl, I think," Thomas announced.

"Leave her alone, Thomas!"

"She's not just yours, Daphne," Agatha said. She had risen too and was scratching the cat behind its ears.

"She is so mine! Ian said so! You're mine, mine, mine, you little sweetums," Daphne said, nuzzling the cat's nose with her own. "Oh, what kind of monstrous, mean person would just ditch you and drive off?"

All of a sudden Ian had an image of Agatha, Thomas, and Daphne huddled in a ditch by the side of a road. They were hanging onto each other and their eyes were wide and fearful. And far in the distance, almost out of sight, Ian's car was vanishing around a curve.

But then immediately afterward, he felt such a deep sense of loss that it made his breath catch.

His mother was truly disabled now. Oh, she still hobbled from room to room, she still insisted on standing over the stove and creeping behind the dust mop, but the arthritis had seized up her hands and the finer motions of day-to-day life were beyond her. Folding the laundry, driving the car, buttoning Daphne's dress down the back—all that was left to Ian and his father. And Ian's father was not much help. Any task he began seemed to end in, "How the dickens . . .?" and "Ian, can you come here a minute?" In the old days Claudia had stopped by once or twice a week to see what needed doing, but she had moved to Pittsburgh when Macy found a better job; and first they'd returned for holidays but now they didn't even do that very often.

Meanwhile, these children were a full-time occupation. They were good children, bright children; they did well in school and never got in serious trouble. But even nonserious trouble could consume a great deal of energy, Ian had learned. Agatha, for instance, was suffering all the miseries of adolescence. Every morning she set off for school alone and friendless—the earnest, pale, studious kind of girl Ian had ignored when he himself was her age, but now he cursed those callow high-school kids who couldn't see how special she was, how intelligent and witty and perceptive. Thomas, on the other hand, had too *many* friends. Tall and graceful, his voice already cracking and a shadow darkening his upper lip, he was more interested in socializing than in schoolwork, and one or another of the Bedloes was always having to attend parent-teacher conferences—most often Ian, it seemed.

As for Daphne, she wound through life sparkling at everyone and lowering her long black lashes over stunning blue-black eyes; but any time you crossed her there was hell to pay. She was *fierce*, that Daphne. "I think she had a difficult infancy," Ian was always explaining. "She's really a good kid, believe me. She just feels she's got to fend for herself," he told a teacher. Yet another teacher. At yet another parent-teacher conference. (His second of the year, and school had been in session only ten days.)

Cicely was living out in California now with a folk guitarist. Pig Benson's family had moved away while he was in the army. Andrew was in graduate school at Tulane. And anyhow, the last time Andrew came home it turned out he and Ian didn't have much to talk about. At one point Andrew had referred to the "goddamned holiday traffic," and then reddened and said, "Sorry," so Ian knew he'd heard about Second Chance from someone. And then Ian had to take Daphne for her booster shots, and that was that. Andrew had not suggested getting together again.

Bachelor. What a dashing word. Ian the bachelor. He would live in an apartment all his own. (A bachelor pad.) He'd have friends his own age dropping by to visit. Young women going out with him. And no one trailing behind to ask, "But how about *us*? Who will see to us? Who will find our socks for us and help with our history project?"

At work, he was putting the final touches on a drop-front desk. He was rubbing linseed oil into the wood, while Bert, one of the new men, worked on a bureau across the room.

Their kitchen-cabinet days were over, thank heaven. Now rich young couples from Bolton Hill showed up at Mr. Brant's shop to commission one-of-a-kind furniture: bookcases custom-fitted to Bolton Hill's high ceilings, stand-up desks made to measure, and Shaker-looking benches. Everything was built the old way, with splines and rabbets and lap joints, no nails, no stains or plastic finishes. Orders were backed up a year or more and they'd had to hire three new employees.

You'd think this would delight Mr. Brant, but he remained as morose as always. Or was that only his deafness? No, because whenever his wife dropped by—a much younger woman who'd been deaf from birth, unlike Mr. Brant—she would sign to him with flying fingers, her face lighting up and clouding over to go with what she said; and Ian could see she lived a life as full and talkative as any hearing person's. Mr. Brant would watch her without altering his expression, and then he would make a few signs of his own—clumsy, blunt signs, stiff-thumbed. Ian wondered how on earth they had courted. What could Mr. Brant have said that would win such a woman's heart? When Mrs. Brant watched his hands, her eyes grew very intent and focused and all the animation left her. Ian had the feeling her husband was somehow dampening her enthusiasm, but maybe it only seemed that way.

One of the new employees was Mrs. Brant's niece, a rosy, bosomy girl named Jeannie who'd dropped out of college to do something more real. (They were seeing a lot of that nowadays.) Jeannie said Mrs. Brant was a regular social butterfly. She said Mrs. Brant had dozens of friends who'd gone to Gallaudet with her, and they would sit around her kitchen talking away a mile a minute, using their special sign language with lots of inside jokes and dirty words; but her husband had come late to sign and could barely manage such basics as "Serve supper" and "Mail letter" (like Tonto, Jeannie said), so of course he was left in the dust. He was neither fish nor fowl, Jeannie said. This made Ian feel fonder of the man. He had long ago given up all hope of befriending him, or of seeing any hint of emotion in that handsome, leathery face; but now he regretted dismissing him so easily. "He must be awfully lonesome," he told Jeannie, "watching his wife enjoy herself with her friends."

"Oh, he doesn't care," Jeannie said. "He just stomps off to his garden. None of us can figure why she married him. Maybe it was sex. I do think he's kind of sexy, don't you?"

Jeannie often talked that way. She made Ian feel uncomfortable. Several times she had suggested they go out together some evening, and although he did find her attractive, with her streaming hair and bouncy peasant blouses, he always gave some excuse.

This afternoon she was helping Bert with his bureau. (She didn't know enough yet to be entrusted with a piece all her own.) Her job was to attach the drawer knobs—perfectly plain beechwood cylinders—but she kept leaving them to come over and talk to Ian. "Pretty," she said of the desk. Then, without a pause, "You like nature, Ian?"

"Nature? Sure."

"Me and some friends are taking a picnic lunch to Loch Raven this Sunday. Want to come?"

"Well, I have church on Sundays," Ian told her.

"Church," she said. She rocked back on the heels of her moccasins. "But how about *after* church?" she said. "We wouldn't be leaving till one or so."

"Oh, uh, there's my nephew and nieces, too," Ian said. "I sort of have to keep an eye on them on weekends."

"Why can't their parents do that?"

"Their parents are dead."

"Their grandparents, then," she said, instantly readjusting.

"My mother's got arthritis and my dad is kind of tied up."

"Or the other grandparents! Or other aunts and uncles! Or baby-sitters! Or can't the older ones watch the younger ones? Or maybe you could call the mothers of some of their school friends and see if—"

"It's kind of involved," Ian said. He was surprised at the number of options that could be produced at such short notice. "I guess I'd just better say no," he told her.

"Christ," she said, "what a drag. Why, even chain gangs get their Sundays off."

Then Mr. Brant called, "Jeannie!" He towered over the bureau, glaring in her direction, and she said, "Oops! Gotta go."

She skipped away, a juicy morsel of a girl, and Ian noticed how her long hair swung against the tight-packed seat of her jeans.

He had made it up about the children, of course. They were well past the stage when they needed sitters. But somehow he began to believe his own alibi, and as he watched her he thought, *Right! Even chain gangs,* he thought, *are allowed a little time to themselves.*

Well, no one had ever said this would be easy.

But then why didn't he feel forgiven? Why didn't he, after all these years of penance, feel that God had forgiven him?

The little black cat settled in immediately. She was very polite and clean, with a smell like new woolen yarn, and she tolerated any amount of petting. Daphne named her Honeybunch. Thomas named her Alexandra. Any time one would call her, the other would call louder. "Here, Honeybunch." "No, *Alexandra*! Here, Alexandra, you know who you love best." Agatha stayed out of it. She was abstracted all that weekend, moping because a classmate had thrown a party without inviting her. The reason Ian knew this was that Thomas announced it, cruelly, during Saturday night supper. Agatha had told Thomas he was piggish to chew with his mouth open, and Thomas said, "Well, at least I don't have to buy my clothes in the Chubbette department. At least I'm not so fat that Missy Perkins wouldn't ask me to her slumber party!" Then Agatha threw down her napkin and bolted from the table, and Daphne said, in a satisfied tone, "You're a meanie, Thomas."

"Am not."

"Are so."

"She started it."

"Did not."

"Did so."

"Quit that," Ian said. "Both of you may be excused."

"Why do *I* have to go when he's the one who—"

"You're excused, I said."

They left, grumbling under their breaths as they moved into the living room.

Supper was more or less finished, anyhow. Ian's father had already pushed away his plate and tilted back in his chair, and his mother was merely toying with her dessert. She hadn't taken a bite in the last five minutes; she was deep in one of her blow-by-blow household sagas, and it seemed she would never get around to eating her last half-globe of canned peach.

"So there I was in the basement," she said, "looking at all this water full of let's-not-discuss-it, and the man pulled a kind of zippery tube from his machine and twined it down the . . ."

Ian started thinking about the comics. It was childish of him, he knew, but one thing he really enjoyed at the end of every day was reading "Peanuts" in the *Evening Sun*. It made a kind of oasis—that tiny, friendly world where everybody was so quaint and earnest and reflective. But what with Good Works, and the weekly grocery trip, and shopping for the kids' new gym shoes, he hadn't had a chance at the paper yet; and now he could hear the others mauling it in the living room. By the time he got hold of it all the pages would be disarranged and crumpled.

"The total bill came to sixty dollars," his mother was saying. "I consider that cheap, in view of what the man had to deal with. When he was done he had me look down the floor drain. Big dark echoey floor drain. 'Hear that?' he said, and I said, 'Hear what?' He said, 'All along the line, your neighbors flushing their toilets. First one here and then one far, far away over there,' he said, 'all connected by this network of pipes.' 'Well, fine,' I said, 'but left to my own devices I believe I could manage to live out my life *not* hearing, thank you very much.' "

In the living room, quarrelsome voices climbed over each other and Ian caught the sound of paper tearing. They were demolishing "Peanuts," he was certain. He sighed.

Suppose, he thought suddenly, his boyhood self was to walk into the scene at this moment. Suppose he was offered a glimpse of how he had turned out: twenty-six years old and still living with his parents, tending someone else's children, obsessed with the evening comics. *Huh?* he'd say. *Why, what has happened here? What has become of me? How in heaven's name did things ever get to this state?*

• • •

"Give me one good reason I should have to go to church," Agatha said on Sunday morning. "It's hypocritical to go! I'm not a believer."

"You can go to Grandma and Grandpa's church if you prefer," Ian told her.

"Listen carefully, Ian, I'll only say this one more time: *I am not a believer.*"

He wrapped an elastic around Daphne's ponytail. "How about this," he said. "You attend till you're eighteen, and then you stop. That way, I won't have to feel guilty you didn't get the proper foundation."

"You don't have to feel guilty even now," Agatha told him. "I absolve you, Ian."

He drew back slightly. Absolve?

"Maybe she could go to Mary McQueen," Daphne suggested.

Agatha said, "Mary Our Queen is for Catholics, stupid."

"Agatha, don't call her stupid. Let's get moving. Thomas is already downstairs."

They descended to the living room, Daphne clattering in the patent leather Mary Janes she liked to wear to church. The sound of Sunday morning, Ian thought. He told his parents, "We're off."

"Oh, all right, dear," his mother said. She and his father were reading the paper on the couch.

"Take that business of the fig tree," Agatha said as she let the front door slam behind her. "Jesus cursing the fig tree."

"Where's Thomas?"

"Here I am," Thomas said from the porch swing.

"Let's go, then."

"Jesus decides He wants figs," Agatha said. "Of course, it's not fig *season*, but Jesus wants figs anyhow. So up He walks to this fig tree, but naturally all He finds is leaves. And what does He do? Puts a curse on the poor little tree."

"No!" Daphne breathed. Evidently she hadn't heard about this before.

"Next thing you know, the tree's withered and died."

"No."

Ian knew that Agatha was just passing through a stage, but even so he minded, a bit. Over the years he had come to view Jesus very personally. The most trite and sentimental Sunday School portrait could send a flash of feeling through him, as if Jesus were . . . oh, one of those older boys he used to admire when he was small, someone he'd watched from a distance and grown to know and love without ever daring to engage in conversation.

Also, Agatha was seeding doubts in the other two.

"Doesn't that seem petty to you?" she was asking Daphne. "I mean, doesn't it seem unreasonable? If *we* behaved like that, we'd be sent to our rooms to think it over."

"Agatha," Ian said, "there's a great deal in the Bible that's simply beyond our understanding."

"Beyond yours, maybe," Agatha said. She told Daphne, "Or Noah's Ark: how about that? God kills off all the sinners in a mammoth rainstorm. 'Gotcha!' He says, and He's enjoying it, you know He is, or otherwise He'd have sent a few sample rains ahead of time so they could mend their ways."

Picture how they must look from outside, Ian thought. A cleaned and pressed little family walking together to church, discussing matters of theology. Perfect.

From outside.

"Or Abraham and Isaac. That one *really* ticks me off. God asks Abraham to kill his own son. And Abraham says, 'Okay.' Can you believe it? And then at the very last minute God says, 'Only testing. Ha-ha.' Boy, I'd like to know what Isaac thought. All the rest of his life, any time his father so much as looked in his direction Isaac would think—"

Ian said, "Agatha, it's very bad manners to criticize other people's religion."

"It's very bad manners to force your own religion on them, too," Agatha told him. "Shoot, it's very *unconstitutional*. To make me go to church when I don't want to."

"Well, you're right," Ian said.

"Huh?"

"You're right, I shouldn't have done it."

By now, they had stopped walking. Agatha peered at him. She said, "So can I leave now?"

"You can leave."

She stood there a moment longer. The other two watched with interest. "Okay," she said finally. "Bye."

"Bye."

She turned and set off toward home.

But without her it seemed so quiet. He missed her firm, opinionated voice and that little trick she had of varying her tone to quote each person's remarks. No matter how imaginary those remarks might be.

"I the Lord thy God am a jealous God," Reverend Emmett read from Exodus, and Ian could almost hear Agatha beside him: "Any time *we* act jealous, people have a fit." He shook the thought away. He bowed lower in his seat, propping his forehead on two fingers. Next to him, Daphne tore a tiny corner off a page of her hymnal and placed it on her tongue. Thomas was sitting behind them with Kenny Larson and his family. A fly was crawling up the front counter.

Reverend Emmett called for a hymn: "Blessed Assurance." The congregation rose to sing, standing shoulder to shoulder. Everyone here was familiar to Ian. Or at least, semifamiliar. (Eli Everjohn and his wife were sitting with Sister Bertha, and Mrs. Jordan had brought her cousin.) "This is my story," they sang, "this is my song . . ." Ian put an arm around Daphne and she nestled against him as she sang, her voice incongruously husky for such a little girl.

The sermon was on the Sugar Rule. Recently a committee had approached Reverend Emmett suggesting that the rule be dropped. It was just so complicated, they said. Face it, they were eating sugar every day of their lives, one way or another. Even peanut butter contained sugar if you bought it from a supermarket. Reverend Emmett had told them he would meditate on the issue and report his conclusions. What he said this morning—pacing behind the counter, running his long fingers through his forelock—was that the Sugar Rule was *supposed* to be complicated. "Like error itself," he said, "sugar creeps in the cracks. You tell yourself you didn't realize, you were subject to circumstance, you forgot to read the list of ingredients and anyhow, it's everywhere and it can't be helped. Isn't that significant? It's not that you'll be damned forever if you take a grain of sugar; nobody says that. Sugar is merely a distraction, not a sin. But I feel it's important to keep the rule because of what it stands for: the need for eternal watchfulness."

The children—those who were listening—sent each other disappointed grimaces, but Ian didn't really care that much. The Sugar Rule was a minor inconvenience, at most. So was the Coffee Rule; so was the Alcohol Rule. The difficult one was the Unmarried Sex Rule. "How can something be right one day and wrong the next?" Cicely had asked him. "And what's done is done, anyway, and can't be undone, right?"

He had said, "If I thought that, I wouldn't be able to go on living." Then he'd told her he wanted them to get married.

"Married!" Cicely had cried. "Married, at our age! I haven't seen the world yet! I haven't had any fun!"

He covered his eyes with his hand.

In his daydreams, he walked into services one morning and found a lovely, golden-haired girl sitting in the row just ahead. She would be so intent on the sermon that she wouldn't even look his way; she had grown up in a religion very much like this one, it turned out, and believed with all her heart. After the Benediction Ian introduced himself, and she looked shy and pleased. They had the most proper courtship, but he could tell she felt the same way he did. They would marry at Second Chance with Reverend Emmett officiating. She would love the three children as much as if they were hers and stay home forever after to tend them. The Church Maiden, Ian called her in his mind. He never entered this building without scanning the rows for the Church Maiden.

After the sermon came Amending. "Does somebody want to stand up?" Reverend Emmett asked. But standing up was for serious sins, where you confessed to the whole congregation and discussed in public all possible methods of atonement. Evidently none of them had strayed so grievously during this past week. "Well, then," Reverend Emmett said, smiling, "we'll amend in private," and they bowed their heads and whispered their mistakes to themselves. Ian caught snatches of "lied to my husband" and "slapped my daughter" and "drank part of a beer with my boss." "Thursday I stole my sister's new bra and wore it to gym class," Daphne said, startling Ian, but of course he should not have been listening. He averted his face from her and whispered, "I was snappish with the children three different times. Four. And I told Mr. Brant I was sick with the flu when really I just wanted a day off."

Unlike the other denominations Ian knew of, this one had nothing against sinning in your thoughts. To think a sinful thought and not act upon it was to practice righteousness, Reverend Emmett said—almost as much righteousness as not thinking the thought in the first place. Jesus must have been misquoted on that business about committing adultery in your heart. So Ian left unspoken what troubled him the most:

I've been atoning and atoning, and sometimes lately I've hated God for taking so long to forgive me. Some days I feel I'm speaking into a dead telephone. My words are knocking against a blank wall. Nothing comes back to show I've been heard.

"Let it vanish now from our souls, Lord. In Jesus' name, amen," Reverend Emmett said. He looked radiant. Whatever had weighed on his own soul (for his lips had moved with the others', this morning) had obviously been lifted from him.

They sang "Sweet Hour of Prayer," in a tone that struck Ian as lingering and regretful. Then Reverend Emmett gave the Benediction, and they were free to go. Daphne shot off to join a friend. Ian wove his way through the other members' greetings. He answered several inquiries about his mother's arthritis, and politely refused Mrs. Jordan's offer of a ride home. (She drove like a maniac.) Near the door, Eli Everjohn stood awkwardly by in a brilliant blue suit while his wife talked with Sister Myra. "Morning, Brother Eli," Ian said. He started to edge past him, but Eli, who must have been feeling left out, brightened and said, "Why, hey there! Hey!"

"Enjoy the service?" Ian asked.

"Oh, I'm sure your pastor means well," Eli said. "But forbidding ordinary white sugar, and then allowing your young folks to listen to rock-and-roll music! Seems like to me he's got his priorities mixed up. I don't know that I hold with this Amending business, either. Awful close to Roman Catholic, if you ask me."

"Ah, well, it's a matter of opinion, I guess."

"No, Brother Ian, it is *not* a matter of opinion. Goodness! What a notion."

That more or less finished the conversation, Ian figured. He gave up and raised a hand amiably in farewell. But then he paused and turned back. "Brother Eli?" he said. "I wonder. Do you think you could locate a missing person for me?"

"Why, I'll do my best," Eli told him.

He didn't seem at all surprised by the question. It was Ian who was surprised.

"His name was Tom Dean," he told Eli. "Thomas Dean, Senior. He was married to my sister-in-law before she married my brother, and he's the only one who might be able to tell us who my sister-in-law's family was."

He and Eli sat on the couch in Sister Bertha's living room. No doubt Sister Bertha was wondering what business Ian could possibly have here, but she stayed out of sight, ostentatiously rattling pans in the kitchen and talking to her daughter. Her house was a ranch house with rooms that all flowed together, and Ian distinctly heard her discussing someone named Netta who had suffered a terrible grease fire.

"I don't know where Tom Dean grew up," Ian said, "but sometime in the spring of 'sixty-five he wrote to Lucy from Cheyenne, Wyoming. Or maybe he phoned; I'm not sure. *Somehow* he got in touch, asking her to send him his things."

"How long had they been divorced?" Eli said.

"I don't know. The kids were still small, though. It can't have been too long."

"And what state was this divorce granted in? Maryland? Wyoming? What state of the Union?"

"I don't know that either."

Eli surveyed him mournfully. He had taken off his suit coat and the armpits of his white shirt showed a faint bluish tinge.

"It was only mentioned in passing," Ian said. "You don't discuss your divorce in detail with the family of your new husband. So when my brother died, and then Lucy died, there was no one we could ask. She had left behind the three children and we were hoping some of her relatives could take them, but we didn't know if she had any relatives. We didn't even know her maiden name."

Beyond the plate glass window, Sunday traffic swished along Lake Avenue. Sister Bertha said Netta had escaped unburned and so had her husband and baby and her dear, darling, wonderful, incredible little dog.

"Still," Eli said, "your sister-in-law must have had some kind of document. Some certificate or something, somewhere among her papers."

"She didn't leave any papers. After she died my dad went through her house and he couldn't find a one."

"How about her billfold? Driver's license?"

"She didn't drive."

"Social security card?"

"For Lucy Dean. Period."

"Photos, then. Any photos?"

"None."

"Your family must have photos, though. From after she married your brother."

"We do, but my mother put them away so as not to remind the children."

"Not to remind them? Well, land sakes."

"My mother's kind of . . . she prefers to look on the bright side. But I can find them for you, I'm sure."

"Maybe later on," Eli said. "Okay: let's talk about your sister-in-law's friends. You recall if she had any girlfriends?"

"Not close ones," Ian said. "Just a couple of women she waitressed with, back before she married Danny. One of them we never tracked down, and the other my mother ran into a year or so after Lucy died but she said she really didn't know a thing about her."

"Didn't no one ever *ask* this Lucy anything?"

"It does sound peculiar," Ian said. This was the first time he'd realized exactly how peculiar. He was amazed that they could have been so unaware, so incurious, living all those months alongside another human being.

Eli said, "Tell what was in her desk."

"She didn't have a desk."

"Her topmost bureau drawer, then. Or that ragtag drawer full of string and such in her kitchen."

"All I know is, my dad went through her house and he didn't find anything useful. He talked about how people don't write letters anymore."

"So: no letters."

"And no address book, either. I remember he mentioned that."

"How about her divorce papers? She couldn't have throwed them away."

"Maybe after she remarried she did."

"Well, then, her marriage certificate. Her marriage to your brother."

"Nope."

"You know she would've kept that."

"All I can say is, we didn't find it."

"She must've had a safe deposit box."

"Lucy? I doubt it. And where was the key, then?"

"So you are trying to tell me," Eli said, "that a person manages to get through life without a single solitary piece of paper in her possession."

"Well, I realize it's unusual—"

"It's impossible!"

"Well . . ."

"Had her place been burglarized recently? Did the drawers look like they'd been rifled?"

"Not that I heard of," Ian said.

"Was anybody else living in the house with her?"

"No . . ."

But a dim uneasiness flitted past him, like something you see and yet don't see out of the corner of your eye.

"Anyone suspicious hanging about her?"

"No, no . . ."

But wary, suspicious Agatha pushed into his mind—her closed-off face with the puffy lids that veiled her secret thoughts.

"Now, I don't want you to take this wrong," Eli said, "but you are about the most *unhelpful* client I ever had to deal with."

"I realize that. I'm sorry," Ian said. "I shouldn't have wasted your time."

Eli shook his head, and his cowlick waggled and dipped. God's arrow with no place to go, Ian couldn't help thinking.

Monday noon, he told Mr. Brant he was eating at home today. He drove home and let himself into the house, announcing, "It's me! Forgot my billfold!"

"Oh, hello, dear," his mother called from the kitchen. Then she and his father went on talking, no doubt over their usual lunch of tinned soup and saltine crackers.

He climbed to the second floor and onward, more stealthily, to the attic, to Daphne and Agatha's little room underneath the eaves.

Girls tended to be messier than boys, he thought. (He had noticed that in his college days.) Agatha's bed was heaped with so many books that he wondered how she slept, and Daphne's was a jungle of stuffed animals. He went over to Agatha's bureau, a darkly varnished highboy that had to stand away from the wall a bit so as not to hit the eaves. The top was littered with pencil stubs and used Kleenexes and more books, but the drawers were fairly well organized. He patted each one's contents lightly, alert for something that didn't belong—the rustle of paper or a hard-edged address book. But there was nothing.

He knelt and looked under her bed. Dust balls. He lifted the mattress. Candy-bar wrappers. He shook his head and let the mattress drop. He tried the old fiberboard wardrobe standing at one end of the room and found a rod of clothes, half Daphne's and half Agatha's, packed too tightly together. Shoes and more shoes lay tangled underneath.

He bent to poke his head inside the storage room that ran under the eaves. In the dimness he made out a dress form, a lampshade, two foot lockers, and a cardboard carton. He crawled further inside and lifted one of the carton's flaps. The musty gray smell reminded him of mice. He dragged the carton toward the door for a closer look: his mother's framed college diploma, a bundle of letters addressed to Miss Beatrice Craig . . . He pushed the carton toward the rear again.

Turning to go, he saw a faded, fabric-covered box on the floor—the kind that stationery sometimes comes in. He flipped up the lid and found a clutter of barrettes and hair ribbons and junk jewelry. Agatha's, no doubt. He let the lid fall shut and crawled on out.

In the bedroom, he paused. He reached back and pulled open the drawer in the box's base.

Right away, he knew he'd hit on something. The contents were so tidy:

flattened papers stacked in order of size, and on top of them a few pieces of jewelry, no less junky than those in the main compartment but obviously dating from an earlier time. He pushed the jewelry aside and removed the papers.

A savings booklet from Mercantile Safe Deposit and Trust, showing a balance of $123.08. The title to a Chevrolet owned by Daniel C. Bedloe. A receipt from Morehead TV Repair guaranteeing all replacement parts for thirty days. A marriage certificate for Daniel Craig Bedloe and Lucy Ann Dean. (Ian paused a moment over that one. Was there any remote possibility that Ann could be a last name?) A birth certificate for Daphne Marie Bedloe. A pamphlet of instructions for filing health insurance claims. A birth certificate for Agatha Lynn Dulsimore and then one for Thomas. A receipt for—

Agatha *who*?

Agatha Lynn Dulsimore, born April 4, 1959. Father's full name: Thomas Robert Dulsimore. Mother's maiden name: Lucy Ann Dean. And Thomas Robert Dulsimore, Junior; same parents.

Why, Dean was not Lucy's married name but her maiden name. She must have changed back to Dean after the divorce, and changed her children's names too—at least by implication. All this time, the Bedloes had been hunting a man who didn't exist.

Ian sifted through the few remaining papers—a hazy, unflattering photo of Lucy and the older two children, an auto insurance policy, a recipe for banana bread—but the birth certificates were the only items that told him anything. Both listed the parents' home address as Portia, Maryland. Both carried definite dates, and a doctor's name, and a hospital's name in a town called Marcy, which if Ian recollected right lay not far from Portia, just below the Pennsylvania line. He had enough to track a man down by, provided a person was halfway skilled at tracking.

He slipped the papers inside his shirt and went off to see Eli Everjohn.

"Have some mashed potato, Honeybunch," Daphne said. She held her spoon out to the little cat, who was sitting on Daphne's lap with her front paws folded primly beneath her. First the cat peered into Daphne's eyes, as if checking to make sure she really meant it, and then she leaned forward and lapped daintily. When she was finished, the spoon gleamed. She sat up to wash her face. "Good girl," Daphne said, and she dipped the spoon back in her plate and took a mouthful for herself.

"Ooh, revolting!" Agatha said. "Ian, did you see what she did?"

"What? What'd I do?" Daphne asked.

"You ate from a spoon the cat licked!"

At the other end of the table, Thomas gave an elderly cough. "Well, actually," he said, "the cat's the one who should worry. Mr. Pratt says human spit carries more germs than any other animal's, because humans have these fingers they keep putting in their mouths."

Ian laughed. The others looked at him.

"I was just, ah, thinking," he told them.

They looked away again.

You could never call it a penance, to have to take care of these three. They were all that gave his life color, and energy, and . . . well, life.

What he would do was, once he got Eli's report he would file it in a drawer someplace. Then when they grew up and started wondering about their origins he would hand it over to them; that was all. He would certainly not use the information himself in any way.

People needed to know their genetic backgrounds—what diseases ran in their families and so forth. Also this would help him apply for guardianship. Social Security. That sort of thing.

He rose and started clearing the table. It was a relief to have all that settled. He was glad he hadn't told anyone what he was doing.

But at work the next day, he did tell someone. He told Jeannie. He was teaching her how to select the right grain of wood and she asked if he'd like to go to a movie that night at the Charles. "I can't," he said.

"What, are movies against your religion?"

"No, it's my turn to car-pool for Brownies."

"Hey," she said. "Ian. How long you going to go on living like this, anyway?"

So he told her about Eli. He didn't know why, exactly. It wasn't as if finding Thomas Dulsimore would change his situation. Maybe he just hoped to prove he wasn't as passive as she supposed. And she did seem gratifyingly interested. When he mentioned the stationery box she said, "Naw! Go on!" She asked, "What-all was in it?" and she even wanted to know about the jewelry.

"It wasn't the kind of jewelry that would give you any clues," he said. "I honestly didn't pay much attention."

"And the photo?"

"Oh, well, that was . . . well, the detective was glad to see it, of course, so's he'd know more or less what she looked like, but it didn't show a street sign or a license plate or anything like that. Just Lucy."

"Was she pretty?"

"Sure, I guess so."

For some reason, he didn't want to tell her *how* pretty.

Lucy's image swam into his mind—not the real-life version but the version in the snapshot: out of focus, too young, still unformed, nowhere near as finely chiseled as she had seemed later. One hip was slung out gracelessly to support Thomas's weight, and one hand was reaching blurrily to gather Agatha closer. Against all logic (he knew he was being ridiculous), he started resenting Agatha's disloyalty in keeping her mother's likeness. There you are: you give up school, you sacrifice everything for these children, and what do they do? They secretly hoard their mother's photo and cling to her and prefer her. She hadn't even taken proper care of them, willfully dying and leaving them as she did; but evidently blood motherhood won over everything.

Jeannie said, "I'm really glad to hear you're doing this, Ian."

"Well, it's only so we can get straight," he told her. "I certainly don't plan to hand the three of them over to strangers or anything like that."

"What are you, crazy?" she asked. "You've got a life to live! You can't drag them around with you forever."

"But I'm responsible for them. I worry I'd be, um, sinning, so to speak, to walk away from them."

"You want to know what I think?" Jeannie asked. She leaned forward. Her face seemed sharper now, more pointed. The hollow between her collarbones could have held a teaspoon of salt. "I think you're sinning *not* to walk away," she said.

"How do you figure that?"

"I think we're each allowed one single life to live on this planet. We'll never get another chance in all eternity," she said. "And if you let it go to waste—now, *that* is sinning."

"Yes," he said, "but what if I'm honor bound to waste it? What if I have an obligation?"

He worried she would make him explain, but she was too caught up in proving her point. "Even then!" she said triumphantly. "You put your regrets behind you. You move on past them. You do not commit the sin of squandering your only life."

"Well, it *sounds* good," he said.

It did sound good. He really had no argument to offer against it.

At Prayer Meeting the following night he looked for Eli Everjohn but didn't find him, or the strawberry blonde either. He spotted Sister Bertha's dark red pompadour and he sat down next to her and asked, "Where's your daughter this evening?"

"She went home."

"Home?"

"Her and Eli both, home to Caro Mill. Eli said to give you a message, though. What was it now he said? He said not to think you had slipped his mind and he would be in touch."

"Thanks," Ian told her.

Then Reverend Emmett announced the opening hymn: "Work for the Night Is Coming."

Every time Ian attended Prayer Meeting, he thought of his first visit here. He remembered how he had felt welcomed by the loving voices of the singers; he remembered the sensation of prayers flowing heavenward. Coming here had saved him, he knew. Without the Church of the Second

Chance he would have struggled alone forever, sunk in hopelessness.

So when Prayer Meeting seemed long-winded or inconsequential, when the petitions had to do with minor health complaints and personal disputes, he controlled his impatience. Tonight he prayed for Brother Kenneth's colon to grow less irritable, for Sister Myra's husband to appreciate her more fully. He listened to a recitation from Sister Nell that seemed not so much a request for prayers as an autobiography. "I learned to stop blaming myself for everything that went wrong," one of her paragraphs went. "I had all the time been blaming myself. But really, you know, when you think about it, mostly it's other people to blame, the godless and the self-centered, and so I said to this gal on my shift, I said, 'Now listen here, Miss Maggie. *You* may think I was the one in charge of the . . .' "

Till Reverend Emmett broke in. "Ah, Sister Nell?"

"What?"

"What would you like us to pray for, exactly?"

"Pray for me to have strength," she said, "in the face of fools and sinners."

Ian prayed for Sister Nell to have strength.

The closing hymn was "Softly and Tenderly," and when they sang, "Come home! Come home!" Ian felt he was the one they were calling.

"Go ye now into the world and bear witness to His teachings," Reverend Emmett said, raising his arms. Almost before his "Amen," people were stirring and preparing to leave. Several spoke to Ian as they passed. "Good to see you, Brother Ian." "How're the kids?" "Coming to paint with us Saturday?" They filed out. Ian hung behind.

Often it seemed to him that this room itself was his source of peace. Even the flicker of the fluorescent lights heartened him, and the faint chemical smell left over from when the place had been a dry cleaner's. He found reasons to loiter, first collecting the hymn pamphlets and then stacking them just so on the counter. He paused at the edges of a conversation between Reverend Emmett and Brother Kenneth, who was offering further details about his colon. He rolled down his shirtsleeves and carefully buttoned his cuffs before, at long last, stepping out the door.

Then behind him, Reverend Emmett said, "Brother Ian? Mind if I walk partway with you?"

Ian felt his shoulders loosen. Possibly, this was what he'd been hoping for all along.

They walked north on York Road through a summerlike night, Reverend Emmett swinging his Bible. He was taller than Ian and took longer strides, although he kept trying to slow down. Occasionally he hummed a few notes beneath his breath—"Softly and Tenderly" again. Ian thought of an evening back in his Boy Scout days, when the scoutmaster (a young, athletic man, a former basketball star) had given him a ride home, filling him with a mixture of joy and self-consciousness. He knew Reverend Emmett merely acted as God's steward, and that for someone who was the church's founder and its sole leader he seemed remarkably unimpressed with his own importance. Still, Ian always felt tongue-tied around him. Tonight he considered discussing the weather but decided that was too mundane, and then when the silence stretched on too long he wished he *had* discussed the weather, but if he brought it up now it would seem strained. So he kept quiet, and it was Reverend Emmett who finally spoke.

"Some Prayer Meetings," he said, "are like cleaning out a closet. Clearing away the dribs and drabs. Necessary, but tedious."

And Ian said, as if making a perfectly apt response: "Is there such a thing as the Devil?"

Reverend Emmett glanced over at him.

"I mean," Ian said, "does someone exist whose purpose is to tempt people into evil? To make them feel torn one way and another so they're not sure which way is right anymore?"

"What is it you're tempted to do, Brother Ian?" Reverend Emmett asked.

Ian swallowed. "I'm wasting my life," he said.

"Excuse me?"

He must have mumbled the words. He raised his chin and said, almost shouting, "I'm wasting the only life I have! I have one single life in this universe and I'm not using it!"

"Well, of course you're using it," Reverend Emmett said calmly.

"I am?"

"This *is* your life," Reverend Emmett said.

They faced each other at an intersection. A woman swerved around them.

"Lean into it, Ian," Reverend Emmett said. Not "Brother Ian," but "Ian." It made what he said sound more direct, more oracular. He said, "View your burden as a gift. It's the theme that has been given you to work with. Accept that, and lean into it. This is the only life you'll have."

Then he clapped Ian on the shoulder, and turned away to cross York Road.

Ian resumed walking. For a while he pondered Reverend Emmett's message, but he didn't find it much help. To tell the truth, the man had disappointed him. And besides, he hadn't answered Ian's question. The question was: Is there such a thing as the Devil?

Ian had been referring to Jeannie, of course—Jeannie sitting forward compellingly, the hollow deepening at the base of her throat as she tempted him from his path. But the face that came to his mind at this moment was not Jeannie's. It was Lucy's. It was the tiny, perfect, heart-shaped face of Lucy Dean.

"Honeybunch has worms," Agatha told Ian.

"How do you know that?"

"You really want me to say?"

"On second thought, never mind," Ian said. "So, what? We have to take her to the vet?"

"I made an appointment: tomorrow afternoon at four."

She and Thomas sat on either side of Ian in the porch swing, enjoying the last of a golden autumn day. Down on the front walk, Daphne was playing hopscotch with the Carter girl and the newlyweds' five-year-old. "You did step on the line, Tracy. You did," she said in her raucous little voice.

Ian said, "Maybe Grandpa could drive you. I could leave the car with him tomorrow and take the bus."

"We like it better when *you* come," Agatha said.

"Well, but I have work."

"Please, Ian," Thomas said. "Grandpa drove us when we went to get her cat shots and he yelled at her for sitting on his foot."

"His accelerator foot," Agatha explained.

"We like it better when you're there, acting in charge," Thomas told him.

Ian looked at him a moment. His mind had drifted elsewhere. "Thomas," he said, "remember that big doll you used to carry around?"

"Oh, well, that was a long time ago," Thomas said.

"Yes, but I was wondering. How come you named her Dulcimer?"

"I don't even know where she is anymore. I don't know why I named her that," Thomas said.

He seemed embarrassed, rather than secretive. And Agatha wasn't listening. You'd think she would suspect; she was the one who'd kept that box hidden away. But she stirred the porch swing dreamily with one foot. "Suppose we got bombed," she said to Ian.

"Pardon?"

He saw the stationery box in his mind: the dust on the lid, the congealed sheaf of papers. She must not have glanced inside for years, he realized. She might even have forgotten it existed.

"Suppose Baltimore got atom-bombed," she was saying. "Know what I'd do?"

"You wouldn't do a thing," Thomas told her. "You'd be dead."

"No, seriously. I've been thinking. I'd break into a supermarket, and I'd settle our family inside. That way we'd have all the supplies we needed. Canned goods and bottled goods, enough to last us forever."

"Well, not forever," Thomas said.

"Long enough to get over the radiation, though."

"Not a chance. Right, Ian?"

Ian said, "Hmm?"

"The radiation would last for years, right?"

"Well, so would the canned goods," Agatha said. "And if we still had electricity—"

"Electricity! Ha!" Thomas said. "Do you ever live in a dream world!"

"Well, even without electricity," Agatha said stubbornly, "we could

manage. Nowadays supermarkets sell blankets, even. And socks! And prescription drugs, the bigger places. We could get penicillin and stuff. And
some way we'd bring Claudia and them from Pittsburgh, I haven't figured
just how, yet—"

"Forget it, Ag," Thomas told her. "That's ten more mouths to feed."

"But we *need* a lot of kids. They're the future generation. And Grandma
and Grandpa are the old folks who would teach us how to carry on."

"How about Ian?" Thomas asked.

"How about him?"

"He's not old. And he's not the future generation, either. You have to
draw the line somewhere."

"Gee, thanks," Ian said, lazily toeing the swing. But Agatha turned a
pensive gaze on him.

"No," she said finally, "Ian comes too. He's the one who keeps us all
together."

"The cowpoke of the family, so to speak," Ian told Thomas. But he
felt touched. And when his father called from the doorway—"Ian?
Telephone"—he rested a palm on Agatha's thick black hair a second as
he rose.

The receiver lay next to the phone on the front hall table. He picked it
up and said, "Hello?"

"Brother Ian? Wallah," a man said from a distance.

"Pardon?"

"This is Eli Everjohn. Wallah, I said."

"Wallah?"

"Wallah! I found your man."

"You . . . what?"

"Except he's dead," Eli said.

Ian leaned one shoulder against the wall.

"Appears he didn't live much past what your sister-in-law did. Hello?
Are you there?"

"I'm here."

"Maybe this is a shock."

"No, that's all right," Ian said.

The shock was not Tom Dulsimore's death but the fact that he had
lived at all—that someone else in the world had turned up actual evidence
of him.

But Eli started breaking the news all over again, this time more delicately. "I'm sorry to have to tell you that Thomas Dulsimore, Senior has
passed away," he said. "Had himself a motorcycle crash back in nineteen
sixty-seven."

" 'Sixty-seven," Ian said.

"Seems he was one of those folks that don't hold with helmets."

So Tom Dulsimore was not an option anymore—not even in Ian's
fantasies.

"Reason I know is, I phoned his mother. Mrs. Millet. She'd remarried, is the reason it took me a while. I told her I was a buddy of Tom's wanting to get in touch with him. I didn't say no more though till I got your say-so. Should I go ahead now and pay her a visit?"

"No, never mind."

"She's bound to know the kids' relatives. Small-town kind of lady; you could just tell she would know all about it."

"Maybe I should get her address," Ian said.

"Okay, suit yourself. Mrs. Margie Millet. Forty-three Orchard Road, Portia, Maryland. You need to write that down?"

"I have it," Ian said. (He would have it forever, he felt—chiseled into his brain.) "Thanks, Eli. I appreciate your help. You know where to send the bill."

"Aw, it won't amount to much. This one was easy."

For you, maybe, Ian thought. He told Eli goodbye and hung up.

From the kitchen, his mother called, "Agatha? Time to set the table!"

"Coming."

Ian met Agatha at the door and stepped past her onto the porch. She didn't notice a thing.

The evening was several shades darker now, as if curtain after curtain had fallen in his absence. Thomas was swinging the swing hard enough to make the chains creak, and down on the sidewalk the little girls were still playing hopscotch. Ian paused to watch them. Something about the purposeful planting of small shoes within chalked squares tugged at him. He leaned on the railing and thought, *What does this remind me of? What? What?* Daphne tossed the pebble she used as a marker and it landed in the farthest square so crisply, so ringingly, that the sound seemed thrown back from a sky no higher than a ceiling, cupping all of Waverly Street just a few feet overhead.

"Lucy Ann Dean was as common as dirt," Mrs. Millet said. "I know I shouldn't speak ill of the dead, but there's just no getting around it: she was common."

They were sitting in Mrs. Millet's Pennsylvania Dutch–style breakfast nook, all blue painted wood and cut-out hearts and tulips. (Her house was the kind where the living room waited in reserve for some momentous occasion that never arrived, and Ian had caught no more than a glimpse of its white shag rugs and white upholstery on his journey to the kitchen.) Mrs. Millet slouched across from him, opening a pack of cigarettes. She was younger than he had expected, with a very stiff, very brown hairdo and a hatchet face. Her magenta minidress struck him as outdated, although Ian was not the last word on fashion.

He himself wore a suit and tie, chosen with an eye to looking trustworthy. After all, how did she know he wasn't some knock-and-rob man?

He hadn't phoned ahead because he hadn't fully acknowledged he was planning this; he had dressed this morning only for church, he told himself, although he almost never wore a tie to church. After services he had eaten Sunday dinner with his family and then (yawning aloud and stretching in a stagy manner) had announced he was feeling so restless, he thought he might go for a drive. Whereupon he had headed north without consulting a map, relying on the proper road signs to appear or else not, as the case might be. And they did appear. The signs for Portia, the signs for Orchard Road. The giant brass 43 glittering, almost shouting, from the lamppost in front of the redwood cottage. "My name is Ian Bedloe," he had said when she opened the door. "I hope I'm not disturbing you, but I'm Lucy Dean's brother-in-law and I'm trying to locate some of her family."

She hadn't exactly slammed the door in his face, but her expression had frozen over somehow. "Then maybe you better ask *her*," she told him.

"Ask who?"

"Why, Lucy Dean, of course."

"But . . . Lucy's dead," he said.

She stared at him.

"She died a long time ago," he told her.

"Well," she said, "I'd be fibbing if I said I was sorry. I always knew she was up to no good."

He was shamed by the rush of pleasure he felt—the bitter, wicked pleasure of hearing someone else agree with him at long last.

Now she said, "First off, her parents drank." She took a cigarette from her pack and tamped it against the table. "How do you suppose they had that car wreck? Three sheets to the wind, both of them. Then her aunt Alice moved in with her, and she was just plain cracked, if you want my honest opinion. I don't think the two of them had anything to do with each other. It's more like Lucy just raised herself. Well, for that much I give her credit: she'd come out of that run-down shack every morning neat as a pin, every hair in place, every accessory matching, which heaven knows how she did on their little pittance of money . . ."

She stole it, is how. Shoplifted. Not even you know the worst of it.

". . . and she'd sashay off to school all prissy and Miss America with her books held in front of her chest. The boys were fools for her, but my Tommy was the only one she'd look at. You should've seen my Tommy. He was movie-star handsome. He could pass for Tony Curtis, ought to give you some idea. He and Lucy went steady from ninth grade on. Went to every dance and sports event together. Well, excepting Junior Prom. They had a little disagreement the week before Junior Prom and she went with Gary Durbin, but Tommy beat Gary to a pulp next morning and him and Lucy got back together. At their Senior Prom they were King and Queen. I still have the pictures. Tommy wore a tux and he looked good enough to eat. I said, 'Tommy, you could have any girl you wanted,' but then, well, you guessed it."

She lit her cigarette and tilted her head and blew out a long stream of smoke, all the while staring defiantly at Ian. He said, "I did?"

"Lucy went and got herself pregnant."

"Oh."

"I said, 'Tommy, you can't be certain that baby's even yours,' and he said, 'Mom, I know it. I just don't know what on earth I'm going to do,' he told me."

Ian said, "What?" He felt he'd missed something. "You mean it could have been someone else's baby?" he asked.

"Well, who can say?" Mrs. Millet said. "I mean life is all so iffy, right? I said, 'Tommy, *don't* fall for this! You could be anything! You could be a male model, even! Why saddle yourself with a wife and kid?' But Lucy talked him into it. She had him wrapped around her little finger, I tell you. It was the kind of thing that just breaks a mother's heart."

"So . . . but this aunt of hers," Ian said. He seemed to be losing track of the purpose of his visit. "Alice, you say."

"Alice Dean. Well, she had nothing against it. She was delighted to marry Lucy off. Meant she could get back to wherever she came from and her old-maid ways. So Tommy and Lucy set up house in this crummy little trailer over at Blalock's Trailer Park and Tommy started work at Luther's Sports Equipment, but when Lucy told him she was expecting *again*—two babies in three years!—he left her. I don't blame him, either. I do not blame him. He was just a boy! 'When you going to do this, when you going to do that?' she was always asking, but he hadn't had him any kind of life yet! *Naturally* he wanted to roam a bit. She claimed he was irresponsible and she fretted about the least little thing, so of course he stayed away even more and when he did come home they'd fight. Twice the police had to be called. Then thank the Lord, he finally had the sense to leave. Got shed of her and asked for a divorce. And wouldn't you know she hired herself a big-shot city lawyer and sued for child support. Proves what I'd been telling him: all as she was after was his money. Someone to support those kids; by then she'd had the second one and she was always yammering about, 'I can't feed these kids on yard weeds,' and such. I told Tommy, I said, 'She should just go to work, if she needs money so bad.' "

"But then who would watch the children?" Ian asked.

"Lord, you sound just like her. 'Then who would watch the children?' " Mrs. Millet mimicked in a high voice. She flicked her cigarette into a tin ashtray. "She should've got a sitter, of course. That's what I told Tommy. 'And don't expect *me* to sit,' I told him. I never did like other people's children much. So anyhow, Tommy hung around here awhiles but there wasn't all that much for him in Portia, and so finally he hitchhiked to Wyoming. He had in mind to find work there, something glamorous having to do with horses. Well, that didn't quite come through like he had hoped and so of course he couldn't send money first thing, but he was planning to! And then we hear Lucy's run off."

"Run off?"

"Run away with some man. That lawyer that handled her divorce. It was Mr. Blalock called and told me, down at the trailer park. She owed him rent. He said her trailer was empty as last year's bird nest, door flapping open in the wind and everything hauled away that wasn't nailed down. Said her neighbors saw a moving van come to take her belongings. Not a U-Haul; a professional van. The man was loaded, was what they guessed. She must've went with him for the money."

"Went with him where?" Ian asked.

"Why, to Baltimore, but at first we didn't know that. At first we had no idea, and I told Tommy he was better off that way. 'The slate has been wiped clean,' I told him on the phone. 'I do believe we've seen the last of her.' But *then* guess what. She calls him up a few months later. Calls him in Cheyenne. Tells him she's in Baltimore and wants the money he owes her. Oh, I just wish I'd have been on the other end of the line. I'd have hung up on her so fast! But Tommy, I will say, he was a whole lot smarter by then. He says, 'I thought you had yourself some rich guy now,' and she says, 'Oh,' says, 'that didn't work out.' Well, I just bet it didn't work out. I bet the fellow was married, was what. That's the kind of thing you see happen every day. Tommy tells her, 'I can't help *that*, I met somebody here and we're planning on a June wedding. All I got is going for the wedding,' he says. Then he says, 'And anyhow, where's my things? You took every blasted thing I left in that trailer,' he says. 'Stuff I was coming back to fetch someday you packed up and hauled away like it belonged to you.' 'Tommy, I need money,' she says. 'I'm in a awful fix right now.' He says, 'First you send me my things,' and signs off. You see how he'd got wise to her. Oh, she aged him, I tell you. She hardened him. She callused him."

Mrs. Millet stubbed out her cigarette and sat staring into space. Over the stove, a plastic clock in the shape of a cat ticked its long striped tail back and forth.

"It was the winter of 'sixty-seven he had the accident," she said. "Motorcycling on icy roads. His wife called me up and told me. I will never hear the phone ring again as long as I live without going all over cold and sick."

Ian said, "Well, I'm sorry."

But it was only the most detached and courteous kind of sorry. He would never have left the children with such a man, even if the man had been willing.

"Of course, that second wife was pretty no-account herself," Mrs. Millet said.

Ian stood up. (No use staying on for more of this.) He said, "Mrs. Millet, I appreciate your talking to me. I guess what you're saying is, there was only that one aunt."

"That's all as *I* ever heard of," she said.

"And no brothers or sisters, or cousins, or anything like that."

"Not as I know of. Chances are the aunt has passed on too, by this time. Lord, lately it seems the whole world has passed on."

It did seem that way, at times. At times, it really did.

At Prayer Meeting the ghostly smell of dry-cleaning fluid mingled with Mrs. Jordan's cologne. "Pray for me to accept this cross without complaint," Sister Myra said. Accept what cross? Ian hadn't been listening. He bowed his head and felt the silence wrap around him like a clean, cool sheet that you reach for in your sleep halfway through a hot night.

"For our Sister Myra," Reverend Emmett said at last.

"Amen."

"Any other prayers, any other prayers . . ."

In a row toward the rear, Sister Bertha stood up. "I am troubled in my heart for another person tonight," she said. She spoke pointedly to the empty chair in front of her. "I know of someone here who seems to be experiencing a serious difficulty. I was waiting to see if he'd ask for our prayers but so far he hasn't."

He? There were only three men present: Reverend Emmett, Brother Kenneth, and Ian.

"I know," Sister Bertha said, "that this person must be feeling very overworked, very beset with problems, and he's casting about for a solution. But it doesn't seem to occur to him that he could bring it up at Prayer Meeting."

She sat down.

Ian's cheeks felt hot.

Surely private detectives were sworn to secrecy, weren't they? Just like lawyers, or doctors. Weren't they?

Reverend Emmett looked uncertain. He said, "Well . . ." and glanced around at the other worshipers. His eyes did not linger noticeably on Ian, although of course he must suspect. "Does this person wish to ask for our prayers?" he said.

No response. Just a few rustles and whispers.

"In that case," Reverend Emmett said, "we won't intrude. Let us pray, instead, for *all* of us. For all of us to know that we can bring our problems to God whenever we feel ready to let go of them."

He raised his arms and the silence fell, as if he had somehow cast it forth in front of him.

Sister Bertha is a nosy-bones, Ian thought distinctly. *And I hate that tomato-soup color she dyes her hair.*

After the Benediction, he was the first one out the door. He left behind even Mrs. Jordan, who most likely would want to walk home with him, and he set off at a brisk, angry pace. So the last thing he expected to hear was Reverend Emmett calling his name. "Brother Ian!"

Ian stopped and turned.

The man must have run the whole way. He must have left his flock unattended, his Bible open on the counter, his church lit up and unlocked. But he wasn't even breathing hard. He approached at a saunter, seemingly absorbed in slipping on a cardigan the same color as the dusk.

"May I tag along?" he asked.

Ian shrugged.

They set off together more slowly.

"Of course, it does come down to whether a person feels ready to let go," Reverend Emmett said in the most conversational tone.

Ian kicked a Dixie cup out of his path.

"Some people prefer to hug their problems to themselves," Reverend Emmett said.

Ian wheeled on him, clenching his fists in his pockets. He said, "*This* is my life? This is all I get? It's so settled! It's so cut and dried! After this there's no changing! I just lean into the burden of those children forever, is that what you're saying?"

"No," Reverend Emmett told him.

"You said that! You said to lean into my burden!"

"But those children will be grown in no time," Reverend Emmett said. "*They* are not the burden I meant. The burden is forgiveness."

"Okay," Ian said. "Fine. How much longer till I'm forgiven?"

"No, no. The burden is that *you* must forgive."

"Me?" Ian said. He stared at Reverend Emmett. "Forgive who?"

"Why, your brother and his wife, of course."

Ian said nothing.

Finally Reverend Emmett asked, "Shall we walk on?"

So they did. They passed a lone man waiting at a bus stop, a shopkeeper locking up his store. Each footstep, Ian felt, led him closer to something important. He was acutely conscious all at once of motion, of flux and possibility. He felt he was an arrow—not an arrow shot by God but an arrow heading toward God, and if it took every bit of this only life he had, he believed that he would get there in the end.

7

Organized Marriage

It was Agatha who came up with the notion of finding Ian a wife. Agatha
was graduating that June; she'd had word she'd been accepted at her first-
choice college; she would soon be leaving the family forever. And one
night in April she walked into the living room and told the other two,
"I'm worried about Ian."

Thomas and Daphne glanced over at her. (There was a commercial
on just then, anyhow.) She stood in the doorway with her arms folded, her
tortoiseshell glasses propped on top of her head in a purposeful, no-nonsense
manner. "Who will keep him company after we're gone?" she asked.

"You're the only one going," Daphne told her. "He's still got me and
Thomas."

"Not for long," Agatha said.

Their eyes slid back to the Late Late Movie.

But they knew she had a point. In a sense, Thomas was already gone. He
was a freshman in high school now and he had a whole outside existence—
a raft of friends and a girlfriend and an extracurricular schedule so full that
he was seldom home for supper. As for Daphne, well, their grandma liked
to say that Daphne was eleven going on eighty. She dressed like a tiny old
Gypsy—muddled layers of clothing, all tatters and gold thread, purchased
on her own at thrift shops—and was generally off in the streets somewhere
managing very capably.

"Pretty soon all he'll have will be Grandma and Grandpa," Agatha
said. "He'll be taking care of them like always and shopping and driving
the car and helping with the housework. What kind of life is that? I think
he ought to get married."

Now she had their attention.

"And since he doesn't seem to know any women, I think we'll have to
find him one."

"Miss Pennington," Daphne said instantly.

"Who?"

"Miss Ariana Pennington, my teacher," Daphne said.
It was just that easy.

Miss Pennington had been teaching fifth grade for only the past two years, so neither Thomas nor Agatha had had her when they were fifth-graders. Thomas knew her by sight, though. Every boy in the neighborhood knew her by sight. Not even the youngest, it seemed, was immune to her hour-glass figure or her mane of extravagant curly brown hair. Agatha, on the other hand, had to be shown who it was they were talking about.

So on a Friday afternoon just before the last bell, when Thomas was supposedly in a Leaders of Tomorrow meeting and Agatha had study hall, they met at the old cracked porcelain water fountain behind Poe High and walked the two blocks to the grade school. Almost no other students were out at this hour, but Thomas greeted by name the few who were—those excused early for dental appointments and such. "Thomas!" they said, and, "Yo, man, what you up to?" Agatha merely stalked on, blank-faced. She wore a bulbous down jacket over a skirt that stopped in the middle of her chunky bare knees—not an outfit any of her classmates would have been caught dead in, but then Agatha never concerned herself with ap-pearances. She was supremely indifferent, impervious, striding on without Thomas until he ran to catch up with her.

At Reese Elementary Thomas took the lead, choosing a side door in-stead of the main entrance and climbing the stairs two steps at a time. Outside Room 223 he paused, turned toward Agatha, and beckoned.

Through the small window they saw rows of fifth-graders bent over their books. Miss Pennington walked among them, tall and willowy, paus-ing first at this desk and then at that one to answer questions. You would never take her for a woman of the seventies. In an era when teachers had started wearing pants to work, Miss Pennington wore a silky white blouse and a flaring black skirt cinched tightly at the waist, sheer nylon stock-ings, and high-heeled patent leather pumps—the sexy, constricting clothes of the fifties. Her hair was shoulder-length and her fingernails were sharp red spears, and her makeup—when she turned as if by instinct and glanced toward the door—was seen to be vivid and expertly applied: deep red lipstick emphasizing her full lips, and plummy rouge and luminous blue eyeshadow. Thomas and Agatha stepped back hastily, out of her line of vision. They looked at each other.

"Well?" Thomas asked.

"She's kind of . . . brightly colored, isn't she?"

"Oh, Agatha, you don't know anything. She's gorgeous! Women are *supposed* to look that way. That's the type guys dream about."

"Oh," Agatha said.

"She's perfect," Thomas told her.

"All right," Agatha said crisply. "Let's get this thing rolling, then."

. . .

Daphne told Ian he needed to make an appointment for a parent-teacher conference. "Conference?" Ian said. "*Now* what'd you do?"

"I didn't do anything! How come you always think the worst of me? I just want you to talk to my teacher about my homework."

"What about it?"

"Well, like, are you supposed to help me with it, or let me do it on my own?"

"But I already let you do it on your own. What are you saying, you need help?"

"It might be a good idea."

"Why don't I just go ahead and help, then? We'll set aside a time each evening."

"No, first I think you should ask Miss Pennington," Daphne told him.

He gazed down at her. He and she were doing the supper dishes (she had offered to dry) while the other two sat at the kitchen table, ostensibly studying. Now Agatha said, "It wouldn't hurt to show the teacher you take an interest, Ian."

"Well, of course I take an interest," Ian told her. "Good grief, I'm one of the grade mothers. I baked six dozen cookies for Parents' Night and delivered them in person."

"You never went in for a private conference, though," Daphne said.

"I thought that was an improvement. Your first full year in school I haven't been issued a summons."

"Well, all right," Daphne said sorrowfully. "If you don't want to keep the lines of communication open . . ."

"Keep the what? Lines of what? Well, shoot," Ian said, setting a stack of bowls in the sink. "Fine, I'll go. Are you satisfied?"

Daphne nodded. So did the other two, but Ian had his back to them and he didn't see.

Daphne reported that the parent-teacher conference went very well. "He was wearing that grown-up shirt we bought him for Christmas," she told Thomas and Agatha, "the one he has to iron. He came to school straight from work and he had his wood-chip smell about him. I'm pretty sure she noticed."

"Maybe he should've worn a suit," Thomas said. "Miss Pennington's always so dressy. We don't want her to think he's just a laborer."

"He *is* just a laborer," Daphne said. "What's wrong with that?"

"Yes, but first she should see he's intelligent and all," Thomas said. "Then afterwards she could find out what he does for a living."

"Well, too late now. Anyhow: so I used their first names in the introductions, just like Agatha told me. I said, 'Ian Bedloe, Ariana Pennington. I believe you-all have met before.' "

"It should have been the other way around," Agatha told her. " 'Ariana Pennington, Ian Bedloe.' "

"Oh, big deal, Agatha. So then they shook hands and Miss Pennington asked Ian what she could do for him. They sat down at two desks in the back of the room and I stood next to Ian."

"You were supposed to leave them on their own."

"I couldn't. They sort of, like, included me. Ian said, 'Daphne, here, wanted me to discuss with you . . .' and all like that."

"Well, I don't guess it matters much at this stage," Thomas told Agatha. "They wouldn't right away start making out or anything."

"Miss Pennington wore her blue scoop-necked dress," Daphne said. "We all just wait for that dress. It's got a lacy kind of petticoat showing underneath, either attached or not attached; we never can make up our minds. And usually she pins this heart-shaped locket pin to her front but not this time, and I was glad. We think there may be a boyfriend's photograph inside."

"You mean she might already have somebody?" Thomas asked, frowning.

"Who cares? Now that she's met Ian."

"She liked him, then," Agatha said.

"She had to like him. He was sitting where the sun hit his hair and turned it almost yellow on top, you know how it does. He kept his cap off and he didn't say anything religious, not once. Miss Pennington kept smiling at him and tipping her head while he talked."

"Gosh, this is going better than we'd hoped," Thomas said.

"And when he called her 'Miss Pennington,' she put her hand on his arm and said, 'Please. Ariana.' "

"Gosh."

"She told him I was one of her very best students and she didn't know why I was concerned about my homework, but she appreciated his coming and she just thought it was so refreshing to see a man involve himself in his children's education."

"She did understand we're not *really* his, didn't she?" Agatha asked. "She knows he's not married, doesn't she?"

"She must, because she had my file opened out in front of her. And besides, Ian told her, 'It's not only me who's involved. Both their grandparents used to be teachers, and they help quite a bit, too.' "

"Well, I wish he hadn't of said that. It's *mostly* him, after all."

Thomas said, "No, this way is better. Now she doesn't think she'll be totally saddled with kids when she marries him."

"Everyone in my school is going to die of jealousy," Daphne said. "Boy! I can't wait to see DeeDee Hutchins's face, and that stuck-up Lolly Kaplan."

"So get to the end," Agatha told her. "Did you do like we planned about dinner?"

"I did exactly like we planned. When Ian got up to go he said, 'Well, I really do thank you, Miss Pennington—' "

"Not 'Ariana'?"

" 'Miss Pennington,' he said, and I said, 'Me too, thanks; and Ian, can't we ask her to dinner sometime?' "

"That did it," Thomas said. "No way to back out of that."

"Well, he tried. He said, 'Oh, Daph, Miss Pennington has a very busy schedule,' but she said, 'Please, it's Ariana. And I'd love to come.' "

"Goody," Agatha said.

"Except . . . Ian is so backward."

"Backward?"

"He said, 'To tell the truth, our family's not much for entertaining.' "

The other two groaned.

"But Miss Pennington told him, 'Oh, I wouldn't expect a banquet!' and then she laughed and put her hand on his arm again."

"She's nuts about him," Thomas said.

"Except Ian moved his arm away. In fact every time she did it he moved his arm away."

"He's playing hard to get."

That made Daphne and Agatha look more cheerful. Thomas was the social one, after all. He was almost frantically social; he could skate so deftly through any situation. He was the one who knew how the world worked.

On the night Miss Pennington came to dinner, their grandma fixed roast beef. (The Bedloes confined themselves now to foods that didn't require much preparation: roasts and baked chicken and burgers.) She had trouble holding utensils, and so she let Agatha make the gravy. "Pour in a dab of water," she instructed, "and now a dab more . . ."

Thomas was setting the table, arranging the good silver on the place mats their grandma had already spread around. He came to the kitchen with a fistful of forks and said, "How come you've got nine place mats out?"

"Why, how many should we have?" their grandma asked.

"It's only us and Miss Pennington: seven."

"And also Mr. Kitt and the woman from your church," their grandma said. "That comes to nine."

Mr. Kitt needed no explanation; he was the authentic, certified vagrant who'd been more or less adopted by Second Chance last winter. But the woman? "What woman?" Thomas asked.

"Why, I don't know," their grandma said. "Some new member or visitor or something, I guess. You'll have to ask Ian."

The three of them looked at each other. "Rats," Daphne said.

"I'm sure we'll like her," their grandma told them. "Ian said as long as we were going to all this trouble, we might as well invite her. And we've never had Mr. Kitt once; Ian says you're the only people in church who haven't."

"Yes, but . . . rats," Daphne said. "This was supposed to be just Miss Pennington!"

"Oh, don't worry, we won't neglect your precious teacher," their grandma said merrily.

Last week they'd heard a new neighbor ask their grandma how many children she had. They'd listened for her answer: would she say two, or three? What *did* you say when a son had died? But she fooled them; she said, "Only one that's still at home." As if the people who stuck by you were all that counted, as if anybody not present didn't exist.

She probably thought it was fine for Ian to grow old all alone with his parents.

The first to arrive was Mr. Kitt. Mr. Kitt wasn't really a vagrant anymore. He had a job sweeping floors at Brother Simon's place of business and he lived rent-free above Sister Nell's garage. But people at church still traded him proudly back and forth for meals, and he continued to look the part as if he felt it was expected of him. Gray whiskers a quarter-inch long shadowed his pale face, and his clothes always sagged, oddly empty, even when they were the expensive tailored suits handed down from Sister Nell's father-in-law. On his feet he wore red sneakers, the stubby kind that toddlers wear. These made him walk very quietly, so when he followed Daphne into the living room he seemed awed and hesitant. "Oh, my," he said, peering around, "what a family, family type of house."

"Ian's not home from work yet," Daphne told him. The three children had been asked to make conversation while their grandma changed. Thomas said, "Won't you sit down?"

Mr. Kitt settled soundlessly on the front four inches of an armchair. "Last night I ate at Mrs. Stamey's," he told them. (Sister Myra's, he must mean. He refused to go along with the "Sister" and "Brother" custom.) "She served me a porterhouse steak her husband had cooked on the barbecue."

"We're just having roast beef," Agatha said.

"That's okay."

Their grandpa came down the stairs. In the doorway he stopped and said, "Why, hello there! Doug Bedloe."

"George Kitt," Mr. Kitt told him. He rose by degrees and they shook hands. Of the two men, Mr. Kitt was the more dressed up. Their grandpa wore his corduroys and the wrinkled leather slippers that had no heels. "Can I fix you a drink?" he asked Mr. Kitt.

"No, thank you. Drink has been my ruin."

"Ah," their grandpa said. He studied Mr. Kitt a moment. "You must be the fellow from Ian's church."

"I am."

"Well, my wife will be down any minute now. She's just putting on her face."

He took a seat on the couch next to Agatha. Agatha hadn't dressed up either—Agatha never dressed up—but Thomas and Daphne had taken special care. Thomas's heathery pullover matched the blue pinstripe in his shirt, and Daphne wore her favorite outfit: a purple gauze skirt that hung to her ankles and a man's fringed buckskin jacket. She was twisting the silver hoop in one earlobe, a nervous habit she had. One of her crumpled black boots kept jiggling up and down. "Did you remind Ian to come straight from work?" she asked Agatha.

"I reminded him at breakfast."

"I sure hope Miss Pennington doesn't get here before he does."

"Who's Miss Pennington?" their grandpa asked.

"My *teacher*, Grandpa. We *told* you all this."

"Oh. Right."

"My fifth-grade teacher."

"Right."

"Fifth grade?" Mr. Kitt asked, looking anxious. "I detested fifth grade."

"Well, you won't detest Miss Pennington," Daphne told him.

"Fifth grade was long division," Mr. Kitt said. "I used to erase holes in my paper."

"Miss Pennington's super nice and she lets us bring in comic books on Fridays."

The front door opened. "Here he is!" Daphne cried. But the first to enter the living room was a heavyset young woman in a business suit. Ian followed, carrying his lunch pail. He said, "Sorry if we're late."

We? The children looked at each other.

"This is Sister Harriet," Ian said. "She's new at our church. Harriet, this is my father, Doug Bedloe. You know Mr. Kitt, and I guess you've seen Thomas and Daphne at services. Over there is Agatha."

If Sister Harriet had seen them, they had not seen her; or else they'd forgotten. She was extremely forgettable. Her lank beige hair hung down her back, gathered ineptly by a plastic barrette at the nape of her neck. Her face was broad and plain and colorless, and her suit—a straight jacket and a midcalf-length skirt—was made of some cheap fabric without texture. Also she didn't seem to be wearing stockings. Her calves were blue-white, chalky, and her bulging black suede flats were rubbed smooth at the widest part of her feet.

"Oh, Mr. Bedloe," she said, "I'm so pleased to meet you at last. And Mr. Kitt, it's good to see you again." Then she went over to the children. "Thomas, I sat right behind you in church last Sunday. I'm Sister Harriet."

She held out her hand to each of them in turn—a square, mannish hand, with the fingernails trimmed straight across. There was a moment when the only sounds were shuffles and sheepish murmurs. "Um, how do you . . . nice to . . ." Then their grandma arrived. She was always slow on the stairs, gripping the banister heavily as she descended, but she must have guessed this evening that she was needed; for before she'd even entered the living room she was calling out, "Hello, there! Sorry I took so long!" This time the introductions went the way they were supposed to, with everyone talking at once and little compliments exchanged. "Isn't that a lovely pin!" Grandma told Sister Harriet, picking out the one attractive thing about her, and Sister Harriet said it used to be her great-aunt's. Then the doorbell rang and Ian went to admit Miss Pennington.

Miss Pennington looked just right. She was one of those people who seem to know exactly what to wear for every occasion, and tonight she had not overdressed, as other women might, nor did she make the mistake of shocking them with something excessively informal and off-dutyish. She had on the flowered shirtwaist she had worn all day at school, with a soft flannel blazer added and a double strand of pearls at her throat. The way she moved through the group, greeting everyone so pleasantly, even Mr. Kitt and Sister Harriet, made the children grin at each other. When she came to Daphne, she gave her a little hug. She might as well be family.

The talk before dinner, unfortunately, centered on Sister Harriet. It appeared that Sister Harriet came from a small town near Richmond, and at first she'd found Baltimore a very hard place to make friends in. "The company where I work is as big as my whole town," she said. "At home it was a tiny branch office! Here they have so many employees you just can't hope to get to know them all."

"What company is that?" Miss Pennington asked her.

"Northeastern Life. They handle every type of insurance: not only life but auto, disability—"

"Insurance? But aren't you a nun?"

"Why, no," Sister Harriet said.

Mr. Kitt started laughing. He said, "Ha! That's a good one. Nun! That's a good one."

"It's just what we call each other in church," Sister Harriet told Miss Pennington. "Ian's and my church. We call each other 'Sister' and 'Brother.' But you can say 'Harriet,' if you like."

"Oh, I see," Miss Pennington said.

The three children looked down at their laps. How irksome, that "Ian's and my." As if Ian and Sister Harriet were somehow linked! But Miss Pennington kept her encouraging expression and said, "I imagine church would be an ideal place to make friends."

"It surely is," Sister Harriet told her. And then she had to go on and on about it, how nice and down-home it was, how welcoming, how in some ways it reminded her of the little church she'd grown up in except that there they'd held Prayer Meeting on Tuesdays, not Wednesdays, and they didn't approve of cosmetics and they believed that "gosh" and "darn" were cuss words; but other than that . . .

While Sister Harriet talked, Ian smiled at her. He was sitting on the piano bench with his long, blue-jeaned legs stretched in front of him and his elbows propped on the keyboard lid. One last shaft of sunlight was slanting through the side window, and it struck his face in such a way that the peach fuzz on his cheekbones turned to purest gold. Surely Miss Pennington would have to notice. How could she resist him? He looked dazzling.

At dinner Mr. Kitt offered an account of his entire fifth-grade experience. "I do believe," he said, "that everything that's gone wrong in my life can be directly traced to fifth grade. Before that, I was a roaring success. I had a reputation for smartness. It was me most often who got to clean the erasers or monitor the lunchroom, so much so that it was whispered about by some that I was teacher's pet. Then along comes fifth grade: Miss Pilchner. Lord, I can see her still. Brassy dyed hair curled real tight and short, and this great big squinty fake smile that didn't fool a person under age twenty. First day of school she asks me, 'Where's your ruled paper?' I tell her, 'I like to use unruled.' 'Well!' she says. Says, 'In *my* class, we have no special individuals with their own fancy-shmancy way of doing things.' Right then and there, I knew I'd hit hard times. And I never was a success after that, not then or ever again."

"Oh, Mr. Kitt," Miss Pennington said. "What a pity!"

"Well now, I, on the other hand," their grandpa said from the head of the table, "I was crazy about fifth grade. I had a teacher who looked like a movie star. Looked exactly like Lillian Gish. I planned to marry her."

This was a little too close for comfort; all three children shifted in their chairs. But Miss Pennington merely smiled and turned to Ian. She said, "Ian, I hope *you* have happy memories of fifth grade."

"Hmm? Oh, yes," Ian said without interest. He didn't look up from his plate; he was cutting his meat.

"Did you attend school here in Baltimore?" she asked him.

Her voice was so bendable; it curved toward him, cajoling, entwining. But Ian merely transferred his fork to his right hand, seeming to move farther from her in the process. "Yes," he said shortly, and he took a bite of meat and started chewing. Why was he behaving this way? He was acting like . . . well, like a laborer, in fact.

Finally their grandma spoke up in his place. "Yes, indeedy! He went all twelve years!" she said brightly. "And you know, Miss Pennington—"

"Ariana."

"Ariana, *I* was a teacher, back about a century ago."

"Oh, Ian mentioned that."

"I taught fourth grade in the dark, dark ages."

"Me too," Sister Harriet said suddenly.

Everyone looked at her.

"I taught seventh," she said. "But I wasn't very good at it."

Ian said, "Now, Harriet. I bet you were excellent."

"No," she said. "It's true. I just didn't have the—I don't know. The personality or something."

Well, *that* was for sure. The three children traded amused sidelong glints.

Leaning forward so earnestly that her bolsterlike bosom almost grazed her plate, Sister Harriet said, "Every day I went in was such a struggle, and I had no idea why. Then one night I dreamed this dream. I dreamed I was standing in front of my class explaining conjunctions, but gibberish kept coming out of my mouth. I said, '*Burble*-burble-burble.' The students said, 'Pardon?' I tried again; I said, '*Burble*-burble-burble.' In the dream I couldn't think what had happened, but when I woke up I knew right away. You see, the Lord was trying to tell me something. 'Harriet,' He was saying, 'you don't speak these children's language. You ought to get out of teaching.' And so I did."

"Well, my goodness," their grandma said, sitting back in her chair.

But Ian was regarding Sister Harriet seriously. "I think that was very brave of you," he told her.

She flushed and said, "Oh, well . . ."

"No, really. To admit the whole course of your life was wrong and decide to change it completely."

"That does take courage," Miss Pennington said. "I agree with Ian." And she sent him a radiant smile that he didn't appear to notice.

Was he blind, or what?

This past Easter, one of the foreigners had dropped by with his younger sister who was visiting from her college. She might have stepped out of the *Arabian Nights*; she was dark and slim and beautiful, with a liquid, demure way of speaking. Twice her brother had made pointed references to her eligibility. "High time she find a husband and settle down, get herself a green card, develop some children," he said, and he told them it was up to him to locate a suitable husband for her, since his family still believed in what he called organized marriage. But Ian hadn't seemed to understand, and later when Daphne asked if he'd thought the sister was pretty he said, "Pretty? Who? Oh. No, I've never cared for women who wear seamed stockings."

They should have known right then that no one would ever meet his qualifications.

"Seconds, anyone?" their grandpa was asking. "Mr. Kitt? Miss Pennington? Ian, more roast beef?"

"I wonder," Ian said, "how many times we dream that kind of dream—something strange and illogical—and fail to realize God is trying to tell us something."

Oh, perfect. Now he was turning all holy on them. "Ariana," their grandma said hastily, "help yourself to the gravy." But Miss Pennington was watching Ian, and her smile was glazing over the way people's always did when the bald, uncomfortable sound of God's name was uttered in social surroundings.

"It's easier to claim it's something else," Ian said. "Our subconscious, or random brain waves. It's easier to pretend we don't know what God's showing us."

"That is so, so true," Sister Harriet told him.

Miss Pennington's smile seemed made of steel now.

"Damn," Daphne said.

Everybody looked at her. Their grandma said, "Daphne?"

"Well, excuse me," Daphne said, "but I just can't—" And then she sat up straighter and said, "I just can't help thinking about this dream I had a couple of nights ago."

"Oh, tell us," their grandma said, sounding relieved.

"I was standing on a mountaintop," Daphne said. "God was speaking to me from a thundercloud." She looked around at the others—their polite, attentive faces, all prepared to appreciate whatever she had to say. " 'Daphne,' He said—He had this big, deep, rumbling voice. 'Daphne Bedloe, beware of strangers!' "

"And quite right He was, too," their grandma said briskly, but she seemed less interested now in hearing the rest of it. "Doug, could you send the salad bowl this way?"

" 'Daphne Bedloe, a stranger is going to start hanging around your uncle,' " Daphne bellowed. " 'Somebody fat, not from Baltimore, chasing after your uncle Ian.' "

"Why, *Daphne*!" their grandma said, and she dropped a clump of lettuce on the tablecloth.

Later, Daphne argued that their grandma was the one who'd hurt Sister Harriet's feelings. After all, what had Daphne said that was so terrible? Nothing. She had merely described a dream. It was their grandma who had connected the dream to Sister Harriet. All aghast she'd turned to Sister Harriet and said, "I'm so sorry. I can't imagine what's got into her." Then Sister Harriet, white-lipped, said, "That's okay," and sipped shakily from her water glass, not looking at the others. But she wouldn't have taken it personally if their grandma had not apologized, Daphne said; and Thomas and Agatha agreed. "She's right," Agatha told Ian. "It's not *Daphne's* fault if someone fat was in her dream."

This was after their guests had departed. They had left at the earliest acceptable moment—Miss Pennington reflective, Mr. Kitt bluff and unaware, Sister Harriet declining with surprising firmness Ian's offer to walk her home. As soon as they were gone, the grandparents had turned and climbed the stairs to their bedroom.

"Daphne was only making conversation," Thomas told Ian, but Ian said, "Yeah, sure," in a toneless voice, and then he went into the dining room and started clearing the table.

They followed, humble and overeager. They stacked plates and took them to the kitchen, scraped leftovers into smaller containers, collected pots and pans from the stove while Ian ran a sinkful of hot water. He didn't say a word to them; he seemed to know that all three of them were to blame and not just Daphne.

They couldn't bear it when Ian was mad at them.

And worse than mad: dejected. All his fine plans come to nothing. Oh, what had they done? He looked so forlorn. He stood at the sink so wearily, swabbing the gravy tureen.

Last month he'd brought home a saltcellar shaped like a robot. When you pressed a button in its back it would start walking on two rigid plastic legs, but they hadn't realized that and they hadn't paid it much attention, frankly, when he set it among the supper dishes. He kept asking, "Doesn't anyone need salt? Who wants salt? Shall I just pass the salt?" Finally Agatha said, "Huh? Oh, fine," and he pressed the robot's button and leaned forward, chortling, as it toddled across the table to her. His mouth was perked with glee and his hands were clasped together underneath his chin and he kept darting hopeful glances into their faces, and luckily they'd noticed in time and put on amazed and delighted expressions.

"Dust off the fruitcake, it's Christmas again," he always caroled in December, inventing his own tune as he went along, and on Valentine's Day he left a chocolate heart on each child's breakfast plate before he went off to work, which tended to make them feel a little sad because really all of them—even Daphne—had reached the stage where nonfamily valentines were the only ones that mattered. In fact there were lots of occasions when they felt sad for him. He seemed slightly out of step, so often—his jokes just missing, his churchy language setting strangers' eyes on guard, his clothes inappropriately boyish and plain as if he'd been caught in a time warp. The children loved him and winced for him, both. They kept a weather eye out for other people's reactions to him, and they were constantly prepared to bristle and turn ferocious on his behalf.

One vacation when they were little he took a swim in the ocean and told them to wait on the shore. He swam out beyond the breakers, so far he was only a dot, and the three of them sat down very suddenly on the sand and Daphne started crying. He was leaving them forever and never coming back, it looked like. A man standing ankle-deep told his wife, "That fellow's *gone*," and Daphne cried harder and the other two grew teary as well. But then Ian turned and swam in again. Soon he was striding out of the surf hitching up his trunks and streaming water and shining in the sun, safely theirs after all, solid and reliable and dear.

He lowered a serving bowl into the sink. He swished it back and forth.

Daphne said, "Ian? Want for us to take over now?" but he said, "No, thanks." The others sent her sympathetic looks. Never mind. He wasn't the type to carry a grudge. Tomorrow he would view this in a whole new light; he would realize they hadn't meant to cause any harm.

All they had wanted, he would see, was somebody wonderful enough to deserve him.

8

I Should Never Tell You Anything

When Reverend Emmett had his heart attack, the Church of the Second Chance was forced to manage without him for most of the month of October. The first Sunday a retired Baptist minister, Dr. Benning, gave the sermon, but Dr. Benning had to leave immediately afterward for a bus tour of the Sun Belt and so the second Sunday Sister Nell's uncle filled in—a nondenominationalist named Reverend Lewis who kept mixing up his "Thy" and his "Thou." "We beseech Thee to flood Thou blessings upon this Thou congregation," he intoned, and Ian was reminded of the substitute teachers he'd had in grade school who had always seemed just the slightest bit lacking. The sermon was based on Paul's first letter to Timothy. Many might not realize, Reverend Lewis said, that it was *love* of money, and not money alone, that was held to be the root of all evil. Ian, who had never had much money or much love of money either, held back a yawn. *All* evil? Wasn't that the phrase to examine?

On the third Sunday not even Reverend Lewis was available and they skipped the sermon altogether. They sang a few hymns and then bowed their heads for a closing prayer delivered in an uncertain voice by Brother Simon. "Dear God," Brother Simon said, "please give Reverend Emmett back to us as soon as possible." The fourth Sunday Reverend Emmett returned, gaunter and paler than ever, and preached a message of reassurance. Afterward, while shaking Ian's hand at the door, he asked if they might have a little talk.

So Ian sent Daphne on home without him and waited at one side, listening to each member inquire after Reverend Emmett's health. When the last of the congregation had departed he followed Reverend Emmett through the door behind the counter, into what passed for an office. Tangled pipes ran overhead and giant bolt holes marred the floor. In the center of the room stood an antique desk and swivel chair that must have come down from Reverend Emmett's family, with two blue velvet armchairs facing them. Reverend Emmett gestured Ian into one armchair but he himself remained on his feet, distractedly running a hand through his hair. As usual, he wore a white shirt without a tie and skinny black trousers. Ian guessed he must be in his mid-forties by now or maybe even older, but he still had that awkward, amateurish air about him, and his Adam's apple jutted above his collar like a half-grown boy's.

"Brother Ian," he said, "while I was in the hospital I did some serious thinking. It's unusual to have a heart attack at my age. It doesn't bode well for the future. I've been thinking I should face the fact that I'm not going to live forever."

Ian opened his mouth to protest, but Reverend Emmett raised a palm. "Oh," he said, "I don't plan on dying tomorrow or anything like that. Still, this kind of thing makes you realize. It's time we discussed my replacement."

"Replacement?" Ian asked.

"Someone who'll take over the church when I'm gone. Someone who might help out before I'm gone, even. Ease my workload."

Ian said, "But—"

But you ARE the church, he wanted to say. Only that sounded blasphemous, and would have distressed Reverend Emmett.

"I believe you ought to start training for the ministry," Reverend Emmett told him.

Ian wondered if he'd heard right.

"You know our congregation is fairly uneducated, by and large," Reverend Emmett said, finally sitting in the other armchair. "I think most of them would feel the job was beyond them. And yet we do want someone who's familiar with our ways."

"But I'm not educated either," Ian said. "I've had one semester of college."

"Well, the good thing about this heart attack is, it serves as advance warning. It gives us a chance to get you trained. I realize you might not want to follow my own route—university and such. I was younger and had more time. You're what, thirty-four? Still, Lawrence Bible School, down in Richmond—"

"Richmond! I can't go to Richmond!"

"Why not?"

"I have responsibilities here!"

"But surely those are just about finished now, aren't they?" Reverend Emmett asked. "Shouldn't you be thinking ahead now?"

Ian sat forward, clamping his knees. "Reverend Emmett," he said, "Daphne at sixteen is more trouble than all three of them were at any other age. Do you know her principal has me picking her up at school every day? I have to take off work and pick her up and drive her home in person. And it has to be me, not my father, because it turns out my father believes anything she tells him. Both my parents: they're so far behind the times, they just don't fully comprehend what modern kids can get into. You honestly suppose I could leave her with them and head off to Richmond?"

Reverend Emmett waited till Ian had wound down. Then he said, "What grade is Daphne in in school?"

"She's a junior."

"So two more years," Reverend Emmett said. "Maybe less, if she straightens out before she graduates. And I'm certain that she will straighten out. Daphne's always been a strong person. But even if she doesn't, in two years she'll be on her own. Meanwhile, you can start with a few courses here in Baltimore. Night school. Towson State, or maybe community college."

Ian said, "But also . . ."

"Yes?"

"I mean, shouldn't I hear a *call* to the ministry?"

Reverend Emmett said, "Maybe I'm the call."

Ian blinked.

"And maybe not, of course," Reverend Emmett told him. "But it's always a possibility."

Then he rose and once again shook Ian's hand, with those long, dry fingers so bony they fairly rattled.

When Ian arrived home, Daphne was talking on the kitchen telephone and her grandmother was setting various dishes on the table. Sunday dinner would apparently be leftovers—tiny bowls of cold peas, soggy salad, and reheated stew from a tin. "Cool," Daphne was saying. "We can get together later and study for that Spanish test." Something artificial and showy in her tone made Ian flick a glance at Bee, but Bee missed his point and merely said, "Well? How was church?"

"It was all right."

"Could you tell your father lunch is on?"

He called down to the basement and then beckoned Daphne from the phone. "I gotta go now," she said into the receiver. "My folks are starting brunch."

"Oh, is this brunch?" Ian asked his mother.

She smiled and set a loaf of bread on the table.

Once they were seated Ian said the blessing hurriedly, conscious of his father drumming his fingers on his knees. Then each of them embarked on a different meal. Doug reached for the stew, Ian put together a peanut butter sandwich, and Daphne, who was a vegetarian, dreamily plucked peas from the bowl one by one with her fingers. Bee finished anything the others wouldn't—more a matter of housekeeping than personal taste, Ian thought.

He missed the two older children. Thomas was away at Cornell and Agatha was in her second year of medical school. Most meals now were just this makeshift, often served on only half the table because Daphne's homework covered the other half. And most of their conversations felt disjointed, absentminded, like the scattered bits of talk after the main guests have left the room.

"Me and Gideon are going to study Spanish at his house," Daphne announced into one stretch of silence.

"Gideon and I," her grandmother said.

Ian asked, "Will Gideon's mother be home?"

"Sure."

Ian scrutinized her. Gideon was Daphne's boyfriend, an aloof, chilly type. Evidently his mother, a divorcée, had a boyfriend of her own. She was often out somewhere when Ian stopped by for Daphne.

"Maybe you could study here instead," he told her.

But Daphne said, "I already promised I'd go there." Then she picked up her empty bowl and licked it daintily, like a cat. Everyone noticed but no one objected. You had to select your issues, with someone like Daphne.

It unsettled Ian, sometimes, how much Daphne reminded him of Lucy. She had Lucy's small face and her curly black hair, although it was cut short and ragged. She had her froggy voice. Even in voluminous army fatigues, her slender, fine bones seemed so neatly turned that they might have been produced by a lathe. Her eyes were her own, though: still a dense, navy blue. And her own native scent of vanilla underlay the smells of cigarettes and motor oil and leather.

At the end of the meal Ian's father rose and brought a bowl of instant pudding from the refrigerator. He wiggled it at the others inquiringly, but Bee said, "No, thanks," and Daphne shook her head. "All the more for me, then," Doug said cheerfully, and he sat down and started eating directly from the bowl.

Was it because of the Sugar Rule that Daphne had declined? No, probably not. This was a girl who drank beer in parked cars during lunch hour, according to her principal. But she did continue to go to church every Sunday, singing the hymns lustily and bowing her head during prayers, when most other young people lost interest as soon as they reached their teens. And she flung herself into Good Works with real spirit. Whether she was actually a believer, though, Ian couldn't decide, and something kept him from asking.

There was a knock at the kitchen door, a single, surly thud, and they looked over to find Gideon surveying them through the windowpanes. "Oops! I'm off," Daphne said. No question of inviting Gideon in; he didn't talk to grownups. All they saw of him was the tilt of his sharp face and the curtain of straight blond hair, and then Daphne spun through the door and the two of them were gone. "Daph? Oh, goodness, she'll freeze to death," Bee said.

Ian wished Daphne's freezing to death were the worst he had to worry about.

Doug and Bee went upstairs for their Sunday nap and Ian did the dishes. Scraping the last of the pudding into a smaller container, he thought again about Reverend Emmett's proposal. Bible School! He had a flash of himself packing the car to leave home—participating in the September ritual that he had watched so often from the sidelines. The car stuffed to the ceiling with clothes and LP records, his parents standing by to wave him off. Maybe even a roof rack, with a bike or a stereo lashed on top. Or a butterfly chair like his former roommate's. Provided they still made butterfly chairs.

Over the years he had often wondered whatever had become of his roommate. He had imagined Winston proceeding through school and graduating and finding a job. By now he would be well established, probably in some field involving creative thought and invention. He had probably made a name for himself.

Ian glanced down at the pudding bowl and realized he had been eating each spoonful as he scraped it up. The inside of his mouth felt thick and coated. An unfamiliar sweetness clogged his throat.

At work he was training a new employee, a stocky, bearded black man named Rafael. He was giving his usual speech about the importance of choosing your wood. "Me, I always go for cherry if I can," he said. "It's the friendliest, you could put it. The most obedient."

"Cherry," the man said, nodding.

"It's very nearly *alive*. It changes color over time and it even changes shape and it breathes."

Rafael suddenly squinted at him, as if checking on his sanity.

The shop had seven employees now, not counting the high-school girl who came in afternoons to type and do the paperwork. (And they probably *shouldn't* count her; sometimes her order sheets were so garbled that Ian had to sit down at the typewriter and place his fingers wrongly on the keys so as to figure out what, for instance, she'd meant by "nitrsi.") All around the room various carpenters worked on their separate projects. They murmured companionably among themselves but left Ian alone mostly. He knew they considered him peculiar. A couple of years ago he had made the mistake of trying to talk about Second Chance with Greg, who happened to be going through some troubles. Forever after that Greg kept his distance and so did all the others, apparently tipped off. They were polite but embarrassed, wary. As for Mr. Brant, he was even less company than usual these days. It was said that his wife had left him for a younger man. The one who said it was Mrs. Brant's niece Jeannie, who didn't work there anymore but sometimes dropped by to visit. Mr. Brant himself never mentioned his wife.

Last spring, Mrs. Brant had paused to admire a bench Ian was sanding and she had softly but deliberately laid a hand on top of his. Her husband was in his rear office and the others were taking a break. Mrs. Brant had looked up into Ian's eyes with an oddly cool expression, as if this were some kind of test. Ian wasn't completely surprised (several times, women who knew his religious convictions had started behaving very forwardly, evidently finding him a challenge), and he dealt with it fairly well, he thought. He had merely slid his hand out from under and left her with the sandpaper, pretending he'd mistaken her move for an offer to help. And of course he had said nothing to her husband. But not two months later Jeannie announced that she was gone, and then Ian thought maybe he should have said something after all. "Mr. Brant," he should have said, "it seems to me your wife is acting lonely." Or, "Wouldn't you and Mrs. Brant like to take a trip together or something?"

But *telling* was what he had promised himself he would never do again.

Oh, there were so many different ways you could go wrong. No wonder he loved woodwork! He showed Rafael the cherrywood nightstand he had finished the day before. The drawer glided smoothly, like satin, without a single hitch.

While the other men took their afternoon break, Ian grabbed his jacket and drove off to fetch Daphne from school. He could manage the round trip in just over twenty minutes when everything went on schedule, but of course it seldom did. Today, for instance, he must have left the shop too early. When he parked in front of the school he found he had several minutes to kill, and even longer if Daphne, as usual, came out late or had to run back in for something she'd forgotten. So he cut the engine and stepped from the car. The air was warm and heavy and windy, as if an autumn storm might be brewing. Behind him, another car pulled up. A freckled woman in slacks got out and said, "What, we're early?"

"So it seems," Ian said. Then, because he felt foolish just standing around with her, he put his hands in his pockets and ambled toward the building. Scudding clouds glared off the second-floor windows—the art-room windows, Ian recalled, and Miss Dunlap's world-history windows, although Miss Dunlap must have retired or even died by now. Two boys in track suits jogged toward him on the sidewalk, separated around him, and jogged on. He wondered if they guessed what he was doing here. ("That's Daphne Bedloe's uncle; she's on suspended suspension and has to go home under guard.") It occurred to him that Daphne would be mortified if anyone she knew caught sight of him. He circled the school, therefore, and kept going. He passed the little snack shop where he and Cicely used to sit all afternoon over a couple of cherry Cokes, and he came to the Methodist church with its stained-glass window full of stern, narrow angels. One of the church's double doors stood open. Almost without thinking, he climbed the steps and went inside.

No lights were lit, but his eyes adjusted quickly to the gloom. He made out rows of cushioned pews and a carved wooden pulpit up front, with another stained-glass window high in the wall behind it. This one showed Jesus in a white robe, barefoot, holding His hands palm forward at His sides and gazing down at Ian kindly. Ian slid into a pew and rested his elbows on the pew ahead of him. He looked up into Jesus' face. He said, *Would it be possible for me to have some kind of sign?*

Nothing fancy. Just something more definite than Reverend Emmett offering a suggestion.

He waited. He let the silence swell and grow.

But then the school bell rang—an extended jangle that reminded him of those key chains made from tiny metal balls—and his concentration was broken. He sighed and stood up. Anyhow, he had probably been presumptuous to ask.

In the doorway, looking out, he saw the first of the school crowd passing. He saw Gideon with a redheaded girl, his arm slung carelessly around her neck so they kept bumping into each other as they walked.

Gideon?

There was no mistaking that veil of blond hair, though, or the hunched, skulking posture. Almost as if this were Ian's love, not Daphne's, he felt his heart stop. He saw the redhead crane upward for a kiss and he drew his breath in sharply and stepped back into the shadow of the door.

By the time he reached the car, Daphne was waiting in the front seat. The car's interior smelled of breath mints and tobacco. "Where've you *been*?" she squawked as he got in, and he said, "Oh, around." He started the engine and pulled into the crawl of after-school traffic. "No Gideon?" he asked.

"It's his day to go to his dad's."

"Oh."

Daphne slid down in her seat and planted both feet on the dashboard. It appeared she was wearing combat boots—the most battered and scuffed he had ever laid eyes on. He hadn't realized they came that small. Her olive-drab trousers seemed intended for combat too, but the blouse beneath her leather jacket was fragile white gauze with two clusters of silver bells hanging from the ends of the drawstring. Any time she moved, she gave off a faint tinkling sound and the grudging creak of leather. How was it that such an absurd little person managed to touch him so?

He thought of Gideon's blond head next to the coppery, gleaming head of the girl in the crook of his arm.

Daphne, he should say, *there's something I have to tell you.*

But he couldn't.

He pulled up in front of their house and waited for her to get out, staring blankly through the windshield. To his surprise, he felt a kiss on his cheekbone as light as a petal. "Bye," she said, and she slipped away and shut the car door behind her. He could almost believe she knew what he had spared her.

• • •

One day last summer, while sitting with Honeybunch in the veterinarian's waiting room, Ian had noticed a particularly sweet-faced golden retriever. "Nice dog," he had told the owner, and the owner—a middle-aged woman—had smiled and said, "Yes, I've had a good number in my day, but this one: this is the dog of my life. You know how that is?"

He knew, all right.

Daphne, he felt, was the *child* of his life. He wondered if he would ever love a daughter of his own quite so completely.

It was true the older two were easier. In a sense, he even liked them better. Thomas was so merry and winsome, and Agatha had somehow smoothed the corners off that disconcerting style of hers—the bluntness transformed into calm assurance, the aggressive homeliness into an intriguing, black-and-white handsomeness. He enjoyed them the way he would enjoy longtime best friends who found the same things funny or upsetting and didn't need every last remark explained for them. In fact, you could say they were his *only* friends. But Daphne was the one who tugged at him most deeply.

And Daphne had always relied on him so, had taken it for granted that he would stand by her no matter what. He still had an acute physical memory of the weight of her infant head resting in the cup of his palm. Even now, sometimes, she would lean against him while they watched TV and artlessly confide her secrets and gossip about her classmates and recount her hair-raising adventures that he had had no inkling of, thank heaven, while she was undergoing them. (She knew the city inside out, and slipped without a thought through neighborhoods that Ian himself avoided.) But if he showed any concern she would say, "I knew I shouldn't have told you! I should never tell you anything!" And when her friends came over she grew visibly remote from him, referring to him as "my uncle" as if he had no name and rolling her eyes when her girlfriends tried to make small talk or (on occasion) flirt with him. When he said he was off to Prayer Meeting, she told her friends he was "speaking metaphorically." When he enforced her curfew, she announced she was running away to live with her mother's people, who—she claimed—were worldly-wise and cosmopolitan and wouldn't *think* of making her return to their mansion at the dot of any set time. Ian had laughed, and then felt a deep, sad ache.

That was what Daphne brought out in him, generally. Laughter and an ache.

Reverend Emmett invited him to supper. "Just the two of us," he said on the phone, "to talk about the matter of your vocation." Ian gulped, but of course he accepted.

Reverend Emmett warned him that he wasn't much of a cook (his mother had died the previous fall) and so Ian asked if he could bring something. "Well," Reverend Emmett said, "you know that cold white sauce that people serve with potato chips?"

"Sauce? You mean dip?"

"It has little bits of dried onion scattered through it."

"You mean onion soup dip?"

"That must be it," Reverend Emmett said. "Mother used to make it whenever we had guests, but I haven't been able to find her recipe. I thought maybe you could ask *your* mother if she might fix it for us."

"Shoot, I'll fix it myself," Ian said. "I'll bring over the ingredients and show you how it's done."

"I'd appreciate that," Reverend Emmett told him.

So Tuesday evening, when Ian rang the doorbell, he was carrying a pint of sour cream and an envelope of the only brand of onion soup mix on the market that didn't contain any sugar. He had washed up after work but (mindful of the sin of superficiality) kept on his everyday clothes, and Reverend Emmett answered the door in jeans and one of his incongruously jaunty polo shirts. "Come in!" he said.

Ian said, "Thanks."

To tell the truth, he felt a bit apprehensive. He worried that Reverend Emmett labored under some false impression of him, for how else to explain his plans for Ian's future?

The living room was small but formal, slightly fussy—the mother's doing, Ian guessed. He had seen it on several occasions but had never gone beyond it, and now he looked about him curiously as he followed Reverend Emmett through a dim, flowered dining room to a kitchen that seemed to have been turned on end and shaken. "I thought I would make us a roast of beef," Reverend Emmett told him, and Ian said, "Sounds good." He wondered how a roast could have required all these pans and utensils. Maybe they'd been used for some side dish. "Would you like an apron to work in?" Reverend Emmett asked.

"It's not that complicated," Ian said. "Just a mixing bowl and a spoon will do."

He emptied the sour cream into the bowl Reverend Emmett brought him and then stirred in the soup mix, with Reverend Emmett hovering over the whole operation. "Why, there's really nothing to it," he said at the end.

"A veritable snap," Ian told him.

"Would you mind very much if we ate this in the kitchen? I'll need to keep an eye on the roast."

"That's fine with me."

They pulled two stools up to the counter, which was puddled with several different colors of liquids, and started on the chips and dip. Reverend Emmett gobbled chips wolfishly, a vein standing out in his temple as he chewed. (Had his doctor not warned him off fats?) He told Ian to call him Emmett. "Oh. All right . . . Emmett," Ian said. But he could force the name out only by imagining a "Reverend" in the gap, and he thought, from the way Reverend Emmett paused at each "Ian," that he was mentally inserting a "Brother."

"The fact is, um . . . Ian, hardly anyone I know calls me just plain Emmett anymore," Reverend Emmett said. "The fact is, this is a lonely profession. Oh, but not for *you*, it wouldn't be. You would be training among our own kind from the start. You would be making your friendships among them, and whoever you marry will know she shouldn't expect a half-timbered rectory and white-glove teas."

"But . . . Emmett," Ian said, "how can I be certain I'm cut out for this? I'm nothing but a carpenter."

"Our Lord was a carpenter," Reverend Emmett reminded him. He rose and went to peer inside the oven.

"Maybe so," Ian said, "but that might have been made a little too much of."

"Excuse me?"

"Well, we don't seem to hear about anything He built, do we? I wish we did. Sometimes when I look at paintings of Him I try to see what kind of muscles He had—whether they're the kind that come from hammering and sawing. I like to think He really did put a few bits of wood together; He didn't just stand around discussing theology with His friends while Joseph built the furniture."

Reverend Emmett set the roast on the counter and cocked his head at him thoughtfully.

"Or camel barns, or whatever it was," Ian said. "I hope I don't sound disrespectful."

"No, no . . . Could you bring in that salad, please?"

"But anyhow," Ian said. He picked up the salad bowl and followed Reverend Emmett into the dining room. "I'm getting off the track here. What I'm trying to say is, I'm not sure someone like me would be able to give people answers. When they had doubts and serious problems and such. All those ups and downs people go through, those little *hells* they go through—I wouldn't know what to tell them."

"But that's what Bible School teaches," Reverend Emmett said.

"It's not enough," Ian said.

They had both taken their seats now at the lace-covered table. Reverend Emmett was brandishing a bone-handled carving set. He paused and looked at Ian.

"I mean," Ian said, "*maybe* it's not enough."

"Well, of course it is," Reverend Emmett told him. "How do you suppose *I* learned? No one is born knowing."

He started slicing the roast. Plainly it was overdone—a charred black knob glued fast to the pan it had been cooked in. "When I began seminary," he said, sawing away manfully, "I had every possible misconception. I thought I was entering upon a career that was stable and comfortable, my father's career—a family business like any other. I envisioned how Father and I would sit together in his study over sherry and ponder obscure interpretations of the New Testament. Finally he would think well of me; he would listen to my opinions. But it didn't happen that way. What happened was I started reading the Bible, really reading it, and by the time I'd finished, my father wasn't speaking to me and my fiancée had left me and all my classmates thought I was some kind of mental case."

He laid down his knife. "Oh, dear," he said, "*that's* not the point I was trying to make."

Ian laughed. Reverend Emmett glanced at him in surprise, and then he laughed too.

"Also, this meat is inedible, isn't it?" he said. "Let's face it, I'm a terrible cook."

"We could always fill up on salad," Ian told him.

"We could, but you know what I'd really like? I'd like to polish off that dip, your onion dip. That was excellent!"

"Let's do it, then," Ian said.

So while he helped himself to the salad, Reverend Emmett went out to the kitchen for the chips and dip. "No," he said, returning, "that wasn't my point at all, believe me. No, my point was . . . well, the ministry is like anything else: a matter of trial and error. I've made so many errors! In the hospital it seemed they all came back to me. I lay on that bed and looked at the ceiling and all my errors came scrolling across those dotted soundproof panels."

"*I've* never seen you make an error."

"Oh, Ian," Reverend Emmett said, shaking his head. He noticed a blob of dip on his finger and reached for a linen napkin. "When I was starting out, my church was going to be perfect," he said. "I figured I was setting up the ideal doctrine. But now I see how inconsistent it is, how riddled with holes and contradictions. What do I care if someone drinks a cup of coffee? Wouldn't I have done better to ban TV? And here's the worst, Ian: the thought of doing that did cross my mind, back in the beginning. But then I said, no, no. And never admitted the reason, which was: how would I get any members, if I didn't let them watch TV?"

Ian didn't know what to say to that. He supposed it would have been nearly impossible to get members, come to think of it.

"And then there's tithing," Reverend Emmett said. "Who am I to tell them they have to give a tenth of their income? Some of those people are dirt poor. Not a one of them is wealthy. Now I see that's why I dispensed with the ritual of collection. I said, 'Slip your envelopes through the mail slot, no return address,' because secretly I hoped they *wouldn't* tithe, even when the heating bill had to come out of my own pocket; and I didn't want to have to deal with it if they didn't. I preferred to be looking the other way. There's so much I've looked away from! I see everyone has made Second Chance his own, adapted it to suit his own purposes, changed the rules to whatever is more convenient, and I pretend not to notice. I know Brother Kenneth smokes! I can smell it on his clothes, although I never say so. I know Daphne smokes too, and also drinks beer, and Sister Jessie has never given up her evening cocktail, not even the day she joined the church, which rumor has it she celebrated with a split of champagne after services. But I've never so much as mentioned it, because the awful truth is I find I don't mind. I find as I get older that it all seems just sort of . . . endearing, really: this little flock of human beings who came to me first to atone for some sin, most of them, and then relaxed and settled in and entirely forgot about atonement. How long since you've seen someone stand up at Public Amending? And Christmas! Three-quarters of the congregation marks Christmas with trees and Santa Claus, don't you think I know that?"

Ian stirred guiltily.

"But the silliest," Reverend Emmett said, "is the Sugar Rule."

"Oh, well . . ." Ian said.

It wasn't as if this subject hadn't come up before, here and there.

"I knew almost from the start I'd made a mistake on that one. I just didn't know how to get out of it. And truthfully, I never felt sure that I wasn't merely rationalizing, once I'd seen how hard the rule was to follow. But in the hospital I was reading this book Sister Nell brought me. This nutrition book. I was trying to learn how to eat more healthily. Although," he said, waving a hand toward the potato chips, "I may not always act on what I've learned. Well, I came upon a discussion of sugar, and do you know what? It's not a stimulant."

"It's not?"

"It's a tranquilizer."

"It can't be," Ian said.

"It's a tranquilizer. Oh, it gives you energy, all right. *Physical* energy. But as far as the mental effect: it lulls you."

"Well, uh . . ."

"Want to know what *is* a stimulant?"

"What?"

"Milk."

Ian thought about that. He started grinning.

"See?" Reverend Emmett said. He was grinning too. "How could you give answers any more wrong than mine have been, Ian? Why, you could be a better minister with one hand tied behind you!"

"No one could be a better minister," Ian said.

He meant it with all his heart. Reverend Emmett must have realized that, because he sobered and said, "Well, thank you."

"But I'll think about Bible School, um, Emmett."

"Wonderful," Reverend Emmett said. Then he reached for another potato chip. His eyes seemed no longer brown but amber. "Oh," he said, "it would be so wonderful to have somebody working at my side and calling me Emmett!"

And he popped the entire chip into his mouth and chomped down happily.

• • •

Bert was telling the new man, Rafael, how Mr. Brant had discovered his wife had left him. "First he claims she's kidnapped," Bert said. "He shows Jeannie the closet: 'See? All her clothes still hanging here. She can't have left on purpose.' 'Uncle,' Jeannie goes. She goes, 'These clothes are her very least favorites. Where's her silk blouse with the poppies on it? Where's her turquoise skirt? These are just the extras,' she goes."

Rafael tut-tutted. He said, "Womens always got so many emergency backups."

"Tell about the neighbor," Greg said, nudging Bert in the ribs.

"Jeannie goes, 'Uncle, your neighbor Mr. Hoffberg is missing too. His wife is just about frantic.' Know what he says? Says, 'Why!' Says, 'Why, it's a *rash* of kidnaps!' "

The three men chuckled. Ian frowned at the bureau he was working on. He should have given Mr. Brant some warning. He wished he had it to do over again.

Unexpectedly, Gideon and the redhead strolled through his memory. Framed by the church's doorway, they kissed, and Ian all at once straightened.

What if that was the sign he had prayed for inside the church?

But if it was, he had no idea what it meant.

The others went for their break and Ian drove off to pick up Daphne. It was a crisp, glittery day, and the leaves were at their brightest. He found the ride so pleasant that when he reached the school, it took him a moment to notice the place was deserted. Not a single car sat out front; not a single student loitered on the grounds. He got out of the car and went to try the main entrance, but it was locked. A janitor pushing a broom down the hall saw him through the glass and came over to open the door. "School's closed," he told Ian. "There's a teachers' meeting. Kids got out at noon."

"Oh. Great," Ian said. "Thanks."

He walked around to the phone booth at one side of the building and called home. "Mom?" he said. "Is Daphne there?"

"Why, no, I thought she was at school."

"They got out at noon today."

"Well, you might try calling the Locklear girl," she said. "Shall I look up her telephone number?"

"Never mind," Ian said.

He wondered how his mother could stay so naive. She must work at it. She still thought the biggest issue confronting a teenaged girl was whether or not to kiss on the first date, and the answer (he'd heard her tell Daphne) was no, no, no. "You have years and years to do all that. You don't want them saying you're cheap."

He drove to Gideon's—a sagging, unpainted house on Greenmount—and parked sloppily and crossed the porch in two strides and rang the doorbell. No one answered, but he sensed a sudden freezing of movement somewhere inside the house. He opened the screen and knocked on the inner door. Shading his eyes, he peered through the windowpane. He saw a threadbare rug, part of a banister, and then Gideon lumbering down the stairs, tucking his shirt into his jeans. For a moment they faced each other through the glass. Gideon yawned. He opened the door and stuck his head out.

"I'd like to speak to Daphne," Ian told him.

Gideon considered. "Okay," he said finally.

He had a burnt, ashy smell, as if his skin were smoldering. And although his shirt was more or less tucked in now, it wasn't buttoned. A slice of his bare chest showed through. "Daph!" he called. "Your uncle's here." He went on facing Ian. Up close, his hair was brittle as broom straw. The color must come from a bottle.

"Ian?" Daphne said. She came clomping down the stairs in her combat boots. Her face looked puckered, the way it did when she first woke up, and her eyes were slits. "What are *you* doing here?" she asked, arriving next to Gideon.

"I might ask you the same," Ian told her.

"We had a half day. I forgot to mention."

"Did you also forget the way home?"

She adjusted an earring.

"Let's go," Ian told her. "I'm running late."

"Can Gideon come?"

"Not this time."

She didn't argue. She tossed Gideon a look, and Gideon gazed back at her expressionlessly. Then she unhooked her leather jacket from the newel post. She shrugged herself into it, slung her knapsack over her shoulder, and followed Ian out to the car.

When they'd been driving a while she said, "You didn't have to be rude to him."

"I wasn't rude. I just want to talk to you alone."

She clutched her knapsack to her chest. Now that she sat so close, he realized she too had that burnt smell. And her lips were swollen and blurry, and a red splotch stretched from her throat to the neckline of her Black Sabbath T-shirt.

"Daph," he said.

She hugged her knapsack tighter.

"Daphne, some things are not what they seem," he said.

"Watch out for that car," she told him.

"I mean some *people* aren't what they seem. People you imagine you'll be with forever, say—"

"That car's edging over the line, Ian."

She meant the dark green Plymouth that was wavering a bit in the right-hand lane just ahead. "No doubt some teenager," Ian grumbled.

"Prejudice, prejudice!" Daphne scolded him. "Nope, it's an old man. See how low his head is? Some white-haired old man just barely peeking over the steering wheel and hanging on for dear life."

Ian said, "What I'm trying to tell you—"

"He's showing off for his girlfriend."

"Girlfriend!"

"See the lady next to him? Probably this hot-and-heavy pickup from the Senior Citizens' Center. He's showing her how in-charge he is, and reliable and steady."

Ian snorted. He applied his brakes and fell behind, allowing the Plymouth more room.

"You think I don't know what I'm up to, don't you," Daphne said.

"Pardon?"

"You think I'm some ninny who wants to do right but keeps goofing. But what you don't see is, I goof on purpose. I'm not like you: King Careful. Mr. Look-Both-Ways. Saint Maybe."

"*Now* look," Ian said. "The Plymouth is slowing down too. Seems he's set on staying with us."

"Mess up, I say!" Daphne crowed. "Fall flat on your face! Make every mistake you can think of! Use all the life you've got!"

Ian glanced over at her, but he didn't speak.

"Let's pass," Daphne told him.

"Pass?"

"Speed up and pass. This driver's a turkey."

He obeyed. He whizzed through a yellow light, leaving the Plymouth behind, while Daphne rolled down her window and squawked out: "Attention! Attention! Lady in the green car! Your date's been spotted on an FBI's Most Wanted poster! I repeat!"

"Honestly, Daphne," Ian said. But he was smiling.

He turned down Waverly Street, pulled up in front of the house, and sat there with the engine running. He said, "Daph?"

"Thanks for the lift," she told him, and she hopped out.

He watched her cut across the front lawn—her knapsack bouncing, her ragged hair ruffling. The sole of one combat boot was working loose, and at every step she had to swing her left foot unnaturally high off the ground and stamp down hard. It gave her a slapdash, rollicking gait. It made her seem glorious. He was still smiling when he drove away.

At Prayer Meeting, the church always felt even smaller and cozier than it did ordinarily. It was something to do with the darkness closing in around it, Ian supposed. This was especially true tonight, for he was early and the fluorescent lights had not yet been switched on. He made his way through the rows of dimly gleaming metal chairs. He stepped behind the shop counter and tapped on the office door, which showed a thin line of yellow around the edges.

"Come in," Reverend Emmett called.

He was sitting in one of the armchairs with his legs stretched out very long and straight. He was thumbing through a hymn pamphlet. "Why, Ian!" he said, smiling, and he rose to his feet in his loose-strung, jerky manner.

Ian said, "Reverend Emmett—"

He probably could have stopped right there. Reverend Emmett looked so crestfallen, all of a sudden; he must have guessed what Ian was about to say.

"It's not only whether I'd be *able* to give people answers," Ian told him. "It's whether I'd want to. Whether I'd feel right about it."

Reverend Emmett went on waiting, and Ian knew he should explain further. He should tell him about the sign from God. He should say what the sign had finally recalled to him: Lucy rushing home out of breath, laughing and excited, and his own arrogant certitude that he had an obligation to inform his brother. But that would have opened the way for debate. (When is something philosophical acceptance and when is it dumb passivity? When is something a moral decision and when is it scar tissue?) He wasn't up to that. He just said, "I'm sorry."

Reverend Emmett said, "I'm sorry, too."

"I hope we can still be friends," Ian told him.

"Yes, of course," Reverend Emmett said gently.

Out in the main room, Ian lowered himself into a seat and unbuttoned his jacket. His fingers felt weak, as if he'd come through an ordeal. To steady himself, he bowed his head and prayed. He prayed as he almost always did, not forming actual words but picturing instead this spinning green planet safe in the hands of God, with the children and his parents and Ian himself small trusting dots among all the other dots. And the room around him seemed to rustle with prayers from years and years past: *Let me get well* and *Make her love me* and *Forgive what I have done.*

Then Sister Myra arrived with Sister Edna and flipped the light switch, flooding the room with a buzzing glare, and soon afterward others followed and settled themselves noisily. Ian sat among them, at peace, absorbing the cheery sound of their voices and the gaudy, bold, forthright colors of their clothes.

9

The Flooded Sewing Box

The spring of 1988 was the wettest anyone could remember. It rained nearly every day in May, and all the storm drains overflowed and the gutters ran like rivers and the Bedloes' roof developed a leak directly above the linen closet. One morning when Daphne went to get a fresh towel she found the whole stack soaked through. Ian called Davidson Roofers, but the man who came said there wasn't a thing he could do till the weather cleared. Even then they'd have a wait, he said, because half the city had sprung leaks in this downpour. So they kept a saucepan on the top closet shelf with a folded cloth in the bottom to muffle the constant drip, drip. Of course they'd moved the linens elsewhere, but still the upstairs hall smelled of something dank and swampy. Ian said it was him. He said he had mildew of the armpits.

Then along came June, dry as a bone. Only one brief shower fell that entire scorching month, and the yard turned brown and the cat lay stretched on the cool kitchen floor as flat as she could make herself. By that time, though, the Bedloes hardly cared; for Bee had awakened one June morning unable to speak, and two days later she was dead.

Agatha and her husband flew in from California. Thomas came down from New York. Claudia and Macy arrived from Pittsburgh with their two youngest, George and Henry; and their oldest, Abbie, drove up from Charleston. The house was not just full but splitting at the seams. Still, Daphne felt oddly lonesome. Late at night she cruised the dark rooms, stepping over sleeping bags, brushing past a snoring shape on the couch, and she thought, *Somebody's missing.* She poured a shot of her grandfather's whiskey and stood drinking it at the kitchen window, and she thought, *It's Grandma.* In all the flurry of arrivals and arrangements, it seemed they had lost track of that.

But after everyone left again, Bee's absence seemed almost a presence. Doug spent hours shut away in his room. Ian grew broody and distant. Daphne was working for a florist at the moment, and after she closed shop she would often just stay on downtown—grab a bite to eat and then maybe hit a few bars with some friends, go home with someone she hardly knew just to keep occupied. Who could have guessed that Bee would leave such a vacancy? Over the past few years she had seemed to be diminishing, fading into the background. It was Ian who'd appeared to be running things. Now Daphne saw that that wasn't the case at all. Or maybe it was like those times you experience a physical ailment—stomach trouble, say, and you think, *Why, I never realized before that the stomach is the center of the body*, and then a headache and you think, *No, wait, it's the head that's the center . . .*

July was as dry as June, and the city started rationing water. You could sprinkle your lawn only between nine at night and nine in the morning. Ian said fine; he just wouldn't sprinkle at all. It just wasn't worth the effort, he said. The grass turned brittle, like paper held close to a candle flame. The hydrangeas wilted and drooped. When Davidson Roofers arrived one morning to hammer overhead, Daphne wondered why they bothered.

Late in August a gentle, pattering rain began one afternoon, and people ran out of their houses and flung open their arms and raised their faces to the sky. Daphne, walking home from the bus stop, thought she knew how plants must feel; her skin received each cool, sweet drop so gratefully. But the rain stopped short ten minutes later as if someone had turned a faucet off, and that was the end of that.

Then summer was over—the hardest summer in history, her grandfather said. (He meant because of Bee's death, of course. He had probably not even noticed the drought.) But fall was not much wetter, or much more cheerful either.

October marked the longest Daphne had ever held a job—one entire year—and the florist gave her a raise. Her friends said now that she was making more money she ought to rent a place of her own. "You're right," she told them. "I'm going to start looking. I know I should. Any day I will." No one could believe she still lived at home with her family.

That Thanksgiving was their first without Bee. It wasn't a holiday Agatha usually returned for—she was an oncologist out in L.A., with a very busy practice—but this time she did, accompanied of course by Stuart. When Daphne came home from work Wednesday evening, she found Agatha washing carrots at the kitchen sink. They kissed, and Agatha said, "We've just got back from the grocery. There wasn't a thing to eat in the fridge."

"Well, no," Daphne said, leaning against a counter. "We thought we'd have Thanksgiving dinner at a restaurant."

"That's what Grandpa said."

As usual, Agatha wore a tailored white blouse and a navy skirt. She must have a closetful; she dressed like a missionary. Her black hair curled at her jawline in the docile, unremarkable style of those generic women in grade-school textbooks, and her face was uniformly white, as if her skin were thicker than other people's. Heavy, black-rimmed glasses framed her eyes. You could tell she thought prettiness was a waste of time. She could have been pretty—another woman with those looks *would* have been pretty—but she preferred not to be. Probably she disapproved of Daphne's tinkling earrings and Indian gauze tunic; probably even her jeans, which Daphne did have to lie down to get into.

"You know what Grandma always told us," Agatha said. "Only riffraff eat their holiday meals in restaurants."

"Yes, but everything's been so—"

Just then, Stuart came through the back door with a case of mineral water. "Hello, Daphne," he said, setting the case on the counter. He shook her hand formally. Daphne said, "Well, hey there, Stuart," and wondered all over again how her sister had happened to marry such an extremely handsome man. He was tall and muscular and tanned, with close-cut golden curls and eyes like chips of sky, and away from the hospital he wore the sort of casual, elegant clothes you see in ads for ski resorts. Maybe he was Agatha's one self-indulgence, her single nod to the importance of appearance. Or maybe (more likely) she just hadn't noticed. It was possible she was the only woman in all his life who hadn't backed off in confusion at the sight of him, which would also explain why *he* had married *her*. Look at her now, for instance, grumpily stashing his bottles in the refrigerator. "Really, Stu," she said, "you'd think we were staying till Christmas."

"Well, someone will drink it," he told her affably, and he went to hold open the door for Doug, who was hauling in a giant sack of cat food.

Ian arrived from work earlier than usual, and he hugged Agatha hard and pumped Stuart's hand up and down. He was always so pleased to have everyone home. And after supper—mostly sprouts and cruciferous vegetables, Agatha's doing—he announced he'd be skipping Prayer Meeting to meet Thomas's train with them. Ian almost never skipped Prayer Meeting.

He was the one who drove, with his father up front next to him and Daphne in back between Agatha and Stuart, her right arm held stiffly apart from Stuart's suede sleeve. (*She* could not take his looks for granted.) The dark streets slid past, dotted with events: two black men laughingly wrestling at an intersection, an old woman wheeling a shopping cart full of battered dolls. Daphne leaned forward to see everything more clearly, but the others were discussing Agatha's new Saab. So far it was running fine, Agatha said, although the smell of the leather interior kept reminding her of adhesive tape. Agatha probably thought of Baltimore as just another city by now.

At Penn Station all the parking slots were filled, so Ian circled the block while the others went inside. "What's happened to Ian?" Agatha murmured to Daphne as they walked across the lobby.

"Happened?" Daphne asked.

But then their grandfather caught up with them and said, "My, oh, my, I just never can get over what they've done to this place." He always said that. He made them tip their heads back to study the skylight, so airily delicate and aqua blue above them, and that was what they were doing when Thomas discovered them. "Gawking at the skylight again," he said in Daphne's ear. She wheeled and said, "Thomas!" and kissed his cheek and passed him on to Agatha. Lately he had become so New Yorkish. He wore a short black overcoat that picked up the black of his hair and the olive in his skin, and he carried a natty little black leather overnight bag. But when he bypassed Stuart's outstretched hand to give him a one-armed bear hug, Daphne could see he was still their old Thomas. He had this way of assuming that people would just naturally love him, and so of course they always did.

Now they had to crowd together in the car, and since Daphne was smallest she sat in front between Doug and Ian. As they drove up Charles Street, Thomas told them all about his new project. (He worked for a software company, inventing educational computer games.) None of them could get more than the gist of it, but Ian kept saying, "Mm. Mm*hmm*," looking very tickled and impressed, and Stuart and Agatha asked intelligent-sounding questions. Doug, however, was silent, and when Daphne glanced up at him she found him staring straight ahead with an extra, glassy surface in front of his eyes. He was thinking about Bee, she knew right off. All of the children home again but Bee not there to enjoy them. She reached over and patted his hand. He averted his face and gazed out the side window, but his hand turned upward on his knee and grasped hers. His fingers felt satiny and crumpled, and extremely fragile.

It wasn't till late that night, after Doug and Ian had gone to bed and the others were watching TV, that Agatha had a chance to ask her question again. "What's happened to Ian?"

"Nothing's happened," Daphne said.

"And Grandpa! And this whole house!"

"I don't know what you're talking about."

"Thomas, you know, don't you?"

Thomas gave a light shrug—his favorite response to any serious question. He was seated on Agatha's other side, flipping channels with the remote control. Stuart lounged on the floor with his back against Agatha's knees. It was after midnight and Daphne was getting sleepy, but she hated to miss out on anything. She said, "How about we all go to bed."

"Bed? In California it's barely nine o'clock," Agatha said.

"Well, *I'm* ready to call it a day," Stuart announced from the floor. "Don't forget, we flew the red-eye."

"I come home and find this place a shambles," Agatha told Daphne.

"The grass is stone dead, even the bushes look dead. The front-porch swing is hanging by one chain. The house is such a mess there's no place to set down our bags, and the dishes haven't been done for days and there's nothing to eat in the fridge, nothing in the pantry, not even any cat food for the cat, and when I go up to our room both mattresses are stripped naked and all the sheets are in the hamper and when I take the sheets to the basement the washing machine doesn't work. Grandpa told me it's been broken all fall. I asked him, 'Well, what have you done about it?' and he said, 'Oh, any time one of us goes out we try to remember to gather a little something for the laundromat,' and then he said we're eating our Thanksgiving dinner in a restaurant. A restaurant! On St. Paul Street!"

"Well, it's not as bad as it looks," Daphne told her. "There's been a drought, for one thing. I mean, the grass isn't really our fault. And the swing is probably fine; it's just that Ian needs to check the porch ceiling-boards that buckled in the floods."

But she could hear how lame this was sounding—drought and floods both. And to tell the truth, she hadn't realized about the mess. She looked around the living room (newspapers so outdated they'd turned yellow, dead flowers in a dusty vase, cat fur from the carpet clinging to Stuart's corduroys) and she felt ashamed. A memory swam back to her of her most recent drop-in visit to the laundromat, during which she had spotted, on one of the folding tables, a hardened mass of Bedloe plaids that some stranger had removed from a washing machine and left to dry in a clump, possibly several days back.

"Also, Ian needs a haircut," Agatha told her.

"He does? But I *gave* him a haircut," Daphne said. (Ian hated barbershops.) "I gave him one just last—"

Oh, Lord, way last summer. All at once she saw him: the long, limp tendrils drooping over his collar, dull brown mixed with strands of gray, and the worn lines fanning out from his eyes.

"He looks like some eccentric, middle-aged . . . uncle," Agatha said.

"He does not!" Daphne protested, so loudly that Stuart, slumped against Agatha's knees, jolted upright and said, "Huh?" and Thomas raised the volume on the remote control.

"And Grandpa has food stains down his front," Agatha said, "and you've got dirty fingernails."

"Well, I do work in a florist shop," Daphne told her. She darted a glance at her left hand, which rested on the arm of the couch.

"Is it Grandma?" Agatha asked. "But it can't be, can it? I know we all miss her, but Ian's been in charge of the house for ages, hasn't he?"

"It's true we miss her," Daphne said, and just then she heard Bee calling her for supper on a long-ago summer evening. "*Daaph*-ne!"—the two notes floating across the twilight. Surreptitiously, she started cleaning her nails. "But we get along," she said. "We're fine! And no way is Ian middle-aged. He's forty; that's not so old! He's even got this sort of girlfriend. Clara. Have you met Clara? No, I guess not. Woman at our church. She's okay."

"Is she coming for Thanksgiving dinner?"

"Who, Clara?" Daphne asked stupidly. As a matter of fact, she had never given the woman much thought. "Well, no, I don't believe he invited her," she said.

"How about you?"

"How *about* me?"

"Are you seeing anyone special?"

"Oh. No," Daphne said, "I'm between boyfriends at the moment."

"What happened to . . . was it Ron?"

"Rich," Daphne said. "He was getting too serious. I think I'm more the one-night-stand type, if you want the honest truth."

She didn't know why she had this urge to shock, sometimes, when she was talking to Agatha. It wasn't even that effective, for Agatha merely raised her eyebrows and made no comment.

The TV said, "Drop us a postcard stating—female deposits her eggs in—not *thirty*-nine ninety-five, not *twenty*-nine ninety-five, but—"

"Stuart does that too," Agatha told Thomas. "Just hand him a remote control and he turns sort of frantic. It must be hormonal."

"Say what?" Stuart asked, snapping his head up.

"Tomorrow afternoon we clean house," Agatha told Daphne.

"All right," Daphne said meekly.

"We'll have a regular, normal, home-cooked Thanksgiving dinner; I bought an eighteen-pound turkey at the grocery store, and I've invited Mrs. Jordan and the foreigners. Then afterward we'll start cleaning and sorting. Discarding. Do you know Grandma's cosmetics are still on her bureau?"

"Maybe Grandpa likes them there," Daphne suggested.

"Her arthritis pills are still in the medicine cabinet."

"Maybe—"

"Past their expiration date!" Agatha said, as if that settled it.

Stuart said, "Aggie, can't we go to bed now?"

"Now?" Agatha said. She checked her watch. "It's not even nine-thirty."

Daphne was so sleepy that the room was misting over, and Thomas had been yawning, but they all settled back obediently and fixed their eyes on the screen.

Thursday afternoon Agatha and Daphne washed all the dishes, even those in the cupboards, and Thomas vacuumed downstairs while Ian tried to reduce the general disorder. Stuart, who turned out to be fairly useless around the house, watched a football game with Doug.

Thursday night at ten they had turkey sandwiches (in California it was seven) and then Agatha dusted the downstairs furniture, Daphne scrubbed the woodwork, and Thomas polished the silver.

Friday Daphne went back to Floral Fantasy, and by the time she got home the upstairs had been vacuumed and dusted as well and the washing machine repaired and all the laundry done. Bee's little walnut desk in the living room stood bare, its cubbyholes dark as missing teeth; and when Daphne opened the drawers below she found only the essentials: a box of envelopes, a photo album whose six filled pages covered the past twenty-two years, and the document transforming those two strangers, Thomas and Agatha "Dulsimore," into Bedloes and tucking them into Ian's safe-keeping along with Daphne herself. This last was so familiar she could have quoted it verbatim, but she scanned it yet again and so did Agatha, breathing audibly over Daphne's left shoulder. "What's disturbing," Agatha told her (not for the first time), "is we don't know a thing about our genetic heritage. What if we're prone to diabetes? Or epilepsy?"

Diplomatically, Daphne refrained from pointing out that she herself did know her heritage, at least on her father's side. She shook her head and put the document back in the drawer.

Saturday Ian went to Good Works, but Daphne stayed home to continue with the cleaning. "Grandpa," Agatha said, "today we're sorting through Grandma's belongings. Anything you want to keep, you'd better let us know now."

"Oh," he said, and then he said, "Well, her lipstick, maybe. Her perfume bottles."

"Lipstick? Perfume?"

"I like her bureau to have things on top of it. I don't want to see it all blank."

"Couldn't we just put a vase on top?"

"No, we couldn't," her grandfather said firmly.

"Well, all right."

"And I'd like her robe left hanging in her closet."

"All right, Grandpa."

"But you might ship her jewelry to Claudia. Or at least what jewelry is real."

"Well, you're going to have to tell us which is which," Agatha said, for of course they wouldn't know real from Woolworth's.

But later, when they had packed all Bee's limp, sad, powdery-smelling lingerie into the cartons Thomas brought up from the basement, they called for Doug to advise them on the jewelry and he didn't answer. They'd assumed he was watching TV, but when they checked they found only Stuart, channel-hopping rapidly from golf to cartoons to cooking shows. Daphne said, "I bet he's at the foreigners'."

"Honestly," Agatha said.

"The foreigners have a VCR now, did you know? They own every Rita Hayworth movie ever made."

"Run get him, will you?" Agatha asked Thomas.

But Thomas said, "Maybe we should just let him stay there."

"Well, what'll we do about the jewelry?"

"Send Claudia the whole box, for heaven's sake," Daphne said. She told Thomas, "Wrap the whole box for mailing. You'll find paper and string in the pantry."

"But it isn't just the jewelry," Agatha said. "We need him here to answer other questions, too."

"Agatha, will you drop it? He doesn't want to be around for this."

"Well. Sorry," Agatha said stiffly.

They went back upstairs to their grandparents' bedroom, and while Thomas bore the jewelry box off to the pantry Daphne and Agatha started on the cedar chest at the foot of the bed. They had assumed this part would be easy—just sweaters, surely—but underneath lay stacks of moldering photo albums Daphne had never seen before. "Oh, those," Agatha said. "They used to be downstairs in the desk." She picked up a manila envelope and peered inside. Daphne, meanwhile, flipped through the topmost album and found rows of streaky, pale rectangles showing ghostlike human faces with no features but pinhead eyes. "Polaroid, in its earliest days," Agatha explained.

"Well, darn," Daphne said, because the captions were so alluring. *Danny at Bethany Beach, 1963. Lucy with the Crains, 8/65.* Her father, whom she knew only from a boringly boyish sports photo hanging in the living room. Her mother, who was nothing but the curve of a cheek above Daphne's own newborn self on page one of her otherwise empty baby book.

She turned to the albums below. The pictures there were more distinct, but they documented less interesting times. Claudia, thinner and darker, married a plucked-looking Macy in a ridiculous white tuxedo. Doug stood at a lectern holding up a plaque. Claudia and Macy had a baby. Then they had another. People seemed to graduate a lot. Some wore long white robes and mortarboards, some wore black and carried their mortarboards under their arms, and one, labeled *Cousin Louise*, wore just a dress but you could see this was a graduation because of her ribboned diploma and her relatives pressing around. All those relatives attending all those ceremonies, sitting patiently through all those tedious speeches just so they could raise a cheer at the single mention of a loved one's name. It wasn't fair: by the time of Daphne's own graduation, most of those people had vanished and Claudia and Macy had moved out of state. The family had congealed into smaller knots, wider apart, like soured milk. Their gatherings were puny, their cheers self-conscious and faint.

"Thomas and me with Mama," Agatha said, thrusting a color snapshot at Daphne. "I wonder how *that* got here."

She had pulled it from the manila envelope: a slick, bright square that Daphne took hold of reverently. So. Her mother. A very young woman with two small children, standing in front of a trailer. Probably she and Daphne looked alike—same shade of hair, same shape of face—but this woman seemed so long ago, Daphne couldn't feel related to her. Her dress was too short, her makeup too harsh, her surroundings too tinny and garish. Had she ever cried herself to sleep at night? Laughed till her legs could no longer support her? Fallen into such a rage that she'd pounded the wall with her fists?

Daphne used to ask about her mother all the time, in the old days. She had plagued her sister and brother with questions. They never gave very satisfactory answers, though. Agatha said, "Her hair was black. Her eyes were, I don't know, blue or gray or something." Thomas said, "She was nice. You'd have liked her!" in his brightest tone of voice. But when Daphne asked, "What would I have liked about her?" he just said, "Oh, everything!" and looked away from her. He could be so exasperating, at times. At times she imagined him encased in something plastic, something slick and smooth as a raincoat.

Agatha held out her hand for the snapshot, and Daphne said, "I think I'll keep it."

"Keep it?"

"I'll get it framed."

"What for?" Agatha asked, surprised.

"I'm going to hang it in the living room with the other family pictures."

"In the living room! Well, that's just inappropriate," Agatha told her.

Daphne had a special allergy to the word "inappropriate." A number of teachers had used it during her schooldays. She said, "Don't tell me what's appropriate!"

"What are you so prickly about? I only meant—"

"She has just as much right to be on that wall as Great-Aunt Bess with her Hula Hoop."

"Yes, of course she does," Agatha said. "Fine! Go ahead." And she passed Daphne the manila envelope. "Here's all the rest of her things."

Daphne shook the envelope into her lap. Certificates. Receipts. A date on one read 2/7/66. She didn't see any more photos. "Put them away; don't leave them lying around," Agatha said, delving into the chest again. Her voice came back muffled. "We're trying to get organized, remember."

So Daphne took them across the hall to her room. It used to be Thomas's room, and although Thomas had to sleep on the couch now he kept his belongings here during his visits. His toilet articles littered Daphne's bureau and his leather bag spilled clothing onto her floor. Daphne suddenly felt overcome by *objects*. What did she need with these papers, anyhow? Except for the snapshot, they were worthless. And yet she couldn't bear to throw them away.

When she returned to her grandparents' bedroom, she found Agatha looking equally defeated. She was standing in front of Bee's closet, facing a row of heartbreakingly familiar dresses and blouses. Crammed on the shelf overhead were suitcases and hatboxes and a sliding heap of linens—

the linens moved last spring from beneath the leaky roof. It showed what this household had descended to that they'd never been moved back, except for those few items in regular use. "What *are* these?" Agatha asked, taking a pinch of a monogrammed guest towel.

"I guess we ought to carry them to the linen closet," Daphne said.

But the linen closet, they discovered, had magically replenished itself. The emptied top shelf now held Doug's shoe-polishing gear and someone's greasy coveralls and the everyday towels not folded but hastily wadded. And the lower shelves, which hadn't been sorted in years, made Agatha say, "Good grief." She gave a listless tug to a crib sheet patterned with ducklings. (How long since they'd needed a crib sheet?) When they heard Thomas on the stairs, she called, "Tom, could you bring up more boxes from the basement?"

She pulled out half a pack of disposable diapers—the old-fashioned kind as stiff and crackly as those paper quilts that line chocolate boxes. From the depths of the closet she drew a baby-sized pillow and said, "Ick," for a rank, moldy smell unfurled from it almost visibly. The leak must have traveled farther than they had suspected. "Throw it out," she told Daphne. Daphne took it between thumb and forefinger and dropped it on top of the diapers. Next Agatha brought forth a bedpan with an inch of rusty water in the bottom—"That too," she said—and a damp, cloth-covered box patterned with faded pink roses. "Is this Grandma's?" she asked. "I don't remember this."

Both of them hovered over it hopefully as she set the box on the floor and lifted the lid, but it was only a sewing box, abandoned so long ago that a waterlogged packet of clothing labels inside bore Claudia's maiden name. There were sodden cards of bias tape and ripply, stretched-out elastic; and underneath those, various rusty implements—scissors, a seam ripper, a leather punch—and tiny cardboard boxes falling apart with moisture. Clearly nothing here was of interest, so why did they insist on opening each box? Even Agatha, common-sense Agatha, pried off a disintegrating cardboard lid to stare down at a collection of shirt buttons. Everything swam in brown water. Everything had the dead brown stink of overcooked broccoli. It was amazing how thorough the rust was. It threaded the hooks and eyes, it stippled the needles and straight pins. It choked the revolving wheel of the leather punch and clogged each and every one of its hollow, cylindrical teeth.

Daphne thought of the dress form in the attic storeroom—Bee's figure but with a waist, with a higher bosom. Once their grandma had been a happy woman, she supposed. Back before everything changed.

"Will these be enough?" Thomas asked, arriving with two cartons. But Agatha flapped a hand without looking. "Shall I pack these things on the floor?" he asked.

"Oh, don't bother," Agatha told him, and then she turned and wandered toward the stairs.

"Just *leave* them here?" he asked Daphne.

"Whatever," Daphne said.

In fact they remained there the rest of the day, obstructing the hall till Daphne finally stuffed them back in the closet. She piled everything onto the bottom shelf, and she set the cardboard cartons inside and closed the door.

"I dreamed this high-school boy was proposing to me," Agatha said at breakfast. "He told me to name a date. He said, 'How about Wednesday? Monday is always busy and Tuesday is always rainy.' I said, 'Wait, I'm . . . wait,' I said. 'I think you ought to know that I'm quite a bit older than you.' Then I woke up, and I laughed out loud. Did you hear me laughing, Stu? I mean, older was the least of it. I should have said, 'Wait, there's another thing, too! It so happens I'm already married.' "

"I dreamed I was going blind," Thomas said. "Everyone said, 'Oh, how awful, we're so sorry for you.' I said, 'Sorry? Why? I've had twenty-six years of perfect vision!' I really meant it, too. I sounded like one of those inspirational stories we used to read in Bible camp."

"I dreamed I was seeing patients," Stuart said. "They all had some kind of rash and I was trying to remember my dermatology. It didn't seem to occur to me to tell them that wasn't my field."

Agatha said, "I'd never go into dermatology."

They were having English muffins and juice—just the four of them, because it was ten-thirty and Doug and Ian had eaten breakfast hours ago. Doug was in the dining room laying out a game of solitaire, the soft flip-flip of his cards providing a kind of background rhythm. Ian was moving around the kitchen wiping off counters. When he passed near Daphne he smiled down at her and said, "What did you dream, Daphne?" Something about his crinkled eyes and the kindly attentiveness of his expression made her sad, but she smiled back and said, "Oh, nothing."

"Dermatology's not bad," Stuart was saying. "At least dermatologists don't have night call."

"But it's so superficial," Agatha said.

"You should see Agatha with her patients," Stuart told the others. "She's amazing. She'll say straight out to them, 'What you have can't be cured.' I think they feel relieved to finally hear the truth."

"I say, 'What you have can't be cured at this particular time,'" Agatha corrected him. "There's a difference."

Daphne couldn't imagine that either version would be as much of a relief as Stuart supposed.

"Speaking of time," Ian said, draping his dishcloth over the faucet, "when exactly does your plane take off, Ag?"

"Somewhere around noon, I think. Why?"

"Well, I'm wondering about church. If I wanted to go to church I'd have to leave right now."

"Go, then," she told him.

"But if your flight's at noon—"

"Go! Grandpa can drive us."

Ian hesitated. Daphne knew what he was thinking. He was weighing Sunday services, which he never missed if he could help it, against the possibility of hurting Agatha's feelings. And Agatha, with her chin raised defiantly and her glasses flashing an opaque white light, would most definitely have hurt feelings. Daphne knew that if Ian did not. Finally Ian said, "Well, if you're sure . . ." and Agatha snapped, "Absolutely! Go."

He didn't seem to catch her tone. (Or he didn't want to catch it.) He rounded the table to kiss her goodbye. "It's been wonderful having you," he said. She looked away from him. He shook Stuart's hand. "Stuart, I hope you two will come again at Christmas."

"We'll try," Stuart told him, rising. "Thanks for the hospitality."

"You planning on church today, Daphne?"

"I thought I'd ride along to the airport," Daphne said.

"Well, I'll be off, then."

In the dining room, they heard him speaking to Doug. "Guess I'll let you do the airport run, Dad."

"Oh, well," Doug said. "Seems I'm losing here anyway."

"And another thing," Agatha told Daphne. (But what was the first thing? Daphne wondered.) "This business about you not driving is really dumb, Daph."

"Driving?" Daphne asked.

"Here you are, twenty-two years old, and Grandpa has to drive us to the airport. As far as I know you've never even sat behind a steering wheel."

"How did my driving get into this?"

"It's a symptom of a whole lot of other problems, any fool can see that. Why are you still depending on people to chauffeur you around? Why have you never gone away to college? Why are you still living at home when everyone else has long since left?"

"Maybe I *like* living at home, so what's the big deal?" Daphne asked. "This happens to be a perfectly nice place."

"Nobody says it isn't," Agatha said, "but that's not the issue. You've simply reached the stage where you should be on your own. Right, Stuart? Right, Thomas?"

Stuart developed an interest in brushing crumbs off his sweater. Thomas gave one of his shrugs and drank the last of his orange juice. Agatha sighed. "You know," she told Daphne, "in many ways, living in a family is like taking a long, long trip with people you're not very well acquainted with. At first they seem just fine, but after you've traveled awhile at close quarters they start grating on your nerves. Their most harmless habits make you want to scream—the way they overuse certain phrases or yawn out loud— and you just have to get away from them. You have to leave home."

"Well, I guess I must not have traveled with them long enough, then," Daphne told her.

"How can you say that? With Ian doddering about the house calling you his 'Daffy-dill' and spending every Saturday at Good Works—Good Works! Good God. I bet half those people don't even *want* a bunch of holy-molies showing up to rake their leaves in front of all their neighbors. And marching off to services come rain or shine; never mind if his niece is here visiting and will have to go to the airport on her own—"

"He gets a lot out of those services," Daphne said. "And Good Works too; it kind of . . . links you. He doesn't have much else, Agatha."

"Exactly," Agatha told her. "Isn't that my point? If not for Second Chance he'd have much more, believe me. That's what religion does to you. It narrows you and confines you. When I think of how religion ruined our childhood! All those things we couldn't do, the Sugar Rule and the Caffeine Rule. And that pathetic Bible camp, with poor pitiful Sister Audrey who finally ran off with a soldier if I'm not mistaken. And Brother Simon always telling us how God had saved him for something special when his apartment building burned down, never explaining what God had against those seven others He didn't save. And the way we had to say grace in every crummy fast-food joint with everybody gawking—"

"It was a silent grace," Daphne said. "It was the least little possible grace! He always tried to be private about it. And religion never ruined *my* childhood; it made me feel cared for. Or Thomas's either. Thomas still attends church himself. Isn't that so, Thomas? He belongs to a church in New York."

Thomas said, "It's getting on toward eleven, you two. Maybe we should be setting out for the airport."

"Not to change the subject or anything," Daphne told him.

He pretended he hadn't heard. They all stood up, and he said, "Then driving back, you and Grandpa can drop me at the train station. I'll just get my things together. You want me to put my sheets in the hamper, Daph?"

"Are you serious?" Daphne asked. "Those sheets are good for another month yet."

Agatha rolled her eyes and said, "Charming."

"You have no right to talk if you're not here to do the laundry," Daphne told her.

"Which reminds me," Agatha said. She stopped short in the dining room, where their grandfather was collecting his cards. "About the linen closet and such—"

"Don't give it a thought," Daphne said. "Just go off scot-free to the other side of the continent."

"No, but I was wondering. Isn't there some kind of cleaning service that could sort this place out for us? Not just clean it but organize it, and I could pay."

"There's the Clutter Counselor," Daphne said.

Stuart laughed. Agatha said, "The what?"

"Rita the Clutter Counselor. She lives with this guy I know, Nick Bascomb. Did you ever meet Nick? And she makes her living sorting other people's households and putting them in order."

"Hire her," Agatha said.

"I don't know how much she charges, though."

"Hire her anyway. I'll pay whatever it costs."

"What?" their grandfather spoke up suddenly. "You'd let an outsider go through our closets?"

"It's either that or marry Ian off quick to that Clara person," Agatha told him.

"I'll call Rita this evening," Daphne said.

Rita diCarlo was close to six feet tall—a rangy, sauntering woman in her late twenties with long black hair so frizzy that the braid hanging down her back seemed not so much plaited as clotted. She'd been living with Nick Bascomb for a couple of years now, but Daphne hadn't really got to know her till just last summer when a bunch of them went together to a rock concert at RFK Stadium. They'd had bleacher tickets that didn't allow them on the field, where all the action was; but Rita, bold as brass, strode down to the field anyway. When an usher tried to stop her she held up her ticket stub and strode on. The usher considered a while and then spun around and called, "Hey! *That* wasn't a field ticket!" By then, though, she was lost in the crowd. Daphne hadn't seen much of her since, but she always remembered that incident—the dash and swagger of it. She thought Rita was entirely capable of yanking their house into shape.

On the phone Rita said she could fit the Bedloes into that coming week, so she dropped by Monday after work to "case the joint," as she put it. Wearing a red-and-black lumber jacket, black jeans, and heavy leather riding boots, she ambled about throwing open cupboards and peering into drawers. She surveyed the basement impassively. She seemed unfazed by the smell in the linen closet. She did not once ask, as Daphne had feared, "What in hell has *hit* here?" She poked her head into Doug's bedroom and, finding him seated empty-handed in his rocker, merely said, "Hmm," and withdrew. This was tactful of her, of course, but Doug's room had urgent need of her services; so Daphne said, "Maybe after Grandpa's gone downstairs . . ."

"I got the general idea," Rita told her.

"That's where Grandma's closet is and so—"

"Sure. Clothes and stuff. Hatboxes."

"Right."

"I got it."

She climbed the wooden steps to the attic, which had a stuffy, cloistered feeling now that it was no longer in regular use. She bent to look into the storeroom under the eaves. When she plucked one of Bee's letters from a cardboard carton, Daphne felt a pang. "I guess these . . . personal things you'll leave to us," she said, but Rita said, "Not if you want this done right." Then she added, "Don't worry, I don't read your mail. Or only enough to classify it. Stuff like this, for instance: too recent to have historical interest, no postage stamps of value, and the return address is a woman's so we know it's not your grandparents' love letters. I'd say ditch them."

"*Ditch* them?"

Rita turned to look at her. Her face was tanned and square-jawed; her heavy black eyebrows were slightly raised.

"But suppose they told us what young women used to think about," Daphne said. "Politics, or feminism, or things like that."

Rita shook a piece of ivory stationery out of the envelope. Without bothering to unfold it, she read off the phrases that showed themselves: ". . . *tea at Mrs. . . . wore my new flowered . . . self belt with covered buckle . . .*"

"Well," Daphne murmured.

"Ditch them," Rita told her.

They went back downstairs. Daphne felt like a little fairy person following Rita's clopping boots. "What I do," Rita said, "is sort everything into three piles: Keep, Discard, and Query. I make it a practice to query as little as possible. Everything we keep I organize, and what's discarded I haul away; I've got my own truck and two guys to help tote. I charge by the hour, but I generally know ahead of time how long a job will run me. This place, for instance—well, I'll need to sit down and figure it out, but offhand I'd say if I start tomorrow morning, I could be done late Thursday."

"Thursday! That's just three days!"

"Or four at the most. It's a fairly straightforward house, compared to some I've seen."

They were back in the kitchen now. She opened one of the cabinets and gazed meditatively at a collection of empty peanut butter jars.

"It doesn't look so straightforward to *me*," Daphne told her.

"Well, naturally. That's because you live here. You feel guilty getting rid of things. This one old lady I had, she could never throw out a gift. A drawing her son made in nursery school—and that son was sixty years old! A seashell her girlfriend brought from Miami in nineteen twenty—'I just feel I'd be throwing the *person* out,' she told me. So what I did was, I didn't let her know. Well, of course she knew in a way. What did she suppose was in all those garbage bags? But she never asked, and I never said, and everyone was happy."

She slammed the cabinet door shut. "I've seen houses so full you couldn't walk through them. I've seen closets totally lost—I mean crammed to the gills and closed off, with new stuff piled in front of them so you didn't know they existed."

"Your own apartment must be neat as a pin," Daphne said.

"Not really," Rita told her. "That Nick saves everything. I *would* end up with a pack rat!" She laughed. She hooked a kitchen chair with the toe of her boot, pulled it out from the table, and sat down. "Now," she said, drawing a pencil and a note pad from her breast pocket. The pencil was roughly the size of a cartridge. She licked its tip and started writing. "Six rooms plus basement plus finished attic. Your attic's in pretty good shape, but that basement . . ."

Ian appeared at the back door, lugging a large cardboard box. "Open up!" he called through the glass, and when Daphne obeyed he practically fell inside. Whatever he was carrying must weigh a ton. "Genuine ceramic tiles," he told Daphne, setting the box on the floor. "We're replacing an antique mantel at a house in Fells Point and these were just being thrown out, so—"

"Will you be putting them to use within the next ten days?" Rita asked.

He straightened and said, "Pardon?"

"Ian, this is Rita diCarlo," Daphne said. "My uncle Ian. Rita's here to organize us."

"Oh, yes," Ian said.

"Do you have a specific bathroom in mind that's in need of those tiles within the next ten days?" Rita asked him.

"Well, not exactly, but—"

"Then I suggest you walk them straight back out to the trash can," she said, "or else I'll have to tack them onto my estimate here."

"But these are from Spain," Ian told her. He bent to lift one from the box—a geometric design of turquoise and royal blue. "How could I put something like this in the trash?"

Rita considered him. She didn't give the tile so much as a glance, but Ian continued holding it hopefully in front of his chest like someone displaying his number for a mug shot.

"You see what I have to deal with," Daphne told Rita.

"Yes, I see," Rita said.

Oddly enough, though, Daphne just then noticed how beautiful that tile really was. The design looked kaleidoscopic—almost capable of movement. She couldn't remember now why stripping the house had seemed like such a good idea.

Rita did do an excellent job, as it turned out, but Daphne hardly had time to notice before something new came along for her to think about: Friday afternoon, she was fired.

It wasn't entirely unexpected. Ever since she'd got her raise, she seemed to have lost interest in her work. She had shown up late, left early, and mislaid several orders. The messages people sent with their flowers had begun to depress her. "Well, I think I'll say . . . well, let me see," they would tell her, frowning into space. "Why don't we put . . . Okay! I've got it! 'Congratulations and best wishes.' " Then Daphne would slash *CBW* across the order form. "To the girl of my dreams" was *G/dms*. "Thanks for last night," *Tx/nite*. She felt injured on their behalf—that their most heartfelt sentiments could be considered so routine. And when they were not routine, it was worse: *I am more sorry than I can tell you and you're right not to want to see me again but I'll never forget you as long as I live and I hope you have a wonderful marriage.* "With delivery that comes to twenty-seven eighty," she would say in her blandest tone.

The way Mr. Potoski put it was, she could either leave now or stay on for her two weeks' notice, but she could see he was eager to get rid of her. He already had a new girl lined up. "I'll leave now," Daphne told him, and so at closing time she gathered her few possessions and stuffed them into a paper sack. Then she slipped her jacket on and ducked quietly out the door, avoiding an awkward farewell scene. On the way to the bus stop she found herself composing messages to Mr. Potoski. *Tx/fun: Thanks, it's been fun. TK: Take care.* Not that she had anything against Mr. Potoski personally. She knew this was all her own fault.

Her bus was undergoing some heater problems, and by the time she reached home she was chilled through. Still in her jacket, she went directly to the kitchen and lit the gas beneath the kettle. Ian must be working late this evening. She could hear her grandfather down in the basement, rattling tools and thinking aloud, but she didn't call out to him. Maybe there was some advantage to living alone after all—not dealing with other people, not feeling responsible for other people's happiness. Although that was out of the question, now that she had no salary.

She took a mug from the cupboard, where everything sat in straight rows—eight mugs, eight short glasses, eight tall glasses. The mugs that didn't match and the odd-sized glasses had been sent to Good Works. The cereals that people had tried once and never again had disappeared from the shelves. In just three days Rita had turned this house into a sort of sample kit: one perfect set of everything. But Daphne hadn't quite adjusted yet and she felt a little rustle of panic. She wanted some extras. She wanted that crowd of cracked, crazed, chipped, handleless mugs waiting behind the other mugs on the off chance they might be needed.

She ladled coffee into the drip pot and then poured in the boiling water. Coffee was her weakness. Reverend Emmett said coffee clouded the senses, coffee stepped between God and the self; but Daphne had discovered long ago that coffee *sharpened* the senses, and she loved to sit through church all elated and jangly-nerved and keyed to the sound of that inner voice saying enigmatic things she might someday figure out when she was wiser: *if not for you, if not for you, if not for you* and *down in the meadow where the green grass grows* . . . She waited daily for caffeine to be declared illegal, but it seemed the government had not caught on yet.

She poured the coffee and sat down at the table with it, warming her hands around the mug. Now her grandfather's footsteps climbed the basement stairs and crossed the pantry. Daphne looked up, but the figure in the doorway was not her grandfather after all. It was Rita. Daphne said, "Rita! Aren't you done with us?"

Well, she *was* done. She had finished yesterday afternoon and even presented her staggeringly high bill, which Daphne was going to mail on to Agatha as soon as she figured out where the stamps had been moved to. But here Rita stood, flushed from her climb, looking a bit better put together than usual in a flowing white shirt that bloused above her jeans and a tan suede jacket as soft as washed silk. "Daphne," she said flatly. "I thought you were Ian."

Ah.

Daphne had been through this any number of times. Back in high school, girlfriends of hers showed up unannounced, wearing brand new outfits and carrying their bosoms ostentatiously far in front of them like fruit on a tray. "Oh," they'd say in just such a tone, dull and disappointed. "I thought you were Ian."

But Rita already had somebody, didn't she? She was living with Nick Bascomb. Wasn't she?

"It just occurred to me," Rita said, "that I ought to try once more to sort out your grandpa's workbench. Not that I'd charge any extra, of course. But I didn't feel right allowing it to stay so . . ."

Her voice dwindled away. Daphne, sitting back in her chair and cupping her mug in both hands, watched her with some enjoyment. Rita diCarlo, of all people! Such a tough cookie. Although Daphne could have warned her that she was about as far from Ian's type as a woman could get.

"But it seems your grandpa's sticking to his guns," Rita said finally.

"Yes," Daphne said. She took a sip from her mug.

"So I'll be going, I guess."

"Okay."

In another mood, she might at least have offered coffee. But she had troubles of her own right now, and so she let Rita see herself out.

Daphne started reading the want ads over breakfast every morning. A waste of time. "What *is* this?" she asked her grandfather. "A city where nobody needs anything?"

"Maybe you should try an agency," he said.

When it came to unemployment, he was her best listener. Ian always said, "Oh, something will show up," but her grandfather had been through the Depression and he sympathized from the bottom of his heart every time she was fired. "You might want to think about the Postal Service," he told her now. "Your dad found the Postal Service *very* satisfactory. Security, stability, fringe benefits . . ."

"I do like outdoor exercise," Daphne mused.

"No, no, not a mailman," her grandfather said. "I meant something behind a desk."

She hated desk work. She sighed so hard she rattled her newspaper.

In the afternoons she would take a bus downtown to look in person—"pounding the pavement," she called it, thinking again of her grandfather's Depression days. She gazed in the windows of photographic studios, stationery printers, record shops. A record shop might be fun. She knew everything there was to know about the current groups. However, if customers asked her assistance with something classical like Led Zeppelin or the Doors, she'd be in trouble.

Thomas told her she ought to come to New York. She phoned him just to talk, one evening when she felt low, and he said, "Catch the next train up. Sleep on the couch till you land a job. Angie says so too." (Angie was his girlfriend, who had recently moved in with him although Ian and their grandfather were not supposed to know.) But Daphne couldn't imagine living in a city where everyone came from someplace else, and so she said, "Oh, I guess I'll keep looking here."

One Sunday she even phoned Agatha—not something she did often, since Agatha was hard to reach and also (face it) inclined to criticize. But on this occasion she was a dear. She said, "Daph, what would you think about going to college now? I'd be happy to pay for it. We're making all this money that we're too busy to spend. You wouldn't have to ask Ian for a cent."

"Well, thank you," Daphne said. "That's really nice of you."

She wasn't the school type, to be honest. But it felt good to know both her brother and sister were behind her. Her friends were more callous; they were hunting jobs themselves, many of them, or waitressing or tending bar till they decided what interested them, or heading off to law school just to appear busy. Nobody in her circle seemed to have an actual career.

At the start of her third week without work, her grandfather talked her into going to a place called Same Day Résumé. He'd heard it advertised on the radio; he thought it might help her "present" herself, he said. So Daphne took a bus downtown and spoke to a bored-looking man at an enormous metal desk. The calendar on the wall behind him read TUES 13, which made her nervous because an old boyfriend had once told her that in Cuba, Tuesday the thirteenth was considered unlucky. Shouldn't she just offer some excuse and come back another time? It did seem the man wore a faint sneer as he listened to her qualifications. In fact the whole experience was so demoralizing that as soon as she'd finished answering his questions she walked over to Lexington Market and treated herself to a combination beef-and-bean burrito. Then she went to a matinee starring Cher, her favorite movie star, and after that she cruised a few thrift shops. She bought two sets of thermal underwear with hardly any stains and a purple cotton tank top for a total of three dollars. By then it was time to collect her résumé, which had miraculously become four pages long. She had only to glance through it, though, to see how it had been padded and embroidered. Also, it cost a fortune. Her grandfather had said he would pay, but even so she resented the cost.

All the good cheer she had built up so carefully over the afternoon began to evaporate, and instead of heading home for supper she stopped at a bar where she and her friends hung out on weekends. It gave off the damp, bitter smell that such places always have before they fill up for the evening, and the low lighting seemed not romantic but bleak. Still, she perched on a cracked vinyl stool and ordered a Miller's, which she drank very fast. Then she ordered another and started reading her résumé. Any four-year-old could see that she hadn't gone past high school, even if she did list an introductory drawing course at the Maryland Institute and a weekend seminar called New Directions for Women.

"Hello, Daphne," someone said.

She turned and found Rita diCarlo settling on the stool next to her, unbuttoning her lumber jacket as she hailed the bartender. "Pabst," she told him. She unwound a wool scarf from her neck and flung her hair back. "You waiting for someone?"

Daphne shook her head.

"Me neither," Rita said.

Daphne could have guessed as much from Rita's shapeless black T-shirt and paint-spattered jeans. Her hair was even scruffier than usual; actual dust balls trailed from the end of her braid.

"I had my least favorite kind of job today," Rita told her. "A divorce. Splitting up a household. Naturally the wife and husband had to be there, so they could offer their opinions." She accepted her beer and blew into the foam. "And they did have opinions, believe me."

"Too many jobs get too personal," Daphne said gloomily.

"Right," Rita said. She was digging through her pockets for something— a Kleenex. She blew her nose with a honking sound.

"Like this florist's I was just fired from," Daphne said. "Everybody's private messages: you have to write them down pretending not to know English. Or when I worked at Camera Carousel—those photos of girls in bikinis and people's awful prom nights. You hand over the envelope with this smile like you never even noticed."

"Look," Rita said. "Did Ian tell you he and I have been seeing each other?"

"You have?" Daphne asked.

"Well, a couple of times. Well, really just once. I guess you wouldn't count when I accidentally on purpose ran into him at the wood shop."

No, Daphne wouldn't count that.

"I went to Brant's Custom Woodworks and ordered myself a bureau," Rita told her.

"I don't believe he mentioned it."

"Do you have any idea how much those things cost?"

"Expensive, huh?" Daphne said.

She glanced again at her résumé. Page two: Previous Employment. Here the facts were not padded but streamlined, for the man had suggested that too long a list made a person look flighty. "What say we strike the framer's," he had said, his sneer growing more pronounced.

"Another example is picture framing," Daphne told Rita. "People bring in these poor little paintings they've done themselves, or their drawings with the mouths erased and redrawn a dozen times and the hands posed out of sight because they can't do hands, and all you say is, 'Let me see now, perhaps a double mat . . .' "

"Then after we talked about my bureau awhile I asked if he'd come look at my apartment," Rita said, "just so he'd have an idea of the scale."

Daphne pulled her eyes away from the résumé. She focused on Rita's face for a moment, and then she said, "Don't you live with Nick Bascomb?"

"Well, I did, but I made him move out," Rita said.

"Oh? When was this?"

"Wednesday," Rita said.

"Wednesday? You mean this Wednesday just past?"

"See," Rita said, "Monday I went to visit Ian at the wood shop, and that night I asked Nick to move out. But I let him stay till Wednesday because he needed time to get his things together."

"Decent of you," Daphne said dryly.

"So then Friday Ian came by and we settled on what size bureau I wanted. I invited him to supper, but he said you-all were expecting him at home."

Daphne tried to remember back to Friday. Had she been there, even? She might have gone out with her usual gang and forgotten supper altogether.

"So when was it you saw him the second time?" she asked Rita.

"Well, that was it. Friday."

"You mean the second time was when he came to measure for your bureau?"

"Well, yes."

Daphne sat back on her stool.

This Rita was so *big*, though. She had that angular, big-boned frame. You'd expect her to be immune.

"Um, Rita," she said. "Ian's kind of . . . hard to pin down, sometimes. Also, I believe he has this sort of girlfriend at his church."

"So what? I had a boyfriend, till last Wednesday," Rita said.

"Yes, but then besides he's very, let's say Christian. Did you know that?"

"What do you think *I* am, Buddhist?"

"He's unusually Christian, though. I mean, look at you! You're sitting here in a bar! Drinking beer! Wearing a Hell Bent for Leather T-shirt!"

Rita glanced down at her shirt. She said, "That's not exactly a sin."

"It is to Ian," Daphne told her. "Or it almost is."

"Daphne," Rita said, "you get to know folks when you rearrange their belongings. Ian's belongings are so simple. They're so plain. He owns six books on how to be a better person. The clothes in his closet smell of nutmeg. And have you ever honestly looked at him? He has this really fine face; it's all straight lines. I thought at first his eyes were brown but then I saw they had a clear yellow light to them like some kind of drink; like cider. And when he talks he's very serious but when he listens to what I say back he starts smiling. He acts so happy to hear me, even when all I'm talking about is drawer knobs. Okay: so he does that to everyone. I don't kid myself! Probably it's part of his religion or something."

"Well, no," Daphne said. She felt touched. She was seeing Ian, all at once, from an outsider's angle. She said, "I didn't mean to drag you down. I was just thinking of back in school when some of my friends had crushes on him. They used to end up so frustrated. They ended up mad at him, almost."

"Well, I can understand that," Rita said. She took a hearty swallow of beer and wiped the foam off her upper lip.

"And he is a good bit older than you," Daphne pointed out.

"So? We're both grownups, aren't we? Anyhow, in some ways it's me who's older. Do you realize he's only slept with two women in all his life?"

"What?" Daphne asked.

"First his high-school sweetheart before he joined the church and then this woman he dated a few years ago, but he felt terrible about that and vowed he wouldn't do it again."

Daphne didn't know which shocked her more: the fact that he'd slept with someone or the fact that he and Rita had discussed it. "Well, how did . . . how did *that* come up?" she asked.

"It came up when I invited him to spend the night," Rita said calmly.

"You didn't!"

"I did," Rita said. "Bartender? Same again." She met Daphne's eyes. "I invited him when he came about the bureau," she said, "but he declined. He was extremely polite."

"I can imagine," Daphne said.

"Then all last weekend I waited to hear from him. I haven't done that since junior high! But he didn't call, and so here I sit, drinking away my sorrows."

He wasn't ever going to call, but Daphne didn't want to be the one to tell her. "Gosh! Look at the time," she said. She asked the bartender, "What do I owe?" and then she made a great to-do over paying, so that when she turned back to say goodbye, it would seem the subject of Ian had entirely slipped her mind.

• • •

Agatha and Stuart didn't come home for Christmas. Stuart was on call that weekend. Thomas came, though, and they spent a quiet holiday together, rising late on Christmas morning to exchange their gifts. Ian gave Daphne a key chain that turned into a siren when you pressed a secret button. (He was always after her about the neighborhoods she hung out in.) Her grandfather gave her a ten-dollar bill, the same thing he gave the others. Thomas, the world's most inspired shopper, gave her a special crystal guaranteed to grant steadiness of purpose, and Agatha and Stuart sent a dozen pairs of her favorite brand of black tights. Daphne herself gave everybody houseplants—an arrangement she'd made weeks ago when she still worked at Floral Fantasy.

For Christmas dinner they went to a restaurant. Daphne viewed this as getting away with something. If Agatha had been home, she never would have allowed it. But Agatha might have a point, Daphne thought as they entered the dining room. The owner kept his place open on holidays so that people without families had somewhere to go, and at nearly every table just a single, forlorn person sipped a solitary cocktail. Across the room they saw Mrs. Jordan, which made Daphne feel guilty because if Bee were still alive she would have remembered to invite her. But then Ian and the owner conferred and they added an extra place setting and brought her over to sit with them. Mrs. Jordan was as adventurous and game as ever, although she must be in her eighties by now, and once they'd said grace she livened things up considerably by describing a recent outing she'd taken with the foreigners. It seemed that during that peculiar warm spell back in November, she and three of the foreigners had driven to a marina someplace and rented a sailboat; only none of them had ever sailed before and when they found themselves on open water with a stiff breeze blowing up, the one named Manny had to jump over the side and swim for help. After they were rescued, Mrs. Jordan said, the marina owner had told them they could never take a boat out again. They couldn't even stand on the dock. They couldn't even park on the grounds to admire the view. By now she had them laughing, and she raised a speckled hand and ordered a bottle of champagne—"And you must join us, Ezra," she told the owner—along with a fizzy apple juice for Ian. It turned out to be a very festive meal.

In the evening Claudia and her family telephoned from Pittsburgh, and Agatha from California. Agatha didn't seem as distressed about the restaurant as she might have been. All she said to Daphne was, "Did Ian bring Clara?"

"Clara? No."

Agatha sighed. She said, "Maybe we'll just have to marry *Grandpa* off, instead."

"Actually, that might be easier," Daphne told her.

· · ·

In January Daphne started working at the wood shop, performing various unskilled tasks like oiling and paste-waxing. She had done this several times before while she was between jobs, and although she would never choose it for a permanent career she found it agreeable enough. She liked the smell of sap and the golden light that the wood gave off, and she enjoyed the easy, stop-and-go conversation among the workmen. It reminded her of kindergarten—everyone absorbed in his own project but throwing forth a remark now and then. Ian didn't join in, though, and whenever he said anything to Daphne she was conscious of the furtive alertness in the rest of the room. Clearly, he was considered an oddity here. It made her feel sorry for him, although he might not even notice.

The Friday before Martin Luther King Day, Agatha and Stuart flew in for the long weekend and Thomas came down from New York. Agatha toured the house from basement to attic, checking the results of the Clutter Counseling. She approved in general but pointed out to Daphne that a sort of overlayer was beginning to sprout on various counters and dressers. "Yes, Rita warned us that might happen," Daphne said. "She offers a quarterly touch-up service but I swore I would do it myself."

Agatha said, "Hmm," and glanced at the cat's flea collar, which for some reason sat on the breadboard. "I wonder how much one of these touch-ups would cost."

"I could probably get a bargain rate," Daphne told her. Shoot, she could probably get it for free, if Rita still had her crush on Ian. But maybe she had recovered by now. Daphne hadn't seen her since that evening in the bar.

Saturday Agatha and Stuart attended an all-day conference on bone marrow transplants, and that night they had dinner with some of their colleagues. This may have been why, on Sunday, they agreed to go to church with the rest of the family. They had barely shown their faces, after all, and tomorrow they would be flying out again. Ian was thrilled, you could tell. He talked his father into coming along too, which ordinarily was next to impossible. Churches ought to *look* like churches, Doug always said. He was sorry, but that was just the way he felt.

It was coat weather, but sunny, and so they went on foot—Doug and Ian, then Thomas and Stuart, with Agatha and Daphne bringing up the rear. As they passed each house on Waverly Street, Agatha inquired about the occupants. "What do you see of the Crains these days? Does Miss Bitz still teach piano?" It wasn't till that moment that Daphne realized how much had changed here. The Crains, no longer newlyweds, had moved to a bigger house after the birth of their third daughter. Miss Bitz had died. Others had gone on to condominiums or retirement communities once their children were grown, and the people who took their places—working couples, often, whose children attended day care—seemed harder to get to know. "All that's left," Daphne said, "are the foreigners and Mrs. Jordan."

"Where *is* Mrs. Jordan? Shouldn't we stop by and pick her up?"

"She has to drive now, on account of her rheumatism."

"This is depressing," Agatha said.

It did seem depressing. Or maybe that was just the season, the thin white light of January; for in spite of the sunshine the neighborhood had a pallid, lifeless look.

The church was barely half full this morning, but there weren't six empty chairs in a row and so they had to separate. The men sat near the front, and Daphne and Agatha sat at the rear next to Sister Nell. Sister Nell leaned across Daphne to say, "Why, Sister Agatha! Isn't this a treat!" Daphne felt a bit jealous; she was never called "Sister" herself. Evidently you had to leave town before you were considered grown.

Two years ago Sister Lula had willed the church her electric organ—the very small kind that salesmen sometimes demonstrate in shopping malls— and Sister Myra was playing "Amazing Grace" while latecomers straggled in. Under cover of the music, Agatha murmured, "Show me which one is Clara."

Daphne looked around. "There," she said, sliding her eyes to the left. Clara sat between her father and her brother—a slim woman in her mid-thirties with buff-colored hair feathered perfectly, dry skin powdered, tailored suit a careful orchestration of salmon pink and aqua.

"Why isn't she sitting with Ian?" Agatha asked.

"Because she's sitting with her father and brother."

"You know what I mean," Agatha told her. But just then the music stopped and Reverend Emmett rose from behind the counter to offer the opening prayer.

He was getting old. It took Agatha's presence to make Daphne see that. He was one of those people who hollow as they age, and when he turned to reach for his Bible his back had a curve like a beetle's back. But his voice was as strong as ever. "Proverbs twenty-one: four," he said in his rich, pure tenor. " 'An high look, and a proud heart, and the plowing of the wicked, is sin.' " Then he announced the hymn: "In the Sweet Bye and Bye."

Daphne loved singing hymns. She had forgotten, though, what a trial it was to sing with Agatha, who *talked* the words in a monotone and broke off halfway through to ask, "Where are the young people? Where are the children?"

Daphne wouldn't answer. She went on singing.

The sermon had to do with arrogance. Nothing was more arrogant, Reverend Emmett said, than the pride of the virtuous man, and then he told them a story. "Last week, I called on a brother whose wife had recently died. Some of you may know whom I mean. He was not a member of our church, and had visited only a very few times. Still, I was surprised to see him bring forth a bottle of wine once I was seated. 'Reverend Emmett,' he said, 'you happen to have arrived on my fiftieth anniversary. My wife and I always promised ourselves that when we reached this day, we would open a bottle of wine that we'd saved from our wedding reception. Well, she is no longer here to share it, and I'm hoping very much that you will have a glass to keep me company.' "

Daphne held her breath. Even Agatha looked interested.

"So I did," Reverend Emmett said.

Daphne started breathing again.

"I reflected that the Alcohol Rule is a rule for the self, designed to re- move an obstruction between the self and the Lord, but drinking that glass of wine was a gift to another human being and refusing it would have been arrogant. And when I took my leave—well, I'm not proud of this—I had a momentary desire for some sort of mouthwash, in case I met one of our brethren on the way home. But I thought, 'No, this is between me and my God,' and so I walked through the streets joyfully breathing fumes of alcohol."

Agatha fell into a fit of silent laughter. Daphne could feel her shaking; she had a sidelong glimpse of her white face growing pink and convulsed. In disgust, Daphne drew away from her and folded her arms across her chest. She didn't hold with the Alcohol Rule herself, but she almost wished now she did just so she could make a gesture like Reverend Em- mett's. In fact, maybe she already had. Couldn't you say that *every* social drink was a gift to another human being? She played with that notion throughout the rest of the sermon, deliberately ignoring Agatha, who kept wiping her eyes with a tissue.

At Amending, Daphne confessed in a low voice that she had spoken rudely to her grandfather. "I told him to quit bugging me about a job," she said, "and I called Ian an old maid, and I said Bert could go to hell when he showed me where I'd skipped on a bookcase." Sister Nell was murmuring something long and involved about a dispute with a neighbor. Agatha said nothing, wouldn't you know. This meant she got to hear everyone else's sins and pass judgment. "Talk about an high look!" Daphne whispered sharply, and then Reverend Emmett said, "Let it van- ish now from our souls, Lord. In Jesus' name, amen." After that they stood up to sing "Love Divine, All Loves Excelling."

The Benediction was hardly finished before Agatha was in the aisle, making her way toward Clara as she put her coat on. Daphne followed, but then Brother Simon stopped her to talk and so she arrived at Agatha's side too late to introduce her. "I'm Agatha Bedloe-Simms," Agatha was saying. (Only the rawest newcomer mentioned last names within these walls, but no doubt she wanted to establish her connection to Ian.) "I be- lieve you must be Clara."

"Why, yes," Clara said in her ladylike, modulated voice. "And this is my father, Brother Edwin, and my brother, Brother James."

She was probably making a point, with all those "Brothers," but if so it passed right over Agatha's head. "It's a pleasure to meet you," Agatha told them. "Clara, Ian has talked so much about you."

"Oh! Has he?" Clara asked, and a blush started spreading upward from her Peter Pan collar.

Daphne felt confused. Had he really? Before she could find out, though, Reverend Emmett reached their group. "Sister Agatha," he said, "I'm so glad to see you here."

He gave no sign of recollecting that Agatha had spurned his church for years and insisted on a city hall wedding. And Agatha herself seemed unabashed. "So tell me, Reverend Emmett," she said, "what does a fifty-year-old bottle of wine taste like, anyhow?"

"Oh, it was vinegar," he said cheerfully.

"And don't you think mentioning it to us was another form of mouth-wash, so to speak?"

"Ah," he said, smiling. "Something to confess at our next Amending."

He turned to Stuart, who had shown up behind her with Ian. "You must be Agatha's husband," he said.

"Brother Stuart," Stuart announced, with the prideful smirk of some-one speaking a foreign language.

There was a bustle of introductions and small talk, and then Reverend Emmett moved off to greet someone else and Agatha whispered to Daphne, "Do we have enough lunch for three extra?"

"Three?" Daphne asked.

"Her father and brother too?"

They didn't, but that wasn't the issue. Daphne said, "Agatha, I really don't think—"

Too late. Agatha turned to Clara and said, "Won't the three of you come home with us for lunch?"

Clara was still blushing. She looked over at Ian. "Oh, we wouldn't want to inconvenience you," she said.

"Right," Ian said. "Maybe some other time." And he took Agatha's arm and propelled her toward the door. Daphne and Clara were left gap-ing at each other. Daphne said, "Um . . ."

"Well, it was lovely seeing you," Clara said melodiously.

"Yes, well . . . so long, I guess."

Daphne hurried to catch up with the others. Ian still had hold of Agatha, who was looking cross. Outside, when they regrouped—Agatha walking next to Daphne once again—Agatha muttered, "What a dud."

"Who, Clara?"

"Ian."

"Maybe they've had a fight or something," Daphne said.

"More likely they've just withered on the vine," Agatha told her.

Up ahead, Stuart was asking all about the Church of the Second Chance. He wanted to know how sizable a membership it had, when it had been founded, what its tax status was. You could tell he was only making conversation, but Ian answered each question gladly and at length. He said that Second Chance had saved his life. Doug, walking in front with Thomas, coughed and said, "Oh, well, ah . . ." but Ian insisted, "It did, Dad. You know it did."

He told Stuart, "Sometimes I have this insomnia. I fall asleep just fine but then an hour or so later I wake up, and that's when the troublesome thoughts move in. You know? Things I did wrong, things I said wrong, mistakes I want to take back. And I always wonder, 'If I didn't have Some-one to turn this all over to, how would I get through this? How do other people get through it?' Because I'm surely not the only one, am I?"

They had reached an intersection now, and they waited on the curb while a spurt of traffic passed. Agatha clutched her coat collar tight and glanced over at Daphne. There was something meaningful in the way she narrowed her eyes. *And you didn't want me to invite a girlfriend for him,* she must be saying.

"You know that clock downstairs that strikes the number of hours," Ian told Stuart. "And then it strikes once at every half hour. So when you hear it striking once, you can't be certain how much of the night you've used up. Is it twelve-thirty, or is it one, or is it one-thirty? You have to just lie there and wait, and hope with all your heart that next time it will strike two. Or what's worse, some nights it starts striking one, two, three and you say, 'Ah!' And then four, five and you say, 'Can this be? Have I really slept through till dawn?' And then six, seven and you say, 'Oh-oh,' be-cause you can see it's not *that* light out. And sure enough, the clock goes on to twelve, and you brace yourself for another six hours till morning."

The street was clear now and they could have crossed, but instead they stood watching him. It was Agatha who finally spoke. "Oh, Ian," she said. "Oh, damnit. How much longer are you going to be on your own?"

"Why, not long at all," he told her.

They squinted at him in the sunlight.

"I wasn't planning to bring this up yet," he said. "But anyhow. Since you ask. I believe I might be getting married."

Somewhere far off, a car honked.

Agatha said, "Married?"

"At least, we're talking it over."

Stuart said, "Hey, now!" He punched Ian in the shoulder. "Hey, guy. Congratulations!"

"Thanks," Ian said. He was grinning.

"This is you and Clara," Agatha said.

"Who? No, it's Rita," he said. He told Daphne, "You know Rita."

Daphne's mouth dropped open.

"Rita who?" Agatha asked. She tugged Daphne's jacket sleeve. "Who's Rita?"

Their grandfather was the one who answered. "Rita the Clutter Coun-selor," he said. "Hot dog!"

"But who is she?" Agatha demanded. They started crossing the street, with Ian leading the way. "Have *you* met her, Thomas?"

Thomas said, "Nope." But he was grinning too.

"We've only been going out a month or so," Ian told them. "When I first got to know her I held back, for a while. I was afraid we were too different. But then finally I said, 'I just have to do this,' and I called her up. By the end of that first evening it seemed we'd known each other forever."

"You must have at least suspected," Agatha told Daphne.

"I swear I didn't," Daphne said.

She was in that stunned state of mind where every sound seems unusually distinct. Of course she liked Rita very much, and yet . . . "This is so sudden," she said to Ian. "Shouldn't you go more inch-by-inch?"

He stopped in the middle of the sidewalk and turned. "Look," he said. "I'm forty-one years old. I'm not getting any younger. And you all know my beliefs. You know I can't just . . . live with her or anything. I want to get married."

"Right on!" Stuart cheered.

"Besides which, you're going to love her. Aren't they, Dad?"

"Absolutely," his father said, beaming. "She let me keep my workbench just the way I wanted. She let me keep Bee's lipstick on the bureau."

"She's very tall and slim and beautiful," Ian told Agatha. "She could easily be Indian. She has beautiful long black hair and she moves in this loose, swinging way, like a dancer."

Daphne looked at him.

As a matter of fact, every word he had said was true.

"There's something honest about her, and just . . . right," he said. "I've never met anyone like her."

Agatha stepped forward, then. She put both hands on his shoulders and kissed his cheek. "Congratulations, Ian," she said.

"Me, too," Daphne said, and she kissed his other cheek, and Thomas clamped his neck in a rough hug. "Mr. Mysterious," he said.

Their grandfather touched Ian's arm shyly. Ian was trying to get the grin off his face.

They started walking again. Agatha asked all about the wedding, and Doug described how Rita admired his baby-food-jar system for sorting screws. But Daphne strolled next to Stuart in silence.

She was thinking about the dream she had dreamed at Thanksgiving. It wasn't so much a dream as a feeling—a wash of intense, deep, perfect love. She had awakened and thought, *For whom?* and realized it was Ian. But it was Ian back in her childhood, when he had seemed the most magnificent person on earth. She hadn't noticed till then how pale and flawed her love had grown since. It had made her want to weep for him, and that was why, at breakfast that day, she had said she hadn't dreamed any dreams at all.

10

Recovering from the Hearts-of-Palm Flu

She asked if he thought he might ever want children and he said, "Oh, well, maybe sometime." She asked how long he figured they should wait and he said, "A few years, maybe? I don't know."

They'd been married just four months, by then. He could see his answer came as a disappointment.

But why should they rush to change things? Their lives were perfect. Simply watching her—simply sitting at the kitchen table watching her knead a loaf of bread—filled him with contentment. Her hands were so capable, and she moved with such economy. When she wiped her floury palms on the seat of her jeans, he was struck with admiration for her naturalness.

"I had been wondering about sooner," she told him.

"Well, no need to decide this instant," he said.

He watched her oil a baking pan, working her long, tanned fingers deftly into the corners, and he thought of a teacher he had had in seventh grade. Mrs. Arnett, her name was. Mrs. Arnett had once been his ideal woman—soft curves and sweet perfume and ivory skin. He had found any number of reasons to bicycle past her house. Her front bow window, which was curtained off day and night by cream-colored draperies, had displayed a single, pale blue urn, and somehow that urn had come to represent all his fantasies about marriage. He had imagined Mrs. Arnett greeting her husband at the door each evening, wearing not the bermudas or dull slacks his mother wore but a swirly dress the same shade of blue as the urn; and she would kiss Mr. Arnett full on the lips and lead him inside. Everything would be so focused. No distractions: no TV blaring or telephone ringing or neighbors stopping by.

Certainly no children.

You couldn't say Ian and Rita lived that way, even now. They were still in the house on Waverly Street—partly a matter of economics, partly to keep his father company. (Daphne had a place of her own now.) His father still occupied the master bedroom, and Rita's widowed mother was forever dropping by, and Rita's various aunts and cousins and a whole battalion of woman friends sat permanently around the kitchen table waiting for her to pour coffee. Where would children fit into all this?

"Next birthday, I'll be thirty," Rita told him.

"Thirty's young," Ian said.

Next birthday, Ian would be forty-two.

Forty-two seemed way too old to be thinking of babies.

At the wood shop, one of the workers had a daughter smaller than his own granddaughters. He was on his second wife, a manicurist named LaRue, and LaRue had told him it wasn't fair to deprive her of a family just because he had already had the joy of one. He had reported every detail of their arguments on the subject; and next he'd discussed the pregnancy, which seemed so new and exciting to LaRue and so old to Butch, and finally the baby herself, who cried every evening and interrupted dinner and caused LaRue to smell continually of spit-up milk. Now the baby was two and sometimes came along with her mother to give Butch a ride home after work. She would toddle through the shavings, crowing, and hold out her little arms until he set aside his plane and picked her up. "Ain't she a doll?" he asked the others. "Ain't she a living doll?" But the sight of his grizzled cheek next to that flower-petal face was disturbing, somehow, and Ian always turned away, smiling falsely, and grew very busy with his tools.

Ian and Rita went to church on foot that next Sunday because the weather was so fine. Besides, Ian liked the ceremony of it: the two of them holding hands as they walked and calling out greetings to various neighbors working in their yards. Rita wore a dress (or at least, a long black T-shirt that hit her above the knees), because she'd grown up at Alameda Baptist and considered jeans unsuitable for church. Her braid was wound in a knot at the nape of her neck. Ian couldn't help noticing the unusually attractive way her hair grew, hugging her temples closely and swooping down over her ears in ripples.

"Did I tell you Mary-Clay went in for her ultrasound?" she asked. "Her doctor said she's having twins."

"Twins! Good grief," he said. A shadow fell over him.

"Two little girls, her doctor thinks. Mary-Clay is just tickled to bits. Girls are easier than boys, she says."

"Rita," Ian said, "neither is easy."

She glanced at him. He hadn't meant to sound so emphatic.

"At least," he said, "not according to my limited experience."

They turned onto York Road. Ahead they could see a cluster of worshipers standing in front of the church, enjoying their last few moments of sunshine before they stepped inside. Rita said, "Well, now that you mention it, your experience *was* limited. Those children weren't your own. You weren't even solely responsible for them!"

"Right," Ian told her. "I had both my parents helping, and still it wasn't easy. A lot of it was just plain boring. Just providing a warm body, just *being* there; anyone could have done it. And then other parts were terrifying. Kids get into so much! They start to matter so much. Some days I felt like a fireman or a lifeguard or something—all that tedium, broken up by little spurts of high drama."

Rita gathered a breath, but by then they'd reached the others. Sister Myra said, "Why, hello, you two!" and kissed them both, even Ian. She had never kissed Ian before he was married. Marriage changed things a good deal, he had learned.

They were the church's only newlyweds at the moment, and almost the only ones ever. Their wedding had taken place at Alameda Baptist, but most of Second Chance had attended and Reverend Emmett had helped officiate, even donning one of Alameda's flowing black pastoral robes so when he raised his arms to pray he had resembled a skinny Stealth bomber. Now they were passed from hand to hand like babies in an old folks' home, with Rita saying those just-right things that women somehow know to say. "Brother Kenneth, how's that sciatica? Why, Sister Denise! You've gone and lightened your hair." Ian was impressed, but also disconcerted. This never seemed to be *his* Rita, who spent her weekdays bluntly informing customers that most of their lifelong treasures belonged in the nearest landfill.

They went inside and took two seats halfway up the aisle. Sister Nell was passing out hymn pamphlets. When Ian opened his he found the top corner of each page torn off as if gnawed by a mouse, and he smiled to himself and looked around for Daphne. (She must have some kind of deficiency, Agatha always said, to eat paper the way she did.) But he didn't see her. The fact was that she attended less and less, now that she lived downtown. Just about all you could count on her for was Good Works on Saturday mornings.

Rita was talking with her neighbor on the other side, Brother Kenneth's son Johnny, who used to be a little pipsqueak of a boy but now was studying for the ministry. Sometimes lately he had assisted with the services. Today, though, Reverend Emmett rose alone to deliver the opening prayer. Rita faced forward obediently and bowed her head, but Ian sensed she wasn't listening. She failed to straighten when Reverend Emmett said, "Amen," and she chewed a thumbnail edgily during the Bible reading. Ian reached over and captured her hand and tucked it into his, and she relaxed against him.

"Thus concludes the reading of the Holy Word," Reverend Emmett said. "We will now sing hymn fourteen."

The little organ wheezed out the first notes and Ian let go of Rita's hand. But she didn't draw away. Instead she looked directly into his face as they stood up, ignoring the hymnal he held before them.

"Listen," she said in a low voice. "I think I might be pregnant."

He had already opened his mouth to start singing. He shut it. The congregation went on without them: "Break Thou the bread of life . . ."

"It wasn't on purpose," she said. And then she whispered, "But I intend to be glad about this, I tell you!"

What could he say?

"Me, too, sweetheart," he said.

They faced front again. Stammering slightly, he found his place and joined the other singers.

That was in July. By September, she was having to leave the waistband of her jeans unsnapped and she wore her loosest work shirts over them. She said she thought she could feel the baby moving now—a little bubble, she said, flitting here and there in a larking sort of way. Ian set a palm on her abdomen but it was still too early for him to feel anything from outside.

She bought a book that showed what the baby looked like week by week, and she and Ian studied it together. A lima bean. A tadpole. Then finally a person but a clumsily constructed one, like something modeled in preschool. They were thinking of Joshua for a boy and Rachel for a girl. Ian tried the names on his tongue to see how they'd work in everyday life. "Oh, and I'd like you to meet my son, Joshua Bedloe . . ." His son! The notion brought forth the most bewildering mixture of feelings: worry and excitement and also, underneath, a pervasive sense of tiredness. He told Rita about everything but the tiredness. That he kept to himself.

Now it seemed the household was completely taken over by women. Rita's batty mother, Bobbeen, spent hours in their kitchen, generally seated not at the table but on it and dangling her high-heeled sandals from her toes. With her crackling, bleached-out fan of hair and snapping gum and staticky barrage of advice, she seemed electric, almost dangerous. "You're insane to go on working when you don't have to, Rita, stark staring insane. Don't you remember what happened to your aunt Dora when *she* kept on? You tell her, Ian. Tell her to quit hauling other folkses' junk when she's four and a half months gone and all her pelvic bones are coming off their hinges." But she didn't actually mean for Ian to say anything; she didn't leave the briefest pause before starting a new train of thought. "I guess you heard about Molly Sidney. Six months along and she phones her doctor, says, 'Feels like somebody's hauling rope out of way down low in my back.' 'Oh,' her doctor says, 'That's normal.' Says, 'Pay it no mind,' and the very next night guess what."

She could recite the most bizarre stories: umbilical cords kinked off like twisted vacuum-cleaner hoses, babies arriving with tails and coats of fur, deluges of blood in the lawn-care aisle at Ace Hardware. If Rita's two married girlfriends were around they would tut-tut. "Hush, now! You'll scare her!" they'd say. But their own stories were nearly as alarming. "I was in labor for thirty-three hours." "Well, they had to tie *me* down on the bed." Serenely, Rita circulated with the coffeepot. Ian retreated to the basement, where his father was repainting the family high chair. "Women!" Ian said. "They're giving me the chills."

"You want to close that door behind you, Ian," his father said. "It was paint fumes caused your cousin Linley's baby to have that little learning problem."

In October Ian started building a cradle of Virginia cherry—a simple slant-sided box without a hood because Rita wanted the baby to be able to see the world. He obtained the materials at no cost but of course he had to contribute his own time, and so he fell into the habit of staying on in the shop after it closed. His metal rasp, zipping down the edge of a rocker slat, said *careen! careen!* Often he seemed to hear the other workers' voices echoing through the empty room. "Drove a spindle wedge too hard and split the goddamn . . ." Bert said clearly, and Mr. Brant asked, "Why the hell you choose a plank with the sapwood showing?" Ian stopped rasping and ran a hand along the slat's edge, trying to gauge the curve. All his years here, he had worked with straight lines. He had deliberately stayed away from the bow-backed chairs and benches that required eye judgment, personal opinion. Now he was surprised at how these two shallow U shapes satisfied his palm.

And all his years here he had failed to understand Mr. Brant's prejudice against nails, his insistence on mortise-and-tenon and dovetails. "You put a drawer together with dovetail, it stays tight a century no matter what the weather," Mr. Brant was fond of saying, and Ian always thought, *A century! Who cares?* It was not that he opposed doing a thing well. Everything that came from his hands was fine and smooth and sturdy. But you could manage that with nails too, for heaven's sake; and if it didn't last forever, why, *he* would not be there to notice. Now, though, he took special pride in the cradle's nearly seamless joints, which would expand and contract in harmony and continue to stay tight through a hundred steamy summers and parched winters.

Early in December Rita and Ian went with Daphne and her new boyfriend, Curt, to a bar downtown that featured pinball machines. Daphne had developed a passion for pinball. Rita was beginning her seventh month and she had lately cut her work hours in half, which left her with too much time on her hands. Any outing at all struck her as preferable to staying home. This was why Ian agreed to go to the bar, even though he didn't drink. And Rita, of course, couldn't drink, and Curt turned out to belong to A.A. So there the three of them sat with their seltzers while Daphne, merrily sloshing her beer, toured the various games. Her favorite, she said, was the one called Black Knight 2000, which she wanted the four of them to try if only the others would give them half a chance. She hoisted herself onto a stool and glowered at the crowd. There were so many people here that Ian couldn't even see what kind of room it was.

Curt was telling Rita about his sister's breech baby. (Did people actively *collect* these tales?) He didn't look like much, in Ian's honest opinion—a bespectacled and bearded type in clothes too determinedly rustic. Also, something unfortunate had happened to his hair. It stuck out all over his head in rigid little cylinders. Ian said, "What . . . ?" He leaned closer to Daphne and said, "What would you call that kind of hairdo, exactly?"

"Do you like it? I did it myself," she said. "You braid dozens and dozens of eentsy braids and dunk them in Elmer's glue to make them last. The only problem is when he jogs."

"Jogs?"

"He claims they bobble against his head and bang his scalp."

Ian snorted, but all at once he felt old. In fact he was very likely the oldest person present. He looked down at the hand encircling his glass—the grainy skin on his knuckles, the gnarled veins in his forearm. How could he have assumed that old people were born that way? That age was an individual trait, like freckles or blond hair, that would never happen to him?

He was older now, he thought with a thud, than Danny had ever managed to become.

Rita was laughing at something Curt had said, unconsciously cradling the bulge of her baby as she leaned back against the bar. Daphne was humming along with the jukebox. "Madonna," she broke off to tell Ian.

"Pardon?"

" 'Like a Prayer.' "

"I beg your pardon?"

"The *song*, Ian."

"Oh."

He took a gulp from his glass. (This seltzer smelled like wet dog.) "So anyhow," he said to Daphne, "where did you and Curt meet?"

"At work," she said.

Daphne had a job now at a place called Trips Unlimited. Ian said, "He's a travel agent?"

"No, no, he came in to reserve a flight. By profession he's an inventor."

"An inventor."

"He's got this one invention: a Leaf Paw. This sort of claw-type contraption you hold in your left hand to scoop up the leaves you're raking. We think it's going to make him rich."

Ian glanced over at Rita, hoping she'd heard. (They often considered the same things funny.) But Rita was staring fixedly across the room. He followed her eyes and saw a small, pretty girl in a Danzig T-shirt playing the Black Knight 2000 machine. An old friend, maybe? But when he turned back to ask, he realized Rita's stare was unfocused. It was the glazed and inward stare of someone listening to faraway music. He said, "Rita?"

"Excuse me," she said abruptly. She stood and made her way through the crowd, disappearing behind the door marked LADIES.

Ian and Daphne looked at each other. "Think I should go after her?" Daphne asked.

"I'm not sure," he said. "Well, she's probably okay."

Although he was nowhere near as confident as he sounded.

They fell silent. Even Curt seemed to know better than to try and make small talk. Now Ian noticed the noise in this place—the laughter and clinking glassware and the hubbub from the pinball machines, which whanged and burbled and barked instructions in metallic, hollow voices. Everyone was so carefree! Two stools over, a young woman with long hair as dark as Rita's nonchalantly swung her pink-and-turquoise mountain-climbing shoes. A young man in a red jacket and a straight blond ponytail passed her one of the beers he'd just paid for. The jukebox had stopped playing, but some people in a booth were singing "Happy Birthday."

Then Rita was back, white-faced. All three of them stood up. She told Ian, "I'm bleeding."

He swallowed.

Curt was the first to react. He said, "I'll get the check. You three head out to the car," and he dropped a set of keys into Ian's palm.

Ian had forgotten that they'd driven here in Curt's Volvo. "Let's go," he said. He shepherded Rita toward the door. Daphne followed with their wraps. When they reached the sidewalk he stopped to help Rita into her jacket. She shook her head, but he could hear how her teeth were chattering. "Put it on," he told her, and she submitted, allowing him to bully her arms into the sleeves.

Curt caught up with them as Ian was unlocking the car door. "Which hospital?" he asked, sliding behind the wheel, and he started the engine in one smooth motion. He drove as if he'd dealt with such crises often, swooping dexterously from lane to lane and barely slowing for red lights before proceeding through them. Meanwhile Ian held both of Rita's hands in his. Her teeth were still chattering and he wondered if she was in shock.

At the Emergency Room entrance, Curt pulled up behind an ambulance. Ian hustled Rita out of the backseat and took her inside to a woman at a long green counter. "She's bleeding," he told the woman.

"How much?" she asked.

Instantly, he felt reassured. It appeared there were degrees to this; they shouldn't automatically assume the worst. Rita said, "Not a whole lot."

The woman called for a nurse, and Rita was led away while Ian stayed behind to fill out forms. Insurance company, date of birth . . . He answered hurriedly, scrawling across the dotted lines. When he was almost finished, Daphne and Curt came in from parking the car. "They've taken her somewhere," he told them. He asked Daphne, "Do you know her mother's maiden name?"

"Make one up," Daphne said. She looked around at the faded green walls, the elderly black man half asleep on a molded plastic chair. "Not bad," she said. "Usually this place is packed."

How often did she come here, anyway? And Curt, standing behind her, said, "Lord, yes, there've been times I've waited six and seven hours."

"Well, we might have a wait this evening, too," Ian said. "Maybe you should both go home."

"I'm staying," Daphne told him.

"Yes, but," Ian said. He slid the form across the counter to the woman. He said, "But, um, I'd really *rather* you go. To tell the truth."

He could see she felt hurt. She said, "Oh."

"I just want to . . . concentrate on this. All right?" he asked.

"I could concentrate too," she said.

But Curt touched her sleeve and said, "Come on, Daph. I'm sure he'll call as soon as he has anything to tell you."

When he led her away, Ian felt overwhelmingly grateful. He felt he might even love the boy.

Rita lay on a stretcher in an enclosure formed by white curtains. No one had come to examine her yet, she said, but they'd phoned her doctor. She wore a withered blue hospital gown, and a white sheet covered her legs and rose gently over the mound of her stomach. Ian settled on a stool beside the stretcher. He picked up her hand, which felt warmer now and slightly moist. She curled her fingers tightly around his.

"Remember our wedding night?" she asked him.

"Yes, of course."

"Remember in the hotel? I came out of the bathroom in my nightgown and you were sitting on the edge of the bed, touching two fingers to your forehead. I thought you were nervous about making love."

"Well, I was," he said.

"You were praying."

"Well, that too."

"You were shy about saying your bedtime prayers in front of me and so you pretended you were just sort of thinking."

"I was worried I would look like one of those show-off Christians," he said. "But still I wanted to, um, I felt I ought to—"

"Could you pray now?" she asked him.

"Now?"

"Could you pray for the baby?"

"Honey, I've been praying ever since we left the bar," he said.

Really his prayers had been for Rita. He had fixed her firmly, fiercely to this planet and held her there with all his strength. But he had prayed not only for her health but for her happiness, and so in a sense he supposed you could say that he'd prayed for the baby as well.

She spent one night in the hospital but was released the following morning, still pregnant, with orders to lie flat until her due date. At first this seemed easy. She would do anything, she said, anything at all. She would stand on her head for two months, if it helped her hang onto this baby. But she had always been the athletic, go-getter type, and books didn't interest her and TV made her restless. So every evening when Ian came home from work he found the radio blaring, and Rita on the telephone, and the kitchen bustling with women fixing tidbits to tempt her appetite as if she were a delicate invalid. Which, of course, she wasn't. "I don't care if it takes major surgery!" she'd be shouting into the phone. "You get those moldy old magazines *away* from her!" (She was talking to Dennis or Lionel—one of her poor frazzled assistants.) Her hair flared rebelliously out of its braid and her shirtsleeves hiked up on her arms; nothing could induce her to spend the day in her bathrobe. And constantly she leapt to her feet on one pretext or another, while everybody cried, "Stop! Wait!" holding out their hands as if to catch the infant they imagined she would let drop.

Ian's father, who kept mostly to the basement these days, told Ian this was all a result of a misstep in evolution. "Human beings should never have risen upright," he said. "Now every pregnant woman has gravity working against her. Remember Claudia? Same thing happened to Claudia, back when she was expecting Franny."

"That's true, it did," Ian said. He had forgotten. All at once he saw Lucy in her red bandanna with her hair hanging down her back. "Just, you know, a little bleeding . . ." she informed him in her quaint croak. Lucy had been pregnant herself at the time. She had been pregnant at her wedding, most likely, and only now did Ian stop to think how she must have felt going through those early weeks alone, hiding her symptoms from everyone, trying to figure out some way to manage.

"It won't be real fancy," she said.

And, "Twenty twenty-seven! Great God Almighty!"

She said, "Do you think Danny will mind?"

That evening while he and Rita were playing Scrabble, he rose and wandered over to Lucy's framed photo above the piano. Daphne had hung it there some time ago, but he'd hardly glanced at it since. He lifted it from its hook and held it level in both hands. "I'll trade you two of my vowels for one consonant," Rita said, but Ian went on frowning at Lucy's small, bright face.

Of course, she struck him as preposterously young. That was only to be expected. And everything about her was so dated. That leggy look of the sixties! That childish, Christopher Robin stance grown women used to affect, with their feet planted wide apart and their bare knees braced! She resembled a little tepee on stilts. A paper parasol from a cocktail glass. One of those tiny, peaked Japanese mushrooms with the thready stems.

He was noticing this to gain some distance. Surely he was able to see her clearly now. Wasn't he? Surely he had the perspective, at last, to understand what Lucy's meaning had been in his life.

But Rita said, "Okay, *three* of my vowels. For one lousy consonant. You drive a hard bargain, you devil."

And Ian replaced the picture on its hook, no wiser.

This was going to be the first Christmas of their marriage and Rita had big plans. She sent Daphne on mysterious errands with shopping lists and whispered instructions. She phoned Thomas in New York and Agatha in L.A., making sure they were coming. She drew up a guest list for Christmas dinner: Mrs. Jordan and the foreigners and her mother and Curt. Ian had once mentioned how the Bedloes' holiday meals used to be all hors d'oeuvres, and she decided to revive the practice even though it meant cooking from the living room. For days she lay on the couch with a bread-board across her lap, rolling pinwheels and stamping out fancy shapes of biscuit dough and mincing herbs that Doug obligingly toted back and forth for her. Ian worried she was overdoing, but at least it kept her entertained.

Christmas fell on a Monday that year. Thomas arrived in time for church on Sunday morning, and Daphne met them there, carrying her knapsack because she'd be sleeping over. Agatha and Stuart flew in that afternoon. For the family supper on Christmas Eve they had black-eyed peas and rice. Everybody was puzzled by this (they usually had oyster stew), but Rita explained that black-eyed peas were an ancient custom. Something to do with luck, she said—good luck for the coming year. Almost immediately a sort of click of recognition traveled around the table. Coming year? Then wasn't that *New Year's* Eve? They sent each other secret glances and then applied themselves to their food, smiling. Rita didn't notice a thing. Ian did, though, and he was touched by his family's tact. Lately he'd started valuing such qualities. He had begun to see the importance of manners and gracious gestures; he thought now that his mother's staunch sprightliness had been braver than he had appreciated in his youth. (Last summer, laid up for a week with a wrenched back, he had suddenly wondered how Bee had endured the chronic pain of her arthritis all those years. He suspected that had taken a good deal more strength than the brief, flashy acts of valor you see in the movies.)

"To the cook!" Thomas said, raising his water glass, and they all said, "To Rita!" Rita grinned and raised her own glass. Probably for decades of Christmas Eves to come the Bedloes would be loyally eating black-eyed peas and rice.

It was afterward, in front of the fire, that Thomas announced his engagement. "You two won't be the newest newlyweds anymore," he told Ian. This wasn't exactly a shock—he'd been dating the same girl for some time now—but they had been hoping he would get over her. They all felt she bossed him around too much. (He kept falling for these managerial types who didn't have any softness to them; they might as well be business partners, Daphne had once complained.) Still, the women hugged him and Doug said, "What do you know!" and Ian suggested they call Angie and welcome her to the family. So they did, lining up in the hall to tell her more or less the same thing in several different ways. While Ian was waiting his turn at the phone he had a sudden memory of Danny presenting Lucy in this very spot. What was it he had said? "I'd like you to meet the woman who's changed my life," he had said, and then as now the family had received the news with the most resolute show of pleasure.

On Christmas morning they opened their presents—most of Ian's and Rita's relating to babies—and then cleared away the gift wrap and started getting ready for the dinner guests. Rita directed from an armchair Ian had dragged into the dining room, except that she kept jumping up to do things herself. Finally Agatha put Stuart in charge of diverting her. "Show her your card tricks, Stu," she said. "Oh, please, no," Rita groaned. Ian and his father fitted all the leaves into the table, and the women added last-minute touches to the dishes Rita had prepared. Everyone was entranced to find nothing but hors d'oeuvres. "Look! Artichokes," Doug pointed out. "Look at this, kids, my favorite: Chesapeake crab spread. It's just like the old days." Rita beamed. Stuart told her, "Pick a card. Any card. Come on, Rita, pay attention."

The current foreigners' names were Manny, Mike, and Buck. They were the first to arrive—they always showed up on the dot, not familiar with Baltimore ways—and Mrs. Jordan followed, bearing one of her sumptuous black fruitcakes with the frosting you had to crack through with a chisel. Then Bobbeen appeared with an old-fashioned crank-style ice cream freezer, fully loaded and ready for the ice, and last came Curt, looking as if he'd just that minute rolled out of bed. Those who were guests had to have the hors d'oeuvres explained for them—all but Mrs. Jordan, of course, who'd been through this year after year. Mrs. Jordan said, "Why, you've even made Bee's hearts-of-palm dish!" And later, once they'd taken their seats and Doug had offered the blessing, she said, "Rita, if Ian's mother could see what you've done here she would be so pleased."

"Remember the first time we tasted hearts of palm?" Agatha asked Thomas.

"Was that when we had the flu?"

"No, no, this was before. You were really little, and Daphne was just a baby. I don't think she got to try them. But you and I were crazy about them; we polished off the platter. It wasn't till five or six years later we had that flu."

"Ugh! Worst flu of my life," Thomas said.

"Mine too. I couldn't eat a bite for days. But finally I called out, 'Ian, I'm hungry!' Remember, Ian? You were flat on your back—"

"*I* was sick?" Ian asked.

"Everyone was, even Grandma and Grandpa. You said, 'Hungry for what?' And I thought and thought, and the only thing that came to me was hearts of palm."

"So then we all wanted hearts of palm," Thomas told him. "They just sounded so *good*, even though I'd forgotten them and Daphne'd never had them. We said, 'Please, Ian, won't you please bring us hearts of—' "

"I don't remember this," Ian said.

"So you got up and tottered downstairs, holding onto the banister—"

"Put your coat on over your pajamas, stepped into somebody's boots—"

"Drove all the way to the grocery store and brought back hearts of palm."

"I don't remember any of it," Ian said.

They regarded him fondly—all but the foreigners, who were giving the hors d'oeuvres their single-minded attention. "My hero!" Rita told him.

"I said, 'Ian, thank you,' " Agatha went on, "and you said, 'Thank *you*. Until you mentioned them,' you said, 'I didn't realize that's what I'd been wanting all along myself.' "

Stuart said, "Maybe they contained some trace element your bodies knew they needed."

"Well, whatever," Curt said, "these here taste mighty good. You should go into the catering business, Rita."

"Oh, I believe I've got enough to do for the next little bit," she told him. And she patted her abdomen, which Ian's borrowed shirt could barely cover.

Daphne said, "Have you heard? After this baby's born, Rita and I are planning to be partners. Half the time I'll do clutter counseling while she stays home with the baby, half the time I'll stay with the baby while *she* does clutter counseling."

Ian raised his eyebrows. He knew Rita had been considering various strategies, but she hadn't mentioned Daphne. He said, "What about Trips Unlimited?"

"That's not really working out," Daphne told him. "It's too personal."

"A travel agency is personal?"

"Mr. X and Mrs. Y book two flights to Paris and one hotel room, say, and I can't let on I've noticed. Or they cheat on their expense accounts with first-class reservations to—"

No one suggested that this new job would surely be even more personal— that she seemed to *search out* the personal. Finally Curt said, "Well, if you ever get tired of clutter counseling you could always become a scribe."

"Scribe?" Daphne asked, perking up.

"You could rent a stall at Harborplace and offer to write people's letters for them."

Daphne looked perplexed. The only person who laughed was Ian.

There was a little wait before dessert because they had to freeze the ice cream. Bobbeen said, "You realize we don't have a single child here? No one begging to turn the crank for us." But the foreigners, it emerged, would love to turn the crank. They rushed off to the kitchen while Daphne and Agatha cleared the table. Rita stayed seated at Ian's left, debating baby names with Mrs. Jordan. Curt was attempting to break into the fruitcake, and Thomas was telling his grandfather about his latest computer game. The idea was, he said, to show how dislodging one historical event could dislodge a hundred others, even those that seemed unrelated. "Take slavery," he said. "Students would tell the computer that the U.S. has never had slavery, and then they would name some later event. The computer goes, 'Beep!' and a message flashes up on the screen: *Null and void.*"

"But why would that be any fun?" Doug asked.

"Well, it's not supposed to be fun so much as educational."

"I wonder whatever became of Monopoly," Doug said wistfully.

Rita took Ian's hand and placed it palm-down on a spot just beneath her left breast. "Feel," she whispered. A round, blunt knob—a knee or foot or elbow—slid beneath his fingers. It always unnerved him when that happened.

Last week he had signed the papers for Rita's hospital stay. She'd be in just overnight, if everything went as it should. On the first day he was liable for one dependent and on the second, for two. Two? Then he realized: the baby. One person checks in; two check out. It seemed like sleight of hand. He had never noticed before what a truly astonishing arrangement this was.

"So I took a shortcut through a side street," Daphne told him, "or really more of an alley, and it was starting to get dark and I heard these footsteps coming up behind me. Pad-pad, pad-pad: gym-shoe footsteps. Rubber soles. I started walking faster. The footsteps walked faster too. I dug my hand in my bag and pulled out that siren you gave me. Remember that key chain with the siren on it you gave me one Christmas?"

They were heading down to the shop together to bring home the cradle. Ian was driving Rita's pickup, which had a balky gear shift that was annoying him to no end. When the light turned green he had to struggle to get it into first. He said, "Very smart, Daphne. How many times have I warned you not to walk alone at night?"

"I spun around and I pressed the button. The siren went *wow! wow! wow!* and this person just about fell on top of me—this young, stalky black boy wearing great huge enormous white basketball shoes. He was shocked, you could tell. He backed off and sort of goggled at me. He said, 'What the hell, man? You know? What the hell?' And I was standing in front of him with my mouth wide open because I realized I had no idea how to switch the fool thing off. There we were, just looking at each other, and the siren going *wow! wow!* until bit by bit I started giggling. And then finally he kind of like shook his head and stepped around me. So I threw the siren over a fence and walked on, only making sure not to follow him too closely, and way far behind I could still hear *wow, wow, wow . . .*"

"You think it's all a big joke, don't you," Ian said, turning down Chalmer.

"Well, it was, in a way. I mean I wouldn't have been surprised if that boy had said, 'Oh, man, that uncle of yours,' while he was shaking his head. Like we were the old ones and you were the young one. You were the greenhorn."

"At least I won't end up dead in some alley," Ian told her. "What were you doing in that part of town? How come you're always cruising strange neighborhoods?"

"I like newness," Daphne said.

He parked in front of the wood shop.

"I like for things not to be too familiar. I like to go on first dates; I like it when a guy takes me someplace I've never been before, some restaurant or bar, and the waitress calls him by name and the bartender kids him but I'm the stranger, just looking around all interested at this whole new world that's so unknown and untried."

They got out of the truck. (Ian didn't ask how come she still lived in Baltimore, in that case. He was very happy she lived in Baltimore.) He walked around to the rear end to lower the tailgate, and he reached in for the folded blanket he'd brought and spread it across the floorboards.

"If I were a man I'd call up a different woman every night," Daphne said, following him. "I'd like that little thrill of not knowing if she would go out with me."

"Easy for *you* to say," Ian told her.

He didn't have to use his key to get into the shop, which meant Mr. Brant must be working on a weekend again. He ushered Daphne inside and led the way across the dusty linoleum floor, passing a half-assembled desk and the carcass of an armoire. Through the office doorway he glimpsed Mr. Brant bending over the drafting table, and he stepped extra heavily so as to make his presence felt. Mr. Brant raised his head but merely nodded, deadpan.

When they reached the corner that was Ian's work space, he came to a stop. He gestured toward the cradle—straight-edged and shining. "Well?" he said. "What do you think?"

"Oh, Ian, it's beautiful! Rita's going to love it."

"Well, I hope so," he said. He bent to lift it. The honey smell of Wood-Witch paste wax drifted toward him. "You take the other end. Be careful getting it past that desk; I spent a long time on the finish."

They started back through the shop, bearing the cradle between them. Mr. Brant came to the office doorway to watch, but Daphne didn't even glance in his direction. She was still talking about newness. "I'd call some woman I'd just seen across a room or something," she said. "I would *not* say, 'You don't know me, but—' That's such an obvious remark. Why would she need to be informed she doesn't know you, for goodness' sake?"

All at once it seemed time slipped, or jerked, or fell away beneath Ian's feet. He was fifteen years old and he was rehearsing to ask Cicely Brown to the Freshman Dance. Over and over again he dialed the special number that made his own telephone ring, and Danny picked up the receiver in the kitchen and pretended to be Cicely's mother. "*Yell-*ow," he answered in fulsome, golden tones, and then he'd call, "Cicely, dahling!" and switch to his Cicely voice, squeaky and mincing and cracked across the high notes. "Hello? Oooh! Ian-baby!" By that stage Ian was usually helpless with laughter. But Danny waited tolerantly, and then he led Ian through each step of the conversation. He told Ian it was good to hear from him. He asked how he'd done on the history test. He spent several minutes on the he-said-she-said girls always seemed to think was so important, although in this case it was, "He said mumble-grumble and she said yattata-yattata." Then he left a conspicuous space for Ian to state his business, after which he told him, why, of course; you bet; he'd be thrilled to go to the dance.

Daphne said, "Ian?"

He balanced his end of the cradle on one knee and turned away, blotting his eyes with his jacket sleeve. When he turned back he found Mr. Brant next to him. "Hot," Ian explained. It was January, and cold enough in the shop to see your breath, but Mr. Brant nodded as if he knew all about it and opened the front door for him. Ian and Daphne carried the cradle on out.

Rita started labor in the middle of a working day. Envisioning this moment earlier, Ian had expected it to be nighttime—Rita nudging him awake the way women did on TV—but it was a sunny afternoon in late February when Doreen came to the office door and said, "Ian! Rita's on the phone." The other men glanced up. "Sure you don't want to change your mind, now," one said, grinning. They'd acted much less guarded around him since the news of the baby.

On the phone Rita said she was fine, pains coming every five minutes, no reason to leave the shop yet unless he wanted. By the time he reached home, though (for of course he came immediately), things had speeded up and she said maybe they should think about getting to the hospital. She was striding back and forth in the living room, wearing her usual outfit of leather boots and maternity jeans and one of his chambray shirts. His father paced alongside her, all but wringing his hands. "I've *never* liked this stage, never liked it," he told Ian. "Shouldn't we make her sit down?"

"I'm more comfortable walking," Rita said.

For the last two weeks she had been allowed on her feet again, and Ian often felt she was making up for lost time.

It was the mildest February ever recorded—not even cool enough for a sweater—and Rita looked surprised when Ian wanted to bring her coat to the hospital. "You don't know what the weather will be like when you come home," he told her.

She said, "Ian. I'm coming home *tomorrow*."

"Oh, yes."

He seemed to be preparing for a moment far in the future. It was unthinkable that in twenty-four hours they'd be back in this house with a child.

At the hospital they whisked her away while he dealt with Admissions, and by the time they allowed him in the labor room she had turned into a patient. She lay in bed in a coarse white gown, her forehead beaded with sweat. Every two minutes or so her face seemed to flatten. "Are you all right?" he kept asking. "Should I be doing anything?"

"I'm fine," she said. Her lips were so dry they looked gathered. The nurse had instructed him to feed her chips of ice from a plastic bowl on the nightstand, but when he offered her one she turned her head away fretfully.

She used to seem so invulnerable. That may have been why he had married her. He had seen her as someone who couldn't be harmed, once upon a time.

It was dark before they wheeled her to the delivery room. The window-panes flashed black as Ian walked down the hall beside her stretcher. The delivery room was a chamber of horrors—glaring white light and gleaming tongs and monstrous chrome machines. "You stand by her head, daddy," the doctor told him. "Hold onto mommy's hand." Somehow Rita found it in her to snicker at this, but Ian obeyed grimly, too frightened even to smile. Her hand was damp, and she squeezed his fingers until he felt his bones realigning.

"Any moment now," the doctor announced. Any moment what? Ian kept forgetting their purpose here. He was strained tight, like guitar strings, and all his stomach muscles ached from urging Rita to push. Couldn't women die of this? Yes, certainly they could die. It happened every day. He didn't see what prevented her from simply splitting apart.

"A fine boy," the doctor said, and he held up a slippery, angry, squalling creature trailing coils of telephone cord.

Ian released the breath that must have been trapped in his chest for whole minutes. "It's over, sweetheart," he told Rita. He had to raise his voice to be heard above the racket.

The doctor laid the baby in Rita's outstretched arms and she hugged it to her, cupping its wet black head in one hand. "Hello, Joshua," she said. She seemed to be smiling and weeping both. The baby went on wailing miserably. "So, do you like him?" she said, looking up at Ian.

"Of course," he told her.

It wrenched him that she'd felt the need to ask.

Eventually the baby was carted off somewhere, and Rita sent Ian to make phone calls. In the waiting room he shook quarters from the envelope she had prepared weeks earlier. He called each of the numbers she'd written across the front—first Bobbeen, and then his father, and then Daphne, Thomas, and Stuart (Agatha was still at work), and Rita's two best friends. They all sounded thrilled and amazed, as if they hadn't understood till now that an actual baby would come of this. Bobbeen wanted to drive right over. Ian persuaded her to wait, though. "You can visit her tomorrow," he said. "But stop by early. They're letting her go home right after lunch."

"Modern times!" Bobbeen marveled. "When Rita was born I had to stay a week, and they didn't let Vic in the delivery room, either. You-all are lucky."

It was on Rita's account that he'd asked Bobbeen to wait till morning; he assumed she would be exhausted. But when he went to her room he found her sitting upright, looking ready to spring out of bed. Her hair was combed and she wore her flannel pajamas in place of the hospital gown. "Eight pounds, four and a half ounces," she said. She must be talking about the baby, who wasn't there yet. They kept them in the nursery for the first few hours. "He's got your mouth: those little turns at the corners. And my dad's Italian hair. Oh, I *wish* they'd bring him in."

"Ah, well, you'll have him for the next eighteen years," Ian said.

Eighteen years; merciful heavens.

He sat with her awhile, listening to her rattle on, and then he kissed her good night. When he left, she was dialing her mother on the phone.

At home, a single lamp lit the front hall. His father must have gone to bed. It was after ten o'clock, Ian was amazed to see. He trudged up the stairs to his room.

Already Rita's pregnancy seemed so long ago. The pillow laid vertically to ease her backache, the opened copy of *Nine Months Made Easy*, and Doug's pocket watch, borrowed for its second hand—they struck him as faintly pathetic, like souvenirs of some old infatuation.

He sat on the bed to take off his shoes. Then he realized he would never manage to sleep. He was tired, all right, but keyed up. Padding softly in his socks, he went back downstairs to the kitchen and switched on the light. He poured milk into a saucepan and lit a burner, and while he waited for the milk to heat he dialed Reverend Emmett.

"Hello," Reverend Emmett said, sounding wide awake.

"Reverend Emmett, this is Ian. I hope you weren't in bed."

"Goodness, no. What's the news?"

"Well, we have a boy. Joshua. Eight pounds and some."

"Congratulations! How's Sister Rita?"

"She's fine," Ian told him. "It was a very easy birth, she says. To me it didn't look easy, but—"

"Shall I go visit her tomorrow?"

"They're sending her home in the afternoon. Maybe you'd like to come see her here."

"Gladly," Reverend Emmett said. "Why, we haven't had a new baby at church since Sister Myra's granddaughter! I may have forgotten how to hold one."

"You're welcome to brush up on your skills with us," Ian told him.

"God bless you for thinking to call me, Brother Ian," Reverend Emmett said. "I know absolutely that you'll be a good father. Go get some rest now."

"I believe I will," Ian said.

In fact, all at once he felt so sleepy that after he hung up, he turned off the stove and went straight to bed.

He stepped out of his shirt and his jeans and lay down in his underwear, not even bothering to pull the covers over him. He closed his eyes and saw Rita's glowing face and the baby's expression of outrage. He saw Reverend Emmett attempting to hold an infant. *That* would be a sight. It intrigued him to imagine the incongruity—to try and picture Reverend Emmett in this new context, the way he used to try picturing his seventh-grade teacher doing something so mundane as cooking breakfast for her husband.

Apparently, he thought, there were people in this world who simply never came clear. Reverend Emmett, Mr. Brant, the overlapping shifts of foreigners . . . In the end you had to accept that the day would never arrive when you finally understood what they were all about.

For some reason, this made him supremely happy. He pulled the covers around him and said a prayer of thanksgiving and fell headlong into sleep.

"This is proper gift," the foreigner named Buck told Ian. Or Ian *thought* he told him; then a moment later he realized it must have been a question. "This is proper gift?"

He meant the white plastic potty-chair resembling a real toilet, a pink ribbon tied in a bow across the seat like one of those hygienic paper bands in hotel bathrooms. Buck and Manny held it balanced between them on the top porch step. If Ian answered, "No," they seemed ready to spin around and take it home with them. He said, "Of course it's proper. Thank you very much."

"In America, every what you do is proper," Manny said to Buck. They appeared to be resuming some previous argument. "Why you are always so affrighted?"

"Wrong," Buck said. "They *tell* you is proper. Then catch your mistake. Ha!" he cried, startling Ian. "Pink ribbon. For boys should be blue."

"We already have been discussing this," Manny told him severely. "It is no problem." He turned to Ian. "Pink or blue: is all the same to you. Correct?"

"Correct," Ian assured him. "Come on inside."

He stood back, holding open the door, and they carried the potty through the front hall and into the living room. Rita sat in the rocker with a large pillow beneath her. Daphne and Reverend Emmett shared the couch. "This is proper gift," Buck told them. He and Manny set the potty on the floor.

"Well, certainly," Rita said, "and it's exactly what we wanted. Thank you, Buck and Manny."

"Is also from Mike. Mike has been arrested."

"Arrested?"

But before they could get to the bottom of this, Bobbeen called, "Yoo-hoo!" and let herself in. Her heels clattered across the hall and then she appeared in the doorway, wearing an orange pantsuit with a flurry of silk scarf tied artfully at her throat. She held both arms out at her sides; a vinyl purse dangled from one wrist. "Well?" she said. "Where is he? Where'd you put him? Where's that precious little grandbaby?"

"Hi, Ma," Rita said. "You remember Buck and Manny here, and Reverend Emmett."

"Oh! Goodness *yes*, I do," Bobbeen said, directing her squinty grimace solely to Reverend Emmett. He was standing now, looking uncomfortable, and Bobbeen stepped forward to grasp his hands in hers. "Wasn't it Christian of you to take this time from your duties," she said. Ian always suspected her of harboring a romantic interest in Reverend Emmett, but maybe she was just exceptionally devout. "Hey there, Daphne hon," she added over her shoulder. She sat in the center of the couch, pulling Reverend Emmett down beside her. "I can't believe I'm a grandma," she told him. "Isn't it a hoot? I sure don't *feel* like a grandma."

She didn't look like one either, Reverend Emmett was supposed to say, but he just smiled hard and clutched both his kneecaps. Bobbeen studied him a moment. She patted the ends of her hair reflectively and then turned to Rita. "So where's that little sweetie pie?" she asked.

"Ian was just on his way to bring him down," Rita told her.

He was?

Before the foreigners arrived, Reverend Emmett and Daphne had been about to follow him upstairs and peek into the cradle. But now there were too many of them, Ian supposed, and so he nodded and left the room. He was a little out of practice, was the trouble. He wasn't sure he remembered how to support a newborn's head.

As he started up the stairs he heard Bobbeen say, "Now tell me, Reverend Emmett, do you-all hold with christening? Or just what, exactly?"

"We believe christening to be a superficial convention," Reverend Emmett said.

"Well, of *course* it is," she told him in a soothing tone.

"Not to say there's anything wrong with it, you understand. It's just that we don't consider infants capable of . . . but if *your* church favors christening, why, I certainly—"

"Oh, what do I care about christening?" Bobbeen cried recklessly. "I think it's real holy of you to cast off the superficial, Reverend."

Ian went into his and Rita's bedroom, where they were keeping the baby for the first few nights. It lay facedown in one corner of the cradle with its knees drawn up to its stomach and its nose pressed into the sheet. How could it manage to breathe that way? But Ian heard tiny sighing sounds. Long strands of fine black hair wisped past the neckband of the flannel gown. Ian felt a surge of pity for those scrawny, hunched, defenseless little shoulders.

He knelt beside the cradle and turned the baby over, at the same time gingerly scooping it up so that he held a warm, wrinkled bundle against his chest as he rose. This didn't feel like any eight pounds. It felt like nothing, like thistledown—a burden so light it seemed almost buoyant; or maybe he was misled by the softness of the flannel. The baby stirred and clutched two miniature handfuls of air but went on sleeping. Ian bore his son gently across the upstairs hall.

"In fact I've been thinking of joining your congregation," Bobbeen was telling Reverend Emmett. "Did Rita happen to mention that?"

"Um, no, she didn't."

"I just feel you-all might have the answers."

"Oh, well, *answers*," Reverend Emmett said. "Actually, Mrs.—"

"Bobbeen."

"Actually, Mrs. Bobbeen . . ."

Ian grinned.

He was halfway down the stairs when he felt a kind of echo effect—a memory just beyond his reach. He paused, and Danny stepped forward to present his firstborn. "Here she is!" he said. But then the moment slid sideways like a phonograph needle skipping a groove, and all at once it was Lucy he was presenting. "I'd like you to meet the woman who's changed my life," he said. His face was very solemn but Lucy was smiling. "Your what?" she seemed to be saying. "Your, what was that? Oh, your *life*." And she tipped her head and smiled. After all, she might have said, this was an ordinary occurrence. People changed other people's lives every day of the year. There was no call to make such a fuss about it.

Anne Tyler was born in Minneapolis, Minnesota, in 1941, but grew up in Raleigh, North Carolina. She graduated at nineteen from Duke University and went on to go graduate work in Russian studies at Columbia Univeristy. Ann Tyler has written thirteen novels. *Breathing Lessons* was awarded the Pulitzer Prize in 1988. She is a member of the American Academy and Institute of Arts and Letters. She and her husband Taghi Modarressi, live in Baltimore, Maryland.